A STREET & SMITH PUBLICATION
10¢ CLUES
APRIL
DETECTIVE
STORIES
BRIDE OF THE RATS
An Ivy Frost Story
BY
DONALD WANDREI
NRA
CODE
THE
DRAGON'S
SHADOW
Introducing
PAWANG ALI
by E. HOFFMAN PRICE
8 COMPLETE STORIES

DETECTIVE
STORIES
THE ARTIST
OF DEATH
An Ivy Frost Story
by DONALD WANDREI
NRA
CODE
ONE HOUR TO LIVE
A Jaffray Story by Harry Lynch

10¢ CLUES
DECEMBER 1935
DETECTIVE
STORIES
I. V. Frost's phone rang at 3 a. m.
"This is the watchman at Platinum Park," shouted a man's voice. "There's a skeleton riding a griffin on a merry-go-round! The cops say I'm drunk or crazy. Do you?"
"I'll be there in twenty minutes," the professor answered, and hung up.
MERRY-GO-ROUND
BY DONALD WANDREI
FURY
A Jaffray Story
BY
HARRY LYNCH

10¢ CLUES
FEBRUARY 1936
DETECTIVE
STORIES
VISION OF VIOLET
A VIOLET McDADE STORY
By CLEVE F. ADAMS
"So strange things move in Eden!"
Professor Frost's eyes glittered as he lighted one of his long, pungent cigarettes. Jean Moray watched him closely.
"Change your clothes," he snapped suddenly, "——riding suit——we're going into the country——quick——"
GIANTS IN THE VALLEY
AN IVY FROST STORY
BY DONALD WANDREI

BOOKS BY DONALD WANDREI

Novels

The Web of Easter Island
Dead Titans, Waken! / Invisible Sun

Collections

The Eye and the Finger
Strange Harvest
Colossus:
  The Collected Science Fiction of Donald Wandrei
Don't Dream:
  The Collected Fantasy and Horror of Donald Wandrei
Frost
A Donald Wandrei Miscellany
The Complete Ivy Frost

Poetry

Ecstasy and Other Poems
Dark Odyssey
Poems for Midnight
Collected Poems
Sanctity and Sin :
  The Collected Poems and Prose Poems of Donald Wandrei

THE COMPLETE IVY FROST

Donald Wandrei & Howard Wandrei
New York City, July 3, 1935

Photograph courtesy of David Rajchel

DONALD WANDREI

Introduction by
D. H. Olson

Interior art by
Chris Kalb

Edited by
Stephen Haffner

HAFFNER PRESS
ROYAL OAK, MICHIGAN
2020

FIRST EDITION

The acknowledgments on page 701
constitute an extension of this copyright page

HAFFNER PRESS
5005 Crooks Road Suite 35
Royal Oak, Michigan 48073-1239
www.haffnerpress.com

ISBN: 978-1-893887-61-9 (Trade Edition)
ISBN: 978-1-893887-62-6 (Limited Edition)

Library of Congress Control Number: 2012934778

Printed in the United States of America

PUBLISHER'S ACKNOWLEDGMENTS

The publisher wishes to thank the following for their assistance in the preparation of this book:

Zuma Coffee House in Birmingham, Michigan and Bean and Leaf Cafe in Royal Oak, Michigan (both now consigned to history).

Dennis Weiler and the late Philip Rahman of Fedogan & Bremer for their collection of the first eight "Ivy Frost" stories in *Frost* (2000).

David Rajchel for the photograph of Howard & Donald Wandrei from his Arkham House collection.

The staff at the Library of Congress and Bowling Green State University.

Ariana Quesada for digital restoration of the endsheet images.

Lauren Hoepner for proofreading the manuscript.

Chris Kalb for creating the cover titles and interior artwork.

Raymond Swanland for his incredible cover artwork.

D.H. Olson—custodian of the legacy of Donald Wandrei and without whose guidance and patience this book would not exist.

CONTENTS

INTRODUCTION
D. H. OLSON

WHEN DONALD WANDREI was approached by the editors of *Clues Detective* he was still a relatively little-known writer whose work had scarcely ventured into mystery at all. They'd seen something in him, however. A knack for the uncanny, perhaps? A penchant for novelty which could add some zest to their product? A youthful talent, no doubt, who could be counted upon to deliver a steady flow of wordage for as long as the market might last. Though any details are lost, the tale of I. V. Frost's creation, development, promotion, and even the series aftermath, makes for interesting reading indeed.

Donald Albert Wandrei was born in St. Paul, Minnesota in 1908. His early life was genteel and bookish, financially comfortable. His father, Albert, was an editor at West Publishing, then, and now (as part of Thomson-Reuters), one of America's preeminent publishers of legal tomes and volumes of case law. As such, the Wandrei children grew up in an environment that fostered both reading and association with the children of the Capitol City's movers and shakers. They were also able to witness, first hand, the darker side of Prohibtion Era St. Paul, a gangster haven where mobsters and gunsels, prostitutes and bootleggers mingled freely with the crème de la crème of polite society.

Donald Wandrei's tastes were more literary than realistic, however, and his bent toward the poetic and outré soon led him in directions that were hardly mundane. The fixation of Poe and Bierce. The poetry of De Le Mare, Sterling, and the Romantics. The writings of Wilde and the Decadents. Some tendencies were further enhanced during his University of Minnesota days.

He tried his hand at Weird Fiction and poetry, managing to sell some to professional publications like *Weird Tales.* He began to correspond with fellow authors such as Clark Ashton Smith and H. P.

Lovecraft, neither of whom were exactly household names at that time. These contacts encouraged him and provided entré into a cycle of further literary influence beyond that of his upbringing alone. Wandrei, in turn, shared those influences among his classmates and the University and became a major player in the campus literary scene. His contemporaries were future judges and politicians as well as budding authors, artists, and poets. They fancied themselves decadents and trangressives. The atmosphere was electric but, not unsurprisingly, short-lived.

Wandrei was also adventurous. He traveled, hitch-hiking cross-country to visit correspondents and publishers, even staying for some time with H. P. Lovecraft in Providence. After graduation, he moved to New York where he took a job as an editor while also pursuing a career as a free-lance author after hours. Then he moved back to Minnesota to pursue a more advanced degree.

In 1934, he moved back to the Big Apple with his brother, Howard, both intent on writing full-time. For Donald, success came quickly and he became a permanent resident of New York until the Nazis, and World War II, intervened. His earliest stories were mostly geared to genre magazines like *Weird Tales,* where he had an in, and *Astounding Stories,* which proved an even better market in terms of both steady payment and demand. Not really enough to live on, though, given both publications' notoriously low rates. To correct this, Wandrei began to try his hand at better and more varied markets. He started to dabble in mysteries, a more popular and upscale market, then and now. F. Orlin Tremaine and Desmond Hall at Street & Smith liked his work and when he began to speak of crossing over into a new genre—from *Astounding Stories* to *Clues Detective,* as it were—they encouraged the shift. It's possible they even inspired it, though those details remain unclear. Their main interest lay in series characters, literary creations who could be branded and promoted. Interesting protagonists who would pull the readers in and fuel newsstand sales. Given Wandrei's bent for the outré, it seemed a promising venture indeed.

Wandrei, Hall, and Tremaine met for lunch on April 30, 1934 to go over what Don had come up with. They liked the character and the ideas presented but found the initial proposal rather cluttered and over-long. 15,000 word novelettes were the goal. Wandrei would need to pare back the length and save some of the ideas for later installments. Don obliged. On May 13th, Hall asked for a few minor changes. On the 18th, these changes had been made. Street & Smith paid Donald Wandrei $157 for that initial Frost adventure—originally titled "Advertise for Death"—and scheduled it for September publication. Still, even then, there remained certain contractual matters to contend with. Hall and Tremaine had high hopes for the character and wanted to keep Wandrei happy. They demanded exclusive "first serial" rights to all subsequent Frost adventures but, in return, allowed Wandrei to retain all other rights to the stories and characters, including book and movie sales. Such high hopes were not unreasonable. Though no Frost books or movies were published in Don's lifetime, Hollywood and serialization inquiries were being made before the fourth Frost installment had hit the stands, with more offers and potential book deals to follow. Sadly, none ever progressed beyond the negotiation stage.

In the meantime, Frost became an instant hit with *Clues* readers, boosting sales just as Tremaine and Hall had hoped. It garnered copycats too, most notably in *Dime Detective.* Wandrei was, by turns, both amused and annoyed by such back-handed praise. At the time it hardly mattered, however, for Don was enjoying the work, and appreciative of the steady income being provided.

Between September 1934 and September 1937, Wandrei wrote eighteen I.V. Frost adventures for *Clues.* Though his paychecks varied, most were purchased for slightly more than $200 apiece. His income was further supplemented by other writings in both the Mystery and SF/Weird Fiction fields. During one period in January 1935, for instance, he cranked out three stories in ten days. One of these, "The Siege of Mr. Martin," was also published by *Clues,* albeit under the pseudonym of "Clyde B. Ashton," to provide the reader some disconnect from the author of "Frost." Nor did Wandrei show any signs of exhaustion during the bulk of Frost's run. He found the work easy. Very few changes were ever asked for in the manuscripts he turned in, and once in the habit of producing most of those stories could be banged out in less than a week. One story, "Nightmare" (later retitled "Giants in the Valley"), was even "written straight through" in a single draft.

In time, however, frustration grew. When early serialization deals fell through, Street & Smith toyed with the idea of doing such a project themselves. It never happened. Nor did the longed-for book deals materialize. Knowing that publishers preferred novels to stories, Tremaine suggested that Wandrei try his hand at an I.V. Frost novel. While Don plotted such a work out, in 1936, the press of other engagements and responsibilities prevented him from doing much more. He was also, by then, turning his eye toward the stage, becoming interested in playwriting, rather than on something exclusively in the pulps.

What killed Frost eventually is unclear, but can probably be explained in a variety of ways. The novelty had worn off for the readers, the author, and publisher alike. The latter was feeling some pressure financially and began to compress its pulp line. Wandrei, for his part, had too many irons in the fire, his eyes still on Broadway. Freed of his commitment to Frost, he could concentrate on playwriting. Solo plays and collaborations alike, including work with his brother Howard and a certain Douglas Wood Gibson who would later have some small success in television. Moreover, H.P. Lovecraft had died in March of that year. Earlier, Wandrei had used his influence with Tremaine to get a Lovecraft story published in *Astounding*. Now, with his friend's passing, he'd teamed up with August Derleth to preserve Lovecraft's legacy. And not just the fiction either . . . Wandrei and Derleth were collecting Lovecraft stories and manuscripts from wherever they could find them. They were contacting HPL correspondents, transcribing letters, assembling a collection and marketing it to publishers, while also trying to clear rights from a literary estate that had become unnecessarily confused. As the details have been covered elsewhere and from many divergent viewpoints, there is no reason to delve into it here. It is, I think, sufficient to say that, between Lovecraft and playwriting, Don simply had no time left to continue with Frost.

To facilitate a meaningful exit, Wandrei agreed to write one final Frost adventure, which would bring the series to a close. At Street & Smith's request, however, there had been some uncertainty built into the ending, a literary trap door of sorts, from which Frost could eventually reemerge should both publisher and author choose to have him return.

And that's where it ended, more or less.

Street & Smith went through a period of upheaval after Donald Wandrei departed their stable. Tremaine left *Clues* and was replaced by Frank E. Blackwell. The upper levels of the corporation were likewise in flux, especially following the death of executive George Campbell Smith. The contraction continued while editorships and editorial policies were changed month by month. In November 1938, Blackwell was replaced by Anthony Rud who, having fond memories of Professor Frost, invited Wandrei back into the fold.

And Wandrei, by then, needed the money. His playwriting had made him no income. Though he was making sales to upscale markets like

Black Mask and *Esquire,* such was not enough to offset the costs of the H. P. Lovecraft transcription project he'd initiated. Nor was his involvement with *The Outsider* yet done. After its rejection by three major publishing houses, Don had already come to the conclusion that, if a collection of Lovecraft's stories were to be issued in hardcover, he and Derleth would have to finance it themselves.

So, at Rud's urging, Wandrei returned to *Clues.* Not wanting to simply resuscitate Frost however, he insisted on a new character, Cyrus North, a captain of industry, not in New York, but in a fictionalized version of his native St. Paul. The money was good. A lot of it went to transcription and more was put aside to provide seed money for what eventually became Arkham House, but the new character was cursed from the start. With Tremaine and Hall no longer involved, and Rud having only partial control of the magazine's focus, Wandrei could never be clear of what they wanted. There were constant rewrites and policy changes. The character never gelled. The first adventure was rejected outright. Further policy changes eventually killed the series entirely, after a mere six adventures. As I've covered the details elsewhere (*Pulp Vault* #14), I won't duplicate them here, save to mention that the final cancellation, after the rejection of a 25,000-word novella Street & Smith had requested, threw Wandrei into a fit of despondency and near-bankruptcy that almost scuttled publication of *The Outsider* as well.

Thankfully the story doesn't end there. In 1989, the specialty publisher Fedogan & Bremer released *Colossus: The Collected Science Fiction of Donald Wandrei,* marking the beginning of a revival of Wandrei's writings. This revivial included a collection the first eight I. V. Frost stories in *Frost* (Fedogan & Bremer, 2000).

The book you're holding now is a labor of love, and I am thankful to Haffner Press for making the complete adventures of I.V. Frost available to new readers after a multi-decade hiatus. I hope you enjoy them as much as I, and that they will lead you to seek out other Wandrei writings if you haven't already. It was another era, another world, but good work really does stand the test of time . . . as those readers unacquainted with Professor Frost will now see . . .

D. H. Olson
Minneapolis, Minnesota
April 23, 2016

FROST

He had a gaunt, hatchet-thin face, excessively high cheek bones, and a nose like the beak of an eagle. His eyes were inscrutable.

A **GIRL TURNED** the corner into State Street. Keeping to the inside, she walked swiftly. Only a trained observer would have seen anxiety in her hurrying stride. To the average passer-by she would merely have given the appearance of a young woman walking briskly.

At this fairly late hour, State Street was almost deserted. Doormen lounged inside the entrances of huge apartment buildings that lined the first half of the block. A couple of cars were parked along the curbing. The last half of the block was occupied by private houses, half a dozen mansions of the sort that require moderate wealth to keep them up, each isolated from the others by iron grille fences or stone walls, each set in its own small grounds.

The girl hurried past a street light. It shone briefly on a velvet wrap clasped at her throat. The slinky lines of a glowing red evening gown flowed below the wrap. Her pumps were flame, dusted with gold. They were costly things that she wore, but lifeless, negligible compared with her lithe beauty of figure and the strikingly individual loveliness of her face.

Her gray-green eyes were a trifle wide. They gave her an expression of cool and determined intelligence. Her cheek bones were a bit high; her cheeks held only a faint curve. The corners of her slightly full mouth turned in. Her complexion was a shade from that warm color of ripe wheat which only the sun can give. Not even the expert hands of the hairdresser could have concealed the willful poise of her head. No cosmetician's art could have created in her face its distinctive but indefinable natural quality; the bloom was still on the grape.

Hurrying past street lights, keeping to shadow whenever possible, the girl continued walking toward the Hudson. The drone of riverside traffic grew louder. When she reached the second mansion, she slipped quickly through an iron grille gate.

A weak, overhead bulb shone on the engraved nameplate: I.V. Frost, Sc.D. The girl hesitated, hovering for a moment in the shadows at the side of the porch. All windows were shuttered. From one on the groundfloor left, emerged bars of light. They permitted no glimpse of the interior when she came up the walk.

She stared back at the street, listened a full minute. Then she stepped forward and rang decisively, insistently. The stone retreat was well built. She could not hear the ring of a bell. Having no means of telling whether the bell was working, she rang again, waited a few seconds, and knocked on the door.

It opened silently. The girl stared at an odd hall, neither long nor wide, but occupied by an amazing number of objects—table, oriental vases, small settee, pictures, umbrella stand, book-and-magazine rack, a couple of singularly carved chairs, and a few miscellaneous items. Most singular of all was the fat and benign Buddha that squatted in a niche at the end of the hall, some twenty feet from her.

But there was not a person in sight. Tense, the girl stood in the doorway. Her face showed alertness, but neither fear nor perplexity.

"Please step inside, Miss Moray," an oddly muffled voice suggested. "There is nothing to fear, and you will be perfectly safe while you are here."

THE GIRL entered. It must have required extraordinary self-possession to conceal her surprise that her name was known. She returned to her purse an envelope that she had half removed.

The voice continued: "If Miss Moray will be so kind as to leave her automatic on the table—"

The visitor's poise was admirable. She betrayed no emotion as she took the weapon from her purse and obeyed instructions. It was an authoritative but not unpleasant voice.

"Thank you," the hollow voice spoke again. "Now, if you would be obliging enough to remove the pearl-handled toy from your right thigh."

The girl lifted her gown, took the tiny automatic from its sheath just above her knee, and laid it beside its companion. Not even a start, or a glint of eyes, indicated any reaction. She looked with apparently naïve interest at the Buddha. To all appearances, she accepted it as a matter of fact that some one she had not yet seen knew in some magical fashion what weapons she had and where she concealed them, as well as who she was.

"Thank you," the muffled voice said. "Will you kindly walk to the end of the hall and enter the first door on your left, where Professor Frost will receive you?"

The girl followed directions. When she was three feet from the door, it sprang open with a *clup* of compressed air and without visible agency. The door, like the front door through which she had first passed, slowly closed behind her.

THE GIRL entered a library complete in sumptuous furnishings, from Astrakhan rug to built-in bookcases lining every wall to the ceiling, from mahogany table to Minoan amphora. The only unoccupied wall space lay between the two front windows, and there an antique print of Sir Francis Bacon overlooked a pedestal on which stood a bust of Socrates. Yet the room was so spacious that it did not seem crowded, in spite of its furnishings, objects, and thousands of books.

A man had been leaning back in a huge overstuffed chair with an air of abstraction, chin resting on interlaced fingers. He unfolded like a gaunt specter when she entered, until he stood fully six feet four. The girl was convinced that he could not possibly have been sitting in that chair for more than thirty seconds, yet he rose with the reluctance of one who had been comfortably meditating for a long while.

He was about as unlovely a specimen as the girl had ever seen. He had a gaunt, hatchet-thin face, excessively high cheek bones, an ascetic mouth, and a nose like the beak of an eagle. His eyes were inscrutable under immense black eyebrows. He towered like a loose-jointed scarecrow, of large bone and little flesh, and his beautiful, almost feminine, hands were a startling contrast to the rest of him and to his nondescript clothes. Corduroy trousers that looked as though they had not been pressed since he bought them—and that might have been a decade ago—blue shirt past its prime, and a leather jacket bearing the scars and stains of many a mishap, clad the specter.

In spite of his appearance, he smiled one of the most engaging smiles the girl had ever seen as he bowed her to a seat; and in spite of his impersonal manner, his air of scientific and emotionless detachment, there lay, deep underneath, the impression of some great human dream. Even the mission that drove her and dominated her thoughts could not prevent her from feeling slightly piqued; there simply was no response to her personal beauty. She might have been an old hag or a lump of inanimate stuff.

"Allow me to introduce myself. I am Professor Frost."

"It doesn't seem necessary to tell you that I am Jean Moray. And I presume you know that I came in answer to your advertisement?"

She took out of her purse an oblong strip torn from the "Help Wanted—Female" columns of a newspaper. The advertisement asked for the services of an:

> Assistant for criminal investigation; young woman of exceptional appearance, personality, courage, health, intelligence, without close ties, for dangerous but exciting work with private criminologist. Reply in detail. High salary to right person. Box Z, 149.

The girl also removed a sealed envelope, addressed to the professor, which she handed him. He laid it aside without opening it, saying:

"Your reply made a very favorable impression which my attorneys inform me was amply confirmed by the appointment they arranged. In fact, you are only the fifth applicant recommended to me out of some five thousand replies."

"Thank you. May I inquire just what the nature of the position is?"

The professor laced his fingers. The lids half drooped over his eyes. The girl's glance strayed toward the windows, and she edged forward in her chair, listening in vain for sounds from outside that could not penetrate within. The window slid part way up as if to answer her wish. Her gaze darted back to the professor. If his hands had moved to some hidden button, they had done so instantly when her attention wandered, for they were again laced under his chin.

Professor Frost spoke slowly and precisely, each word the result of cautious selection: "I am seeking an assistant to further my researches and to help carry on various criminal investigations. In addition to the qualifications listed in my advertisement, the successful applicant should have a scientific background and an unusually analytical mind. Since I hold no official positions, I am acting entirely upon my own initiative. For that reason, the position entails more than ordinary danger and personal risk.

"However, some of my work has started at the request of friends in office who desired aid in solving obscure cases. I have begun other investigations for private individuals, though I prefer as a rule not to handle such matters. Much of my analysis is voluntary, involving problems abandoned by others as hopeless of solution, or peculiarly puzzling affairs cited by the newspapers, in which events I offer my services if desired.

"Laboratory study of material clues, microscopic analysis of data, the trailing and even apprehension of criminals, are only a few phases of the work. I have as many bitter enemies as friends. The danger cannot be minimized."

"I see. Can you mention a specific instance? A case or two that you've worked on? That would give me a more definite idea of what to expect."

THE PROFESSOR drew a special cigarette from a case, offered the girl one from a different pack of common brand, which she declined in favor of her own. He exhaled a cloud of sharply pungent smoke. A peculiarly hard glitter entered his eyes.

"Not long ago, State Senator Kyle was killed, apparently by a hit-and-run driver, on the eve of pressing for passage of important labor legislation. The laws died in committee, with his influence removed. Several large industrial plants in that State are now having violent labor disturbances as a direct result. Unless there is a special session of the legislature, riots of the most serious character are likely to occur. There were circumstances suggesting criminal planning behind the occurrence. This is typical of the lines that my research follows."

The professor's face was grim. The girl sensed in his carefully chosen phrases an ulterior motive, a deeper mystery.

"It sounds as if all these, at least, might be linked to a single source," she suggested, with a rising inflection.

"Possibly. My purpose is not to theorize, but to prove."

"I should think that you would find masculine aid more valuable."

"No. A man could only offer qualities that I already possess. I want a woman who must be alert, intelligent, a keen analyst, one who can circulate in places where a man could not, and who through her beauty and magnetism of personality can quickly obtain information that it might require even the most brilliant of men longer to acquire. No; my assistant must be a woman because she will have the only additional qualifications of value in my work, those springing primarily from the difference between the sexes.

"For instance, she should be of such striking beauty that if we were seated at a table, and some one entered intending to kill me, her appearance would attract admiration for just a brief moment. That fractional second would be all I need. The position, I repeat, is full of constant peril. My assistant would never be free of danger. The salary, one hundred dollars a week and all living expenses, is small compared to the menace. Incidentally," he asked with seeming irrelevance, "how much do you weigh?"

"123 pounds, stripped."

"That's correct."

"Of course it's correct," she exclaimed. "Why, how did you know?"

"When you entered the front door, you stepped on an electrical weighing device which registered your weight as one hundred and twenty-five and one half pounds. Allowing a pound for clothing and a pound and a half for your hardware, the result could be only a few ounces off."

"And what's the good of that?"

The criminal investigator shrugged. "It enables me to find out, for instance, whether truth or vanity predominates when I ask a simple question."

"I see. And the same device is sensitive to the presence of metals, which told you I was armed?"

"Your reasoning faculties bear out the report of my attorneys. Yes; the presence of metals being established, I press a button which sets the Buddha X-ray at work. In thirty seconds, I know the exact position of every weapon my visitor has."

"I gather that your visitors are well prepared to defend themselves?"

"If you wish to put it that way. But I have outlined the nature of the position. Perhaps you would now like to tell me a little more about yourself and why you think you are qualified."

"Since my parents died, I've been on my own for several years. I have no close relatives. A little money was left me, and I finished my college education, receiving my B.A. and M.A. I majored in science—chemistry, physiology, and psychology. Then I decided I didn't want to teach. I wasn't interested in business, but tried various jobs for a while. Up to a month ago, I modeled until the art school term ended. Then when I saw your ad—"

WHILE the girl rattled on, the professor's eyes, as they had ever since she arrived, continued searching her from head to foot, as if she were a human book, or a fly under the microscope. She felt that keen scrutiny rove over each feature, register it indelibly, read its meaning, extract each secret.

He produced another of his pungent cigarettes and exhaled a cloud of smoke. He drawled with a crooked smile: "That is a very interesting little speech, Miss Moray. It seems to say much about you, but actually it is couched in the broadest and most general terms which convey a minimum of information. You did not come here to tell me that pretty fable?"

The girl's face tensed. "Is that a hint for me to go? I presume you would not be interested in employing some one whose word you did not trust."

"True; but truth is a relative matter. A trained observer can extract truth from mere appearances and actions. Then, too, any one's private life is a matter of his own concern, about which he is at liberty to keep silent or tell any evasion he prefers. It does not concern me what your private life has been or your reasons for concealing it.

"I already know that you possess the requirements I wish, are completely trustworthy, and cool in emergency. You are quick-witted and intelligent. The part of your story concerning your educational background and scientific bent is true. You have the major qualifications for the position. Are you able to accept it?"

He studied her intently as she thought over his unusual proposition. "I wouldn't worry about it, if I were you," he remarked. "No one will ever see the scar, and one vaccination mark is all that is necessary to provide the one flaw which will emphasize your otherwise perfect figure."

The girl stared at him, started to ask a question, then looked down. While listening, she had unconsciously been rubbing the spot above her right knee.

She looked up at Professor Frost with a glint of admiration. "That is good observation."

"It is nothing of the sort, though I compliment you on your quick understanding. It is good observation, analysis, and synthesis. Observation tells me that you are in splendid health, possess a most enviable figure, and a very beautiful face. I observe your hair which is the color of a rare rye whisky. I analyze it and discover that it is a natural color. Observation presents only the surface of things. Analysis goes to their heart. Synthesis takes their real significance and relates it to other objects, events, or patterns of existence.

"I observe your formal attire. You will admit that it is distinctly unusual for a young woman to apply for a job in such clothing and at this rather late hour. Furthermore, while costly, even attention-arresting, the color harmony is not quite suitable to your personal characteristics. Analysis, synthesis, induction, and deduction, all convince me that you wear this particular raiment by somebody else's specifications, and that you came not so much to apply for the position as to ask for aid, if you could convince yourself of the advertiser's good faith.

"I can assure you without fear of contradiction that your story was largely fabrication, that you have been in this city less than a month, that you came from Minneapolis, that you have just been through a strange experience, and that you are right now in great fear. May I suggest—"

The girl sprang up. "It is true! I did not come here primarily for the position. I came because I had heard about your success in solving mysteries that baffled other experts, but I had to make sure I was not letting myself in for more trouble of the sort I got from answering the other advertisement. I'll make a bargain with you, Professor Frost. You want my help, and I need yours. Solve my mystery, and I'll go my limit in aiding your work."

"Suppose you tell me about it?"

II.

THE GIRL moved closer to the window, began speaking rapidly. "Perhaps I have delayed too long already. I may not have time to finish. If I suddenly break off and go, don't try to stop me or follow me immediately. The rest will be up to you.

"I *am* in danger, but I don't yet know from whom or why. I arrived here two weeks ago with only enough money to last a week. The first thing I did was buy a paper. As you probably know, there were two identical advertisements. I wrote the same answer to both. I received an answer from both. The first came two days before the answer from your lawyers.

"I had an interview at what purported to be another law firm. It was in a small office on Broadway near Forty-second, and there was only one ferret-looking man there when I called. I got the job. I was paid a week in advance. I was to do nothing but follow a few simple orders. He explained that the first week would be a test of my courage, ability to follow orders, and general merit. He gave me some further instructions and told me not to come back to that office.

"Nevertheless, I did go back the next morning. I had thought it all over and become suspicious. The office was empty. I found it had been rented only a week before. Right then and there, I decided to go through with it and see what it was all about. Besides, I had a queer feeling I was being followed, and I didn't know what might happen if I failed to do what I was told."

The professor lighted another of his peculiar cigarettes without shifting his gaze. From the intensity of the look that enveloped her, she sensed a more than casual interest.

"Following the ferret-faced man's instructions, I went to a jeweler's window near Fifth Avenue and Forty-second Street, at ten o'clock. A neatly dressed man, whom I never saw before or since, stopped to look at the trays and gave me further instructions together with five hundred dollars. I was to purchase some gowns and other things, turn myself into as seductive a siren as I could, go to Mardi's restaurant at three o'clock, take the table reserved for me, and at three thirty—but I'll tell you when I come to that.

"The man disappeared in the morning crowd. By this time I was more mystified than ever and determined to see the thing through. I've always loved excitement, and this promised plenty of thrills. I bought some lovely things and went to the best beauty experts. When I entered Mardi's at the cocktail hour, there wasn't a man in the place who didn't forget about his companion, though there were dozens of wealthy and attractive girls around."

"Yes; I can well imagine it. You would shine even among the stars," Frost agreed in a tone as if he had said: "Albany is the capital of New York."

The girl gave him an exasperated glance. "At three fifteen, a distinguished-looking man with a very florid face and a mole on his left cheek—"

Frost said: "Did he also have a triangle of white hair in his left eyebrow?"

"Yes! Do you know him?"

"Go on."

"He and his companion, a dizzy young thing with a sugar-face, took a table reserved for them next to mine. At three thirty, making sure that no one was looking in my direction, I carried out the fantastic part of my instructions. I lighted a cannon cracker in my lap and tossed it under the table so that it slid under the next table. It exploded like a gunshot. The young thing screamed, the man leaped to his feet with the whitest and most scared face I've ever seen, waiters came rushing up, and the place was in an uproar.

"I rose like several others and called for my check. The head waiter made profuse apologies to me as I left. A good many people looked at me, but I don't think any one connected me with the incident."

The professor leaned forward in his chair. "Very interesting," he murmured. "Go on."

"I'll have to hurry. Ever since, I've been given instructions from time to time, always at a different place and by different people. More than ever, I began to feel—I *knew*—that I was being followed, though not once have I been able to identify any pursuers. I even changed my address. But no matter where I am, I know that some one or some ring of persons is constantly near by. It's an intuitive feeling that I haven't much real basis for proving except the one possible clue of a sound."

"What sort of sound?"

"Just an automobile horn of a peculiar pitch. It's the first of the four notes that French horns have. Sometimes it comes merely as a honk at a pedestrian or a traffic snarl, but other times it sounds in short and long notes and pauses, like a definite pattern. I've heard it many times, but I've never been able to tell what automobile it comes from. Maybe it hasn't anything to do with the mystery, but it's distinct from other horns if I listen hard, and it seems strange that it should always be near, since I took the position.

"After the firecracker farce, I had nothing further to do that day or the next, except to round out my wardrobe. But the next evening I went to a theater, was met in the lobby by a man I never saw before or since, and escorted in. His tickets were in the sixth-row center. He made no effort to talk with me, except to whisper further instructions, and to say that my employer was satisfied with my work thus far. When the curtain rose he excused himself for a minute, but left a package on the seat which he asked me to watch. He did not return."

"OF COURSE," Frost muttered. "Personal escort—to see that you not only went in but took the exact seat specified. Departure—to prevent suspicion from falling on him, and to make sure, in safety from the back of the orchestra, that you carried out everything to the dot."

Jean stared at him. "If I hadn't so much confidence in you, I would almost suspect you of having planned this. Anyway, some late arrivals took seats in front of me. In ten minutes, a wild clatter burst from the package. It was obviously an alarm clock. I leaned over and whispered: 'Everything is set, if you raise the ante.'

"The man in front of me whirled around with wide, scared eyes. He was the same man of the firecracker incident. Then I seized the package and made my way out. The play fumbled along. The whole audience was restless. Two ushers hurried down the aisle toward me. All in all, I don't suppose there's been a madder audience or a more harassed woman on Broadway this season.

"It then seemed clear to me that my strange assignments were concerned with the man I had twice seen, but who he was I hadn't any idea, or what was behind this fantastic rigmarole. And I didn't have any friends here close enough to take into my confidence.

"For the next three days, I had only insignificant things to do. I did try giving my unseen shadowers the slip by dodging into a motion-picture house and leaving by a side exit. For half an hour I felt free, and then—I heard the horn.

"Yesterday, after the three days of trifling around, I had another curious assignment, the most disconcerting of all. Early in the morning, a singular bird was delivered to me. It had beautiful colors of green, gold, purple, and scarlet, looked somewhat like a macaw or parakeet, and possessed a flowing tail of pastel feathers at least a yard long.

"I strolled down Fifth Avenue with this extraordinary creature perched on my shoulder, and you can imagine the sensation we created. Still obeying orders, I walked along until a taxicab drew up at the curb beside me. It honked twice and then once. I climbed in. The taxi moved on slowly. It circled a block and slid into a parking space just off upper Fifth Avenue. After a while, someone came out of the nearest big apartment house and entered a waiting limousine.

"We followed it down Fifth Avenue. Below Thirty-eighth Street, my driver swung out in front of the limousine. It was skillfully done. The two cars locked and banged against the curb. My driver nonchalantly got out and vanished among the passers-by I waited until the limousine door opened and the owner came forth. He was the same man of the firecracker and alarm-clock scenes. I stepped from the cab and said: 'Make it a million, or else—'

"His face turned positively green. A second man came threateningly toward me, but the first man shook his head. The bird on my shoulder cackled harshly. I pushed my way through the gathering crowd. A cab, waiting around the corner for me as promised, took me across town before the nearest policeman arrived. I saw by the evening paper that the wrecked cab had been stolen. I was surprised that only the chauffeur of the limousine was mentioned by name.

"That is the whole story so far, except that I think I succeeded in giving my pursuers the slip twice more—once when I went to your attorneys, and a while ago before I came here. But I feel that the mystery is coming to a head any hour now, and I'm worried. This is the last day of my trial week. I'm in too deep to draw back, but I'd stay, anyway, just to satisfy my curiosity.

"My last instructions were whispered to me this afternoon by another stranger."

"What were you told to do?" Frost asked.

"To-night at midnight," she said slowly, "I am to—"

The girl's voice broke. Through the window had come the sound of an oddly pitched automobile horn.

The girl dashed for the door.

The criminologist rose.

"No! Don't try to follow until I'm clear!" the girl cried. "They're catching up with me again. I've got to get out of here before you're drawn into it directly. I'll try to telephone you soon. But it's a bargain—clear this mystery, and I'll join forces with you. Yes?"

She spoke with breathless haste. From the doorway she gave him a quick look, provocative, challenging, questioning—an expression of diverse moods, her face glowing with a more hectic beauty from the fever of the chase.

"Yes." The professor smiled, and she was gone, snatching her weapons as she fled.

FROST watched her through the window, after adjusting the shutter so that he had a clear view. She melted like a shadow into the other shadows of trees, then into the sidewalk shadows of buildings. She darted to a parked taxi. It immediately sped off, whirled around the nearest corner. A sedan raced in the same direction, sloughed around the same corner.

Ivy Frost strode across the room, passed through a door opposite the windows.

His laboratory gleamed with the instruments of science. One entire wall was shelved with thousands of bottles of chemicals, pure and in compound, of drugs, acids, and alkalis. The tables were strewn with microscopes, slides, retorts, furnaces, Bunsen burners, electrical equipment of every kind, a great variety of sensitive measuring instruments from micrometer calipers to interferometer, complete sets of draftsman's, surgeon's, and carpenter's tools, radio materials, photographic supplies. Long rows of filing cabinets stood against the walls. There was an immense quantity of miscellaneous items that appeared to cover every conceivable category of science.

Frost moved without hesitation to a short-wave television set and turned on the power current. He watched a metal screen into which a room gradually swam and focused.

"F calling JV, F calling JV," he intoned into a microphone.

Within a half minute, a man wearing a lounging robe hurried into the other room and moved to a duplicate set.

"Hello, F!"

"I want the address of the girl who—"

John Vogel, senior partner of Vogel, Vogel, and Brant, attorneys, interrupted with a chuckle. "I thought she would make an impression. Just a second, I have it in my coat." He left, reappeared in a moment. "She gave it as 609 West 75th."

"Thank you. She's moved, but I'll have to start from there. Good night!"

He lifted the receiver from a telephone and dialed the central telegraph office. "I'd like the following message delivered in exactly twenty minutes. Can it be arranged? Good! To Jean Moray, 609 West 75th Street, City."

Frost picked up a telephone directory as soon as he had given his telegram message, hunted another number, and called it. He heard central buzz repeatedly before an answer came.

"May I speak to Mr. Hastings?"

"Mr. Hastings is not in. Whose name shall I give him?"

"Professor Frost. Can you tell me where I can reach him? It is urgent that I communicate with him at once."

"I am sorry, sir, but Mr. Hastings did not say where he would be this evening. However, if you wish to leave a message—"

"Which is a plain lie," the criminologist muttered as he hung up.

He dialed another number. "Jerry? Ivy talking. Glad I found you in and sober—what, you're not sober? Sorry I cast aspersions. I want some information as fast as possible. Can you find out where Sam Hastings is to-night? Yes—the power behind Coin Machines, Inc. It's very important. Leave his home out—I just tried there."

"Absolutely!" the answering voice said. "If nobody on the *Press* staff knows, some of my columnist friends will. It'll take a while. Want me to call you back?"

"No; I'll be on the move. Can you find out by telephoning around? Fine! I'll call you again at fifteen-minute intervals. Also, find out who's in charge at the central station to-night. Calper? You're positive? Thanks! Call you later."

He passed from section to section of his laboratory. Into a small valise he carefully placed his selections. From the gleaming apparatus and stoppered vials of science, he made his choices instantly, without hesitation.

Within five minutes he took the wheel of his car. It purred out of the basement garage. He sped downtown and at Eightieth Street halted to phone Jerry Travis again from a drug-store booth. Travis reported Hastings' movements up to nine o'clock and was still on the trail.

At the West Seventy-fifth Street address, Frost climbed the steps of a grimy brownstone house near the river road. Prolonged ringing brought a hag, reeking of beer, and wrapped in a greasy, torn kimono.

"Is Miss Moray at home?" Frost asked suavely. "I'm sorry to intrude at this late hour, but I've only now arrived from out-of-town."

The harridan stared at him sullenly, suspiciously. "No one here by that name."

"She has moved? Where can I find her?"

"I don't know, mister. Write her a letter." The door banged.

Frost returned to his car and waited. In five minutes, a messenger wheeled, up with his telegram and roused the crone. He argued with her for a moment, then jotted a notation on the envelope he carried. He remounted his bicycle and pedaled downtown, with Frost following. In West Sixty-third, the messenger stopped at another brownstone. He talked to someone, left a delivery notice, and then wheeled back toward his office with the telegram.

The professor made a quick selection from the contents of his valise. Carrying a bundle under one arm, he mounted dilapidated steps that were grooved from the tread of generations. A red-eyed hunchback answered his ring and studied him overtly with glittering pupils when he inquired for Miss Moray.

With a shrug as if it was none of his funeral, the dwarf mumbled: "Third-floor front, No. 31." Then he scuttled back to a dimly lighted rear recess.

Frost climbed the worn stairs. Stillness enveloped the rooming house. Not another person except the hunchback seemed awake. There were no lights shining through transoms or under the bottom of any door that he passed. The silence was uncanny.

At the head of the stairs on the third floor, he paused and listened, but still heard no sound. No. 31 was in the front. The scientist made his preparations with precision and speed that required only seconds. He unrolled the bundle, pocketed a few items, and donned an all-protective garment. He carried no firearms.

Frost strode soundlessly to the door of Room 31 and gently tried the knob. The door was unlocked. He opened it and faded inside.

III.

BY THE WEAK light filtering in through the single grimy window could be seen a typical cheap, furnished room. Frost twisted his head sharply aside. The blackjack raked the left side of his head, and a dark blob closed in on him. He raised his two forefingers and jabbed the blob. An explosive cry jerked from its throat. It doubled over, straightened again, stiffened rigidly as though in the convulsions of epilepsy, and jackknifed against the wall. From a chair tipped backward against the far corner of the room, a second dark shape raised a silenced automatic and fired with cold-blooded aim. They were all direct hits. The first *whammed* against the scientist's chest, one *panged* his forehead; the whole clip was fired and wasted on the bulletproof metallized cloth of his protective suit. The only damage was bruises from the force of impact.

When the shots ended, Frost acted. The second blob grunted in surprise as the strange specter plowed in, unharmed by six direct hits at close range. The second man yanked at another gun, but never used it.

The scientist knocked him clear out of the chair. The would-be killer could take it, if only because he had to.

As he came up, the first hoodlum groaned on the floor. The professor's long arms were as deadly as pile drivers. As calmly, carefully, and methodically as if he was perfecting an experiment, the criminologist broke the second man's nose, laid open his right cheek, stuffed a few teeth down his throat, and sent him to oblivion with a smash that sounded as if it cracked his jawbone.

The first victim was still groggy when Frost returned and plunged a hypodermic needle into his arm. He treated the more badly damaged killer with a similar dose. As the stiff injections of morphine took effect, the breathing of the two men became regular and they passed into a state of deep coma from which they would not emerge for many hours.

They were gangsters, two of Joe Blake's gorillas. It was a rule of Blake's that his men keep away from dope. The rule was rigidly enforced. Death was the penalty.

Frost dragged one of the bodies in front of the door. He pulled down the window curtain and then turned a light on. He hauled a good-sized suitcase from under the bed. Next he went through the room with swift but minute care, packing all the girl's belongings in the suitcase. If he had needed any corroboration of her strange story, it was partly borne out by the amazingly gaudy bird that perched in a tall cage and cocked a sleepy eye at him.

There were no interruptions. Frost removed the protective cloak and hood which he rolled into a bundle. He scrutinized the insulated caps for each forefinger, from which the needles had been broken off when he jabbed the first man. He removed the caps, loosely bunched the wires that led from them, and stuffed them into his pockets beside the powerful, compact batteries to which they were connected.

Frost's face wore the expression of a man satisfied with a job well done. After dragging the body out of the way, he turned out the light and raised the window shade. He carried the suitcase with him when he left.

On the ground floor, he summoned the dwarf. "You have an extra room to rent now. Miss Moray will not be back."

The hunchback squinted evilly

"Also, there are a couple of uninvited callers in Room 31 who need attention." Frost's features hardened. He bluntly ordered the crooked man: "I think you had better move—fast."

The dwarf glared, turned without a reply, and padded up the stairs.

The bundle and the suitcase went into the rear of Frost's car. Three blocks away, he stopped long enough to use a coffeepot phone booth to call Travis.

"Hello!" came the reporter's slightly worried voice. "Everything O.K.? That's good. You're ten minutes late in calling, and I was beginning to wonder if something happened. I got the dope all right, from Win Morro. You know, the human keyhole. He says he got it by calling some of his girl friends at the hot spots. Hastings blew in at the Golden Goblin twenty minutes ago with John T. Dellener, the political boss, and a couple of Eves in tow. I can't guarantee that he's still there, but when Win says something is so, I'd hate to put up money against him. Anything else I can do?"

"That's all, thanks. I'll see that you get some of your favorite Scotch to-morrow."

BACK in his car, Frost drove to the Golden Goblin, a gyp-joint nude-review rendezvous in the blistering Fifties, before twelve thirty. He parked at the nearest space and hurried inside.

The hat-check siren stared at him in disgust as he sauntered along the lushly carpeted and ornate lobby without even having noticed her. Several people glanced his way in surprise. It was a tribute to his impressive carriage that, however startled strangers might be by his disreputable clothes, they never smiled.

A hostess hurried toward him with polite but firm intentions. "I am sorry, sir, but it is one of the rules of the club—your clothing is—"

Frost looked through her. She suddenly stuttered, lost the power of speech, lapsed into silence.

In the main room, an orchestra was evoking low music, wearily feverish. The floor show had gone on. As he entered, a chorus of platinum blondes, flood lights spotting only the upper half of their bodies, undulated through involved patterns.

The head waiter approached, eyeing the gaunt intruder doubtfully.

Frost dismissed him with a gesture. "No table, I'll be here only a few minutes."

He lounged by an enormous rubber plant. After a few seconds he shifted his position and scrutinized the booths beyond the floor show.

Frost smiled a crooked smile as he spotted Jean Moray. She was outstanding even in this haven of beauty. Her mobile, intelligent face expressed something original. She struck a new note. Her rye-whisky hair was a welcome exception to the run of artificial blondes and smoky brunettes. For an instant his gaze lingered on her, as she sat alone, in a small wall booth. She was flirting outrageously with every man in the place.

His scrutiny advanced. Hastings and his three companions occupied the next booth to Jean.

The professor's searching analysis reached across tables to the wall booths diagonally apart from Miss Moray and Hasting's party. A man and a moon-faced doll sat in one of the booths. They seemed no different from other patrons. Only Frost in all that crowd saw the barrel of the gun that crept in the direction of Hastings' booth from apparently folded hands. Even waiters glanced at the review while the orchestra wailed to a saxophonic triumph.

The woman rose, passed in front of the booth, walked away. There was a quiver of recoil from the stranger's gun at almost the same instant that Frost fired from the hip. Neither *sput* of the silenced automatics was loud enough to attract attention, but the killer yelped. A few waiters stared. Holding his shattered hand, he rose, hurried after the girl friend, vanished through a door near his booth.

Dellener wabbled and slumped over his table. The lights went out, stayed out for what seemed ages while Frost plunged across the room. Someone screamed. A weird chatter swept up from blackness, a babbling staccato of inquiries and forced banter.

Frost jerked out a flashlight as he ran, bumped into a table, collided with some one before the beam stabbed forth. Three other beams sprang into existence from other parts of the floor.

The lights flickered on. Jean Moray lay sprawled upon her table, a red streak searing eye to ear across her left temple. Her purse was open. An automatic rested at her finger tips. Frost dived for her, saw instantly that she was only stunned from a minor scalp wound. He whisked around to Hasting's booth. The Eves, wise in their way, had vanished. Hastings, white-faced, was trying to claw his way past Dellener from the inside of the booth. Blood trickled from the unconscious man's head. A deep gash laid open the top of his skull. Frost grabbed a clean napkin, wrapped it over the wound. He had shot barely in time to spoil the killer's aim.

"Out of the way, you!" grated a harsh voice. "I'm taking charge here."

It was a plain-clothes detective. Another was reviving Jean Moray. A third ran up. The Golden Goblin burst into an uproar of babbling guests and scurrying people.

"Certainly, take charge," Frost said, "but this man is injured if not dying. He must be taken to a hospital immediately."

"I'll take care—"

"I'm taking him now. Come along if you wish."

He lifted the unconscious man and carried him out. The detective hesitated, issued crisp orders to the two others, and trotted after Frost.

"How the hell do you get in this?" the detective demanded.

"The name is Frost—I.V. Frost."

"I've heard of you." The detective's attitude stiffened in the wary fashion of the man who bagged a black panther and didn't know what to do about it.

Frost honked a couple cars out of his path and stepped on the accelerator. His car swung from the curb. He sped to the corner and turned left.

The detective opened his mouth.

"Clinic Center Hospital," Frost drawled. "Keep an eye open for traffic police. If we're flagged, flash your badge."

"What the hell!" the detective exploded, but followed instructions.

"Did you trace the telephone call to headquarters?" asked Frost. "By the way, I didn't catch the name."

The detective squinted. "Seeley. Say, what do you know about that call?"

"Nothing. But there's no reason why three extra plain-clothes men should be detailed to the Golden Goblin. Some one must have phoned in that something was going to happen."

"You know too much for a guy who just wandered along in time for the fireworks."

"The fact that some one phoned headquarters doesn't mean it was the only place he called. I'm doing some investigating, too."

THE CAR shot up to the receiving ward of the hospital, a fifteen-story masterpiece of architecture set in its own block of ground, one of the most celebrated and progressive medical units in America, with lawns and landscaped shrubbery on all sides. It occupied a short cliff bordering the river road.

The interne made a rapid examination of Dellener, summoned a night surgeon who treated the wound. He shook his head.

"The patient has an even chance of recovery. Hemorrhage may occur. Concussion of the brain is undoubtedly present. A trepan may be necessary later, but there is nothing more to be done now but keep the patient absolutely quiet."

Frost turned to Seeley. "Want to stay here in case he regains consciousness? Or come with me?"

"I'm sticking."

The scientist asked the surgeon: "Are there any escape-proof rooms here, aside from the psychopathic wards?"

"The best and safest of the private rooms are on the eighth-floor rear. The windows are not barred, but, even so, there is not enough bedding by which any one could conceivably make a sheet rope long enough to reach the ground, and it is impossible to scale the wall. But there is no chance of the patient's recovering consciousness for hours."

"Take Dellener to one of those rooms. If you stay with him, Seeley, keep a guard outside the door. If you leave the room, see that some one else stays inside with Dellener. A double guard must be kept."

Seeley glowered. "You kind of like to give orders, don't you?"

"One attempt has already been made at murder. There may be another because it failed. Whoever is behind this has brains and uses them. If Dellener vanishes from the hospital, I would regret being in your shoes when headquarters heard about it. I can't waste any more time here now. I'll be back later."

As the injured man was wheeled down a spotless corridor, Frost went out to his car. Five minutes later he was well on the way to the central station.

The city's night life had begun to subside fast. Theaters long dark were joined by the dimming lights of restaurants and taverns that closed. Traffic was so diminished that the harried pedestrian could cross streets in safety at almost any point. Even the inevitable cruising taxis became of reasonable infrequency, after one o'clock. The roar of noises, traffic and miscellaneous, passed from a loud confusion to a separate intermittency, as subdued as they ever were in midtown.

Frost parked by police headquarters. It was now nearly an hour after the Golden Goblin mess. A clock chimed one-fifteen as he climbed the steps.

The captain at the night desk was an elderly, slightly florid, rather thick-featured man. Calper had gone up and down in the ranks during long service. He played politics. When his party was in, his fortunes and promotions went up. When a rival administration held power, he generally found himself reduced or transferred to the sticks. He had been on the carpet several times, for investigation or censure. Like many men on the force, he had a general dislike of private investigators and a particular grudge against Frost.

Calper stared over the desk top with bland interest as Frost entered.

"Good evening, Captain Calper."

"What can I do for you?"

"A friend of mine, Miss Jean Moray, has been detained, I believe, in connection with some incidents at the Golden Goblin an hour ago. I would appreciate her release."

"Would you? That's interesting. Any more friends of yours around that I can turn loose for you?"

"It is only by mistake that my friends spend even an hour here."

"I'm afraid that you'll need a better excuse, perfessor. The lady knows plenty about what happened in that joint."

"I presume she's held both as a material witness and under direct suspicion?"

"So you're in the guessing game now?"

Frost leaned over the desk. "Calper, that young lady happens to be my assistant. She was there for the sole purpose of helping me not only prevent what happened, but of catching the criminals on the spot. That the police arrested my assistant while the guilty escaped wouldn't look so well in the papers, would it? And I don't suppose it would help certain reputations."

"If that's so, she should 'a' told us to begin with. And if she does know something, she better put it in the hands of the proper authorities."

To Captain Calper, it seemed as if the figure of the scientist suddenly expanded, achieved a more towering stature and a more implacable power.

Frost's dark eyes burned with the fire of an irresistible will. "Calper, I want that woman. *I want her now.*"

He got her. In that uncompromising ultimatum, backed only by the strength of Frost's personality, Calper read the finish of his career unless he yielded. Without another word, he issued the order for Jean's release.

IV.

THREE MINUTES later, the abrasion on her temple taped, but otherwise looking cool and self-possessed, Jean sat beside Frost in the car.

As it swung north, she asked: "Where to, now?"

"Clinic Center Hospital, where I left Dellener."

"Who is he?"

"Political boss of his party—didn't you know?"

"I'm afraid I'm still pretty much in the dark. After I left you, I followed the instructions that had been given me by my employers and went to the Golden Goblin where I took a booth that they had reserved for me. As I expected, the man I had already been thrown against three times was in the next booth with a party. The time hadn't arrived for the stunt I was to do when the lights suddenly went out. Something hit me on the head.

"The next thing I knew, detectives were rushing me off. They claimed I had shot somebody and the gun was at my finger tips. But they wouldn't tell me anything more. They tried to make me confess that I knew who was shot, and why I did it, whereas it's still as much a mystery as when I came to you. But you know what it's all about, don't you?"

"It was a fairly simple problem," Frost admitted. "If you had lived here for a longer period, I am sure you would have seen the answers yourself."

Jean looked at him curiously. "How did you know I came so recently?"

"If your story had been true, and you had been in town a month ago looking for a position, you would have answered the first advertisement which appeared in the Sunday papers three weeks ago. That was no advertisement of mine, however. For reasons of my own, I inserted a duplicate notice in the following Sunday's papers, when a repetition of the first also was printed. You answered those two, thus indicating that you had begun looking for a job between three and two weeks ago.

"Your accent, even your use of words, was sectional. New England, the South, the Mid-West, the Far West, all have regional peculiarities of language, and within these districts speech may be further localized by its varying degree of colloquiality. Your usage was definitely Mid-Western.

"Furthermore, young women here do not carry new purses with the label of a Minneapolis store. It might have been a gift, but considered with the two facts I mentioned and a half dozen others that I won't bother detailing, it was evident that you had bought a new purse in that city just before you came East less than three weeks ago."

The professor stopped for traffic lights, kept the motor idling.

Jean remarked: "It seems like a miracle that you picked up my trail so quickly, especially since I left without telling you where I would be."

"As a matter of fact, you need not have left so suddenly when you heard the horn. That was a deft bit of psychology on the part of your employer. Impress on the mind of any given individual a certain factor, such as this sound, which is associated with another factor, such as fear of pursuit, and if that individual eludes watch, one merely needs to repeat the factor at random. The victim, by association, believes that he has been caught up with and is startled from cover."

The car leaped on again as the lights changed.

"You could have stopped me"—Jean began, then interrupted herself—"but of course not. If you had, you would have prevented the plot from coming to a climax, but by letting me go, you stood the best chance of catching the people behind it."

"Exactly! And I was confident I knew who they were. It was mainly a matter of identification. Your remarkable story suggested criminal activity in the first place. Legitimate affairs are not conducted by such fantastic means. Your description of the man identified him as Sam Hastings, owner of Coin Machines, Inc., and not generally known as a leading public enemy and one of the most influential racketeers in the country. His company controls ninety per cent of all slot machines, with an estimated 'take' of some ten million dollars monthly.

"The second major clue was your statement of the number of strangers who issued instructions to you. That indicated a large but well-organized group, which could only be Joe Blake's gang, whose twenty-three members, now twenty-one, dominate the city's underworld. The third important point was your phrase, 'Make it a million.' That of course referred to dollars.

"The slot-machine racket cannot thrive without political protection. A law is now in committee before the legislature to outlaw slot machines. That law will fail or pass according to the wish of the State boss, John Dellener, the man who was shot. Add to these the fact that the man who shot Dellener was Sam Orny, a paid killer, and you have the main essentials. Now do you understand?"

Jean wrinkled her brow. "Partly. Hastings was evidently dickering with Dellener, bribing him to use his influence to defeat the slot-machine bill. In return, Dellener would get a million for himself or to build up his party's power."

"A million a month," Frost corrected grimly.

"But I don't see where I fit into the picture. There is no reason why Blake's gang should use me to annoy Hastings. It's plain, though, that my mysterious assignments were meant to draw attention. Dozens of people would remember me in connection with Hastings. It looks as if somebody intended to railroad me and Hastings for the killing of Dellener.

"But why? And if a rival gangster did the shooting, there must have been a double cross somewhere. Why shoot Dellener with Hastings around? Whether he lives or dies, the newspapers are bound to raise so much trouble that the slot-machine law will be passed. And that will be killing the goose that laid the golden egg. It begins to seem as if there is a deeper mystery behind this."

"Come in and we'll have a look at Dellener," Frost said as the car halted at the hospital.

They had scarcely entered when the scientist exclaimed: "Seeley! What are you doing down here?"

"I have to report to headquarters now and then, see? I'm keeping track of developments at the other end."

"Is any one guarding Dellener?"

"Of course somebody's watching him. I know my business. The door's locked, and there's a guard outside."

"How long have you been gone?"

"Say, can the Sherlock Holmes stuff! I haven't been gone more'n a half hour. Dellener won't come to for a long while yet, the doc said. Nobody can get past the guard without permission, and I hope you don't think some bird is going to hop through an eighth-floor window."

"A half hour!" Frost groaned. He tossed the keys of his car to the girl. "Keep the motor idling for a quick start." He raced to the self-service elevator.

Seeley snarled: "Listen, Frost, I don't like your airs, see? The guy can't get out because he's unconscious, and nobody can get in through the door because the guard's there, and nobody can get in through the window because it's eight floors up. Is that clear? Or want me to draw a diagram?"

Frost gave Seeley one short glance. Seeley squirmed and subsided. It was strange how that raking gaze made him feel like an inferior bug on a pin. Frost wore an air of abstraction until the elevator stopped.

WHILE Seeley puffed after him, the lank scientist raced down the hall to the one door in front of which a guard was lounging. "Quick—open the door!"

The guard hauled out a key and inserted it. He swung the door open. His eyes took on a queer, baffled look. Seeley opened his mouth and remained on the verge of speaking. Frost alone swept the room with a glance.

It was empty.

"I knew Dellener would be gone. You should have carried out my directions." It was less a rebuke than a simple statement of fact. Frost turned and sprinted for the elevator.

Seeley found his voice: "Hey, you! Come back here! How'd the guy get out? Where you going?"

"There are at least four means by which he might have left. I'm going where he is now. I gave you all the instructions you needed an hour ago, and you didn't follow them. Now find out for yourself what happened." He slammed the elevator door, punched the starting bell, and dropped while Seeley fumed behind.

He tore through the ground-floor corridor. Jean, with beautiful teamwork, had the car under way and shifted to high before he climbed in. She deftly slid out of the driver's seat, and he took the wheel.

"What's the trouble?" she asked.

"Everything! Because an obstinate detective wouldn't remember the alphabet, Dellener is gone, and we've got to start all over." He sketched the situation rapidly.

"It sounds impossible, but I suppose the guard might have been bribed or doped," she speculated.

"That's one possibility."

"A helicopter plane could have landed on the roof, and some one slid down a rope to the eighth floor."

"Number two."

"And a human fly with suction cups like the man who walks upside down at the circus might have scaled the side of the building."

"Good alternative number three," Frost approved. "You have at least three hundred per cent more brains than that unimaginative ass behind, which I'll admit isn't much of a compliment."

"What's the fourth? I can't think of any other reasonable explanation."

"The kidnaping was maneuvered in a highly ingenious manner. One man with a coil of strong, light rope carried a balloon, or more likely a duralumin shell filled with gas under high pressure, the lifting power of which equaled his weight. Dellener's room was in the rear of the hospital facing the Hudson. The kidnaper, unnoticed in the dark night and at this late hour, stood under Dellener's window and leaped straight up.

"Guiding himself by pressing his hands down on the wall, using suction tips on his fingers, he simply drifted up to the eighth floor, lowered Dellener to his confederates, then stepped out of the window and floated to the ground. It could be done easily in five minutes,"

The girl objected. "It sounds plausible enough—except for the fact that the balloon had to be made, prepared, and filled, even before it was taken to the hospital. The feat could not possibly have been accomplished in the short time since you left Dellener here."

"The balloon was ready. The mind that engineered this coup was not trusting anything to chance. He had foreseen and prepared for everything."

"No mere gangsters could be as clever as that and so well equipped with scientific supplies—"

Frost interrupted: "Can't discuss it any more now. I'll be gone three or four minutes. That gown you're wearing would be a fatal hindrance. You'll have time to change before I return."

"Change? To what? Where?"

"In the car. I forgot to tell you I took everything out of your room. Your things are in the suitcase on the floor behind us. Your life would be worthless if you ever returned to the Sixty-third Street address. I own both the houses adjoining my State Street address. They are rather crowded with material of all sorts, but you are welcome to the use of either one."

The car shrilled to a stop in front of Frost's laboratory. He hurried inside without waiting for a reply.

The girl moved as if she was trying to rival the speed of light. She was on pins and needles for fear that Frost might be back before she had changed. She sensed that feminine appeal was wasted on him. Though men succumbed to her, she knew that the professor considered her only as an added impersonal quantity to be fitted into his plans.

She flung open the suitcase, wriggled from the gown, slipped into a tweed suit, and changed to sport shoes. The transformation was completed just as Frost came running out with a load of apparatus which he set carefully on the rear seat.

Gathering speed, the car streaked north toward the outskirts of the city.

"Where are we going now?" Jean asked.

"Why don't you try telling me?"

"Because I still don't see where I fit—" she began, but her voice trailed off. Sudden enlightenment brought a startled expression to her face.

FROST, watching the girl from the corner of his eye, nodded agreement. "Now you understand it. For the time being, call X the agency behind all this. X has larger plans in view, but works through Blake's gang to have them kidnap Hastings, fasten suspicion on you, and leave you to face the music. Then X hires a killer to accomplish one of the real aims—the murder of Dellener, leaving both Hastings and you to answer in court.

"You can imagine what would happen if you told your story in court. Your beauty attracts attention, even without such bizarre elements as that tropical bird. Dozens of people would remember your behavior at Mardi's, the theater, and in the cab collision. It would be as sensational front-page stuff for days as the press has ever had.

"Murder, the mysterious woman, fantastic explanations, crime and politics involved, suspicion of mental derangement—at least I can admire the imaginative audacity of that plot. And while the papers issued reams of this spectacular stuff, X could put across crooked schemes that would slide unnoticed by the public while it devoured the murder mystery of the century. Unfortunately, I spoiled the schedule."

"Then X must have been in the Golden Goblin at the time of the shooting!" Jean took up the thread excitedly "By now he must know that you are in the picture. When he saw his plans miscarry, he had you trailed to the hospital. But there doesn't seem to be any reason for kidnaping Dellener, except for the sole purpose of drawing you on so that X and Blake's gang have a chance to remove us once and for all, using Dellener as bait. If they caught us, they could again fasten suspicion on me, and they would be free of a dangerous enemy by killing you."

"It is disconcerting to have one's sudden departure from this existence discussed in so casual a fashion, but for a young woman you have a very good head. The most dangerous part of our work lies immediately ahead.

"In the course of a lifetime devoted to criminal investigation, I have accumulated a vast mass of information and data, much of which even the police do not possess. I doubt whether they know that the house on Tucker Lane where we are headed is the clearing point for all Blake's activities. Dellener has unquestionably been taken there.

"It is strategically situated off the main highway, and a mile from the nearest habitation. It stands in a clearing so that a surprise raid is impossible. It can be surrounded, but it has three long underground tunnels leading into the adjacent woods, so that, if ever raided, the gang could still escape in safety."

The everlasting lights that streamed toward them as they sped through the outskirts of the city became more infrequent. A wall of wind seemed to be pressing against the car with a roar. They shot beyond the city limits, racing northward along a deserted highway. Only their headlights pierced the darkness.

"Ah! The first attack—and just about where I thought it would be!" Frost breathed.

He shot past a crossroad. The lights of another car suddenly blazed out. A long, powerful limousine swung after them. Frost stepped on the accelerator. His car leaped faster, but the pursuers roared faster still. Two radiating series of cracks spread across the rear window of Frost's car. The *pang* of metal came repeatedly. Fifty—fifty-five—sixty—sixty-five—seventy—

"The tires!" Jean cried.

"Built-in and protected. This car is armored, and the glass is bulletproof. Let them shoot all they wish—it's the last time they ever will shoot."

"They're still catching up! Can't you go faster?"

"Certainly! I could leave them out of sight in five minutes, but I want them to catch up. The best way to meet a threat is not to run away from it but to eliminate it altogether. Less than a mile ahead, the road is elevated over a cross-highway. If you're not used to sudden, violent death, you'd better not watch."

The girl watched.

Frost's car zipped down the middle of the road. The pursuing car raced nearer, nearer, swung clear over to the left side of the road, edged on foot by foot as the scientist let them catch up. The wind droned past as in a gale. The girl looked into the death car, saw three murderous faces in the rear seat, another in front beside the driver, and all four men armed with submachine guns.

A blast raked the whole side of Frost's car. The flaming gun was followed by a spitting clatter that raised a dozen round spots with radiating cracks on the windows. The bridge loomed ahead. The limousine edged closer to Frost's car, forcing him farther to the right.

Then his hand flicked to the dashboard, punched a button. At the same time he swerved his car sharply to the right, and for a moment it rocked wildly along the edge of the road. To Jean, his face in profile seemed as stern as destiny itself.

The two right tires of the limousine exploded. Its front plowed toward Frost's car, fell a foot short. Its rear sloughed away. It careened, rolled sidewise over and over, slanting left across the road. It mounted the slope at a tangent and piled into the concrete retaining wall. It stood on its nose for a sickening second, and a dark, limp figure hurtled through its smashed top and sailed down like a grotesque bird. Then the limousine toppled to the lower roadbed, while Frost's car sped across the bridge.

Jean, white-face and wordless, wrenched her eyes away, stared at the road ahead as they raced on.

Frost snapped: "Don't waste any sympathy on them. That was a service to society. Did you notice the swarthy-faced man sitting beside the driver? He was Spike Leone, one of three members of Blake's gang who specialized in kidnaping. The others in the car were more of Blake's gang—strong-arm men, killers."

"What did you do?"

"Perhaps you noticed that the front bumper is tubular? I merely released one of two springs. It ejected a couple of quarts of tacks, nails, broken glass, and scrap iron from the left side of the bumper. Momentum did the rest."

V.

TEN MILES north of the city, Frost cut his speed. He halted just before a curve, and told the girl to await his return. He vanished noiselessly into the darkness, came back ten minutes later. A pleased expression hovered on his face.

"The second waiting committee sleeps," he remarked, as he drove around the bend and approached a semiprivate side road that wound through the woods. He left the arterial highway and followed it. "A lookout was posted at the juncture. He made the mistake of smoking a cigarette." Frost commented, as if that explained everything.

The headlights dimmed and, progressing at scarcely more than a walking pace, he drove at last off the rough road into a thicket.

He lifted a pile of apparatus from the rear seat. "I'll need your help. Move as quietly as you can," he cautioned and led the way into the forest.

She followed silently in his path.

"Where did you learn the woodsman's art?" he whispered.

The girl's answer, almost voiceless, came with a hint of laughter: "One doesn't spend summers on canoe and camping trips through the Ten Thousand Lakes district without learning a few things."

Frost halted. Ahead of them, in the midst of a clearing two hundred yards across, loomed a house, dark save for one window on the ground floor which was open to a brightly lighted room.

Frost climbed a tree and perched on a limb. "Hand me the things," he whispered and leaned down.

The girl passed up to him the camera, plates, and telescopic lens.

While he busied himself for several minutes, Jean studied the house. She could make out the head and shoulders of a seated man. He looked powerful, ruthless. He had a crooked nose and a frog's face and his hair was whitish. A shadow might have been thrown by a second man, or an article of furniture. She could hear no voices, and the quiet of night remained unbroken except for the faint, mechanical sounds made by Frost. They were inaudible more than a dozen feet away.

The professor at last lowered his materials to her and cautiously descended.

While again transferring the things to him, she whispered: "Did you see Dellener?"

"He is lying on a couch, still unconscious. Beside him is Stocky Mason, chief lieutenant and killer of Blake's gang."

"Who is the third man? Or is the shadow only—"

"Quiet!" the professor insisted impatiently. "Stay here until I return. But if you see any one leave the house, come back to the car and let me know. Have you a gun? Then take this. I shall be gone for twenty-five minutes."

Carrying his equipment, Frost melted into the blackness of the woods. The minutes dragged on, doubly long now that she kept vigil. The girl centered her gaze on the lighted window. Mason hardly moved. He sat half facing the window. She wondered why he did not shift his position or raise his hands into view even once. He seemed to be waiting, so far as she could tell.

Keyed-up and alert though she was from the tension of the night, and from her feeling that the strange events in which she had become enmeshed through answering advertisements were coming to a head, she wondered if there might not be more at stake than the criminologist had yet explained to her. She felt privileged to have become his assistant in games where death was always a part—until a flash of insight destroyed her pleasure.

The first advertisement had been inserted by some one who deliberately sought to make her a victim of circumstantial evidence in a crime of far-reaching results. But Frost had inserted a duplicate advertisement a week later. Why? Because inevitably one or more applicants who at least had an interview with the agent of the first advertiser would also come to Frost.

Yet she could not be sure. Had Frost duplicated the first advertisement primarily because he recognized the germ of a deep plot? Had he actually wanted an assistant and simply used the opportunity to serve both purposes?

And who was the X, the unknown quantity, that Frost had postulated? Was he hunting bigger game than gangsters, or had he merely used the symbol to designate some grafting politician who protected Blake's gang, or even to designate Joe Blake?

Frost was gone a long time, fifteen minutes, a half hour—Jean could not tell. Her eyes began to ache from the strain of watching. She wondered what Frost was up to. She consoled herself by thinking that, whatever the motivation, Frost had definitely offered and she had just as definitely accepted the position. But then, positions may only last a week, she thought wryly.

No one emerged from the house, and no unusual sound broke the silence.

She tensed and almost ran when the professor suddenly stood beside her like a bleak specter from the darkness. Then she felt a sense of absolute security, so strong was the force of his personality.

The scientist handed her some things and whispered his last instructions: "The trap is set for us, all right, and we are going to spring it. Slip into this bulletproof cloak and hood. They will protect you against ordinary pistol fire when we rush the house. Keep this shield in one hand. The suit is not proof to submachine gun or rifle bullets, but the armor-plate is.

"Drop this automatic in the outside pocket of the cloak and keep the other gun in hand. You'll need both. Above all, shoot at any lights that appear outside of the house. Now put the gas mask on and keep it on. Are the instructions clear? We won't be able to talk after the masks are in place."

The girl nodded. They made the transformation in silence. The atmosphere became electric. She felt the thrill of imminent and all-powerful danger. Yet her nerves remained steady, and she liked the way in which she had been accepted as a working partner.

Frost made no idle chivalrous gesture, did not try to persuade her to stay behind or to back out. She liked, too, his positive methods; his bold counterstrikes, the scope of his analytical imagination that enabled him to make definite and sure preparations for any eventuality.

ONE ON EACH side of the lighted window, they broke from the woods and stole toward the house. There came an almost inaudible click, a sudden faint hissing, when they were still eighty yards from their goal. At fifty, the grounds sprang into blinding radiance from flood lights on the roof. A rifle cracked above. Frost staggered.

The girl calmly aimed at the spot of the flash on the roof and fired.

A scream pierced the night. The figure of a man spun from the roof and toppled, twisting, to earth. The girl flung herself face-down, held the protective shield in front of her. The light in the window vanished as Mason's hands came up with a submachine gun. Flame spurted to the accompaniment of a staccato bark. Bullets clipped the ground, whined overhead, *panged* and flattened against the shield. Her hand stung from the vibration.

Frost picked himself up, warily advanced, running low behind his shield. The more infrequent but deadlier bark of a rifle again sounded from the roof. Through a slit in the shield, the girl emptied one gun and two of the four flood lights shattered into darkness. A startled rabbit bounded across the grass. Suddenly it wabbled and fell inert. Jean thought it had been hit, but there was no trace of injury. Then she remembered the hissing noise, and Frost's insistence on the gas mask.

The girl raked the remaining flood lights with her second weapon, Crash of glass and *zing* of metal. The grounds plunged into blackness. The roof sniper fired again, and Jean jerked as a slug tore off a heel.

From the darkened window, the submachine gun poured its livid spurts; the air whistled and the shield quivered. Jean sensed rather than saw the professor run toward the house. His arm swept back, curved forward, three times, almost as fast as the eye could follow. The gas bombs hurtled through the window and broke with dull plops. Some one cried out, whether in warning or fear or pain was impossible to tell. The firing abruptly ceased. Jean reloaded both automatics and raced after the professor.

His long, loose-jointed form swung easily through the window as she ran up. He produced a flashlight from his pocket and played it around the room. Mason lay sprawled on the floor. A faint, thudding noise, as of a dead weight being dragged, came from far away. Dellener had been abandoned. Frost stooped, lifted the unconscious man, and returned to the window. He lowered Dellener to Jean who sturdily supported him while the professor dropped down to her side. He cast one quick glance at the huddled figure of the man who had toppled from the roof.

Dellener's breathing was so faint as to be almost indetectable. Frost carried the body again and stumbled off in an obvious but unexplained hurry. Jean took the cue and ran beside him. They were scarcely forty yards from the house when a terrific explosion blasted the night. Frost immediately dropped to the ground, but the girl was blown from her feet.

A wall of wind roared from where the house had stood. Plaster, bricks, debris began to rain everywhere. Frost staggered to his feet and carried Dellener to the protection of the woods. Jean, stunned, slowly regained her senses and followed.

The sight of a stain spreading down the professor's shoulder brought her sharply back to reality. She tore off her mask. She swayed dizzily, then recovered. The scientist removed his own mask.

The girl cried: "You're hurt!"

"Just a flesh wound, painful but not serious. The bullet passed through, and I have already staunched the flow. Miss Moray, hereafter, in the presence of anaesthetic gases—"

"Please, Professor Frost, credit me with enough intelligence to know that an explosion as strong as that one must have blown the gases away. Are we safe now?"

"Not entirely. Keep your automatic ready while I carry Dellener to the car."

"Then you don't think the blast killed them all?"

"Rather, it was intended to destroy us. Mason, who was probably gassed by the bombs I tossed in, must have died, as well as the second sniper on the roof. It's just as well. The law has been saved from the necessity of prosecuting Mason and the first sniper—the two other kidnapers. But the mind that planned to-night's work may have got away. When we entered, did you hear the sound of some one's dragging a body? He had time to reach the underground passageways, and thought we would search the house or delay long enough to be blown up with Dellener."

"How were they warned so quickly? I thought we were very quiet when we started across."

"Do you remember hearing a faint click?" Frost asked, as they approached the road. "We crossed the beam of a photo-electric eye and thus announced ourselves by breaking the circuit."

"That's strange. I didn't see any beam of light."

"There are several kinds of photo-electric cells, including one that works only by infra-red rays which are invisible to the eye. If we have time, I'll make a survey of the grounds, but I really see no need for it. That is the only automatic way by which our advance in the darkness could have been recorded. The cell-operated relay was undoubtedly connected with the buried gas containers.

"The mistake lay in thinking that we might escape the death car, the lookout, and even the gas, but not the shooting. They overlooked the possibility that I might go them one better by not only coming prepared for defense but also by bringing my own gas bombs."

"I should think they would have worn masks, if only because their own gas might drift back into the house."

"The wind drift, what little there is, is away from the house. Even so, they counted on shooting us in mere seconds and then closing the one open window until the gases had dissipated. The plan was thorough—but not thorough enough."

FROST strode from the woods and went toward his car. The gray dusk of dawn was just beginning to lighten the air. Frost stopped abruptly and laid Dellener on the ground.

"Is something wrong?" Jean asked anxiously.

"Just one of the precautions I took when I left you at the clearing."

He searched along the roadside until he found the wire he had left connected with the ignition of his car and pulled it. It was still fastened. He unscrewed the bulb of his flashlight and scraped the wire across the exposed battery. It sparked.

Forty feet away, his automobile leaped into the air in a cascade of flame and exploding debris.

Frost's eyes were grim. "Some one has been active while we were gone. Now—"

The motor of a car purred to life farther down the road. Frost raced to one of the two hiding places where he had concealed the plates of the photographs he took and returned with three in hand.

A car gathering speed swung around a curve fifty yards off. The glare of headlights fell on them. Low, powerful, and armored, the car swept ahead and glided to rest a dozen feet away, its motor idling with a deep-throated purr.

"Professor Frost and Miss Moray, I believe? Be so good as to drop your weapons." The soft, triumphant voice slurred from the impenetrable blackness in the car.

"The pleasure is mutual; one encounters you so seldom."

Frost's sardonic answer had the hardness of metal. He and Jean dropped their guns. The girl felt as if she were in a nightmare that went on and on, but, even now, her nerves did not crack, though she faced death. She had confidence that the dominant figure in the nightmare was still the scientist, weird in his protective garments.

The bodiless voice continued: "Your automobile appears to have been wrecked. That is a pity. It was such an ingenious little laboratory in itself."

"And a greater pity that we were not in it when the unfortunate accident occurred?"

"Not necessarily, for there might be an unexpected but altogether satisfactory pleasure in silencing your efficient, but annoying, partnership, now and for ever."

To the girl, the personal antagonism underneath this polite interchange was like a lighted fuse, crackling swiftly to the final explosion that would end the nightmare.

"Wish-fulfillments do not often occur in life," Frost replied suavely.

"But frequently by death."

"Before that sad event takes place, perhaps you would be interested in viewing some most unusual photographic plates I have here."

Silence from the car for only a moment. Then a single shot came from the interior of it. The three plates burst into fragments, and the bullet flattened against Frost's cloak.

The voice murmured with mock regret: "What a pity! I am sure that the plates would have been most entertaining."

Jean, staring at the sinister car, felt that a sardonic smile must have crossed the professor's face when he drawled:

"Fortunately, those were the spoiled plates, though the figure of Dellener was clear enough. The three others, the perfect three, the most compromising three, clearly showing Dellener, Mason, and a third person, will doubtless be of remarkable interest to the police and the press."

"They would be, indeed—if they reached such hands. But, of course, it is difficult to extract information from a corpse. And those who do not know what or where to hunt, do not hunt."

Frost's voice took on a slur of satisfaction, as if he and he only controlled the situation: "Surely, if you were thoughtful enough to plant a bomb in the ignition system of my car, you were observant enough to notice the built-in developing outfit, and the wireless transmission set under the rear seat? Nor should it be necessary to remind you of the high-tension wires a hundred feet from here which furnish ample power for sending.

"It was close to an hour ago that I wirelessed the location of this place and of those valuable plates. I should say that fifteen minutes at most would suffice for the arrival of certain persons who would think nothing of spreading those pictures on the front page of the nation's press. The least of results, of course, would be the utter ruin of one hitherto brilliant career."

"Your imagination is far-sighted," the voice from the car answered, "but in fifteen minutes, one may investigate a considerable area."

"True! The problem is quite simple. You may kill Miss Moray and me, then hunt for the plates. If you do not find them, and I can assure you that you will not, you may be trapped on the scene, which would be most unfortunate, or if you departed, your own legal execution would be only a matter of limited time as a consequence of the incriminating plates.

"Much as I regret doing so, I am afraid that I must give you an opportunity to escape," Frost remarked with cool and ironic effrontery. "Since it is undeniable that you could destroy us now, I shall, before my friends arrive, be so careless as to smash the plates. You will be considerate enough to continue on your way. The mutual profit of the action should be immediately evident to an intelligent mind. I might add that instant action is desirable. Fifteen minutes was my maximum estimate, not the minimum."

The voice from the car spoke for the last time: "I have always held a high opinion of your extreme resourcefulness, Professor Frost, and of your gifted mind. I trust, indeed, I anticipate meeting you again. It is both a liability and an asset that you have the one weakness of always fulfilling your promises."

THE MOTOR roared. For an instant, Jean had an impression that she had reached the permanent end of the nightmare, that the drone of the engine would drown the spitting racket of a submachine gun. The car swept past and disappeared around a bend. Its deep purr suddenly died down. There was silence for a minute, then a burst of shots. The motor faded away.

"What did that mean?" Jean demanded.

Frost shrugged. "The lookout will never awaken, now. Those who sleep on guard duty, no matter what the cause, have no place in Blake's gang."

"It was not Blake who spoke from the car?"

"It was the voice of the mind behind to-night's work, a mind that conceived a perfect plot," Frost replied. "Whatever happened at any point, he could still turn the developments to his purposes. Even now, though this case is closed."

"How can he profit now? We have Dellener. The kidnapers are dead. You have made it impossible for them to make me the victim of circumstantial evidence as they planned."

"Yes; but to-day's papers will carry headlines on the attempted murder, the kidnaping, the rescue, and the persons involved. Under the glare of publicity, public opinion will force the passage of the anti-slot-machine law."

"But that means that an immensely profitable source of revenue will be cut off from crooks and racketeers. Grafting politicians will lose some of their easiest money"

"Precisely! They won't surrender fat profits as readily as that. With bootlegging gone, and the enormous slot-machine income erased, only one result can occur: a great increase in burglaries, bank robberies, kidnapings, business racketeering, hijacking, blackmail, and other criminal activities. But this is no time for a post-mortem. Let's be off."

"Aren't you going to wait till your friends arrive?"

A mirthless smile twisted the professor's lean features. "I am afraid it would be a waste of time. I neglected to inform our recent visitors that when I used the wireless some time ago, I was unable to obtain any answer. But let us account for the other plates."

Jean's hair, tousled and wind-blown, framed a face all the lovelier for its glint of admiration at the successful bluff, as she accompanied Frost to the second cache, where he had left the remaining plates under leaves near a great boulder.

A piece of twisted metal from the wrecked car lay over the hiding place. The plates had been shattered into bits.

Chuckling silently, the scientist lifted Dellener. The girl walked beside him as he strode slowly toward the lightening east and the main highway to hail a car.

GREEN MAN —CREEPING

The bullet plowed true into the thing's forehead.
No blood oozed. The thing crept on.

AS HIS ALTOGETHER too good-looking assistant entered, Professor I.V. Frost continued to stare indifferently at a point somewhere beyond the ceiling.

"Here is the mail—if I'm not disturbing you." Jean Moray hoped she was, but knew perfectly well that hopes were futile so far as the rangy, beak-nosed criminologist was concerned.

He did not bother to turn around. "Is there anything of consequence in it?"

"A Mr. Blane, of various corporations, offers a retaining fee of five thousand dollars. His idea seems to be that substantial proof, to be acquired by you, will be needed of his wife's indiscretions for divorce proceedings."

"Not interested. I do not handle such cases."

"The Women's City Club wants you to address them on the fifth. The topic suggested is 'The Solution of Crime.' "

Frost massaged the tip of his nose. "Tell those good ladies that unfortunately I shall be in Peoria on the fifth. And, if necessary, I *will* be in Peoria."

Jean glanced at another letter. "A kid at the General Hospital says he heard about your work in the Golden Goblin affair, and when he gets out he wants to see you so that he can tell you he thinks you're a swell sleuth."

Frost shifted his position. "Disillusion him."

"Here's a terse message. Somebody who signs himself 'Ishmael' writes that you have interfered with the destined order of things and are therefore marked for death. Upon him has fallen the honor of being the agent."

"Let me see it."

The girl handed him the note. He tossed it back after studying it for a few seconds.

"Well?" she suggested.

"Fairly interesting, but not important. It bears out a belief of mine that deductive logic is almost worthless by itself."

"Why?"

"The threat is written on cheap, soiled, ruled paper, with a scratchy pen. The last part is in pencil. Various words are misspelled. Deduction would indicate that the letter was written by a poor, illiterate man who was munching a sandwich held in his left hand, and who had biblical delusions. But the matter is not so simple as that. A highly intelligent man could have written the letter. He might have gone to great pains to obtain just such a piece of cheap, dirty paper. The misspellings could have been the result of deliberation rather than ignorance. However, there is no need to waste further time on a trifling note."

He unfolded from the chair, slouched to a window. Even when half stooping, Frost seemed taller than the average man. He hooked a heel on the radiator cover, rested an elbow on his knee, and bent over, cupping his hand under his chin while he stared moodily outside. Lines of boredom creased his lean features. His black eyes looked lusterless.

"Little things, odds and ends that any competent police force or detective agency could manage," he fretted. "Why do people bother me with these run-of-the-mill affairs? There surely must be strange, terrible, and almost incredible crimes taking place in the world every day. A city of this size must be rotten with them.

"But where are they? Nothing unusual has come to my attention in a fortnight. Either the perplexing riddles are not occurring, which is contrary to human nature and to all probabilities for a city as large as this, or they are taking place but not coming to light, which also stretches the laws of probability.

"If I am exposed to these dull episodes much longer, I may be compelled to invent or arrange bizarre events. There might be some stimulus in watching others attack a knotty problem."

"I hope you don't," Jean returned. "If you did start something, nobody would ever find the answer. So what fun would there be in that?"

FROST continued to stare moodily out of the window. A sport roadster turned the nearest corner, rolled slowly along State Street, and came to rest in front of No. 13. A hectic young woman in her middle twenties stepped out. Frost's glance raced over her. His boredom dropped away like magic. A glitter entered his eyes. His sagging frame tautened, and animation returned to his face. He whirled around.

"Stuff those letters out of sight. Empty the ash trays and powder your nose in ten seconds flat," he ordered crisply.

As Jean flitted to obey, she complained: "It might help if you'd tell me what part of the house is on fire. Maybe the world was made in a day, but you can't expect me to polish it off in a second even if the enemy is coming."

"Miss Mae Ellen Hollister is almost here. She has just come through a remarkable experience. It was so terrifying that she decided not to ask police aid for fear of disbelief. Her nerves have gone completely to pieces. She is not only distressed. She is in such a state of hysteria that she may collapse with a nervous breakdown. I want you to admit her. And, by all means, stay at her side and use every last gram of feminine understanding you have while she is here, or at least until she has had time to tell her story."

Mingled expressions held a field day on Jean's face. When she did manage to straighten her thoughts, the bell rang sharply before she could speak.

As she left, with a last glance at her compact and a pat for her already perfectly arranged hair, Frost plucked a cigarette from an ivory case. It was one of unusual length and emitted smoke of a peculiar and stimulating aroma. While he inhaled, his frame took on a deceptive repose, but his eyes glittered more brightly under the bushy black brows, and his features lost their pallor.

Jean introduced Mae Ellen Hollister. The visitor, fighting for control, dropped limply into the nearest chair. Her face was bloodless. Her eyes hardly seemed to see the criminologist. She was obviously near the end of her resources. She acted like a person in a dream or suffering from shock, with mechanical motions, blazed pupils, countenance alternately quivering and then set in a mask of stone. She was attractive in the way of her kind—expensive clothes, slim figure, a wise, thin curve to her mouth, sophisticated hazel eyes, the discontent of having so much that there is nothing left to want.

Frost took one look at her and disappeared into his laboratory.

The visitor sat trembling, unable to speak, exerting the full strength of her will to keep from going over the edge. Frost emerged with a glass of pinkish fluid that he handed her. She gulped it down. In five minutes, an indefinable change took place. The shock and the terror remained, but her manner became calmer, more detached. She seemed just a trifle drowsy.

"It was a terrifying experience, wasn't it?" Frost meditated coolly. "But the explanation is so simple that you will wonder how you were ever frightened so badly."

"Do you think so, really?" The girl looked up with anxious hope.

"Of course! The strangest things in life are often easiest to explain. I remember a time years ago when my car broke down on a lonely road late at night. I started walking, and when I came to a cemetery I knew that a town would be not much farther on, but I was tired and leaned on the fence for a rest.

"While I was looking at the tombstones, a white figure suddenly rose, a misshapen, ghostly thing that seemed to issue straight from the ground. If I had been frightened and ran away, I would have sworn to this day that I saw a ghost at least eight feet tall rise out of the ground. But I went over to investigate and discovered that some tramp had wrapped himself in an old sheet and gone to sleep. He became cramped and stood up to stretch about the time I happened along. Your experience will prove to have just as natural an explanation, once all the facts are known."

"I hardly know what to say or where to begin," Mae Ellen Hollister replied slowly.

She fumbled with a small package and stared at it with the fascination of horror before nervously sliding it onto a table. Her eyes continually strayed to it while she talked.

"I've lived a pretty fast life," she went on at last. "I've never thought much about anything except what my crowd went in for—parties, sports, clothes, and the rest of it. A pretty pleasant and carefree sort of life with plenty of everything. Now, I don't know what to believe. Half the time I think I'm going mad; the rest of the time I feel that some awful force actually exists in a form ever so much more worse than just ghosts. If it was only something supernatural, I could pretend it was a dream. But it's the hideous reality of this that sent me to pieces."

"Suppose you start at the beginning and tell me what happened," Frost urged.

"It began shortly after my father died, four years ago. He was very wealthy, and when the stroke carried him away, he left most of his property to my mother. We were away cruising in the Caribbean at the time, and the interment had taken place before we returned or even had word of it. Separate trust funds were established for my sister, my brother, and myself. In addition, there was a big annual income in royalties from some mining and manufacturing patents that my father owned.

"After his death, we continued living in the town house, except Paul, my brother, who married an adventuress and set up a place of his own more than a year later. Paul of course dropped in to see us from time to time."

The visitor took a deep breath. Her voice trembled.

"My father died on April 9, 1930. Nearly a year later, on April 6th, before Paul left, I was awakened long after midnight by a shriek from my sister's bedroom. I won't call it a shriek. It was a continuous sound, appalling. Of course I jumped out of bed. I could hear the servants already pattering down from upstairs. I heard the door to my mother's room open. How I heard is a mystery to me because that cry never stopped.

"I was the first to reach Ann's room. The door was locked. She never locked it for any reason at any time that I know of. When the servants came up, they broke the door in. The lights were on. The window was wide open. Ann was out of her head, staring at the open window and still screaming, but in a raw sort of voice now.

"She kept on screaming. We called our physician, had her taken to a sanitarium. She never recovered, never talked. She died two weeks later. Her voice was only a dull whisper by then."

Mae Ellen Hollister closed her eyes, as if to forget an unforgettable memory. Jean leaned forward, all sympathetic attention. "Ivy" Frost puffed his cigarettes with the peculiar aroma. The lids drooped over his eyes, but they glittered keenly under the black brows.

THE VISITOR resumed, speaking in a low monotone:

"If it will help, I can give you a general idea of our town house. It is three stories high, built in the early years of the century, of stone exterior, and surrounded by lawns, trees, and shrubbery. The ground floor contains the reception room, tea room, ballroom, conservatory, library, dining room, and kitchen. On the second floor are our bedrooms and the guest rooms, eight in all, and some closets and storerooms. On the third floor are the servants' quarters. None of the second-floor rooms have adjoining doors. You must go out into the hall to reach another room."

"At the time, none of you had the least inkling about what frightened your sister, but you discovered later," Frost remarked.

"Yes; I am coming to that. Naturally we were alarmed and mystified. We couldn't imagine why her door was locked. The best guess seemed to be that some intruder had entered, locked the door, and done something that terrified Ann. But we looked at the ground under her window, and there was no trace of anything there, not even the marks of a ladder."

"He who comes by the roof leaves no trace on the ground," Frost murmured, exhaling a cloud of smoke.

"We even thought my sister might have been the victim of a hallucination, but though we were all a pretty high-strung, nervous family, she had never shown any such tendency before. We thoroughly examined the house, but nothing was missing.

"After the interment, we gradually returned to our usual mode of living.

"A year passed. The depression grew worse, but it did not affect us nearly as much as it did many of our friends, partly because of sound investments, and partly because the companies leasing father's mining and manufacturing patent rights found them so valuable that they could not stop payment of royalties without losing the leases to rival companies and perhaps being forced out of business. We had that fixed income so we kept our town house open and went on pretty much as usual.

"One night, on April 15, 1932, mother asked me to go shopping with her the next morning. Of course I said I would. She said she was tired, though, and would I mind waiting until she wakened.

"For some reason, I didn't sleep well. I heard mother moving around at one time in the night and decided she hadn't been as tired as she thought. I rose early for me, about eight o'clock, had breakfast, and was surprised when mother still had not come down by ten o'clock. I don't know why I didn't ask a maid to look in her room, but I suddenly decided to run up. I tapped on her door. There was no answer, but instead of turning away, I tried the door. It was locked. My heart felt so heavy I thought I would faint. I called the servants and had them break the door open.

"Mother was dead. There was an awful look on her face. The doctor said that it was a case of heart failure, and her expression was simply the result of muscular contraction and *rigor mortis.* Perhaps he was right, but why did she have heart failure? She was not subject to heart trouble. Why was her door locked when I had never before known her to lock it? And that awful look on her face—it reminded me only too closely of the fate that had taken my sister. But there were no signs of an intruder, except the wide-open window, and nothing was missing. I had no tangible evidence to support my suspicions.

"I thought many times of moving from the house. I began to feel as if a curse hung over it. But I stayed on for sentimental reasons, and, after all, one must stay somewhere. It was a good place to entertain in, too, and I often had friends for week-end parties. After this, my brother Paul began to drop in more frequently, and his scoffing at what he called my wild ideas made it easier for me to stay. He was having his own troubles.

"His marriage soured. His wife turned out to be a greedy little gold digger, played fast and loose with other men, and constantly nagged him for ever larger sums and more expensive things, to a point that brought a definite financial strain. A divorce became inevitable. I believe there was a pretty bad scene the night of the break. The upshot was that Paul abandoned his apartment and moved back into the family mansion.

"I felt a greater sense of security then. Time slipped by, and I began to be my old self. I convinced myself that mother's death had been from natural causes."

The girl paused, fumbled in her purse. Frost offered a case of cigarettes, but she preferred her own. Inhaling nervously, she resumed her story.

"In April of 1933, I was invited down to Washington to spend a week with friends. I left Paul in charge of the house.

"When I returned on the morning of April 11th, I knew something was wrong the minute I drew up at the house. I hurried from the cab. There were police around. Winton, the oldest of our servants in term of service, had even telephoned to Washington to make sure I didn't extend my stay.

"Paul had disappeared. According to the servants' stories, they heard a scuffle and cries in his room about two in the morning. Then there was a bumping sound. They came down to investigate, found the door locked, and pounded on it. After a short interval, they heard what they described as a stirring within, then Paul answered in a faint voice and said everything was all right; that he had been walking in his sleep and tripped over a chair.

"But as they were leaving, the door opened and Paul raced out of the house, jumped into his roadster, and sped away. He did not speak or give any clue to his actions. The servants say his face was dead-white and that he had a nasty bruise on his forehead.

"When he had not returned by morning, they called the police and gave the license number of his car. An hour later, the car was found abandoned at Elmwood Cemetery. That is the site of our family crypt. The police of course made a careful examination of the grounds. They found Paul lying in the partly opened crypt. He had been killed by a blow that crushed the top of his head. It might have been struck from the front or behind or either side.

"Who, if any one, had been in his room? What was the scuffle? Why did he run wildly out of the house in the dead of night without a word of explanation? Why did he go straight to Elmwood Cemetery as he apparently did? For what possible reason was he trying to open the vault? Who killed him and why? Did he accidentally discover some one else trying to enter the vault? Or did some one know that he was coming and lie in wait for him? Did he have an appointment there, for some unguessable reason? What inexplicable purpose lay behind his actions, if they were rational at all?

"Why? Why? Why? I nearly went mad asking questions. I found no answers. There were no clues, no weapons found at the vault, no positive evidence of who the murderer could have been, no signs in his room to indicate the cause of the scuffling sound or the presence of a second person.

"There was trouble with the servants. Two of them left, though they had been generously remembered in the family's wills.

"This last death, the fourth in the family in three years, almost finished me. I was now absolutely alone. I felt I could not remain any longer in the house; that a fatal destiny had settled on it. Yet neither could I quite bring myself to sell it; it had been my home for so long, and I had so many memories connected with it. At last I left it in charge of the servants and took a month's cruise.

"That did me a lot of good. I came back determined to stay put. As I said, I was the only remaining member of the family. If there was some malign purpose behind the deaths, it would be next directed against me. But also I felt reasonably sure that I had nothing to fear for a while at least. It seemed to me to be significant that the fatalities had all occurred around the anniversary of my father's death. On that assumption, I would not need to worry until this month.

"I busied myself in a hectic round of activities, morning, noon, and night. Parties, dances, teas, luncheons, bridge, theaters, travel, sports—anything to keep me busy. Maybe I shouldn't have gone the pace so hard. It left me little enough time to think and that prevented me from worrying, but I don't suppose it helped my health any.

"This year, as April approached, I began to grow nervous. Time and again, I thought of leaving on a long cruise, but I've never been one to run away from things. Better to face the issue and either prove my fears were groundless, or find out what the trouble was, I decided. So I stayed. I bought an automatic pistol, though, and kept it under my pillow. Father's old six-shooter I put in my vanity table for extra protection.

"There was even a heavy old sword in the den, which I took to my room. I bought a couple of flashlights. There is a high, iron fence around our grounds, but I was taking every precaution I could think of, so I bought a pair of police dogs and turned them loose each night. I felt pretty secure then. I was still nervous, but confident I could handle any situation that might rise."

II.

THE LAST of the Hollisters paused and drew a deep breath, as if about to plunge into icy waters. Her face was bloodless. Her voice sank to a lower monotone. Her eyes roved restlessly from her lap to the package on the table, from Frost to Jean Moray. The pupils of the professor's eyes seemed brighter in a blacker fashion. He had smoked at least a dozen of his pungent cigarettes.

Jean listened in rapt attention. She hung on every word of their client as if she was living the narrative and intuitively placing herself in Mae Hollister's place. It was a keen, sympathetic response that obviously served as a sustaining chord for the visitor.

Mae Ellen Hollister resumed speaking: "Through the early days of this month, I felt an increasing tension. I would lie awake for hours, but nothing happened, and I would drift off into a troubled sleep. Because nothing happened, I would feel more strongly that something would take place the next night. When I kept the lights on, I couldn't sleep. When I turned them off, I pictured all sorts of terrible things coming toward me in the darkness. I thought of asking one of my girl friends to stay with me. But if she did, and something happened, I would have deliberately drawn an innocent person into danger. I did nothing more about it.

"Yesterday, April 9th, the strain reached a point where I saw my physician. He gave me a prescription which he said was a sedative. When I took it, I would quickly fall into a deep sleep. I didn't take it last night. I couldn't. I kept thinking about all the things that might happen if I was in a drugged sleep. I could die without ever knowing how or why, but no matter how much it hurt, I wanted to fight the battle out.

"So I went to a dinner party, theater, and dance, with some friends. I got home after one. The dogs barked when I came in. I was pretty tired and took to bed almost at once. Every one else seemed to have retired. The house was absolutely still.

"I didn't sleep well, I thought of the prescription and decided against it. I opened a dull book on sociology. I counted sheep. Nothing seemed to help. I tossed around for what dragged like ages. I must have dozed off.

"I don't know when I woke up. I had a drowsy feeling that the window was wide open. Then I became fully awake. I distinctly heard a weight fall on the floor. I strained my eyes, but I couldn't see a thing. I stared and stared, but there was no moon, and it was very dark. I reached over to the light-switch and clicked it, but nothing happened. I grew alarmed, and a panicky feeling swept over me. Some one was crawling across the floor. I sat up and fumbled around until I found the flashlight under my pillow and turned it on."

Again the girl took a deep, nervous breath. Her eyes remained fastened now on the little parcel.

"I don't know if I shrieked when the beam leaped forth. I don't think so. I was too paralyzed by the shock of horror such as I never dreamed of.

"A green thing, like a man, was creeping toward me. It resembled the corpse of my father, Franklin Hollister, only bigger, more—more—enormous. The thing was dead, as dead as anything can ever be that has been buried four years. It crept toward me, slowly, the stiff limbs hooking crab-fashion on the floor, a few inches at a time. I felt my scalp prickle, and I shivered I was so cold. I had the strangest roaring in my head, yet I could hear every little sound that the thing made.

"It was halfway to me when I moved, but I couldn't seem to control myself. I sprang clear out of bed in a single leap. I pulled the door, but it was locked, and I couldn't find the key. I jumped for the automatic, but I was trembling so badly that I knocked it off the bed.

"And still the green man crept toward me, its dead eyes shining dully, its face set in the dreadful rigidity of death. The noise in my head swelled to a great roar. I have a vague memory of clutching the sword on the wall and trying to wield it. Then I sank into infinities of blackness."

The girl was shuddering again now. Not even the powerful bromide that Frost had mixed could counteract the terrific shock she had received.

Her voice came faint and trembling: "I don't know how long I was out, but I don't think it could have been very long. The first thing I realized was that I was clutching a sword. I couldn't remember why. I got up and turned on the lights in a heavy sort of way as if I was numb all over.

"There was a hand lying on the floor—a green hand. For a long time, I couldn't bring myself to go near it. I noticed in a mechanical kind of fashion that the window was wide open. Then I wondered why the lights worked when they didn't earlier. I tried the door. It was still locked. That scared me. I went around the hand to shut and bolt the windows. I found the door key lying on the floor. I don't know how it got there.

"I stared at the gruesome thing in the middle of the room until I thought my eyes would pop out. I was going to call the servants, but, for the first time in my life, I was up against something so abnormal and appalling that no ordinary help would do. I thought of calling the police, but I could predict in advance what stock they would take in my story. I racked my brains, and the one person I had heard of who might help in getting to the bottom of this was you.

"So I mustered up courage and took some stockings which I dropped on the hand. I simply couldn't bring myself to touch it directly. Even so, I could feel its awful reality when I dropped it into a box.

"Then I began wondering why the dogs hadn't barked. It was getting light now. How I ever found strength enough is beyond me, but I threw on a robe and went downstairs. It was dreadfully quiet. I slipped outside. Bingy and Carl had been poisoned.

"I went back and sat in my room for hours. I can never express all that this terrible experience did to me. I would sit in a sort of mad ecstasy of horror, drifting midway between unconsciousness and insanity. Again and again, the memory of that frightful scene when I turned the flashlight on congealed me in a waking stupor. Then my thoughts would veer crazily back and forth across the years.

"I knew now what frightened Ann to death, what caused mother's heart to stop beating, why Paul rushed from the house a year ago. I could not believe, I would not believe, yet I had to believe against all the reason I could summon. Reality and unreality spun around me. I would pretend I was dreaming, wait to wake up, only there was no waking.

"Time and again, I started to call the servants, to call the police. I tried to get up enough courage to drive out to Elmwood Cemetery to see if—to see—" Her voice broke. She stared straight into the eyes of Frost. The utter demoralization and appeal in her face outweighed everything she had said.

FROST straightened a little in his chair. "During the latter years of you father's life, do you recall that he ever made a point of disappearing for a period in April?"

The visitor thought hard. "No; not that I remember. But, then, I wouldn't know. We always took a Caribbean cruise in April. Father insisted it was good for our health."

"He accompanied you?"

"His business affairs kept him here."

"Excuse me for a few minutes."

Frost rose and took the parcel, with which he vanished into his laboratory. Miss Hollister, her face bloodless, sat with staring eyes. She looked numb, crushed.

The criminologist came back in less than five minutes, wearing a faint and enigmatic smile of grim significance.

Mae Ellen Hollister clutched the arms of her chair as if to keep from screaming. Her voice rasped in a shrill and rising plea: "Isn't there anything you can do to help me? Isn't there anything—"

Frost bent over and laid an extraordinarily slender, almost feminine, hand on the young woman's clenched knuckles. "Do? There is a great deal to be done, Miss Hollister. You did a splendid job in putting me in possession of all the information I need. I know how the atrocity was committed. I know why it was committed. Within twenty-four hours, I shall identify the persons behind this and bring them to justice. I shall say nothing more now because only in this way can I prevent any mischance and avoid even the least inadvertent motion that knowledge might cause you. I can assure you that the explanation is simple, through not pleasant. Cease worrying."

The girl relaxed a little. The lines on her face sagged from released tension.

Frost continued, speaking in a matter-of-fact manner: "Does your household know you came here?"

"No; I told them nothing."

"Good! Then go back and act as naturally as possible. You have hired a new servant. Her name is Jean Moray, but you will hire her as Jane Armstrong. She will arrive about an hour after you return to your home. You will carry on an extended conversation with her about her previous employment, her references, what she can do, and so on. Try to have at least one of the servants within earshot. You will then take her on for a trial, assign her to her quarters and duties, and introduce her to the staff. You will also take her over the entire house from cellar to roof. Have you bought any dogs to replace Bingy and Carl?"

"No; but I thought—"

"Do not do so. To-morrow you may if you wish."

Mae Ellen Hollister gave him a queer look. "You seem to know what I am thinking even before I have a chance to tell you. You said your assistant would be coming to the house shortly. May I expect you, too?"

Frost mused, with an air of abstraction. "No; not until considerably later. Let me see, the library will require several hours, then it will take an hour or two for the drive out and back, and I may need to spend as much as two hours at the circus. All in all—"

"The circus!" Mae Ellen Hollister rose, her face white and furious. "I come to you for help when I need it most, and you talk about going to a circus! Why, you would think—I think—" But her voice trailed off.

The air of abstraction had vanished from Frost the moment she exclaimed. She stared into eyes blackly glittering and deep, with pupils so expanded that the iris virtually disappeared. The effect was hypnotic.

Yet Frost spoke with a calm authority that instantly restored the woman's confidence.

"You have been through a frightful experience, Miss Hollister, and it is a miracle that you have controlled yourself as well as you have. In the circumstances, I can understand how irrelevant my actions may seem to you.

"I am attacking the problem with my own methods. My visit to the circus is absolutely necessary. It has a direct and vital bearing on your welfare. You are in very great danger of death, or were, as you must have realized. The terror that has been menacing your family ought to be eliminated now. I shall accept the responsibility only on the condition that I have an absolutely free hand to do exactly what I deem best, however incongruous or fantastic it may sound. As I remarked before, I do not care to tell you more now, simply because there will be no slip-up in my plans so long as they are known to myself alone.

"Now, return to your home. Do not worry. Jane Armstrong will arrive soon. I shall announce my presence when I come."

Jean accompanied the last of the Hollisters to the door.

Bursting with curiosity when she reentered, Jean demanded: "Why in the world are you going to the circus?"

Frost flung over his shoulder: "Come into the laboratory."

IN SPITE of air conditioning and the ozonator, the place smelled of acids, reagents, chemicals, and solutions. Microscopes and slides, X-ray machine and spectrographs and fluoroscope occupied the first table. Mae Hollister's parcel also lay upon it.

The professor, donning a pair of rubber gloves, and inhaling continually his private cigarettes, tossed aside some hose that Jean looked at enviously. They must have cost ten dollars a pair—beautiful things. She would have loved to wear them. Then the criminologist, his graceful fingers holding it as if it was a work of art, lifted from the bottom of the box a severed, green hand.

"Here," he remarked, "is the answer to your question."

Jean did not take the loathsome object while she studied it. That it had been detached from a corpse long dead was too gruesomely clear. The yellowing finger nails, the greenish color of the skin, the film of mold that had begun to develop, the faint odor of formaldehyde and embalming fluid, the purple-black hue of arteries and veins, the stagnant aspect of flesh and muscle—all were unmistakable evidence of the grave. The hand may have been attractive during the life of its owner. In death and decay it was only repulsive, a detestable relic, a thing of ugly and sinister nature.

"What does it suggest to you?" Frost inquired.

"Why ask? I think you know already."

"I should like to hear you tell me."

Jean shuddered. "It is so obviously what Miss Hollister said it was that I'll have to believe the rest of her story, incredible as it sounded. There is nothing imaginary about that hand. I wish there was. It is so real that it makes the affair more horrible than I ever thought anything could be. Like Miss Hollister, I believe it, and yet it is unbelievable. It cannot be, but it is. It's so strange and abnormal and so much beyond anything I've come across before that I simply can't think of a reasonable explanation."

Frost replaced the relic in its container. "You have as much information as I have. All the clues necessary to provide the motive and explanation of the crimes, and to indicate the course to follow in trapping the fiends behind this, lay in the woman's story and in a scrutiny of the hand. Eliminate the impossible answers and what remains must be true, however unlikely or improbable or exceptional it may seem.

"When you are installed in the Hollister place, make a note of every room and every individual in the house. Take any action you think best, until you hear from me. I do not know when I shall arrive, but not until I have completed the outside work."

Frost's shaggy brows were knit as in contemplation of some perplexing and abstract problem. Jean, feeling both mentally and physically dismissed, started on her way. Her last glimpse of the professor showed him still rapt in his thought, but walking about and selecting with unhesitating choice various items from the immense and exhaustive stocks of his laboratory.

III.

JEAN, installed in the Hollister house as second maid, had surveyed the entire place from cellar to attic by late afternoon. Mae Ellen Hollister showed her through. Still suffering from the effects of shock, she moved with tired but nervous steps, keyed-up, jumping at the least sound. She made an effort to repair the ravages of strain and loss of sleep; cosmetics helped little. Jean had taken pains before she came to remove her make-up; but, even so, her natural beauty of face and figure obviously impressed the mistress of the house.

That was a help. Envy and a slight irritation of jealousy tended to bring the Hollister woman back to the petty, familiar things of life.

"Make-up is *such* a help," she remarked in the basement.

"I'll take care of mine when I reach my purse," said Jean.

"Oh, that wouldn't do at all! My maids do not use cosmetics," Mae Ellen hastily replied.

In the living room, the last of the Hollisters inquired: "Just who is Professor I.V. Frost? I've heard a good deal about him and his work, and he seems like a rather strong and confident person, but then I don't know whether I can count on anything after last night. Is he all he's said to be? What sort of man is he?"

"That," Jean sagely commented, "is a question to which no one will ever really know the answer. He doesn't talk much about himself, doesn't say much, but you can consider the mystery just about solved right now. He has his own methods of working. He always seems to be a couple of jumps ahead of everybody else."

In her second-floor bedroom, Mae Ellen fidgeted, ill at ease. Merely being in the room caused added strain, so overwhelming had been the shock of the previous night's horror. Jean's vitality and positive manner afforded the only support that kept Mae Ellen from breaking. Jean led the way out after a quick survey.

The servants' quarters on the third floor, and the roomy attic with its ladder to a roof skylight, completed Jean's once-over. It fixed the exact location of rooms and windows on her memory, but offered little to enlighten her. From Miss Hollister's own narrative, it had been evident that entrance and exit could have been accomplished in a number of ways. The house as a whole was a great capacious thing of large rooms and long corridors, the sort of structure that was built around the turn of the century. It had front and rear staircases.

More interesting than the house were its occupants, a curious ménage. Mrs. O'Linn, the cook and general housekeeper, was a quiet old soul who seemed lost in dreams of Irish hills. Miss Hollister's personal maid, Adrienne Gallis, looked frustrated. Winton, the butler, resembled a certain type of clergyman. He had a round face, placid blue eyes, an air of pompous dignity and self-righteous virtue. He looked twice when Jean passed.

The housemaid, Winton's wife, was a morose, pudgy person who would have disliked Jean because of her youth even had she been completely lacking in beauty. The caretaker and gardener, Olaf, appeared incomprehensible and stolid. He had colorless hair, vacant eyes, and knotty fingers.

Of this singular group, not the least noticeable was William Gallis, the chauffeur, who devoted most of his time to taking cars apart, putting them together again without the loss of a piston ring, building short-wave radio sets, and reading all the science and aviation magazines.

So far as Jean could determine, these individuals, including the Wintons and the Gallises, lived separate lives and might have been so many persons brought together by mere chance in a rooming house. Yet Winton had dwelt here for twenty years, his wife twelve, and the others from nine down to the chauffeur, who had come only a year previously.

The more Jean thought about it, the more baffled she became. The terrifying picture of a dead, green man creeping absolutely paralyzed rational action. It was so utterly at variance with reality as she knew it; so gruesome a thought that even yet she could scarcely believe. Yet there rose in her mind the image of Ann Hollister, screaming her life away in an asylum; Mrs. Hollister, dead from shock; Paul Hollister, found murdered in a cemetery after inexplicable incidents behind the locked door of his room.

Had this same dreadful nightmare afflicted them all? Was there a legend, a curse, a taint, or a psychopathic strain in the family? Or—and Jean faced the thought with dismay—was some new and infinitely evil force, of another realm entirely, bringing the dead back from the grave?

She wished Frost would come or call. There was no word from him. What could he possibly have meant by his cryptical allusions to his plans for the day?

The hours dragged. The house was like a tomb, an inhabited tomb. The frequent jangle of the telephone seemed an alien, discordant note. The servants attended to their tasks with noiseless and secretive efficiency. Mae Ellen Hollister went out in the afternoon to a cocktail tea, returned as sober as when she left. Neither stimulants nor narcotics would affect her much until the profound first effects of her grisly experience had begun to wear off. From shock such as she had received, she would never fully recover, whatever the answer might be.

Mae Ellen Hollister summoned Jean at six thirty to her boudoir. She seemed nervously distraught, unable to reach a decision. Her face was haggard. Yet a slow lassitude accompanied her hectic and overwrought condition. "I had decided to spend the night with friends," she began abruptly. "I can't make up my mind. I don't want to stay here another night. It will be hard on me to stay, just as bad to leave. What can I do?"

Jean answered quietly: "I've already thought of that. Professor Frost would never have insisted on my coming here as a member of the staff if he hadn't been sure that our investigation should be as indirect as possible. If you leave and I remain, it will be obvious to any interested person that there is a connection between the two events. Aside from that, it might prove more difficult or impossible to take action if you went elsewhere and were again menaced.

"It will be better if you act as though nothing had happened. If there is no word from Frost by ten o'clock, retire to your room. As soon as the servants are asleep, I'll slip down and tap four times on your door."

The Hollister woman seemed relieved, content to let some one else assume her burden of worry.

DINING with the staff was an experience that Jean had no desire to repeat. Mrs. O'Linn looked at her with a wistful air that she could not quite analyze. The Irish came out only to the extent of a few impersonal questions, a kindly interest in seeing that the new member had enough to eat. Adrienne Gallis, staring with depressed fascination at her husband and at Jean alternately, volunteered no remarks. William Gallis rattled on about connecting rods and piston rings, compared different makes of cars, gave a résumé of the last science-fiction story he had read, studied Jean with direct and observant eyes, and appeared pleased with his contributions to life.

Winton ogled Jean, tried to be agreeable and managed to be unctuous while Mrs. Winton maintained a stony silence. Olaf peered blandly at every one, his big, pale eyes serene and vacant as an idiot baby's.

In the midst of this ill-assorted, curious, and secretive group, whose talk was purposeless and awkward, Jean felt as much a stranger as if she had intruded upon the private habits of so many newly arrived visitors from alien lands who spoke no language but their own. She doubted whether Freud had ever encountered a finer set of neuroses, or whether Bellevue ever had a better assortment of psychopathic cases. That these people had lived in the same house, however spacious, for years without being more intimate was as inexplicable a vagary of human aberration as that, preserving this isolation, they had not plotted each other's death long before.

Jean welcomed the end of this trying meal. She went directly to her room where she wasted an hour in a vain attempt to get a start somewhere in unraveling the weird mystery of the green man and the queer reticence of the servants. She merely succeeded in working herself into a state of exasperation. About nine, she took a shower and felt refreshed. Studying her face in a mirror, she decided to improve it, but could not find her compact. She recalled that she had had it during dinner.

Descending the rear staircase, she met Adrienne Gallis.

The maid frowned. "If you hear of another opening, take it," Her voice rattled like dry peas in a pod.

"Why?" Jean's voice expressed curiosity rather than the surprise that the maid's unexpected remark caused.

"You won't like it here."

The maid went her way without another word.

Jean, still wondering what the maid had in mind, reached the second floor just as Winton strutted along the hallway.

"Ah, Miss Armstrong!"

"Yes?" Jean practiced a meaningless inflection.

Winton purred: "Couldn't we have a talk? It is just possible that I might be able to tell you some very interesting things."

"Yes?"

"Not here, of course. Oh, in strict privacy. How would—"

"To-morrow. I'm very tired to-night."

"Very good!" Winton seemed not at all taken aback as she continued on her way.

Mrs. O'Linn was drying dishes when Jean entered. She looked up. "If you came for your compact, it's there on the table. I was going to bring it to you when I finished here."

Jean took the compact. "It was good of you to think about it. Can I help you with the dishes?"

Mrs. O'Linn polished a plate. "No; I'll get along all right." She appeared to be thinking about other and far-away matters. Jean moved toward the door.

Mrs. O'Linn spoke softly: "Miss Armstrong, you are new here. You aren't used to our ways. If I were you, I wouldn't walk around after ten. I wouldn't leave my room."

Jean stopped. "I don't understand. Why?"

Mrs. O'Linn carefully dried a saucer. Her face was hidden by the back twist of her gray hair. Her voice, reflected from the sink, had a muffled sound. "When you leave your room, lock your door, Miss Armstrong. But don't lock it when you are inside. Good night!"

Jean almost stayed, but Mrs. O'Linn, busy with her work and her thoughts, gave no further explanation of her enigmatic words. Frost's assistant, after a few seconds' hesitation, departed, a bewildered and puzzled young woman.

Closing the door behind her as she left the kitchen, Jean thought she heard the sound of receding footsteps. She listened, ran lightly and rapidly through the dining room and living room to the front staircase. In the dark area of the turn, she was sure she caught a glimpse of a figure, or the shadow of a figure.

She hurried noiselessly up the thick-carpeted steps. She heard something like the faint sound of far footfalls, but they died away. She cautiously explored the second floor and the third floor, but saw no one.

Had there been an eavesdropper? What did Mrs. O'Linn mean by her cryptic warning? What sort of household was this, where each individual appeared to lead a private life, separate and isolated from the others? Where was Frost?

IN HER ROOM, Jean undressed, donned black pajamas. Black would be least conspicuous if she had to do much wandering through the halls.

A thousand suspicions and speculations ran through her head as she sat in darkness, waiting till the household was asleep. Dominating every thought, the image of the creeping green man clung like an evil incubus. What had Adrienne Gallis meant? What was Winton's purpose in furtively accosting her? How much did Mrs. O'Linn know?

At eleven, she palmed a tiny automatic, a deadly and efficient weapon that she could handle better than a .32. She carried a flashlight in a pocket of her blouse. She opened the door and slipped through. From long experience on summer trips in forest and lake wildernesses, she moved with the soundless ease of a phantom.

As she passed the door of Mrs. O'Linn's room, she paused. The woman, apparently the only kindly member of the staff, seemed to possess suspicions or knowledge that must have been well-grounded, or she would never have mentioned them. Perhaps if Jean could speak to her in the privacy of her room, she would give more specific information.

On impulse, Jean twisted the knob, wafted silently inside, whispered: "Mrs. O'Linn!"

She heard no answer. She moved to the bed, played the small beam of her flashlight around. The room was empty.

Puzzled, she returned to the hall, melted wraithlike along the black corridor.

Why was Mrs. O'Linn not in her room? Where was she? Why had there been no word from the professor?

On the second floor, about to go toward Mae Ellen Hollister's boudoir, Jean hesitated. Again she changed her immediate goal. She descended the rear staircase to the kitchen. The darkness made her progress slow. She did not wish to use the flashlight except when absolutely necessary.

She heard no sound. The eerie silence and the darkness got on her nerves. She felt like a ghost in a catacomb, as she trod with noiseless steps, listening for creaks that did not come, for sounds of people stirring, for any sign of human presence.

She waited till she had felt her way into the kitchen before she flicked the button of her flashlight.

"Mrs. O'Linn!" she gasped.

Mrs. O'Linn did not reply. The Irish cook made no answer because she was leering at the open window. Her dress ran red with blood from the gash that sliced her throat. Her spirit had returned to the Irish hills.

For a long interval, Jean stared at the lolling head and leering face of the dead woman. An appalling silence pervaded the house. With a great effort, she mastered an impulse to cry out, to run away. Silently she advanced and studied the corpse. It was cold. Mrs. O'Linn must have died an hour ago, without a struggle or scream.

Had she surprised some one or something in the act of entering the house? That seemed unlikely, for she would have had time to give the alarm. Had some one she knew entered and taken her utterly off guard with a sudden attack? A possible answer.

But the more Jean thought, the more she became convinced that Mrs. O'Linn had been murdered to silence her. If this was so, it implied that some one had overheard her talking to Jean, and Jean's thoughts flashed back to the retreating footsteps she had tried to follow at the time. The set-up became clearer. Mrs. O'Linn had been caught off guard and slain brutally, without warning. The placing of the body and the open window were plants to throw investigators on a wrong trail.

But who? And why? All the servants profited handsomely through Hollister wills. And any one of them might be a homicidal maniac—Mrs. Gallis, jealous, frustrated, neurotic; Olaf, the incomprehensible ox; Winton, the self-righteous and pompous, with a flair for young women; Mrs. Winton, sour, taciturn; William Gallis, skilled mechanic, ingenious at making things. As fine a crew of potential cutthroats and nervous wrecks as ever manned a house.

Jean did not dare rouse the household or summon the police. If she did, Frost's plans, whatever they were, would be ruined. She feared to disturb the body, could not take it upon herself to do more than spread a napkin over the hideous face for the sake of Mrs. O'Linn's kindly efforts to warn her.

Knowing now that some one had been watching her, wondering how much of her other brief talks had been overheard, she strained her ears to make sure that no one was at hand before she carried out her next move. Here she felt stymied. She originally started out for Miss Hollister's room, must still go there, but the murder of Mrs. O'Linn threw a new and major interference in her schemes. The cold-blooded ferocity of the murder was proof enough that she faced a criminal dangerous and swift to strike. The knife-wielder plunges for the heart. The man or woman in this case struck with deliberate reason for the throat—so that any cry would be choked.

Afraid to use her flashlight in the hallways lest she give herself away, so anxious to breathe silently that her heart pounded, redoubling her caution, she paced slowly, apprehensively, up the stairs. Her senses became preternaturally keen. She heard the faint swish of silk against her own ankles. And suddenly she felt sure that she was followed.

The one thing she must not do was to make any move toward Miss Hollister. Whatever peril she met, she must not drag it straight to the woman she was trying to protect. Thinking fast and coolly now that she sensed a definite encounter, she determined that the wisest course was to return to her room. She could leave the door ajar. There she could listen, find out if she was being shadowed, and slip quietly to Mae Ellen Hollister's room in half an hour or an hour.

JEAN reasoned while she climbed. Softly and as quickly as she could, she mounted the stairs and glided down the third-floor hall in almost total blackness. The feeling of being observed grew on her—an unpleasant enough sensation in daylight or in a crowd, a morale-shattering impression in darkness and alone.

Solely because of the accuracy with which she had studied the house, she sensed when she was opposite her room. She listened, imagined a dozen sounds, but heard nothing definite. She groped along the wall and found her door. She opened it slowly, without creak or protest, and melted within.

A hand closed her mouth. She fought like a demon. She bit, kicked, clawed. She flicked her right arm up to fire over her shoulder. Fingers like steel springs tore the automatic from her palm. A sweetish odor filled her nostrils. She held her breath. She twisted and wrenched. Her pajama-top tore with the sleazy sound peculiar to silk. Her feet kicked vainly. If only she had worn pumps, she could have brought a yelp of pain with a dig of their sharp heels. The hand pressed harder, relaxed. She bounded away. A dull, tremendous weight fell on her head. Cushioned into flame-split blackness, she went out like a burst shell.

From nightmares and dreams, from visions of vast armies of dead, crawling green men swarming toward her out of crimson and infinite hells, Jean struggled to consciousness. Her head throbbed. She tried to raise a hand. It would not move. She tried to lift her other arm. Then it dawned on her that her wrists were knotted beneath her back; as thoroughly knotted as if bound with steel and set in glue. She attempted to open her mouth. It was plastered with adhesive tape. She tried to roll over, but her legs were tied to the foot of the bed. A rope encircled her neck and held her to the head upright.

She ceased her attempts in momentary panic when the knot tightened around her throat. Struggle only made her precarious position worse. She was as effectively out of the running as if she had been set in plaster. But she refused to give up. She could not call for help. She could not make use of teeth or feet. She could not double over. She could not bring her hands around. Yet she determined to free herself.

More angry than frightened now, her mind working swiftly and methodically as her head cleared, she concentrated on the problem of escaping from apparently unescapable bonds. She moved her hands tentatively. She arched her back, swung her bound hands a few inches sidewise. This was the only action she could take without garroting herself. It was enough.

With numb fingers, she plucked at the sheet, thread by thread. She split a finger nail, tore through the sheet in a few minutes.

The mattress was harder going. She gritted her teeth. Her arms wearied. Her fingers felt raw. She broke two more nails before she opened the mattress. Bit by bit, she plucked the wadding out. Her back became a solid ache from the strain of taut muscles. The rope around her neck tightened a little more. It was difficult to breathe. Bit by bit, a piece of wadding between thumb and forefinger, out, drop it to one side, down into the hole again, bit by bit, minute after minute.

Then the bottom of the mattress, and another finger nail gone as she shredded through the tough fabric. With a hole in the mattress just large enough for her hands, she had little play in this awkward position, but she moved them an inch from side to side until her sharp middle finger nails cut through.

Her heart beat exultantly. The spring consisted of rough, parallel wires composed of several smaller strands tightly twisted. The parallel wires, an inch or so apart, were fastened in pairs by metal clips at intervals of a foot. She dropped her wrists on a wire, forced her hands through the inch-wide space on either side, slid them toward the foot of the bed, drew them back. The wires scraped her skin, cut into her flesh; but the wire between her wrists frayed the rope slowly.

The effort proved agony. Pain dwelt in every part of her body. Her hands felt like raw fire. Patiently sawing her wrists down and back, tortured by every motion, hurrying lest her assailant return, Jean persisted though will alone now kept exhausted muscles working.

She had no idea how long she had been out, or of the real lapse of time since she began her efforts. It seemed hours. Actually, it might have been little more than a half hour before the bond snapped, and with cramped, throbbing arms she drew her bleeding hands out.

Another minute or two, and the neck and ankle ropes came free. The tape proved more resistant. She wasted several minutes peeling it from sensitive skin.

She did not turn the lights on. Accustomed to gloom now, she hunted in darkness for her flashlight and automatic, found them lying on a bureau. With difficulty she made out the hands of a clock. It was nearly twelve thirty. She wondered if the sheets would tear into enough strips to reach the ground, since she expected to find the door locked from the outside, but it opened without trouble. Surprised, she slipped into the deserted hallway.

Her bare feet made no sound on the carpet as she sped along the hall and hurried down to the second floor. Miss Hollister alone lived on the second floor, but Jean took no chances. Fading along the corridor, she did not even attempt to knock as she had promised, but silently entered Mae Ellen's bedroom.

JEAN had fears of what she might find—anything from a strange corpse or a green man to a dead Hollister; but the reality proved so mystifying that she stood just inside the door for at least a minute trying to think straight.

Mae Ellen Hollister had vanished. Her clothing lay tossed over a chair. The bed, mussed, had obviously been occupied recently. But Mae Ellen Hollister was gone.

Jean searched the room, examined closets, peered in corners and under the bed, in all likely and unlikely places for some clue to what had happened. She ended as perplexed as she began.

Had the Hollister woman lost her courage and suddenly departed from the house for the night or for good? Had she lost her mind and wandered away at random, on irrational impulses? For that matter, was the last of the Hollisters already deranged, a psychopathic case who might herself be responsible for her fantastic story and these puzzling occurrences? Had she worried over Jean's delay in coming and left to find her? Had she been murdered here, or lured elsewhere to death, and her body hidden? Above all, where was Frost?

Tormented by doubts and haunted by fears and utterly unable to find a starting point for untangling the weird, sinister, and complicated web of mystery that enveloped her, Jean began a half dozen different schemes, but abandoned each in turn. She thought of exploring the house again; the risks seemed great, the potential profit small. She considered going to her own room and awaiting the almost certain return of her assailant. She would have got in touch with Frost if she had the slightest inkling where the professor could be reached.

She remained where she was because she saw no better course. If the Hollister woman had left for some temporary reason, her return might come momentarily. If Mae Ellen had been slain, Jean could do nothing for her, except try to trap the criminal. All factors considered, it seemed better to stay put. Some one or something, unaware of her absence, might make another attempt on her life here.

Jean flopped on the bed. Her nerves ragged, her body weary, she hung between the sleeplessness of mental excitement, the oblivion of exhaustion. She could not get out of mind the memory of the dead woman still keeping a leering vigil in the kitchen; the attack in her own room, as unexpected as it was savage; Mae Ellen Hollister's astounding narrative; the green hand; and now this inexplicable disappearance of the last of the Hollisters.

Jean dozed, waked into apprehension, walked around. She sat in a chair, nodded. She returned to the bed and slept fitfully while deciding to remain awake. At one thirty, she poised in a detached, sleepy mood. Her aching muscles demanded rest. She was too healthy a young animal to resist. She stirred vaguely with the idea of walking around again, but she drowsed. She did not dream.

She wakened suddenly, fully. She wakened because she heard a sound and knew she was no longer alone. She wakened because all her faculties shrilled a warning of immediate and deadly peril. She wakened and stared, and for one freezing, timeless moment felt the impact of such panic as had swept Mae Ellen Hollister to the verge of collapse.

A great, dark blob sprawled on the floor by the window. The blob moved toward her. She turned her flashlight on it, and it sprang into hideous reality. Edging forward, creeping, slithering along the floor, bloated and dead, a greenish corpse inched toward her. Its left hand was missing. The light wavered as the flash trembled in her nerveless fingers. It flickered on dead eyes and glistened on corrupt flesh that belonged to the grave.

Sick and appalled, weak with horror, Jean crept out of bed, aimed, fired. The bullet plowed true into the thing's forehead. No blood oozed. No sound came after the bullet's plop. The thing, remorseless, evil, horrible, crept on.

The door opened behind her. Jean whirled. A flying form bowled her to the floor, hurtled across the room. The flashlight was shattered. She lay stunned, unable to move, pain flashes streaking her vision. A powerful figure leaped on the green thing, struggled, heaved. Something misshapen, repellent, like a gigantic rat, scuttled away. The dim figure lunged after it. It poised on the window sill, leaped. A wail pierced the air, and then followed the sickening sound of a body smashing.

The figure turned, raced across the room, dashed out of the door as Jean struggled to regain vision and consciousness. She had managed to sit up when she heard what sounded like two quick, distant shots. She was on her feet when racing steps approached. She had her gun ready when the figure plowed in.

"Frost!" she cried. She had never been so glad to see any one.

"Quick!" he whispered. "It's all over, but I want this out of sight before the servants arrive."

He hurried to the gruesome object on the floor, bent over, opened something he carried. There was the shuffle of feet on the floor above. Frost straightened, heaved. A bag slung over his back, he strode toward the door.

"This won't be a pleasant job, but you had better come along," he told Jean. "The police will be here before I return. You might not have an easy time of it if you stay. I'll straighten things out when we return."

He spoke without emotion, without ego. They were statements of fact and made solely as such. He did not slacken his pace, did not wait for any debate on Jean's part.

IV.

JEAN trotted along beside him. There was more scuffling of feet, growing activity, cries, far away. Jean opened the front door and walked with Frost to the street. The professor turned, walked a block, turned again, stopped at a parked car.

A disheveled drunk, staggering down the street, stared owlishly at a curious illusion. He thought he saw a towering, hatchet-faced person, with eyes like black coals and an immense sack swung over his shoulder, walking beside a ravishing vision in the shredded remnants of pajamas. The lank person dumped the sack in the rear seat of a car. He climbed in, and the dream followed. The car sailed away. The disheveled drunk reeled after it, muttering incoherently until a fire hydrant reached up and bit him.

The car gathered speed. Jean relaxed, took a cigarette, inhaled, and let out a thankful sigh.

"The grand-stand finish was simply swell," she said. "I don't know who won or what the score was or what it was all about, but it was a swell finish."

Frost smiled faintly. "As Alice might have said, your speech grows curiouser and curiouser," he observed. "How did you make out at the Hollister house?"

His thoughts seemed to be elsewhere, yet he listened intently. He nodded approvingly at one or two points in her narrative.

"Exactly what you should have done," he agreed when she spoke of not disturbing the corpse of Mrs. O'Linn.

"In the circumstances, that was a careless way to enter your room," he remarked with disapproval when she was telling of her flight from the unknown pursuer. Jean's voice became meeker, less enthusiastic. But when she described her escape from apparently fool-proof fetters, he drawled:

"Ingenious! Not all people would have had sense enough to see what could be done, or perseverance enough to do it."

Jean's voice became excited again as she continued her story.

"So there you are," she finished. "Maybe I'm dumb and don't know it, but the Hollister affair is a big, nasty mess as far as I'm concerned, and I'll admit it. I don't know what it's all about, and I can't believe half of it yet."

The car hummed on. Frost, his eyes glued to the road, did not turn his head.

"That admission does you credit," he said. "Estimating reality at its face value is a gift that few persons have. The frank statement of one's ignorance is often a sign of intelligence."

Jean pouted. "I don't want a lecture on philosophy I want to know who and why. Maybe the case is ended in your opinion. It isn't in mine. How in the world did you get started and what magic did you use?"

Frost settled lower in the seat. Driving with one hand, he pulled a cigarette out of his pocket, lighted it, and exhaled a patch of pungent, aromatic smoke. His eyes took on a deeper gleam.

"When Miss Hollister arrived yesterday she gave all the information needed to deduce the broad outlines, the explanations, the course of action to take, and the probable solution of the case—"

Jean interrupted: "How did you know who she was? You mentioned her name before she arrived."

"I make a point of remembering the names and faces of prominent, wealthy, or important people, and members of their families. Certain types of crime, including blackmail, extortion, bribery, and kidnaping, are most prevalent in this group.

"Even before she reached the house, it was obvious that terror brought her. Her extreme agitation, strained features, nervous actions, and other indications were so plain that it required no very alert mind to read them. If she had already asked police aid, there would be no necessity for coming to me. Since she could have employed the services of a detective agency at a fraction of my fee, it was evident that money meant nothing, and that her experience had been of so extraordinary a nature that ordinary assistance would not help.

"Accepting her complete story as an accurate presentation of the case, analytic reasoning then broke it down into probable cause and result. Let us begin with the most striking part of her narration—the creeping green corpse.

"In general, only three theories were tenable. Her story might have been pure invention or delusion or dementia. That category I discarded because of her serious condition. Her collapse was not responsible for hallucinations; but something was responsible for her collapse.

"The second category was that of a supernatural occurrence, not subject to known laws and explanations. This I also dismissed. There may be supernatural manifestations, but I have never witnessed any connected with crime. I would have recourse to such an alternative only if all other methods, approaches, and investigations utterly failed.

"The third possibility was that she *had* actually seen what she claimed, that a corpse *had* crept toward her, that it was the body of her father, though dead four years, and that a logical purpose and human motives lay behind the outrage.

"Several suggestions about how the phenomenon was achieved occurred to me. I was convinced I knew the truth, but I desired further investigation and objective proof to substantiate the theory I had formed."

Jean grabbed the door handle, steadied herself as the car turned a corner and sped on over an almost-deserted highway.

FROST continued speaking in a calm, lucid, incisive fashion: "Discarding for the moment the various ways in which the seemingly impossible could have been brought to reality, and accepting a rational explanation as certain, let us consider Miss Hollister's recital in the light of motives.

"First, why was the green man creeping? The answer is apparent. Miss Hollister stated that she came of a high-strung, neurotic family, some of whose members were subject to heart trouble. Such individuals are usually short-lived. They die of apoplexy, overexertion, hemorrhage, or shock. Only a ruthless and cunning mind, plotting murder, knowing the victims well, would create so novel a device for achieving his purpose.

"If the device failed, more direct means could be employed. It failed on Paul Hollister. Seeking the truth, he was beaten to death. If the device succeeded, as it did in two instances, a murder without clues and without physical violence was committed.

"Now we have a result to be achieved; the death of Hollisters and a method for achieving it—the animated corpse, with more direct and violent means in reserve. But we have also a weakness in the plan. A corpse *walking* would be infinitely more paralyzing, outrageous, and terrible than a corpse slowly *crawling*. An astute observer, after the first shock would conclude that the corpse did not walk, because it could not; that it had nothing to do with the realm of the supernatural; that dead it was and dead it would be; and that its semblance of life appalling had no inexplicable basis. Consideration of this detail added further support to the theory I had formed.

"The means and the result having assumed a logical sequence, I next turned to the cause or motive. It should hardly be necessary to point out the purposes that were deducible and obvious in Miss Hollister's narration. By her own statement, the servants were generously remembered in Hollister wills. Every death meant a direct, worthwhile, financial gain to them. Furthermore, Paul Hollister had married a shrew and a spendthrift.

"There were now nine or ten suspects in the case. By elimination, I reduced the number to six. Paul Hollister's wife could immediately be dismissed as having no connection with the affair, since he did not marry her until *after* the death of Ann Hollister. The servants who had left could also be dismissed, since the crimes continued *after* their departure. Since they were under no suspicion, there was no need to leave; and, by leaving, they sacrificed bequests from subsequent wills and would not profit by subsequent deaths. The criminal, therefore, should be sought among the remaining staff of six."

His body relaxed, but his gaze fastened on the highway and, zest in his drawling, educated voice, Frost pursued his résumé with relentless logic: "The more I thought about it, however, and taking into account other elements of the situation, the more evident it became that the solution was by no means as simple as this. Money, even in a large amount, did not seem sufficient to justify the remarkable circumstances, the extreme and fantastic lengths, to which the criminal had gone. I was convinced, then, that there must be not one, but two motives; not one, but two criminal units working together; that this was both an inside and an outside job.

"It was significant that Franklin Hollister sent his family away in April during the latter years of his life. Why? It was significant that the corpse of Franklin Hollister made its appearance in April around the anniversary of his death. Why? It would have been more effective if the manifestations had come on the exact anniversary.

"Here another statement of Mae Hollister's offered a clue, and the case rapidly became clearer as the details filled in. Miss Hollister asserted that her father's wealth came chiefly from some valuable patents that he controlled. Not that he *invented* but that he *owned.*

"A tentative theory at once offered itself. Franklin Hollister obtained the rights to, or patented, the inventions of some one else. He got them illegally, or did not pay for them in proportion to their worth, or did not pay for them at all. The unknown person tried repeatedly to gain some part of the fortune to which he was, or felt he was, entitled. He came in April because he was in town only in April. Franklin Hollister knowing that the person would be in the city every April and would see him or try to see him and wrangle over the patents, sent his family away.

"When Franklin Hollister died, the inventor lost all chance of obtaining redress for the wrong done him. It must have preyed on his mind, demented him, until for revenge he determined that the Hollisters should never enjoy the ill-gotten fruits of his labors. And Franklin Hollister himself, dead and buried, was to bring ironic justice, be the terrible instrument of vengeance, the curse and destroyer of his own heirs.

"This demoniacal scheme would be difficult to carry out by one not intimately familiar with the Hollisters and their habits, or by one limited to short visits to the city in April. It would require coöperation, inside help, from some one who stood to profit by the action. Presumably, the unknown person and one of the servants came to know each other during the former's successive visits at the Hollister house."

The look of admiration growing on Jean's face vied with expressions of absorbed attention and marveling as the tale unfolded.

"WITH THIS theoretical outline from which to start," Frost continued, "the next step was a matter of taking action in the most effective way. If the previous sequence of events continued, it would be a year before the next apparition of the corpse. But I had excellent reason to believe that the sequence was broken and that another visitation would occur to-night.

"Consider the green hand. It lent not only physical confirmation to various phases of my working hypothesis, but also gave circumstantial support to other parts. Close scrutiny showed it to be in a state of deterioration assignable to a body long dead. At one time, but not recently, it had been treated with theatrical grease paint, the green type which is generally used for shadows. In addition, the hand was covered with a fine layer of greenish mold.

"I must digress for a moment. There are a great number and variety of molds, fungi, films, and sporous growths which may accompany decay. Even in thoroughly refrigerated storage rooms of medical colleges, the cadavers will develop such growths unless they are treated with alcohol, formaldehyde, or other chemical substances. The green mold on the hand might have been such a spontaneous growth, but it was most unlikely. The mold was more likely to have been artificially developed. A chemist could easily have done so, and not merely on a hand, but over an entire body.

"These interpretations were of major importance. The grease paint indicated some one familiar with stage make-up. The mold suggested some one familiar with chemistry. The Hollister patents were of a chemical nature. Of the different performers who use grease paint, the class that fitted must be one which came here every April. Legitimate actors, motion-picture actors, concert artists, and so on, are here the year around. But every April, the circus pays us a visit before swinging around the country. You may have noticed the current advertisements and publicity about it.

"I now had a good picture of the outside criminal. He was a former inventor who knew something about chemistry. He had so limited means that he had to accept employment and had been connected with the World Circus in recent years.

"Now, to return to the severed hand. Why had it been left behind when the corpse disappeared? It could have been by accident or design. It seemed incredible that the loss of the hand was not noticed when the sword amputated it. Therefore the abandoning of it must have been intentional. Why?

"To the criminal, Mae Hollister had fainted. When she recovered consciousness, she might go to pieces, she might have hysteria, she might persuade herself that she was the victim of a nightmare. But if she saw the hand, the sight might finish her. If it did not, it would prey on her mind. If she went to the police, she would very likely be turned over to a psychopathic ward for observation.

"If the police did investigate, there was no one upon whom to fasten suspicion. If Mae Hollister departed, another indirect or direct attempt on her life could be made later. If she remained, the best time to strike, from a psychological or any other viewpoint, was to-night. The inside criminal could check up on her actions. The partnership had much to gain and nothing to lose by abandoning the hand.

"Concluding that another atrocity would be committed to-night, if conditions were favorable, I saw to it that they were. If I had gone to the Hollister house, the warning would instantly have been given. Nothing would have happened. But it was necessary that Miss Hollister return to her home, and that she have protection and some feeling of security. Going as a servant, you would be suspected, but even the criminal is prone to look with favor upon beauty. As a woman, you would not be regarded as dangerous as a man. There was a good chance of your being accepted for what you were supposed to be."

Jean made a noise in her throat. The car streaked toward less congested parts of the city.

Frost, engrossed in his analysis, and absorbing a curious excitation from his peculiar cigarettes, approached the climax. "After Miss Hollister and you had gone, I took a few things from the laboratory.

"I first stopped at the library and checked a number of records and files. I examined the reports of the patent office. I found the application of Franklin Hollister for three patents. Exception was taken, some months later, by one Kurt V. Raim. Exception was denied, and final patent was granted to Hollister.

"I studied the April files of all the newspapers here. I found that in each of the last ten years, the World Circus arrived in the second week in April and left at the end of the month for its tour of the country. Among the publicity and advertising, I discovered a reference to Kurt V. Raim seven years ago, another two years ago.

"Having substantiated parts of my theory, I then drove out to Elmwood Cemetery and talked to the caretaker. I got a key to the Hollister vault and entered it. The casket of Franklin Hollister was empty, further proof that I had made a correct analysis.

"I returned to the city and made some arrangements with a mortician. I then spent a couple of hours at the World Circus. I discovered that Raim was still associated with the circus.

"It was then dark and time to set the trap."

Jean broke in: "Haven't you eaten since breakfast?"

Frost replied indifferently: "It didn't occur to me. The case was so unusual that it held my attention exclusively.

"I LEFT my car a little distance from the Hollister house and entered the grounds," Frost went on. "Light shone from a second-floor window, thereby identifying Mae Hollister's bedroom. Directly under the window, I placed the battery I carried. The light-bulb was screened so that only infra-red rays formed the beam which, of course, was invisible.

"In the rear of the house I found an open window. I discovered the body of Mrs. O'Linn when I entered. A brief inspection produced ample proof of what had happened. The murder also testified that one of the criminals was becoming desperate, and that another attempt on Mae Hollister's life was scheduled for to-night.

"I ascended the rear staircase to the attic, thence to the roof. The light had gone out in Miss Hollister's bedroom, but I had accurately fixed its location. Under the eave, and directly over the bulb on the ground, I placed a small photo-electric cell, sensitive to infra-red rays. I pressed a couple of thumb tacks in to hold it. I ran a wire around under the eaves to the opposite side of the house and let the loose end hang down to the room opposite Miss Hollister's.

"Working in silence and encountering no one, I reëntered the house. In the unoccupied room opposite Miss Hollister's, I fixed the wire to a simple relay. The contact was closed. It would open the moment anything tried to enter her room and interrupted the beam.

"It had been apparent from her own story how entrance for the manifestation was effected. The slain dogs, the lights that failed at crucial moments, the very avoiding of detection, were indicative of an operator inside the house. There were no tracks on the ground. Entrance must have come from inside the house or from the roof. The Hollisters did not lock their doors. In two instances, the corpse came down by way of a rope from the third floor, in the other instances it came down from the roof.

"The crimes could have been prevented. But Ann Hollister, crazed, could not tell what she saw. Mrs. Hollister died of heart failure. Paul Hollister was not so easy a victim. He advanced to the corpse, struggled with it, and was knocked out. Finding nothing when he regained consciousness, he rushed out to Elmwood Cemetery. The inside member of the crime partnership was no fool. He could easily guess where Paul was headed, and warn the outside member, who thereupon took cruder means of preventing Paul from finding the truth, and of satisfying his bloodthirsty vengeance. Mae Hollister fainted long enough for the corpse to disappear.

"All I needed to do was wait until the contact broke, allow enough time for entrance to be accomplished, then go in and trap the guilty. There was, however, very real danger that another shock might finish the woman. I decided that she should not be exposed to the risk.

"She was sleeping very lightly when I entered. I administered enough anæsthetic to put her in a deep coma, before carrying her across the hall. She continued to sleep soundly while I waited by the relay.

"After a while, I heard the door to her room open and close so faintly that it would have escaped detection if I had not been keenly concentrating. You did an expert piece of work. It was obvious that it must have been you, since the visitor did not come out. Your presence there admirably suited my plans. If the criminals checked up before acting, you would, in darkness, be taken for granted as Mae Hollister. The criminals made one fatal error—they thought you were securely tied. They did not make sure by a second visit. The rest you know."

V.

THE CAR slowed down, halted. Frost took a small parcel from the rear seat, got out, and slung the large sack over his shoulder as Jean joined him beside the entrance to Elmwood Cemetery. A figure rose out of darkness.

"Hello, Johnson! Everything's all right."

An anxious voice answered: "Did you succeed, Professor Frost?"

"Yes. Is Connolly here?"

"Waiting inside."

"Good! Have him come to the vault. Give me the key. If you don't mind, I think it would be better for you to keep watch here and see that we are not molested."

The caretaker handed a key over, glanced dubiously at Jean. "But the young lady—"

"She is my assistant."

"Well, I mean—" The man hesitated.

Frost looked at Jean, his glance encompassing her for the first time. "Do you generally go around wearing as little as that?" he inquired, curious.

Jean defended herself. "Well, you told me to come along and you didn't give me time to change or grab anything," she began, but Frost was already striding through the cemetery.

Slightly peeved, she nevertheless trotted meekly after him. She didn't feel that he was at all properly appreciative of beauty.

Frost flashed the beam of his light on the Hollister vault. They entered and descended. An eerie sensation crept through Jean as she looked at the caskets in the gloomy interior.

"I still don't know the rest," she whispered. "You practically knocked me out when you barged in."

"Kurt V. Raim fell to his death. I reached the third floor in time to see Winton shoot his wife in a last effort to save himself. He was a trifle slow in aiming at me. He died."

Frost opened the sack, grasped it by the bottom, eased its contents out. "There is the answer," he remarked.

Jean shuddered. The entire front torso of the corpse had been removed. One look was more than enough for her. She felt ill.

"Now do you understand? Franklin Hollister was a large man, but Kurt V. Raim was a midget, a strong midget, but one of the smallest dwarfs of our time. It was his crazed brain that conceived this fiendish means of revenge. It was Winton's greed that made him help. It was Winton who killed Mrs. O'Linn and assaulted you, and whose wife was a tacit partner to his evil. It was Winton who lowered the corpse and Raim, once from his bedroom, once from his wife's bedroom, which were directly above the rooms of two of the dead Hollisters, and twice from the roof.

"It was Raim the dwarf who, protected by a rubber sheet from direct contact with the body, was willing to endure what must have been a ghastly experience for the sake of satisfying his insane desire for vengeance. It was Raim the inventor who conceived so weird a revenge. It was Raim the chemist who doctored the corpse to make it more gruesome, and who built the air-tight, chemically refrigerated box underneath the surface clothing in that big chest in Winton's room."

STEPS SOUNDED. A man of untroubled composure entered, followed by another bearing a load of clothing and materials.

"Hello, Connolly! This won't be a pleasant task, and it must be done fast. Can you use some assistance?"

"Thank you, but it won't be necessary, Professor Frost. I brought another member of our firm. We shall be through in an hour. You understand that it is a delicate matter for a house as respectable as ours to handle."

"I understand perfectly. Here is the key. Be sure to send the bill to me, and go to any expense necessary. The hand is in the small parcel."

As they left, the two morticians were already at work with the undertaker's magic that transforms a mutilated corpse into a dignified and unblemished body, seemingly asleep.

"To-day," Frost prophesied, while the car gathered speed, "we shall bring Miss Hollister here, if she wishes, and show her the casket containing Franklin Hollister. We will tell her a fable about wax dummies and mechanical contraptions that make them move. If necessary, we shall make a wax hand looking real but decayed, and return it to her as the one she brought. The guilty are dead. The police will be mystified, and after much speculation they will call it a case of attempted burglary and murder, which just happened to occur in the same house during the same night as a suicide pact."

The bright glitter of his eyes was beginning to wane. Jean, drowsily curled up and about to fall asleep, knew that days of boredom lay ahead for him, now that the case was closed.

THEY COULD NOT KILL HIM

The killer vanished. Frost walked forward.
A fearful scream tore up through the trapdoor—

WHEN JEAN MORAY tripped up the steps of 13 State Street, entered, and threw off her wraps, she powdered her nose and gave a fluff to her hair. She surveyed herself critically in the hall mirror. She approved what she saw, from immaculate complexion on a wise, youthful face to the nonchalant tilt of her head, from hair the color of an old rye whisky to hands that would have graced a nail-polish ad.

She was young and beautiful and sophisticated and full of the devil, with just enough of naïveté to perplex an observer. She was exceptional even in a city noted for its attractive women. Her face glowed.

She held the evening paper in one hand and floated into the library. She felt like humming. Had not her escort paid every compliment to her beauty over the dinner table at a night club? His admiration lingered in her heart. But she had deftly turned aside every advance, checked him on the verge of proposing, taken the fruits of victory while granting nothing. She liked the sensation of being loved, but conquests came easy, too easily. With perverse reaction, she would never respond save to some one completely indifferent to her appeal.

She danced through the library and into the laboratory.

Professor I.V. Frost did not look up as she entered.

The criminologist, carelessly dressed in old corduroy, blue shirt open at the throat, and the stained leather jacket that he always wore around his laboratory, was studying an object on a table. His back, half turned to Jean, concealed the object.

His sharp, hawklike features were etched against a table light. The immense and shaggy black eyebrows stood out in ridges. Bent over though he was, slouched toward the object, he yet conveyed an impression of latent power in every part of his long, spare figure.

It was obvious that the professor's immediate interest lay elsewhere. Nettled, Jean decided to get some attention.

"Can I help? Am I intruding?" she asked with sweet innocence.

Professor Frost straightened and glanced at her. She felt herself raked by eyes that pierced and probed. He smiled faintly

"Perhaps you will not always have the good fortune to obtain as dinner companions men who are gentlemanly enough to let you parry their advances, even to the extent of thwarting an intention to propose," he observed calmly.

"Well, I size 'em up pretty well first," Jean began defending herself. Then she flushed. Rattled by this man who studied her and told her where she had been and what she had been doing, she burst out: "You talked to him?"

Frost shook his head. "No. Nearly every person carries on his features and in his actions the impress of his recent doings, and even of his thoughts. I doubt whether there are half a dozen individuals alive who can successfully disguise or conceal their character and habits from the trained analyst.

"But tell me what you make of this. I found it lying on the sidewalk."

He handed her the object. It was a woman's purse. She scrutinized it carefully. The contents were a mess—powder case open, coins and compact and handkerchief and lipstick and miscellaneous girl-things jumbled together. Jean tried to get a mental picture of the owner.

"To begin with, the woman was slovenly and untidy," she guessed.

"Wrong. Go on," Frost placidly contradicted her.

"These things are about the most expensive you can buy. The gloves would be fifteen dollars a pair, the perfume forty-five an ounce, and the platinum compact at least fifteen hundred. She was a wealthy woman."

"Wrong, but continue."

Jean pouted. "She was a blonde. A natural blonde. Hair about the color of clover honey."

"Right."

"And she didn't have enough money for a cab, so she was walking to a bank to cash a check when she dropped the purse."

"Wrong."

Jean gazed at him steadily.

Frost's cool voice had no reproof or pride. He stated facts and corrected errors, so far as Jean could tell, with the same merciless, impersonal, and accurate logic by which he tracked criminals and solved the most baffling of mysteries.

She returned the purse. "I don't seem to be doing so well," she commented with a trace of irritation.

FROST continued in his detached manner: "Do not let it worry you. Your method is correct, and if you carried it far enough you would arrive at the truth. Logic, whether inductive or deductive, can be one of the most powerful aids to the scientific investigator. It can also be a source of profound error and confusion when improperly used, or when employed without possession of all the facts. Logic is not only an aid to science. It is a science in itself.

"I told you I found the purse on the sidewalk. You began with the assumption that it had fallen from the arm of its owner. You then made other deductions which would have been true had the initial premise been true. But the starting point of your analysis should have been—how did the purse come to be lying on the sidewalk?"

"How else could it get there if it didn't fall? It certainly wasn't deliberately placed there."

"I did not say it did not fall. I merely challenged your assumption that it fell from its owner's arm: If you examine the end of the clasp closely, you will find it scraped and twisted. The gleam of the metal combined with the presence of a few embedded grains of concrete indicate that the dent is fresh and was caused by the purse falling with considerable force to the ground. The logical explanation is that it was accidentally knocked from a window ledge several stories above the sidewalk.

"In falling and striking, its contents became jumbled. Far from being a slovenly person, the owner was actually fastidious and possessed of great pride in her personal appearance and in the neatness of her belongings."

Explanations were easy, Jean thought, when Frost made them.

"Again," he went on, "your deduction that she was a woman of means and that she was on her way to a bank was incorrect. Obviously she could not have been on her way anywhere if the purse was dislodged from the window ledge of her apartment.

"You next determined that she must be wealthy because her belongings were costly. You thought she was on her way to a bank because she had no bills and only a few coins in her purse, but did have an uncashed check for one hundred dollars.

"Now, if you had examined the check carefully, you would have noticed that it was made out to 'Cash.' If you had thoroughly investigated the signature, you would have discovered that no such person as 'T. J. Williams' exists. The woman's initials, 'M. M.,' you of course noticed on her handkerchief.

"Husbands are not in the habit of signing fictitious names on checks for their wives; neither, as a rule, do they make out such checks to 'Cash.' The conclusions are inescapable that 'M. M.' was kept, that the valuable belongings were gifts, and that she had only such means as her friend allowed, through an account set up for safety's sake under a fictitious name. I will have the purse delivered to her to-morrow.

"Is there anything unusual in the paper?"

Jean tossed it on the table. "Just the usual run. Gangster killings, suicide pacts, a love murder. They haven't found a trace of the gang that got away with the four hundred and thirty-five thousand dollars haul at the Midtown Bank yesterday. Nothing that sounds as exciting as the case of the Green Man, or even the Golden Goblin affair. Do you suppose we shall ever hear anything more about that?"

"Possibly. Joe Blake and the remnants of his gang are still loose," Frost replied in a perfunctory voice. "That was a clever raid on the Midtown. While crowds gathered at the fire a block away, the gang entered the Midtown, scooped up the cash, and got away without a shot being fired. They took the teller at the R-Z window with them. The fire, of course, was incendiary."

"That's what the fire and insurance investigators announced tonight. But to return to the raid, the police have given up hope of finding the kidnaped cashier alive. They think he was slain to prevent his identifying the criminals."

"Or to avoid giving him his share of the loot," Frost suggested.

Jean looked at him intently "You think he was in league with the gangsters?"

"At the angle of his cage, he could not have been shot from the point where the leader trained a submachine gun on the place. The teller in that particular cage could have ducked and set off the burglar alarm."

JEAN wondered about the professor's expression of returning boredom as he slouched from the laboratory. Only in the grip of some knotty or abstruse problem did his features light up.

From the amazing knowledge that he sometimes displayed in the most offhand manner, Jean guessed that pursuits of the pure intellect afforded him the stimulus that lesser men found in simpler ways. Yet she had not elicited a single item about his life, or obtained anything from him that he did not choose to give, or learned anything except what he allowed. His was as enigmatic a nature as that of the great stone Sphinx.

In the months that she had served as his assistant, she had discovered little even about his habits. He sometimes disappeared, leaving no clue to his destination when he left and volunteering no information when he returned days later. He had no detectable schedule. In the solving of strange and perplexing crimes, he went without food and sleep until he had answered the riddle, whether it took one day or three.

During these periods he appeared to subsist on nervous energy. The only stimulus he received at such times seemed to be the peculiar cigarettes that he smoked incessantly then, but never on other occasions. He made them himself. Jean did not know what they were or what he put into them.

Of what he thought, or how his mind worked, she knew absolutely nothing. When he chose to explain the steps and processes by which he arrived at his deductions, they seemed surprisingly obvious. But when he did not explain, she floundered in darkness. She felt, with unreasonable irritation, that she would never penetrate beyond his external appearance.

For all his indifference to what he wore, his striking but unlovely aspect, the long, lank figure of the professor possessed an extraordinary fascination.

She could not specify or isolate even this quality—whether it came from his personality, or from his latent power and his inexhaustible reserves of nervous energy, or the hyperneurotic complexity of his nature, or from the compelling strength of his features.

The hatchet-thin face, with its high cheek bones and sharp features, its shaggy eyebrows, and the black eyes that on different occasions varied from a listless lackluster to a hypnotic intensity, had stamped itself indelibly on her memory the day she came. A strange man. A remarkable man. A personality more baffling and incomprehensible than any problem she had yet seen him solve.

A curious sound broke her chain of thought as she followed him from the laboratory.

An alarm clock was ringing stridently. She halted in surprise. The sound rasped from somewhere outside, buzzed through the partly open latticed windows, made a harsh undercurrent to the noise of late evening traffic. Why would an alarm clock be going off, apparently on the grounds of 13 State Street, at this hour of approximately eleven P.M.? Was it something for which Frost had been responsible? She watched him.

He had paused and listened intently for just the briefest of moments. The next instant, he plunged for the door faster than she had ever before seen him move. She raced after him.

THE DRONE of traffic swelled louder as Jean darted into the cool night air. The glow of the sky, the reflected glare of the city, the illumination from street lights, would have been more than enough even without the beam of the flashlight that Frost turned on the thing at his feet in the middle of the lawn.

Jean felt sick. She experienced a nausea in which revulsion and horror and pity left her weak. For once in her life, she could have done without all the light on earth. The buzz of the alarm clock came with sinister harshness while it was running down. And neither the alarm clock nor the noise of traffic could drown out the indescribable bubbling bleat that issued from the man on the lawn.

Dark blood spouted from his severed hands and feet. It crept from the raw stubs of his ears. It dribbled from his tongueless mouth. His inarticulate, writhing agony became more dreadful because no pain could be expressed by his eyes. There were only gaping sockets where his eyes had been. An alarm clock, tied to the victim's waist, lay face up on the ground.

Jean's hand flew to her mouth. She bit a white, clenched knuckle to stifle a scream.

The hands of the clock pointed to five minutes to twelve. The significance was hideous. The tortured man had only five minutes to live—five minutes to die. A challenge to Frost had been flung at his doorstep for reasons unknown, by persons unknown. Was it a gesture of brutal contempt? How could any one, even Frost, extract information from a deaf, dumb, blind, limbless, dying man with less than five minutes to live?

II.

FROST snapped, in a voice harsh and cold: "Search the grounds for any possible clue."

He knelt and in one continuous motion scooped the alarm clock on the dying man's chest, lifted the body, and hurried toward his laboratory. Gouts of blood dribbled to the ground. The dying man's head lolled, rolled feverishly. The blood bubbled and frothed on his lips, clotted in his ears, bathed his sockets with ebbing life. His wordless gurgle held a more awful and sickening plea than any shriek Jean had ever heard.

In the faint light—or was it an illusion or distortion of her overwrought nerves?—Frost's features took on an expression of stern, implacable, and relentless purpose. Yet even now, in the presence of a gruesome crime, Frost's reaction seemed less emotional than rational; as if the laws of reason had been violated, so that the ultimate resources of mind, the acid bite of logic, must be summoned to restore the true pattern of things. And while wondering what demons they were who had flung this wreckage at Frost's door, Jean experienced a shudder at the thought of the fate awaiting them if Frost caught up with them.

His long, spectral form, bent from the weight of his burden, erased the distance to his laboratory in great strides.

With the flashlight that he had left, Jean began a systematic and minute search of the lawn, foot by foot, in an ever-widening circle around the spot where the body had been found. She hunted for footprints, for crushed blades of grass, for cigarette butts, scraps of paper, anything that might prove helpful.

She found only Frost's and her own footprints, and one curious fact. There were glistening drops of blood in a line extending away from the spot and toward the sidewalk. The last of the splashes was approximately eight feet from the stained area where the body had rested. The sidewalk was twenty feet distant. But the grass was not trampled at any point between the body and the sidewalk.

How had the drops of blood come there, in that line extending from the body? It was incredible that the man had threshed around in such a fashion that a trail of blood had been flung out in a singularly straight line. Why did the trail end or begin at that particular point? If it marked the direction from which the stranger had come, why were there no signs of his struggle? And if others had brought him, why were there no footprints?

By what agency had he arrived, and why? What sinister purpose lay behind his mutilation? How could even Frost, in spite of his immense resources, solve this riddle, unravel the mystery of the tortured stranger, and bring the guilty to justice?

Jean's exhaustive survey of the grounds revealed no clues. With a last swing of the flashlight, she abandoned further search and returned to the house.

Frost had just emerged from the laboratory. He carried a valise. His expression was inscrutable. By the long, pungently aromatic cigarette that he smoked, Jean knew he had found a crime worthy of his attention. The hunt was on. Wherever it might lead, into whatever danger it might hurl them, there would never be a moment's let-up in Frost's remorseless pursuit.

"Remain here until I return or until you hear from me," he commanded as he strode toward the cellar garage. "Did you find any clues?"

"No. No footprints, nothing. The only suspicious fact was a trail of blood extending from the spot toward the upper sidewalk for about eight feet. The man—"

"Died a few minutes after I brought him in."

Jean's face fell. "Then there is nothing to go on," she said in a disappointed tone.

Frost flatly contradicted her: "On the contrary, there is a great deal to go on. I know his identity, why he was mutilated, where he lived, how he came here, why he was brought, and who is responsible."

Jean looked incredulous. "Did he carry all that information with him?"

"His pockets had been emptied and every mark of identification removed."

"But you said—how in the world could—"

Frost cut her short, and stated calmly: "I obtained the information I needed from the man himself before he died."

Jean burst out: "But he could not talk! He could not hear or see or write! He—"

The door closed on Frost's departing figure. Behind him he left a bewildered assistant who floundered around in mental dead-ends in a hopeless attempt to visualize the magic by which Frost elicited all the information he wanted from a tongueless, earless, eyeless, limbless, dying man.

Frost climbed into his car. Driving out of his garage, he turned north on Broadway. He watched in the mirror the headlights of a sedan that swung along behind. Sometimes he speeded up for short bursts, sometimes he drifted along at twenty or thirty miles an hour. The sedan kept pace a block behind him.

The professor settled into a more comfortable position. He drove toward upper Manhattan, his eyes occasionally flicking to the mirror to watch the trailing sedan. He made no effort to elude it, and it made no attempt to overtake him. A bleak, mirthless smile hovered on his features. He smoked one cigarette after another.

He turned into West 180th Street. He stopped in front of a cheap apartment building. The sedan sidled to the curb, still a block behind.

Frost entered the vestibule and punched a button marked "E. L. Troff." The latch clicked almost immediately.

THE PROFESSOR climbed one flight and rapped on the door of apartment 2C. A lock turned and the door opened cautiously.

"Who are you? What do you want?"

A worried-looking woman in her passing thirties faced him. She was plain-faced and a bit plump. She looked like the average, middle-class housewife. Though midnight had passed, she was fully dressed.

"I came to talk to you about your husband."

"I've already told the police all I know."

"I am Professor I.V. Frost, a private investigator. I have been drawn into the case. I can and will help you."

Frost was halfway in when the woman said: "Come in."

The professor did not sit down.

"Do you know where Everett is? Have they found him?" the woman asked anxiously.

Frost did not reply directly. "We are on the trail. Can you tell me offhand who some of his best friends were?"

The woman rattled off several names. Frost listened idly until she named "Ganther."

"The former district attorney?" he interrupted.

"Yes. It was mostly his recommendation that got Everett the job."

"Let me use your telephone."

Frost reached the instrument without waiting for a reply and dialed a number. A full minute passed before the intermittent buzz in the receiver was broken.

"Who is it? What do you want? What do you mean by disturbing a man's sleep at this hour of the night?" an irate voice exploded.

"Frost calling."

"Oh! Why didn't you say so? Where have you been hiding all these months? Get a fellow out of bed at this hour. You ought to be ashamed of yourself. What are you up to? Where are you? Why don't you say something?"

Frost wore an amused expression. "What's your opinion of Everett Lucius Troff?"

"Did you phone just to ask me that? Are you on the case? What the devil difference does it make? Where are you? Have you—"

"What do you think of Troff?"

"Don't believe a word of it. Can't trust the papers nowadays. Everett's a fine fellow. One of the best. I got him that job. I'll stake my reputation on him. It's a lot of stuff and nonsense. It's—"

Frost broke in: "I merely asked. The papers say he was kidnaped. Why spring to his defense when he is under no suspicion?"

"You should ask me that. You wouldn't be calling if his name was clear. Where is he? What have you found? Anything I can do? Why—"

"You'll get the details later. Right now you need the rest of that sleep you were sputtering about."

When he hung up, Mrs. Troff, who had been anxiously listening to his side of the conversation, stammered: "Everett—do you know—is he—"

Frost replied, gently: "I cannot say. If he has not been heard from before this, I would be prepared for bad news."

The woman, dull-eyed, despondent, sank into a chair as Frost left.

The hall was clear. He went down the rear stairway to the back entrance of the building. He studied the dark areaway. After a moment, he slowly and silently opened the door and put a wedge under it.

Flattened against the wall, he waited while minutes dragged. A cat meowed. A rat scampered in the black shadows. The sound of faint breathing came from beyond the door.

Frost struck first and eased the inert body to the ground. One look at the thug's face sufficed. The professor handcuffed the killer's hands to his ankles behind his back.

Swiftly crossing the areaway, Frost entered the building opposite and emerged in 179th Street. He headed for Broadway where he hailed the first cab he saw.

A few blocks downtown, he halted at an all-night restaurant. His first telephone call went through to the night desk of police headquarters.

"Let me speak to Inspector Frick. . . . Hello, Frick? . . . Frost calling. Will you take a couple of men and meet me at the Midtown Bank? . . . No. I'm merely doing some investigating. The bank will be opened by its president, in our presence. Time is important. It might be too late if we waited till morning. . . . Fine! In three quarters of an hour."

He dialed another number. "Tell Mr. Stafford that Professor I. V. Frost is on the phone." Frost listened. His voice hardened. "Tell Mr. Stafford that Frost wants to speak to him. Now."

A long pause. Then, "Yes?" came a noncommittal answer.

"Professor I.V. Frost speaking. I—"

A suave voice interrupted: "Sorry, but you must have made a mistake. I have not the pleasure of—"

Frost drawled: "You will have, within an hour."

The suave voice sounded hostile: "I am not accustomed to being disturbed by strangers at this hour. You may speak to my secretary in the—"

"The police are waiting for us at your bank. I am working with them on the Midtown Bank robbery. As president of the bank, you will be there in three quarters of an hour to open it in our presence."

"But I'm—"

"Then get dressed."

"But I haven't—"

"Get the keys. Be there in three quarters of an hour. We appreciate your coöperation," Frost sardonically finished.

He glanced at his watch. Returning to the cab, he ordered: "Drive slowly uptown."

He peered out of the window as the cab rolled along. At 180th Street, he suddenly commanded: "Turn left here."

THE SEDAN was gone. Frost's car stood where he had left it. Making sure that the street was clear, he dismissed the cab. He entered the vestibule of the apartment building again. The glass of the front door had been shattered over the knob. Frost shrugged his shoulders and departed.

After a quick inspection of his car for bombs, Frost drove downtown. On his way, he stopped at the same restaurant to call headquarters again.

"Has Inspector Frick left yet? . . . Let me speak to him. . . . Frost calling. There is the body of a murdered man in West 180th Street. . . ."

The professor talked for a minute. He then drove leisurely toward central Manhattan, his shaggy brows frowning while he hunched low in his seat. The air in the car became thick from the fumes of his odd cigarettes. Whatever stimulus they gave showed in the brightness of his eyes and in his deceptively dreamy expression.

A squad car already waited at the curb in front of the Midtown Bank when he arrived. A wiry, crisp little man with a military carriage bounced out of the car.

"Hello, Frost, glad to see you again. What's the news on the stiff? When did you find him?"

"I didn't find him."

"What the heck! You called in, didn't you?"

"On my way to that address an hour ago, I was trailed by a sedan. It parked a block behind me. It was supposed to be curtains for me when I came out. They planted the man in the rear entrance, just in case. I left by the rear entrance and knocked him out. I left him handcuffed. After calling you the first time, I went back to get my car. The sedan was gone. The glass in the front door of the building was knocked in. You know the rules in Blake's gang—the penalty of failure is death. I didn't need to go back to the areaway."

A car drew up behind them. A huffy gentleman emerged. He wore impeccable clothes. His face was of the bland, confident kind that makes small depositors believe that God's in His heaven and all's well with the world of banking.

He greeted Inspector Frick politely and bowed coldly to Frost. The professor eyed him searchingly and lighted another cigarette. Frick sniffed dubiously. He started to speak, but held his words.

Frost looked up at the burglar alarm. He drove his car onto the sidewalk underneath it. Vaulting to the top of his car, he stood up and removed the alarm casing. With the aid of a flashlight, he inspected the mechanism.

Leaving the casing off, he dropped to the sidewalk.

"What's the idea of that?" Frick asked.

"I'm going to test the alarm, without making any more racket than necessary." To Stafford, he suggested: "Now open the doors."

The squad-car men kept guard outside while Frost, Stafford, and Frick entered the bank. Stafford threw a light switch, and the floor sprang into desolate clarity—long marble aisles, deserted cages, untenanted desks. The bank, by night, seemed only less dismal than a tomb.

"Which was Troff's cage?" Frost demanded.

Stafford pointed out the teller's window.

"And where did the first gunman issue orders?"

Frick took a position. "Right about here, from what the witnesses said."

Frost studied the two spots. He walked over to the teller's cage and stood inside, facing an imaginary line of depositors. He faced the door. Then he turned his attention to the burglar alarm, worked by foot pressure, that jutted from the floor of the cage. He pressed it. The mechanism outside whirred. If the casing had been on, there would have been a terrific clangor.

"If I hadn't fixed it up at headquarters, the place would be swarming with radio cars right now," Frick remarked, with an element of pride at the efficiency of the service.

Frost halted the alarm, tried it out a couple of times. With a thoughtful look, he knelt by the foot button. He took a couple of instruments from his valise and dismantled the object. Lifting the top part off, he stared down. With a few swift motions, he made some adjustments and then replaced the top part.

He rose, holding an innocent-looking metal-and-composition gadget, with a couple of springs on it. "Here is the answer."

Frick and Stafford inspected it curiously.

"What in blazes is it?" Frick asked, frowning.

"A simple type of interference spring, with an automatic catch so that it locks after one shift."

Stafford wrinkled his forehead. "I do not quite follow you."

Frost explained: "When the floor button was pressed, with this thing under it, the button pushed against the composition. The composition is a nonconductor. The burglar alarm would not ring. But when pressure was released, this spring automatically pulled the metal part into position and locked at the same time. The metal being a conductor of electricity, the alarm would go off every occasion thereafter."

Light dawned on Frick. "How long would it take to install the thing?"

"Anywhere from two to ten minutes, depending on the skill of the workman."

Frick asked Stafford: "Would it be possible, during banking hours, for the teller in the cage to install this thing without attracting attention?"

Stafford nodded slowly, with grave features. "I am sorry to agree, it would be entirely possible."

Frick pocketed the gadget. To Frost, he stated: "It looks bad for Troff. He installs this, makes a phony play at pushing the alarm and goes through a phony kidnaping. He splits with them and lights out, or he turns up in a day or two, goes back on the job, and takes the gadget out when he has time. But the chances are he's flown, with his share of the split."

"It sounds possible," Frost admitted.

"I wouldn't have believed it." Stafford shook his head ruefully. "And now, if you gentlemen have finished your business—"

Outside, after Stafford had left, Frick said, with a note of genuine regret: "The force could use you, Frost. Any time you wish, you can just about name your own position and pick your own cases."

"The police are efficient. I prefer freedom of action and the use of my own methods."

"You find out things that even we don't know, Frost. Any time you need us, call me at headquarters. Good luck!"

The squad car moved off.

THE HUM of the city was at its low ebb. Skyscrapers and gigantic buildings raised their dark towers to the always faintly luminous sky. At infrequent intervals, a lone passerby hurried on his way. From time to time a car roared down the wide avenue. The pulse of life never wholly ceased in the great metropolis, but it had become as quiet as it ever was.

Seated in his car, the professor opened the valise and made some quick changes. They took but a minute. When he had finished, he drove uptown.

He had not gone two blocks, and was still gathering speed, when a tire blew out. Frost did not seem in the least surprised, as he eased the car to the curb. He climbed out and surveyed the damage.

"Stick 'em up!" snarled a harsh voice.

Frost's hands rose slowly as he turned. Out of the black shadows of doorways emerged two men with submachine guns. A sedan streaked to a halt in front of Frost's car.

"Get in!" barked the leader.

Another submachine gun poked its ugly muzzle through a window to emphasize the command.

"You aren't afraid of me, by any chance, are you?" Frost ironically asked. "By the way, did you know that army officials figure one machine gun as equal to the attacking power of two hundred troops? I believe I see three submachine guns."

The leader viciously jabbed a gun in his back. "In, or you'll get it here!"

Frost entered, a strange, tight smile on his features. The car picked up speed, roared north.

III.

THEY were rats. They looked like rats. Behind a spitting submachine gun, they could be brave. They could even be brave if they merely had a sawed-off shotgun to train on an unarmed man. They were brave now. Did not a man sit on each side of Frost with muzzles aimed at him? Did not a third killer keep him covered point-blank from the front seat? They were taking him for a ride, and the driver's foot stepped with relish on the accelerator.

"Pull those side curtains down!" barked the leader. "We don't want any dumb cops lookin' in."

The curtains were drawn. The car shot on toward the outskirts of the city.

"The great Ivy Frost goin' for a ride!" jeered the swarthy killer on his right. "Just another fall guy."

The professor made no reply. He sat still, hands folded, the strange, enigmatic smile still on his face.

"Wipe that grin off your mug!" the swarthy gangster growled with an angry prod.

"Cut it out!" the leader curtly ordered. "It's the last chance he'll ever have to smile at anything."

"Let's give it to him here."

"Orders are orders. He'll keep."

The car roared on, and still Frost sat with that puzzling, mirthless expression, as if he enjoyed some huge joke. His lips were tightly compressed. He seemed to have a little difficulty breathing through his nose. The car streaked out of the city limits and off to a little-traveled road.

"Bulletproof clothes, huh? They don't help much when your mug gets riddled. Won't talk, huh? You don't need to. You're never gonna talk again. Ivy Frost takin' a ride like any punk," the swarthy rat mocked.

The car wabbled.

"Keep your eyes on the road, Sam!" clipped the leader.

The driver shook his head, muttered: "Aw, what's eatin' ya? Can't miss all the bumps."

The swarthy man jabbed Frost again. "So you were gonna find out what happened to Troff, huh? Save your time. We'll tell you. We did the job. Anything else you'd like to know?"

The car lurched wildly.

"Say, I got a headache," moaned the man on the left.

"What the hell!" muttered the leader. His voice was thick. His eyes had a peculiar look.

The expression on Frost's face did not change. His features were rigid. There was something almost unearthly in his bearing and implacably menacing in his silence.

The swarthy killer opened his mouth to speak and talked incoherent syllables. The gangster at Frost's left moved a hand to his collar, but the gesture was listless. The driver suddenly slumped in his seat and his hands slipped off the wheel. The car lost momentum, skidded crazily out of control. The leader made no protest, no effort to seize control. The gun fell from his hands. His head lolled. His dying eyes stared with a look of reproach into Frost's glittering black pupils.

And now the professor bent forward with a swift motion and grasped the steering wheel. The driver did not stir. The leader had slumped beside him. The man to the left of Frost sat hunched over, head and knees on the floor. The dark-faced rat tried to keep the submachine gun trained on Frost, but he had trouble holding it. It wabbled around. His finger hung on the trigger, but the finger was nerveless. His jaw sagged. He gaped at Frost with dull bewilderment and strove to rise. He lurched and slid dizzily to the floor, gasping.

Tight-lipped, the mirthless smile gone like a prophecy the meaning of which the killers would never know, now, Frost straightened the car and guided it till it came to rest. The motor choked and died. As coolly as if he was completing a common experiment, the scientist stooped, shifted the gears from high to neutral, and pressed the starter. The motor idled.

With swift, expert fingers, so nimble that they seemed possessed of a life of their own, Frost searched the four gangsters. His nostrils quivered and his breathing was slow.

The pockets of the four yielded large sums in bills which he inspected briefly and stuffed in his coat. He glanced at papers and memoranda, but did not keep them, and did not take time to copy even the important numbers he observed.

He left the car, motor still idling, and shut the door. The moment he emerged, he gulped a deep, satisfying breath of air, and for some minutes, as he strode along the rutty road to the main highway, he enjoyed the night air with keen zest. His gaunt, spectral figure, striding down the lonely road, would in itself, and by its forbidding nature, have been defense enough against most mortal assaults.

Fifteen minutes brought him to the highway. A pair of headlights streaked toward him. He planted himself in the middle of the road and hailed it. The car sped on. When hardly a dozen yards distant, its brakes squealed, it veered sharply, and accelerated. Frost made a flying leap to the running board as it attempted to pass him.

A white-faced driver cringed, slammed on the brakes. "D-d-d-don't shoot. I-I-I was only foolin'."

"Drive on!" Frost briefly ordered as he climbed in. "I merely want a lift. I'm on police business."

The fat-faced driver did not seem much reassured. He glanced doubtfully at his newly acquired passenger. "Going far, mister? I'm kind of in a hurry, and you see, the way you jumped on, I thought—"

"I'll tell you when to let me off," Frost silenced the man. Volunteering no further explanations, he maintained an air of abstraction until they entered the city limits.

"I live in the Bronx," the driver began.

Frost looked out. "All right. Let me off here."

The stranger, relieved, did not wait to accept the bill Frost was fishing for, but drove off in a remarkable hurry.

The professor entered a restaurant and telephoned his own private number. There was no answer. He hung up, tried again. Still no answer.

He frowned and dialed the listed number of his assistant. Still no answer. He tried a different number, and this time got a reply.

"J.V.? Frost calling."

THE SLEEPY voice of John Vogel, an old friend and his personal attorney, answered plaintively: "Don't you ever sleep?"

"This is urgent, J.V."

"Everything you do is urgent. I wish my life was as exciting."

"Try the television set and see if you can get any response from my house."

Protracted silence. Frost deftly flipped a cigarette from deep down in a pocket, produced a match, and lighted it, in a continuous movement born of long habit, with one hand.

Vogel's voice at last came through, "There's no answer and I can't get anything on the screen."

"I expected as much. As soon as possible in the morning find out and send these over—the serial numbers of any or all bills known to have been taken in the Midtown Bank robbery; the market quotations on Midtown stock for the past two weeks; the credit rating of Stafford, and whatever else you can dig up about his financial affairs."

Hurrying out, Frost took the first cab available. "State Street and Riverside Drive. As fast as you can make it!" he flung at the driver.

The car shot downtown, clipping through light changes, screeching around curves and corners. Frost brooded, but the driver, occasionally glancing into his mirror, was unable to tell what went on behind the inscrutable expression of his fare.

The driver wasn't sure he wanted to know what those thin, sharp features concealed. He felt, on the whole, that he would not even care to make an issue of a tip. There was something about the passenger that made him leery. He had handled tough birds and hard customers in his time, but never one with quite the peculiar character of Frost, or one who proved so difficult to size up. He would be a bad one to tangle with.

"Quite right," Frost spoke aloud, and lapsed back into silence.

Badly shaken, the driver pushed his cab for all it was worth. As a rule, he didn't care much one way or another about fares, but he was damned glad to beat it after dropping Frost.

The professor melted into the shadows along the inner sidewalk, and faded into the grounds of the house at 15 State Street. Moving warily, his keen eyes probing every place of concealment, he crossed to the grille fence inclosing No. 13. He went through a section that suddenly opened at his touch.

No. 13 was dark. Satisfied that no one watched him, he crossed the lawn, stepped lightly across the driveway, and stopped at an ornamental pillar on the side of the porch.

Again he listened intently before touching the pillar. It opened noiselessly and revealed a compact mechanism. From a tray at the bottom, he lifted several wet films which he studied by holding them against a tiny red bulb set in the mechanism.

The first negative showed two masked men crouching on each side of the door. A third man, erect, unmasked, had one foot forward toward the opening door.

The second negative showed both masked men still crouching. The door was closed. The next film showed both entering. The fourth was merely a picture of the doorway. The fifth outlined the two masked men emerging. They carried the body of Jean Moray, who might have been unconscious or dead. The sixth was another blank.

The seventh negative showed four husky thugs carrying a huge crate. Number eight blank, on number nine the four were coming out empty-handed. Ten blank, eleven saw the same four entering with smaller parcels. Twelve was a blank, but thirteen indicated four of the gang leaving. The last film was a blank.

Eyes narrowed, face drawn into tight, hard lines, Frost dropped the wet films back in the tray. He tore off a strip of paper from a spool. It was stamped with figures that ranged from 12:58 to 1:33 in fourteen separate notations.

Jean Moray had been kidnaped between 12:58 and 1:33 A.M. by a gang numbering at least five persons.

IV.

FROST straightened. From the upper compartment of the pillar, he lifted a small earpiece with one hand and pulled out a tiny disk with the other. He pressed two buttons almost simultaneously.

"Drop the gun and throw up your hands!" he ordered in a low voice.

He listened, heard nothing. He replaced the items and closed a power switch, before sliding the movable section so that the pillar looked as innocent as before.

Speed now marking every action, he vaulted over the porch railing and reached the door in a few strides. He whipped an automatic from his coat. He inserted a key and turned it with his left hand. He shoved the door open and kept his automatic trained into the brightly lighted hall.

The heavy brute stared up. He gave a last tug at his gun that lay curiously immovable on the floor. The gun slid only a fraction of an inch. The killer scrambled to his feet, face working, hand streaking to his pocket. It all happened in fractions of time, but Frost, slouching outside, a sardonic twist on his face, did not fire.

"Hands up and come out," he threatened, "or I shoot!"

The ugly one made a final, desperate tug at his second weapon. He could not seem to budge it from his pocket. His eyes bulged. Sweat popped out on his forehead.

He gave up and marched forward as commanded, his features twitching. Frost turned him around and handcuffed him.

"Get inside."

The killer entered. As Frost followed and closed the door, he clicked a button. He removed the captive's second gun. He walked over and picked up the fallen weapon.

The gangster's eyes stared. He ran his tongue over dry lips. His face had the sickly color of old cabbage. His mouth twitched, and the muscles of his throat corded. Frost strode toward him.

The prisoner's voice broke out: "Whatcha gonna do? Whatcha gonna do? I ain't done nothin'! Honest, I ain't done nothin'! I'll talk! Lemme go an' I'll tell ya all ya wanna know. I'll tell ya where the girl is! I'll—"

Frost's words cut like lashes: "Shut up! You can tell me nothing that I do not already know."

The captive shrank unnerved against the wall. He could face any human opponent. With gun in hand, he could meet any ordinary emergency. But he had waited in darkness, waited for hours, with those other things all around, until his nerves got fidgety, and nothing happened.

Then the hallway had been mysteriously flooded with light. From the walls, the ceiling, nowhere, came a muffled voice commanding him to drop his gun. As he peered around in amazement, the gun was suddenly torn from his hands with a terrific jerk. He dived for it, but could no more lift it than he could have budged the Statue of Liberty. And even while his wits, trained in the gutter school of crime, tried to fathom events wholly beyond his comprehension, the door opened, and it seemed to his panicky gaze that a nightmare had become real.

The prisoner cowered against the wall. His handcuffed hands clawed. He cringed, knew the terror of silence. Frost came on, wordless. The criminologist taped his captive's lips, shackled his feet, and left him lying on the floor.

Then he spoke: "You'll have plenty of time to think things over, Squinty. When I want you to talk—talk!"

Ignoring the gangster, Frost faced the door of his library and studied it speculatively, as if debating a problem. He walked toward it. "Squinty's" eyes took on a momentary crafty gleam, then went white with terror.

Frost laid his automatic on a table. He broke the chamber and extracted the first bullet. He roughened its nose and smeared it with some paste that he took from a vial in his pocket. He replaced the cartridge.

Gun in hand, he stooped by the soundproof door to his library. Squinty twisted and squirmed on the floor. A weird, nasal moan shrilled from his nostrils, and blood trickled from his torn lips as he tried to open his mouth to scream.

But Frost flung the door wide, pressed the light switch on the wall within, and threw himself flat on the floor. The entire motion was completed in a second.

The panther sprang, eyes blazing. It sailed overhead with a mad snarl. Frost fired from the floor. The bullet tore into the great cat's neck. It landed in the hallway and for a split second glared at Squinty. The helpless thug quivered in the paralysis of horror.

The beast whirled and leaped savagely at Frost. But the professor had whipped into his library and flattened himself against the wall inside the door.

The jungle cat, its leap oddly short for its power and the fury to kill in its hunger-maddened eyes, sprawled on the rug, pawed crazily, and spun around. A scream poured from its throat. It shook and tried to leap. It went limp after a last contortion in a death agony.

The professor inspected the carcass. Even in death, the giant cat was a thing of beauty, in its own sleek, savage fashion.

In Frost's harsh features was no sign of relief or surprise as he walked to the door of his laboratory.

HURLING it open, he switched on the light and dashed to a wall panel. He closed a control. The hum of a powerful air-conditioner arose. The stagnant, chemical-sodden air stirred and cool drafts circulated. Still holding his breath, Frost paused just long enough to grasp an empty bottle and stopper it before racing from the laboratory. Ten minutes would allow an ample margin of safety.

The rear entrance to his house led to the kitchen, from which also led the stairs to his basement garage. The kitchen could be reached both through the laboratory and from the hall. Conserving time, Frost returned to the hallway. Squinty Maginess' eyes rolled, still wide with the unnerving terror that had swept him when the panther seemed ready to pounce.

Frost, every movement exhibiting the calculation characteristic of the scientist who tackles a problem to which only one solution is ultimately possible, walked to one of the doors beside a stone Buddha. Its fat face had a placid smile.

The door, unlocked as he had left it hours ago, yielded readily to his shove. He pushed the light switch. His eyes probed into corners and nooks, studied every inch of floor, walls, and ceiling. He took a step forward.

From under a cabinet, something small and coral streaked like a flame. Before its venomous head struck, it was buried under the folds of the garment that Frost dropped. Methodically he trampled on the cloth, crushed the writhing snake into pulp.

Out of the radiator coils ran something tiny, black, and hairy. Sprayed by the liquid pump that Frost turned upon it, it was dead before it reached him. Its mate never left the coils into which he wafted death.

One task remained in the process of repossessing his house—the most dangerous task of all. They were innocent-looking parcels that rested, precariously balanced, on horizontal wooden laths that had been nailed to the jamb of the cellar door and the outside kitchen door. The strips of wood jutted halfway across the door. Had the door been pushed even slightly open—

Frost gingerly lifted the parcels, one at a time. He carried them outdoors. Nothing was ever handled more gently. Darkness still remained, though dawn was not far distant. Picking his way carefully, avoiding every possible tripping point with unerring accuracy, the professor set his parcels in the middle of the lawn behind his house.

Using a shaded flashlight, he unwrapped the parcels with sensitive fingers. After a painstaking study of its construction, he dismantled one box. The second parcel proved less difficult. It contained a bottle. This he opened, tilted, and let the yellowish fluid seep gradually into the ground. He had completed a task as deadly as it was simple.

Returning inside the house, he tore off the wooden strips. Then he lighted a cigarette and inhaled deeply. His eyes glittered.

For some minutes, he was busy collecting things. A trail of pungent smoke swirled after him. He made a detailed examination of all rooms. A half hour later, in the gray of coming dawn, he lowered himself to an easy-chair in his library and surveyed a remarkable assemblage.

These specimens comprised: one Squinty Maginess, alive; one panther, dead; a large, iron-barred cage, and its crate; a coral snake, dead; a small wire-mesh cage, and its crate; two black-widow spiders, defunct; a tiny wooden box with perforations in the lid; a heavy metal container that had once held gas under pressure; one stoppered bottle with a sample of cyanide gas; parts of a dismantled dynamite bomb; a bottle to which only a bare trace of nitroglycerin adhered; fourteen wet films; a piece of tape on which fourteen time indications were stamped; eighty-seven thousand dollars in bills; the shrouded corpse of a mutilated man; and a couple of automatic revolvers with silencers.

To these might be added the cards on each of the crates, which merely bore the stenciled address: "To Professor I.V. Frost, 13 State St." On a sheet of paper, Frost jotted the significant numbers he had seen among pocket memoranda of four gangsters who had raised no objection to his search.

"They are an interesting lot, aren't they?" he remarked to Squinty. "Remember what you have just seen. Think hard about what might happen to you. And when I tell you to talk—talk!"

V.

FOR HOURS, Frost sat in a reverie. The captive's eyes were closed. Frost seemed unaware of his presence. He smoked incessantly. The air grew hazy. The ash trays overflowed with butts. Ashes sprinkled his jacket, his old corduroy trousers, littered the floor. He looked dreamy, almost benign, and quite without worry. If anything, so far as observable, his features expressed the same detached air, the same attitude of serene contemplation, that was chiseled on the marble bust of Socrates upon a pedestal at one end of the library.

Occasionally the professor shifted into an easier position, but always with his legs doubled up on an ottoman.

If the mysterious appearance by mysterious means of a dying man outside his house caused him any perplexity, it did not show. If the pursuit of the black sedan and the episode of the waylayer waylaid in a building on 180th Street were cause for speculation, no one could have guessed.

If the ride that ended in death, but not for the intended victim, motivated whatever plans he had, he gave no indication of it. If the kidnaping of Jean Moray, or her subsequent fate, commanded his attention, only he knew it. And he must already have dismissed from his calculations, so Squinty thought, these recent occurrences in his house, since the professor plainly took no notice of the considerable array of objects around him.

The telephone rang. It was not yet seven o'clock. Frost reached out a slim hand and lifted the instrument.

"Frost? Thank Heaven!" came the relieved voice of Inspector Frick. "Your car was picked up on Fifth Avenue and I thought—"

Frost cut in sharply: "Let no one know that you have talked to me. Hold the car until I call for it. Do not give out any information. This is highly important. I'll call you later in the day."

The professor sank back in his chair and studied the long ash of his cigarette. He stretched for an ash tray. The ash fell to the floor. It was ever thus.

Fifteen minutes later, the phone ran again.

"What the hell!" exploded the voice of Inspector Frick. "We got a report from a guy in the sticks of a stranded car. And what do we find when we get there? Four stiffs and a note in one mug's lap, 'Call Frost immediately.' "

"Thanks for calling," the professor replied. "Can you keep it out of the papers for a couple of hours?"

Frick protested: "I'm going off duty at eight. How did four of Joe Blake's gang come to die way out there? And from what looks like carbon monoxide? Understand, we aren't shedding any tears, but just the same, there'll have to be some routine stuff."

"That can wait. Can you withhold the information from the court reporters and from the papers until ten o'clock? . . . Good! No; it isn't necessary, but if you're going to stay on the job I'll drop in around noon."

An hour passed. Squinty made a poor pretense of sleeping, but at last abandoned the effort.

A BELL tinkled. Frost sprang from the chair. In his laboratory, he closed a power switch. Minutes later, the round face of John Vogel blurred into the television screen and focused.

"Hello, Frost! I have the information you wanted."

The professor glanced at a clock. "You needn't have stayed up all night. Mid-morning would have been time enough."

"Yes," replied the senior partner of Vogel, Vogel & Brant, attorneys, "so you said. But your cases have a habit of ending rapidly the minute you possess all the facts. Here are the serial numbers of the bills." He read them off.

"Now, as for the price range of Midtown stock, it held steady all last week at thirty-one. On Monday it opened at thirty-one but spurted up to thirty-six. Tuesday it opened off, dropped to thirty, and on Wednesday slid to twenty-six where it has stayed since."

"Did you find any reason for the fluctuation?"

"Yes. The Midtown had applied for a government loan. There were rumors Monday that the loan had been approved, but after the market closed, it was announced that the loan would not be granted."

"Exactly!" Frost agreed.

"Eh? You knew this?"

"No; but it was the only theory that the facts could have fitted," Frost drawled.

Vogel floundered. "Don't you mean it the other way round? Theories fit facts, don't they?"

"Sometimes they do," Frost conceded. "But any fact, merely as such, is worthless. It has no value unless it bears a relation to some other fact. It has no meaning except in so far as it concerns other truths. The interpretation of facts, truths, and series of events is a matter of mind and logic, which analyze them and understand them in terms of ideas, concepts, or theories.

"Thus far, the process is inductive. But from there on, the light of pure, analytic, deductive logic comes into play. It must, or the facts never would have significance. Therefore I say, and agree with a celebrated English scientist and philosopher, that facts must be tested and proved by theory."

"Many an innocent man has died from a good theory." Vogel's eyes twinkled.

"Circumstantial evidence never yet convicted an innocent man; wrong interpretation of such evidence has, or failure to discover all the evidence has, but those miscarriages of justice are the fault of facts, not of theories, and the fault of incorrect or inferior reasoning. But let us save the discussion for an evening next week. I shall be finished with this case before then.

"You might drop into a pawnshop Tuesday afternoon and purchase a number of old trinkets. We shall use those things, those facts, to discover solely by logical analysis and deduction the one true theory that presents us with an understanding of their previous owner or owners, the habits and characteristics of those owners, and the reasons whereby the trinkets found their way to the pawnshop.

"But there is a matter that I must attend to this morning. What else did you find out?"

John Vogel complained: "Just when the discussion becomes exciting, you abandon it. Stafford, in a dummy account carried in the name of a friend, speculated heavily in Midtown stock, expecting a rise after the government loan. It was a complicated business involving some skullduggery. He lost heavily on the decline. His affairs were further complicated by the fact that his bank has made some questionable loans that might not stand investigation, and that he himself has a large indebtedness to meet to-day."

"Which he is ready to meet," Frost observed.

And John Vogel added wryly: "The facts appear to confirm your theory in every detail."

"You did an excellent job of obtaining valuable and not readily available information in a short time at unfavorable hours."

Vogel stated simply: "The legal and the medical professions have traditions pertaining to the confidences of clients. Those traditions can work for injustice as easily as for justice. There is only one living person to whom I would freely divulge everything I could, for I know that such information will be devoted only to the attainment of justice."

The face of John Vogel, bland and approving, faded from the screen when Frost and he cut off power from the duplicate transmitters.

VI.

THE ATTITUDE of repose sloughed from Frost like a discarded coat. The inactivity of hours vanished. The air of abstract meditation disappeared. In no single, definable, specific way did the change come. It was more than a matter of motion. It represented the difference between potential and kinetic energy.

The professor came out of the laboratory with a number of tools and appliances. He wore rubber gloves. The telephone received his concentrated attention for a few minutes. Testing the results, he found them wholly satisfactory.

Returning to the laboratory, he strode to a maze of switches, controls, screens, dials, and electrical equipment. He pressed a button and a small section of wall opened. Another, and the fat Buddha lost part of its anatomy. Another, and the front door swung open. Frost threw a switch. Satisfied with what he saw, he closed all portals.

Taking further instruments, he descended to the basement and worked for several minutes on the wiring of an electrical switchboard.

His task completed, he plowed through an accumulation of odds and ends from which he took a battered trunk. He carried it upstairs.

Walking to the front door, he pushed the bell button. The action accomplished, he returned to the library and put through another phone call.

"Let me speak to Mr. Ransome. . . . All right. I'll hold the wire." A minute passed. "Hello, Pete! Frost calling."

"Say, why'n hell didn't ya tell the dumb cluck it was you? I'd 'a' been here in two jiffs."

"Night school, as I have observed before, would, on the whole, improve your vocabulary, but, on the other hand, it would eliminate a certain picturesque quality indigenous to one phase of the American scene."

"That's swell, chief, but whaddaya mean? I don't get them six-bit words."

"Never mind, Pete. Can you get away for an hour or so with the truck? Just starting out? Good! I want you to stop at my house, 13 State Street, and pick up a trunk. When you arrive, do not ring the bell. You will find the door open. I shall be gone before you arrive. Remember, *do not ring the bell.* Walk in. A trunk is standing just inside the door. The address where it is to go will be on it. Close the door tightly as you leave and take the trunk straight to the address. Just leave it there. Is that clear? Repeat it."

The professor listened. "That's the idea." He looked at a clock. "It's nine twenty-five now. Can you manage to be here exactly at ten? Good! The envelope on top of the trunk is for you."

The gaunt figure of the criminologist vanished into the mysteries of his laboratory. When he emerged, with an assortment of objects, the hands of an ancient grandfather's clock stood at nine-forty.

Frost stood over the prisoner. "Squinty, I told you to talk when the time came. That time is now. Do precisely what I tell you, but say it in your own words."

He stripped the tape from Squinty's mouth with a deft motion. He unlocked the handcuffs. His eyes, inscrutable black slits, burned into the thug's. He toyed with an automatic.

"Now, listen carefully. The bullets in this gun are explosive. One false move, one change made from what I tell you, and you die in pieces."

Frost issued orders. Squinty moistened his lips. Frost finished: "And remember the password, 'Frost and thirteen.' "

Squinty's eyes, imbued with a brief crafty gleam, turned dull again. "O.K.," he mumbled. His right hand went shakily to the phone. He dialed a number.

Frost lifted the receiver of the duplicate phone he had just installed, and listened. He kept the gun point-blank on Squinty.

"It's Maginess. Lemme speak to the boss," the thug mouthed.

"It's about time you called. Hold the wire," a disagreeable voice snarled.

The line went dead. Frost aimed at the crook's face.

A soft voice slurred over the wire: "Yes?"

"Listen, boss, it's Squinty. I want—"

"Aren't you forgetting something?"

Frost's finger quivered.

Squinty hastily mumbled: "Frost and thirteen. I got 'im as he was comin' in just now. Nope; I dunno what took him so long. He was alone. He's out cold and sewed up."

Frost groaned through his nose.

"What was that?" the voice asked sharply.

"He's comin' to. I got 'im handcuffed and taped his mug just in case. Want me to finish the job?"

"If you do, you'll die the way Troff did, and it won't be pretty. Finishing Frost is a pleasure that's going to be all mine, understand? Stay there. I'll send four or five of the boys over. Don't pay any attention from now on to the phone or doorbell until they get there. Four short rings will be their signal."

The line went dead.

The criminologist snapped: "Now address this card as I tell you."

Frost glanced at the clock. Ten minutes to ten. It was nine minutes to ten when the gangster lay on the floor, more securely tied than before. The professor took the card and the items he had selected from the exhaustive stocks of his laboratory. He did not look back at Squinty, or the panther, or at any of the queer assortment of objects in the confusion of his library as he strode to the hallway door.

The gangster watched the door close. He was left alone with dead things, a musty animal odor, and air full of stale cigarette smoke that made him giddy.

VII.

PETE RANSOME stopped his truck in front of 13 State Street and lumbered up the sidewalk. He was a tremendous person. He had a bull neck, a flat nose, and crazy ears. He had been a prize fighter once, until he got in a jam. He had been framed on a murder charge, but a guy named Frost had proved that Pete simply did not have brains enough to commit murder by the use of spoiled antitoxin serum. Pete always admired him for that.

Pete thumped up the steps and across the porch, and was about to jab the bell when he remembered Frost's instructions: "Do not ring the bell." He pushed the door open.

A battered old trunk stood in the hallway. A heathen idol squatted in a niche at the end of the hall. A nutty piece of junk. There was an envelope on the trunk. It contained ten ten-dollar bills. The card tacked on the trunk read: "From I.V. Frost, To Oversea Export Co., 227 Front St." The trunk was so worn that part of the lock had gone.

Pete shouldered it and plowed out. What was it the brainy guy had said? "Be sure to close the door." Pete pulled it shut with a bang and without bothering to set the trunk down.

His delivery route lay in another direction, but Pete drove the truck south. A big car with some tough-looking customers swung into State Street as Pete turned the corner.

"I'd hate to have those guys sore at me," he thought.

He cut across town and headed down the East Side. He passed Fourteenth Street and ran through slum districts where the streets swarmed with dirty brats. The air was full of exhaust fumes, the stench of refuse and litter, food smells.

Driving through the tenement section, Pete swung over to Front Street, almost at the East River, and followed it toward the tip of the island.

No. 227 proved to be a dingy place with windows so covered with grime that Pete could see nothing inside. The building had not been painted since the year one. It was only three stories high. If it had been four, it would have collapsed. The gilt letters on the window had long ago faded, and some had peeled off entirely, but the legend was still plain—"Oversea Export Co." in a half moon over the numerals "227."

Hardly anybody was around. Most of the buildings in this section had gone to ruin and were deserted. All were run-down. They had a depressing effect, though the roar of traffic surged loud only a couple of blocks away. Pete climbed out. He took the trunk and shouldered his way in through a filthy door that creaked.

It was a dim, musty room that he entered, a small room that had once been an office. Paper peeled off the walls in scabby splotches. The floor was bare. Dust lay around. Some rickety chairs and the wreckage of a desk might have been discarded by the last tenants.

A pasty-faced tough got up with cold, venomous eyes. "What the hell you doing here?"

"I got orders to deliver this. Here it is." Pete dropped the trunk and turned to leave.

"Who's it from? Wait a sec, guy." The pale tough looked at the address card, scowled. "From Frost? That guy is poison. Squinty's writing. Come on, punk; march upstairs and tell it to the boss."

Pete hesitated.

The evil-looking one yelped, clapped a hand to his neck. "You damned rat!" he snarled. "Try to get funny, will you? Maybe this'll teach your ugly mug a lesson."

His hand snaked to his hip. Midway in the action, he crumpled to the floor. A tiny sliver was sticking from his neck. A drop of blood oozed out.

Pete did what he had wanted to do—took Frost's advice and lammed.

The lid of the trunk came up. Frost stepped silently out and went to the rear of the room. A door on the left opened on a flight of stairs leading up. A door on the right was locked. After listening, Frost went to work on it. In less than a minute, he had it open.

The dark interior contained old boxes, papers, junk. Frost played a flashlight on the ceiling. When it reached one spot, he turned it down to the floor opposite. The floor was bare there and filmed with dust. Frost scrutinized the area intently, prowled around a section about four feet square. He found a couple of loose knots in the floor strips, and dusty holes where other knots had sunk. He probed these with a forefinger.

When he poked into the third knot, a section of the floor swung down, noiselessly. He caught the section as it was swinging back and shoved against it with a heel.

The beam of his light played into a cellar. A pile of rags lay below him. He gauged the distance and dropped. Holding the trapdoor with one hand, he kicked away the pile of rags. Only smooth concrete lay underneath them. He swung the flashlight around. Débris, cobwebs, furnace, pipes, rubbish, dank walls, sprang into fleeting view. A staircase. A rear door.

He hoisted himself through the trapdoor and continued to force it down against the steady pressure of the electrical device. He squeezed thumb and forefinger in the knot hole beside it, and twisted the wires free. Skin and flesh tore but the trapdoor suddenly hung perpendicular, stayed down.

There was a rear door to the room. He tried it. Locked. When he finished working on it, he looked into a rubble-strewn areaway. Soundlessly, he devoted a minute to his task before locking the door.

He avoided the yawning hole and locked the front door of the first room when he went out. The front and rear doors were the only entrances to the room.

The pasty-faced savage lay where he had fallen. Frost crossed toward the staircase and opened the door.

HE MOUNTED, a step at a time, examining the walls carefully before each step. The light was only short of darkness, but he did not use his flash. Less than a third of the way up, he halted and assumed a curious posture. He lay flat on the steps and inched himself up for approximately a yard. Then he carefully stood erect once more.

There was a door at the landing. The staircase continued up. Frost mounted as painstakingly as before. Again he flattened and edged his way up for a short distance. He trod with the precautionary ease that eliminates squeaks.

The stairs ended at the third floor landing. A vertical iron ladder reached to the roof. A single door faced him. Frost remained on the landing for a brief interval. When he descended, as phantomlike as before, he again lay flat on his back, rigid, and slid down with slow care at the same spot as previously.

On the second-floor landing, he listened. The sound of voices came from behind the door. He kept an automatic in his right hand. With his left, he gently turned the knob and tried the door. It was unlocked. He flung it open and stepped inside.

The room was large and almost empty. There was no rug on the floor. The varnish had long ago worn away. A dozen cheap chairs stood around a couple of tables. Toward the rear of the room, a desk put up a tawdry front all by itself. A dozen feet beyond it, the only window, frosted glass over a wire mesh, was so covered with the grime of years that light could not pierce through. An overhead bulb emitted a blinding flood.

A curious man wearing spectacles sat behind the desk. He looked like a scholar or student, with deep eyes, an intellectual forehead, a wedge chin, thin lips, and a frown on his face. He might have been thirty. His hands were not visible. He looked up and stared at Frost with something of the interest that might be expected of a fossil expert who had discovered the bones of an unknown species.

The only other person in the room had been leaning back in a chair. Dapper in appearance, cruel of face, he had the strange look that dwells in the eyes of the irresponsible killer. Joe Blake, for years a crime lord, racketeer, mobster, public enemy, and menace to society, the leader of a gang notorious for its ruthlessness, butchery, and cold-blooded efficiency, let his chair tilt forward and stood up.

The action had no rational basis. It resulted from hatred—hatred of the man who had ruined his immensely profitable slot-machine racket during the Golden Goblin affair. It rose from a desire to be free of his hampering position, a lust to kill. It rose from surprise and anger and fury. Above all, it rose from fear, the fear of the trapped and doomed rat caught in its hole, faced by its most dangerous enemy at the moment it felt most secure.

In that interval of electrical tension, no word was spoken. Ivy Frost towered in the doorway like a hawk about to strike. The man behind the desk looked up like a college instructor interrupted in the midst of a lecture. Blake stared at Frost with slitted eyes. His lips twitched as if to speak.

No use speaking. No use arguing with Frost. Nothing was any use while that hound remained alive. He got you in your own hide-out when you thought you had him out of the picture somewhere else. And in that menacing attitude, Blake sensed something tougher and more inflexible than anything he had ever before faced or any one he had ever put on the spot.

Nothing soft in that guy. Frost didn't need to speak. Blake's gorillas never gave a break, never took a chance. They killed for efficiency and ruled by terror. Four of them had been told to erase Frost. They hadn't yet come back. Frost's house had been turned into chambers of death.

The rest of the gang was over at Frost's place now. No telling what was happening there. But they wouldn't come back. Blake knew they wouldn't come back. And what about Tony Valency downstairs? But Frost didn't need to speak. Joe Blake knew. It was take it or give it. Something fell into the palm of Joe's right hand. The hand lifted at the wrist, imperceptibly.

"Your arrival was most opportune, Professor Frost," the man at the desk spoke in educated tones.

Frost was not staring directly at Blake. Blake shot. The bullet smacked into the floor. That was strange. That wasn't where he wanted to send it. And Joe Blake, dying, like the rats he had taken for rides, realized only that the sound of his gun had blended into the sound of Frost's and that the room was spinning into eternal blackness.

From the floor above came a cry and a sound, the sound of a thud, like that of a body falling.

"Nice work, Frost," said Gordon, guessing the downfall of the guard. "You always were a jump ahead of the game."

The implacable aspect of the professor's face remained, as unyielding as Gibraltar.

"It is perhaps unfortunate, Gordon, that society does not give to its sores precisely what it gets from those sores."

Gordon seemed indifferent. "I suppose you are referring to our work on Troff. He was an easy out for Stafford and me. It doesn't look so good now."

Frost prophesied: "Stafford will commit suicide to-day."

A TRACE of petulance entered Gordon's face. "It seemed like a novel idea at the time. I've hated you, Frost, ever since you half wrecked the organization and spoiled our profits. I should have killed you that night at our country place. I've planned ever since to kill you. Troff was innocent and a stranger to you and it struck me as a bright idea. He made a lot of noise when we—er—prepared him in the balloon. Useless things, balloons."

The satanic perversity of the man showed in his casual tones. "I wanted to give you a riddle you couldn't solve, Frost. Just to satisfy myself that I could think up something you couldn't answer. I would be ready for you and kill you if you did get the answer. By the way, how did you work it so fast? Or did Troff live longer than the few minutes I allowed?"

Frost answered harshly: "I shall tell you nothing, Gordon, except that you are going to die by your own hand."

"Really! I think not. It doesn't matter. When you left your house, we trailed you to see if you were on the right track. You were. But you got out of the trap on 180th Street. Too bad that Sam slipped up on his end of the job. It was his last slip. So we lost your trail, but I sent the boys over to your house, Frost, and fixed it up for you in case you returned. And we got that kid assistant of yours. I wish we had gone to work on her, Frost. I had pretty things planned for her and for you. But I was frankly afraid of you, afraid of what you might do when you found out, and if you escaped us. She's upstairs, you know."

"I know all this. I am merely waiting for you to destroy yourself."

Gordon mused: "We picked up your trail again when Stafford got in touch with us and told us you had just ordered him to the bank. I suppose you found what we did to the burglar alarm. Stafford thought he was safe. He thought his tracks were covered. To-day he was to get his part of the loot, but in other money of course, not the 'hot' bills. I didn't bother to disillusion him. He won't commit suicide, Frost. He was the kind who'd squeal. We took care of him."

The complacency of the criminal had something inhuman, something fiendish. Blood and death and torture and crime all appeared to be simply parts of some mathematical problem in his twisted mind.

"You are wasting time," Frost drawled.

"Perhaps. It looked like a good set-up. Four of the boys were told to shoot your tires and take you for a ride. If you got out of that trap, you would either be caught by Squinty or killed in your own home. Good work, Frost. I don't know what happened to the four. I presume you eliminated them. When Squinty called, I sent the rest of the boys on. Except the four of us, here. I figured on playing safe. I don't know how you got past Squinty or what you did. I don't know how you got by Tony downstairs, or why the infra-red photo-electric cells on the stairs didn't warn us you were here. But it doesn't matter, now."

"It doesn't matter, for now you are going to kill yourself."

Gordon murmured: "Am I? You're clever, Frost, damned clever, but even the best of us can't guess right all the time. I don't think I will be so obliging as to do what you ask."

The killer vanished. Frost walked forward. A fearful scream tore up through the closing trapdoor, a sickening smash followed. Frost held the trapdoor open a moment and looked down along the beam of a flashlight, down through the trapdoor that he had sprung and left open on the first floor, down onto the concrete basement where pulp lay.

"I told you," he echoed grimly, "that you would have the pleasure of killing yourself."

He gave only a passing glance to the desk, and the button that operated the trapdoor, and the signal light connected with the invisible eyes that he had avoided on the staircases. He paused upstairs only long enough to free the girl. Not much the worse for rough handling, she eased the tape off her mouth.

"Say, I didn't think you'd ever come." She bounced up. "Let's go."

VIII.

ON THE WAY out, Frost tied Valency. In the cab, he sat silent, almost morose.

Jean rubbed her wrists, chafed her ankles to restore circulation. She felt her lips gingerly. Pulling adhesive tape off did not help a skin or complexion any.

"Here a girl gets herself knocked out and kidnaped and tied up and things," she complained, "and she practically doesn't get any attention and nobody even wants to know if she's all right. I bet if I got shot and was practically dying and blood just pouring out and things, you'd just stand there and go into a lecture on how many kinds of blood there are and—"

"As a matter of fact," Frost remarked, "the analysis of blood is a special study. Biochemists have not done nearly enough in exhausting its possibilities. When the science is sufficiently advanced, it will be possible, by microscopic and chemical analysis, to determine from a single drop of blood the sex, health, and racial admixture of the person from whom it came. Furthermore when—"

"There you go!" Jean sighed, exasperated. "I don't want to hear about blood. I want to know how you get information out of people who can't give any information, and what this is all about, and why I get knocked out and carried off by a lot of men I never saw before and don't ever want to see again."

Frost straightened, a little less morose. "For a while, it was rather interesting," he returned. "But it seems strange that Gordon with his intellect and you with your good mind could not guess the answer to so simple a question."

"Who's Gordon?"

"De Lancey Gordon was a brilliant protégé of Henderson, the noted physicist and chemist. But Gordon, like occasional other brilliant men, had a mental quirk, a distortion, a warp that turned his abilities toward evil ends. There is something about crime that fascinates the most intelligent minds.

"There is a challenge, a lure, that can overpower the restraints of sane thought. Gordon was such a person, gifted with a keen mind, of scientific bent, an excellent student, but with a taint. Most scientists are poorly paid. Few of them receive the thanks or the appreciation of the world that they do so much to improve.

"Gordon used the help and the aid and the knowledge he had got from Henderson to turn on him. Henderson would have nothing more to do with him and withdrew all support. Gordon, then, devoted all his talents to the pursuit of crime. He had a delusion that he was the arch-genius of crime, that he could combine the tools of science with the ambitions of the gangster. He enlisted Joe Blake's gang, because it was the strongest in the city. He became the brains behind its operations.

He was the one who plotted the Golden Goblin affair. He was the mysterious voice you inquired about."

"But about the dying man?" Jean persisted.

"From the first, I suspected that it was the work of Blake's gang. Blake and Gordon and part of the gang escaped from the Golden Goblin episode. It was inevitable that they would strike back. The singular circumstances surrounding the finding of the dying man, Troff, were indicative that he had been placed there as a challenge and gesture. Blake and Gordon were the two who had most reason to wish me out of the way.

"Because of the man's condition, it was hopeless to try to save his life. Considering the limitations of time, I did the best possible thing. I took him into my laboratory and spoke into an amplifier that literally blasted sound through his blood-filled eardrums. Then I simply asked him questions which he could answer with a nod or shake of his head."

Jean looked admiring and disgusted simultaneously. "It's so darned plain I could kick myself for not guessing."

Frost went on: "I first asked him if his last name began with a letter in the first half of the alphabet. A shake. Then I raced from M down the line until he nodded at T. When I had T-R-O-F-F, which sounded as if it might be a name, I asked him if there were more letters. A shake. I asked him if he was listed in the telephone directory. A nod. I asked him if his residence was Manhattan. A nod.

"I then found out the numerals of his address. I inquired if he was connected in any way with a recent crime. A nod. I discovered, by this process, that he was not a criminal, but was concerned with the Midtown Bank robbery. He died then, but I had all the information I needed to bring his murderers and the robbers to justice. The rest, of course, is evident." He gave a resumé of subsequent events.

"No; it isn't plain," Jean contradicted. "I never listened to such a disconnected story. I'll admit you succeeded, but I don't see the explanations. Why did you go to Troff's place first of all?"

Frost began to look bored. "I went primarily to draw the criminals into the open, to test the validity of my deductions, and to find out whether Troff's replies were all truthful. Since the sedan made no attempt to attack on the way uptown, it was logical to assume that they were ready to act when I came out. They would have the rear entrance guarded for safety's sake."

JEAN pouted. Frost's logic was an exact science, merciless. He gave the only answers possible. And yet the answers were always obscure until he explained them.

"I had the bank opened because, on the basis of the knowledge I had accumulated, Troff appeared to be innocent. He would have, must have, touched off the burglar alarm. It failed. I wanted to know why. The only answer possible, of course, was that the mechanism had been tampered with in such a way that Troff could try to give warning and fail, but all subsequent attempts would succeed. The device I discovered was precisely what I expected.

"It was now clear that the bank robbery had been more than a raid by Blake's gang. There had been inside assistance. It had not come from Troff. For subtle reasons so detailed that I won't go into a long explanation, but involving actions, reactions, attitudes, and so forth, my suspicions fastened on Stafford. If Stafford was the man, then he undoubtedly had got in touch with the gangsters immediately after I called him. Naturally I prepared for another attempt on my life. The attempt came a short distance from the bank when one of my tires was shot. As I expected, the hoodlums were not anxious to get rid of me there, with a radio car in easy hearing distance. I was taken for a ride."

Jean exclaimed: "And you came back! It sounds incredible."

Frost remarked: "It was quite simple. To escape detection from even chance observers, gangland cars keep the windows up and sometimes the curtains down as well, in such circumstances. Carbon monoxide gas is odorless and deadly in as little as seventeen parts in one thousand of air. The interior of an automobile may contain anywhere from sixty to two hundred or more cubic feet of air. Assuming a high average of one hundred and fifty, only 2.6 cubic feet of carbon monoxide gas would be dangerous in a closed car. I carried four cubic feet under pressure in a special vest the valve of which I loosened when I stepped out of my car."

"But how could you foretell so exactly what method or procedure they would use?" Jean burst out.

"I am surprised that you ask. I was not prepared for one particular emergency. I was prepared for all emergencies. So long as I had the saturated cotton wads in my nostrils, the gas could not harm me; and if I had not been taken along, I was ready for other methods. A trained analyst, knowing that he is to be murdered, can forestall any attempt."

"So—" breathed Jean. "But tell, tell me—how ever did you get out of the traps set in the house."

"That was a problem involving many possibilities and probabilities," Frost admitted. "There again I was prepared for several emergencies. And yet the pattern became clear, under the scrutiny of analytic logic. It was evident from the films—one exposure each time the door was opened or closed, a purely automatic process of infra-red photography—it was evident that one member of the gang remained behind. It was also evident that other traps had been set if that failed.

"The presumption was that I would enter through the front door, as most people do. Therefore the gangster would be waiting for me there, in the hope of possibly capturing me alive. I turned the hallway floor into an electromagnet. The gangster's weapons became useless.

"That danger past, the others became simpler of solution. The large crate suggested an animal. I threw myself on the floor when I opened the library door, because an animal springing would pass overhead; because any other concealed crook would shoot overhead; because the force of an explosion would be upward and outward; and so on.

"But explosives, if used at all, must logically be at the outside doors of the kitchen, so that if I entered, the force of the explosion would not extend to the front hall where Squinty waited. And if I escaped Squinty and entered the kitchen through the hall, the presumption was that I would notice the explosives, walk toward them, and be struck by the snake or spiders while my attention was diverted. But if I avoided Squinty and killed the panther, the presumption was that I would expect some other living thing in the laboratory. I would be killed by the gas while I was searching for something else."

JEAN mused: "And of course you used Squinty as the means of splitting the rest of the gang into two parts. And I suppose the ones who started out for your house killed Squinty."

"No," Frost told her; "they didn't kill Squinty. They joined him. The only one who escaped was the driver of the car. The others hurled themselves into an escape-proof, stone-walled room the moment the doorbell was pushed. If they haven't killed each other by now, Frick may have the personal pleasure of carting them away.

"And with the enemy divided, the last step was carrying the battle into the heart of their camp. At most, there could be not more than four or five gangsters remaining. I employed the most efficient method of entering their headquarters without observation. It was then an easy and instantaneous matter to render Valency, the lookout man, unconscious by blowing through a tube and through a broken lock of the trunk a dart tipped with an aconite paste.

"The logical steps from there on must be self-evident. When I found a trapdoor in the ceiling directly over another in the floor, the obvious answer was that it was an ingenious mode of escape, which in turn informed me that Blake or Gordon or both must be directly overhead. The building had but three stories. Therefore, you and a guard would be on the third floor. Thus, in case of a raid or of being surprised, the leaders would drop out of sight through the trapdoors, and the man on the third floor would have time to kill you and leave by way of the roof."

Jean grimaced. "The way you talk about the most depraved spectacles, you'd think I was a cat or something that the humane society ought to put out of misery."

Frost ignored the interruption. "When I reached the third-floor landing, only one problem, of course, remained. I could not risk the chance of creating any disturbance in eliminating the guard, or the leaders on the floor below would be warned. The solution, naturally, was to make such arrangements that when I entered the den of the leaders, a disturbance would be created there, and the man upstairs, drawn out to investigate or to try a flank attack, would be automatically felled."

The cab slid into the curb. Frost got out.

"And what earthly means did you use so that he would obligingly take himself out of the picture?" Jean demanded.

Frost replied: "I have some matters to talk over with Inspector Frick. It seems to me that I am doing all the explaining. I will leave you to cope with that little problem. I may remark that it is capable of more than one solution."

Jean had a bright idea. "You know what?" she called after the professor's retreating back. "I bet I don't even guess one!"

BRIDE OF THE RATS

Jean turned back in time to see Ivy Frost's arm stop moving. Hossner went head-first into the pit.

JEAN MORAY wore a frown of irritation on her lovely face as she skipped up the steps of No. 13 State Street. Adversity could not change nor displeasure mar the breath-taking eloquence of her features, even though everything had gone wrong this morning.

She was quite capable of suppressing her feelings, with that exasperating flair for deception that is a native talent in most women. But being young and beautiful, possessed of a lithe and luscious figure, with a face the more strikingly attractive for its combination of naïveté and sophistication, and independent in a willful fashion because she usually got what she wanted without the necessity of doing anything about it, she took no pains to hide her annoyance.

Anyway, what was the use of trying to conceal her feelings? Men were easy to handle—but not Frost. She had originally become his assistant in the investigation of crime as the readiest way out of a mystery in which she had become hopelessly entangled. She expected, then, to cut loose and drift on her way.

But she stayed. The cases he handled were of so fascinating and frequently bizarre a nature that they made life as exciting as the "Arabian Nights." And the character, the remarkable personality, of Professor I.V. Frost, both challenged and baffled analysis.

He didn't give a damn about the way he looked. Every time she saw the old corduroy trousers and the chemical-stained leather jacket that clad his lean, unlovely figure, she suffered qualms. He was long and thin. He had a hatchet-shaped head with a hawk nose, shaggy eyebrows, and piercing black eyes. Any one could notice these externals. No one ever got beyond them or found any more about his thoughts and methods than he himself chose to tell.

But Jean at the moment was irritated past caring much what even he thought. Little things had upset her, the little things that do not count but that upset empires. She twirled her hat in her fingers, idly.

Frost, lolling in an easy-chair and with his hands interlocked under his chin, shifted his gaze from the bust of Socrates and surveyed her with what appeared to be a casual glance as she entered the library.

"You ought to be grateful to the dentist for saving that dying tooth," he drawled.

"Well, I'm not. It hurt like sin and it'll keep aching for a while. I almost wish I'd told him to extract it."

"We are sometimes ungrateful to those who help us," the professor mused. "And it is really too bad that you don't like the hat you bought, but of course you can return it to-morrow."

"To-day," Jean decided.

"If I were you, I would forget about the man who seized your arm when you were leaving the subway train. Such incidents will happen, but it is seldom worth while making an issue of them."

Jean complained: "Sure; but that doesn't change it any from being a disagreeable experience."

"It is also unfortunate that you didn't enjoy the chocolate malted milk at Mardi's, but, then, it would naturally start the tooth aching again."

"It was worth it, and I had some aspirin along," she returned. "Except at Mardi's, the malteds are as thin as milk in this neck of the woods. I wouldn't think of getting one anywhere else."

Frost dangled a leg over the arm of his chair, swung it indifferently. "Ill luck sometimes runs in streaks. I can sympathize with you over the loss of your purse. Annoyed and upset as you were, it was an easy thing to forget when you left Mardi's, but no doubt they are holding it for you at the counter. Naturally, worked up as you were, and having decided to walk back here, you didn't miss it until you had arrived almost at the door."

Jean pouted. "At that, I darn near went back. Everything's gone wrong."

A look of surprise and exasperation suddenly drew her face into a grimace. She opened her mouth, only to click her teeth as if biting something with relish. She blurted out at last: "Have you been having me trailed? How did you know what I've been doing?"

Frost smiled. "The facts and evidence indicated that certain events had occurred. I deduced them and found them supported by your answers and testimony." He made it sound as if she was the all-important key in a chain that would have been useless except for her proofs.

She looked somewhat mollified but argued: "There doesn't seem to be much point in carrying on a conversation with you. You know all the right answers. I might just as well sit here a couple of hours and then listen to you tell me what I've been thinking. It's uncanny. How did you know I had a dying tooth? I didn't say anything about it. How did you know the dentist filled it instead of pulling it out?"

Frost relaxed. "Nothing could be simpler. There was a slight swelling in your upper right cheek when you went out. You took an aspirin tablet. Aspirin is one of the fastest known agencies for the relief of toothache. An extraction would be followed by a small flow of blood until the clot had formed. Some gesture, if only the use of a handkerchief, would be natural. You have taken no such action. Furthermore, definite traces would remain if any local or complete anæsthetic had been given. In the absence of these, I conclude that the dentist filled the tooth."

"It does sound easy," Jean admitted. "I should have guessed."

Frost calmly contradicted her: "It isn't a matter of guessing."

"Well, it's good observation." Jean attempted to minimize the ingenuity of the rational masculine mind by reducing it to a merely sensory basis.

The professor shrugged. "Observation? Yes; but only as a starting point. Any one can observe day and night; then, like Ptolemy, offer the simplest explanation. It takes a man like Copernicus to evolve a true theory of celestial motions. Daily life is crowded with facts and incidents that need not only to be observed, but also to be interpreted, related, and compared with other truths until their absolute value is apparent. Observation, synthesis, analysis, induction, and deduction are equally necessary in the process.

"The hat you hold will serve as a good illustration. And one who observed it casually would assume that it was part of your wardrobe. Only if he noticed its unspotted and uncrinkled newness, its fresh label, its failure quite to harmonize with your ensemble, the fact that you carry it instead of wear it, and that it is not the hat you had when you left, would he conclude it had been newly bought. It would also be evident that while you walked along the street, looked at your reflection in shop windows, and noticed the critical expression of passers-by, you decided it was not quite suitable after all."

JEAN nodded slowly. "What made you think a man grabbed my arm on purpose? How do you know I didn't stumble and somebody was only trying to help me?"

Frost interlaced his fingers at the back of his head. "If you had tripped, the tips of your shoes would be scuffed, and there would be other corroboratory evidence. But your shoes are in impeccable condition. The sleeve of your upper left arm is both mussed and soiled. The palm of your right hand is slightly reddened. It must have been a hard slap to leave an impression that still lasts.

"The facts suggest that some one accosted you when you were on the way to the dentist. Such an encounter would be unlikely on the street at that hour, or when you were entering a subway car. The best opportunity would be at the point of leaving the train. Then, if the advance was successful, the stranger could accompany you, but if repulsed or if you made any outcry, he could easily vanish in the crowd."

The telephone rang. Frost lazily lifted the receiver. "Yes? . . . Speaking. . . . Yes. . . . Excellent. . . . Thank you, and good-by." He frowned slightly as he hung up.

Jean tossed her head, " 'Yes and thank you,' " she echoed. "If I said that over the phone while you were listening, you'd promptly tell me who I was talking to and what was said. It sounds easy when you do it, but neither I nor anybody else could get to first base given the same lead."

Frost objected mildly: "Your diction is as confused as your figures of speech. In baseball, it is impossible for the batter to have a lead. After he is safe upon first base, and when he has become the runner—"

Jean's eyes gleamed, but all she said when she interrupted was: "What about the malted milk and the purse I lost?"

"The evidence behind those deductions was, I admit, of less tangible nature and more nebulous except for the spot on your cuff. The spot is of a creamy color, fresh, and obviously has passed unnoticed. It alone, considering the usually fastidious care you take of your attire, would imply that you were upset to the point of overlooking details, and consequently that it must have followed the incidents that annoyed you.

"Dental pastes have a whiter color, milk has a thinner consistency, and while various fluids or chemical compounds might have left such a spot, they are rare in daily life. A chocolate malted milk would leave just such a spot; and if this deduction was true, it followed that you must have gone to Mardi's which you once said was the only place you would go for the beverage."

"Do you ever forget anything you see or hear?" she asked perfunctorily.

The professor glanced at a clock. "When you entered the library, you unconsciously held your left arm as if you were holding a purse, in the manner you have always used. If you had deliberately set the purse on the hall table, or left it near by, your mind would be at rest. Furthermore, you felt a twinge of pain from the tooth a few minutes ago. You grimaced. Your right hand moved toward the spot where your purse would normally be, and which would contain aspirin tablets. Also, the pocketless ensemble you wear would absolutely require the presence of a purse at all times for common necessities like a handkerchief and cosmetics and change.

"Your failure to have a purse is subject to three different explanations. You could have purposely left it somewhere, you could have lost it, or it could have been stolen. If you had left it near by, you would have gone for it before now. If it had been stolen—"

The doorbell rang.

"Bring Mrs. Hossner in," Frost murmured.

II.

FOR A MOMENT, Jean looked as if she would refuse unless he divulged the magic that enabled him to predict who stood outside, but she turned around without speaking. Seconds passed. Voices sounded in the doorway, indistinguishable words. The door closed. Click of heels, then a woman entered ahead of Jean.

She was passing from her twenties and inclined to be a bit plump, but still on the voluptuous side. She had a roundish face, but her eyes were set close and possessed a peculiar, stony blankness in their pupils of mottled gray. She had neither coat, hat, nor purse, and her clothing was soiled. Her plain brown hair needed a few hairpins and some attention. She breathed unevenly and walked jerkily, with uncoördinated movements.

"Be seated, Mrs. Hossner," Frost gently urged.

The visitor betrayed no surprise that he knew her name. She did not ask how he knew it. She did not seem to care whether he knew it or not. She sat down stiffly and said, abruptly:

"The alienist Clehr sent me to you. I started to tell him what was wrong. First he thought I was crazy. Maybe he still does. He said it might be a case for investigation. He told me to see you. You are Professor I.V. Frost? He told me to come back after I talked to you."

The woman spoke in clipped sentences, jerkily, like her motions. There was no continuity of thought. Frost studied her with a deceptively careless glance that passed for merely interested attention. She kept her hands tightly clasped. Her whole attitude had something wooden and unnatural, even psychopathic. The far-away look in her eyes bordered on the abnormal and partook of invisible worlds.

Frost helped her along: "Clehr is exceptional. He would not have sent you to me unless he believed your story and thought it worthy of investigation. By all means, continue."

The woman did not move, showed no emotion, and persisted in her trancelike state. Her lips barely moved as she stated tonelessly: "I began breakfast with an antelope."

Frost sat up, tense and alert. He reached into a satinwood container and extracted a cigarette of unusual length. By that gesture, and the sharply spiced fumes that he exhaled, Jean knew he had found a case to his liking, a mystery with fantastic overtones.

"Did you say canteloupe?" Jean demanded, thinking she might not have heard correctly.

Mrs. Hossner repeated "Antelope," and stopped.

She began and ended with that preposterous statement. She sat with impassive disregard of what effect her words had. Jean stared at her, incredulous, skeptical, wondering what sort of lunatic they now had on their hands. Frost waited, a bright glint in his eyes, until it became obvious that further information would have to be pried out of her.

The professor inquired: "Have you ever before had breakfast with this or any other antelope or any other animal?"

"No. I never want to see the creature again."

"Just where did the incident occur?"

"I reached across the table for some grapes. The door opened and the antelope came in. It was a beautiful creature."

The visitor again ceased speaking. Jean tried in vain to extract some grain of meaning from these absurd and irrational assertions.

Frost persisted: "Where did this happen?"

"In the castle. The antelope and I were in the castle."

"What castle?"

"I don't know."

"Where is it?"

"I don't know."

"How did you come to be there?"

"I don't know."

"How did you leave it?"

"I ran away."

"Why?"

"It was bad enough when the rats kept me awake. I couldn't stand it any longer when the organ played as the antelope came up to me."

"Why did the organ annoy you?"

"Because there was no organ in the castle."

And in this baffling manner, this group of apparently unrelated dream-images like a nightmare and a fairy tale combined, this queer jumble of contradictions and meaningless ravings, began one of the strangest riddles that Professor I.V. Frost was ever called upon to solve.

JEAN, listening with growing exasperation to the toneless statements of Mrs. Hossner, nevertheless felt pity for the woman who was either suffering from dementia or had been made the victim of some savage hoax.

But Frost, sitting forward, firing questions like bullets as if to jolt the woman out of her daze, and inhaling whenever possible the fumes of his odd cigarettes, showed no skepticism whatever. He exhibited only deep interest and curiosity in the information he was eliciting.

"Would you recognize the route by which you ran away from the castle?"

"No."

"Why not?"

"I couldn't see because of the tears."

"You were crying?"

"I don't know why."

"But you ran away and left the antelope in the dining room?"

Mrs. Hossner replied: "I was frightened. I ran into the hall. The organ music frightened me. It sounded like demons muttering. I ran to the door. The first door I saw. I had my hand on it when something hit me with a plop. I couldn't scream. There was no one to scream to.

I cried so hard that the tears blinded me. I ran outside and ran and ran. I thought I heard steps. I bumped into bushes and trees. I tripped and got up. I ran and ran.

"Then I heard a squeal of brakes. Somebody said 'What's the trouble, lady?' I said 'Take me to New York.' Somebody said 'Sure, but stop crying.' I think it was a truck. We rode a long time. After a while I stopped crying. I looked out. We were on Fifty-seventh Street. 'Let me out here,' I said. They stopped the truck and I jumped out and walked to Dr. Clehr's office.

"I thought I was going crazy. I had heard his name somewhere; I didn't know him. I looked him up. I had to talk to somebody. He gave me money to come here."

The woman stopped. Jean, hopelessly mystified, but inclined to ascribe the whole story to the ravings of an unbalanced mind, squirmed uneasily. Did Frost believe these incredible assertions?

He asked: "You said there was no one to scream to. Were you alone in the castle?"

"I don't know. I saw no one. I heard no voices. But there was fruit on the table when I came down. I was hungry and wanted breakfast. Or I think I saw fruit. I wouldn't swear to it now. I must be mad. No; I didn't see any breakfast or antelope. It was all a dream like all the rest."

"Stop that!" Frost's voice cut with a harsh and stern command. His eyes glittered like black stars.

The woman stiffened.

"Mrs. Hossner, there is truth in your story. Tell me that truth without further doubts. You are unquestionably sane in spite of a terrifying experience. There must be and is a perfectly rational explanation. Give me the facts and I will find you the answers.

"When you left the castle, you ran along a path or road that you remembered?"

"I don't recall. Maybe I had a vague memory of it from the night before. I don't know."

Frost suddenly abandoned Mrs. Hossner's story: "Where were you yesterday?"

She showed some surprise. "Why, with my husband, of course. I suppose I was kidnaped and held for ransom. No. That doesn't account for the antelope."

Frost snapped: "Forget the antelope. Have you seen or talked to your husband to-day?"

"No. We had no phone. I had to tell somebody my story first. Somebody who wouldn't think I was crazy. I wasn't sure of myself. I didn't know what I might find. Maybe he's gone, too. Maybe I dreamed it all."

"Have you tried to communicate with friends or relatives?"

The woman sighed. "I have none here."

The criminologist inhaled more deeply than ever of acrid smoke while a gleam of what looked like keen relish dwelt in his black eyes. He ceased his questions for the moment and wore an air of meditation, as though putting together the parts of a verbal jig-saw puzzle. He flipped a glance at Socrates, and Socrates placidly gazed across the room with calm and dispassionate inquiry in the eternity of marble.

Frost resumed the Socratic method: "You mentioned rats. Did you see any rats?"

"No. I only heard them. They kept me awake. Running, running, running. I heard them in the walls and halls. Maybe they were part of the dream."

"How do you know there was no organ?"

"Because the chords were just as loud when the dining-room door was open or shut. They must have come from the room I was in. I looked. There were no pipes or keyboard or organ."

Frost nodded approval, though of what Jean had not the slightest idea. If the matter was in her hands, she would have summoned an alienist. Yet Clehr had sent this patient to Frost. And Frost did not waste time chasing rainbows. In spite of herself, the eerie feeling grew on her that she was wrong, that the woman told truths, impossible truths, baffling truths, truths that bore some unknown relation to each other and to some unknown crime of gnarled and devious nature.

FROST took up another tack: "You are positive you were with your husband yesterday?"

"As usual, we spent the whole day together. We had breakfast in, but went out toward noon. We had lunch, tea, and dinner at different places, all new ones to me, of course. We went to the zoo in the afternoon and a movie in the evening."

"What happened last night?"

Mrs. Hossner looked weary. "Nothing."

"The most trivial detail may be more important than you think. Exactly what happened after you got home?"

"We talked about the day. He said that when the weather got cold and I got tired of the city, we could fly down to Florida or Cuba."

"Your husband, I take it, has no regular occupation?"

"No. He's retired. He has plenty of money. We turned in about eleven. I had a headache. I took an aspirin and a glass of water. I fell asleep after a while. There were strange, blurry dreams, but I can't remember them clearly. I half awoke and thought I was somewhere else. I did not recognize it. It was dark. I thought I was alone, but I was terribly tired and dozed off.

"It was lighter when I became conscious again. I listened and heard rats running, rushing, scampering in the walls and floors. I was afraid to cry out. It was all too strange. I dozed and half awakened from time to time. It is hard to tell what was dream and what was real. I wanted to move but didn't. It was so easy to stay in bed. And always I heard the rats scampering.

"When I next opened my eyes, it was much lighter. I saw I was in a big, dark room like a prison. With an effort I went to the window and looked out. The window had bars. What I could see of the building made it look like a prison or castle. Yes; I wondered then if maybe I hadn't been there a long time; if maybe there had been something wrong with me. I saw the sea. The sea was blood-red."

"From the rising sun?" asked Frost.

"No. The sun wasn't up high enough. But the sea was blood-red just the same, by itself," Mrs. Hossner insisted. "I went back and slept again. It was daylight when I got up. I went to the door and opened it. I didn't see or hear any one. I crept downstairs and opened the first door I saw. There was fruit in a big bowl. I suddenly realized how hungry I was. I went in and took an orange from the bowl. Then I heard a sound by the door and I whirled around. The antelope was coming in. The door was closing. I heard the organ thunder. I guess I lost my mind and began running."

Antelope and rats—blood-red sea and organ music without organ—disappearing home and mysteriously appearing castle—these were the material of fantasy.

But Frost stared at the woman with ever-deepening interest. His first eager attention had given way to an air of abstraction, and now something grim, ominous, entered his attitude. The lids drooped half over his eyes. However crazy the narrative sounded to Jean, it must already have assumed some definite pattern for him.

He suddenly demanded; "Where was your apartment?"

"At 16 Logan Street."

"Tell me more about your husband. Who is he?"

"Fritz Hossner."

Frost shifted impatiently. "Have you been married long?"

"No, for only about—"

The doorbell rang sharply. The woman broke off in mid-sentence, made a wild dash for the laboratory, but Frost was there first.

"Delusions of persecution on top of all the rest!" Jean thought as she went to answer the ring.

Looking in the hall mirror as she passed, she approved of her lovely self. Nevertheless, she reached for her compact, remembered that it lay in the lost purse, and continued toward the door with a feeling of irritation. She firmly believed that nature was never so good that it could not be improved.

A CURIOUS little man stood on the porch. He couldn't have weighed more than a hundred pounds. He looked like an idiot gnome. He had vacant eyes of pale, watery blue and skin the color of a grub. A tuft of fuzzy hair, lemon-yellow in hue, sprouted from his chin like the whiskers of a goat. His cranium was barren of shrubbery, foliage, or the least sign of life—a naked plain stretched tightly over bone. His hands made fluttering motions in the air. Though his lips moved, he spoke not a word, but peered vacuously at Jean.

"What do you want?" she demanded.

His fingers did odd bends and dances, as if possessed of separate lives. And Jean realized that he was a deaf mute.

The stranger magically produced paper and pencil. He scrawled a note, in handwriting as devious as the worm tunnels in rotten logs.

"Let me have that," Frost ordered.

She had not heard him approach, but there he suddenly was, beside her.

The note read: "Is Professor I.V. Frost in?"

Frost looked at the little gnome whose lips moved and whose fingers danced. Frost shook his head with a frown. He wrote: "Who are you? Who sent you here? What do you want?"

The dwarf scrawled a reply. As Frost took it, the stranger's hands made a few last flutterings, and, as if of their own volition, his lips writhed.

Jean ventured to the professor: "Well, it's some comfort to know that you're at least partly human and can't do everything, such as reading lips and sign language."

The dwarf peered at Jean, peered at Frost.

The professor lifted his eyebrows in a calm manner that made his assistant feel like a fly on a pin. He turned his attention to the note. It said: "I am D. S. Higgs. Dr. Clehr sent me. A dead man has been threatening my life. Will you accept the case?"

Frost wrote in answer to this extraordinary communication: "Previous engagements make it impossible to discuss the matter now. At four this afternoon?"

Mr. Higgs nodded, bowed, and departed. A hat came out from under his arm and concealed the painfully bare, bobbing cranium of that retreating personage.

Jean mused: "Clehr must have taken to sending all the screwy ones here. Or else he seems to be becoming a regular gold mine of freak cases."

"Doesn't he?"

Something in Frost's tone made her look up sharply. "Why did you send him away? Threatened by a dead man. It isn't any goofier than Mrs. Hossner's yarn. It sounds like a honey, just up your alley."

"Doesn't it?"

Jean bit her lip. "Higgs is crazy, she's crazy, I'm crazy, everybody's crazy," she chanted.

Frost wore a sardonic smile as he turned away from the door. Jean did not see what amused him. He reëntered the library, strode across to the laboratory door, and pushed. The door stuck. He heaved it open far enough to slip through. The smile vanished from his face, to be replaced by a grim tightening of cheek bones. Jean raced after him, her heart pounding.

It had been a mad morning, mad events, anything could happen, but she knew what had happened, what must have happened, to set those implacable lines on Frost's features.

She squeezed through the aperture. "What's wrong?" she asked anxiously.

She did not need an answer. Trained in the hard school of life and reality, having seen death in violent forms, she neither screamed nor fainted. She stood stoically regarding the corpse while Frost clipped the words out savagely:

"Mrs. Hossner has been murdered."

III.

THE WOMAN lay face up, with contorted limbs, her body still warm. An expression of agonized surprise was fixed in her wide-open eyes. She had been telling her incoherent narrative only a few minutes before. She had dashed for concealment in the laboratory when the doorbell rang. No one could have entered through the fortified windows of the laboratory. Mr. Higgs, the visitor, had not for a moment been out of sight. He had never got beyond the outer doorway where she and Frost met him.

Mrs. Hossner could not have been murdered. Of that Jean felt sure. But dead the woman was, and it seemed no more unnatural than the preceding events, which had no relation or reason and possessed no connection with each other or with this.

Frost snapped: "Get Clehr on the phone for me. Initials L. S. In the Crayman Building."

Jean stepped back into the library. She returned after a minute and reported: "Clehr has not come back from lunch yet. I left word with his secretary to call you as soon as he came in."

Frost nodded, continued his careful, detailed study of the body. He missed nothing. Whatever caught his special interest immediately underwent inspection and enlargement to a hundred diameters through a lens he had taken from his equipment. He studied the woman's hair, eyes, mouth, make-up, every spot on her clothing. He examined her hands as if they were a masterpiece of art. He gave her shoes the care that a connoisseur would bestow on a newly discovered painting by Ryder. Even the slight grime under her finger nails received attention.

"Could it have been heart failure? Or did she commit suicide?" Jean suggested.

Frost straightened. "Neither. She killed herself without knowing it. She was murdered as definitely as if a bullet had been put in her heart. It was simply an accident, an unfortunate accident, that the place happened to be here, and the time had to be now. It might as easily have occurred before, in which event I would have lost a most unusual case, or it might have occurred later, in which event I would have obtained more information, perhaps prevented this death, and certainly shortened the time requirements. No matter. It is done. And I have all that I need to bring her murderers to justice."

"And just how was she so obliging as to murder herself without knowing it?"

Frost pointed to an open aspirin tin. It was empty and lay near the body. "Don't touch it!" he warned.

Jean frowned. "It doesn't mean much to me."

"Look at the thumb and forefinger of her right hand. Look at her face and position."

Jean looked. "Yes; the white powder certainly indicates that she took the tablet, but I don't see how she died from aspirin."

Frost almost groaned. "Because she took a tablet from an aspirin box, does it follow that it was an aspirin tablet? Isn't it significant that the box contained only one tablet? She took what she thought was an aspirin; she had a terrible convulsion and met death instantly. So would any one who took five grains of strychnine.

"In her blouse, I found this key. Does its presence strike you as having any significance?"

Jean glanced at it before handing it back. "Not particularly," she decided.

It was a serrated key of common type, evidently for an apartment door.

Frost said: "The woman came here with an extraordinary tale. She came without a purse. By her own words, she had no money. She borrowed from Clehr in order to reach us. Yet her pocket contained a key, unquestionably to her apartment, and a box the one tablet in which was sufficiently deadly to kill several persons."

Jean protested: "It would only be natural for her to keep the key on her person—" Then she caught herself.

"Exactly! Your mind is beginning to function," Frost agreed. "She retired in one place and awakened in another. From her story, it was not clear whether she found herself dressed or still in her nightrobes when she awakened. The point is unimportant.

"Most women keep keys in their purses. But even if Mrs. Hossner had some exceptional habit of carrying a key and a box of aspirin on her person, you will notice that hers is a sport blouse of the slipover kind. Her jacket has no pockets. She could not conceivably pull the blouse off without spilling the contents of the pocket.

"It is just as inconceivable that she would put them back, or that she would keep on spilling them out at night and replacing them in the morning. But if, when she put the blouse on in the morning, something fell out, she would automatically put it in the pocket; and if nothing fell out, she might not know for a considerable period that anything was in her pocket. Her mind would be preoccupied by her nerve-racking mystery."

"It's too much for me. Shall I call the police?"

"No; not yet. In the interests of a larger justice, we'll have to accept responsibility for any difficulties that may arise. Bring me Throckmorton's 'Historic Sites of Long Island.' Tenth book from the left, third shelf from the top, second section in the library."

WHEN Jean brought the desired volume, she found Frost absorbed over a microscope.

"Drop the book on the table. Get the missing-persons bureau and find out if a Mrs. Hossner has been reported as missing within the last day or two, and if so, by whom," he ordered, without looking up.

The sunlight, sliding through western windows, chiseled his features into bleak profile. In some intangible way, some invisible manifestation of personality, he suggested relentless power; not a merely physical energy; not the strength of those who live by brawn alone; not the smugness of those who by wealth or influence control other destinies; but the power of that most merciless weapon ever at the disposal of the mind of man—the use of pure logic based upon an exact knowledge of facts in the quest for absolute truth.

He was a strange one, Jean sighed, a rare one. He took no one, not even her, his assistant, into his confidence, admitted no one to his thoughts, and divulged only as much as he cared to, if the spirit moved him. The smoke of his nameless cigarettes eddied about him, cast a pungent disguise over the smell of chemicals and acids in the laboratory.

Jean reported: "The missing-persons bureau by its Sergeant Hays says Mrs. Hossner was listed as missing early this morning. Her husband, Fritz Hossner, gave the alarm."

"What!" Frost exclaimed, whirling toward her.

"That's what they told me," Jean repeated. "Mr. Hossner expressed the fear that his wife had either been kidnaped for ransom or taken away to a fate unknown for reasons unknown. He awoke in the middle of the night, saw a stranger in the room, started to get up, and was slugged unconscious. When he came to, he was alone.

"The police sent a detail over, taped a bump on his head, and promised to keep hands off until he got some word from the kidnapers. The thing has been kept out of the papers so far. I got the information only by using your name. Hays wants to talk to you. He's still on the line."

Frost strode out, returned after a few seconds, his face expressionless. He picked up the Throckmorton guide and skimmed it swiftly till he found what he wanted. He opened a closet and took out a couple of garments, looking somewhat like leather jackets, one of which he tossed to Jean.

"We've a great deal of ground to cover in a rather short time," he explained. "Take this. It's a bullet-proof vest. Perhaps you won't need it, but wear it.

"Here's fifty dollars. Take a taxi to Clehr's office first. If he isn't there, talk to his secretary and find out anything she knows about Mrs. Hossner's appointment and his conversation with her. Find out who his patients and all other visitors were to-day.

"Then run out to the zoo and get some antelope hair. On your way back, stop at the Chemical Products Co.'s main office and buy a flask of liquid air. It will be heavy, but I think not too heavy for you to manage. Handle it with the greatest care and bring it here."

Jean mulled over this diversity of errands. "Anything more?"

"That's all." Frost was already striding toward the door.

"Will you be here? Or where can I get in touch with you if necessary?"

Frost paused briefly, mused. "First the library, then the marriage-license bureau—"

Jean interrupted. "Don't tell me you are going to take out a license?" she inquired maliciously.

As if sprung from a catapult, Frost bolted out of the room with an expression of pure horror on his face.

IV.

AT THE MAIN library, Frost called for Landon's "Architecture of Old English Manors." The library's sole copy resided in the reference room from which the President and an Act of Congress together could not have removed it. Impatient at the delay, he carried the volume, a large folio, to a table for perusal. In the back was a series of folding plates through which he rapidly flipped until he came to the one he sought. He studied this minutely and read every bit of descriptive detail which lay in the text proper.

From the library, he continued his way downtown to the City Hall. In the marriage-license bureau, it took him less than ten minutes to rifle through the records, retrogressing day by day, until he obtained the information he was after.

Leaving the City Hall, he drove to police headquarters and entered the offices of the missing-persons bureau.

Sergeant Hays had nothing to add to the information he had given over the phone, but gave the gist of the report again.

At the conclusion, Frost nodded ambiguously. "Is any watch being kept over Hossner?"

The sergeant, a rugged, ruddy-faced individual with square jaws and a ponderous manner, shook his head. "No. As the thing stands, we don't know what we've got on our hands. Kidnaping, maybe. Maybe another man in the case. Or maybe she herself just slugged him and walked out in the middle of the night. Sounds goofy, but you never can tell, and of course he isn't much help. Anyway, he asks us to lay off just in case a ransom note does turn up.

"Hell," he fumed, "you know how it is, Frost, and what we're up against. If we tail the guy and it is a kidnaping, sure as fate we queer the negotiations, the victim gets hurt or killed, and then we've got the whole damn press as well as the family hollerin' about the way we messed things up.

"Besides, there's no phone in the place. For all we know, they may both have been slugged by a burglar. She comes to, sees her husband out cold, and goes tearing for a doctor. Meanwhile, he comes to, and hot-foots out to report that his wife has vanished.

"Come to think of it, you haven't yet told us how you're in on the case."

"She was a client of mine," Frost truthfully replied.

"Client of yours, eh? What's the set-up?"

"That," Frost drawled succinctly, "is precisely what I am interested in discovering."

He abandoned the missing-persons bureau in favor of the homicide-squad offices.

"Is Inspector Frick around?" he asked the man at the desk.

"No; he went out on a call. Due back any minute, though, if you want to wait."

"I'll wait." He took a seat and consumed two of his cigarettes, by which he deduced that approximately twelve minutes elapsed before Frick bustled in, to find Frost surrounded with an aura of pleasantly pungent fumes.

The inspector, a wiry, crisp little man with a decidedly military carriage, immediately trotted over to Frost.

"For cripes' sake," he whispered anxiously under his breath, "why do you want to take chances smoking those infernal things in here of all places?"

Frost crushed the butt absently. "I hadn't thought about it. I've got something I want to talk over. Busy?"

Frick nodded his head. "I'll say I am. Can't you let it wait?"

"It's important. How long will you be occupied?"

"That's hard to say. This Clehr mess is as bad as the Lingle case."

THE ABSTRACTION disappeared like magic. Frost snapped: "What Clehr mess?"

"Where have you been hiding? Clehr was murdered this noon."

"What!" the professor barked.

"I said murdered. The papers have been yelling it all over town. Thought everybody knew by this time. Interested in the details?"

"Go on!"

"Clehr left his office in the Crayman Building at twelve fifteen according to his secretary. He must have mingled in the noon crowd and turned south on Fifth Avenue. Somebody let him have it as he started to cross the corner of Forty-eighth Street on a traffic change, at twelve twenty-three. No witnesses so far found, and no clues except the slug which we turned over to a ballistics expert.

"He just crumpled over. For a couple of seconds, they thought he had stumbled. Somebody stooped to give him a hand and let out a squawk. Then the panic was on. He stopped just one slug, but he stopped that with his heart, and it came from behind. Coat powder-burned. Whoever did it simply stood right behind him and walked off in the crowd. It's going to be messy."

"Why?"

"Clehr was a big man in his field, psychiatry and that sort of thing.

Nervous old ladies and society dames could run in and tell him all about the big bad dreams they had after eating too many chocolates or soaking up too many Martinis," Frick said dryly.

"He had some big clients, some of the biggest names in town. They told him stuff about their private lives, and what they did, and what they thought they were going to do, that they'd never think of telling us. Confidential stuff, love affairs, family skeletons, and the rest of it. And Clehr kept it all card-indexed, case history for each.

"We took a look at those files when we went over his office. There were plenty of cranks of all sorts who came to Clehr. It's entirely possible that some one turned sour on him, or decided he'd given away too much dangerous information. We're working on that angle, hoping we can pick some leads up, because so far we haven't a thing to go on. Chances are he had made enemies, too.

"That makes it messy enough. But, on top of that, there've been a dozen people, powerful people, who've already pulled strings and brought pressure to bear not only on the higher-ups but on the papers and anywhere else it might do some good. We're sitting on a powder keg."

Frost nodded serenely. "That makes it much easier."

"Easier!" Frick snorted. His already perspiring face took on a somewhat redder hue. The clouds of wrath gathered.

"Easier all around," Frost added genially. "The murder of Clehr is solved. Those who are quaking lest their sins be discovered and broadcast," he continued in a lightly mocking tone, "can rest in peace until they feel the need of telling all about their latest fixations and complexes to another psychiatrist.

"However, while solving the mystery of why the highly important Dr. Clehr was murdered, I'm afraid that at the same time I must present you with the mystery of why a hitherto obscure, unknown, and unimportant Mrs. Hossner was killed."

"Any connection between the two? Where?" Frick asked impatiently.

"There you have the answer," Frost agreed. "In my laboratory."

"What! In your l-lab—" Frick stammered in his haste. It was his turn to be astonished.

"I would suggest," Frost urged, "that we lose no time. We'll need the photographer, coroner, and the rest of the crew. And have them do the job as fast as they can."

V.

THE BUSTLE of police headquarters was gone. The noise of mid-afternoon traffic was gone. The corpse was gone, and with it the photographer, the fingerprint expert, and the rest of the homicide squad.

Only Frick remained with Frost in the restful quiet of his library, while Frost told precisely as much as he chose, and no more, of the circumstances in which the dead woman had come to him and the circumstances in which she had died.

"Hence it is plain," Frost concluded, "that Clehr was murdered because the woman had told him some or all of her experience, and because some one as yet at large did not want that experience to be investigated. It was a needless murder, in many respects, and indicates that the killer is becoming panicky."

"You should have phoned us the moment you found she was dead," Frick said. "There'll have to be a lot of explaining now. It might have saved Clehr's life."

"Nonsense!" Frost exclaimed. "Your own examiner places the time of death for the woman at approximately one o'clock. As a matter of fact, it was exactly fourteen minutes and twenty-one seconds before one o'clock according to my watch. And, by your own testimony, Clehr had already left his office at twelve fifteen."

Frick yielded the point. "I still don't see why the woman picked your laboratory of all places, intentionally or otherwise."

"Why not? She was so wrought up and nervous that it is probable she never knew she had the aspirin box in her pocket. Remember, she had been wandering around, until she went to Clehr, who sent her to me. When some one rang the doorbell, she made a dive for the laboratory, as if she was afraid of being seen, or of being pursued. I told her she would be absolutely safe there, that she had nothing to fear, and that the laboratory was soundproof. Then I went to see who was at the door.

"In the meantime, she experienced a relief of tension and found the box in her pocket with the poison tablet. It appears that she did not even think about a glass of water. She could have got one from the laboratory faucet, but the indications are that she swallowed the tablet as soon as she found it."

The inspector frowned. "You think some one put the box in her pocket without her knowing it? Some one who thought that she would take the tablet sooner or later and that the death would be checked off as suicide?"

"Exactly!"

"But why? Why? If it's a case of kidnaping, nothing is gained by killing the goose that might have laid a golden egg. And if Clehr was killed because of knowledge he might possess about the woman, why aren't you and Miss Moray in danger of the same fate?"

"We are."

"Have you been attacked? Do you know them? What's behind this, Frost?"

The professor replied: "I don't know them. I know the cause and result, the motivation, even the identities of one or two persons involved. The identity of the real criminal remains to be found. I have my suspicions, but I want proof. Rather to my surprise, no attempt has been made on my life. In the absence of any other explanation, I am inclined to believe that my assistant was the object of an attempt that failed, and the criminal or criminals then decided on a change of tactics."

"Don't you think it would be wise to pay a call on Mr. Hossner at his apartment?"

Frost glanced at his watch. "I have merely been waiting for my assistant. If she is not here within two minutes, we shall leave without her."

"Why two minutes?"

"Greater delay would enable some one from the missing-persons bureau to be ahead of us. I should like to arrive there first, for reasons of my own."

"You haven't told me anything very definite about why the woman came to you or what she told you," Frick recalled.

"For the good reason that you would declare her crazy. I will repeat it when I have definite, physical evidence to substantiate it."

"Come now, Frost, you can at least give me an idea of what she told you."

Frost answered, with a gleam in his eye: "Of course, since you insist, inspector. She had breakfast with an antelope this morning in a castle by a bloody sea to the accompaniment of organ music from an organ that did not exist."

Frick glowered suspiciously. "Are you kidding me?"

"Certainly not!" Frost denied with a bland air. "That was her story and, in the vernacular, we are stuck with it."

"She was crazy as a loon!" Frick grunted in disgust.

"That is precisely what I told you your reaction would be," Frost remarked. "Time to go."

AS THEY left the house, a cab drew up in front. Jean popped out, breathless and excited, but anger only made her the lovelier. Frost ran down, took the container of liquid air, and deposited it in his laboratory. He rejoined Frick and Jean in the official car.

"I see I was right," Frost observed.

Jean glanced at him. "You probably are, whatever you're talking about. Listen to this. I took a cab to the Crayman Building, I got out at the corner and was walking toward the entrance when I felt a stiff jolt in the middle of my back. I jumped into the doorway and looked around, but I couldn't find any one whose actions were suspicious. There was the usual crowd on the sidewalk. I felt around, and if it hadn't been for that bulletproof vest—" She shivered slightly. "I pulled the slug out—here it is."

Frost pocketed the pellet.

Jean continued: "I suppose you know about Clehr. The cops had already been there and gone before I arrived. The secretary was all excited and not much help. Maybe she'll remember better when she calms down. I did find out that Mrs. Hossner was the only patient who came without appointment to-day."

"What floor is the office on?"

"Tenth."

Frost mused: "He could have got off the elevator at the same time and sauntered along as if looking for some particular office until he discovered which one she entered. Perfectly easy, since she would not know him."

"What are you talking about?" Frick cut in.

Frost said to his assistant: "What else did you find out?"

"Nothing of any help. His secretary had never before seen Mrs. Hossner, did not know the purpose of her visit, did not hear a word of the conversation, and could not find any record of it. Clehr apparently decided the case was outside his province and did not keep his usual index card. That's all. You already have the liquid air. Here are the antelope hairs."

Frick looked as if he was about to have convulsions, "Do you mean to tell me that all this stuff ties up?"

"I do not recall making any such statement," Frost replied. "This, I believe, is 16 Logan Street."

Frick parked the car directly in front of the address.

IT WAS a noisy street. Trucks continually pounded its pavement with heavy loads from the wholesale market not far away. This block, however, aside from the noise, appeared to be a fairly respectable residential district of three-and-four-story stone buildings. According to the owners' whims, each building, though contiguous, had been painted a different color to distinguish it from the others; but the browns, reds, blues, and greens merely lent the street a pied effect, since all the buildings but one were more or less newly painted, and that one was 16 Logan Street, which thus distinguished itself by default.

Frost scanned the directory. Hossner was listed in Apartment 1A. The superintendent dwelt in subterranean crypts, the basement rear to be exact. Frost poked the Hossner button, received no answer.

He tried the entrance door, the lock of which proved to be out of commission. They entered a rather decrepit hallway, none too clean, and found the apartment to their right in the front of the building.

Frick looked down the hall, but out of the corner of his eye watched Frost insert a key in the lock and open the door. It did not open fully. That was because dead men do not care whether doors are pushing against them or not. And the dwarf was as dead as any one could be who had a hole in his forehead.

But even the dead are sometimes not lonely. Another man sat across the room facing the doorway from a swivel chair, his back to a desk. He did not, however, rise to greet the visitors. That was because dead men do not care whether they have visitors or not. And the second man was as dead as any one could be with a bullet in his heart.

VI.

THE DIM LIGHT of the autumn afternoon, straggling through the edges of the lowered curtains, cast a gloom not greatly less than that eternal darkness which the two had entered. The rumble of trucks had a muted sound, here in the chamber of death. The stage was set and the curtain ready, but the leading characters had already taken their last bow.

Jean was first to break the momentary silence of shocked surprise. "Higgs!" she cried out, staring at the nearer corpse. "It's the man who called on us this noon!"

Frick turned to the professor accusingly. "You didn't tell me about Higgs."

"No; I didn't," Frost agreed. "Miss Moray, if the superintendent and his wife are in, bring them up."

Frick hesitated, seemed to debate many matters, then announced to Frost: "There's no phone here. I'll have to go out and put in a call for the homicide squad. Keep a close watch over everything."

Jean walked out with him. She gave him an appraising glance. "Isn't the procedure a bit irregular for a murder case?"

Inspector Frick did not give a direct answer, but there was a note of finality in his voice: "Once in a great while, somebody comes along who stands head and shoulders above the rest of us. Whatever his line is, he's got what it takes, whether he's an inventor, a poet, or anything else. When you spot a genius, my dear young woman, give him all the room to play in that he wants. Rules and regulations aren't for men of that caliber. They make their own rules. They don't play the game according to Hoyle, but they always come out winners. Frost knows what he's doing. And he'll do it better if he has the chance before half a dozen other people go tramping around the room."

The inspector strode briskly toward the nearest telephone in a corner drug store.

Jean found the superintendent's wife in, while the superintendent achieved a doubtful distinction by being both in and out. He was sprawled in bed, and out completely from a successful attempt to decorate his interior with a new coat of whisky. The wife, whose slovenly appearance was rivaled by her sour disposition, glared suspiciously when Jean told her she was wanted upstairs, but finally plodded in the girl's wake.

Frick and another man were entering the front door as Jean headed down the hall from the rear-basement stairway.

"Lieutenant Flaherty of the missing-persons bureau. He was here this morning when Hossner reported his wife as missing," Frick explained.

Frost lounged just inside the door to Apartment 1A, as if he had remained there during the whole of the two or three minutes that the others were gone.

Flaherty let a low whistle escape him. The superintendent's wife, Mrs. Wod, launched the first gasp of what had the earmarks of a three-octave screech, which Frick stopped with a curt:

"Cut out the noise. They're dead and neither you nor anybody else can raise 'em."

He gave the room a rapid inspection. He bent over the man at the desk for several seconds, eyes glued to something he saw there. He strolled back to the group in the doorway with a more positive bearing than he had hitherto worn.

"You," he pointed an accusing finger at Mrs. Wod, "ever see this man before?" He indicated the body of Higgs.

Mrs. Wod shook her head.

"Ever see the fellow sitting in the chair?"

She peered across the now brightly lighted room. "Yes. That's, let me see, the chap who moved into 1A. What was his name? Hossner, that's who it is."

"You're sure?"

"Positive."

Frick asked Flaherty: "Did you ever see that man before?"

Flaherty inspected the corpse briefly, answered: "Yes. It's Fritz Hossner. There's the patch we put on that bruise on his head."

Frick turned to the professor. He demanded and received what information Frost possessed about the late Mr. Higgs. He asked Mrs. Wod if she had heard the shots fired, which she flatly denied.

Frost offered a suggestion: "It's a noisy street, with heavy truck traffic. Any one who heard the shots would undoubtedly ascribe them to back-firing and pay no attention to them or to the time."

"The police surgeon can probably fix the time of death pretty accurately," Frick decided.

"Approximately an hour and a half ago, for both of them," Frost stated.

"You saw the note Hossner was writing just before he was killed?"

"I saw a note on the desk," Frost admitted. "If I remember correctly, it read: 'To whom it may concern—I have carefully thought it over. I have decided not to pay the ransom. The kidnaping racket must be stopped. I will try to capture him when he returns and force him to tell me where my wife has been taken. It may be foolish but—' The note abruptly terminates. There is a spatter of ink where the pen was dropped."

Frick announced, looking at the professor: "Well, it looks as if the case is clear now, motive and all."

Frost said: "An unfinished note lying on a desk need not necessarily have been penned by a dead man found at the desk."

Frick's face fell. He asked grumpily: "Mrs. Wod, would you know Hossner's handwriting if you saw it?"

"Spare yourself the trouble," Frost cut in. "I can identify the handwriting. It is identical with that on an application for a license to wed, made out by Fritz Hossner."

"That clinches it."

"Indeed?"

Frost's inflection conveyed nothing but interest. He had been smoking cigarettes incessantly, and with such speed that the lighted tip seemed to race toward the butt, which he then used to ignite another cigarette. A cloud of spicy fumes eddied around him. All his faculties seemed to be keyed up, and while the fumes appeared to make the others a trifle giddy or drowsy, the only visible effect upon him was a brightening of his eyes, a sharper alertness to every detail—word and action.

IN SPITE of his announced conviction, Frick spoke rather as if he was on the defensive. "Hossner is sitting at the desk writing the note. He has his automatic ready. He hears a sound at the door, whirls around, sees Higgs, and fires. Higgs sees what's coming and fires at the same time. It's a double killing. They've happened before."

"I believe the door was locked when we arrived," said Frost.

"What of it? Hossner may have left it ajar. If you notice the lock, you'll see it's the kind that automatically works when the door is shut, so that anybody inside could get out just by turning the knob, but anybody outside could get in only with a key."

"Precisely what I observed," Frost agreed. "Did you happen to observe that the weapon beside the man at the desk has been discharged once, whereas the automatic in Mr. Higgs' hand has been fired thrice?"

"I expect the ballistics expert to certify that Hossner's bullet is in Higgs' head, and one of Higgs' bullets in Hossner's heart."

Frost persisted: "And the other bullets? I failed to find a trace of them in the room."

Frick hesitated a moment. "That puzzled me at first, but I wouldn't be surprised if one of them turned out to be the bullet that got Clehr."

"I would be not only surprised but positively astonished if one missing bullet was not found in Clehr's body and the other stopped by my assistant," Frost said. "And I am confident that Higgs' fingerprints will be found on the gun in his hand, and Hossner's on the gun beside him."

"What the devil else would you expect?" Frick snapped with some exasperation.

"When Mrs. Hossner left Clehr's office, only she and Clehr knew that she was coming to me. If Higgs trailed her all the way, it is most improbable, aside from time limitations, that he then immediately rushed back to ambush Clehr, and promptly returned, after the murder, to my address."

Frick argued: "Higgs could have followed her and loitered by the taxi. He could have overheard the address she gave. Or he may have had an accomplice. Snatches are seldom the work of one man, usually two or more. He could have told the accomplice, if he had one, to follow the woman while he took care of the doctor. Better still, if he was deaf and dumb as you say, he wouldn't even need to be close to the woman. He could read her lips from a little distance and see the address she gave."

Frost exhaled a cloud of smoke. "Ingenious!" he commented, in a noncommittal manner. He dropped the idle remark: "Did you note that only five of the sixteen apartments in this building are rented?"

"What of it?"

"The building doesn't seem to be well-kept-up. I presume you are aware that this is on the ground-floor front, and that the superintendent's quarters are in the basement rear?"

"What are you driving at?"

Frost suddenly turned to Mrs. Wod. "You don't find much to do around the building, do you?"

The woman yapped: "None of your business."

There was an acid, withering effect in Frost's drawl: "The voice and the attitude are exquisitely true to the nature of their proud owner. By the way, you frequently saw Mr. Hossner?"

"No; I didn't." The woman's attitude had become a good deal more helpful. She developed a profound respect for and fear of that lean, towering, dominant person. "I saw him when he came to look at the apartments. And one morning I saw him and his wife go out."

"How long have they lived here?"

"He rented the apartment five or six weeks ago."

Frost said irrelevantly: "I believe the apartment has been recently cleaned. Vacuum-cleaned, in fact."

Frick put in: "It's a quaint modern custom."

Frost mused, with an imperturbable air: "How bright the woodwork and furniture! What a truly excellent job of polishing even the brass fixtures!"

The inspector wore a harassed face with acute discomfort.

Frost added: "I am sure that you will find the fingerprints of your Mr. Hossner upon the alarm clock that I observe on a table by the bedside. I am likewise confident that Mrs. Hossner's prints will be found on the empty water glass standing beside the alarm clock. Furthermore, I would be most astonished if the fingerprints of your Mr. Hossner were not found on the barrel of the fountain pen lying beside the unfinished note."

Frick looked fit to be tied, when a rush of feet announced the arrival of the homicide squad.

Frost declared: "Miss Moray and I must leave for some important research. We would appreciate your getting the routine questions over with. If you forget any, you will find me at home to-morrow."

Frick gave him a keen but wasted glance and obliged. The squad was hard at work when the professor and his assistant left.

"Will you be at home in case we want to call you this evening?" Frick inquired.

"In other words, what am I up to? I am going to descend into the dwelling place of rats," Frost cryptically replied.

VII.

THE PROFESSOR, in his laboratory, drove with smooth and unerring precision toward some objective that Jean had not yet fathomed.

He slipped something under a microscope, darkened the lights, connected the microscope with a projector. On the wall screen the image of what looked like a huge, fuzzy needle swam into view and focused.

He inserted other tiny things under the microscope, and other images sprang into enormous magnification an the screen.

"What are they?" Jean asked.

"Hairs—antelope hairs. Three of them, you will note, are identical in appearance. The first I found on Mrs. Hossner's skirt. The second came from the sleeve of Fritz Hossner. The third was embedded with some dust and grime on the instep of Higgs' right shoe. The last is one of the specimens you brought from the zoo. You will notice that it is of identical type with the three others, thus establishing proof that the others *are* antelope hairs, but that its coloring is darker and that it differs in minor characteristics."

"And what does this prove?"

Frost snapped: "Simply that Mrs. Hossner, Fritz Hossner, and Higgs have all been, and recently, at a particular place where a particular antelope was kept, probably as a pet."

He replaced the hairs in carefully marked envelopes, inserted new items under the microscope. Again fuzzy forms, like tree trunks, leaped out on the screen with giant enlargement. Frost studied them with a relish that was neither pride nor elation, but rather the eagerness with which a scholar, thirsty for knowledge for its own sake, pounces upon a new fact which is utterly useless by itself but of importance in relation to other facts.

"They're different in type from the others, and not all alike among themselves," Jean commented.

"They are human hairs. I took the first from Mrs. Hossner. It is identical with the second which came from the crossbar at the head of the bed in 16 Logan Street. The third was one of a few short remaining wisps that lived at the base of the almost totally bald skull of the late Mr, Higgs. The fourth I plucked from Fritz Hossner's head, while the last also came from the crossbar of the bed. The first and second are not only identical. Watch!"

Frost removed the twin hairs, inserted them in a spectroscope, focused a beam of light, adjusted delicate mechanism of micrometrical graduation. "Look at the bands!"

Jean stared at a series of lines that sprang into view. "They're lines in the spectrum—meaning what?"

"Aspirin! If all other proofs were lacking, those bands alone would indicate that the person from whom the hairs came was a chronic user of aspirin. The body, among other means, attempts to eliminate absorbed aspirin through the follicles of the hair. Those bands help to explain why Mrs. Hossner would unthinkingly swallow any tablet that came out of an aspirin box."

Frost returned the hairs to the slide under the microscope. "The third hair, from Higgs, has striking differences from the first two. Cross sections from all of them would show the differences even better, but I can't take time to prepare them now. They would tell the exact age of the individuals to which they belonged.

"The fourth hair, from Fritz Hossner, is likewise different from the others, you will notice. And the fifth, one of several similar ones that I found on the crossbar of the bed, also differs from the preceding four. In other words, there are five specimens from four individuals of whom only three, all dead, are known."

Jean's face lightened as understanding dawned. "I get it!" she cried out excitedly. "The hairs prove that Mrs. Hossner *did* live at 16 Logan Street and that some one else lived there who was not Higgs and who was not the man identified as Fritz Hossner."

Frost said: "There is evidence in quantity—dirt, grime, stains, hairs, scratches, and other marks and materials—to substantiate my interpretation in a dozen ways. Logic told what the truth must be, but logic is not enough for juries. The tools of science have supplied the incontrovertible evidence to solve these murders and have woven a web from which the criminal cannot escape. Now we shall use logic and the tools of science for another purpose.

"Bring me the metal flagon with the clamp top. It's over there, in the corner."

He disconnected the projector, switched the laboratory lights on again, replaced the evidence in individual envelopes. He took the container that Jean brought and into it carefully poured the liquid air from its original flask.

"Get the bottles of porcelain cement and binder from the second section of the chemical cabinets," Frost ordered.

Jean laid them on the worktable while Frost brought out a small machine and cylinder.

"Bring all the explosives in Drawer C," he said.

He took solutions and jars from shelves laden with powders, compounds, extracts, fluids, and chemicals of infinite variety.

Jean trotted off and returned gingerly carrying four sticks of dynamite.

"Not enough, but they'll have to serve," Frost remarked. "Don't be afraid of them—they won't explode unless you drop them."

Jean promptly got the jitters and almost spilled them all.

When she had safely deposited them, Frost said "Get the long cloaks from the closet," while he himself turned to other tasks.

Jean remembered them well—they were the garments, bulletproof, except to high-powered rifles, that had protected their lives the night of the Golden Goblin affray, when they raided the hide-out of Blake's gang in woods north of the city.

She paused for a moment, puzzled, before she laid them with the rest of the paraphernalia.

FROST was amusing himself in a singular fashion. He had a glass gun. Except for the fact that it was made of glass, it looked much like the water squirt guns that small boys play pranks with. It worked with a plunger action. The end of the barrel was sealed except for a tiny hole in the center. At Frost's elbow stood a pitcher of water. The professor dipped the glass toy in the water, held it there until the chamber was full, then aimed at a spot on the ceiling and squirted the stream at it. Three tries hit the spot every time.

"Good enough!" The professor seemed satisfied.

"Let me play, too," the girl chided.

"That toy may serve to get us out of a tight predicament." Frost did not elaborate his mystifying remark. "Have you anything like a blouse or sweater and shorts in your wardrobe?"

Sheer astonishment almost petrified the girl. "Why, yes. I also have the loveliest tweed outfit—"

"The devil take the tweed outfit! Sweater and shorts will do, just so you get out of the clothing you are wearing."

"Undress? Here?"

"I don't care where. I am interested only in your legs," Frost flung over his shoulder as he strode toward a section of trays and drawers.

"Goody, goody!" Jean called brightly. "I hope it's going to be assault even if it does sound merely aesthetic."

"Guess again," Frost retorted.

He opened a section, pulled out an immense tray, and lifted from it some sheets that gleamed with a silvery, metallic luster. He brought them back to the worktable.

The girl lay on the unoccupied side of the table, lazily stretching her arms and looking up with frank impudence. She had taken Frost's suggestion literally. Shoes, hose, and dress lay in a little heap. What little she wore was a theory rather than a fact and might just as well have been added to the pile.

"Nice legs, aren't they? You'll never see a better pair," she gayly prophesied.

"Fifty million women in this country alone have the same appendages," Frost dryly commented.

"But I'm not fifty million, thank goodness!"

"A sentiment in which I heartily concur."

Frost set to work. He took a sheet of the gleaming stuff, wrapped it around the girl's ankle and leg, molded it to form, clamped it in back and clipped it. Jean subsided momentarily in the fascination of watching his long, supple fingers, so graceful and symmetric that they seemed almost feminine, work nimbly at their task.

"What are you doing this for?" she asked at last when curiosity got the better of her.

"Time will tell."

The gleaming stuff flowed up ankle, calf, and thigh.

" 'So the captain said, I'll sail alone. And he set his course for the torrid zone,' " Jean hummed.

Frost ignored the levity, finished the leg, set to work on the other.

The girl looked at the first critically, approved of herself, and cocked an eye at Frost. "You'll have to admit it's a swell figure, one of the best. It has everything," she modestly declaimed.

"Thin, flexible, and tough," Frost mused, and added as his assistant opened her mouth: "I was speaking of the metal."

He finished the job. "Try walking and tell me if it bothers you any."

She slid off the table, pranced experimentally, paused in front of a mirror. She looked at her reflection and laughed with glee. "I can see the headlines: 'Nude woman picked up on street. Claims silver-plated legs are latest style.' No; the stuff doesn't bother me to speak of. Next? What's left?"

"You'll be left unless you hurry," Frost threatened.

The girl gathered her things and skipped out, to return a few minutes later to find Frost ready to leave. The long cloak enwrapped his form.

"Take some of the smaller stuff. I'll handle the explosives and other materials," he ordered.

Jean was piqued as she donned the protective garment. He might at least have commented on how weirdly beautiful she looked with her blue blouse, white shorts, silvery gleaming legs, and her whole splendid figure emphasized by the impertinent young wisdom of her face. There must be a way. There ought to be a way. Or else there ought to be a law against men like Frost.

She trotted, not too meekly, after him toward the car.

VIII.

THE LIGHTS of the city retreated behind them, and behind them lay the colossal glow that always hung over it by night, the reflected glare of all its millions of lights. The seemingly endless skyscrapers and the interminable blocks of apartments at last gave way to houses. Traffic lessened, they sped through outlying towns, and at length they emerged on a south-shore road.

Now came the distant surge of the sea and the ebb and beat of waters in the Sound. A stiff on-shore wind was blowing. It rushed through the trees and screamed into every crevice of the car that ambled along at a steady fifty.

They had left the city shortly after eight. It was now nearly ten. A haggard moon hung far down on the eastern horizon and crept higher with weary slowness.

Jean admitted: "It's a good thing I had some sandwiches this afternoon. As it is, I'm hungry enough to eat turkey and caviar. Where are we going? You get me all ready for the tropics and then go batting off toward the polar regions."

"We are not far from the castle now."

"Do you mean to tell me that you took the dame's whole story? That there is really a castle here?"

Frost did not take his eyes off the road. "There are a good many castles in America. Some have been built here, others have been purchased abroad, taken down stone by stone, and carried across the Atlantic to be reërected on this continent.

"Lind Castle is among the latter group. A wealthy eccentric bought it in England more than twenty years ago and shipped it to its present site on Long Island. It attracted some attention as a curiosity, but he died, the heirs sold it, and it was forgotten by a public more interested in the War.

"The woman's story of course brought it back to mind. I refreshed my memory about its location and other characteristics by reference to a couple of volumes, one of which was in my library."

Frost suddenly slowed the car on a curve. "Look off there, between the trees, into that bay."

Jean peered in the northerly direction he pointed. Farther out, the waters of the Sound were dark, and even in the margins of the bay seemed black, but pale and faint rays from the rising moon made a path across the wind-riffled bay, and the wave crests rose from depths the color of old blood and broke with eerily crimson tips.

"Why—why the sea looks as if it was bloody!" Jean gasped.

"That is the woman's blood-red sea. In daylight, you would find the sight even more impressive. It is caused by a variety of marine vegetation, algae which sometimes multiply and concentrate in such quantity in local areas that the result you see is brought about."

"If all this was planned in advance, the killer must be something of a genius."

"Not particularly. He has a certain kind of low cunning. He is shrewd enough to take advantage of most factors. He uses opportunism. But first and last he is a rat, and when the chase grows warm he will be found, like rats, hiding in his lair."

Frost drove on, more slowly now, the lights dimmed. They had not passed a house or met a car in miles. Frost as usual kept his thoughts to himself, and when Jean glanced at his profile, she found it inscrutable.

But to-night there was a difference, an intangible quality that she sensed intuitively rather than saw. Frost was neither annoyed nor angry, neither moved by hatred nor revenge; not disgusted and not ruthless, yet a mood that suggested all these hovered in him.

Jean hoped that something she had done disturbed him, but in self-honesty she decided that the source lay elsewhere. Something, somewhere, past or yet to come in the tortuous windings of murder and mystery, had made him a close companion of the destroying angel.

Frost halted the car and extinguished its lights in a clump of bushes off the road. He divided the equipment into two unequal piles, the larger of which he carried. They trod noiselessly along a private road, obviously little used, that wound through woods. Only the faint moonlight illuminated their course. Frost led and hugged the shadows. The dim light passed into total darkness from time to time when clouds scudded across the moon.

They walked for several minutes before they came to a clearing. In its center stood a castle, Lind Castle, strangely anachronistic, a relic of medieval architecture, transplanted in alien soil. There were no lights shining in its iron-grilled windows, and it seemed to be deserted. It loomed like the dark towers of legend. It flung its casements and scarps against the sky, stood silhouetted against the bay beyond, where the waves endlessly beat.

Frost whispered: "Wait here."

He vanished in the darkness that a cloud cast. Jean thought she saw him move toward the rear of the structure. She heard nothing. The wind made confusion. Frost moved among shadows like a shadow itself.

He was gone for ten or fifteen minutes. He reappeared as silently and swiftly as he had melted away. "Wear the hood," he whispered.

She slipped it over her head.

They walked unchallenged to the front door, a massive thing of hewn oak. Frost tested it gently, and, to Jean's surprise, it opened. Frost pushed it only far enough for her to slip through. He attached something to its outside handle, then stepped inside and closed it with infinite pains. He locked it behind him.

He pressed the button of a flashlight, swung it. The circling beam picked out a great stone hall, with the solid furniture of a much-older generation. The hall had one doorway in each wall, and all the doors were closed,

Frost let Jean hold the flashlight while he pulled from the front door the iron key that rested in its lock. From the inner folds of his cloak, he took the porcelain powder, mixed it with the binder, poured the stuff into the keyhole. It hardened almost as fast as he rammed it in with the key.

The girl did not raise questions. It was not the time. All she knew was that Frost had made it impossible for them or any one else to leave by way of the front door without spending hours prying the rigid porcelain out, or bursting the door from its hinges. She could have understood his doing something to make escape easier, but she could think of no reasonable explanation for his present maneuver.

CATLIKE, Frost stalked to the door in the left wall, listened, and softly opened it. Soundlessly Jean followed.

The swinging flashlight picked out a smaller room, sturdily paneled, and containing stiff-backed chairs against the walls, with an oak dining table in a corner.

Frost strode toward the table, inspected it swiftly, then bent over and played the flashlight on its under side. Jean caught a glimpse of heavy braces and what looked like a cigar box, but which might have been merely another supporting block.

The professor whispered, in words difficult to distinguish through the thin slit in the hood: "Whatever happens, take your cue from me. We are approaching the lair of the rat."

He walked to a door in the rear of the room. Like the others, it opened to his touch. They entered without sound, halted again to listen. Frost played the beam around—

Light suddenly flooded the room, brought the kitchen into full view.

A thick, emotionless voice ordered: "Do as I say or I will kill you." The words sounded slow, labored, and held a trace of accent.

The barrel of a rifle was trained squarely on Frost. It projected from the partly opened door of a closet across the kitchen. The bullet from a high-powered rifle would penetrate their cloaks.

Jean thought of many things. She thought that if one of them made a break, the other might conceivably drop the hiding killer before he could bring the barrel around for a second shot. She thought ruefully of the loaded automatic in a pocket of her cloak. But much as she wished she had been holding it in her hand, she knew she could never have sighted the rifle barrel or possibly have hit the man behind it before he shot first.

Frost drawled: "Moderation is an excellent quality in using that instrument. You may find our aid indispensable in getting out of here before other persons arrive."

The voice commanded, in slow, distinct gutturals: "You will please walk straight ahead. Do not walk fast. Do as I say."

Frost obeyed, Jean at his side.

The professor replied, with a calmness and conviction of mastering the situation that made Jean wonder, and with something akin to a sardonic gibe: "It might possibly interest you to know that the front and rear doors are the only exits to the castle. If you so much as disturb either one, you will have the pleasure of blowing yourself into food for rats. However, do not take my word for it. I would enjoy your finding out for yourself."

The voice, more hesitant, said: "Walk. Do not talk."

Frost mused: "Iron bars are most effective. They serve to keep strangers out. On the other hand, they also keep those inside from getting out. It will take time to remove enough bars for escape. I have not allotted you as much time as you will need."

"Halt where you are!" the thick voice answered.

The floor dropped from under them. Jean gasped aloud. It was all she had time for in the second of that sickening plunge through Stygian blackness. She heard a throaty chuckle, far away, and a grinding of metal and stone. She had a horrible fear of falling through endless blackness to unfathomable depths. But all her terrifying near-thoughts were stopped by the abrupt end of her fall.

Jarred to her hands and knees, she inhaled a sickening stench as dreadful as anything she had ever known, an odor of decay and death and animal smells, overpowering in its nausea.

Then they were upon her with a rush of tiny feet and sharp teeth that tore at her, worried her hands and ankles. Furry bodies flung themselves at her. In the midst of darkness and terror, she thanked with all her heart the foresight of Frost that saved those ravenous teeth from ripping her limbs to shreds. She staggered upright.

"Miss Moray!" Frost's voice cut steellike through the darkness. "There is nothing to fear! Are you all right?"

The flashlight swept around and she gasped without replying.

Walls. Stone walls. A chamber eight feet high, twelve in length and breadth. Rats. Hundreds of rats, lean rats, gaunt rats, hungry rats, giant, rats, swarming and rushing and snapping with the ferocity of starvation. A mound of débris, terrible in its implications. Skeletons, long picked clean of flesh, inextricably piled together with litter and refuse that had accumulated for unknown years.

Jean's head swam. She wanted to faint but could not. She could only stare, in unnerved horror, at those gaping eye sockets and finger bones, those cavernous ribs, the wild horde of rats that surged at her with savage desperation, while her very breathing was poisoned by an indescribable, loathsome stench.

Nothing to fear? Only death by rats, or starvation, or slow suffocation in the stone walls of a prison as impregnable as Gibraltar. And outside—if by some miracle they did escape—a homicidal maniac.

IX.

FROST leaped in front of Jean. His hand flashed into a pocket, came out instantly, and swung in a swift circle, in one of those graceful, continuous motions so characteristic of him. He sprayed a fine stream, and in that deadly strychnine solution, the rats died as they leaped.

He flung a gray monster from his arm, kicked others clear to the opposite wall. He crushed the life from more than one, fought them with a weapon of science and with bodily skill alike, stemming their rush and beating them back with an efficiency more murderous than their attack.

As if by some strange, mysterious communion, they suddenly swarmed off, with squeaking and cries and the patter of myriad feet. There were holes in the walls, where the cement had been furrowed out between stones. They retreated, but they left dozens of carcasses among the débris that had nourished them. Some of them scampered around, or waited beyond range of the deadly spray. Their vigil held an ominous prophecy.

Frost turned the sprayer over to his assistant. "Use it if the rats return in numbers or attack."

He removed his hood, an example that she followed. The stench in the cell smote her like a blow.

The professor immediately trained the flashlight on the ceiling and played it over a small area. Even Jean, accustomed to his peculiarities, was surprised by the appearance of his face in faint profile against the light. Of fear, worry about their fate, alarm over the rats, or awe of the mysterious skeletons, there was none. He showed only curiosity, the curiosity of a chemist analyzing an unknown substance.

"That's interesting," he muttered.

"What is?"

"The trapdoor that dropped us here. I thought we might find something of the sort." He pointed to a block of stone in the ceiling, recessed, and with its visible face at a slant. A piece of rusty metal jutted over its lowest tip. "The block has been cut like a cube diagonally bisected. It is pivoted on a bar, part of which you can see on two sides in those crevices between it and adjacent stones.

"Normally it would hang with its wide, heavy side down and its narrow side up, but the catch prevents the heavy side from swinging down. It is controlled by electrical or spring action, probably both. Our hidden enemy simply pressed a button that withdrew the catch. The stone instantly pivoted of its own weight, and we fell. The catch then returned to position, forcing the block back to its original state."

Even while he was talking, Frost drew a stoppered bottle from his pocket, together with the glass gun. He uncapped the bottle and dipped the barrel into a brownish fluid within. As the chamber filled, an inkling of the toy's purpose entered the girl's head.

Frost raised the gun, aimed at the catch-piece, and squirted the fluid on it. He repeated the performance on the two crevices where the pivot bar was visible.

"Concentrated nitric acid, one of the most powerful corrosives known. It is attacking the metal already," he explained. "Don't let even a drop fall on you."

His voice echoed hollowly through the chamber. The damp, fetid air added a clammy weight to the semidarkness. There was never complete silence, because of the restless rats, but there were eerie quasi silences at times. A slimy film covered the great stone blocks, and the cement that the rats had dug out lay in scattered damp patches. How far their runways extended was impossible to tell. If Mrs. Hossner was right, the house must be honey-combed with tiny tunnels. Perhaps those tunnels would at least save them from suffocation.

Frost drenched the metal parts with acid again. The gruesome mass of skeletons looked on with grins that would never vary, save as the slow encroachments of time and dissolution turned bone to powder and fleshless, mocking jaws back into original dust. There must have been seven or eight human skeletons in that pile. The bones of countless rodents were intermingled with them and littered all over the floor. On top of all lay the freshly picked bones of one large animal.

The professor asked: "Does anything about the human skeletons impress you as unusual?"

Jean shuddered. Her low answer had a tinge of exasperation: "No. Of course it's perfectly natural that they happen to be here and the only surprising thing is that there aren't more."

Among ghostly relics, Frost murmured with the mirthless ghost of a smile: "You may be more accurate than you think."

"If we ever get out of here, and aren't killed by that maniac above, and get out of the castle after that, all of which I have some doubts about, maybe you would give me an idea of why three and six add up to nothing," she retorted.

Frost bathed the iron with more of the concentrated acid. "Shall I start at the beginning? And yet, in the final analysis, there is really little to say. Everything has been said. All the clues were at hand. Words and events needed only comparison in order for the truth to appear."

"Yes? The truth is about as plain as the nose of a fish. For instance, just what did Mrs. Hossner's ravings mean to you?"

"It signified much by itself, and it implied more," the professor began. "At the outset there was a choice of alternatives—either the woman had gone through some mystifying experiences, or she had not. It was quite evident from her manner, and from various of her statements, that she was telling truths.

"The nature of those facts next came under consideration. What were they but a series of fantasies and improbabilities? How many persons would believe them or believe her if she told exactly what she had experienced? The answer could only be that those experiences were designed and planned for the very reason that the woman and her story would be discredited.

"This interpretation further implied that it was the police who would be expected to put her in a psychopathic ward rather than investigate the case if it came to their attention. On the other hand, it also seemed that the police were intended not to hear her at all, but that some one had planned with such cunning that if she did escape she would not find an audience."

WITHOUT pausing, Frost emptied another chamber of acid to attack the metal. "I say 'escape' because from her own story it was evident that she had been drugged, and that it had been planned to keep her in the castle for some ulterior purpose. But her own constitution and her habitual use of aspirin combined to counteract the sleeping potion to a limited degree. She was not carefully guarded. When she ran for the front door, a tear-gas bomb was thrown at her, blinding her. The door must have been unlocked, otherwise she could hardly have had time to fumble for the key and twist it before she would be caught.

"But surely it would be oversight of the most flagrant kind if some one made elaborate preparations for a crime and then left the door unlocked so that the victim escaped from an almost impregnable stronghold. That fact alone was ground for suspicion that, while a specific crime had been prepared, it was only one of a series, and that the criminal or criminals had grown somewhat careless from constant and easy success. It was taken for granted that she would remain in a helpless stupor.

"So far, of course, there was no certainty that any crime had been committed. But the very nature of the circumstances indicated that, regardless of this specific instance, it might lead to the discovery of hitherto unsuspected crimes. What could be the nature of such crime or crimes, and who was responsible for them?"

Frost stopped long enough to light one of the curious cigarettes of his own make and to exhale a stream of smoke that helped to disguise the intolerable odor of the cell.

"Kidnaping, abduction, extortion, and other types of criminal intention occurred to me, and also that, whatever the truth, there must be at least three persons involved. If the woman's husband was the schemer, it would be necessary for many reasons to have an accomplice in the castle, two accomplices for steady vigil. If the woman's husband was not involved, it would still require two persons for the actual kidnaping, and a third at the castle. The arrival of Higgs at the door, though indirectly responsible for the woman's immediate death, was directly responsible for giving me positive evidence of the identity of the criminals."

Frost wore a crooked smile. "In the first place, Clehr has always personally telephoned on the occasions when he has sent clients to me. Higgs stated that Clehr had sent him, but Clehr had not called me. It was presumptive evidence that he had followed the woman to Clehr's offices and trailed her from there.

"In the second place, Higgs made the mistake of assuming that, since I looked puzzled when his fingers and lips moved, I could not read either lips or sign language. I am thoroughly acquainted with both. I watched him while I was scanning his written message. As is not uncommon, his lips and hands were both eloquent, perhaps unconsciously.

"His lips said: 'So it's two here. Well, Fred ought to be done with his job by now, and the three of us can take care of you two in a hurry. And this time we'll see to it that the dame gets curtains for good.'

"His hands talked: 'The game is getting too hot. Whether he likes it or not, I quit after this one. Fred and I should have turned thumbs down. No one would have believed her, and we're taking a big chance this way. Still, if it's all going to smash, a couple more bump-offs can't make it any worse.' "

Jean gave Frost a hard glance. So he read lips and sign language? Well, it would be a long time, practically forever, in fact, before she again assumed his ignorance of anything.

Frost continued: "I let Higgs go on his way because I knew I could find him when necessary. When I found the body of Mrs. Hossner, the hitherto missing crime became a reality, and at the same time the case entered, like a spreading disease, what might be called its malignant stage. Some one had arranged a plot. The plot had failed because the woman escaped. But it had been so carefully laid that no one would believe her anything but insane, and the chances were that she would unwittingly kill herself before she had an opportunity to talk.

"I now had a secondary crime, so to speak, but not the primary crime. I knew that three persons were implicated, of whom one was Higgs, one the man called Fred, and the third either Fritz Hossner or an unknown.

"Surveying in detail each statement made by the dead woman, I resorted to logic to explain some anomalies and to eliminate others. Deliberate staging had to be separated from accidentals and incidentals. The motive and the nature of the crime must be, and were, elicited."

Frost kept his gaze intently fixed on the pivot stone now, while he repeated the acid spraying at intervals. "The antelope was undoubtedly a pet. Whether it wandered along by accident at the time the woman entered the dining room, or whether it was directed there, was immaterial. It served its function. It could be dismissed as unimportant except in so far as it contributed to the fantasy of her narrative and to the unbalancing of her mind. This was efficient planning.

"The blood-red sea I also dismissed as a natural phenomenon known to science. The organ music was part of the staging and constituted one of the apparently inexplicable or hallucinatory stratagems employed to cast skepticism on the woman's story. You saw how it was done."

"I did not," Jean contradicted him.

"You saw the box under the table upstairs. That was the organ, actually a pipeless pipe organ. The box contained thyratron tubes about three inches long. The tubes are essentially radio tubes with a small percentage of added mercury. Each of the tubes was electrically connected to one of the keys on a toy console elsewhere in the house, probably in the kitchen closet. The console undoubtedly has a dial to regulate volume. Different tones are produced by adding electrical resistance, more resistance giving lower frequency and lower notes.

"When any one manipulated the console keys, chords with the full volume of an organ would thunder forth in whatever room the thyratron tubes were placed. The woman may have looked, may have seen the box, but ignored it as being only a part of the table's supporting blocks. As she said, she literally listened to organ music from an organ that was not there.

"The rats that she heard in such numbers in the walls impressed me as having a deep and sinister significance. It was possible but highly improbable that the occupants of the castle would ignore so great a nuisance. Was it not likely that the rats themselves were cultivated for a definite reason?

"FROM this point on," Frost continued, "the case rapidly became clear. Why had not the woman gone straight to the police, or to her husband, when she reached the city? The answer lay in her statement that she had not been married long. I verified that by the city records. Fritz Hossner took out the license on September 26th, only five weeks ago. He rented the apartment at 16 Logan Street on September 23rd, only three days earlier.

"Furthermore, the woman stated that she had no friends here; that she was a stranger. She spent the whole of her time with Fritz Hossner, exploring the city, moving from spot to spot. He introduced her to no one. His wife disappeared the night of October 30th. On November 1st, he intended giving up the apartment and moving to another address.

"All the indications were that the marriage was one arranged through a matrimonial agency. Most of the persons utilizing the services of such agencies have sincere intentions, but crooks are found everywhere."

Frost lighted a new cigarette from the butt of the old, as he continued: "The entire design was now evident. Fritz Hossner surveyed the lists of prospects until he found one who was lonely, friendless, and possessed of a worth-while sum in cash, negotiable securities, or jewels. This last assumption I made, not on the base of anything the woman had said, but as the sole motive that would explain the intended crime.

"If this motive and interpretation proved correct, then the sequence of events was plain. Fritz Hossner corresponded with the woman, had her come to the city to meet him. If the meeting was successful, he married her. If not, he tried correspondence with another potential victim. In this case, the meeting was successful. He married the woman.

"He lived with her for a month, became familiar with her habits, found out whether she had friends or was keeping in touch with them. He had rented the apartment only for a month, and when they both left, there would be no questions asked. He had picked the apartment carefully so that he could even control the matter of exits and entrances to a considerable degree and avoid attracting attention.

"Two nights before the month was up, he gave his wife a sleeping potion and took her by automobile to the castle. If he was noticed as he carried her out late at night, he could explain that his wife was ill and, there being no telephone at hand, he was rushing her to a doctor or a hospital. He was legally married. There would be nothing upon which he could be held.

"Having got her to the castle, he deposited her with his accomplices while he returned, collected all belongings in the apartment, and further made sure that his actions had not been reported or observed. If they had been, and he found himself under surveillance, you may be sure he had a prearranged plan with his two partners for release of the woman in some distant spot.

"But the woman escaped. Higgs and Fred trailed her to the city. One of them continued trailing her, the other went to Hossner's apartment. Hossner, realizing that the woman had confounded his plans by neither swallowing the tablet nor going to the police nor returning to him, but by visiting first Clehr and then us, knew the game might be up. He took a desperate chance in deciding to kill all persons concerned, except himself."

THE STORY unfolded, and Jean almost forgot the grim setting, the killer still at large or perhaps free of the castle by this time, as Frost fitted the details into the larger pattern.

"Fred shot Clehr. Hossner had already made his own fake report to the police. Higgs' arrival at our door was a blunder. His purpose was, presumably, either to gain entry and learn what had happened to the victim; or to hope for an opportunity to kill us if the circumstances were favorable. I am inclined to believe that he was acting on his own initiative, but the point is a minor one.

"Hossner, meanwhile, had prepared everything for his own purposes, by removing all identifying characteristics from the apartment, such as fingerprints and stray hairs, vacuum-cleaning it thoroughly, and then spraying it.

"All this, and the clues I called Frick's attention to, plus the identification of the dead man as Fritz Hossner, was proof to me that the dead man was not Fritz Hossner, but actually the person called Fred. The two were either close relatives, or Fritz had hired the other because of a striking personal resemblance.

"It must have been Fred who trailed you and tried to duplicate his earlier performance in the slaying of Clehr. He failed. He returned to my residence in the hope of breaking in, or finding out what had happened to Mrs. Hossner. I did not take time to look for his footprints outside the laboratory window, but knowledge of the woman's death must have been present in order to account for what followed. The position of the bodies, among other signposts, indicated that it was Fred who made the discovery of Mrs. Hossner's death."

Frost filled the gun and directed acid against metal for perhaps the last time. The fluid was almost exhausted. So far there was no indication that the quantity he had brought would suffice. The pivot stone held. The dank, miasmal odors assailed their nostrils even through the aromatic smoke of Frost's cigarettes.

Frost went on: "Fred returned to the Logan Street apartment to inform Hossner of the wife's death. Hossner kept him there until Higgs arrived and rang the buzzer or tapped on the door. Hossner then knocked Fred out with a blow on the head. He opened the door a mere slit, stepped back, and shot Higgs as the deaf mute entered. He took Fred's gun, shot the unconscious man with it, wiped it clean of fingerprints, and pressed it into Higgs' fingers. He wiped his own gun clean and put it in Fred's hand. He wrote the note found on the desk, and put Fred's fingerprints on the barrel of the pen. He took the patch off his own head and affixed it to the bump he had raised on Fred's skull, in almost the identical spot where he had slugged himself. He carried Higgs' gun away with him when he looked out of the window, peered through a crack in the door, and found that the way was clear.

"He had thus accomplished directly or indirectly the cowardly murder of Clehr, the double-crossing of both his partners and their deaths, and the killing of his wife. If there was no unexpected development, a totally different interpretation of the crimes would be made, the interpretation that Frick and the police were advancing when we were in the Hossner apartment. He not only would not be hunted. He would be listed as dead. He alone would enjoy and spend the profits of murder.

"But his cunning was limited. His best recourse was flight. Instead of departing elsewhere, he returned to the castle. There were incriminating clues that could be destroyed, others—"

Whatever Frost intended to say was never completed. He listened sharply, flattened himself against the wall. "Back!" he commanded his assistant. "Follow these instructions carefully!" He spoke a few swift, concise sentences.

From the ceiling came a sudden grinding tear and scream of tortured metal. From far away rose the quick, instinctive patter of countless feet, a rushing sibilance of rats. The great pivot stone settled, sheared through the acid-weakened bar, and smashed to the floor, crushing débris and bones alike as if they were so much mush.

Frost bent, lifted the girl by her thighs until her straining fingers caught the edge of the floor above. Half pulling herself, half boosted, she went through the opening. She sat on its edge, leaned down, and caught Frost's hand. She hauled until his own hands caught the edge and he chinned himself up.

The kitchen was still fully lighted. Frost raced to a wide window at one side and reached his hand through the iron bars. Immediately after this curious action, he raced back to the opening in the floor. He sat with his legs over the edge of the hole, his back to the door, his body bent down as if he was helping some one up.

Jean ran to the inside kitchen door and flattened herself against the wall the moment she was free. She held her loaded automatic.

The door opened wide suddenly, swiftly. The barrel of a rifle swung into view, and a hand was upon the trigger. Without warning, without compunction, now that she knew what cold-blooded murderer they had trapped in his lair, she followed Frost's instructions and fired. The rifle wabbled, discharged at a tangent, fell to the ground.

Frost was on his feet, around, and training his own gun at the doorway in one fluent motion. "Walk in. Make a false move and I will perform a service to humanity," the professor ordered with deadly sincerity.

Holding his shattered right wrist, blood dribbling down his fingers, a man stepped into view, a man who at first sight seemed like the corpse that had recently lain in a room at 16 Logan Street.

X.

THERE he stood at last, the rat cornered in his lair, the killer who preyed on the helpless and unsuspecting, who used emotions and dreams as the tools for enriching himself, who promised happiness and delivered death; the missing Fritz Hossner who had been identified as the dead Fritz Hossner; a perfect twin.

He was stocky in build like the dead man, with the same stolid face, the same small eyes, the same thin mouth, the same appearance of almost peasantlike simplicity combined with an impression of animal cunning. He had not made a cry or sound when the bullet plowed through his wrist. He made not a sound now, as he came, holding the wrist, his features emotionless.

"Stop where you are!" Frost snapped, and the captive halted ten feet away. "I told you I had not allowed you time enough to escape. You might have succeeded in wrenching the bars out or filing through them in another fifteen minutes. Before I deliver you to a justice that will send you to the electric chair, but will never begin to punish you for your crimes, you may utilize those fifteen minutes by divulging some information I wish to know. What day is this, Miss Moray?"

"Why, it's now the early morning of November 1st," she replied with a slight frown of puzzlement.

"For how many years have you been carrying on your marriage-murder racket?" Frost flung the question at Hossner.

No answer.

"Is your real name Fritz Hossner?"

Sullen silence.

"What were the names of these women whose skeletons lie in the cell? Those whom you made brides of the rats?"

No answer.

Frost's whole manner, as he stood on the edge of the pit, had been stiffening and tensing. Now, with a look of hawklike and ruthless determination, towering as if he longed for the captive to continue his stubborn silence or to make some break that would furnish excuse for giving the killer what the killer had given to his victims, Frost stated savagely:

"I want those names. I want them now. If necessary, I will get them by other means, the same means that enabled me to identify you by hairs that you overlooked on the crossbar of the bed at 16 Logan Street, hairs that will send you to the chair.

"I will photograph every set of teeth on those skeletons and circularize every dentist in the country until some are identified by bridges and fillings. I will gather up every scrap of metal, every button, every remaining piece of cloth, no matter how rusty or moldy, and place them under the microscope. I will study the bones and analyze them, until I have built up an accurate picture of the height, weight, appearance, and, characteristics of the woman of whom they were part.

"I will set handwriting experts at work on the records of the license bureau, comparing your recent signature with every signature on every application for the last twenty years, until all the false names you have ever used are brought to light, and the names of all your victims.

"I will have all the files of all the matrimonial agencies in the country examined in detail for records of your handwriting, your photograph. I will have the police departments throughout the country compile, if necessary, a list of all women missing and never found. It will take time, but I will build up a web of evidence and mute testimony from which you will never escape the chair, if you escape mob vengeance. You can believe me.

"You may sit silent through trial, and I will send you to the chair. You may lie and deny everything, and I will send you to the chair. Plead insanity, and I will prove you sane beyond any doubt whatsoever. Now talk!"

The prisoner talked. He mentioned names and years, a woman from Okmulgee, another from Denver, one from Iron City. The first three he had buried in the grounds of the estate, but success came easy, the extra work seemed needless. Thereafter he simply turned the bodies over to the rats. No; he had not always used the same technique. He drove one of his brides to the castle, murdered her as she slept. In other cases, his technique was much like that employed on the latest victim. The obscurity of the victims, and his own reticence, were his best protection.

Yes; Fred was related to him, a half brother. Higgs had been hired more than twelve years before, included in the plan partly because of his physical defects. Higgs and Fred occupied the castle. Fritz went there eventually only to deliver the drugged brides.

Yes; he had always planned to get rid of Higgs and Fred when the need arose. No; his real name was not Fritz Hossner. Yes; the proceeds had been split—half for himself, half to be divided between Fred and Higgs.

"And you thought this would be a favorable opportunity to eliminate those two and to retire from activity?" Frost asked him. "The prize must have been unusually attractive. How much did the woman have? Five thousand? Fifty thousand? One hundred thousand?"

"Twenty-seven thousand dollars in bills. She did not trust banks," came the slow, stolid reply.

The man shifted slightly on his feet. Frost held the gun at his side, not troubling to keep it trained on the killer.

The captive showed no emotion, no feeling, no regret. The crimes were only so much cash business so far as he was concerned. They served his perverted nature well and gave him an easy living.

Jean listened with a repugnance and loathing greater than anything she had felt, even over the rats, as he admitted the fiendish murders in a voice of brutal complacency.

The occurrences at 16 Logan Street had taken place just as Frost reconstructed them. From there, Fritz had gone direct to the castle. He killed the antelope and tossed it to the rats. He did not expect to be pursued, but he was taking no chances. He had long planned where to hide and what to do in case some one came to the castle in search of him. It was incredible that Frost and the young woman had escaped from the cell. He had removed two bars from one of the smallest windows when he heard a crash and ran to the kitchen to find out what had happened.

"That is all," Frost abruptly terminated his questions. "Now we can be an our way."

The captive stepped forward.

"The other direction," Frost commanded.

The man moved—like a catapult, head down, hurtling straight on. Jean cried out, swung her automatic, knew in that fleeting moment that whether she fired or not, the hurtling body would still topple Frost into the pit. The professor neither side-stepped nor shot. There was no time for one and nothing to be gained by the other. Jean stared. One moment the professor had been standing—the next he was sitting on the floor, cross-legged; in some instantaneous fashion, his legs folded under him, he was down.

Hossner's head battered free space where Frost's shoulders had been, but Hossner's legs hit where Frost's shoulders now were. The killer went over head-first into the pit.

He uttered one bull-like cry before a sharp snap and a thud sounded from the cell underneath. Then there remained only the patter and scurry and squeaking and gnashing of hundreds of ravenous rats.

SICK, appalled, Jean looked away.

"Save your sympathy for a better cause. One is tempted to believe in cosmic justice," Frost remarked coldly. "The man was dead when he landed—that snap came from a broken neck."

Jean shuddered. "It's a pity he didn't live, if only to clear up the old murders."

Frost walked to the window, reached a hand out, "I can turn the dictaphone off now," he informed her.

He stopped the machine that he had suspended on suction disks outside and above the window, and returned carrying a small parcel.

Jean ventured: "And now how are we going to get out of here? Why can't we leave by the front or rear door?"

"Because if the front door is burst from its hinges, or bullets are fired through the clogged lock, the dynamite which I attached to the outside handle will explode. And if the rear door is opened, a weighted stopper will drop into the flagon of liquid air, and the clamps will then snap shut, holding it in place."

Jean frowned. "What of it?"

"Liquid air is a gas in an abnormal state. It constantly tries to return to its natural state by evaporating, expanding, and warming. In doing so, tremendous energy is released. Liquid air must be shipped and handled in uncapped flasks. A full flask will evaporate in a day's time. If the door is opened, the evaporation and expansion will almost instantly build up the pressure for a violent explosion."

He placed his parcel at the base of the door. "Wait in the dining room," he said.

He rejoined his assistant there a few seconds later.

"Now what? Some hard work prying or sawing bars out?" she asked.

Frost shook his head. "I left part of the dynamite with the dictaphone. I just lighted its fuse."

A dull boom came from the rear of the castle, followed seconds later by a second, sharper blast and splintering thuds.

Frost strolled to the kitchen, examined it with interested eyes. "I would like to have watched it," he said. "The dynamite of course blew the door out, and the explosion of the liquid air blew it back in."

Jean sighed. "It's uncanny the way you predict and prepare for what is going to happen."

"No," Frost answered, striding toward the spot where he had left the automobile. "I did not prepare for what was going to happen. A wise man does not prepare for a specific emergency. He prepares for all emergencies. A sequence of events occurred and was faced. If it had been any other sequence of events in the castle, it would have been met in other ways."

Jean kicked an unoffending pebble. There ought to be a way, she thought, or else there ought to be a law.

THE ARTIST OF DEATH

Two men stood in the rear door. For a minute, sick with self-criticism, Jean thought of taking a chance and turning with the automatic still clutched in her hand—

IT WAS A COLD, blustery morning, more like early winter than early spring. Gray clouds shrouded the sky. The wind whipped in from the Hudson. It whirled eddies of dust and bits of paper debris along the Drive. It blew around corners with great, irregular gusts that made walking hazardous. A man hiked after his gray fedora that skimmed away in long arcs like a jack rabbit. A woman started to turn the corner from State Street but the wind blew mightily. Her coat bellowed and she was forced back a few steps. She leaned against the wall of wind. It stopped blowing suddenly and she almost fell. She reached the turn and staggered weirdly as the wind yowled again.

The police car nosed along State Street and eased to the curb in front of Number 13. A blown sheet of newspaper slapped against the windshield, lay flat there for a moment under the pressure of wind, then peeled off and slanted away.

"Wait here, I'll be back in a few minutes," Inspector Frick ordered the driver. He climbed out and huddled his overcoat closer as the raw wind bore down. He hurried briskly toward the old mansion.

Inspector Frick was in no particular rush but he had a wiry appearance and a crisp, military stride that always made him seem to be in a hurry. He approached the door as though the wind drove him, or some urgent and important mission. But if it had been a mild day and if he didn't have a care in the world, he still would have hastened to the house in exactly the same manner.

Frick hesitated briefly before ringing the bell. After all, he had come, partly on impulse, with nothing of very great consequence to tell Frost. He might be disturbing the professor in some important work. Frost might be a little amused or a little annoyed at such an interruption, and the devil of it was that Frick never would know Frost's attitude. The professor, when he chose, which was almost constantly, could be as cold, impassive, and inscrutable as a sphinx, allowing no one a hint of what lay behind the enigmatic exterior.

The door swung open, silently. Frick shrugged as though relieved of a burden and entered. He hadn't pushed the bell, and there wasn't any one in the hallway. It had happened thus before, and it would doubtless happen again. Frick knew something of the precautions, and wonders of modern science with which the professor had protected his house, but each occasion impressed the inspector anew, and he took care to touch nothing, however harmless it seemed.

Another door, leading off the hallway, swung open without sound and Frick walked into the library room. "Good morning, Ivy—hello, Jean," he added as the professor's assistant, Miss Moray, entered from the laboratory door.

Professor I.V. Frost was sitting sidewise in an armchair, his legs dangling over one arm, his back against the other. He didn't seem to be watching anything in particular and he looked vaguely bored. Most men would have found his assistant excitement enough, for Jean was young, beautiful in an exotic fashion, intelligent, and contradictory, but Frost ignored her as she gave a bright response to Frick's greeting.

His quick glance encompassed Frick, and he spoke with a certain detachment, in the purely observational manner of a statistician stating facts.

"I perceive that you still have monkeys on your mind. I would also hazard the opinion that the volume on the subject which you were unable to obtain at the library would not have proved helpful."

"Perhaps so," Frick conceded, "But I thought I might as well get a line on the different kinds. It's a queer business. It doesn't make sense. I don't suppose it's very important, but—the devil!" He looked perplexed. "What ever gave you the idea that I had monkeys on the brain or that I'd been checking up on them?"

"Nothing could be simpler," Frost remarked in an offhand manner. "Any one who reads the newspapers must have noticed the brief account in yesterday's papers stating that both police and the proprietor were puzzled by the actions of a thief who broke into the Acme Pet Shop and killed two baboons. There was a second item this morning to the effect that the body of an ape had been found in a vacant lot.

"When you entered this room, your glance was caught by an ivory monkey which you have seen dozens of times, but which, nevertheless, caused you to give a barely perceptible start. You frowned slightly and your left hand made a vague, unfinished motion toward your left coat pocket. There I observed the corner of a paper slip, with the letters 'i-c-k.' The slip is of the kind, color, and nature in use at the library call desk, and the letters suggest your name, 'Frick.' The inference follows that you called for a book which was either in use or already loaned, hence the slip was returned to you and you put it in your pocket."

The inspector said ruefully, "Right. The answers certainly do sound easy—after you've made them. I suppose I might as well just stand here without saying a word and let you tell me all the details of why I came and what's on my mind."

Frost shook his head. "Be seated and tell me about it. Deductive logic is a valuable tool at times, but like all methods, it has limits beyond which its usefulness does not extend. The time factor alone is its greatest weakness. Logic enables me to study you now and to infer certain truths concerning your current activities; but it would be worthless, except under extraordinary circumstances, for enabling me to determine what you had done a month ago, or what your views of the gold standard are.

"What is so puzzling about those anthropoids?"

Frick hesitated before replying. "I'm not sure that anything is. If you're busy, I won't bother you."

FROST waved him to a chair, but Frick remained standing. "I only intended to stop for a minute or two. You're right about the newspaper stories, but what the papers haven't printed yet is that four more apes were found dead in various places this morning. That makes a total of seven that we know of. There may be others."

The criminologist shifted position slightly. There was no apparent change of expression in his gaunt features, but he had developed a marked interest. Jean, scanning his impassive face from shaggy black eyebrows to hawk nose and stern chin, his thin face seeming fuller in three-quarter profile, decided that his eyes were a trifle less lackluster than they had been a few minutes ago. She kept a keen watch on his hands, but so far he had made no motion toward the box of special cigarettes which he invariably and continuously smoked, from the moment he became interested in a mystery to the minute when he had solved it, but at no other time.

"What are the details?" Frost asked.

Frick took some photographs from his pocket. "Here are a few pictures I had made of the last four when I got interested in the affair. The thing began night before last when somebody broke into the Acme Pet Shop and killed a couple of baboons. Owner claimed about two hundred dollars was missing from the cash register. We decided the apes started raising a rumpus and the burglar shot them so he could loot the place in peace.

"The third ape was found by some boys in a vacant lot last night. We don't know where that one came from.

"This morning, the keepers at the Whitney Zoölogical Gardens found that one of their three apes had been killed. The real massacre occurred in the spring quarters of the Haney Circus up at Ringdale. There they keep all the monkeys in a separate series of inclosed cages which look something like a rambling one-room house. The night watchman was slugged by somebody he never saw. When he came to and looked around, he found that three apes had been chloroformed and the biggest of the three knifed in a dozen places."

Frost mused, as he glanced up from the photographs that he had been studying, "Chimpanzee, baboon, and two mandrills. Did the first three apes resemble any of those in the pictures?"

Frick nodded and indicated one of the bodies.

"They were undoubtedly baboons," Frost stated.

The inspector asked, "What do you make of it? It's cockeyed, unless some nut on the subject is going around killing every ape he can find."

The professor straightened his long, thin form and looked at Frick with new intensity. "Was there any similarity in the nature of the killings, or the animals involved? Think of even the most obvious resemblances."

Frick said, "None that I know of except color. The dead animals were all dark brown or black. The first four were shot. The next two were chloroformed, and the last one was chloroformed and slashed."

"Do you happen to know if gorillas were kept at any of the different places involved?"

"I can't say for the others, but I did see one at the Haney quarters."

Frost remarked, "Good. What do you know about the two apes which were not molested at the Whitney Zoölogical Gardens?"

"Well, I only noticed them in passing, but I would say they were the same size, appearance, and color as the one that was killed."

Frost glanced at a photograph. "That's strange. If your memory is correct, the live ones are chimpanzees. What has happened to the carcasses?"

"Most of them have gone the way of the city garbage by now. There's a chance that the one in the Whitney Gardens won't be picked up until to-morrow morning. You think there may be more to this than appears on the surface?"

"It's too early to say. There are some interesting angles I would like to investigate. You may be right in your suspicion that this is the work of a crank, but suppose we visit the Whitney Gardens. Miss Moray, I will be back in an hour."

He slipped into a long ulster and pulled a battered old black fedora down over his forehead.

The wind whooped as they went out. Frick turned up his collar, but Frost seemed to be wrapped in meditations that made him oblivious to the weather.

They were halfway to the sidewalk gate when it opened and a stranger came through. He eyed the two men diffidently, looked hesitant as though of a mind to turn back, then asked, "Is one of you Professor I.V. Frost?"

Frost nodded his head. The stranger said, "I have an unusual request to make. It is really most unusual, but then, if you are busy—I could come back later—I would rather speak to you in private—"

The professor said to Frick, "Don't bother to wait. Meet me at the Whitney Gardens in a half hour if you like, otherwise I'll give you a ring at headquarters later."

"I'll be at the Gardens," Frick promised.

Frost studied the stranger with an oblique glance that seemed merely casual while they walked back to the house. Jean regarded them in surprise as they entered. The stranger was a nervous, emaciated individual of meek appearance. Pain burned in his eyes. He looked about forty-five, stood approximately five feet eight, and had a pale, tired face. Lines of worry creased his forehead. With his upper teeth, he continually chewed his lower lip.

The professor tossed his hat on a table.

The stranger eyed the girl with distinct disfavor. "I prefer to speak in private," he insisted in a worried voice that was not unpleasant.

Frost's disturbingly good-looking assistant smiled in ready acceptance and went out like an efficient secretary. The stranger seemed a bit relieved. What he did not know was that she had gone into the laboratory and pressed a button that accomplished two functions. It recorded every word of the conversation on a dictaphone, and also brought the speakers' voices to her through an earpiece. She had been with Frost for some months now, and was familiar with many of the electrical, photographic, photo-electric, and other devices that honey-combed the house at 13 State Street, but even she could not say that she knew them all.

When she left the library, the stranger fidgeted for a few seconds, stirred uneasily, and finally blurted, "I might as well get it out at once. I will pay you five hundred dollars to kill me."

Pure astonishment almost caused the girl to relax her hold on the earpiece.

II.

FROST countered with, "Yours is a peculiar request. Why do you make it?" He reached out a hand whose fingers, in striking contrast to the rest of his gaunt, unlovely figure, were slender and feminine in their beauty. He opened the container on a stand and picked up a cigarette that was longer and thicker than standard brands. He lighted it in the same continuous motion and exhaled a cone of fragrantly pungent smoke. His black eyes took on a brighter glitter. Like all great men, Frost was a neurotic, but one whose indulgences were designed to sharpen to their highest thin precision his already brilliant faculties.

The visitor said, "I can't tell you."

"You mean you won't tell me. Why?"

"Well, I won't tell you because I can't tell you."

Frost remarked, "You could go into any underworld hang-out and have yourself killed for fifty dollars, or even ten."

The stranger answered ambiguously, "That wouldn't do. It wouldn't be the same at all."

"Why do you come to me? Who sent you?"

"Nobody. I've read about some of your work. I only came as a last resort. I don't know of anybody else who could to the job just the way I want it."

"There is some particular manner in which you prefer to be killed?"

"Oh, no. Any way will do just so you make sure it can't possibly be considered suicide. Can you accept the offer?"

"No."

The stranger's face fell. "Isn't it possible? Couldn't you plan a perfect murder that could never be traced to you?"

"Of course. There are a dozen or more ways by which I could kill you without the slightest suspicion ever attaching to myself. I could arrange it to include a splendid motive and with clues pointing to some mythical person, or I could guarantee, if you wished, that the homicide would be absolutely and unquestionably classified as suicide."

The stranger looked more hopeful. "Is it a matter of money? I might be able to borrow a little, but five hundred is all I have to my name."

Frost drawled sardonically, "Many men have paid small or large sums for the death of other men during the course of centuries. Many others have paid heavily to avoid being killed. But your anxiety to purchase violent death is, I think, unparalleled in the history of crime. Who are you?"

The visitor hesitated, then gave an evasive reply, "Wouldn't it be better if you didn't know who I am? Then if you killed me and by some accident you were suspected, you could say you didn't know me."

"Perhaps. The difficulties of arranging the demise would, however, be immensely heightened by lack of knowledge about your life and habits."

The stranger thought this over. "That is so," he admitted. "I hadn't thought about the matter very carefully up to now. My name is Connaugh Wilder."

"That's a rather unusual name."

"It's partly Irish and partly German."

"What is your occupation?"

Wilder answered wearily, "I'm a clerk. With Gridley & Halsted for the past twenty years. No, I haven't embezzled any funds. Or at least nobody knows about it yet." The accountant became confused. "Do these details matter now? Can't you arrange it so that I could leave now or possibly you could come along with me and get the affair over with as soon as possible?"

IF EVER a man was in earnest, Mr. Connaugh Wilder was the prize example. He not only did not boggle at the prospect of his own deliberate, premeditated death by violence. He welcomed it and offered to pay in advance. He was eager to quench at once that precious flame of being which most people want desperately to keep to its last final flicker.

Frost lighted a new cigarette from the stub of the old. "Have you entertained the possibility of suicide?"

"Oh, yes, but I haven't the nerve. The sight of a gun makes me nervous. I simply can't kill myself. I want death to come without my expecting it or knowing it. I'm not at all well-known. I'm really a very unimportant person but if you manage the affair well I'll achieve a sort of posthumous fame as the victim of a perfect murder."

Frost asked, "Have you at any previous time tried to have yourself slain?"

"Only the past couple of days," Wilder admitted. He added as an afterthought, "I've been around killing apes."

If this statement was startling, or if it conveyed any hint of deeper significance, or aroused keener interest, not the flicker of an eyelash or the slightest change of expression was visible on Frost's face. Outwardly, he gave the same appearance of calm, impersonal attention, as though listening to a quite ordinary conversation.

The professor suggested, "I read something in the paper about two or three dead apes. Was that your handiwork?"

Wilder looked unhappy. "Yes. I killed seven altogether but it didn't work. I guess it was a crazy idea. At first I thought I would cause something of a mystery. Then I decided that if I was careless enough in doing the job, I might easily get shot and killed. But nothing happened. Nobody interrupted me. The watchman at the Haney place was asleep and when I made enough noise to wake him up I meant to hit him just hard enough so that he would think I was a desperate character and he would really shoot to kill but as it was I knocked him out. After that I decided they might catch me instead of kill me, and then they might think I was insane. Perhaps I am but I don't want people to think so."

Frost listened intently to the singular assertions of the man who wanted to be killed. The air was becoming misty with fumes.

Wilder asked anxiously, "You won't turn me over to the police, will you? And when can you arrange this thing?" There was an almost childlike trust in his manner.

"I have no intention of turning you over to the police," Frost assured him. "However, I wish to consider your offer carefully before I make a decision. Can you call at four this afternoon? No? Then leave your address and I will communicate with you later."

The criminologist continued his analytic study of the visitor as he scrawled on a piece of paper. No slightest detail of Wilder's dress or appearance escaped that probing glance. Yet the man was unaware of being scrutinized. When he rose, he ran fingers as thin as a bird's claw through his already disordered hair. He rubbed his sunken cheeks, and gnawed nervously on the little finger nail of his right hand. His actions were uncertain, disconnected.

"Stay here if you like," Frost urged. "I would suggest that you take a sleeping powder."

"No, no, I have a good many things to do. I must go," Wilder insisted and started for the door.

Frost walked into the hall with him. The professor stated cryptically, "Go straight to your house and wait there. When you hear from me, I believe you will change your mind about certain matters."

Wilder looked astonished for a moment. He opened his mouth, and chewed his lower lip but suppressed whatever he had begun to say. "Perhaps I will," he muttered, and walked across the stone porch. Frost was closing the door as he started down the steps.

Halfway down, he turned around. As he did so, his body jerked. Two bright fountains of red spurted from his neck. A spat sounded from near by. He opened his mouth, but this time he could not speak no matter how desperately he tried. Frost sprang to his side with a motion as swift as a panther's and caught his slumping body. He whirled him around and eased him back onto the porch. Wilder's eyes were already glazing, and there was neither pain nor terror in his face. Only sadness, and a kind of ghostly, dreamy gratitude dwelt on the dead features, as though the unknown murderer had done him a favor.

III.

JEAN came running. Frost snapped, "The man is dead. Get the homicide squad. Call Frick at the Whitney Gardens."

His assistant vanished. When she returned a minute later, she found the professor deftly and swiftly finishing an inspection of the slain man's pockets. He straightened upright by the time two radio squads sped in quick succession toward the house. The wind whipped his hair, and whooped dustily across the porch, but he ignored its chill blasts. Jean shivered even in the coat which she had hastily wrapped around her when she came out.

Frost walked over to the left side of the porch and examined inch by inch the surface of an ornamental pillar. Jean shuddered in the momentary expectation that the sniper might shoot again, but Frost proceeded as calmly as though he knew exactly what events would befall.

The homicide detail sped into State Street while the prowl-car men piled out. Within five minutes, the street swarmed with police and the inevitable throng of the morbidly curious to whom violent death is a magnet.

Frost gave a staccato summary of the slaying. His coolness remained, but an intangible change had taken place. By the cold flame in his eyes, by the endless cigarettes whose glowing tips were whipped into showers of sparks by the wind, Jean knew that his faculties centered on a new and mysterious puzzle which he would abandon only when solved.

All the resources at his command, the tools of science and the weapons of logic, would shadow the criminal with implacable and relentless pursuit. The manifestation of those resources she would see in actions, she thought ruefully; but she would know nothing of the deductions that motivated them. Frost did not conceal clues or facts. He interpreted them in his own particular fashion, and kept silent until he could demonstrate their truth.

Obviously he was on the trail of a mystery with deep and fantastic windings, but what? She wondered whether he put any stock in the dead man's preposterous tale. Except for the murder itself, what was the significance of the case? Had Wilder told the truth about himself or were his statements irresponsible? If so, what could possibly be the real reason for the slaying of the apes?

Frost finished his brief résumé. "Miss Moray and I have a few things to do inside. Send Frick in when he comes. I'll give you any further details you want then." Without waiting for an answer to his crisp remarks, he hurried his assistant along with him.

"Time and speed are of major importance right now. This thing has already gone so far that we can't afford to sift out all the details." The words flowed automatically. His attention appeared to be elsewhere, but while his mind wrestled with some gnarled problem ahead, he told her what lay behind. "This is one case where investigation of some important phases must be left until after the mystery is solved. Call all the places in which apes were killed. Find out when and where they were obtained."

While Jean burned up the telephone wires, he took the *Who's Who* from its shelf and flipped it to the W's. Under *Wilder, Druo,* he found the notation: "Artist and painter . . . residence . . . single . . . brother, Connaugh, b. 1891. . . ."

He looked up a number in the directory and ordered his assistant to call the number immediately.

Jean tried, reported, "Operator says the line is out of order."

"Continue as before," came Frost's reply. He disappeared into his laboratory and was absent for several minutes. When he returned, Jean had completed her calls. She handed him a slip of paper. "The Animal Import Co. supplied all the apes except two at the Haney place. Those two were purchased more than a year ago from another concern. The Animal Import Co. delivered the others within the past week."

Frost ordered, "Get the company, find out how many apes they had a week ago and the sources of supply. Buy all that they now have in stock."

Jean stared at him in bewilderment, but obeyed instructions without protest. If Frost wanted to enter the wholesale market as a trader in the larger anthropoids, doubtless he could produce some excellent reason for an action that on the face of it seemed extravagant.

She put a call through and talked for some time. While the connection was still open, she informed him, "They had forty anthropoid apes a week ago, including a consignment of thirty-five brought back by the Ditzer Expedition. About thirty of these, for which orders had been placed, were shipped out immediately on arrival. The eight or ten remaining were bought yesterday by a Mr. Jones who paid cash and represented himself as the agent for several zoos. The only apes now in stock are a large number of monkeys. Do you want them?"

"No. Get a list of all the consignees."

Jean had just finished when the bell rang insistently. "That's probably Frick," she guessed, and the inspector strode in a few seconds later.

Frost said, "We haven't time to delay any longer. Miss Moray will give you the record of the dead man's conversation with me. Here is a list of all the places where apes have been shipped the past week. Some of them are out of town. Post a man at every one of these addresses in the city and get the cooperation of the police departments in the other cities. Wilder, the dead man, was the self-confessed killer."

Frick looked baffled. He asked dryly, "You want us to protect some apes from a dead man?"

The professor turned to his assistant. "If you aren't wearing your automatics, get them."

"I'm ready."

Frick protested. "But the dead man—Wilder—haven't you any clues about who killed him or why?"

"Just as many as you have. He was shot by a high-powered weapon, undoubtedly a rifle, from the ambush of a truck less than a block distant. The truck instantly drove off. Have your men question everybody in the district, but the day being what it is, I am afraid they will never find witnesses or any one who noticed the car. The bullet passed through his neck and severed the spinal cord. It ricocheted off a pillar. Judging from the angle of deflection, it now lies somewhere at the bottom of the Hudson."

"In other words, no clues?"

Jean handed the dictaphone record to the inspector and hurried after Frost who was already making for the door. Frick trotted out with them.

The professor said, "See what you can find in his pockets."

"They have already been searched. There was only the usual run of stuff—keys, wallet, letters, small change, receipts for bills, and personal papers. Plenty of identification, but nothing to help us much. We're starting a general check-up, of course, to find out if his books are in order and if he had enemies. But if we can't find the slug and don't locate witnesses who saw the actual shooting, we'll never be able to pin a thing on any suspect we might uncover."

Frost closed the issue. "Examine the evidence and have an autopsy performed. If I discover any new material, I will communicate with you at headquarters."

A minute later, he was driving his assistant downtown as fast as traffic and safety permitted.

IV.

FOR A WHILE Jean kept silent in an effort to assemble a significant pattern from the haphazard, irrational, and seemingly irrelevant occurrence of the past hour. The harder she tried, the more confused she became, and the less relation she was able to discern between pieces which were mystifying by themselves. Finally she ventured, "It is rather a muddled affair, isn't it?"

"Not particularly. The structure is now plain, and all that remains to be accomplished is the capture of the murderer, after which the other details can be filled in." He kept his eyes on the road. In profile, his features looked harsh without specific expression. Whatever his deductions were, or wherever the trail led, he kept them secret.

Jean asked, "Did Wilder tell the truth?"

"He told part of the truth, concealed part of the truth, and added a few fictions. He spoke truthfully when he said he had been killing apes. He gave reasons that were false."

"He was not really sincere about wanting to pay to be killed?"

Frost snapped, "He could not possibly have been more sincere."

Jean, exasperated, added lipstick to an immaculate make-up, before insisting, "Why in the world would any one pay to be murdered?"

The professor had the answer. He always had the answer—several answers, she thought wryly.

"There are many possible reasons, among which I might enumerate six. First, he might be so tortured mentally or physically that death would be preferable. Second, he might sacrifice himself to save the life of another. Third, he might desire death, but own a life-insurance policy with a suicide clause. Fourth, he might be insane. Fifth, he might choose a novel method, by appealing in the right quarters, of ridding himself of an insoluble burden while at the same time calling attention to a greater problem which his death might unravel but which his life would complicate. Sixth, he might make the offer insincerely, for the sole purpose of drawing the person appealed to into an ambush, or into a framed murder charge. There are other alternatives, but these are the most obvious."

"Which is the real answer?"

Frost answered, with a faint, sardonic smile, "You ought to be able to deduce the true motive by taking into account the other crimes."

"The other crimes!" she exclaimed, startled.

"Certainly. It is obvious from the statements and evidence that at least one and possibly two other crimes must necessarily have been committed already. That is why speed is important. We must uncover those crimes, and forestall others by trapping the killer."

Jean prove skeptical. "What was there in anything Wilder said or anything that's happened so far to indicate another crime?"

The professor waited impatiently for a red light to change. "Connaugh Wilder was an obscure, unimportant man with almost no funds or resources. The name was unusual and suggested a somewhat betterknown name, that of Druo Wilder. *Who's Who* proved that the two were brothers. Druo Wilder has made a reputation for his experiments in surrealism in painting. He is also an excellent painter of wild animal life and has been employed by a number of museums.

"Druo Wilder was single. That Connaugh Wilder was married was proved by a couple of letters in his pocket addressed to 'Mr. & Mrs. Connaugh Wilder.' If Connaugh Wilder or his wife became involved in trouble, their natural tendency would be to seek out Druo first of all. But it is less likely that they would be the object of criminal activities than the older brother, the artist, who was better-known and better off.

"Furthermore, most of the dead apes were captured by the Ditzer Expedition. Such an expedition would be very likely to include in its personnel a photographer or a trained artist, or both, to depict wild animals in their natural setting. By proceeding with purely logical and rational methods, therefore, and on the basis solely of the information obtained from Frick and Wilder, we have arrived at the strong probability that Druo Wilder plays a more important part in this affair than Connaugh Wilder does.

"But the fact that it was Connaugh Wilder who appealed to us, and who has ostensibly been the key figure, offers strong evidence that Druo Wilder has already been attacked in some manner, and perhaps killed in the same cowardly way that Connaugh was shot. The inclusion of all possible alternatives permits the suspicion that Connaugh may have brought harm to his brother; but consideration of other factors, too long for detailed analysis now, eliminates that theory and returns us to an unknown killer who is still at large. It is more probable that Druo came to grief which enmeshed the obscure clerk."

Frost spun the wheel and drove into West Ninety-first Street.

Jean half wished that Frost would some day make a mistake, if only to prove that he was human. If only once the incisive, clear patterns that he deduced from the scantiest of information would turn out to be something else; if only once that brilliant mind, working with the cold and cutting accuracy of a micrometer precision instrument, would go astray, she would feel more at ease. It was irritating to be given the same material, the same information, the same clues, and to have the same opportunities that he had, but to make little or no headway with them. She admired the methods and faculty that set him apart. Still, being human and feminine and contradictory, she decided that she wanted him to make an erroneous deduction sooner or later. She glanced covertly at him.

"Perhaps I will," Frost abruptly spoke aloud, in enigmatic tones.

A LITTLE electrical tingle shivered through her. Had Frost's uncanny accuracy of observation, his hypersensitive powers of analysis and deduction, enabled him to answer her inmost thoughts? Had she betrayed her thoughts by gesture or expression? She studied his profile from the corner of an eye but found nothing to support or deny her speculations.

As though there had been no interruption in the general course of her thoughts, she asked, "What about the dead apes? You said that Wilder did not tell the truth in explaining his motives. What other reason could there be for killing apes? And why did you change your mind about buying apes?"

Frost retorted, "I did not change my mind. There were no apes available of the kind I wanted. Remember, Wilder was not killing lemurs, marmosets, or other small monkeys. Neither was he killing gorillas, nor all of the larger anthropoids, though he had the opportunity. True, he slaughtered two apes that had been with the Haney Circus for a year, but all the other carcasses had recently come from the Animal Supply Co. The inference is that he slew those two also because he could not distinguish them from the late arrivals.

"In the case of the Whitney Gardens, the deduction offers itself that he was able to detect the new addition, and killed only that ape. We are thus left with the further inference that he was slaying apes that came from a specific source, the Ditzer Expedition.

"Wilder killed apes that were larger than monkeys and smaller than gorillas—apes of the baboon, chimpanzee, and mandrill species, which all approximate four feet in length when full-grown. Why he did so remains to be proved.

"Aside from the reasons he gave, there are many motives for such an action. The apes may have carried the germs of a deadly, contagious disease. The killings may have served as a blind to detract attention from ulterior purposes. In the history of espionage, secret messages have been conveyed on stranger mediums than the skin of an ape."

"Which do you think is the explanation?" asked the young woman.

Frost said, "Here we are."

He halted the car in front of a narrow, three-story, brownstone house. A flight of six worn, stone steps led steeply up to a dilapidated double door that was unlocked. The wind rattled the mail box which contained a couple of letters. There was no card in the name slot under the single bell button.

Frost punched the button. A bell rang inside. They waited a few seconds and rang again, but obtained no response. Frost walked in. A small entrance lobby, scarcely more than four feet square, separated them from a massive single door. Frost tried it and found it locked. He took a group of blank keys from his pocket, selected one, and inserted it. He twisted it firmly and withdrew it. Jean peered at it and saw nothing, but Frost took a file and wore the notches down to the microscopic nicks his keen eyes must have seen.

Within three minutes he had the door open. A hallway led to a flight of stairs. Beside the stair case was a recess with a door at the end of it. A portiére opened off the hallway on their right at the front of the house. Utter stillness prevailed, a silence unbroken by even the ticking of a clock. The faraway, muted sound of passing automobiles, and occasionally a wail of wind, gave the curious impression of a background that emphasized the quiet.

Frost went through the closed curtains, Jean following in his wake. What had once been a comfortably furnished living room looked now as though vandals driven by vengeance or sheer lust to destroy had rioted through the place. Every chair was smashed to splinters, every pillow slashed and its stuffing strewn around. Vases, tables, and bric-a-brac lay in fragments. Even the walls had been mutilated.

Frost swept the room with a glance and plunged through another curtained partition in the right rear of the room. It led to a short passageway from the left side of which several doors opened. The first door exposed a dining alcove which had escaped unscathed. Frost rapped the table smartly as he passed. It gave off a metallic thump.

The next door opened to a small kitchen strewn with wreckage and debris. Flour, sugar, coffee, and a wide miscellany of foodstuffs littered the floor. Even the garbage pail had been dumped, and the old-fashioned ice box emptied of its contents. The vandals had missed nothing breakable in their destructive fury.

Again Frost took in the scene with a glance and hurried to the next room, a small lavatory which, like the dining alcove, seemed hardly to have been touched. The passageway ended in a door which he opened.

Jean gasped, while the professor towered in the doorway like a gaunt specter come for vengeance on the avengers.

The room looked immense, cathedralesque, because its only ceiling was the skylight roof three stories overhead. Two colossal, narrow windows rose a full thirty feet in the rear wall, windows curtained with drapes that swept to the floor. Paintings by the dozen hung on the walls and were tilted against the baseboards—paintings of living animals in their natural surroundings and of prehistoric monsters roaming through fantastic vegetation of the cycles before man. The majority were of recognizable objects, but other strange, morbid, wildly imaginative scenes suggested nothing so much as the irrational images of nightmare. A model's stand had been demolished. Odds and ends of débris lay scattered around. But the paradoxical note was supplied by the fact that none of the paintings had been harmed.

And the dreadful note was supplied by the corpse. Long dead, and with the ebb of life a dry, dark stain spread around the blackened hole in his head, the artist stared with wide-open, hellish eyes at the visitors he could not see.

V.

JEAN STOOD motionless as Frost hurried into the studio and began a swift, penetrating examination of the corpse and its surroundings. Death always proved something of a shock, and death by violence held an added ugliness. The atmosphere, the silence, the eerie nature of the paintings, the body with its sightless eyes and rigid posture, momentarily shocked her to inaction. But she was not sure whether it was not Frost, most of all, who dominated and caused her reaction.

In the months that she had been associated with him, she had watched him solve difficult and gruesome crimes. She had seen him unravel murder with scientific and unerring methods whose all-inclusive scope left no chance for the criminal to escape. It was one thing, however, to start from a crime and proceed to its solution. What she now witnessed was an altogether different matter. Before Wilder had been murdered, Frost, solely from external evidence and statements, had deduced the existence of another crime, an undiscovered murder which he had promptly brought to light. The feat was an exhibition of rational genius which, more than any other single act of his, placed him in a category of his own in her estimation—a category separate from others, above others, and tinged with something of awe.

The spell snapped. She mentally damned herself for wasting thoughts. Frost was cold, almost inhuman, akin to the mathematician in his impersonal approach to problems. But she grudgingly admitted that she was only guessing. She didn't know. Nobody knew.

She forced herself to walk forward and look at the corpse. Death must have occurred a day or two before. A single shot had entered the brain above the right eye. The body lay in front of an easel which contained an unfinished canvas. The smock the artist wore, and the oil-color stains on his fingers, were testimony that he had been working on his last painting before the interruption that had ended in death. He looked superficially like the man who had visited them, but was older, partly bald, and far less emaciated.

Frost rose from a scrutiny of the corpse.

"What did you find?" his assistant ventured.

He replied, with an abstract air, "He has been dead about forty-eight hours. He was shot at the beginning of a struggle with his assailant. The murderer probed the death wound and extracted the bullet, before ransacking the house. At the time of death, Druo Wilder was convalescing from malaria. He had just returned from tropical Africa which he left about three weeks ago. The only other salient observations I care to make at this point are that the murderer stands approximately five feet ten, weights one eighty, has black hair, possesses tremendous physical strength, is a connoisseur of art but completely without scruples, is a deadly and accurate shot, familiar with all sorts of firearms, will commit murder again and again to obtain his ends, wears a nine shoe, and has blunt finger nails."

Questions sprang to her lips, but Frost had turned to stare intently at the unfinished canvas upon which the artist had been working at the time of his death. She moved to his side to get a better view. She saw now that what she had thought to be a canvas was in reality a painting on wood. The clamps of the easel gripped a large panel of natural mahogany, five feet by four feet in size, and a half inch thick. Upon this unusual base, Druo Wilder had painted a scene of bizarre and cryptic symbols.

A desolate, somber landscape swept to the far horizon. In the lower right foreground rose a clump of palmlike trees, from whose lofty fronds peered the simpering faces of naked men and women. At the base of the trees in a semicircle toward the lower left foreground sat eight white baboons, dressed in tuxedos, and peering sadly at a ninth baboon. The ninth baboon was buried from the waist down in the soil, and white like the others, but lacked a tuxedo. The right half of the visible body was human, the left half simian. In front of the rooted monstrosity lay a pile of coal, above whose top danced a pure flame. In the far background to the upper left rose the sun, enclosed in a glass cage, and giving the impression that it had been imbedded in a cake of ice. The whole fantastic landscape and figures were done in dull-grays, corpse-whites, dead-blacks, leprous-greens, and blood-reds.

Jean looked at other canvases laying around. Many of them exhibited the same crazy juxtaposition of unrelated objects, the same weird coloring and morbid imagination. Some of them looked as though the artist had simply put down whatever ideas emerged from the subconscious, without regard to their relevancy or unity. Others indicated a kind of deliberate opposition to reality, as in the case of two oarsmen who were rowing across a desert, while another painting depicted a nude girl swimming over a valley where a frying pan, two large fishhooks, and a purple orchid rested on the ground.

She turned around, and was surprised to see Frost still standing in front of the unfinished wood panel, a frown of intense concentration on his features. For fully five minutes, he stood motionless as he stared with unblinking, unwavering, rapt attention at the scene.

Jean's own interest began to mount, not because the picture appealed to her artistic appreciations, though she granted it originality and talent of a macabre kind, but because Frost seemed to attach importance to it.

OF ALL the paintings in the room, it was the only one on wood. Did that fact have any significance? Did the scene itself have a deeper meaning than appeared on the surface? Had the artist attempted to convey a message in this last creative work he would ever do? Had fear for his life impelled him to leave a pictorial message, but in such veiled manner as to be hidden from the comprehension of the murderer, but apparent to some one who knew him well? Had Connaugh Wilder seen the painting? Like a flash it came to her—the nine apes; Connaugh had killed seven. But Frost said the Ditzer Expedition had brought back thirty-five apes. The sun inclosed in a glass cage—that might symbolize the bars of a menagerie, inclosing something that was never meant to be shut up. And why was the ninth baboon, the half-human, half-anthropoid monstrosity, rooted to the soil? She abandoned speculation at this stage. She decided that she would have bad dreams enough anyway, and if she thought about it much longer, she might become a good companion for the squirrels.

Frost suddenly snapped out of his reverie. "Wait here until Frick and the homicide squad arrive. I'll report the murder from the nearest phone. After they come, go to Gridley & Halsted, find out what you can about Connaugh Wilder's employment there, and find out especially what was the last day he worked. Then go to any newspaper morgue and see if you can obtain a picture or pictures of all members of the Ditzer Expedition. Ask Frick if any more apes have been killed, and if so, when and where. Stay away from 13 State Street. When you're through, wait for me at police headquarters."

Without a backward glance, the professor hastened from the room. Jean noticed, as he departed, that he still wore an air of abstraction and concentration. She heard his footsteps in the passageway, then the bang of the front door.

The muted silence, with the distant sounds of traffic and city noises seeming miles away, got on her nerves the moment Frost departed. She caught herself staring with morbid intensity at the corpse, half as though she expected it to move. The corpse stared back at her with dead, questioning eyes. She shifted her gaze to the wood painting, and studied it until she felt as if she were being drawn into the swirl of nightmare realms.

She listened, listened, staining her ears and unconsciously tautening for the pounding sounds that would announce the arrival of the police. Somewhere she fancied she heard a board squeak, and she jumped nervously, looking around. She backed away a trifle from the dead body. She hummed the Brahms "Lullaby" softly, but the song disturbed the silence curiously, and her voice broke after a few measures, dying away to stillness. She felt ill at ease and longed for the arrival of the homicide detail.

The indirect lighting of the room, whose illumination Frost had turned on when he entered, cast a soft glow which became secretive in the corners. She fancied shadows that did not exist, and imagined things where there was nothing. She wanted to succumb to an impulse to leave and wait for the police at the front door. She suppressed it because Frost had told her to wait here. He might not have meant this exact spot, but his orders were to be obeyed literally.

The stillness had a ghostly quality, as though the room had partaken of the mysterious borderlands, rooted deep in the subconscious, from which the artist had plucked fantasies for his enigmatic paintings. There was something both incongruous and yet oddly appropriate in the presence of the corpse here. Her imagination began to run riot. She had a creepy feeling that the artist was dead, but that his mind and thoughts lived in the paintings he had left. She stared anew at the last work as though it were indeed the enduring essence of the dead brain.

She was peering at that painting when the lights went out. A timeless and stifling terror welled up within her for the flash of an instant, but even if that immeasurably brief paralysis had not frozen her, she would not have had a chance.

A long, hairy, and powerful arm wedged her neck as in a vise. She clawed. Her finger nails gouged out skin and flesh, raked long scratches from which the blood came. That grip never relaxed. She tried to twist and squirm. She could see nothing, through dimming vision, of who or what held her. She kicked backward, furiously, again and again. The sharp heels of her shoes cut and dug and slashed at the attacker. She struggled for breath, but no air came. Fiery dots began to flicker against a swirling darkness. She swung both knees up in a desperate effort to clutch the automatic that nestled in a special holder on her right thigh. The action only brought all her weight on her neck, and her fumbling arm hung limp.

VI.

FROST raced out of the house toward his car but stopped and swept the street with a glance in both directions. A drug store occupied the nearest corner, slightly less than a half block away. He sprinted for the store, his coat flapping in the wind behind him, a shower of sparks flying from the tip of his cigarette.

"It's pity some folks don't break their necks," muttered a vinegary breeder, fat and forty, as Frost sped by.

A chap bucking the wind, head down and not bothering to give leeway to an approaching postman, swore irritably when a lean specter slid through the margin, dodged in front of him, and ran on while his flapping coat snicked the irritable one's hat off whence it sailed along the street.

Frost vanished into the store and into a phone booth. He dialed for the operator, "Police headquarters!"

He got the connection in seconds. "Is Inspector Frick in? . . . Get him off the other wire and onto this. . . . I don't care how important it is, tell him Frost is calling. . . ."

He opened a pocket case without drawing it out, removed one of the pungent cigarettes with nimble thumb and forefinger, plucked the stub from his mouth with middle and forth digit, inserted the fresh cylinder, and lighted it from the old. The motion was continuous. He crushed the butt underfoot. Acrid smoke poisoned the air in the booth. Frost inhaled with relish and sniffed the air with as much appreciation as if it were the purest breeze across a field of clover. But his knuckles beat an impatient rhythm on the edge of the telephone board.

Frick's voice suddenly came through, "Sorry to keep you waiting but we just got another line on the monkey business. Three more dead apes were found dumped behind some trees below the retaining wall on upper Riverside Drive."

"What!" Frost exclaimed.

"What's more," Frick went on, "one of them appears to have been pretty badly cut up. Damn it all, Frost, what the devil is the meaning of these crazy killings? Why pick on apes?"

"How long have they been dead?"

"How do I know? The report just came in from one of the park patrolmen who found them."

"Give me the approximate location and I'll take a look at them. Here's another murder for you to look into. My assistant and I just found the body of Druo Wilder at his—"

It was Frick's turn to be startled. "What! Why, the men have already checked up on Wilder's apartment and nobody was home. Then they—"

Frost cut him short, impatiently. "I know, but this is Connaugh Wilder's brother, and it's a different address. Take it down. . . . Send the homicide detail over and come yourself. My assistant is waiting there and will explain the circumstances. The man has been dead about forty-eight hours. I don't expect to be on hand when you arrive but I'll get in touch with you later."

He hung up for a few moments, then dialed another number. He got a connection with E. H. Wallace, city editor, brushed preliminaries aside, and asked, "What do you know about Richard Ditzer, the man who just returned from a hunting expedition?"

Wallace appeared surprised by the query. "Why, he's a quiet sort of chap in the fifties. One of the directors of the Anthropological Museum. Financed the last trip partly out of his own pocket. Why?"

"What does he look like?"

"Stands about five feet eleven; grizzled iron-gray hair; rather studious-looking; weighs around one hundred and fifty; walks with a slight stoop—"

Frost broke in. "That's sufficient. Do you know him well? Well enough to vouch for him?"

"Absolutely. He has independent means and makes a hobby of the museum thing. He's on the boards of several charities, and is as square as they come."

Frost closed with, "Thanks. I need some information and time is so valuable that I've got to take short cuts. I'm going to get him on the phone, in case he calls you back as a check-up."

WALLACE'S incipient question went unheard as Frost rang off and put through another call. Time dragged while he waited for Mr. Ditzer to be located in the halls of the museum. Less than a minute actually elapsed before he got his man.

The moment he introduced himself, Ditzer replied, "Professor Frost? You are the criminologist, are you not? I should indeed be happy to make your acquaintance at your convenience."

Frost hurriedly interrupted. "I will call for a few minutes to-morrow afternoon. In the meantime, I am anxious to obtain some information that I believe you are in the best position to supply. Who sponsored the expedition?"

"Well, it was a loose sort of thing. The museum paid for our passage. I financed all other expenses such as hiring native porters, miscellaneous costs of gathering and shipping specimens, and so on, which were directly relevant to our work. Mr. Gairth, who captures wild animals alive for different circuses and zoos, joined our party to assemble a supply of monkeys and anthropoid apes. A friend of his, a big-game hunter named Gensel, also joined the expedition. We three did all the financing."

"How many members comprised the party?"

Ditzer replied, "Eight," and named them, adding, "We jointly assumed the expenses of Druo Wilder, artist and photographer of the expedition."

Frost did not enlighten him as to the fate of the artist, but asked, "What route did you follow?"

"Why, we landed at Cape Town and made our way north through the Transvaal and Rhodesia, on to Tanganyika, then west into the Belgian Congo and northwest to the Gold Coast, Liberia, and Sierra Leone. The whole trip lasted four months."

"Did you happen to notice whether the tropic sun had any noticeably bleaching effect on members of the party?"

Ditzer's voice carried his puzzlement. "That is a curious question. Of course, we all got pretty tanned, but as for bleaching—no, I didn't notice particularly. We were all more or less blond types, except Gairth, Gensel, and young Walkner from the museum here. They are dark in hair and complexion, but I can't say I noticed any change. No, I'm afraid I can't answer the question."

Frost had a thin smile, as he inquired, "Did the party stay together?"

"Why, naturally it did. We joined forces to cut down expenses."

The professor asked patiently in the same urbane tone, "I assume that the party functioned as a unit, but I wondered whether there were side trips en route, or whether it didn't occasionally break up for a day or so into two or three groups in order to cover more ground?"

Ditzer acquiesced. "I see what you mean. Why yes, we often worked that way. Sometimes Gairth would go off to bag apes while I went elsewhere for botanical specimens. Gensel disappeared for three days with Wilder at one point and they came back with films and some rare specimens of eland, fennec, and quagga.

"The longest separation occurred between the Transvaal and Tanganyika. Wilder decided that it would be easier to film and sketch wild-animal life with a minimum of followers. He took three of the black boys and trekked east. He was gone for a week and we were all getting pretty worried when he finally returned with some sketches and mandrills. The country there is unmapped, practically unexplored, and rather rough. After that, we decided against long absences."

Frost's eyes glittered brightly. "Did you have any trouble with your wild cargo?"

"No more that usual. It became something of a job to manage the monkeys and apes, but we had plenty of porters. The apes kept up a terrific chatter. One of them yowled for several days. It had injured itself and we talked about letting it free, but it recovered and stopped whimpering. I shouldn't ramble on like this. Do the details of the trip interest you? By all means, drop in and I'll be glad to reminisce."

Frost persisted, "Just one more question. You all left Africa at the same time?"

"Well," Ditzer admitted, "most of us sailed on the same boat. But Wilder came down with malaria when we got to the Gold Coast. We were going to bring him back with us, but decided it would be better if he waited a few days till the crisis passed, when he had more strength. Gensel and Walkner agreed to stay behind and see that he had proper medical attention. There was another boat a week later. So the majority of the party and all the specimens came back on one boat. Gensel, Walkner, and Wilder returned after us."

"Sorry, sir, but your time is up. Five cents more, please," came the lilting voice of the operator.

"Thank you," Frost interrupted Ditzer's flow and soothed central. "Yours has been a most interesting account. I'll call on you to-morrow. In the meantime, do not mention our conversation to any one."

He hooked the receiver and dashed from the booth. His gaunt figure emerged like a specter from the fog of smoke.

He raced back to his car and was jerking at its handle when a radio patrol slid around the next corner. Frost glanced at the house. As though sprung from a catapult, he leaped across the sidewalk and took the stone steps in two bounds. The inner door halted him but an instant before his self-made key turned.

His eyes narrowed and his face was a mask as he plunged through. He sniffed with flaring nostrils while he dashed across the living room and into the connecting passageway. His long legs sped him on and into the studio.

Jean Moray lay in a huddled heap between him and the corpse of Druo Wilder. The last painting of the artist had vanished forever into the destroying flame of the turpentine that had been poured over it and lighted.

VII.

CATLIKE, Professor I.V. Frost dropped to his knees and accomplished three simultaneous actions. He listened for the beating of the woman's heart. His sensitive, agile fingers felt for a pulse in her wrist. His eyes probed the burning oil panel. Nothing remained of the weird painting. The wood itself, and the easel, gave off thick smoke and the red tongues of a hot fire.

He whisked a tiny hypodermic needle from his pocket, filled it with calculating glance to an exact level from a phial that he unstoppered, and plunged it into the girl's breast. He listened again. The stilled heart suddenly gave a great, convulsive beat, raced irregularly, then settled down to a deep, steady throb far stronger than normal as the adrenalin took effect.

The professor rose and caught up a scatter rug which he tossed over the easel. He beat various burning parts until the flames subsided to a glow that would slowly char out. His eyes searched the room and analyzed the floor and the unconscious girl.

Footsteps stomped from the front of the house, whose door he had left open.

Frost returned to Jean Moray. He watched the flutter of life in her eyelids, saw the red weal, rising like a band around her throat. He slipped a wax envelope from his pocket. With a nail file he deftly removed certain tiny bits of evidence from her finger nails. Those fractional specimens of skin, hair, and blood would be sufficient to convict her assailant.

Her eyes opened and she was struggling to arise when Frick and the homicide detail burst into the room.

Jean mumbled, in a dreamy whisper, "What happened? I was far away—floating off in darkness—I was so cold—and I saw—"

Frick barked, "What in Hades does this mean, Frost?"

Frost said, dryly, "Ask the man who staged it. It obviously signifies that the murderer returned for reasons of his own, that he was in the house when we arrived, and that when I went out to telephone he strangled Miss Moray and set the painting on fire. This is one instance where the time element and the need for swift action defeated their own purpose. I had no time to make a complete search of the house, and as a consequence, the murderer escaped, temporarily."

Whatever annoyance he had felt had passed. Things done were done. Jean knew that he never wasted time on regrets. A new problem had taken the place of the old, with one more score to settle.

The fingerprint expert, the cameraman, the medical examiner, efficiently went about their work. Frick looked puzzled. "Why would he go to all the bother of burning a picture?"

The professor answered, "Try infra-red photography. It may bring out some portions of the painting, though I fear it has been totally destroyed."

"What's the connection between this murder and Connaugh Wilder?"

"That is what must be established."

Frick shook his head. "The whole thing is crazy. Connaugh must have been out of his head. We played the transcript of your conversation. 'I will pay you five hundred dollars to kill me.' Baloney. And this business of killing monkeys—"

"Apes," Frost corrected him.

"—is sheer insanity. And where does this tie in? I don't get it. On top of all that—by the way, I didn't tell you when you called in. After we searched Connaugh's place, and couldn't locate his wife, we sent out a description of her from a couple of photographs we found. She was picked up about an hour ago sitting on a bench, of all places, in a lonely part of upper Central Park. She was out cold, doped, and they haven't succeeded in bringing her around yet. What have you got to say to that?"

"Excellent!" Frost exclaimed. "Splendid!"

The inspector bristled. "Look here, Frost—"

The criminologist stopped him with "Save it. I have no doubt that you will obtain nothing from Mrs. Wilder when she regains consciousness. Her story will be that she was lured from her home two nights ago by a telephone call telling her to hurry to a certain corner where her husband had been injured in an automobile accident. She will insist that she went there, and that is the last she remembers. Her story will be entirely true. I said excellent, because finding her eliminates a step and some necessary calculations from my own investigation." He did not offer to elaborate further.

The inspector eyed him critically. A mixture of reactions ranging from curiosity to utter mystification played across his features. "Suppose you—"

Frost asked the girl, "All right, now?"

She struggled to her feet and gingerly felt her throat. "I—I guess so." Her voice had a husky, raw edge to it. She herself looked surprised at the froglike croak which had replaced her once musical tones.

Frost propelled her toward the passageway.

"Wait a minute," Frick objected.

"Can't stop now. Too much to do and not enough time to do it all," the professor retorted. "Have your men cover the street. It's possible that some one saw the attacker come out and you might get a description of the man. I presume you already have some one constantly beside Mrs. Wilder to take down anything she may say when she regains consciousness. Search the house carefully. There may be clues. If it will prove of any help, this is an accurate description of the burned painting."

He gave a quick description of the scene and departed, leaving behind him some energetic members of the homicide squad, plus one baffled inspector who was becoming fidgety every time any one mentioned the word "ape."

THE PROFESSOR drove toward 13 State Street. Jean complained groggily, "I can't think clearly. He got me from behind. I didn't even get a glimpse of him. All I remember is waiting, with that dead th-thing staring at me and then suddenly the—the arm—"

Frost drawled, in acid tones, "Your voice will be all right in a day or so."

Jean stiffened and spoke hotly through clenched teeth. "I practically get my neck broken and—"

Frost interrupted harshly, "Your beautiful neck will also lose the bruise in a day or two. Really, Miss Moray, you should not let a trifling incident upset you so."

The flame of fury whitened her cheeks and brought a blaze to her eyes. The webs in her brain blew away. At that moment she hated Frost, hated him so violently that everything else was stripped from her thoughts. There remained only the clear, crystallized thought that she hated him.

In a voice quivering with rage, she whispered huskily, "If that is all you have to say, you can let me out here and now. My resignation is effective at once."

The professor smiled in an odd, satisfied sort of way. "Stern measures were necessary, but they sufficed," he placidly commented.

Jean Moray had her hand on the door. "This corner is as good as any."

Frost said, "Sit still. Your usefulness is restored. The fastest way to calm your nerves and bring you out of a daze was to stimulate a violent emotion in you. I regret the measures but I approve of the results."

She protested bitterly, "You'd think I was a brass monkey or something the way I get—"

Frost turned, stared at her with glittering eyes. He shouted in a voice of almost uncontrollable excitement, "A remarkable inspiration! A brass monkey! A stroke of genius! Just the words I wanted! Miss Moray, you are positively brilliant!"

Her cheeks had been white, but now a rush of color added a hectic quality to her beauty. She struggled for words, shook with anger. Her lovely lips parted, and her teeth gleamed as though she would bite. She snapped her head up, and the long lashes of her eyes flew wide open as she glared at him. "Professor Frost, nobody—"

But the violence of her resentment subsided in the presence of the energy that flowed from Frost. It lasted but an instant, that momentary flash of insight and knowledge, yet it overwhelmed her with its irresistible conviction of truth. She knew that she had made some contribution of priceless value to his speculations. She did not know how, what, or why, but she felt mollified in spite of herself.

He deftly swung the car into a space that seemed inadequate, and cut off the ignition.

"Do we get out here?"

His cool, inscrutable surface had returned. "We are going," he answered, "upon a tour of the art galleries."

"Of the art galleries?" she echoed.

"By proxy, so to speak. We will take adjoining booths in this drug store. You will commence with the A's and call every art shop, gallery, and museum in the borough, while I commence with the M's. You will ask each one what paintings or other work of Druo Wilder they have on exhibit, and keep a record of the answers."

VIII.

THE Allerton Art Museum possessed a nude in oil by Wilder. The Carter Galleries offered two water colors and a landscape. A group of animal studies was owned by the Daw Foundation for the Preservation of North American Fauna. Jean had gotten to the Eblin Collections, which listed a number of Wilder prints and etchings. She was about to call the Edgeworth Gallery when Frost pushed the booth door open and told her to hang up.

His eyes gleamed with satisfaction and by the keen zest of his attitude she knew that the trail had taken a new twist that raised still further problems.

"We're on our way to the Paris Studio," he explained as he hurried her toward the door. She stopped to order a couple of sandwiches and got outside just in time to jump in beside Frost as he started the car. She offered him one of the sandwiches but he could not be bothered. A problem and cigarettes were sufficient for his needs.

"The end is near," he prophesied. "I ran into a bit of luck though it wouldn't have made the slightest difference. The woman I talked to wanted to know if I was the gentleman who had called a few minutes ago. Naturally, I said I was. She explained then that she was wrong when she said the studio was closed for the night. She had since consulted the director, who would be pleased to keep the studio open late, or who would open it this evening if I wished to make an appointment. Tell me what you deduce from this information."

Jean hastily swallowed a mouthful of tomato and lettuce. "Well," she began slowly, "I don't see that there's anything to connect the two calls."

"Quite the opposite," said Frost. "It would be stretching coincidence altogether too far to believe that an innocent person just happened to telephone the same place at almost the same time for the same reasons that we did. No, I think we may safely infer that the murderer was off on the wrong track, that he returned to the scene of his crime for another survey of the painting, that he deciphered the riddle, and that he then destroyed the painting in order to check pursuit. We may further conclude that he is becoming desperate, that haste is as imperative for him as it is for us, and that he will not wait until to-morrow before paying a visit to the Paris Studio. The work of Wilder on display there is merely a loan exhibit, and not for sale. All the more reason why the killer is likely to show his hand to-night."

"Who is the murderer?"

"You mean the murderer and accomplice."

His unexpected reply shifted the trend of her thoughts. "And what gives you reason to believe there are two of them?" she demanded, a trifle truculently.

Frost remarked, "If I were shadowing a man, and that man might at any moment commit an action that would endanger my life, I would be prepared to act before he did. In a crowded city, I would not risk an open affray. I would have a small closed truck, driven by my partner in crime. From the interior of that truck, with a high-powered rifle equipped with a silencer or not, I would be ready to shoot the victim. But I would not shoot him while he was accompanied by a criminologist and an inspector of police. I would suspect him of betraying me, but I would wait until he came out alone. Then I would follow him to either a very crowded or a very lonely spot, unless I had urgent reasons for speed, in which case I would shoot him immediately."

It was well for society that Frost indulged in the solution of crime rather than the creation of it, Jean thought. With his talents, he could have been an international menace.

The professor continued, "Yes, I should venture to say that the most recent incident entitles us to several deductions and explains certain small points that were not without interest."

"Such as?" she prompted.

"I had been wondering how Druo Wilder, in spite of the fact that he was closely watched, managed to rid himself of something either dangerous or valuable."

Jean protested, "How do you know he had any such thing? How in the world can you possibly say that he was shadowed?"

Frost went on placidly, "The explanation is absurdly simple. I really should have deduced it some time before this. Druo Wilder simply telephoned the Paris Studio and arranged to have them pick up some items for exhibition. He then left his home and his enemy followed him. While both were gone, the Studio representative arrived and collected the package or packages which Druo had left in the vestibule. Simple, ingenious, and effective. I regret his demise exceedingly. He must have been a person with a clever, distinctive, and no doubt, eccentric mind."

Jean sighed inwardly. Frost was clearing up some points that she had not even known existed. "What else is solved?" she asked in a slightly piqued tone.

"We are now positive of what we only suspected—that Druo Wilder did indeed convey a message in his last painting. There again he was most ingenious. He possessed something which he did not intend to surrender. A demand had been made of him and he had refused. He knew that the demand would be made again, and that he might be killed. He decided to leave a pictorial message that would be more or less meaningless to the murderer and to other people, but whose significance would be apparent to one person. That person would naturally be his brother, Connaugh, who could be presumed to understand the way in which Druo's mind worked.

"Druo, therefore, adopted a novel method of conveying the message. Instead of writing it, he painted it. Instead of hiding it, he left it in open sight. Instead of making it small and obscure, he made it gigantic. Instead of leaving it in portable form, he left it on a huge and unwieldy panel of hard wood. If the murderer attempted to carry off so enormous a thing, he would draw the curiosity of every one he encountered and seal his own death warrant. He would need a good saw to reduce the painting to manageable proportions, and we may be sure that Druo left no such useful tool at hand. There would, furthermore, be not one chance in millions that the murderer would have such an instrument on his person. It was clever, damned clever. I feel a personal grievance against the murderer for depriving me of the potential company of a most unusual mind."

DARKNESS had begun to shroud the city. A fine sleet lashed by the wind stung the faces of pedestrians and made driving perilous. Frost brought the car through the rush of late afternoon traffic and berthed it near the Paris Studio.

The art gallery proved to be on the second floor of an old five-story building.

Frost took the walk-up flight of stairs three at a time. The only door on the landing opened into a comfortable, quiet room of considerable size, occupied by a variety of paintings and art objects, a bespectacled young woman at a desk who poked the keys of a typewriter with disinterest, and a fussy little man. The gentleman looked about forty-five, somewhat stout, and completely impractical. He wore a black toupee and clasped his hands tightly as though he feared one of them would wander off.

The professor conversed in low tones with Mr. Paris Studio, who fussed all over the place. He seemed to be objecting to something with a degree of asperity. Frost did some animated talking. Mr. Paris Studio suddenly began to beam, and finally nodded his head with such vigor that his toupee, unfortunately, slid down over his forehead to the great detriment of his dignity. He then trotted over to Miss Typist and whisked her into her coat.

He trotted back and shook hands with Frost with a singular jerkiness not unlike that of a dying piston in its last gasps. This quaint person then hastened over to Miss Moray, bowed weirdly, and announced, "I am delighted to have made your acquaintance, Miss Moray. Make yourself quite at home. Good day."

"You have done nothing of the sort," she thought, but Mr. Paris Studio was already bounding out with the haphazard typist in tow.

Frost seemed amused.

"What ever did you do to him?" Jean asked.

He chuckled. "I merely introduced myself and stated that I desired to have the run of the place to-night. I told him that an attempt at entrance might be made. He became disconsolate at the prospect of losing prospective purchasers, which he assumed we were. I placated him by commissioning him to purchase a Brueghel wood print which I have long wished to add to my collection. I then engaged him in a discussion of the comparative merits of Gaugin and Modigliani, who of course have nothing in common. When I remarked that Modigliani was the greatest artist of modern times, which he is not, but which Mr. Calyppi thinks he is, our host fairly overflowed. He departed, convinced that we are the only two real appreciators of art in America."

He studied the layout of the gallery. "Ah, the beauties!" he exclaimed, pausing in front of a tall display case that stood against one wall.

The "beauties," Jean thought, were about as repulsive as any work of art she had seen in a long while, but the moment she looked at them, she knew they were tied up somehow with the dark windings of the puzzle. How they tied up, or what their significance was, she could not say, but she appraised them with sharp interest. They were grotesque, stylized in a monstrous fashion, suggestive of savages and the jungle, utterly bizarre. In their deliberate exaggerations and frank symbolism, their cynical lines and artificial distortions, they achieved sophistication from elemental tribal beliefs of a kind alien to the Western world.

Upon the three shelves of the show case squatted nine black images, sculptured in wood. Eight of the strangely fascinating figures were definitely anthropoidal and Negroid. The ninth was a perverse and malignant thing, neither ape nor human; a flight of imagination into the dawn of history; a creature low in the scale of evolution, and vaguely akin to Neanderthal man. All nine statuettes were carved of polished ebony.

A card in the window announced: "Loan Exhibit of African Primitives by Druo Wilder."

IX.

FROST made a quick tour of the gallery rooms which occupied the whole of the comparatively small floor. He returned in a minute and decided, "We will concentrate our defense here, since this room will be the object of attack. I would prefer more elaborate preparations, but I believe a trifling item or two in my car will serve our needs."

"Tell me what you want and I'll get it from the laboratory," she offered.

"No, the presence of both of us is essential. As it is, I regret the necessity of leaving you for even a few minutes. Be on guard, but I believe there is no immediate danger."

There would be no more attack from behind, she decided as she took a position in the corner. This time she kept her automatic ready. Frost locked the room when he went out. She concentrated on the other door in the rear of the room. Nervous apprehensions filled her, but nothing happened until Frost tapped on the door.

He brought a few things with him, and occupied himself for some minutes in various parts of the room. When he had finished, he again paused in front of the display case and scrutinized the little black demons. "What do you think of the beauties?"

Jean promptly retorted, "I suppose they're art, but if they're beautiful, I'm Venus. I'd hate to have them around."

"Beauty is more than a matter of superficial appearances. Which line of argument, if we carried it far enough, would bring us to the old metaphysical proposition of whether beauty is objective or subjective," Frost mused.

He gave the room a last survey "Everything would appear to be in readiness. Before I turn the lights out, I would suggest that you take a position near the door to the adjoining room. I will—"

Footsteps tramped up the staircase to the accompaniment of a badly whistled popular song. Frost listened, frowning.

The footsteps continued up to the first landing and stopped at the entrance door. The whistle ceased. Then came a loud pounding.

"Who is it?" Frost called out.

"Telegram! Telegram for I.V. Frost!"

"Our friend Calyppi must have something on his mind," Frost murmured to his assistant. He walked to the door and opened it a crack, still frowning. There was no doubt of the authenticity of the messenger. He wore the regulation uniform, had the customary receipts, carried a couple of other telegrams, and bore the indefinable stamp which characterizes all telegram messengers.

"Telegram for I.V. Frost," he repeated. "Sign here."

Frost signed, watched him turn about and descend the stairs. He closed the door and started to open the message, still frowning. His face suddenly changed and he whirled about.

"Put 'em up and keep 'em up!"

For a minute, sick with self-criticism, Jean thought of taking a chance and turning around with the automatic that she still held. But Frost's hands were high, and he curtly told her, "Do as they say."

The automatic dropped. She faced about.

Two men stood in the rear doorway, with automatics trained on both Frost and his assistant. The heavier of the two stepped inside. His companion closed the door behind them.

The leader jeered, "Everybody falls for a trick some time or other. If you want to find out if anybody's home, send a telegram. Better still, wait on the fire escape and come through while they're busy with the telegram. Nice dodge, eh? Too bad you'll never have a chance to use it yourself."

Jean paled at the obvious implication. Frost seemed unperturbed. "Really?" he drawled. "Perhaps you flatter yourself."

"Shut up!" the leader snapped. "Both of you line up by the wall. Be quick about it, too."

Frost calmly moved to the side of his assistant.

The leader barked an order to his companion. "Get the thing. It's in the display case. The one that looks like an ape."

He kept the two covered while his partner walked over to the case. The second man opened the door and stooped to pick up the ninth primitive. He kept on stooping. He stooped all the way to the floor and lay there, still, inert.

The dark eyes behind the mask of the leader blazed savagely. "Some more of your damned tricks, Frost? All right. Take your own medicine. Go over and get me that statue."

"Anything to oblige," Frost replied. He strolled to the case, bent over, and lifted the little monster. "What would you like done with it?"

The burglar stared. The glitter in his eyes remained, but he was not so cocksure, now, not so boastful of his prowess. "Set it on the table. Then go back where you were."

Frost obeyed, leisurely. He did not go quite as far as the position he had previously occupied. He rocked on his heels. "May I offer a suggestion?" he asked in a mocking voice. "I would suggest that you start shooting at once."

The killer's glare held murder but he replied cunningly, "Oh, no you don't. I know something about you, Frost. It'd be just like you to fix up some way of striking back even after you're dead. I'll just make damned sure of a clear exit before I take care of you. Keep your hands up!"

He sidled over to the table and crooked his left arm around the carved primitive. He kept his automatic trained on Frost's head. He backed slowly toward the front door. His eyes burned in their sockets with a hard, deadly light. Jean read in every gesture and word the mark of the killer. He would shoot as he had shot before, from ambush, or without warning. He would shoot for any slight pretext, or for the sheer lust to kill. And if he was the hidden sniper who had picked off Connaugh Wilder, he was a lightninglike and accurate shot.

He backed all the way to the door and turned the knob.

Frost shifted his weight.

A great many things happened instantly. The killer's body convulsed. His limbs jerked and his muscles cramped. The contraction of his finger pulled the trigger of the gun. The contraction of his arm swung the automatic toward the ceiling. The powerful electric current which surged through him simultaneously exploded all seven shells in the clip of the automatic. The simultaneous firing of those bullets put a terrific strain on the weapon. It burst into bits, tearing the hand that held it and splashing its owner's face like shrapnel. The sudden flow of the house current into the door latch and knob, which Frost had accomplished by stepping on an open connection which he had left under the rug, blew the house fuses immediately after that momentary flow. The lights blotted out.

There was the sound of racing feet in the darkness, a scuffle near the door.

"Frost!" Jean cried out.

"Got him!" his cool voice clipped through the darkness. "I told him he should have started shooting earlier!"

X.

THE PRISONER snarled, "Maybe you'll succeed in sending me up for a stretch for burglary, but when I get out—"

Frost said softly, "For burglary, Gensel? For assault. For second-degree murder. For first-degree murder. And for kidnaping. You'll never get out, if you escape the electric chair."

Gensel openly scoffed. "You're crazy. Crazy as a bedbug." Blood dripped from cuts in his cheeks. The beam of the flashlight which Frost had given to his assistant played upon the captive. A handkerchief was knotted around his wrist, stemming the flow of blood into his injured right hand. His left hand was handcuffed to the hand of his companion who still slept from the gas he had inhaled upon opening the display case. The heavier man's vitality and strength proved amazing. He had already recovered from the shock that stunned him.

The professor fondled the grotesque little wood sculpture he had rescued. "Yes?" he drawled. "Perhaps you would like to be entertained by a story pending the arrival of the police?"

"Sure. Go on and spill a fairy tale. Spill any number of fairy tales. I've got nothing else to do but listen," the prisoner snapped. His eyes smoldered with a dark, evil blaze, and his white face strained with the effort to suppress the pain of his injuries.

Frost's eyes never wavered from their watch on the prisoner; and though Gensel was manacled, the professor kept his automatic trained upon him.

"The big-game hunter of modern times," he began indirectly, "is a far cry from the primitive hunter of old. He matches brain against brawn. He is favored by long-range rifles, the advantages of ambush, and all the resources which science and civilization supply. The sportsmanship of the game cannot be divorced from the kill, or the thrill of danger. The modern huntsman must steel himself against sympathetic emotions. To him, the charge of a wild-bull elephant, the spring of a tiger, and the flight of a gazelle are the same. The actions of animals may differ, but the huntsman's answer is always the same—a bullet without quarter. In that, lay your undoing.

"The minute that Connaugh Wilder was killed, I knew exactly what type of murderer to seek. A city gangster, or all but one in ten thousand of motivated or psychopathic killers, would use pistol or machine gun in preference to rifle or other methods. A rifle is a cumbersome weapon. It cannot be concealed. Its great accuracy is offset by its physical disadvantages.

"Connaugh Wilder was killed from a distance; not a great distance, but a matter of a hundred yards or more. No one could have known in advance that he was coming to me. Therefore, no one could have rented an apartment and set up an ambush in advance. Therefore, he must have been trailed by his killer. Shooting of such accuracy that a single bullet sufficed to pierce the neck and shatter the spinal cord would be phenomenal at that distance, considering the elements of motion and wind drift, if the marksman employed an automatic, and even if he were an expert shot. Therefore, the killer must have used a rifle, a long-range, high-powered rifle of great accuracy with whose use he was familiar.

"Therefore, he must have been at least familiar with distance shooting. Therefore, he was presumably at home in big-game hunting. Since he could not openly follow Wilder with a rifle, he must have been concealed. Since he was constantly in motion, his best recourse would be to a small, light truck. I have no doubt that the truck employed was built for the transportation of animals, with small barred windows that could be fully or partly closed by hinged panels."

Gensel stared at Frost out of narrowed lids. "Go on. Go on daydreaming as long as you like," he jeered. A new note, a hunted look, had entered his eyes.

There was a glacial quality in Frost's response. "Suppose we shift the scene.

"An expedition winds its way through Africa. Between Rhodesia and Tanganyika, one of the members, Druo Wilder, let us say, disappears for a week. He returns with some film reels and some animal specimens, including an ape that whimpers. The ape is wounded. Gradually it recovers. The expedition proceeds. As the expedition reaches its embarkation port, Druo Wilder contracts malaria. He becomes delirious. He drops a hint that is overheard. Two members volunteer to remain with him and bring him back when the crisis has passed.

"In his fever, Druo Wilder babbles a precious secret; not all of it, but enough to inflame the conspirators. They attend every word of the sick man, but he keeps the important part of his secret. Convalescing, he returns to America. The conspirators wheedle, threaten, exhort, perhaps torture him, but he puts them off. They are mistaken. He has nothing and knows nothing. His possessions have been taken on ahead by the main party. Perhaps, after he reaches America, he can make a deal. It depends on what success he has. Whatever his answer, nothing can be done until after landing.

"But then the victim stalls. He professes ignorance. The plotters threaten to expose him. He laughs. They cannot expose him because they can produce nothing to support their contention. The man is shadowed. Still the plotters learn nothing. In a final effort one evening, when the victim resists, the main conspirator kills him. The murderer searches the house but discovers no clue to what he seeks, with the possible exception of the painting, over which he puzzles in vain. He becomes desperate."

GENSEL moistened his lips. "A great yarn," he muttered, but his face was greenish.

With remorseless logic, Frost continued, "He deciphers the purpose of the painting, but not its meaning. He reasons that Druo Wilder, fearing for his life, may have telephoned his brother and released some inkling of the secret.

"One crook watches until Connaugh goes out alone. He telephones his partner, and either one then telephones Mrs. Wilder. Believing her husband has been injured, she rushes out. She is knocked out or doped, and abducted. Connaugh Wilder is then informed that the price of her release is the full secret of his brother.

"We now approach a remarkable problem in psychology," Frost suggested. Gensel's eyes had become glary. His bravado was melting away.

"Connaugh Wilder does not know his brother's secret, but he has the seal of death upon him in an incurable disease. His life is only a matter of months or weeks. He has an insurance policy with a suicide clause. He is devoted to his wife. Four motivations dominate him. He is doomed to death and knows it. His brother has been murdered and he wishes to avenge him. His wife has been kidnaped and he must release her. In order to accomplish one or all of these purposes, he must interpret the painting.

"He understands how Druo's mind worked, but his own mentality is insufficient to decipher the painting entirely. He goes as far as deciphering the significance of the apes, and kills the apes in his desperate anxiety to effect his wife's release. But meeting only failure on all sides, and seeing no way of extricating himself from complexities that his death may end and which his life will only confuse, he decides to use his last funds to have himself killed.

"That strange, pathetic request was in reality a simple and natural solution arrived at by a mind tortured with grief and the burdens of living. His death would probably mean the release of his wife. The insurance would keep her in modest comfort. He would be free from the pain of his illness. And if he could not avenge the murder of Druo, he at least would do nothing to help the murderers.

"But the conspirators have been shadowing Connaugh. When they see him come to me, they kill him. They think he has been on the right track. They think themselves safe because their identity was unknown to Connaugh. They think they can continue the trail where he left off. Through a dummy agent, they have already purchased the remaining apes from the Animal Import Co. And, as luck would have it, they have purchased the ape that was injured; imbedded in the fleshy posterior of the ape, where Druo's knowledge of anatomy and his possession of the medical outfit which jungle expeditions always carry enabled him to place it, they find, let us say—a piece of roughly carved ivory."

Gensel twitched. Walkner groaned. Gensel ran a tongue over dry lips.

Frost went on, "The piece of ivory baffles them. They cut it open, find nothing, perhaps throw it away in disgust."

Gensel's eyes almost popped, while the professor resumed his story, "You had trailed and killed Connaugh. Thereafter you went alone to Druo's home. You risked discovery but you had to go there immediately or it would be too late. You had to examine the painting again and try to unravel its meaning. You succeeded, partly by recalling the imbedded piece of ivory."

Deftly building his drama to its climax, Frost concluded, "The painting gave its own clue to the riddle. Human beings were in the trees but apes were on the ground. That was a reversal of reality. In other words, everything in the scene was to be taken at its opposite value. Instead of white baboons, black apes should be sought. Instead of being free, they should be sought for in captivity. The upper part of the ninth ape was exposed. Therefore, the object was imbedded in the buried half of its body.

"I was somewhat puzzled by the significance of the half-human, half-anthropoid ninth baboon, a point that my assistant was instrumental in elucidating. The symbolism then became plain. The ninth baboon was rooted to indicate immovability. A dead ape was out of the question. The answer must be either a stuffed ape or a statue of wood sculpture. Since the Ditzer Expedition brought back live animals, I chose the other alternative. Since human beings should normally have been on the ground in the painting, I naturally concluded that they were examining some sort of semianthropoid object. Since Druo was an artist, that object would most likely be in an art museum. Only an African primitive, as it is known in art circles, would answer all the requirements."

Frost twisted at the back of the sculpture. "The lumps of coal, with the flame above them, could have only one significance, for coal is carbon."

The statue opened, under a powerful twist of his fingers, and he removed a tightly wedged object, of a gray-brown hue, dull, like a stone. He surveyed it with appraising eyes, as he murmured, "And diamonds are carbon. This is a raw diamond, weighing at least 700 carats. If it is flawless; it will take its place among the great gems of the world. If its color is good, it will be worth about five hundred thousand dollars as it is, and will approximate three quarters of a million when cut and polished. There will be a tidy sum left for Mrs. Wilder, after I assist her in straightening out certain difficulties with the customs officials."

He looked at Gensel with a reproachful glance. "But this is nothing compared with the fortune you threw away. You should have been on the way to Africa now. You had the opportunity in your hand and you destroyed it in your search for a single diamond.

"On the instep of Druo Wilder's shoes, I found minute traces of a peculiar bluish earth. That piece of ivory could only have been the cleverly carved, topographical map of the route to the diamond soil which he had discovered during the week of his absence in Africa."

When the police took him away, Gensel was raving and screaming.

Frost had stopped smoking. A dullness, suggestive of ennui and disinterest, had begun to replace the glitter of his black pupils. Jean Moray tenderly felt her sore throat.

"I hope you're feeling better," he said as he helped her down the stairs.

That was all. She wished—but her wish would be futile.

DEATH DESCENDING

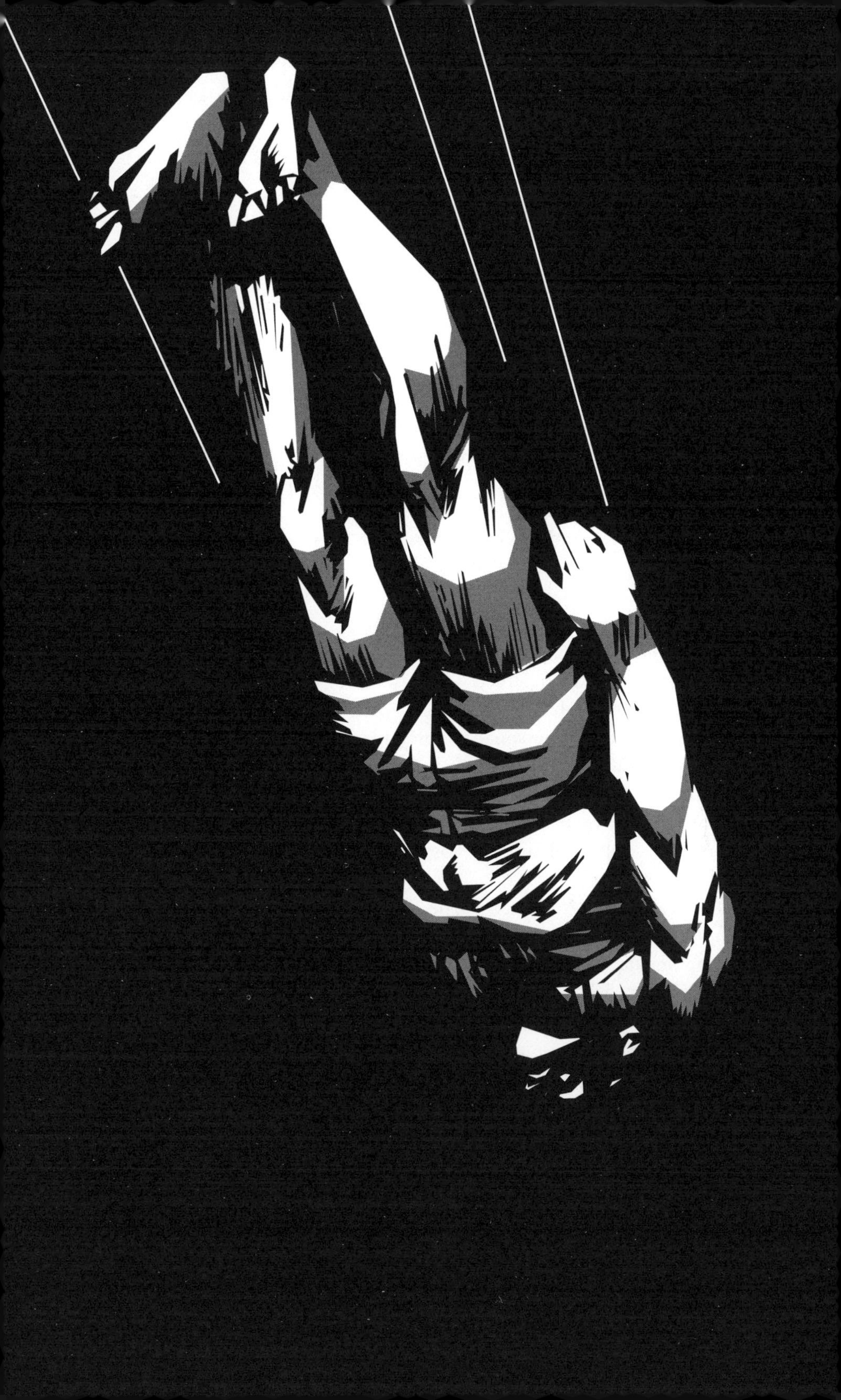

A figure hurtled down—almost on top of them—a figure plunging head-first, body rigid, arms stiffly at its sides, wide-open eyes sightless, glaring in frozen features.

IT HAD BEEN a gay, bright evening except for the fog. It began with a good dinner, continued at the opening of a new play, then after-theater supper and dancing at a night club. The floor show, like the excellent champagne, sparkled. She felt exhilarated, a trifle reckless, and she looked her alluring best.

Jean Moray, endowed by nature with perfect health and body, lived by the principle that what nature bestows can be improved by art. A spirit of tantalizing deviltry dwelt within her face. Her expression seemed constantly on the verge of sophistication, naïveté, aristocratic reserve and easy camaraderie.

Her escort accompanied her to the door of Number 11 State Street. She held out her hand. "A grand evening from start to finish."

He took the impersonal dismissal in good grace. "Sometimes I think you're made of ice. You don't have blood—just ice particles creeping along like the Northern glaciers. Maybe that's why we unfortunates fall for you—the mere fact that you're so far away."

"Isn't it always like that? Easy come, easy go," she answered lightly "Don't most people appreciate things more the harder they have to fight for them? And isn't it true that we generally like some one else more than we are liked in return? Oh dear, we're getting terribly philosophical for two A.M. Call me up soon."

She watched his back retreat through the fog bank that had rolled in during the afternoon. Her glance passed to the house next door. A glimmer of light struggled feebly through the mists. That would be the laboratory window. What was Frost doing in his laboratory at this hour? Had something turned up while she was away, one of the infrequent bizarre cases that were as champagne and caviar to his existence?

It took her but a few minutes to slip into the house, wriggle out of the slinky lines of the pale-pistachio evening gown, that had so subtly and devastatingly emphasized her figure and set off the warm purity of her complexion and her honey-colored hair. She donned practical tweeds, and moments later had crossed to Number 13.

For any other bachelor in New York City, or anywhere else, the employment of an assistant as young and beautiful as Jean Moray would have called out the raised-eyebrow brigade, but Frost's reputation was, unfortunately, her own greatest protection. Jean didn't mind playing the part of a creature of ice, as cool as an Eskimo, but she found herself baffled by a glacier that would not melt.

It was only one of many contradictions in her character that she ignored the admirers she could have won, and reserved everything for the one man who didn't want her, apparently didn't give her a second thought, and had never shown the least sign of personal interest.

It wasn't fair, she decided, to a girl who was perfect, or practically perfect. Maybe if she threatened to resign she would get some action. No; Frost would probably shrug his shoulders and find another assistant, or else he'd raise her salary and let it go at that. Maybe the effect of her entrance would be more stunning if she'd kept on the shimmering gown, but still, Frost might be playing around with acids and chemicals and things by which dresses are likely to be ruined.

The fog eddied around her as her duplicate key admitted her.

She hesitated about knocking on the laboratory door and finally decided just to walk in. She paused on the threshold, closed the door softly behind her.

Professor I.V. Frost, at that hour, and in that place, looked like nothing of the modern world. Instead, he resembled some medieval sorcerer preparing a mysterious and poisonous brew.

Darkness obscured most of the laboratory. An overhead, shaded bulb threw a cone of light around Frost where he sat on a high stool at a table near one of the shuttered windows. He was half facing the door, his features shadowed except for his disheveled hair, the black eyebrows, and the predatory nose. His eyelids flickered up as she entered and she had a fleeting, sinister impression of eyes that burned with knowledge of esoteric secrets. The eyelids drooped, and his gaze returned to his work.

Blue flame flickered from a brazier in front of him. A tripod supported a small, vitreous alembic above the flame. Bottles and phials stood beside the brazier, and a miscellany of strange instruments and objects surrounded it.

Frost remarked idly: "It is pleasant to be admired."

"That's the most egotistic statement you ever made."

He withered her with a look of disgust. "I referred to the expression upon your face when you entered. It was unmistakably that of remembering the most flattering compliment that could be paid you."

Vexed at the rebound of her thoughtless assumption, she hastily changed the subject. "Am I intruding?"

"Of course," Frost admitted with disconcerting candor. "But watch if you like."

She walked to the worktable and observed in silence for a while until curiosity got the better of her. "Might I ask what you are doing?"

"Certainly, you may ask," he agreed, and lapsed into maddening silence.

In a beaker beside the brazier rested a mass of shredded stuff. She noticed a few spilled fibers on the table and picked them up. Some of the shreds were short, dark, and firm; others black, powdery; a few long and golden, fragrant as new-mown hay.

"Dehydrated tobacco," Frost explained. "A mixture of Latakia, Black Walnut, and Sweet Crop."

A colorless fluid simmered in the alembic. With tweezers, he dropped pieces of clove, cinnamon stick, and other spices into the boiling fluid. To the infusion he added a drop of attar of rose, essence of hyssop, and other exotic scents unfamiliar to her. The brew acquired an aromatic character both languorous and sharp, pungent and sweet. From an unmarked phial, he measured a quantity of white powder which he sifted into the beaker and shook vigorously until the tobacco and the powder were thoroughly mixed. He added a number of whole leaves to the liquid, dried leaves of a dark and peculiar plant which she could not identify. The infusion proceeded for five minutes, when he filtered it.

The resulting clear fluid, of a rich, wine color, he drew into an atomizer whose tip he fitted into the beaker. Alternately squeezing the bulb and shaking the beaker, he rehydrated the tobacco with the prepared fluid.

"Tobacco, as you doubtless know, is extremely sensitive to moisture, which it loses readily in dry atmosphere and regains promptly in moist air," he volunteered. "This mixture was dry as desert dust a minute ago. Within ten minutes, it will have completely absorbed the solution, and be ready for the bin." He nodded toward an odd little machine with a hinged receptable attached, a standard device for the home manufacture of cigarettes, with modifications of his own.

"And I had hoped," Jean mourned, "that it was a brand-new mystery that kept you awake at this hour. The perfect crime, maybe."

"If it were a perfect crime, it would never come to our attention. For that matter, there have been thousands of perfect crimes," he drawled.

She knit her brows. "Why wouldn't it be known? What makes you think there have been thousands of perfect crimes? How do you know there have been any, even one?"

The professor seemed surprised. "Isn't it obvious? If a perfect crime were committed, it would never come to our attention, or to any one's attention, for that very reason. Dozens of such crimes are undoubtedly perpetrated every year.

"There are many perfect crimes. Thousands of persons disappear in this city alone. Many are soon located. Some are not found for months or years. A few are never heard from or seen again, and their fate remains a matter for conjecture. They vanish as completely as though they had been transported to another planet. A few among these have doubtless been murdered and their bodies concealed so successfully that the truth is never known."

Jean argued: "How do you know that they haven't committed suicide in some hidden place? Or died a natural death under a different name in another part of the country or abroad?"

"I don't know," Frost admitted, while he watched long, white cylinders drop out of the machine. "No one except the murderer knows. That is the dilemma of the perfect crime: it does not exist except in imagination. It is never known or solved in real life, because it never comes to the attention of authorities. It does not exist in fiction because, if it is solved, it ceases to be a perfect crime, and if it is unsolved, it ceases to be fiction."

The doorbell rang insistently.

"That will be Miss Theresa Wilson," Frost announced. "She is rather late for her appointment."

Jean looked askance, but said nothing. Frost strolled after her into the reception room while she hurried to admit the visitor.

The three-o'clock caller proved to be a slender, smartly dressed young woman with "Junior Leaguer" stamped all over her. She had that peculiar type of bearing which makes society débutantes as characteristic and alike as so many fashion drawings by a given artist, the kind of smooth polish that comes from too much money, nothing to worry about, access to the best circles, and wishes quickly satisfied for the mere asking. But Terry Wilson was worried.

Jean introduced the visitor, who wasted not a second before plunging into the thick of her story. "Sorry I couldn't get here sooner, but after I phoned I decided to go back and see if the body was still scattered around or if it had vanished like the pieces of the statue and the ghost, but it, or I suppose you'd say they, were still there so I started off again and here I am." The amazing statement stumbled out in a breathless rush of words run together.

II.

FROST offered her a pack of cigarettes of a popular brand. She selected one and toyed with it nervously. For himself, he chose one of his own private manufacture. "We'll drive back with you at once." A gleam of interest brightened his eyes as he disappeared into the laboratory. Terry tapped a foot impatiently, gave Frost's assistant a quick appraisal. The professor returned with a valise into which he had hastily crammed some equipment.

"These may prove useful," he observed with cryptical nonchalance.

"But I haven't told you anything yet!" the visitor protested. "All I did was make an appointment!"

"Pardon me, but you told me a great deal the moment you arrived," he informed her. "Pray continue with this strange story."

The heavy fog closed in on them. "I couldn't drive very fast on account of the fog or I'd have been here much sooner," Terry apologized. Her features looked wan and drawn, bore the signs of fast living, but she walked with an athletic stride.

A long, powerful roadster of foreign make stood at the curb. The three climbed in. The fog hung everywhere, limiting visibility to the distance between lamp posts. The lights shone with a sickly glow. Terry threw the car into gear. It leaped ahead with a pur of power.

"The whole business began two nights ago," she explained. "I was driving in from the country and I got the scare of my life when I reached home. Our town house, I should explain, occupies a small block of its own facing the East River. There is a lawn and some shrubbery around the house, and all of it is inclosed by an iron fence. It was about two o'clock, and when I had practically reached home I saw something white in the road. It looked like a human head. Farther on was an arm, and other pieces lay around. I jammed on the brakes, feeling pretty sick, and then saw that a plaster cast had been smashed to bits less than half a block from our house. I decided the vandalism was none of my business and drove home. I kept thinking about the broken statue, and after putting the car up, I walked back to the spot.

"The fragments were gone. A car was roaring off, but I couldn't make out its license number. Only some white powder and a few tiny slivers of the statue remained.

"Why would anybody smash a statue in the middle of a street at night, and then go to all the trouble to pick up the pieces and carry them away?"

Frost listened with signs of increasing animation. "Go on."

"Last night I went to a theater party and got in early, for me. I didn't feel like sleeping, so I sat up reading. Around one-thirty I heard a crash outside. It sounded as if it were on our grounds. I went to the window and looked out. Another statue had been broken up and tossed over the fence. I watched for a while, but no one came. Then I saw something that puzzles me still. The statue was smashed into chunks, and above each separate piece hung a sort of ghost."

"A ghost?" Jean echoed.

"That's what it looked like. A misty ghost above every fragment of the limbs and torso. It was rather quiet, and I sat still, with a creepy sort of feeling. I got the impression that I was seeing things, or dreaming, and that everything would disappear if I waited long enough. Everything did disappear!"

Frost asked, "You mean that all the fragments vanished? While you were watching them?"

"Yes. I couldn't believe my eyes. Finally I dressed and went outside just to prove to myself I wasn't dreaming. I couldn't find a trace of the statue or a single fragment. It had been a fairly warm night. I thought maybe I had seen ice melt, but I know ice doesn't melt that fast. Besides, the ground was hard and not a bit damp, and anyway, why would any one want to throw a lot of ice in our property? I am positive that no one entered the grounds or left them all the while that I watched. I decided to treat the affair as an illusion resulting from a bad case of jitters. I'd seen the ghost of a statue, or the disappearing fragments of a ghost, whichever way you want to put it."

She took a deep breath and tossed the remainder of her cigarette out the window. Fog swirled in. The headlights were almost useless.

"To-day I had a busy schedule—luncheon engagement, cocktail party, dress fitting, dinner, and so on, and my last escort brought me home around midnight. We quarreled on the way, and after he left, I decided to take a run up the Drive. I got the car out and went as far as Van Cortlandt Park, thinking things over. It must have been close to two when I returned. I put the car up—the garage is built onto the house—and walked around to the front.

"The fog was so thick I couldn't see more than ten or fifteen feet. I heard a rush of air and a loud crack. It scared me but I walked on toward the front gate."

TERRY WILSON bit a trembling lip. "I saw something lying there, whitish things scattered halfway between the house and the street. They—they were human, but the body had broken into as many pieces as the statue. It—it was awful. I'll never forget the sight of the—the head—" She clenched the wheel with hands whose knuckles stood out white.

"There was something horribly, horribly wrong about the corpse. I don't know what. It sickened me. It looked as if it had been dead a long time, and it didn't bleed. I turned and ran. I didn't go into the house. I got the car out again and drove off like mad. The fog stifled me. I guess I didn't have any clear idea for a while. I felt caught in a living nightmare. I knew I ought to call the police, but what if they came and didn't find anything, or suppose they did? I started to see our physician but first I feared he might tell me I'd had a breakdown, and then I was afraid it might prove real after all.

"Finally I called our attorney, and Mr. Vogel told me to get in touch with you immediately. So I did, but after I made the appointment I forced myself to drive back and see if the—the thing was still scattered around. It was. I suppose I should have stayed there and told you to come over, but I thought only of getting away as fast as possible."

Frost's brows knitted. His thoughts seemed elsewhere, though he asked a few perfunctory questions.

"You are not alone in the house?"

"Practically. My parents are traveling abroad. I returned early for the wedding of a friend and stayed to open the house. The servants are with the family. There's only the caretaker and my maid here."

"You were engaged?"

"Off and on for the past year," she admitted with candor. "To Fred Devore Allen. We quarrel a lot. He's the one I had the scrap with tonight and right now I guess the engagement's off again."

"I see." Frost's drawl was noncommittal. "He studied to be an engineer, did he not?"

"How did you know? What has that to do with all this?"

"Probably nothing whatever. Do you know of any one who would have real or fancied cause to threaten your life?"

Her face puckered. After a few moments: "No. I've never received any threats, if that's what you mean. I can't imagine why this should happen to me."

"I can," Frost said quietly.

Terry frowned. "You don't think it's just an accident?"

"Ridiculous! There are no limits to coincidence in life, but the laws of probability retain their validity. It is certainly not a coincidence that three similar distressing experiences have occurred in the same place at about the same time on three successive nights. As the Romans would have put it, *ex nihilo, nihil*. I might add that the mystery has only begun, though in progressive stages. Plaster cast—solid carbon dioxide—a corpse—You recognized nothing about the latter arrival?"

"Ugh!" Terry made a wordless grimace. "What I saw of it looked as if it had been buried for ages. What was the phrase you used? It sounded like a chemical."

"Solid carbon dioxide? That was your ghost of a corpse. Nothing else could so adequately answer your description. Commercially, it is known as dry ice. It is extremely cold, with a temperature of -40°C, and evaporates readily when exposed to air temperature."

"But the pieces looked like fragments of a corpse. Why would anybody scatter dry ice around? Or make it in the shape of a body to begin with?"

Frost said: "That is a question whose answer must be proved."

Jean noticed that he did not say "found," but "proved." Had his keen analytic faculties already raced through various alternatives and selected the true answer? His inscrutable features told nothing.

He remarked idly: "You have had other suitors, of course? Have you quarreled with any of them?"

"Suitors?" she repeated cynically. "Any girl nowadays who has good looks and money or money without good looks is swamped. I couldn't even tell you the names of a lot of fortune-hunters I've known."

"No matter. The motive will appear, eventually. In this case, and at this stage, the motive and the identity of our potential criminal are of less importance than the method. The method should lead us to his lair."

"Potential?" queried the driver. "Why do you say potential?"

"Because, if your descriptions are accurate, there has been no crime committed, yet. The crime is to come."

"No crime! Is it no crime to murder a man and dismember the body?"

Frost replied with a laconic paradox. "The fact that a corpse lies in pieces does not mean that it was dismembered. To mutilate and scatter a body that has died of natural causes does not constitute crime in the larger sense of the word. That which is already dead cannot be murdered."

From the blank wall of fog ahead an iron fence with hooked tops became vaguely discernible. Terry cut down her speed. "Here we are," she announced as the car drifted to the curb and stopped.

Through the heavy mist, shapes of men and feeble cones of light grew visible inside the grounds. Another car parked ahead of them could be dimly seen.

Frost frowned. "Did you call the police?"

Terry Wilson shook her head. "I'll question the servants, but I can't imagine why they would even come out on a night like this and I don't see how anybody could have noticed the thing from the sidewalk."

The professor crisply ordered: "Stay here. Better lock the car doors from the inside. Wait till one of us gives you further instructions."

And to Miss Moray: "I hope you won't need this but don it now." His voice sounded grim, imperative. Terry Wilson, accustomed to issue orders but not to receive them, seemed on the verge of rebellion, but for some unaccountable reason subsided meekly.

Jean Moray wriggled into the bulletproof cloak which had saved her life more than once, and followed Frost across the sidewalk. The black, glistening fabric swirled loosely around him. He looked like a bird of prey as he plunged through the fog, his valise in hand.

III.

AS he opened the iron gate, a harsh voice growled: "Hold it! Right where you are!"

A flashlight swept up, poured a thin, weak light on them. An officer in uniform grew clearer from the gray obscurity. "Oh, it's you, Frost? How the heck do you get in on things so fast? And what's the idea of the fancy costume?"

Frost dropped over his face again the slitted hood that he had lifted. "Watch yourself," he warned. "Things, as you express it, haven't even begun to happen yet. Who notified the police?"

Sergeant Conway, whom Frost had met once or twice, answered grudgingly: "Nobody from here, that's a cinch. Some fellow phoned in, said we'd find a body here, hung up without leaving his name or address. Body—phew! I don't think they'll ever get it together again, let alone identify it." He pointed to the grisly fragments that had been collected. "Even the photographer can't do much against this fog."

"You've examined the ground?"

"Yeah, for all the good it did."

"Weren't there any astonishing circumstances?"

"Naw. Not even a footprint."

"That is the astonishing circumstance," said Frost.

The sergeant bristled. "Now look here, there wouldn't be any footprints because somebody threw the stuff over the fence, see? All we got to do is find out why somebody cut up a stiff and threw it here."

The professor stated calmly: "No one did." The sergeant opened his mouth but Frost went on: "Where was that chunk picked up?"

Sergeant Conway pointed to a spot forty feet from the fence.

"That is your answer," Frost observed. "It is the largest fragment and must weight between fifteen and twenty pounds. I suggest that you practice hurling a fifteen or twenty-pound weight and make a careful note of the distance you attain."

He bent low, examined the remains briefly.

"What d'you make of it?" asked the sergeant.

"Obviously it is, or was, a medical-school specimen, some unknown, unclaimed at the morgue."

"You mean some medic cut it up for anatomy and then junked it here as a practical joke?"

"Certainly not. This is in deadly earnest."

"Then what's it doing here?"

Frost answered with grim and ambiguous brevity. "Test. Try-out."

He abandoned his inspection and opened the valise. He moved across the lawn a few paces, like a dark wraith in the fog, and set up a compact apparatus. He adjusted its parts, set a mechanism in motion. It worked automatically. At regular intervals of a minute, then, a subdued click came from the black, squat mass.

"Don't touch it or interfere with it. Tell your men to leave it alone," he warned the sergeant.

Jean, long silent, her curiosity getting the better of her, demanded: "But what is it? It looks like a camera, like a lot of cameras."

"Horizon camera," he replied as though he was already occupied with other matters. "Unlike the ordinary camera, which takes pictures of only a section of the horizon, this one photographs the sky and entire horizon in all directions."

"And what good will it do?"

"Wait and see."

The sergeant scowled. "You can't take pictures in a fog."

"Can't you? I can."

The sergeant made a grunt of objection, said in a voice heavy with scorn: "I suppose next you'll be telling us the corpse fell down from the sky."

"Right!" came Frost's urbane retort. To his assistant: "Get into the house and go through every room and closet. Use Miss Wilson's keys."

Jean nodded silently and slipped off through the impenetrable fog. Frost turned aside on some mission of his own.

WITHOUT WARNING, the muffled sound of an exploding cartridge burst from the wall of mist. A bullet whined.

"Down!" Frost yelled, his voice partly checked by the hood. Another cartridge went off; the hidden marksman shot again, then a burst of firing raked the ground.

The volley seemed to issue from the south. The sergeant whirled and plunged toward his right, service revolver drawn. Elsewhere the shadows that were men blended with the ground. A slug slammed against Frost and flattened. It whirled him part way around. Jean gave a sudden little yelp as a bullet numbed her arm.

"Down! Get down on the ground!" Frost shouted.

Sergeant Conway ignored the warning. He fired blindly at the spot where flashes of fire briefly and faintly split the mist. Somewhere a window splintered, a bullet ricocheted from stone with a low whine.

Doggedly, Conway ran through the curtains of night and mist. Frost raced after him with a muttered curse. Suddenly the firing switched to the north, then it seemed to thunder from behind, from three sides, trapping them in a deadly, crisscross barrage.

Another slug whammed against Frost's bulletproof cloak. Sergeant Conway staggered, tripped again, kept stumbling sidewise. His gun arm hung useless. He clapped his left hand to his right shoulder, slid to the ground.

Either in obedience to Frost's cry of warning, or afraid of hitting their comrades in the darkness and confusion, the rest of the police withheld fire. Only Conway had answered that savage attack.

A burst of shots exploded simultaneously in a dozen places. Windows smashed, glass tinkled; the ugly whine of bullets ripped around them as though a dozen marksmen competed in rapid fire. But no stranger, no skulking forms, no hidden snipers made themselves even faintly visible through that thick curtain.

Frost and Jean raced for the stricken sergeant. A grimace twisted his features. He muttered shakily: "Naw, I'm not dead yet. Busted leg, shoulder, and one in the hip."

With swift, expert fingers, Frost and Jean stopped the flow of blood with strips torn from his shirt. An occasional bullet whined out of the murk, an occasional muffled explosion barked near by.

Sweat stood out on Conway's face. "Good night, how many of 'em are there? A million?"

"Easy," Frost cautioned him. "There's no one here but us."

Conway stared up with vague, puzzled eyes. "Nobody—here—but us? Corpse—from—sky. It's all—screwy—" His eyes closed.

An eerie silence descended, and the fog rolled heavily, ghostily, everywhere. Frost called into the gloom, "The danger's past—you can get up now." Figures detached themselves from the ground, rose from the blobs to shadowy shapes.

Two burly policemen emerged from the sea of gray, lent willing hands to carry the limp weight of Conway.

"Close call. He'll live," Frost answered in their unspoken question.

At the same time, a gruff voice ordered: "Search the grounds!"

Frost shook his head. "They won't find any one."

The two police stared at him searchingly, moved away in the direction of the radio prowl car. The fog swallowed them and their unconscious burden. Pounding feet sounded in the fog. Frost shouted: "Don't shoot at anything or you'll be killing each other! There was no one here besides ourselves!"

His words rang out with a weird, muffled quality. Jean felt a creeping of her scalp. The strange silence that had now desceneded, the fragments of a corrupting body, the phantom bombardment, and the interiminable snipers, must have been hidden behind that pall for such rapid and indisciminate shooting. And yet, now that the surprise attack had ended as abruptly as it had commenced, she felt bewildered. The shooting had seemd to originate on three sides. If that was the case, wouldn't the attackers be caught in their own cross fire? Or had the fog distorted sounds and directions? She recalled having heard of blind shots and curious effects that fogs give rise to.

"How else could there be no one?" she asked.

"The iron fence! See if Miss Wilson is staying in her car, then search along the base of the fence!"

She melted away into the gray density that maddeningly obscured objects and thwarted actions. Terry was still seated at the wheel of her car, nervously tapping her fingers. That she had obediently followed his command in spite of the shooting gave silent testimony to the power of Frost's stern order.

Drawn by the mysterious shots, two radio cars crawled into view, their headlights turned to a dull amber by the moisture-laden vaport.

Jean retuned to the grounds, found the gaunt form of the professor kneeling by the fence left of the gate. He was furiously scooping out sod and dirt. For no reason that she could think of, his action and posture seemed more grotesque than anything that had yet happened.

Corpses might rain from the sky, a dozen men be ambushed in fog, and she would have accepted them as facts; but Frost on hands and knees, rooting around at the base of iron uprights, presented an illogical picture. She drew closer and dropped beside him to see what had attracted his attention.

"Ah!" came his low, pleased exclamation.

HE HAD hammered and gouged out the hard topsoil with the butt of his automatic directly at the base of an upright. The iron railings stood embedded in a narrow flange of concrete that paralleled the sidewalk. Against this concrete base, and tilted diagonally upward at an angle of about thirty degrees, rested the shell of an exploded bullet. The soil was still warm and odorous of powder gases. A wire looped like an armature winding around and around the brass chamber, and wire and shell were hot. The wire continued in both directions along the concrete, buried an inch below ground level.

Frost pulled it up with his gloved hand, followed it to the next upright, and the next. At every other bar, one of the shells wrapped in the tight coil came out. Striding swiftly from rail to rail, he uprooted a line of shells extending to the corner post, and continuing along the side street. The wire and cartridges, after some fifty feet more, turned at right angle to the eighteenth upright, and led to a hedged-in arbor.

The arbor had been wired for electricity, apparently as an evening retreat for summer use. The underground cable that supplied it with current had been tapped; and the wire that Frost pulled up disappeared into a compact little box from whose opposite side another wire emerged and ended at the tapped cable.

"No need to look further," Frost commented softly. There was a biting, chilling edge to his voice.

The new arrivals from the prowl cars stamped through the fog, which had begun to take on a lighter hue from the approach of dawn, but which remained as impenetrable as the blackness of night. A pair of bluecoats loomed toward them.

Jean asked: "What's in the box?"

"Only one thing could be," he replied succinctly, without bothering to pry the box apart. "Remote control."

"How?"

"This contact mechanism must have been buried with an open switch that would close and tap the house current when radio signals on its specific wavelength were sent out by remote control. The cartridges were wound to act as resistance coils. When the current flowed through, they heated until the powder exploded. Differences in the amount of winding made the cartridges explode irregularly. A fiendish and cowardly ambush."

"But why? Why?" Jean cried out. It seemed monstrous, brutal. "How do you know the Wilsons didn't arrange this for their own defense in case of need?"

Frost drawled: "Easy to answer—ask Miss Wilson. I should say it would be protection of a most dubious kind, in view of the fact that the bullets along the front fence shot directly at the mansion."

"But it would take a day to prepare and lay down all this material here!"

"At least a day, if your assumption were true," he admitted. "But if you are implying that this was an inside job, completed while the Wilsons have been away, you are entering the realm of the incredible. To outward appearances, this must have been an inside job. It obviously points to planning or connivance on the part of some one in the household. The obvious and ready explanation is frequently the one most open to suspicion. In this case, the caretaker seems to be so inevitable a suspect that I have already dismissed him from consideration.

"Those cartridges, the wire, the contact-control box, were never assembled here. Prepared elsewhere, some one brought them here. The task of planting them could have been finished in an hour or two. I would suggest that you police question the caretaker. I rather imagine you will find that he was lured away, slugged, and robbed recently; or that he was attacked here and after freeing himself could not find evidence that the house had been burglarized, hence concluded that he had been the sole object of attack. On that occasion, probably a dark, misty, or rainy night, some one buried the phantom snipers."

One of the police growled: "You can't convince me that somebody inside didn't have a hand in it. Come on, Joe, let's find that caretaker."

Frost shrugged his shoulders in an indifferent fashion, as the blanket of gray swallowed their forms.

IV.

"WE'LL TRY the back of the house," Frost snapped, and strode off at a tangent from the disappearing police.

As his assistant hurried at a brisk trot to keep pace with his long strides, she inquired: "Who would go to such trouble to bury bullets? Why plan a mass murder?"

"No one did," he contradicted her. "There were seven persons including us in the line of fire, but only one was injured, and he will recover. The angle and the spacing of the bullets made a fatal hit unlikely. No one who lay on the ground would be wounded unless he chose the base of the fence. You have just seen demonstrated the rarity of fatal injury in symmetric blind firing.

"Terror, not death, is the answer. Some one wanted to terrorize Miss Wilson; some one who didn't care whether she was killed or how many innocent bystanders got hit."

Jean felt chilly. What other menace had been prepared by that murderous unknown? She had an uneasy intuition that the fog might at any moment spawn death in strange and terrifying form.

"It's the worst fog I've ever seen," she remarked abruptly. "Whoever he is, he must have infinite patience if he got everything ready and then waited till a fog like this came along."

"He didn't. The fog is simply an unexpected blessing that nature has bestowed upon him, and an unfortunate hindrance that has been placed in our path. Miss Wilson is the object of his attack. He chose this time when she was separated from the rest of her family. A clear night would have helped us little, in spite of the fact that the fog is a disadvantage." Frost did not elaborate the paradox of his comments.

They skirted the north side of the mansion that loomed dark and mysterious in the fog. Shrubbery and bushes, occasional trees, swam vaguely out of the surrounding gray blanket. It was one of the worst and most persistent fogs that ever struck the Atlantic seaboard, an asparagus soup fog such as London might well have been proud to disclaim. At intervals, the mournful wail of tugboat whistles saddened the air from afar. River traffic had ceased, and the tugs sounded off solely in the melancholy hope of a breeze that would blow away the bank.

In the rear of the mansion lay small flower beds, bird baths, and more lawn. The Wilson mansion must be about the last of the private house-and-garden places left in Manhattan, she reflected; the sort of exclusive, limited estate which is common in the residential sections of cities throughout America, but which has virtually vanished from New York.

Frost interrupted her meditations with: "Try the base of a few uprights. If you don't find anything, look for me along the rear wall of the house."

With a nod of acquiescence, she faded into the dense mists.

Frost prowled along the shrubbery-bordered wall, his flashlight almost useless. Every blade of grass, every bud and twig, dripped with moisture. The dampness of the fog laid a sodden deposit on everything;

its chill crept through clothing. Tiny rivulets ran down the sleek surface of his bulletproof cloak.

In spite of fog and careful concealment, he found something; and he was gingerly dismantling it when his assistant dropped beside him like a phantom materializing from the fog itself.

"Nothing," she reported. "What's that?"

Frost finished his work. "It, too, is nothing, now; originally an efficient little arrangement to crack the gas inlet, thus filling the house with gases which, when they reached sleeping occupants, or came in contact with a pilot light—" He shrugged in lieu of the unfinished thought.

Again Jean shivered. Menace and disaster hovered in the fog. Why? Why? It became increasingly evident that the Wilsons were a doomed family, or more specifically, Terry Wilson. What had she done to bring down upon her head this implacable vengeance?

Frost rose and continued to prowl across the lawn. Jean said: "You found one bomb, or whatever it is. Maybe there are more."

"The police can make a thorough search. The unknown counted upon their doing so. Therefore, he would not waste further time on instruments of death. In addition, he had only a limited period at his disposal, and the chances of being discovered or of the caretaker freeing himself multiplied greatly with every hour that he spent here."

"Then why look further?"

Frost quoted: "He who does not seek, does not find."

Silence and fog and graying, impalpable light. Silence, save for the dismal, infrequent hoot of tugs. Fog that clung like a shroud. Light that made the fog a shade less obscure but did not increase visibility. Jean hunted with Frost; for what, she did not know. Now and again she heard a low, muffled murmur of voices emanating from the police who prowled on their own missions.

FOOTSTEPS came from near by. The feeble arc of a flashlight swinging from side to side grew closer, and a bulky figure emerged.

Frost froze into position, tense, his head cocked in a listening attitude. Jean halted spontaneously. What had he heard? She strained her ears, thought she detected a sound as of a great bird in flight flapping

Frost seized her in a powerful sweep of one arm and leaped backward. The sudden lunge caught her off balance, left her hanging over his arm, her back to the ground, her head facing the sky. Her eyes widened in horror and she slackened, on the verge of a faint. With a violent effort, she controlled her shaking nerves and struggled erect.

A faint, whistling rush of air had come from overhead. A dark figure hurtled earthward, a figure plunging head-first, with fantastically rigid body, arms stiffly at its sides, its wide-open eyes sightless and glaring in its frozen features.

Near the spot where she and Frost had been standing, the thing smashed on the ground. It landed with a sharp smack, and a noise of brittle crackle. Like a fallen icicle, it split into many parts. The body bounced shortly, sickeningly, as it splintered. Its head burst like some horrible egg and the pieces scattered. Arms and legs and torso shattered into queerly shaped wedges, fragments, and chunks with sharp fracture edges.

And no blood came.

In every other respect, those hideous remains seemed undeniably human; flesh and organs, veins, bones, muscles, lay in the appalling shards; and a red darkness as of blood underlay the marble pallor of skin. But not a drop of blood had splashed upon the ground. That which ought to have been gory pulp resembled, instead, the broken pieces of some wonderfully lifelike but mechanical model of a human body.

The policeman, looking sick, stooped toward the débris.

"Don't touch it!" Frost instantly commanded.

"Why not?"

"You'll burn yourself!"

A dull flush crept over the man's whitened face. "This is a hell of a time for jokes," he muttered in threatening tones, and forced himself to examine one of the gruesome hunks as if to convince himself that it could be no part of anything human.

He cried out, jerked his hand away as though fire had scorched it.

Frost simply repeated: "I warned you that you would burn yourself."

The policeman's eyes goggled. He rubbed his fingers on his coat. He showed no further inclination to investigate the remains, stared at Frost with as much awe as he had bestowed upon the broken body.

The professor bent over the ghastly relics and studied them, but avoided contact. A frightful cold emanated from the shattered thing. It was colder than ice, colder than solid carbon dioxide, colder than any subzero temperature that had ever been recorded in the polar regions.

But as it lay there, broken and splintered, it began to adjust itself to air temperature; and slowly, terribly, tiny globules of blood commenced to ooze out like a dreadful sweat.

Though the head and skull had burst like the rest of that which had once been man, enough of the features retained shape to prove that the dead man had originally been dark, swarthy, with slightly slanting eyes—a Eurasian. The skin gradually lost its frosty appearance, turned yellowish, then acquired the mottled color of a bruise. All his finger tips and teeth were missing, and not one specific peculiarity or clue to identity remained.

"In its way, a beautiful job," Frost drawled grimly "Identification will be almost impossible, and even if made, it may never be possible to establish whether the man was murdered or died from natural causes."

"Why not?"

"He may have been killed by a blow that crushed his skull. But his skull was crushed by the impact of landing. He may have been killed by a stab in his heart. But the force with which he hit the ground split his heart. The fact that his finger tips and teeth are missing indicates that some one wished to hinder identification, but is no proof that the victim had not already died from natural causes before his descent."

The policeman muttered: "He fell from the sky. He must have been heaved out of an airplane!"

Frost shook his head in somber denial.

"They must have flown him so high he froze!" the policeman persisted. "I've read that it gets freezing cold the higher you go."

The professor said, with brooding eyes: "He did not fall nor was he thrown out of an airplane, a balloon, or any other sort of aircraft. It is true that extreme cold prevails in the stratosphere, but that cold is nowhere near the temperature to which this body has been subjected. I should like to believe that it came from beyond earth's atmospheric blanket, from the regions of outer space where the bitter cold of absolute zero prevails. Then we would be faced with an extraordinary mystery of truly cosmic horror, a riddle that might never be solved. But I am afraid we cannot have recourse to so tempting a hypothesis until all other possibilities have been exhausted."

The policeman objected strenuously. "Where else could he have come from? Why, damn it all, you saw it fall out of the sky."

"Yes, but it certainly did not get into the sky by itself, nor just happen to fall." He straightened, added briefly, "I'll send the rest of your men here. We've a great deal of work ahead of us, Miss Moray."

THEY VANISHED through the rolling fog without waiting for a reply. Frost sent the rest of the police scurrying for the rear of the house, then made his way to the horizon camera.

It was still functioning with a whir of automatic mechanism and a click that came regularly at the end of each minute. In spite of the men tramping around, it had not been kicked over; and it had escaped the fusillade of shots. Frost stopped its action and took it along with him, issuing instructions as he walked.

"I'll have Miss Wilson drive us back to State Street. I want you to stay with her, then, wherever she goes. Talk to her, obtain any information, however trivial, that may prove useful. I have all the factors needed to identify and capture the guilty, but anything you discover will shorten the time element.

"After daylight she will be safe, and subject to no more attacks until nightfall. Leave her at nine, but see to it that she has a police guard. Make an appointment with Mr. Fred Devore Allen and talk to him. Use any line of questioning you wish. Make sure that he also has police protection or a personal bodyguard. Next comes the longest and hardest task. First, you had better get in touch with Inspector Frick, and you'll probably save time and receive considerably faster action by using a headquarters phone. Call all chemical manufacturing companies and laboratories within a radius of twenty-five miles and obtain a complete list of names and addresses to which liquid air, liquid oxygen, or liquid nitrogen was delivered during the past three days in any quantity. Give a duplicate list to Inspector Frick."

"Why? He hasn't asked for it."

"And very probably he won't know what to do with it," Frost observed urbanely. "That will be his concern, not ours. Find out whether any of the orders represent new business and whether there has been a marked increase in the number of flasks delivered to a regular customer. When you have the complete list, bring it to me. I'll be in before two and after three."

"Where can I find you between two and three?"

"At the Regal Theater, when the first stage show goes on. There is an interesting act billed as 'Shot Before Your Eyes.' A good stunt act works wonders, you know. And I'll spend a little time at the offices of the Astroplane Research Society."

Jean gave him a critical appraisal, in some bewilderment as to whether he was serious or suffered from lack of sleep and too many cigarettes. While death hurtled down from the sky, he talked of idling time away in a Broadway motion-picture palace and at an interplanetary organization. She gave it up. His methods were peculiar to himself.

The fog, if anything, became denser. Its heavy pall enshrouded the city, reduced traffic to a crawling pace, made pedestrians look like shadowy and insubstantial phantoms. But Terry drove with a kind of second sight on the way back to 13 State Street, miraculously escaping half a dozen near accidents.

V.

I.V. FROST sat in a fog in the book-lined living room of his residence. The fog came from endless cigarettes whose butts littered every ash tray in the room. Though past noon, the room was in a half gloom, for he had not troubled to turn lights on, and outside, a wall of mist rolled through the city.

Frost's eyes glowed with a gleam as restless as the fitful rise and fall of fire in the ash; but only the bright smolder in his eyes belied the fierce repose of his features. They were thin, austere features, with sardonic lips and the brow of an ascetic, expressive of an inscrutable but relentless will and an acuteness of perception akin to the mystic's extrasensory powers. Even in rest, they preserved a suggestion of unlimited reserves of nervous energy ready to flash into action instantly upon demand; thus the paradox of explosive calm.

His abstraction persisted in spite of numerous interruptions. He tensed at each ring of the telephone; but the tautness disappeared as soon as the interruption ended. He was the key figure in a series of actions and investigations proceeding on an ever-expanding scale all over the city.

Jean Moray had called at eleven, reported: "Fred Devore Allen is missing. I've talked to his family. They say he's disappeared several times before after scraps with Terry. They aren't worried a bit. What he usually does is register under a different name at a small hotel for a day or two until he cools off. I tried to get a line on his movements after he left Terry last night, but all I found out was that he left his car in their regular garage. He walked into the fog and that's the last that's been seen of him."

"Abandon that line of investigation," Frost instantly ordered. Two minutes later, he was talking to Inspector Frick of the homicide bureau. Ten minutes later, a whole corps of detectives from the Missing Persons Bureau had quietly begun a search for the missing man.

At the morgue, experts in death attempted to reconstruct, against disheartening odds, two whole and recognizable bodies from almost shapeless fragments.

A fingerprint specialist was examining files at police headquarters for a clue to the identity of the first corpse. Another expert went through records of narcotic cases; still another studied thousands of photographs in the rogue's gallery. Investigators canvassed all public and private airports, landing fields, and airplanes over six States.

WHILE the machinery went into motion, and exhaustive research pursued its laborious way, Inspector Frick paid the professor an unceremonious visit.

"I'm completely at sea," he admitted with his usual candor. "As far as we've learned, absolutely nobody made a flight in any sort of an airplane last night anywhere on the Eastern seaboard. There aren't any high buildings near the Wilson place. Nobody saw anybody heave the bodies over the fence. Neither of them's been identified. The caretaker sticks to his story that he was slugged, bound, and robbed a month ago, and it's down in the records—he reported it at the time. There isn't a trace of young Allen. I can't make head or tail of the mess. Why in Hades is your assistant sitting at my desk investigating shipments of chemicals? Have they got anything to do with the condition of the bodies?"

"Unquestionably," Frost replied. "Liquid nitrogen boils at -194°C, liquid oxygen at -181°C, and liquid air below -194°C."

"Did you say boils?"

"As water boils and passes into steam, so they boil and become gaseous again at the temperatures I mentioned. For that reason, I warned one of the policemen not to touch the fragments. He was burned by the contact with terrific cold, burned more severely than if he had touched a red-hot cinder."

"How much liquid air would be needed to freeze a corpse?"

Frost shook his head. "I cannot say with precision. The only way to find out would be to experiment. Unfortunately, I do not happen to have any spare corpses on hand. I should say at least six flasks, and probably more."

"Flasks?" repeat Frick with a puzzled expression.

The professor explained, patiently. "Liquid oxygen and liquid nitrogen are highly explosive and dangerous to handle. They are gases in an unnatural state, created through pressure and reduction in temperature. They cannot be kept in sealed receptacles, because they rapidly absorb heat, revert to gaseous form, attempt to expand, create their own pressure and explode. They are handled commercially in flasks that resemble very large thermos bottles, unstoppered. The evaporating gas escapes through the neck. Liquid oxygen completely evaporates or boils away in a day. It cannot be kept for any length of time. Not many concerns are equipped to manufacture it, and the demand is limited. For these reasons, especially since a considerable quantity would be needed to freeze a corpse to something like the temperature of liquid air, and since the liquid must by the necessity of its own nature be delivered well within twenty-four hours of being used, I set Miss Moray at her task."

Frick chewed his lip. "I see. Does the stuff make things very brittle?"

"Some of the hardest and toughest metals and alloys known will break like dry sticks after they have been exposed to liquid oxygen."

Frick was silent for an interval, while he reviewed in his mind the grotesque incidents. Then he said: "We're checking up thoroughly on the airplane angle, you know. Do you still think the corpses weren't dropped from a plane?"

"I do. In the first place, aviation ceiling is zero because of the fog. No one could pilot a plane over the city in such weather at a low altitude, and blind flying even at a high altitude would be foolhardy. In the second place, skilled marksmen find it almost impossible to score a direct hit upon a ground target of even large size. Under conditions that have prevailed since yesterday, a pilot could not possibly see a ground target, nor estimate within a wide margin of error how close to it he was. Yet the corpses fell less than one hundred feet apart. I repeat, they may have fallen from the sky, but they certainly did not descent from any flying machine of man's invention."

The inspector looked harassed. "For Heaven's sake, Ivy, stop talking riddles and nonsense. How else could the corpses possibly have got where they were?"

"That remains to be proved."

The inspector tried another track. "Why did you tip us off to look through the records of narcotic cases?"

"Because the second body was that of a man who smoked opium. He may have been arrested as a dope addict, or he may have been a dope peddler, or both. The Federal government has lately been making a determined drive against the illicit drug traffic."

"You think that the dope traffic is behind this?"

"Not necessarily."

Frick was fuming. "What the dickens do you think, Ivy? Is this a murder case, or isn't it?"

Frost answered: "What I think is of less importance than what I can prove. I think that the second man was murdered, but I cannot prove it. I think that he was killed by the application of liquid air above his heart, and that his heart immediately froze solid, causing instant death. The rest of his body was then exposed to liquid air. There is absolutely no possibility that you or I or anybody else except the murderer can ever prove that such was the case. It is an ingenious and fiendish crime. The man was dead before he fell. He was dead when frozen from head to foot. Whether he died of heart failure or was murdered by the method I outlined is beyond establishing on the basis of external evidence. Even the removal of the finger tips and teeth to delay identification is no proof of homicide. It is merely cause for suspicion. There is nothing more to say at present."

Frick lingered a few minutes longer, but Frost refused to be drawn into further discussion. The inspector returned to the fog of the outer world. Not long afterward, shortly before two, Frost also went out; but he returned by three, having seen the stage show at the Regal Theater and visited the offices of the Astroplane Research Society.

He resumed his earlier posture, and, looking like some strange, predatory, thin Buddha, remained in abstraction as the hours waned. He was almost as motionless as the bust of Socrates. Outside, the fog persisted, thick, soupy. Inside, the room gradually darkened, and still the professor sat cross-legged, while acrid, pungent fumes spiced the air around him.

IT WAS late afternoon before his assistant hurried in. He glanced at her with a questioning lift of his eyebrows.

"Here's the list." She handed him several pages of typed names and addresses, rattled on breathlessly: "Gee, I'm tired and hungry! Didn't take time for lunch. I'd no idea there were so darned many peanut-sized laboratories in this neck of the woods that use liquid air and chemical companies that make it. My arm's absolutely dead from holding a receiver, so don't be surprised if it falls to the floor any minute now and I bet I hear a buzzing in my ear for the next century. This fog gets me down. What a swell time for a flock of murders! I imagine everybody I bump into is out to kill somebody else, and I can see all sorts of lovely little monsters creeping through the fog like the green man. I'll have an A Number 1 case of jitters if this goes on much longer.

"By the way, Terry is a peach. After we left you, we stopped and had a double chocolate malted and hashed life over pretty thoroughly. Her only trouble is too much money. She told me a lot about herself but nothing that would help any. We had a double Scotch and soda about seven—"

Frost groaned. "Malted milk and Scotch—at seven in the morning! That is the most disagreeable thought I have encountered in some time."

Jean looked surprised. Murder didn't faze him, but mention of malted milk and whisky did. Well, that was only a minor phenomenon in the paradoxes of his make-up. She rushed on: "The kid really doesn't remember the names of nine tenths of the people she's known. She's completely forgotten the names of a couple of men she almost got engaged to at different times, and she can't even recall what they did.

"How'd the pictures turn out?"

Frost answered, with a frown: "They didn't."

"What was the matter? Not enough light?"

"On the contrary, too much light." He handed her a batch of dry films which she glanced through. They were dense, badly overexposed, so black as to be practically worthless.

"I don't understand." She wrinkled her brow in mystification. "I don't understand how you expected to get even a faint picture in that fog and I don't understand where all the light came from that spoiled the pictures. I certainly didn't see it."

"Yes you did," Frost disagreed, "but it didn't register. There are various kinds of light and energy present at all times in the atmosphere.

One of these is infra-red light, which reaches the human eye but which the human eye cannot see in the sense that it sees sunlight. But photographic emulsions and photo-electric cells sensitive only to infra-red light have been developed recently though they are not yet in general use. I used infra-red film, but unfortunately, our clever opponent realized that infra-red rays would pierce the fog and show us the manner in which the corpses fell and whence they came.

"He flooded the Wilson mansion with infra-red rays. They ruined the exposures in the same manner that ordinary film would be spoiled by pointing the camera directly at the sun. He could have done this in various ways, such as using reflectors to concentrate infra-red rays on the property, or sending an electric current through the iron fence which would case it to heat and give off the rays."

Jean mourned: "All that work for nothing."

"By no means!" Frost retorted. "To-night we shall trap him in his lair."

While talking, he had been studying the lists that his assistant had brought. He went through them twice with great care and then put them aside. She was unable to determine his reaction. The list may not have supplied the information he expected. It may have presented new factors not previously taken into account. It may have required a new interpretation to be placed upon preceding circumstances, or yielded the valuable information he sought. Whatever the list meant to him, he made no comment.

Jean, exhausted from the strain of thirty-two hours of continuous activity, waited in silence for Frost to speak, and suddenly passed into dreamless sleep in the chair where she had thrown herself.

She awakened just as abruptly to find the professor gently shaking her. With the quick recuperation of youth, she struggled out of slumber to alert readiness.

"Eight o'clock," he murmured. "Time for us to go."

He had evidently not slept a wink, and by the stale air in the room, and the immense accumulation of butts, and the bright fever in his eyes, she guessed that he had pursued his meditations undisturbed while she slept. He lived upon mysteries and enigmas.

He took a crammed valise with him as they went out.

VI.

THE FOG, damp, depressing, impenetrable, weighted them with a palpable sea. It penetrated clothing, chilled limbs, and settled in lungs. It became a load on the mind, and rolled with a slow and restless motion as though it had come to stay through all eternity. The whistles of river tugs sobbed now with a despairing and wistful infrequency. No liners had entered or left the harbor for two days. No airplanes had taken off or landed. No sign of a breeze had yet come to sweep away that throttling blanket.

The iron fence kept out the curious who came to peer at the Wilson mansion, and they could see nothing of the house. The fog at least served to keep their numbers down to a few stragglers. A police guard remained inside with Terry who had refused to take a hotel room for the night. Jean Moray and Professor I.V. Frost patrolled the grounds.

Once, on the way over, after munching through a couple of sandwiches hastily picked up, she had yawned, thinking of the long sleep that she would get in a cozy bed when the vigil was over. Here, all thought of sleep vanished. The chill of the night came not alone from the all-concealing fog, but from the invisible menace. Everything looked unreal, distorted like images of a dream.

The mansion loomed like an ogre's dwelling, vast and cavernous. The shrubs and trees became the transformed victim of an ancient and evil enchantment. The arbor seemed a nook of legendary twilight regions, and the flower beds lay under a dark and binding spell.

Inevitably, Jean's thoughts turned skyward. The blessed sky and the familiar stars had been absorbed in the persistent empire of fog. The remembered horror of a falling corpse stayed with her, and her thoughts again and again tried to soar beyond the veil. She shivered with each melancholy wail of a foghorn, every dismal honk of an automobile, the dripping of leaves, her own ghostly footsteps on the lawn.

The professor had spoken of the cold of outer space, the absolute zero whose congealing paralysis had never been equaled by man. Did he mean to imply, in spite of the liquid air of chemistry, that the bodies of the Eurasian and the other had descended from those far, unimaginable regions? Like most people, she had read articles on the gulfs between the planets, and separating the stars. She possessed a smattering of information about cosmic laws and astronomical distances. Those tremendous thoughts kept recurring to her, for Frost had insisted that the corpses had not been hurled over the fence, thrown out of the mansion, or dropped from an airplane.

Where else could they have come from except the outer atmosphere, the plaything of little-known forces that swept them away long ago and returned them at random? Though Frost had also said he would consider the outré hypothesis only when all other alternatives had been exhausted, suppose he had already exhausted them?

She prowled around to keep warm, but she seldom drifted far from the professor. He had again set up the horizon camera, and now it clicked, not at the minute intervals of last night, but every ten seconds.

"What good will it do?" she asked, puzzled. "If it failed before, won't it fail again?"

"I've added an infra-red filter to the lens," he explained shortly. "The sun can be photographed with an ordinary camera by use of the proper filter. Same principle as wearing smoked glasses to look directly at the sun. The infra-red filter screens out fifty per cent of the infra-red rays. That, together with a reduction in the length of exposure, should obtain fair results."

He proceeded to arrange additional apparatus, chiefly a black box with a series of what looked like four oversized ear trumpets mounted on its top. He pressed a button and the four horns revolved slowly, steadily, making a complete revolution in a minute.

"What's that?" she inquired.

"Form of sonometer—sound detector and amplifier." Frost picked up a pair of receivers and clamped them over his ears. A wire led from them into the black box. He crouched with an expression of intent concentration. She watched him for a while, then moved around.

Time dragged yet flew in a curious, dual fashion. Each minute lagged with the restless burden of waiting, the everlasting chill of the fog; yet each minute flew with the hush of expectancy, the thrill of imminent danger and death that the fog might spew at any moment. Her own tension mounted as time passed; and for once she experienced a mood of unreasoning irritation against Frost for his calm and stony immobility.

The camera mechanism clicked with unvarying regularity, a monotonous sound as exasperating as the tick of a clock. The four horns revolved in a manner as inevitable as the spinning of earth on its axis.

Ten o'clock went by, ten thirty, eleven, and finally midnight slipped behind. She felt cold and weary and on edge; but Frost stayed by the box. Neither time nor fog nor cramp seemed to have a place in the ascetic discipline of his will.

At some period beyond midnight, when the fog hung like an almost physical entity around them, and when her jumpy nerves had begun to create a threatening monster out of every tree and bush, she was walking a few yards from Frost and sensed rather than saw him tauten. His hands darted to the black box, and the horns ceased revolving. She hurried to his side.

Then, even to her unaided ears, there rose from afar in the fog a strange, raucous, and harshly roaring clamor as weird as the wail of a banshee. It died out, to be replaced almost immediately by a dull blast that boomed through the fog. As the sound faded, a sharp crack issued from somewhere near the top of the mansion. She spun around and darted toward the house in a spontaneous impulse.

FRED DEVORE ALLEN returned from the missing. He made his appearance in broken sections that showered the foundation of the mansion. Shocked into rigidity, she saw his body fall in six fragments—arms, legs, torso, and head. The grisly and whitely pallid parts split further upon impact, severed horribly into still lesser chunks. The fog blanketed them with cold vapor, but they were colder than any fog. She bit her clinched hand to stifle a scream, whirled and ran toward Frost.

The professor had stopped the camera and removed its film holder. He was already feeding the film into a metallic container.

"Ivy!" she gasped. "There's another—"

Frost cut her short. "Stay here. Watch this." He caught up a large carton and raced toward the rear of the house, his face hard, his eyes slitted and flaming like twin, black coals. He carried a pair of tongs with which he collected the fragments of the body and deposited them in the already half-filled carton. One of the tong ends snapped from the terrific cold, the other followed. He continued with the remaining stubs until all the chunks lay upon the solid carbon dioxide in the carton. At -40°C, the dry ice would prevent the shattered body from softening for hours.

He dashed inside the house, put through a call to Frick, and returned to his assistant. He opened the metallic receptacle and lifted out the roll of developed, dripping film. He held it up, his flashlight behind it, and studied it against that illumination.

A minute later, the engine of his car turned over and he swiftly picked up speed toward the Queensboro Bridge.

He must have read his assistant's thoughts. Before she framed the question, he drawled: "You really ought to see the act called 'Shot Before Your Eyes.' It is a most enlightening performance. Picture the stage, the preliminary announcement, the soft background of the orchestra playing. A gentleman in tights inserts himself in the mouth of a cannon. A beautiful girl walks to the breech. Breathless suspense. Only the head of the gentleman protrudes from the cannon. The beautiful girl lights a fuse. There is a concussion, a cloud of smoke, and the gentleman sails forth from the cannon. He describes a perfect parabola and lands on the opposite side of the stage."

Light dawned upon her. "Of course! I saw it done years ago. The man is shot out of a cannon."

"Is he?" Frost inquired.

"Well, isn't he? Didn't you just say so?"

Frost said: "Let us consider the matter more carefully. There is a concussion which the audience assumes to have come from an explosion in the cannon. But the sound may have come from a synchronized, harmless explosion off stage. There is smoke, assumed to be powder gases. On the other hand, it may emanate from smoke-producing chemicals. The man emerges from the cannon, but in spite of the evidence that the audience has seen and heard, the man is not shot out of the cannon."

The lights of the bridge faded behind them, and Frost turned right twice. He now drove toward the seamy factory and manufacturing district that fronted the river. In spite of the fog, he drove as if brilliant sunshine favored him. The car sped through gloomy streets, halted at last in front of a dark and decrepit building.

The dank, miasmal odor of the river assailed their nostrils. They saw no one. The fog swirled around them and hid the upper part of the building. The old edifice stood sandwiched between other grimy structures. A legend on the display window spelled: Suntan Face Powder Co.

"Of all the incredible gall!" Frost exclaimed. He did not stop to elaborate his odd comment.

Two doors made a right angle in the narrow entrance to the building. The door on the right led to the Suntan's offices. The door facing them bore no signs. Solid stone wall rose on their left.

The unmarked door proved locked. Frost took a steel instrument from his pocket and snapped the lock with a sudden, powerful twist. His flashlight probed a worn flight of stairs which he raced up three steps at a time. The second floor was empty save for some cartons stacked in a storage room. Frost kept on climbing past the deserted upper floors, Jean hard at his heels.

An iron ladder led from the sixth-floor landing to the roof. Frost went up it and heaved the hatch cover aside. His assistant followed him out on the flat, dirt-covered roof.

The fog hung even thicker here than at ground level, but not thick enough to cloak the shambles. Blood spattered the roof—fresh blood, in wet, crimson drops and streaked splashes. All around lay bits of gleaming metal, and scattered inextricably among them were the torn and shredded fragments of what had once been human.

VII.

FROST EXAMINED the remains of man and metal, strode from piece to piece, bent low over them in the quick glance that sufficed for his keen perceptions. The only information they conveyed to Jean was that someone had been blown to bits here, recently, along with the metal of the bomb or machine.

He finally returned with a brooding and far-away expression. He peered into the fog whose dense concealment seemed to Jean no more obscure than the riddle of corpses that plunged from the sky or that exploded into shreds. A note of cold anger harshened the professor's voice. "From here, the body of Fred Devore Allen went hurtling across to the Wilson estate; and here lies all that is left of the man who launched it on its way."

She wondered at his tone. He had solved the mystery. Then why feel annoyed? "It is the end of the trail?"

"It is not. That is what we and the police were supposed to believe, when we were expected to discover this days hence. It seems incredible," he burst out, "that the liquid oxygen could have been shipped from some distant point. It could not be transported at all by air express, and even the fastest trains take hours. So much of the stuff would boil away that he would have needed to order great quantities. Yet there is nothing unusual about any of the orders in the list you made up. Are you quite sure that you covered every possible local source?"

Jean insisted: "There is no error. But maybe it wouldn't be possible to locate the source of the liquid air. Suppose that somebody in charge of manufacturing it for some company or research laboratory is the man you're after. He could make more than the orders called for, and store the rest right in his laboratory. It wouldn't show on the sales records, and no one would know if he used it himself at night, because it would have boiled away by morning anyway. Why, I might even have talked to him this afternoon, and he may be laughing up his sleeve at us now because he could truthfully give me the records of sales and—"

Frost seized her and propelled her with such violence toward the open hatch that she almost tripped down it. The hunt was on again; she knew it by the glow in his eyes and the zest in his features. "Miss Moray, if you have only one deduction as inspired as that for every three months that you work, you may consider yourself indispensable."

"Well," she said plaintively as she steadied herself, "you don't need to practically throw me through an open hatch to prove I'm indispensable."

At the second floor, Frost halted just long enough to tear open one of the cartons and pocket a box of face powder. His assistant, breathless from the rapid descent, and perplexed, stifled her curiosity until they were outside. What in the world did Frost want with a box of cosmetics? Back in his car and before starting off, he took out the list of names and addresses, studied them anew with the aid of a pocket map of the city spread open beside them.

A moment later, the car hummed along the route they had recently traversed. Jean could suppress her curiosity no longer. "What happened back there on the roof?"

"Do you remember hearing a raucous noise followed by a muffled boom just before the body of Allen descended? Upon that roof was mounted a short-muzzle light-weight cannon, based upon rocket principles. Some one placed the frozen body in the muzzle. A chamber in the gun contained liquid nitrogen. He poured liquid oxygen into a connecting chamber. The two together have an explosive force many times as powerful as nitroglycerin. The pressure built up to a point where the metal wad upon which the body rested could no longer resist. The body hurtled in an arc to the Wilson house and the wad dropped into the river between. But another chamber had been built into the gun, a chamber that had no safety exhaust and that closed tight the moment the liquid air had been poured. The gas expanded there until the gun exploded from the pressure."

Penciled lines appeared on Jean's forehead. "You mean he committed suicide after killing Allen?"

Frost shook his head. "It looks like an accident. It could have been suicide. It was murder—cold-blooded murder of an underling by a criminal yet to be caught."

"Did all the bodies and dummies come from there?"

"No. The statue and the carbon dioxide mass were shot out as tests from two different places, to determine the accuracy of range. We have just left one of the sources. We will shortly reach the other source, and the final solution."

"Why did you take the box of face powder?"

Driving with one hand at a thirty-mile clip through the fog, Frost took out the box of powder with his free hand and pried the lid off. He poked among the scented talc, drew forth a thin, flat packet whose corner he tore. It contained a white powder.

"Cocaine."

He twisted through fog-hidden streets past fog-shrouded buildings to another district of grimy factories and warehouses fronting the river. He halted in front of one that bore the legend engraved on stone: Chemical and Pharmaceutical Products Co. It covered an eighth of a city block, and though the mist concealed its higher floors, a halo of light shone up there.

Frost rummaged in the valise, took out some things that he dropped in his pockets. His face had grown grim, his attitude as deceptively restrained as an eagle poised to strike. The doors of the building were locked, but a night light burned in the entrance hallway, and Frost rang the watchman's bell.

Less than half a minute passed before a semibald, husky Scandinavian with blue eyes, tanned face, and a prominent gun made his appearance. He looked at the strange pair with a question in his eyes.

Frost said: "We're on police business. There are lights on the top floor—"

"That bane yust Mr. Arthris. He works by night."

"He's the man we want to see." Frost pushed his way in, said something in a low voice to the Swede which Jean missed; but the big watchman nodded and they passed. It was not the first time she had seen him enter without question where almost any one else would have found himself blocked.

They chose the stairs in preference to the elevator; and on the top floor, Frost directed her to await in shadows until he returned. He vanished toward the roof, but was back before she had occasion to feel worried. Off the corridor loomed various doors, dark and locked, and one large double door behind which a light showed.

The professor kept one hand in his pocket, twisted the door handle and pushed his way in with the other.

A long, broad laboratory stretched before them, a room scrupulously clean but filled with tables and equipment, racks of bottles, measuring implements and scientific tools of infinite variety, heavy mechanisms and delicate precision instruments, microscopes and electric furnaces and fantastically shaped devices of conjectural purpose. Jean took them in as a general impression, at the same time that she noticed the dark little man with the thin mouth and crooked nose who, from the table where he worked, glanced toward them in mild surprise.

"May I ask the meaning of this unwarranted intrusion? There are standing orders that I am not to be disturbed," he complained.

"Let this be the first and last. I can safely promise you that you will never again be disturbed—here." Frost said.

"Go away!" said the dark man, and his eyes glittered behind the thick lenses of his spectacles. "I don't care who you are or what you want. Go away. I am performing a delicate experiment and I cannot be disturbed."

He started to turn back to his work, and Frost's voice came with a slurring lash, "Oh, yes you can. Gaino Arthris, you are guilty of the murders of Fred Devore Allen and two other men, to name the more vicious of your crimes."

"But you must be mad! That is ridiculous. I never heard of the man, and why should I want to kill any one?" protested the stranger.

VIII.

"SHALL I refresh your memory?" Frost snapped.

"Refresh my memory? Now I know you must be mad. How can you refresh my memory about something of which I have no knowledge! Go away at once or I will ring for the watchman. I have no time for fairy tales."

Jean felt resentment mount within her, for no reason except the nasty and disagreeable attitude of the obstinate little man, together with an offensive egotism that oozed out of him.

"We have no intention of leaving," Frost drawled, "except with you. Let me implant upon your mind some facts of which it seems to be blank. Possibly you would appreciate it the more in the guise of a fairy tale."

His imperturbable manner, icy, incisive, obviously began to get on Arthris' nerves. He shot Frost a look of venom and opened his mouth, but the professor forestalled him with: "Once upon a time, there lived in the fabulous city a chemical engineer. He was exceptionally clever, but emotionally unbalanced, unprepossessing in appearance, and with a quirk to his mind. Because he proved himself a good chemist, he found his shortcomings overlooked. He obtained a responsible position with a concern of manufacturing chemists.

"Because of his nature and abnormal sensitivity, he lived an essentially solitary life, and in a world largely of his own imagination. He preferred to work alone and at night; and because he had made his services valuable, his wishes were granted.

"Now, in the darkness and silence of night, and as he lived in his distorted world of imagination, he began to acquire delusions of grandeur. He would lead a second life. He would derive from another rôle the thrills and excitement that he visualized. He held a most strategic position for a double life. He could cloak himself behind his position of responsibility and trust. He attached himself to drugs, which he requisitioned from his own company's supplies for legitimate research, but the larger part of which he diverted to his own needs. His ideas expanded. There were profits—enormous profits—to be made in the smuggling and illegal bootlegging of narcotics. He began to inhabit doubtful places in the late hours, after he had finished his work. Since the keen-eyed recognized him as an addict, he had no difficulty making contacts."

The beady eyes behind the spectacles stared at Frost unblinkingly, and Frost returned a gaze of even more hypnotic intensity. "Eventually, proceeding with extreme caution, he had a smuggler and a peddler under him, one of whom was a Eurasian. His double life, his vicarious thrills, progressed rapidly.

"During one of his infrequent attempts at normal, social activities, he met the princess, let us say Miss Theresa Wilson. She became mildly interested in this individual who differed so from the men of her class whom she usually met, but she quickly returned to her customary type.

"The chemist, unfamiliar with emotions, conventions, and the easy-going familiarities of contemporary life, mistook the princess' casual friendship for something more. He felt bitterly resentful. He compensated for his uninspiring personality by developing a hatred for those more fortunate than he. He determined upon revenge for the princess' slight. In the brooding darkness of night and the long hours of seclusion, he decided further that if he could not have her, then neither could any one else."

Arthris stirred restlessly as if to interrupt, but Frost gave him no chance. "His morbid imagination, whetted by injured feelings and rejected attentions, whetted further by knowledge that he meant so little to her that she could not even remember his name, stimulated by drugs and drug hallucinations, and by the announcement that she had become engaged to another, received greater impetus from the growing Federal drive against the narcotic traffic. The fear of discovery sank into his twisted brain, even though his agents did not know his true identity. With discovery, his dual life, his delusions of grandeur, his revenge, his everything would come to an ignominious end.

"There must be a way out. He evolved a plan of fiendish, brutal ingenuity. He would use his two agents for vengeance upon Miss Wilson. He would destroy her fiancé through them, and destroy them afterward, through the resources of modern science and chemistry to which he had access. He would destroy them in a spectacular fashion that would baffle the police, terrorize the princess, and cause the murders to be charged to his own victims. Behind his mask of position, he would revel in the sensational mystery he had launched.

"He planned thoughtfully, with every attention to detail. When his phantom ambush and bomb were planted, he had only to await Miss Wilson's return; for though she might marry and live elsewhere, thus avoiding the buried bullets, his death from the sky could be calculated within a small margin of error to descent upon any site he chose within the city."

Arthris' mouth twitched; his eyes seemed pin points; he found voice at last in shrill, sullen rage. "Haven't I told you you're spoiling an experiment? Get out! Go to the police with your nonsense! I won't listen to any more!"

FROST continued: "Next he built two apparently identical guns; but one was a simple spring catapult of variable tension and recoil, and one worked by the propulsive force of liquid nitrogen and liquid oxygen. He placed the first upon the roof of the laboratory where he worked. Because he could use the freight elevator and delivery entrance to which he had keys, he was able to come and go from the laboratory without the knowledge of the night watchman. The parts of the second gun he carried to the roof of the Suntan Face Powder Co., the building which served as a blind for his traffic in narcotics.

"On successive nights, he checked the accuracy of his calculations by a plaster cast hurled from one cannon and a mass of solid carbon dioxide from the other. He even collected the fragments of the statue to find out in what way and to what degree it shattered.

"He then sent a true body weight, a corpse, after the trial dummies. The origin of the corpse is a minor point—it may have been a medical-school cadaver which he had shipped to him personally at the laboratory, or it may have been filched from a potter's grave by his agents.

"In his grandiose conceptions, nothing could go wrong. The wilder his schemes, the more they appealed to his warped understanding; the deeper he went, the farther he had to go in order to rid himself of all loose ends."

Frost's words echoed hollowly through the long spaces of the laboratory. Arthris licked his dry lips with a small, pink tongue. His forehead had begun to wrinkle.

"Shall I go on with the fairy tale?" Frost asked with a curt, accusing inflection. "I could tell how he arranged to let one of his dupes in through the delivery entrance of the laboratory, where he killed him and sent the chemically refrigerated body upon its last journey. Would you like to hear how, in his crazed jealousy, he trailed Allen, slugged him, and kidnaped him in the fog? Perhaps your conveniently elastic memory would be interested to hear how an appointment was made with your remaining partner in crime at the Suntan Face Powder Co., where he, too, was killed. Then the chemist poured liquid oxygen over the body of Allen, and hurled him upon his way, announced by the noise of the exhaust gases.

"Our chemist immediately left the scene; and he had hardly gotten away from the building before the strange cannon exploded, blasting the dead or unconscious body to bits. It might not be found for days. Investigation would uncover the drug packets in the powder boxes. The crimes would be ascribed to a vice feud, with a verdict of murder and suicide or accidental death by a person unknown. Then, by remote control the chemist would release the bomb that would destroy the princess; but the chemist did not know that the bomb had been discovered and dismantled; and he sat in his laboratory vainly waiting for the sound of the explosion and the fire that would mark her passing.

"He thought himself beyond suspicion, because of the difficulty of establishing a motive, the absence of clues. He did not realize that he left an accurate picture of himself in the way he worked, and that his own methods would inevitably expose the trail to his hiding place. He had never in his worst apprehensions believed that he could possibly be under suspicion before he had time to destroy the last evidence; with the result that, when trapped, he was convicted by his catapult which still stood upon the roof of the building where he worked."

Gaino Arthris shifted his position, and the room plunged into blackness.

Frost's voice bit through the darkness; "Take the roof, Miss Moray."

She whirled, stumbled to the door, but twisted its handle and pushed without result. Arthris had shut them in by some automatic or electric mechanism when he turned the lights out. They themselves were trapped—locked in with a drug-crazed introvert, a madman, who had at his finger tips every chemical, gas, drug, and deadly weapon known to science.

IX.

SHE STOOD, silent, motionless, straining each nerve in the effort to see by ear and to avoid giving her position away. Her heart beat faster, with a thump that sounded as loud as a trip hammer to her own hearing. She tried, hopelessly, to see. Nothing could be discerned in that inky blackness, with the heavy wall of fog pressing against the windows and blotting out even the faint light from stars.

She heard what sounded like softly running feet. There came a rustle from the vicinity of Frost, a thud as if he had tossed something, a flicker of light, then a flood of blue-white sizzling incandescence from the calcium flare. It brought even the far corners of the room into brilliance that only sunlight could have exceeded.

Crouching behind a table yards distant, Arthris was swinging an arm up over his head, and an ovoid object sailed through the air, an object vaguely like a Mills grenade. The little man whirled, sprang toward a high stool a dozen feet away, leaped upon it like a rabbit, with a hooked and cross-barred pole in his hands. He swung the pole through a skylight opening, caught its hook end upon the roof, and climbed up the cross bars.

In that first blur of events, Jean's senses could only register what she saw. She had to comprehend them before she could act. But as the ovoid hurtled toward them, Frost's right hand swung up, and in it nestled a curious weapon with a long, heavy barrel. He fired once, and there came a whang of metal as the powerful, armor-piercing bullet ripped into the ovoid. It stopped, spun backward from the force of impact. A shrill, hissing roar issued from it, and like a thing tortured, it shot around at crazy tangents and unpredictable angles.

The shot broke the spell that had frozen her, and her automatic leaped into her hand. She aimed at the top of the pole up which Arthris was scrambling and emptied the clip. She scored two hits, shot away half the thickness of the pole, and the lower part fell from Arthris' own weight. Like a flash he rolled aside and darted behind the protection of other tables and machines, his face a mask of rage and insane fury.

"Nice shooting!" Frost's cool voice reassured her. "Watch out for that leaping grenade. It could give you a nasty crack but the liquid oxygen that's boiling away and heaving it around is the worst part of it."

The ovoid hopped toward them, hit a chair, sizzled off in another direction, skipped to a table and smashed a microscope. It took another bounce and flew past the man who had hurled it. Again it whirled in its erratic flight and streaked across the floor toward Jean. She jumped. The grenade flew under foot, caromed, and bounded into a jar that it shattered. A bitter odor rose as the fluid spilled over and ran to the floor.

"Keep away from it," Frost warned. "Hydrochloric acid."

A hum swept up, and a drone, a crackle. A huge machine pointing toward them flickered with light. Frost aimed, fired. A wire twanged with a sudden flash of sputtering radiance and the hum died away.

"Pretty little thing," Frost drawled. "A little more of that and we'd have carried scar tissue or cancer for life. High-voltage X-ray, but short-circuited now."

From Arthris' hiding place sailed a small object that Frost did not attempt to hit. While Jean frantically reloaded, the object curved into Frost's hands. He caught it, heaved it away so that its motion did not cease for an instant. It crashed through a window, and exploded as it crashed. A volume of white smoke poured out and mingled with the fog.

Frost said grimly: "This has gone far enough. Tear gas now. Heaven knows what next. He's lost his head and is ready to turn anything loose, whether it hurts him or not in the process."

Arthris' hand shot up again but Frost fired and the missile plowed through table and zinc sheathing. A cloud of choking fumes rolled around the bullet hole.

"Get behind something," Frost curtly ordered, and dropped behind the nearest protection.

Arthris, stooping, dodged between tables toward a rack of tall, glistening containers that resembled thermos jugs. Whether he ran purposely or accidentally toward them, he fumbled with something he carried. He stumbled blindly, his face hideous with ungovernable frenzy. Blood ran down his chin, his hand. He coughed and rubbed his streaming eyes.

The flying ovoid smacked into the rack of containers and one tipped over. A bubbling, colorless, steaming fluid poured out. Arthris did not, could not, see it. He tripped over the fallen container, and clutched wildly to break his fall. The container whose neck he grasped toppled, and the contents splashed over him.

He did not scream, nor cry. Only a sudden gasp clogged his throat as the liquid air froze his head. Death, painless, almost instantaneous, reached for him with fingers as cold as the spaces between the stars.

Frost made a spontaneous movement toward one pocket, extracted the case of his peculiar cigarettes. He opened it, closed it, and returned it to his pocket intact. By that gesture, Jean knew that the mystery had begun to lose interest for him.

His face all at once looked tired, gaunt. The extraordinary brightness in his eyes had started to dim. "If you wish, you can remain here and explain to Inspector Frick, whom I will notify, what happened. But there is nothing to say that cannot equally well be said in the morning. Let's go."

He turned wearily toward the door, had it open in less than half a minute. The watchman was racing down the hall toward them as they emerged. They left him goggling at the fantastically lighted laboratory, with its now dying calcium flare ebbing its radiance upon the débris and an infinitely cold body.

IMPOSSIBLE

Jean's surprise defense trick sent Gordon sprawling to the ground. The others lowered their guns and stared in amazement.

"**IT ALL BEGAN** a little over two weeks ago," said the dark man, shifting his beady bright eyes from Ivy Frost to Jean Moray as if he really didn't expect to be believed. He was not small, but seemed so, in contrast with the lean and towering figure of the professor.

"That was when the advertisement appeared. Frankly, I don't know who my employer is. I don't know where I work. I don't know what I'm doing half the time. Copying Chinese script one day—I don't know Chinese. Talking aloud for hours the next day with nobody anywhere near me. The strange cry like the wail of a banshee. Then the time I had to strip naked and walk up and down the bare room for hours. I'll go crazy if I don't get help soon. I went to the police but they just laughed when I couldn't even tell them the license number of the car. They said I was drunk. When I tried to tell them more, they threatened to put me in the psychopathic ward at Bellevue."

"Start at the beginning," Frost quietly commanded, and his cold, logical approach to the visitor's jumble of words served to calm that jittery caller.

He had come, without warning and without appointment, to the private mansion at 13 State Street where Prof. I.V. Frost preserved a state of chronic boredom until some queer or fantastic crime lured him into winding labyrinths.

Frost held degrees in science, literature, and law. He had taught for a period, and pursued researches into chemistry, physics, biology, and physiology for some years. When he tired of accumulating knowledge, he had turned to utilizing that knowledge and the resources of modern science for the detection and apprehension of criminals.

Private investments—income from several inventions and from publications—plus the occasional large fees that he received enabled him to pick his cases. There were types of investigation which he flatly refused to handle at any fee—divorce cases, political skullduggery, mere swindles and confidence games, fraudulent financial transactions, and so on. Routine work and the messes into which human beings have a genius for miring themselves held no appeal for him. The police could handle such matters in competent fashion.

He specialized in crimes extraordinary, bizarre, and subtle. The case of a "Green Man Creeping," or an "Artist of Death," or a murderer who used such novel instruments of death as solid carbon dioxide and liquid nitrogen, would absorb the whole of his thought, life, and resources until he had solved the puzzle.

His only assistant was Jean Moray, and the two made a partnership as queer as any case they had encountered. Frost, extraordinarily tall and thin, stood six feet four, with gaunt, ascetic features, black eyes, a predatory nose, irresistible will and reserves of nervous energy that seemed never to be exhausted. His hands and fingers, of long, slim beauty, would have been more appropriate to Jean, who was young, lovely in an exotic way, and restlessly full of the devil.

She had a face and figure men stared at—one reason why he employed her. Many a time that sensuous appeal of hers had focused attention, leaving Frost free for priceless seconds of swift action. She was a creature of chameleon moods, provocative or sophisticated; in turn the hoyden, or his gifted understudy. She had courage enough in an emergency, but she was driven more by a reckless thirst for excitement and adventure. She flirted outrageously with most men and then left them for the best of all reasons—no reason. She couldn't make a dent in the impregnable fortress that was Frost, and therein lay the pique of their relationship, a perfect stalemate—the irresistible force and the immovable object. She owned a quick, alert mind, when she wasn't trying to improve her natural beauty, and had proved herself an excellent aid when she wanted to.

She listened now with frank curiosity and skepticism to the statements of one Nick Valmo, who brought a strange tale. She shook her head slightly, rippling hair as warm and golden-brown as ripe wheat, and her full lips pursed. A quick glance at Frost showed him to be lighting a very long and decidedly pungent cigarette. That settled matters. When Frost began to poison himself with those abominations, it was an unfailing sign of his interest.

The dark man said, "Well, a little over three weeks ago, I noticed an ad in the personal columns. I was out of a job and down to my last dollar. It looked made to order for me. Here it is."

He fished a small, crumpled newspaper clipping from a pocket and handed it to Frost, who passed it to Jean. It read:

> Wanted: man, single, 5 ft. 9½", 140-150 pounds, age 26-30, brown eyes, black hair, Latin type, perfect teeth, no physical disabilities, for interesting experimental and research work. Must be prepared to spend days out of town. Good salary to right party. Call in person, Room 1421, Lawyers Bldg., Tuesday after 9:30 A.M.

THE VISITOR continued, "I got there at nine. I thought I'd come early and be one of the first in. About a million other men had the same idea. I never saw such a mob in all my life, and they all looked pretty much alike, because they were all about the same height, age, weight, and color. That was my first general impression. Studying them closer, I could see differences of course. There were silky black-haired ones, coarse brown-haired, and all shades between.

"It was ten before my turn came, even with a constant stream going in the door and coming out a different one farther down the hall. A lot of them must have been rejected on sight. I finally got into the office. A little, leathery-looking, middle-aged chap sat behind a desk. He had shrewd eyes, a half-bald head, and two of his upper front teeth stuck out. It gave him a sort of mousy appearance that I didn't like. He asked me the usual questions about my age, health, background, and so on. I could tell he was definitely interested, though I couldn't tell why. He finally said he thought I might be just the man he was looking for. He wouldn't tell me any more about the job, except that it would involve some very peculiar duties."

Nick Valmo paused to grunt through his nose. "Peculiar! they're about as cockeyed as any I ever heard of. This lawyer, Simon Mord, told me to buy a white gardenia, go to West End Avenue and Ninety-fifth Street, and stand on the northwest corner from two to two-thirty that afternoon. It sounded ridiculous and I told him so. He looked at me very coldly and simply said that if I wanted the job I'd have to follow instructions. He also told me to report back at his office at four and he'd let me know if I had the job.

"So I went through with it, and nothing happened. I bought the gardenia, and I stood at West End and Ninety-fifth from two to two-thirty. I felt pretty silly, just standing there, staring at the few people who passed me and being stared at by them. At two-thirty, I decided to walk downtown a way since I didn't have to be back at the office until four. Well, I started walking down West End Avenue, and darned if I didn't pass five other guys in five blocks, all much the same type, and all wearing different flowers in their lapels, a bachelor's-button, carnation, daisy, and I forget what the other two were.

"I got back to Mord's office at four. Mord told me the job was mine, and that he had been retained by a well-known sociologist or psychiatrist, I forget which. It would be a queer sort of job, lasting two weeks, and paying a hundred a week. If I followed instructions, and tested well, there might be more work at the same salary. Who wouldn't take a plum like that in times like these?"

Again Valmo stopped to shake his head. "I wouldn't blame you if you think I'm daydreaming, but here's what happened.

"The next morning, I followed the instructions that the lawyer, Mord, gave me and went to the corner of Central Park West and Sixtieth Street. At eight A.M. a small truck like an ambulance stopped. The driver told me to hop in the back and I did. Another man was sitting inside. He closed the rear doors. He had black hair, a sandy-colored mustache, and his eyes were a sort of mottled hazel color. He spoke in a drawl. His finger nails were down to the quick from picking them. He said his name was Gordon. He was heavy-set but not very tall.

"Well, he gave me a pencil and pad, and told me to write down from time to time how far I thought we'd gone and how much time had elapsed. I was to do this without taking my watch out. Naturally, since the car was completely inclosed, I had nothing to go on, except the sound of the motor. I couldn't tell when we were doing twenty or fifty, or whatever the speed was. I tried counting but I couldn't tell if ten minutes passed or an hour. My perspective went haywire under those conditions.

"I do know that we rode for a long time. It grew stuffy inside, and I had covered pages with meaningless notations about miles and minutes. Finally the car stopped, and the driver came around to open the rear door. Gordon and I got out.

"We were in front of an old brick house, completely surrounded by woods. The woods came to within a hundred feet of the house. A private dirt road evidently looped off the main road, which must have been some distance away because I couldn't hear any sounds of traffic.

"We entered the house but they didn't show me through it. Instead, we walked into a central hallway and immediately turned left into a large, almost bare room. There was only a desk and a chair in it. I was beginning by this time to wonder what sort of mess I'd let myself in for but there wasn't anything I could do about it, so I kept still. Anyway, curiosity was eating me up.

"Gordon took away the pad with the stuff I'd scribbled on it. He told me to sit at the desk and copy what I found there. Then he turned around and shut the door. I walked over to the desk. A thin book of what looked like Chinese printed on a strange, brownish sort of paper lay there, with some typewriter paper, and pencils."

Valmo took a deep breath. "Then I looked around the room. It had three windows, all of heavy plate glass that you couldn't see through. The windows were spiked shut. A door in another wall had a section of thick glass. I tried the door I had come through. It was locked.

"The only other openings were two small ventilator grilles, one in the ceiling and one in the floor. Finally I went to the table and started work. I tried to copy the stuff in the book and it just about drove me crazy. I had the devil of a time imitating those queer characters with their funny little strokes and lines. I hadn't the slightest idea what they meant, and I didn't know whether they read backward or forward, upward or down. For all I knew, I might be copying the book wrong end first.

"Then I got goose-chills. I can't explain it. I had the feeling that I was being watched, studied like a fly on a pin, and it made me squirm, only I couldn't see anybody and there was no one in the room."

VALMO looked unhappy. The mere recital reminded him too vividly of those queasy sensations. "I suppose I worked about an hour. Then Gordon opened the door, gave me a plate with a couple of sandwiches, declined to answer my questions, and went out again. I worked about an hour more. Then he came back and said we were returning to town. We made the trip in the same manner as before. Gordon told me I'd done well so far. He opened up a little, and said that a noted psychologist was doing some testing, and it had to be done without the subject knowing what it was all about, in order to get natural reactions. He asked me if everything was satisfactory, promised my first week's salary in five days, and gave me more instructions.

"Every day since, I've gone through the same experience. They always pick me up at a different place, sometimes in Manhattan, sometimes in the Bronx. As soon as I'm inside, I get busy with the paper and pad. I know from the different sounds I can hear that we've gone through tunnels, and over bridges, but I don't know whether they're the Queensboro Bridge, George Washington, Brooklyn, Manhattan, or what. Sometimes we've used ferries, but from where to where I don't know. Maybe it's just what they tell me it is. They gave me a hundred dollars a week ago. They gave it to me again yesterday.

"All I know about the brick house is that it takes three hours to get there. We leave at eight and it's around eleven when we arrive."

Valmo paused to fish a pack of cigarettes from his pocket and light one. Frost waited in silence until he resumed his narrative.

"The second day there, I was asked to walk up and down, talking aloud about anything I wished, who I was, what I'd read, what I thought about the New Deal and Communism, just anything that entered my head. They were going to time me, and at the end of a definite interval they would return and test me for various reactions. I rambled on for exactly two hours. Then they came back, Gordon and the driver whom I knew only as Al, and gave me some psychological tests. They followed their employer's instructions, and didn't pretend to understand it themselves.

"The third day, I was told to strip, and walk back and forth, keeping a measured pace to a ticking pendulum.

"The fourth day, I sat alone, the hardest experience of all. I did nothing but sit still. It got on my nerves so after awhile that I could have screamed. I knew somebody watched me, but there was no one around and no way that any one could see me. I just sat there with a bad case of jitters, expecting something to happen, wondering about the location of the place, trying to figure out who and what was behind it all.

"Then I heard something. It came without warning, and it scared me out of a year's growth; a sudden cry, a mournful rising and falling wail, full of agony, that kept on for about a minute. I was covered with sweat when the sound died away. I know that that scream was some one's death cry. But I can't prove it, and I don't know who that some one was." Valmo's forehead beaded with sweat at the memory, his hands shook. He lived again the tension and terror of that moment.

"Gordon came in, after an hour or so, and told me to write down an exact description of anything that I had heard, and guess what caused it. He told me to write in detail. He said he felt sorry he couldn't warn me, but they were testing my memory and power of observation by sounds. Naturally I didn't write what I really thought.

"That's about all I know. Every day I've gone through the same sort of rigmarole. Oh, they've treated me decently enough, but it's the confounded mystery of it all that's got on my nerves. Copying Chinese, talking aloud to myself by the hour, walking up and down as naked as the day I was born. Why? Why?

"Two days ago I heard another cry that ended suddenly; it prickled my scalp. I've never seen anybody die, but only a person dying by violence would shriek like that. I almost went to the police a second time but I was afraid I really would be sent to a psychopathic ward. Yesterday they paid me another hundred dollars, and told me I'd receive new instructions in a day or two. I haven't heard from them yet, and I'm convinced now that I never will hear from them again."

The puzzled, plaintive voice ceased. Valmo looked expectantly at Frost. Jean Moray studied the visitor with sympathetic eyes. He may have been unduly credulous, but she visualized herself in his place. For curiosity's sake she would have done much the same thing, with the same bewildered reaction.

Frost said, "Give me your shoes."

Nick Valmo jumped angrily to his feet. "What the hell!" he exploded. "I get in a jam and you want my shoes! I won't—"

Frost stopped him short, "Sit down! Give me your shoes!"

Valmo opened his mouth, closed it without speaking. He took a look at Frost's suddenly glittering eyes and stern features. He sat down and removed his shoes. Frost left the room with them. Valmo squirmed uncomfortably and tried to hide the holes in his socks. Jean said nothing in that awkward interval.

Frost returned in a few minutes and gave the shoes to their owner. "I will take the case."

He walked with Valmo to the door. "If they communicate with you, call me instantly. Keep to your room and be on guard. Have you a gun and permit to carry it?"

"Yes. Now, about your fee—"

"Forget it," said Frost. "If you were wealthy, I would write my own check. As it is, you bring me a riddle with some peculiar and rather fascinating angles. My mind won't be satisfied until I know the answer. It is like a mathematical problem, or a puzzle, which I will solve for the sheer pleasure of it. You, as a person, do not interest me in the slightest. As one piece of a problem, you are highly interesting.

"However, there is nothing that I can do as yet. You think that one or two persons have been murdered. Proof is lacking. I will make routine investigations, but what I count on most is your notifying me immediately if Al and Gordon communicate with you again. Only then can I act."

II.

"AND WHAT," Frost asked, "do you make of Valmo's adventure?"

Jean Moray answered, "I really don't know. Why would any one want to put on such a mystifying show for somebody as unimportant as Nick Valmo? I'd hate to be in his shoes, though. The poor man is so gullible he's likely to get himself killed before he realizes what's happening."

"Are you telling me that you swallowed his story?" Frost asked in a dry and slightly disgusted tone.

The question startled her. "Well, isn't it true?"

"In almost every detail, yes."

"Then why do you throw doubt on it?"

"Because it happened to Nick Valmo."

Jean's eyes glinted. She felt a surge of exasperation over Frost's curious remarks that seemed to progress in circles. "For goodness sakes, what are you driving at? It's true and it's false; it happened to Nick Valmo so you don't believe in it—why?"

Frost drawled, "The experiences, I have no doubt, did occur to Nick Valmo. But that was not Nick Valmo!"

"Not Nick Valmo! Do you know somebody by that name?"

"I have never before encountered the name anywhere."

She stared at him in open astonishment. "If you don't know the real Nick Valmo, how in the world could you possibly guess that the man who came to us was not what he pretended to be?"

"I did not guess," Frost retorted. "I deduced an obvious truth from factual evidence."

"Well," she hesitated, "if he isn't Valmo, he's a convincing actor. He positively trembled with fear at one point."

"Not for the reasons he gave. In his narrative and appearance, however, there are nine separate indications that he is not Nick Valmo, among which three of the more apparent are his nose, his hands, and his feet. He seemed to have scraped his nose, but if you observed it accurately, you would have noticed a faint scar-line. A similar minute line encircles the first joint of all his fingers. His shoes are well-worn, yet his feet bulge the vamp noticeably, and the shoes are much too long. Furthermore, the hardest wear has occurred in parts where his own feet could not have been responsible. Therefore, he is wearing Nick Valmo's shoes. Therefore, his face and fingers have been altered to resemble Nick Valmo."

"Then why did you tell him you would take the case? Why did you say you wouldn't investigate it until you heard from him again?"

"Because he is a murderer," Frost answered coldly, "and because he was hoping for precisely that reaction. His story is improbable; he offers little evidence, and there is only his belief that a crime was committed. No detective or private investigator would be inclined to take much stock in it, or to investigate it unless there were further developments. Yet he told us how Nick Valmo died, and told it in such a fashion as to make it virtually impossible to locate either the scene of the crime or the body.

"He has lost his identity and stepped into his new rôle of Nick Valmo. He wears Valmo's clothing. Who he is and what compelling motive has driven him to drastic actions are only two of several problems that must be solved immediately."

Jean put on a slight frown. "And just how do you propose to accomplish the impossible, starting with practically nothing?"

Instead of answering, Frost lifted the receiver and phoned for Inspector Frick of the Homicide Bureau. "I.V. Frost speaking. Ask all patrolmen and squad cars to keep a special watch on vacant lots, parks, cemeteries, and isolated spots for the body of a well-dressed man who has a professional appearance and does not look like a criminal. He will be—"

"For heaven's sake, Ivy, what kind of a wizard are you?" came Frick's startled voice. "A body fitting that description was found in Oakview Cemetery less than an hour ago. They've finished the field work and it's on its way to the morgue. Clear case of murder. Fingerprints on the man's collar ought to send some one to the chair."

"Identification?"

"Tentative as C.D. Styker, the wealthy business man who disappeared about a month ago. Member of the family coming down to make identification positive. Want to see the corpse?"

"Not now," Frost replied. "I am going out to read the tombstones in Oakview Cemetery."

Frick's voice seemed to explode. "Going out to read—tombstones by night—say, what sort of a gag is this?"

Frost drawled, "Do you keep fingerprint cards on file after the subject is dead?"

"Why, yes, for a while." The inspector's tone became puzzled. "They sometimes prove useful even a year or two later. After five years, we generally weed out the old ones. Why do you ask?"

"You stated that fingerprints were found on the dead man's collar. I would suggest that you first run through the file of persons who have met death within the past two years."

"Now listen, Ivy, that's ridiculous—"

"I have no time to discuss the matter now. I will get in touch with you again later."

Frost clicked the receiver and turned to his assistant. "Miss Moray, I will be gone all night. I want you to stay behind and sleep. Get all the rest you can. Be ready for a summons at any instant between eight and nine in the morning. It is highly important that you look your best and function most efficiently."

With that he disappeared into his laboratory, for what reason she could only guess. Its seemingly inexhaustible diversity of equipment and supplies had never failed to provide him with exactly what he wanted and precisely when he wanted it. His absence lasted scarcely a minute. He came out with an expression of abstract speculation and did not appear to be aware of her existence, or, for that matter, to be conscious of anything except his own thoughts; and those he kept to himself. He was smoking another of the long, suspicious cigarettes that he manufactured himself. The pungent fumes, sharply aromatic, eddied in his wake.

HE TOOK the *Demon,* as his assistant had nicknamed it. The *Demon* was an automobile which he had assembled from standard parts and parts built to his own specifications. Jean had given it its name on the ground that only a demon could handle it at its top speed of 135 m.p.h. It looked like a cross between a sedan and a limousine, and replaced a similar car that had been demolished by explosives in one of Frost's first cases. The second *Demon,* like the first, had everything—bulletproof glass, armor-protected engine and fuel tank, heavy-tread tires filled with a composition that automatically repaired blowouts and punctures, smoke-screen equipment, racks and compartments for a wide variety of ammunition and accessories, and secret features that came to light only with Frost's need for them.

He ambled along at 35 and 40 most of the way. His air of profound reflection did not change. He looked oblivious to traffic and traffic lights, to pedestrians and crossings. The frequent almost-accidents never became catastrophes. Jean had once said that Frost was at least two persons and probably more—a Protean intellect detached from a physical body with which it frequently coöperated.

The caretaker at Oakview Cemetery said gruffly, "Sorry, but no visitors are permitted after sundown." He stood in front of a small stone structure just inside the entrance.

Frost said, "I know. I would appreciate your keeping an eye on my car. It will not take me long to read the inscriptions. Are there many crypts and mausoleums?"

"No, and they're all grouped around that monument—you can just see it over there. If you'll return—"

"Thank you," the professor nodded as he strode past the caretaker, who stared dubiously at the figure retreating into the darkness that enshrouded the grounds.

The beam of Frost's flashlight winked upon inscription after inscription. Thousands of headstones rose above graves, but crypts and vaults were few. He paused an instant at each of these, until he came to one which stopped him. The beam remained steady, but an oddly shaped tool in Frost's right hand made twisting sounds in the keyhole.

The caretaker sauntered toward him, then ran. "Stop! You can't break into a vault!"

"I already have," Frost stated calmly as the door opened.

The man protested, "Permission from the family and the police are required to open a tomb. I will summon the police—"

"Excellent! I believe they would find it eminently to their advantage to follow me," Frost assented as he led the way to a small crypt. In the crypt lay a coffin, whose name plate had begun to tarnish. It bore the simple legend: Sam Trogg, 1904-1933.

While the caretaker watched him with an air of uncertainty and anxiety, Frost pried up the lid of the casket.

The cadaver of Sam Trogg had not improved with age. His finger nails, through the mysterious alchemy of the grave, had kept on growing. They were long, gnarled, and of a hideous yellowish-gray hue. His hair had matted and twisted beneath his head. His features had gradually shrunk until the bony configurations of the skull showed through the withered skin.

A faint mold had developed unevenly upon the cadaver. It adhered at its thickest to the features, and at its slightest, on the hands. Frost studied the mold with a jeweler's eyepiece. He likewise examined some microscopic granules on the cerements.

"What are you looking for?" asked the caretaker.

Frost led the way out after an ambiguous reply. "Tales told by dead men." He used the same odd instrument to relock the door, and handed the caretaker his card. "In case you wish to consult the police, or if the incident brings further discussion," he finished dryly.

He took long strides to his car. The *Demon* lived up to its name. Twenty minutes later, just before nine, he stopped at the municipal morgue, and asked to view the body found in Oakview Cemetery. Relatives of the dead man, he learned, had already furnished positive identification that he was C. D. Styker.

Frost scarcely glanced at the corpse. He devoted a few moments to scrutiny of three fingerprints in a smear of dust upon the dead man's shirt tabs. When he left, his abstract expression remained, but to it was added the ghost of a sardonic smile.

III.

INSPECTOR FRICK glowered at his desk in police headquarters. The inspector, a wiry, slender, medium-sized individual of ruddy countenance, had a stiff carriage and walked with a crispness that resulted from his years of military service as a major. More persistent and tenacious than keen in his abilities, he nevertheless had been successful in cracking a number of tough homicide cases. His name carried prestige and considerable influence in police circles.

He was Frost's strongest friend on the force. The rivalry that frequently prevails between police and private investigators simply did not exist in their case. Frost got along with the officials better than most private operatives because he ignored fame, cared nothing about publicity, and had often handed to the force a criminal or corpse with air-tight evidence.

Frick frowned up at Mason, a fingerprint expert. "You're positive that there is no mistake? You're certain there hasn't been a slip?"

"Absolutely."

Frick continued to glower at the objects before him. He had ample reason. The enlargement of a photograph showed three clear fingerprints on the collar of a dead man. The other item was the file card of Sam Trogg, with the notation, "Electrocuted at Sing-Sing, Aug. 21, 1933."

The briefest comparison proved beyond question that prints of a man executed in 1933 and prints left by a killer in 1935 were identical!

Frick said, "Do you realize what this means if it gets out?"

Mason nodded. "Fingerprints are an infallible means of identification because no two prints have ever been alike. I've seen apparent exceptions, but they were only partial prints or poorly done, and clear prints later showed the distinctions. Even identic twins show difference in their fingerprints. Yet these three prints are exactly like Trogg's. If this gets out, it means that every criminal lawyer in America will be filing writs for the release of criminals who were convicted by fingerprint evidence. It means a blow to a system of identification built up for half a century."

"Right!" Frick agreed, scowling, "I wish to heavens we'd smeared those damn prints up ourselves. I wish we'd never found Trogg's file card. For once I wish Frost had kept his mouth shut."

"What are you going to do about it?"

"What is there to do? If we publish this, the shysters will spring a bunch of convicts. Not only that, it'll be harder than ever to get convictions against new killers. Maybe we'd better destroy these fingerprints and forget we ever saw them."

Mason said, "It might be a good idea to look into the Trogg angle. I don't remember the case but maybe he escaped or got a pardon and our records are wrong."

Frick phoned Sing-Sing, scowled some more. He called a New York undertaker, and his scowl deepened.

"It's all screwy," he announced irritably. "Trogg was electrocuted all right, and buried—in Oakview Cemetery. Undertaker claims the body was embalmed but we'll have to check. Maybe the guy came to life again by some fluke and let himself out. It seems he had plenty of dough and they put him away in one of those crypts where he could get out by himself. I'm going to get a court order—"

The door opened unceremoniously.

"Frost!" the inspector exclaimed. "I want a talk with you. Something about this Styker bump-off smells. We're going to open the grave of Sam Trogg and—"

"Save yourself the bother. I just came from there."

Frick gaped at him. "You've just come—say, what is this? How the hell did you get in so fast? Damn it, Ivy, we didn't even identify Trogg's prints till fifteen minutes ago and you say you've already been out to the cemetery!"

"And examined the *corpus delicti*. If it will interest you, some one else recently opened the grave and took wax impressions of the fingers, from which a cast was subsequently made."

"Can you prove that?"

"I found particles of wax and the mold is gone from the finger tips."

"But cadavers decay—"

Frost cut in, "A well-embalmed body frequently will show little sign of deterioration for years. Take another look at the fingerprints on Styker's collar. They contain none of the waxy and fatty skin excretions which are always found in genuine fingerprints. They could not have been left by human hands."

Frick's scowl did not noticeably lessen. "So now the fingerprint clue is a dud and we haven't anything to work on. Phooey! What a case!" He ended in disgust. "What are you going to do about it, Frost?"

"I may go walking on the bottom of a lake."

"Oh, sure, sure, that's a hot idea. Guess I'll take another route and go walking through the stratosphere," the inspector said sourly. Nevertheless he eyed Frost with a shrewd appraisal. The professor's unexpected statements had a way of developing into fact.

"My primary purpose in coming here," Frost replied, "was to ask whether the police are particularly anxious to arrest a man with a bulbous nose."

"Oh, nuts," Frick sighed wearily. "Not any more than they are to catch a man with big teeth or one with a full beard."

Frost said curtly, "I am serious."

The inspector shook his head gently, but opened a drawer. "Here's one that came in a month ago—swindler named Coleman wanted in several States." He handed a poster to Frost and dug out a few others. "You'll find plenty of other guys with bulbous noses in the Gallery if you want to run through it."

"These will do." He glanced at the faces, returned the sheaf to the inspector, and departed before Frick could ask more questions.

JOHN VOGEL, senior partner in the law firm of Vogel, Vogel, and Brant, slowly turned the pages of a book he was reading. Many important legal matters had occupied his attention all day, and he had spent the evening preparing an important brief. Now, before retiring, he allowed himself an hour of relaxation, with pipe and text, in his library. The hour was ten. Light from the shaded lamp slanted across his jovial, rather cherubic face. Jovial, except for his eyes, which were astonishingly owl-like and shrewd. The large octavo he read bore the title, "The Toxicology of Mushrooms, Toadstools, and Fungi," by Prof. I. V. Frost. He was both an old friend and legal representative of Frost.

John Vogel, white-haired and past fifty, read with relish. Full-page plates in color illustrated various poisonous mushrooms in their native state. A salty style of writing and a wealth of historical and miscellaneous background material enlivened what easily could have been a dry, scientific treatise.

"The *Amanita Phalloides,"* he read, "has long and rightly been regarded as one of the most highly toxic of North American mushrooms; yet a nation that thrives upon bird's-nest soup makes of this mushroom a quaint and somewhat sinister delicacy. The Chinese employ a process of repeated boiling with native herbs to extract most of the phallin, the characteristic poison of the *Amanita* group. The water in which these mushrooms have boiled is then distilled to yield—"

A buzzer interrupted him. He closed the book, rose and crossed to the telephone stand. He lifted the receiver, listened. Then: "It is weeks since I heard from you, Ivy," John Vogel complained with a smile.

"When I have completed a case that I am investigating, I will pay you a social visit for a change," Frost promised. "J. V., I want some information. I want it fast. Can you tell me anything about a lawyer named Simon Mord?"

A dozen bits of knowledge slipped through John Vogel's mind in a flash: The times he had clashed with Mord as opposing counsel in court; Mord, who defended the sour cream of the underworld in murder cases; Mord, whose brilliantly shady career had never got him disbarred, and against whom two indictments had been quashed; Mord, who used every resource of law to protect the worst leeches of society; Mord, whom even the powerful bar associations had not been able to dislodge.

Could John Vogel give Frost details about Simon Mord? J.V. could—and did.

THE PRIM young woman who wore glasses and had a schoolmarm appearance glanced at the clock and yawned. In fifteen minutes she could close the newspaper reading room and go home. It would be pleasant to leave the musty air of the library, and its inevitable odor of unwashed humanity. She hated her job and she hated the people who used the room.

All the bums and loafers, the ragged-clothed men with unshaven faces, the idle poor who had nothing else to do seemed to concentrate upon the newspaper room. They came and they stayed for hours until the air reeked of their presence. They read to-day's tabloids. And many of them who knew little English buried themselves in queer periodicals of a Hebraic, Russian, Polish, or Italian nature.

"Sorry, but the *Volkszeitung* is in use now . . . No, we don't carry the Fresno *Bee* . . . Tuesday's issue of *Avant?* Sorry, but it hasn't come in yet. It should arrive to-morrow . . . Here is *La Semana*—"

She attended to her duties efficiently, keeping pace with requests and the delivery of papers previously asked for. The demand was now rapidly falling off as closing time drew near.

She opened a drawer to get at her purse. A voice, incisive, crisp, halted her. "I want a complete file of the *Courier* and the *Press* for the past month."

The request was absurd. At this hour—why, it would take till long past closing time for any one to go through those files. She glanced up with a frown of annoyance. An incredibly tall, towering, and determined individual faced her. He didn't frighten her and he didn't attract her. He simply registered power, driving power that would ruthlessly trample her aside if necessary for his ends. Her heart gave a flip-flop, but she said meekly, "I will have them for you in a minute."

Then she was angry with herself for having yielded to his unreasonable request. Her anger, however, did not find words. The rangy man leaned upon the desk, with a faraway look in his eyes. When the files arrived, he took them to the nearest table.

She watched him. The room gradually emptied. He went through the first file with a speed that surprised her. He stopped three times, and copied items. He must have used shorthand, because he halted for seconds only.

Closing time came. All the other visitors had left. For some reason, she dallied about the last details of closing up for the night. The rangy man flipped through pages of the second file as if each page were only a single picture.

"Thank you," he said briefly when he left, and her eyes followed him out the door before she saw the ten-dollar bill on the desk. She looked at his call slip, which was signed, "I.V. Frost."

Though most other offices in the Federal Building were darkened, light showed through the windows of the Topographic Survey. Two clerks toiled, getting out maps, diagrams, and charts, for the benefit of an active man in his middle thirties, who looked exceedingly business-like and practical. It was almost midnight, and the clerks hoped that they would be able to finish their work soon and give to their superior the specific items he was seeking.

They looked up in surprise when an imperious knocking sounded upon the locked door. They glanced uncertainly to the third man, who walked over to the door, stood aside, and opened it, wary caution in every move he made.

Suddenly he opened the door wide. "Frost! What on earth brings you here at this hour?"

"I myself might ask," Frost observed with a smile, "what brings you here at this hour. The division of investigation of the Department of Justice would hardly send its local chief of staff to aid the Topographic Bureau in making surveys. I have a list here of certain soil particles, and I want to know where, within a radius of fifty miles, such soil can be found. I have a special interest in the wilds of northern New Jersey."

For half an hour, Frost pored over files, maps, and geological surveys. When he left, his face was grimmer than when he arrived, and a brooding aspect had entered his eyes. He smoked incessantly his long, self-made, mordant cigarettes. There was a hint of neuroticism in that habit, and in the slender hands, feminine in their beauty, that made so striking a contrast to his lankness and odd appearance.

"SHUT-EYE" Dade was plastered. He knew he was plastered and guessed he ought to be staggering home. He'd dropped over to "Stiffy"

Litescu's shack and a couple of the boys were there, so they opened up a jug. They ran illicit stills in an out-of-the-way part of the northern New Jersey wilds. They all grew roaring drunk on their own stuff, but Vic, who got his nickname from a trick of keeping his eyes half closed and of frequently going by-by from soaking up unbelievable quantities of his own beverage, saw a fight brewing. He didn't feel like a fight.

Shut-eye fell only a couple of times as he headed for the woods in a sort of looping zigzag about 2 A.M. There was a road, but a bad one. He seldom used his car for his social affairs, because shortcuts through the woods and over the hills got him there before a car could creep over the much longer route by road.

Nevertheless, Shut-eye's method of getting home was somewhat circumspect. The trees were particularly nasty. They reached out and bit him several times. Once a tree trunk gave him a biff on the nose and he skinned his knuckles giving it a good hard biff in return, before he discovered that the dastardly assailant was a tree. At another point, a boulder cunningly rose up and pulled him down to earth, so Shut-eye put a few bullets into it to teach it a lesson.

Woozy things kept popping into his head, and sometimes he wasn't sure but what woozy things with peculiar tails and the most extraordinary colors and shapes weren't popping up and down in the woods. He pursued a pair of nine-legged ostriches with heads at each end but he didn't succeed in catching either of those marvelous birds. They somehow got away from him.

Shut-eye reeled blithely on his homeward way. He did not look like a person to be thought of in terms of blithesomeness and conviviality, but gay he seemed and plastered he was. A good five feet eleven, he looked smaller because he walked with a stoop. A young crop of whiskers sprouted hither and yon upon his face, whose other main characteristic was a distinctly glowing nose pushed to the fore by cadaverous cheeks. The entirety of this exquisite person finally arrived, after a series of further minor encounters with recalcitrant nature, in the general vicinity of his farm house.

He managed to get onto the dirt road that straggled toward it, and after a few hundred paces came in sight of his home. The old shack, as he called it, seemed a bit on its uppers, for it did a rather fancy jig in his honor. Then, too, a boulder that he hadn't noticed before seemed possessed of a strange determination to walk like a man.

To Shut-eye's great consternation, the boulder succeeded. It rose to towering proportions. It somehow acquired a pair of glittering black eyes and the beak of a predatory bird. Its profile was etched in sharp and ruthless severity against the sky.

With a yell of pure fright, Shut-eye popped his eyes wide open for the first time in years and sprinted for the house with such determination that he knocked himself cold when the doorknob leaped out and socked him on the cranium.

Prof I.V. Frost, having watched the stranger's eccentric progress with a glint of interest, shrugged. He ceased his examination of the soil and melted into the darkness.

IV.

WHEN JEAN MORAY, fresh as a grape from the vine, emerged from 11 and tripped over to 13 State Street at 7:30 A.M., she found Ivy Frost ruining himself with cigarettes and black coffee. Since he was perfectly content, she insisted upon preparing a breakfast of orange juice, toasted English muffins, bacon and eggs. Frost continued to saturate his system with cigarettes and coffee. Exasperated, she ate what she could and consigned the rest to oblivion.

"What do you make of these?" He read aloud to her the shorthand transcriptions he had made of three newspaper items.

> Chicago, Ill., Aug. 2—Police announced to-day that recent victims of confidence games had failed to identify a suspect using the name Harry Peters as the sought-for swindler. Charges against Peters will be dropped.
>
> Peters at first was thought to be the most notorious and elusive con man ever hunted in this country. His real name and history are unknown, though he is generally listed as Stanley V. Coleman, his first alias. He has never been arrested, nor is his photograph on file. However, victims have supplied police with an accurate description of him, and a full set of his fingerprints has been collected. It was these fingerprints, rushed here from Washington, that furnished final positive proof that Peters was not the wanted fugitive.
>
> The swindler has used a different alias for each of his schemes, and has operated in all parts of the country. He is known to have collected more than a million dollars from fraudulent schemes in the past five years. His actual "take" is believed to be considerably larger, since wealthy and promi-

nent persons frequently do not prefer charges for fear of newspaper publicity.

Albany, N.Y., Aug. 9—Chief of Police Dan Q. O'Reilly to-day announced acquisition of a photograph of Stanley V. Coleman, a fugitive swindler for whom a nation-wide search has been in progress. Coleman has used more than a dozen aliases.

The picture came into the hands of police by accident. A newsreel taken here and showing only at local theaters was responsible for the photograph. The newsreel depicts a shot of the large crowd which gathered to witness the spectacular fire on the water front several days ago. A man in the audience, whose name police withheld by request, positively identified a man in the crowd as the notorious confidence man who swindled him out of a large sum of money at a southern resort two years ago.

Police attach great importance to the photograph. Thousands of copies are being distributed all over the country. From the way the fugitive covered his face immediately after the camera was turned toward the crowd, police believe he knew he would eventually be identified. While a close check-up is in progress, police are certain that he has already departed from this vicinity.

Cleveland, O., Aug. 25—Positive identification of a victim of amnesia found wandering on the streets yesterday as W. O. Byrnes, missing business man of Toledo, was made by relatives to-day, according to police announcement.

Byrnes at first was thought to be C. D. Styker, missing director of the Park Avenue Bank, of New York, for whom an intensive search is in progress. Styker disappeared under mysterious circumstances on August 11. He was last seen in the late afternoon, driving his car toward the George Washington Bridge. The car was found abandoned in Albany on Aug. 12. There were no signs of violence.

The former physician who retired at 30 to devote all his time to the directorships he holds in several companies, is thought to have been a victim of amnesia. He is now 41. A strange circumstance of his disappearance is the fact that, on August 5, a week before he vanished, he withdrew $100,000 in cash from his personal account. No trace of the sum has been found, nor did he give a hint to any of his associates concerning his purpose in withdrawing so large an amount. All his affairs were found to be in order.

The moment he ceased reading, Jean said, "At this stage, I wouldn't even try to guess what it's all about. If you mean to suggest that the three clippings are related to each other and have some tie-up with the fake Nick Valmo, then it's just a fancy mess. Instead of having one puzzle to solve, it looks as if about every kind of crime there is is mixed up in this somewhere."

Frost gave her a thoughtful appraisal. "Your comments, though slangy, are rather apt. And yet, I think one or two small deductions may be made. Arrange the incidents in order of their time.

"August 2: Police are seeking an operator of confidence games; 5: Styker withdraws $100,000 in cash, in New York; 9: Coleman is photographed in Albany; 11: Styker disappears while driving out of New York; 12: Styker's abandoned car is found in Albany; 12: A strange advertisement appears in a New York paper; 13 to 27: Nick Valmo answers the advertisement, and receives a job whose duties are, to say the least, remarkable; 28: Some one claiming to be Nick Valmo comes to us with a story.

"Into the picture, also, must be fitted two gentlemen known as Gordon and Al, and a brick house, location known. From particles of soil adhering to Valmo's shoes, I discovered the nature of the ground surrounding the house, and from U. S. government surveys, I have located the district in northern New Jersey."

Frost glanced at the clock. "I talked to a bank official and found that no record of the serial numbers on the bills withdrawn by Styker had been kept. I visited his residence and discovered several sheets of paper covered with figures, but giving no clue as to their purpose. They are the serial numbers of the missing currency. Come into the laboratory."

He led her to a row of items on a table. Swiftly he went to work upon her hands, incasing them in tight-fitting gloves of a black sheen that reached well past her wrists. Over the back of each hand he affixed a glass phial, swathed it in cotton, and bandaged it securely. "You many need these. Go to Valmo's address, 119 Kaye Street. Use the coupé. Stay in the car and keep low. When Valmo emerges, follow him. Follow him wherever he goes, and remember that you will be in constant danger. Start now; you should reach Valmo's address by nine o'clock."

She had chosen to wear riding breeches, boots, and tuck-in silk blouse. As she passed out of the room, she looked like anything but a student of criminology. She seemed, instead, the loveliest young woman east of the Mississippi, a beauty winner out for a walk, or a star off for a ride.

Frost returned to the library and idled with cigarettes and coffee until nine o'clock. On the hour, he phoned the office of Simon Mord. A secretary answered.

"Tell Mord that I.V. Frost will meet him at his office at 10 A.M. tomorrow for an important conference concerning Nick Valmo."

He repeated the statement. He declined to elaborate or wait for the secretary to consult the attorney. He dropped the receiver in its cradle.

A loaded valise stood on the floor of his laboratory. He took it with him when he rolled out in the *Demon*. It began to live up to its name immediately as he sped downtown.

V.

JEAN MORAY kept her head below the level of the dashboard, and flush against the left front door of the coupé. That was one of Frost's ingenious ideas. She could see the mirror above the steering wheel. It reflected another mirror in the back of the car. The rear mirror reflected the street ahead. Thus she could see, without being seen, unless some passer-by came up to the auto and deliberately peered inside.

The position cramped her, but she wriggled around a little. She craved a cigarette, but did not dare smoke. She glued her vision to 119 Kaye Street. She squirmed from time to time, easing herself into a more comfortable position. Two hours of this slow and tedious waiting passed. Her black-incased hands drew her attention at intervals. Judging from the swellings, any one who looked at them would have said she had broken them.

At 9:15, Nick Valmo came out. He walked swiftly to the corner and turned it. Jean threw the car into gear and followed. She kept about a block behind him. He walked for two more blocks and came to a closed but unlettered truck of the kind that laundries use. He climbed in the front seat. A few seconds later, the truck rolled off.

Then began a long and, at times, difficult pursuit. The truck headed toward lower Manhattan and entered the Holland Tunnel. She almost lost it in Jersey City. For forty miles, sometimes only a block behind when passing through towns, but occasionally dropping as far as half a mile to the rear on the open highway, she kept the car in sight.

She became hungry about 10:30, and contented herself with a bar of chocolate.

Then the vehicle ahead turned on to a macadam side road. Signs of habitation became increasingly rare, and she found herself in a hilly region of second-growth wilderness, a tangle of thick underbrush through which young trees struggled.

By sighting ahead from the crests of hills, she was able to tail the car but remain well behind. Ten miles of this, and the lead car again turned off on what was little more than a dirt road, wide enough for two autos to pass with difficulty, and seldom used. She had encountered other automobiles on the macadam road, but here there was none. The silence of the place made her uneasy She dropped even farther behind, though the coupé made as little noise as any car can.

The dirt road rambled and twisted. She followed it for perhaps three miles, without coming to another road, when she swung around a curve.

There stood the truck, parked at the edge of the road. She let her coupé drift past it, saw that it had been deserted. She stopped around the next turn, and hiked back to the truck. She cut between it and the trees.

"Just a moment," drawled a voice, preceded by a flat automatic.

The door at the rear of the truck opened, and a man dropped to the ground. Although he had no mustache, his appearance otherwise fitted the description that Valmo had given of Gordon.

"Keep your hands high."

He lifted the automatic from her hip pocket, and prodded her ahead of him.

"In," he ordered curtly, nodding to the woods.

A faint trail led through the wild tangle of young growth and trees. Nine people out of ten would never have seen the trail, but Jean had spent so much time on summer canoe trips through forests and streams of the Great Lakes district that she could read nature almost as well as a crack woodsman.

She walked a quarter of a mile and came out on the edge of a lake perhaps a half-mile wide. Al and Nick Valmo stood beside a beached canoe.

Valmo looked at her with a cold and impersonal stare. "Give her the works," he ordered, showing no sign of emotion.

From behind her came Gordon's voice, a slow and stubborn drawl. "Not me. She's too damn good-looking. I always had a weakness for dames. This one's tops. There aren't many like her. Let's take her along."

Valmo said evenly, "That's impossible. The whole scheme has gone wrong as it is. If we keep her, chances are that Frost will come around with some of his poison."

"What more d'you want? You're boss of the show, but we'll be just that much stronger if he does turn up. He won't try anything if he knows we've got the girl."

"I've never heard of that stopping him," Valmo insisted. "If he ever does find her, we'll be so far away that we'll be safe. We can't take her with us for very long, anyway."

"Look at her hands. They're sprained or busted. She hasn't got a chance."

Valmo said, "Give her the works."

Jean's heart did a flip-flop. There was no possible reprieve, judging by his calm insistence. Pride would not let her plead for her life.

"While you gentlemen are trying to decide what to do about my very valuable body, let me change my make-up and fix my hair," she suddenly requested.

They stared at her in momentary astonishment as she patted, arranged, and smoothed her hair. Her right hand flashed out with a trim little automatic. The one shot she fired skimmed above Valmo's head. It went wild when Gordon came up fast from behind with a blow that knocked the pistol out of her hand.

Instantly occurred an action that provided the brief paralysis of surprise. As Gordon ran up, and knocked the gun away, her arms twined behind her and she bent forward. He sailed over her head. It was a defense trick she had practiced upon try-out subjects.

There was no unusual force in her action, but it was an action totally unexpected from a woman. She had a glimpse of Gordon, as though poised sprawled in mid-air, in front of her and facing her, yet falling away. She had a desire to laugh. She noted in the same tense moment that sheer surprise had caused Valmo and Al to lower their guns.

Gordon hit the earth with a thud.

Jean straightened, and remained motionless, her arms hanging free.

She made no attempt to run or to dive for a gun. She stood like a statue as though nothing of consequence had occurred.

Gordon scrambled to his feet. The guns of the two others covered her again, but she simply stared at them as though nothing had occurred.

"Crazy—she's crazy as a loon," Gordon muttered.

"Busted hands!" Valmo snarled and walked toward her.

She uttered no protest when he cracked the butt of his weapon against each hump. There were splintering sounds. He brought out a pocketknife and slit the bandage. The acid spurted and a drop touched him. He let out a yelp of pain.

Valmo sniffed the fumes, and gradually a queer, taut determination settled on his face.

"I get it," he breathed. "Just in case we felt sentimental and tied her up, she'd rub her hands back to back and the acid would eat away at the rope. Swell idea. Now that the acid's gone, that's just what we'll do."

Jean fought and twisted like a cat. Terror produced a strength far beyond her sex and years. The odds were hopeless. They tied her hands behind her back. They knotted her ankles, drew them up tight, and lashed them to her hands. To this they fastened a rope around her neck.

"Now," said Nick Valmo, "you may have the pleasure of signing your own death warrant. Just lie quiet, until you start aching. Then move a little, and garrot yourself. Yell all you want to. So long, sister."

He blew her an ironic kiss. Al and Gordon turned back on the trail and headed for the two cars. Valmo shoved off in the canoe. She could barely see him through the tall reeds that grew thickly along the shore. The canoe faded across the lake.

For a minute, she clung to a desperate hope that they were merely torturing her and would return. The canoe continued on its straight course. She heard the noise of motors starting, and the mesh of gears as Al and Gordon drove the cars away. Then, for a brief interval, sheer panic swept her. She made an inadvertent motion, and the rope tightened inexorably on her throat. She held herself rigid because she had to. If she began to relax, or tried to straighten her already aching limbs, she would garrot herself.

She hoped, half-expected, that Frost would suddenly pop out of nowhere. He had a habit of turning up when the need was greatest. But this time, he could not help her. He had foreseen what might happen, but her own ill-taken action had deprived her of the safeguard.

She had made no plea to Valmo and she uttered no cry now.

Slowly, with infinite pains, she twisted her hands, but the slightest motion tightened relentlessly the rope around her throat. Whatever she did, however she moved, would only result in strangling her. She became acutely conscious of each sound, from the chirp of a cricket and a squirrel's chatter to the song of a meadow lark. Oddly intermingled with these was a far drumming which she recognized, in sudden despair, as a roaring in her own ears. It was the end, the pulse of doom. Since she could not help herself, quick oblivion would be preferable to the delayed agony of fiery gasping for breath. She tautened her body.

VI.

THERE was a swish of branches and crackle of dead leaves. She felt something pounce upon her hands from behind, and all at once, miraculously, she could breathe.

"Take it easy," drawled a cool, confidence-restoring voice. The swimming haze cleared away from her eyes, and she struggled upright to look at the professor.

"Ivy! You came!" she gasped.

"I dislike platitudes and I did nothing of the sort," he snapped. "I have been here all along. I watched the entire proceeding."

Anger flooded her face. "You've been here? You watched?" she blazed in incredulous fury, "You let them do that to me, almost kill me, before you could be bothered about saving my life? You aren't even human! You're a ghoul! You're—"

"Stop it," Frost interrupted in a brusque but insistent tone. "You have not been in any real danger. I deliberately initiated the steps leading to this occurrence. It was necessary in order to force the hand, so to speak, of the murderers and compel them to expose their plot. The inconvenience to you could not be avoided because I wished to give them ample opportunity to depart well out of hearing distance.

"The brick house is on the opposite shore. We shall raid it shortly. Meanwhile, I am going to walk across the lake. I would suggest that you encircle it. Proceed with caution, as you approach the other side. I will meet you by that boulder some two hundred yards to the right of the canoe. Take the valise with you."

He returned to the thicket from which he had emerged. Inside it, he opened his valise and donned more clothing. The suit was a self-sustaining diver's outfit, with oxygen tank, weighted shoes, and a small but powerful lamp in the helmet.

Jean watched him walk into the water until it closed above his head. She rested for several minutes, recovering from the shock of her experience. She looked at the long way around the uneven shore of the lake, and the short, inviting, direct way.

She brought the valise from its hiding place, and found that it was light enough to float. She laid her clothing inside it and struck out across the lake, pushing the valise ahead of her. She leisurely dawdled along, luxuriating in the cool pleasure of the water. It helped to calm her and steady her perspective.

On the other side, she dried herself in the sun.

WHEN FROST strode into the lake, he stopped, as his head went under. He checked every part of the outfit. It was in perfect working condition.

The water proved to be fairly clear. The bottom, sandy and pebble-covered near shore, became rocky farther out. A dozen yards from shore, he could still touch the surface with his hand. A thick patch of weeds grew here. A school of sunfish and a bass swam away. Then the going became rougher, with steep descents and drop-offs. A hundred yards out, the bottom leveled off at about forty feet. Here there were occasional patches of mud and sand among the rocks. Silt eddied up slowly in his wake. Little light filtered down to this depth. He could have discerned nothing in that darkness except for the strong beam from his helmet. He kept swinging his head from side to side, so that the beam cut a semicircle. Even so, visibility stopped at about ten feet.

The water, lukewarm near shore, grew chilly in its deeper places. The pressure was noticeable, but not seriously uncomfortable. His ordinarily swift, decisive movements acquired that peculiar lag which the very nature of under-water work entails.

He passed occasional sink holes. He circled one mud patch which an exploratory test proved treacherous. The bottom remained roughly level. In that strange, soundless, lightless, windless darkness, he prowled like a figure in a picture run off at slow motion. He discovered none of the usual array of tin cans, broken bottles, rusty wheels, and similar junk that lakes have a habit of collecting.

A full half hour went by. He turned toward his right and walked exactly ten paces. He swung around and in doing so the beam of light diffused a ghostly aura upon an object sufficiently grisly of itself.

The object was a human leg. It stood upright. It would have floated to the surface except for the rope around its ankle. A chunk of rusty iron securely anchored the rope.

Frost moved toward it, and the leg swayed gently, with a slow and horrible motion, as though the leg was trying to escape. Then, beyond it, he discovered a second leg, similarly fastened. Near them drifted a pair of arms, socket up, fingers spread wide around the rope as if to clutch it, an arrested motion that would never be completed.

These four gruesome objects were a heavy drag. He walked slowly toward shore, carrying two weights in each hand. A weird figure in the diving suit, he looked like some creature of nightmare, with the extra arms and legs trailing behind him.

Jean Moray, scared speechless, fled into the woods when parts of a corpse suddenly popped to the surface a dozen yards out. She dressed hurriedly and saw the professor deposit his burden. He returned to the lake.

A stream of tiny bubbles marked his under-water trail. Arms and legs as a rule do not mature without a head and torso.

In another half hour, Frost emerged with the remainder of the corpse. He rid himself of the diving suit.

"Some day," he warned, "you will invite death once too often. Against the grays and browns of the soil, the greens and shadows of the woods, your whiteness made a perfect target when you sunned yourself."

"But didn't you think I had a perfect figure?" she asked, instead of showing confusion.

Frost snorted. "Now that I have assembled Nick Valmo, let us add the elusive Stanley V. Coleman to our collection."

She looked at the sickening fragments of the dead man. How Frost proposed to identify him she did not venture to guess. The remains had begun to bloat. The hands had been burned so severely that no fingerprints could be obtained. Only a charred semblance of a face was left.

Frost handed her a long-barreled pistol and extra ammunition. "When we reach the house, watch the rear. I'll skirt around to the front and find out if it is occupied. Stop any one, alive if possible, but shoot to kill if necessary."

He led the way to a faint path that wound away from the lake. A couple of hundred yards at a slight upward slope brought them to the house in the clearing. There, the small truck and coupé were parked.

He separated from his assistant.

Keeping far enough away to be concealed in the underbrush, and moving slowly to avoid making sounds, Frost circled to the front of the house. Lying on the ground, at the edge of the clearing, he slipped a glass projectile into a peculiar gun. Then, aiming carefully at one of the lower windows, he fired. The projectile smashed through the window, and a volume of white smoke rolled up. Loading and firing rapidly, Frost put one of the tear-gas bombs through every window in front.

Suddenly, part of a figure appeared at an upstairs window, and the coughing stutter of a submachine gun chattered through the air. Leaves began slanting from the young trees, spouts of dirt kicked up from the ground, and the whine of bullets was answered by smack upon wood. The swinging gun sprayed the whole front for perhaps fifteen seconds. Then the white smoke eddied around the figure and it stumbled back.

At the same time, the front door opened with a jerk. A man, gun in hand, crossed the porch in a single leap that carried him to the protection of the truck. Frost shouted, "Stop or I shoot to kill!"

He leisurely brought out a duplicate of the revolver he had given his assistant, and sighted accurate. There was a sudden roar as the motor turned over, and the car leaped away in second gear. The professor fired. A trickle of fluid splashed down the hood of the car and a burst of flame roared up. A hand poked through the window and its gun spat flashes. Frost shot once more and the hand went limp. The car slowed down, and rambled erratically, and finally stopped, enveloped in flames.

From the rear of the house came the splutter of the submachine gun, briefly. A single shot ended it. A moment of silence, a savage curse, then the gun coughed again and was answered by the pistol.

The sounds of the shooting died away. The acrid fumes of burned powder mingled with the smell of burning gasoline and paint, the odor of tear-gas. No one else appeared. Silence settled again, save for the crackle from the truck. Frost walked around to the rear of the house, found Jean looking at a sprawled form.

"It's Gordon. He ran out of the house. I ordered him to stop but he began shooting. I hit his leg and he fell. He got up shooting. The second shot I fired went through his heart."

"And Al is dead in front. That leaves Coleman," Frost drawled. "Good work. I would have preferred them alive, but they knew the chair was ready."

They turned toward the house, and entered, protected by temporary masks that Frost had fished from a side pocket of his coat. They found a room, exactly as Nick Valmo described it, almost bare, its window broken from the tear-gas projectile.

Frost pointed to a panel of heavy glass in a door opposite the window. "That is how he was spied upon."

She walked over to study the section and turned around puzzled. "I don't see anything strange about it."

He led the way into the hall, and into the adjoining room. Jean looked through the glass into the room they had just left. She exclaimed, "Why, from this side I can see—"

"Precisely—one-way glass. You can look through it from one side only. It is a recent discovery of science that is just beginning to find commercial use."

They entered a room across the hall.

Jean gasped, "Nick Valmo!"

"Stanley V. Coleman," Frost corrected her.

The man, however, paid no attention to them, It is difficult to speak when you have a bullet in your brain, and are lying face up on a stretcher.

The restless glitter of speculation reëntered Frost's eyes. He knelt beside the body. The dead man's hand still clutched an automatic. Instead of examining it, however, Frost made an unexpected move. He left the room, and came back later with a small box. From the box he took chemical solutions, and from the pocket of the dead man he took a handkerchief. He treated the handkerchief with the chemicals.

Death had woven strange patterns around this house. A gaunt scientist, working in silence, and accompanied by a bright young woman radiating beauty, proceeded to extract its secrets.

VII.

HE WAS a leathery, middle-aged man, semibald, and two of his upper front teeth protruded. They lent him a mousey appearance. He had high cheek bones with pale-yellow skin. He sat with a woman many years his junior, and uncommonly attractive in an obvious fashion. She was a medium blonde, with hair like red mahogany, and of an appearance that suggested the good-looking, well-paid private secretary.

Simon Mord had a curious hold over women. Unattractive physically, he possessed a sharp and nimble mind. He was not only astute; he emanated a sinister influence beneath the smooth conviction of his speech. He had an important if not admirable reputation, and he spent with a free hand. Generally he got what he wanted, and paid for it.

Now, his fingers tapped lightly upon the table and he wore a preoccupied look. The woman sipped an after-dinner cordial, but he barely touched his. Fastidiously dressed, in a manner that never failed to impress juries, he toyed with a gold ring on his left hand.

"You haven't been saying much to-night," she complained. "Is anything wrong?"

"Lawyers always have cases and clients to worry about, among other matters of importance. I will need to return to the office this evening."

"Shall I come with you?"

"You would only distract me."

The woman smiled slightly. "Are you seeing me later?"

"I expect to be through by eleven or twelve."

Simon Mord had a habit of giving indirect answers to questions. A few minutes later, he saw his companion to the door, and into a cab. He watched it roll away from the restaurant, before turning his steps in another direction.

The Lawyers Building was several blocks away. He walked the distance in order to remove some of his after-dinner sluggishness. His face, which usually masked his emotions, showed a certain complacency.

He fumbled for a moment with the key before he managed to open the door to his suite. He pushed a light switch and took a drink from the water cooler after crossing the room. There were two doors to Simon Mord's office—a private one to the hall corridor, and another to the rest of the suite. The arrangement had advantages.

Leaving the reception room, Simon Mord walked past two rooms of file records and desks before he reached his own office. This door was also locked, and it took him a few seconds to enter. He pushed the light switch.

A tall man was seated at Simon Mord's own desk—a stranger of forbidding appearance. He looked at the lawyer without speaking, and the lawyer suddenly felt apprehensive. Could his plans—but no, it was impossible. He stated, in a thin, even voice, "Unless you give me a satisfactory explanation at once of this burglarious entry, I shall summon the police."

"Sit down. The *argumentum ad hominem* is utterly worthless here."

"Since you prefer the police—"

"Sit down! And allow me to introduce myself. Prof. I.V. Frost."

Frost did not rise. Yet Simon Mord, who knew the psychological advantage that a standing person has over one seated, discovered that he was in the presence of a noteworthy exception to the rule. He stepped forward with a slight show of irritation and took the chair facing the desk.

Mord said, "Our appointment was for to-morrow."

The professor's glance flicked over the attorney from head to foot for an instant. The glittering eyes then stared into Mord's with an almost hypnotic intensity. "Many times," he began, "convicts and individuals of more or less evil repute have sat in the chair that you now occupy and have listened to your advice. Now, I believe that you will find it a matter of wisdom to listen carefully yourself, with due attention to details.

"A murder, or a crime, known only to the murderer or criminal, is the only crime that cannot be solved. The moment a crime is discovered, or a dead body found, solution is inevitable and identification of the guilty certain, provided only that the investigator possesses accurate powers of observation, analysis, scientific equipment both mental and mechanical, and patience.

"If the criminal himself admits any one else to his secret, or connives with any one else, that very knowledge is not only one more link against him, but also a powerful motivation for further criminal activity.

"Crime begets crime. Those who harbor knowledge of murder are in as dangerous a position as those who have murdered. They may kill, in order to avoid being killed. A murder case in which a single death occurs is of extreme rarity. Death waits on the gallows or in the electric chair for the killer; and before caught, he frequently kills and kills again—policemen, innocent bystanders, witnesses to his crime, confederates whom he fears may squeal."

"What has all this to do with me?" Mord inquired.

"It is the introduction to a tangle of circumstances in which your part will emerge. It is a complex tangle that began from a simple, single source, but which developed along devious ways until it involved the lives of many people. I entered the snarl in its middle and worked forward to the end and backward to the beginning, but I believe that you, since you are a lawyer, will prefer a straightforward narration of the facts.

"The facts began on August fifth, when C. D. Styker withdrew $100,000 in cash from his personal account. He withdrew that large sum because he had succumbed to the confidence wiles of a swindler called Stanley V. Coleman. He intrusted that money to Coleman, who promptly disappeared.

"Coleman got as far as Albany, where a news-reel photographer took a picture of a crowd in which he stood watching a fire. The picture was identified by an earlier victim of his schemes. Coleman's years of cunning immediately became nullified. With his picture broadcast and the police familiar with his face, he could never operate as successfully as in the past. He was through, unless he in turn could nullify the value of the picture.

"Like other crooks, he decided to alter his appearance, and go through a face-lifting. Unlike the others, he was more thorough in his plans, and more ingenious in their execution. He would not only lose his previous identity. He would become a person already in existence. In order to do this, he must study that person, dispose of his body in a place unlikely to be found, and resume that person's existence in a manner not likely to rouse undue suspicion.

"Coleman first of all got in touch with his latest victim, Styker, told him that the deal had fallen through, and that he would return the sum or look around for some other proposition. Styker had not yet reported the matter to police, partly from fear of newspaper publicity, and partly from fear of a libel and slander suit in case Coleman proved authentic upon investigation. Styker sized at the chance and drove out to meet him.

"Coleman, meanwhile, had been hiding out with Al and Gordon, two of his friends. When Coleman met Styker, he drew a gun and forced him to switch to the truck which Al drove to the brick house, while Gordon ran Styker's car to Albany in order to throw any pursuit off the trail."

Mord said dryly, "A story is always better when backed by proof."

"It grows better. It is backed by physical proofs and that strongest of all evidence, circumstantial evidence," Frost retorted.

"Coleman now had the $100,000 and Styker. Styker had gone willingly across a state line, by himself, but actually it was a clear case of kidnaping. Coleman now promised Styker the return of his money if he would perform an operation. That was the real motive for the abduction of Styker. Coleman remembered that Styker had been a surgeon before he gave up his practice in order to manage his financial affairs. Styker consented for two reasons. He wanted his funds, and he knew he would be killed if he did not obey.

"The swindler next communicated with his lawyer. The lawyer objected to his request but Coleman remained adamant. The penalty of being a lawyer for the underworld is that the underworld itself can doom the lawyer. Coleman had had transactions with Mord before. Thus there appeared the advertisement for a man of Coleman's general appearance, height, and weight. Out of the thousands of applicants, it was easy to pick a half dozen who bore a superficial resemblance to him. They stood upon different corners, and Coleman drove by to examine them. He picked out the most suitable victim and identified him by the flower in his lapel. Thus Nick Valmo received his fatal job."

Mord leaned back in his chair. "I have a great deal of work to do. Your tale is interesting because of its absurdity. My time demands more serious matters. Unless you quickly—"

Frost continued, "Nick Valmo, down and out, with no relatives and few acquaintances, proved an ideal victim. He was Coleman in height, weight, and general appearance. Like Coleman, he possessed a perfect set of teeth, hence could never be identified by dental work if his body should be found. Fingerprints and facial characteristics would be attended to by Styker under Coleman's guidance.

"For two weeks, then, Nick Valmo was under observation. The method of bringing him to the brick house was designed to confuse him about the location of the house, and his own jotted notes proved his ignorance. The method had one drawback. It may convince a man that a goal is farther away than it actually is, but can never convince him that it is closer than it is. The method, the copying of Chinese, and so on, was also a safety factor for the conspirators, for no one would believe Valmo if he carried his tale to the authorities.

"Coleman thus was able to study Valmo's walk, his gestures, his voice, and handwriting. He found out that Valmo had no body scars.

He found out from Valmo's monologues all he needed to know about the victim's life and habits. Coleman had to be a good actor in order to be a convincing swindler. He could easily step into his new rôle.

"It is easier to modify a face than to enlarge it. Styker's task was comparatively simple. He removed the rounded tip of Coleman's nose, and some of the facial tissue, until he sufficiently resembled Valmo to pass examination. The cries that Valmo heard were part of necessary pain; for Styker had lost some of his skill through neglect of his practice.

"As soon as Valmo's usefulness ended, he was drugged, and his finger tips transferred to Coleman. Then Valmo was killed, and his face and hands burned with a blowtorch. To the bottom of the lake went his dismembered body.

"Styker, because of discredit to himself for his own part in it, might not have exposed the plot, but he had to be killed since he knew too much. No one would suspect the real motive behind the murder of a well-to-do business man. Coleman, in addition, had prepared a red herring for the police."

Simon Mord's palms grew damp. He lighted an expensive cigar, and moistened his lips. His mind schemed ahead.

Relentlessly, Frost went on. "Coleman had strolled through cemeteries in search of the red herring. He wanted fingerprints from a cadaver. The grave of Sam Trogg gave him precisely that. It was a crypt, easy of entrance. He intended to clear himself of any possibility of a murder charge in connection with Styker's death. He never expected that the fingerprints would be traced down; but if they were traced down, they could not be connected with him.

"He did not know that fingerprints are made by waxy and fatty body secretions. The casts left fingerprints upon Styker's throat, but there was no such fatty secretion in those prints. The prints could not have been made by human fingers. Therefore, I knew that Sam Trogg's fingerprints had not been duplicated in another, a living human being.

"Coleman now stepped into his new rôle of Nick Valmo, and he stepped straight into death. For under an alias, he had deposited his funds through a power of attorney held by Simon Mord. Part of his latest haul went to Al and Gordon, but $75,000 was turned over to Mord for deposit. Mord, however, kept the money in his safe, pending certification that the numbers of the bills had not been kept. Mord had two powerful incentives to dispose of Coleman. Through the power of attorney, he could appropriate all the funds that Coleman had accumulated, amounting to over $500,000. He had feared Coleman, because if Coleman was caught, his testimony could disbar Mord and send him to the chair for complicity in murder."

Frost regarded the attorney with a brooding eye. "When Coleman, in his new rôle of Valmo, came to me, his story should have proved his greatest protection. In most cases, investigation would have ceased for lack of evidence. Coleman would be sought in connection with Styker's withdrawal of money, his disappearance, and his death. But Coleman had become Valmo and there was nothing to connect Valmo with Styker.

"Coleman's plan was really brilliant; for if, by any chance, the body of Valmo should be taken from the lake before it decomposed, Coleman would claim that it was actually the body of Coleman, who must have died under the knife just as Valmo's fingertips were about to be transferred. Coleman would insist that he was Valmo, and that the conspirators had abandoned the plan just when they had made the primary incision around his fingers. If Al and Gordon were picked up, he would not identify them. If faced with the body of Styker, he would assert that he never saw the man. In other words he would testify to his own death, and no one could prove that he was not Nick Valmo.

"I reasoned that Coleman was acting solely to protect himself, for if he had taken you into his confidence, you as a lawyer would have counseled him against coming to me. Coleman, Gordon and Al would not return to the brick house. Since there was no motive for further action, I supplied that motive by phoning your secretary this morning and making the appointment for to-morrow. I had no intention of keeping that appointment. I knew that you would immediately get in touch with Coleman and dispose of him because he could expose you and send you to the chair for murder conspiracy.

"Therefore after I left my message, you promptly called Coleman and summoned him to come at once to the red brick house, on the logical pretext that you, as an attorney, could certify whether all evidence of the murder had been destroyed. What you could foresee was that Coleman went off on a tangent. He in turn called Al and Gordon to take him there in a small truck. As it happened, Coleman rowed across the lake and reached the house before Al and Gordon.

"There you, first of all, handed over a new pistol to Coleman, and asked for his in exchange so that Coleman could never be identified by bullet grooves. You shot Coleman with his own gun at such close range that there were powder burns. You then wiped the gun and replaced it in Coleman's hand so that it would look like suicide.

"When Al and Gordon reached the house, they found Coleman's body. They had it laid out and were ready to dump it in the lake beside Valmo when I and my assistant interrupted the proceedings."

Mord's hands were sweating. He rose and went to the window and stood in the light breeze to cool off. He walked back to the desk and said, in thin tones, "Only proof and evidence back up any story."

Frost answered grimly, "I have the proof and evidence to support every phase of the story, from the serial numbers on the bills that Styker took out of the bank, to your murder of Coleman. The participants in the chain of crime are dead, save you, who will join them shortly, but the facts remain.

"I can identify Coleman and Valmo by the unburned hairs on Valmo's head, fingerprints, and palm prints in Valmo's room and in the brick house.

"The evidence that damns you, Simon Mord, is complete and final. You did not know that science can now bring out fingerprints not only from polished surfaces, but from paper, cloth and other substances. You wiped Coleman's pistol with his own handkerchief, and I found your fingerprints upon it, together with dust and oil from the pistol. More damning still is the packet of bills, amounting to $75,000, which I found in your safe half an hour ago. Those bills are new. They had few fingerprints, because bank tellers use finger guards. But Styker had handled each bill, in copying down the serial numbers. Coleman had handled the bills in counting them. And you had handled the bills when accepting them from Coleman. Upon those bills alone, is the silent testimony that will send you to the chair."

The professor ceased speaking and laid two objects on the desk. A sudden quiet, and electric tension developed in the room. It was broken by a faint sound, the soft pat of footsteps. A rush of air swept from the window as Simon Mord's body hurtled to the ground.

Simon Mord had committed suicide because of a handkerchief that did not belong to him and a $100 bill intrusted to his keeping.

Frost's face remained impassive. The black glitter in his eyes had already begun to fade as he rose from the desk.

MERRY -GO- ROUND

This man was dead—and in this hall of mirrors there were thousands of Jeans and every Jean accompanied by a corpse.

THE DAY'S HEAT and the high humidity had driven hundreds of thousands of people away from the city and out to near-by beaches. They sought relief in the surf of Jones Beach, cooled off at the Rockaways, swarmed to Coney Island.

Until nightfall, the waters off Coney Island were dotted with bathers, the beach thick with massed humanity.

But with the approach of midnight, the exodus proceeded at full force.

The last dribble of visitors departed from the playlands. Lights winked out. Attendants locked the different premises. The sweepers and cleaning crews finished their work of preparing for the next day's crowds.

Like the other playlands, Platinum Park was deserted, its amusement devices stopped for the night. The turnstiles had been locked; and now, long after three A.M., a deep and desolate hush hung over the park. Its vast interior looked gloomy. Only the vague blurs of revolving tunnels, slides, the whip, and other attractions could be made out against the darkness.

The night watchman dozed. He made the rounds of the park every hour, and between times napped in a chair tilted against a wall of the dance floor.

Nothing had yet happened when he made his tours of inspection. There was no reason why anything should happen. The large sums taken in at the ticket booth were invariably placed by the cashier in the night depository of the nearest bank. The only money kept in the safe was several hundred dollars' worth of change in cumbersome coins. The park contained no readily portable objects of value, hence had little lure for burglars. A night watchman seemed like an unnecessary luxury indulged in by the operators.

The middle-aged, semibald, sleepy-faced watchman, Sam Variss, went methodically about his duties. He could have passed for a business man or a merchant, and gave the impression of having a temper slow to be roused but of bull-dog persistence. His pug nose looked inadequate for his square chin.

He swung his flashlight in arcs around the turnstile. The cone of light traveled across the ticket seller's booth, the wire fence inclosing the park, and the inside entrance to the dance floor. Nothing was wrong. Nothing had ever happened, and probably nothing ever would occur that was out of the ordinary.

He turned away from the entrance and followed the path that ran along the front of Platinum Park. Other paths branched off to open-air attractions like the ferris wheel and roller coaster.

In his ears was the sound of surf, the noise of the hourly surface car, the exhaust of an occasional automobile, but the quiet seemed tomb-like by comparison with the day's racket. Grass and bushes that his beam passed over dripped from the saturated air. The amusement stands loomed dark and vague.

As Variss walked on, flashing the light around in his usual routine, a merry-go-round began playing.

THAT was unusual; not only unusual, but almost unbelievable at this hour. The music, slow and faint at first, swept up louder and faster as the carrousel swung into its full speed. There were four of these devices in Platinum Park. The darkness and muggy atmosphere made it difficult to tell from which direction the sound came, or even whether it originated within the playland.

Variss listened intently. The strains of music blared forth with a startling, eerie quality. He ran along the path to the nearest carrousel. It was at rest. The tinny tune kept on.

The sound began to jangle his nerves. Some drunk must have got into the park through one of the other entrances and started the merry-go-round for a lark. Maybe a party had started out for a midnight spree.

Yet Variss didn't hear shouts or the sounds that even one man would make; and any one running the instrument at this hour ought to be singing at the top of his lungs. The absence of other noises made the clangy tune stranger still.

Variss ran toward the main building which housed two of the carrousels, but as he drew nearer, he heard better, and it became evident that the sound proceeded from the fourth one, on the opposite side of the grounds.

The music, weirdly ominous and out of place, would have made any one's nerves jumpy. He ran along the paths, his flashlight picking a way past attractions whose shapes were queer enough by day, and as unpleasantly real in darkness as the creatures of nightmare.

He hurried through the middle of the park. The music grew louder and closer and monotonously disturbing. He could see the blurry, revolving platform of the merry-go-round now, its triple bank of movable mounts surging upward and forward, downward and backward, while the platform repeated its endless cycle.

The watchman flashed his beam over the control switch. No one was there.

Into the cone of light rode animal steeds—lions, tigers, zebras, camels; and fantastic steeds—unicorns, centaurs, sea horses, griffins. Rising and falling, they mounted into light to the strains of a popular waltz, and without riders. It looked like some one's idle prank, or the mischief of an invisible watcher.

Then, into the diffused glow of the flashlight, bobbed a griffin with a rider, a white rider, gleaming and terrible. The skeleton rose with its steed, and its vacant eye sockets stared at Variss, and it grinned a fixed, tooth-champed grin.

The prickles rose on the back of Variss' scalp. The skeleton's fleshless arms clutched the mane of the griffin, as though urging the steed faster. The bony feet were thrust in the stirrups. The mount and its white rider reached the top of their rise and passed from view.

Variss hastily swept his flashlight around the entire vicinity. He saw no one lurking in the shadows, no figure running off, no sign that anything else had been disturbed.

The beam returned to the merry-go-round and picked out that fleshless rider, rising and falling, advancing and retreating with the griffin in the endless circle of death. The skeleton had slumped lower from the motions of its steed, and seemed to be telling a macabre tale to the griffin, a tale whispered secretly below the metallic din of the music.

Variss walked forward. He didn't feel like hurrying. The flashlight wavered a little. He had advanced almost to the edge of the platform when the skeleton slid off its mount with a horrible crackling clatter; but its right foot caught in the stirrup, and the bones clicked and scraped as the steed progressed through the slow cycle of its motions.

THE WATCHMAN jumped on the platform and worked his way to the rigid center part. He pulled the control stick, and the merry-go-round began to lag. Its musical accompaniment slowed down, became fainter. Finally the sound and motion ceased, but the skeleton rider still had one foot in a stirrup. Cavernous eye sockets stared up, and its jaws retained their hideous grin.

Variss did not disturb the skeleton or go within several feet of it.

His face was clammy when he called the police. "Listen," he blurted, "there's a skeleton riding a griffin around Coney Island—"

"How are the pink elephants doing?" sighed a weary voice from headquarters. "Brother, cut out that stuff and try sleeping it off."

"But I tell you a skeleton on a griffin—" He was talking into a dead mouthpiece. He hesitated for a few seconds, then looked into the Manhattan directory and dialed another number. He received an answer almost immediately.

"I'd like to speak to Professor I.V. Frost."

"You are," came the crisp reply.

"This is the night watchman calling from Platinum Park at Coney Island. You don't know me but I've read about your work on different cases. A queer thing just happened here and when I called the police, they didn't believe me. I found a skeleton riding around on a griffin—"

"I will be there within thirty minutes," Frost cut him short.

Variss, after making allowances for swift dressing and speedy driving from 13 State Street in Manhattan to Platinum Park in Coney Island, didn't see how Frost could make it. If the professor took time to notify his assistant and wait for her, the feat would be impossible.

The night watchman hung around the manager's office for several minutes, wondering whether to summon the police again, and how to phrase a report. He made a second effort. By giving additional details and speaking more calmly, he convinced headquarters that he was not a victim of hallucinations or *delirium tremens.*

II.

IN the lessening darkness that is prelude to dawn, the two patrolmen from a radio car looked down at the skeleton.

"This is just about the limit in crazy publicity stunts," announced

Kerrigan, the bigger and more skeptical of the two. "It beats all the bonehead gags I ever heard of. The management has the watchman fix the set-up, then he pretends to find it. It's so goofy the papers will eat it up. Everybody that comes here to-day will try to get in the park just to see where they found the skeleton. It will make the front pages all over the country, a million bucks' worth of free publicity. You'll need fifty extras to keep things moving."

Variss looked disgusted. "Speaking of dumbness, I had to phone twice before I got any attention."

The third man, Rian, gave him a scowl. "All right, wise guy, why would anybody want to go to all the bother of lugging a skeleton in here and propping it up on a merry-go-round, and start it going? If it ain't a publicity gag, it don't make sense."

"That's your funeral, not mine."

Rian and Kerrigan both started to talk when the drone of a powerful car traveling at high velocity sounded in the distance. The two turned simultaneously toward Ocean Avenue. Headlights shot toward them like twin bullets. Variss glanced at his wrist watch. It was twenty-eight minutes since he had called Frost.

"That guy ought to get about three tickets in a bunch," said Rian, then added grudgingly, "if you could catch him."

A lean, towering figure—at least six feet four—unfolded from the driver's seat as the car stopped. After him came a young woman who had to trot to keep up with his long stride.

Kerrigan momentarily forgot about the skeleton. He watched the approach of the paradoxical pair that he had heard much about but never seen. Frost wore corduroy trousers, a military shirt without tie, an old, chemical-stained, leather jacket; yet they seemed oddly appropriate to him. His thin, ascetic features looked eager. His black eyes smoldered with an almost neurotic tension. A cigarette glowed between two slender fingers.

His assistant, Jean Moray, had an equally arresting individuality. She had come to him a year ago with a bizarre problem which he had solved. Then she had accepted his offer to remain as his understudy.

Her five feet seven was overshadowed by Frost's height, but in contrast with the singularity of his appearance, her matchless figure and the loveliness in her wise young face stood out the more.

Frost, always imperturbable, was the coldly impersonal analyst as completely as any human being could be, while Jean changed her moods as frequently as her wardrobe. She had high cheek bones, a flawless skin, and a beautiful mouth that belied her wide-set, hazel-green eyes. Hers was an exotic face that did not come under any standard type, and that expressed her own distinctive personality.

Frost drooped over the skeleton. For a full minute, he knelt beside it, examining it in minute detail. His eyes glittered, but he showed no more emotion than if he had been glancing at a sack of potatoes. When he stood up, he drawled, "Interesting. A very pretty object for logical analysis."

Jean looked at the thing critically, and with distaste. "I certainly don't think it's very pretty. I'd even go so far as to say I don't ever expect to see an attractive skeleton."

"Yet, to the observing mind, it affords matter for some nice distinctions."

"I wouldn't like it, no matter how nice it was. I don't think I care for skeletons."

"My dear Miss Moray," Frost said acidly, "your attitude may be excellent as I personal philosophy, but it hardly serves to advance the reconstruction of a rather mystifying crime, its solution, and detection of its perpetrator."

"Crime?" echoed Kerrigan, scoffing. "Guess again. Look close enough and you can see the wire supports. It's a museum piece. We'll likely get a report to-day that somebody's pet skeleton was swiped."

"Look closely enough," Frost retorted, "and you will see that the supports are crudely fashioned and not skillfully placed. A novice performed the work."

"I suppose next you'll be telling us the same guy bumped him off."

"Precisely."

Now hostile, Kerrigan gibed, "You wouldn't mind telling us how the guy got bumped off?"

"Not at all," Frost replied with a faint, sardonic smile. "A bullet, probably a .38 or .45 fired from close range, killed him."

The watchman looked at the professor in open astonishment. Rian didn't know what to make of him. Even Jean, accustomed to his feats of pure deduction, watched him with an air of some doubt.

Kerrigan hammered away. "While you're at it, you might as well let us know just about when he got the works."

"I will gladly do better than that," Frost offered. "He got the works, as you picturesquely phrase it, exactly nineteen days ago."

Kerrigan's impatience reached its limit. "Are you trying to kid us? I've seen enough stiffs to know that it just couldn't be as far gone as this in a climate like this inside of three weeks. That's impossible. Nature don't work that fast."

"Right," Frost observed blandly "The processes of nature can be artificially accelerated, however."

Kerrigan snorted, "By the way, you didn't mention who the guy was whose skeleton is here."

The professor tapped a cigarette and lighted it. He exhaled a cloud of acrid fumes with keen enjoyment. "I was coming to that point. The man's name happened to be Werner G. Reisenham, one of the owners of Platinum Park."

The night watchman's jaw fell. He looked pop-eyed. Kerrigan opened his mouth to blurt out some comment. Jean said nothing, but her thoughtful glance passed back and forth between the professor and the sprawled bones.

Rian broke that moment of tense silence. "Haw haw haw!" he exploded in a sudden burst of laughter. "That's the funniest thing I've heard in years!" He gasped. "Sherlock Holmes was a piker compared to this guy! They ought to can the G-men and make him the whole works! He just comes along and looks at a skeleton. Then he announces that the guy was murdered, how he got bumped off, when, and who he was! Haw haw haw! I never heard anything like it! I bet it's the first time in history that anybody looks at a pile of bones and guesses everything and even deduces the name of the guy they came from!"

FROST regarded Rian with a calm, freezing intentness, the black pupils of his eyes grown larger and brighter. Rian stopped laughing. Frost continued to scrutinize him, as though he were a fly stuck on a pin. Rian began to squirm and fidget, unable to turn away from the professor's hypnotic gaze.

"The bones of skeletons in museums and medical schools," Frost stated in a matter-of-fact tone, "are dry if not brittle with age. So also are bones that have weathered, such as the three-year-old skeletons recently found in Vermont. Bones bleach in the sun. This skeleton is unbleached, fresh, the bones moist and far from brittle. The bones very recently were surrounded by flesh. This is deduction of the most obvious kind.

"The fact that the skeleton is wired indicates that some one wanted the police to believe it a laboratory specimen left here as a practical joke or a publicity stunt; which in turn creates suspicion that murder is involved.

"Further examination of the skeleton discloses that the third rib is wired, and the spinal column at the second vertebra. A section is missing from the rib, a larger fraction from the spinal column. The skeleton otherwise is complete, and has been handled with care.

"The bullet of a large-caliber cartridge, fired at close range from the front, would leave just such evidence in shattering the rib and emerging through the spinal column. Since there would be no purpose in firing such a shot after death, it is evident that the shot was the cause of death.

"Studying the skeleton for peculiarities, I note first of all that it contains a perfect set of teeth. The man never had to visit a dentist. Secondly, a small, triangular piece has been cut from the base of the skull, replaced, and allowed to knit, obviously the result of a brain operation. Thirdly, the bones of the feet are excessively long and narrow, and the arches have fallen. Fourthly, the right thumb is misshapen, and the forefinger broken and healed at the second joint. Fifthly, the man must have been between five feet ten and one half inches and five feet eleven inches tall. There are other peculiarities which I need not elaborate.

"Briefly, none of them is of special value; but taken together, they constitute a set of peculiarities that could belong to only one individual, and they identify him as Werner G. Reisenham who disappeared nineteen days ago, and who possessed exactly these characteristics."

Rian and Kerrigan looked stupefied. Variss listened intently. Jean objected, "But that still doesn't explain everything. If Reisenham disappeared only nineteen days ago, he wouldn't have turned into a skeleton by—"

"The stripping of flesh from bones is a little-known and macabre subject upon which it is unnecessary to elaborate," Frost commented dryly. "The process of decomposition can be accelerated by various methods. For instance, many other substances than food have been boiled for specific purposes."

III.

RIAN and Kerrigan exchanged glances.

"I would suggest that you summon the homicide detail," Frost urged impatiently. "Whether you believe it or not, this is a murder case. Tell headquarters to notify Inspector Frick that I am here."

"Get to a phone," Kerrigan ordered the junior member, and as Rian swung off, he turned threateningly toward the night watchman. "You're on a spot, fella. Come clean. You done it, didn't you?"

Variss growled in disgust, "You cops are a pain in the neck. While you stand here jawing, the killer gets farther away. Pick on the nearest guy and give him the works seems to be a police habit."

"You were here, weren't you? You could 'a' done it. How come you're the watchman and didn't see nothing?"

"Listen: I'll probably get sacked because this happened. I might as well kiss my job good-by right now. Even in daylight, you can't see this part of the park from where I was. It's no trick at all for anybody to climb over the turnstile, and they'd have three quarters of an hour to work in between my rounds. It wouldn't take five minutes to fasten a skeleton to the merry-go-round loosely, throw the control lever, and beat it. So far as that goes, sure I could've done it, and had a darn good reason, if that's Reisenham. I hated the guy, and so did everybody else around here."

Frost interrupted with: "How long have you been on night duty here, Variss?"

"About a month. Why?"

"Where were you before that?"

"I was day guard at the Werner Turner—that's the new attraction they just installed this year that's been such a big hit."

"What happened to the night watchman before you?"

"Jepson? Search me. He got canned, I guess. I haven't seen him around since."

Frost drawled to Kerrigan: "Many a man before this has committed murder over labor trouble. Have Jepson picked up for questioning. He had a motive, knowledge of the park, and familiarity with the watchman's duties which would enable him to carry off this coup."

The patrolman admitted, a note of grudging approval beginning to show in his attitude: "You know how to get the answers."

Frost continued: "Also, notify the other two partners of the Platinum Park Corporation. Rout them out of bed, use pressure if necessary, and get them here before the remains are removed."

"What's the point of that?"

"Corroborative identification for one thing. I have other reasons that I do not at the moment care to divulge. The two men are named Leo F. Barburg and Milton Moss."

Frost, who had been speaking in a somewhat mechanical fashion as though his thoughts were elsewhere, walked toward the center of the merry-go-round. The operator's stand and the control lever were situated upon it. This latter object appeared to interest him.

The control, a metal handle that projected about a yard from the floor, worked in a slot a foot long. He stooped and examined the groove, then tested the lever. It took considerable pressure to force it from the stop position at an acute angle to neutral at a right angle.

Then the lever made contact, slid easily the rest of its distance to full speed at an obtuse angle. The platform began to revolve. Frost at once jerked the bar back, stopping the motion and the rising strains of music as Kerrigan yelled a protest. The platform revolved slowly for a few yards upon momentum.

A second lever, parallel with the first, proved to be a safety brake. Its only function was to halt the carrousel in case the first handle jammed while the unit was operating.

"What's the sense of that?" demanded Kerrigan truculently.

"Pure curiosity. I wanted to see how it worked," Frost explained. "And now it might be worthwhile to retrace the route which the watchman would have told you he had followed, if you had thought to ask him about it."

For an instant, Kerrigan looked uncertain. He couldn't be sure if he was on the receiving end of an indirect thrust. "You trying to get us away from this spot? Didn't I see you pick something up?"

"I believe you did," Frost answered with disconcerting candor. He opened his right fist and exhibited a small cylinder of nickel-plated metal. "I was testing the lever to find out whether any one could manipulate it readily. It has been deliberately tightened so that, if left unguarded for any reason, no children and few adults would be able to operate the carrousel. During my inspection, I found this object wedged in the groove."

"What the dickens is it?" asked the puzzled patrolman after turning it over several times.

"A simple timing device. It works by a combination of compressed air and a spring, and consists of a rigid shell with a movable piston inside. Compress the piston and it is caught within the shell. The spring forces a disk against the compressed air, which escapes through a tiny pin point in the shell, and when the air has leaked out, the spring releases the catch which in turn causes the piston to plunge out.

"The complete action requires five minutes. This device explains why Variss did not find any one at the carrousel. Whoever put the skeleton on the griffin also set the control lever upright and slipped the timer into the slot. He then had five minutes to leave the park and be far away, before the piston sprang out and pushed the lever sufficiently to operate the carrousel."

"I thought you said it took a lot of effort to move the lever?"

"I did." Frost frowned impatiently "And it does, up to the point where the lever is in vertical position. At the instant of contact, the lever slides easily and smoothly, and would respond to even less pressure than the timer exerts."

VARISS, who had been on the fringe of the group, staring at the skeleton in fascination, paying little attention to the others, caught the last few sentences. He turned around, said with abrupt interest, "Let me see that gadget."

Kerrigan handed it over, and the watchman studied it briefly. "It's just like mine," he volunteered, and fished an identical timer out of a pocket.

"Well, I'll be damned!" the surprised patrolman burst out. "Where the dickens did you get that? How many of these things are there around here?"

"Plenty," was Variss' terse reply. He added: "I got mine when I was doing duty on the Werner Turner. There's a concession just inside the park, where the suckers toss rings for prizes. A lot of the prizes are timers, which aren't much use to most people, but they're something to play with. Besides that, all the operators of the power attractions have—"

"The which?"

Frost answered for Variss: "The power attractions are those such as the whip, the scooter, the carrousel, the caterpillar, and all those which operate by electrical power, as distinguished from the fixed attractions like the slides, magic chamber, dance floor, and dolls' palace."

"That's right," Variss agreed. "As I was saying, the operators all have these timers. Every now and then, some one falls off and gets hurt. Instead of stopping the attraction, which would let a crowd gather, the operator slips a timer in the lever control and goes over to help. He and the starter put the person on his feet, if he's all right, or carry him away, if he's really hurt. That way, the unit keeps moving, a mob doesn't collect, and the timer automatically shuts off power if the operator is away very long.

"The gadget is used regularly on the scooter because the cars are always jamming and it takes two men to pull them apart and keep them going. So the scooter operator generally slips a timer into the groove and then goes to help out on the floor work."

Kerrigan asked: "How many power attractions are there?"

"Twenty-eight out of the forty-one amusements here," Variss replied.

"Twenty-eight! Plus the two or three we got already only gives us about thirty suspects to work on." He had an inspiration. "We ain't getting anywhere. Supposing you start out and show us the route you followed just before you found the skeleton. Rian, you stay here and wait for the homicide squad."

Frost wore an air of slightly ironic mirth as Kerrigan marched off with the watchman. After several paces, the patrolman looked back in some doubt and called, "Coming along?"

"No."

Kerrigan hesitated, decided to go through with the survey, and disappeared with Variss toward the front of the park.

"Let us try the rear half," Frost told his assistant.

DAWN was approaching; the gray light grew steadily clearer, and tints of orange had crept up in the eastern sky. The air remained sticky and warm, prophetic of another torrid, intolerably humid day.

The professor remarked: "Survey the northern part of the premises while I investigate the southern. Don't bother about footprints. The atmosphere is so saturated that any prints would have filled in long before we arrived, even if the police had not trampled around."

Jean said: "I can't imagine why any one would want to go to all this trouble about a skeleton. There's not only the risk of discovery but just the plain, nasty nature of the thing. Why bring it here? A dozen other places would be better, and with less chance of being caught."

"On the contrary, this is one of the most adroitly prepared crimes that has yet come to my attention. There are no tangible, specific clues. There are innumerable suspects. And in the ordinary course of investigation, the affair would have been dismissed as a prank, with the identity of the victim never known or sought for, and consequently the murder never discovered or search for the murderer launched.

"Yet deductive logic affords us a number of more than tenuous aids. There must have been excellent reason for placing the skeleton upon a carrousel. So many other parts of the grounds would be more accessible that we may assume a particular reason; and it is further significant that the skeleton rode a griffin.

"Reisenham's full name was Werner Grifon Reisenham. Any observer should at once note the similarity between Grifon and griffin. We may deduce another connection between the carrousel and the skeleton. Other attractions were closer to the entrances, yet the merry-go-round was selected. Why? Partly because it was hidden from the streets, and offered greater protection against chance discovery; but, also, the merry-go-round is a symbol for the run-around. We have an additional as yet unexplained connection with Reisenham's name, the new amusement called the Werner Turner.

"Besides these leads, there are four definite suspects with motives, twenty-eight others in reserve, so to speak, and more yet to be found. The problem has subtle and difficult aspects. The murderer may escape by the magnificent ingenuity with which he has involved so large a number of persons."

Jean frowned. "But why Coney Island? Wasn't he taking a long chance?"

"Quite the opposite. He could hardly have picked a safer spot. Among the vast numbers of visitors here, a man could be stabbed and half carried, half supported to a place of concealment without attracting attention. People are constantly bruising and cutting themselves upon the more tough-and-tumble devices, or suffering nose bleeds. Blood spots are so common that no one attaches special significance to them. Again, it would be a simple matter to bring the skeleton in wrapped as a bundle and leave it at the check room. The murderer, if caught while attempting to enter the premises at night, would probably be set free as a mere intruder. In case of a murder actually committed here, there is almost no likelihood that a helpful clue will be found, because the huge numbers of passers-by would destroy any evidence within seconds simply by trampling it."

AT the western end of Platinum Park, Frost separated from Jean. Obedient to his instructions, she began a canvass of the northern side. Frost covered ground even faster than his assistant. His trained eyes seemed to have a photographic quality, to register instantly everything that came within range of vision.

A swirl of faintly aromatic, pungent smoke from the long cigarettes of his own manufacture swirled behind him. He prowled around the different units, peered under the platforms of such as were elevated from the ground, scrutinized the grass and shrubbery, the paths and walks.

Toward the south-central portion of the inclosure, he saw a small, one-story stone shed. The door was locked, but with the aid of an instrument that had a predilection for locks, he entered in short order.

A dynamo stood at one end of the room, and a variety of garden tools, lumber, odds and ends of metal. He descended a stone flight of stairs, and found himself in a much larger room, a workshop with benches, lathes, and other common carpenters' and machinists' equipment. Well-stocked drawers contained electrical supplies, hardware, and spare metal parts in a wide assortment. Portions of scooters, ferris-wheel boats, and caterpillar cars indicated that the shop was used for quick repair of damaged and broken devices.

At the far end of the room, resting upon a series of burners, stood a large and battered copper boiler. It had served many purposes in its day, and was discolored by verdigris, streaks of paint and turpentine, oil smudges, patches of dried tar. A drain lay near it at the bottom of a circular depression in the floor. Not far from the drain a splotch of tar had hardened on the cement. In a basket of junk, he found a silver circlet hammered flat, and the battered pieces of a watch. These he pocketed, and borrowed a trowel with a long, narrow, V-shaped blade.

Emerging from the shed, Frost saw no one in the vicinity, though he heard voices from other points. It had now grown fairly light. He walked slowly along the path, eyes intent upon its surface. He proceeded for ten paces before he stopped and knelt on the cinders. To the average onlooker, there would have seemed no reason why he should stop at that particular spot, for it did not show any apparent difference from the rest of the path. Yet something caught his eye and he went to work without hesitation.

He forced the long, thin blade of the trowel to its full depth and lifted out a scoop of soil. With swift movements, he hollowed a cone two feet deep. A few more efforts and Frost uncovered what he was after.

The trowel struck softer stuff, which happened to be the rest of Mr. Reisenham, in a horrible state.

IV.

FROST replaced the soil and smoothed over the cinder surface. He returned the trowel and locked the door of the shed. He heard a car arrive, the sounds of several men. A babel of voices came from the merry-go-round as the homicide squad went to work.

Frost continued his search. The southern boundary of Platinum Park was the wall of a building that ran clear through from street to street. The park property was open in many places, but toward the front, the dance floor and magic-chamber units were inclosed and adjacent to the dividing wall.

He saw a door on the side of the magic-chamber attraction, a half-hidden, little-used door that swung inward. He entered and found a narrow passage between the wall and the magic chamber. The left side was lined for part of its distance with glass, but pressure caused a panel to swing and he looked directly into the chamber. The mirrors were double-faced and pivoted. At one time, the passageway had served as an exit.

Frost closed the opening and searched on, his flashlight cutting the total darkness. Halfway along the corridor, he saw another door in the wall to his right. Finding it unlocked, he went through.

The step brought him face to face with a gorilla, a spectacle that might have proved a trifle distressing if the animal had not been stuffed. He stood in the dimly lighted interior of a side show, The gorilla was mounted on a pedestal in a kind of alcove nine feet long, which opened directly on the main floor. To his left was a stand, now curtained, bearing the legend: HERMES THE MAGICIAN. The stand to his right screamed: MADAME SERPA.

Investigating the magician's stall, he found a miscellany of crystal globes, wands, turbans, cards, silken scarfs, hollow white balls, and similar paraphernalia, as well as scissors, swords, daggers, and a blankcartridge pistol.

He entered the neighboring stand and surprised a somewhat plump but decidedly personable woman who wore a spangled blouse, a grass skirt, anklets, a head circlet of artificial flowers, and an eight-foot-long python which twined affectionately around her throat and left arm. She had a bold, blond face, voluptuous rather than coarse. Her tawny, golden hair was cut extremely short, and her head festooned with little curls that looked rather silly.

"What's the big idea?" she blurted.

Frost didn't bat an eyelash or show the least surprise. He asked casually, "Why do you hate Reisenham?"

"Because he's a cheap skate, a dirty, four-flushing—" She stopped in mid-sentence. "What's it to you?"

"Suppose you tell me about it."

"Why should I?"

"Because it will do you more good to talk to me now before facing the police later." Frost's flat statement had the force of an inflexible dictum. "Reisenham has been murdered."

Madame Serpa shed nary a tear. "The big slob made a play for me once, but I gave him the gate."

"What about Hermes?"

She hesitated, admitted: "He hasn't any use for Reisenham, either. That's partly because he and I are good pals. Maybe we'll get hitched one of these days. So Reisenham's dead. How'd it happen?"

Frost suggested, "There doesn't seem to be much love wasted on Reisenham among the side-show community."

"There ain't," she snapped. "Reisenham and his two pals tried to buy us out, but Markey—he's the guy that owns the joint—won't sell, and we're all for Markey. There's been trouble ever since the fire here early this spring that almost put us out of business. They never did find out how it got started, but we've had our own suspicions."

"If the two organizations are such rivals, isn't it unusual that the doors between them are not kept locked?"

"Not particularly. Years ago, both outfits were under the same management. After the owners sold out, and a new gang took over the Platinum Park Corporation, the doors were supposed to be locked. They generally aren't. When any of us want to have some fun, we just walk into the park. When any of their operators want to see the side show, they come in through the doors. It's a sort of friendly arrangement we have. The big feud is against the owners. All the park people are poorly paid for long hours and hard work."

Frost looked at a row of daggers.

"I do several numbers," she explained. "Knife-throwing, snake-charming, and the shakes. Some call it dancing, but don't let 'em kid you."

"Thanks for the elucidation," said Frost dryly. "How do you happen to be practicing at this hour?"

"I often get up at dawn. My number is the first one finished at night so I generally hit the hay before any of the others."

"I don't suppose Hermes or Markey would be up yet?"

"Why, yes, they are. Hermes, his real name is Harry Guger, sprained a thumb yesterday and he didn't sleep a wink so he got up. He's been around for the past hour. Markey came down to look over the joint. He's thinking of shifting things around, kind of, and maybe adding a couple of new acts. It's hopeless trying to do any work around here in the day or evening. Crowds are too big. They get in your way."

"Do you live here?"

"Sure. Most of us do. There's a flock of rooms and apartments on the second floor. They're handy and good enough."

Frost left. The snake slid down Madame Serpa's arm and gazed beadily at the departing figure.

THE PROFESSOR, however, made no attempt to question Markey or Hermes. He surveyed the premises with a quick glance. Toward the front, a tall, sallow man with a little mustache and long, black hair was looking at the street. On the opposite end, a plump, shorter man in an eloquent brown suit was fussing around some booths.

Frost returned to Platinum Park.

The merry-go-round swarmed with police. Even Inspector Frick had routed himself out of bed. The inspector, a gray-haired man whose crisp bearing was a hallmark from his years of army service, was an old friend of the professor, and his most influential supporter in the department. He detached himself from the cluster when he saw Frost approaching.

"Look here, Ivy, what's this business about identifying a skeleton just by looking at the bones?" he asked, a bit worried.

"There is nothing mysterious about it. I don't know why your men are making such a fuss over a simple analysis." Frost repeated his earlier observations. "I have three more suspects for you, all with excellent reason and opportunity to have committed the murder," he added, mentioning Hermes, Madame Serpa, and Markey.

Frick was nonplused. "We'll have to have experts check up to make sure the bones are those of Reisenham—"

"Save yourself the bother. Here are his ring and watch. The numbers have been hammered and filed, but acid treatment will bring them out again. It was an expensive watch, and the jeweler who sold it undoubtedly kept a record of its serial number. If you require further proof, you need only dig up the rest of Reisenham. What is left of his more perishable parts lies thirty feet east of the stone shed. He has deteriorated sadly."

The inspector issued prompt orders. "This is going to be one fine mess. Moss left his home at midnight and hasn't returned yet. No one answers the phone at Barburg's apartment. Jepson moved out of his furnished room a week ago and didn't leave a new address. Well, we can start questioning those three birds in the side show, anyway. Ivy, we'll need your help on this. I'll be glad to get anything you pick up or figure out."

"As a matter of record," Frost meditated, "this really is not one of my cases. While Variss notified me because of police inaction, there was no direct commission, and this is strictly a subject for the customary police procedure."

"I know it, but I'll O. K. anything you do even if it does get under somebody's skin at headquarters. This is a weird one, and the way it's breaking, we'll never hang it on the murderers."

"It is not without some tantalizing features," Frost conceded. "Be here at three o'clock. In the meantime, there are a few slight inquiries of my own to be made."

"What's coming off at three?"

"I intend to enjoy the park's excellent facilities for amusement. I will take keen pleasure in riding the roller coaster, for instance."

The professor collected his assistant, whose search had gone unrewarded, and brought her up to date on developments. As they drove away, he explained: "The Missing Persons Bureau sent out an alarm on Reisenham when he disappeared. His wife is in Europe. His partners notified the police. An investigation was launched, but it elicited very little of importance. Reisenham had not received threats, so far as is known, though he appears to have been a disagreeable person whose methods and attitude antagonized almost every one with whom he came in contact. He was last seen in early evening on the night he vanished, when leaving a Manhattan restaurant where he had dined alone. He was believed to have been a victim of amnesia.

"In addition to the bizarre circumstances under which his skeleton came to light, we have several other puzzling questions to answer. Reisenham was killed in Platinum Park. When and how did he get into the park without being recognized, and for what purpose? Thus far, each individual concerned has proved to have a reason and opportunity for murdering him, but the deeper motive has not yet emerged. The murderer has shown remarkable intelligence and subtlety. Instead of trying to protect himself with an alibi, or to cover his tracks, he operated at a time and place, and under circumstances, that cast equal suspicion upon a large number of suspects, most of whom will have great difficulty in establishing even the flimsiest alibi. That will be their main protection and the murderer's immense advantage. There is no conclusive evidence pointing to a specific person. There are no conflicting stories that would enable us to select truth from falsehood."

"Gee!" exclaimed Jean, with wide-eyed interest. "It's a honey! It sounds like he'll get away with it if they ever do suspect who he is!"

"That doesn't sound like you. Your terms are both slangy and not altogether accurate. I know the motive and the identity of the killer. Deductive logic is, however, insufficient evidence. Therefore, I will set a trap for him, and then supply him with motivation to spring the trap."

"How?"

"You will see when the time comes. There is some preliminary work to be done. You possess a rare beauty, Miss Moray, a beauty that immediately arrests the attention of all who see you."

A THRILL of pleasure over his unexpected compliment raced through her. It was the first time since she had been associated with him that he showed a personal interest in her.

"Exactly at three o'clock," Frost continued, "I want you at your ravishing best to stand in front of the Magic Hall and watch the loading platform of the Whirlwind which will be easily visible."

Jean could cheerfully have kicked his shins at this dash of cold water upon her secret hopes. Frost simply didn't fall, but the more he remained dispassionate and aloof, the more piqued she became, and the more determined to employ every wile she had. She flattered herself that she was full of wiles. Only, she thought ruefully, it doesn't help a girl much to be full of wiles and lure and charm and beauty and brains and things if they run smack against an inhuman monster who is mainly interested in logic.

She was brought back to earth with a rude jolt when Frost said abruptly, "You shouldn't waste time on such idle speculations."

V.

WHEN the professor stopped at headquarters shortly before noon, he found Inspector Frick in an irritable mood. The inspector had just come out of his office. "Ivy! I want a few words with you about this Reisenham mess. Have you seen the papers? The news photographers got there just after you left. I tried to hold them down, said the skeleton was only somebody's prank, but it was such a crazy stunt it made the front pages anyway.

"I'll admit it's a hell of a weird picture, probably the sort of stuff the public laps up, but it's putting us on the spot. You were right about the identification. Our experts corroborated it after examining the rest of the remains and bringing out the watch number. Coney Island will be mobbed to-day. There'll be half a million extra people out there just to get a look at the merry-go-round. They'll probably wreck the thing trying to get souvenirs."

"What about Jepson?" Frost asked.

"He was picked up this morning staggering home to a Bowery dump. Admitted he'd been wandering around Coney Island, claims he doesn't remember much of anything that happened. He's sobering off now. Admitted being sore about losing his job, called Reisenham plenty of names before we told him about the murder. That cooled him off, but I don't think we'll get much out of him because he was too drunk to remember what he'd been up to."

"Did you find Moss and Barburg?"

"They're in my office now. Can you beat it? Barburg claims he was in bed all night, and just didn't bother to answer the phone until he finally got up about nine. He lives alone. Moss is a slippery eel, admits he wasn't home all night, but says it's none of our business where he was.

"What gets me is that both Moss and Barburg admit having been at

Platinum Park practically all night the evening Reisenham vanished. It seems they wanted to look over the property to see about repairs and improvements, and couldn't do it in the daytime on account of the crowds.

"But they didn't stay together, and they told Variss to take the night off. On two different occasions, one of which lasted for more than an hour, they were separated. On the night after Reisenham disappeared, a crew of workmen did several jobs around the place, and dug up a depression in the path to fill it with a sand base; they left the excavation for an hour and a half to work elsewhere; and that filled-in patch is where we found the rest of the body.

"We got the same sort of answers from Markey, Hermes, and Madame Serpa. We've questioned half the park's employees, and discovered that they were all underpaid and overworked and down on the management. Any one of these people could be guilty, and not one of them has an iron-clad alibi.

"You'd think"—Frick clipped the words bitterly—"that one, just one of those twenty-eight power operators would have gone straight home after work, or strung along with some one else; but no, they drop in at different places for a couple of beers, so they say, or their car breaks down, or they get a sandwich somewhere, or they decide to walk home at their own sweet time, or they had rooms by themselves, and there's a lost hour somewhere in all their stories.

"The one thing I don't want is another suspect. I'm sick of 'em! I'd like to find just one person involved who offered an air-tight alibi and I'd clap him in jail so fast that he'd see double!"

"And if you found an air-tight alibi, you would have the murderer." Frost soothed the fiery little inspector. Frick had never before been so wrought up over a murder case. The professor continued: "One of these suspects is the murderer. He knew the circumstances well—but so did they all. He had a motive—but so did all the suspects. He had the opportunity—like the others involved. And he had the brilliant audacity to deprive himself of an alibi—because none of the others could produce witnesses to account for all their time.

"I'd like to ask Moss and Barburg a couple of questions."

THEY ENTERED Frick's office. The remaining partners of the Platinum Park Corporation were a sinister pair. Barburg, thin and cadaverous, with hands like claws, resembled a scarecrow. His skin was worm-white, his eyes snaky, his nose as thin as his lips were cruel.

Moss, fat and oily, had Slavic features. His flattened nose went with his moon face. Everything about him seemed round and greasy, from black hair drowned in pomade to fingers like so many plump grubs, and a pudgy figure in a snuff-colored suit.

The professor, raking each with a glance, addressed Barburg. "What did the Platinum Park owners stand to gain by Reisenham's death?"

Barburg peered at his fellow partner with an air of melancholy aloofness. His ophidian gaze returned to the professor, and his voice dripped with self-pity. "A very sad blow. It will cost us money. That it should come at a time like this—"

"Is all to the good," Frost snapped. "The publicity is worth a million. What understanding did you have among yourselves?"

"We? Why should we—"

"Talk," Frost ordered. "The partnership agreement."

Barburg changed his mind and his tactics. Frost's eyes were glittering with a restless, unpredictable, but irresistible purpose.

Barburg talked. "When we bought the park, we put $50,000 apiece into it. The one-third interest was nontransferable. If a partner died or got out, his interest would be purchased at cost and divided between the other two."

"A one-third interest in Platinum Park would sell in the open market to-day for more than a third of a million," Frost drawled. "By Reisenham's death, you divide between you an equity valued at approximately $350,000 for which you pay only $50,000."

Barburg nodded uneasily. "But that—"

"Yeah," Frick interrupted him wearily, "but you were all one big happy family, weren't you?"

Frost turned to Moss. "What is a universal joint?"

The round one looked puzzled. "Should I know? Should I know? I'm asking you," he chirped in an emotional voice.

Barburg answered for him, "It sounds like a place that anybody can get into."

Frost asked, "Why do you keep a night watchman at Platinum Park?"

Barburg replied with reluctance: "There was some trouble early this year. I believe an unfortunate fire damaged the side show. I don't know why we were held to blame. We heard rumors and threats that the park would burn up. So we installed a night watchman."

Frost beckoned the inspector to walk out with him. In the corridor he stated: "There isn't enough evidence to hold any of the seven immediate suspects. Turn them loose, but keep track of them, and see that they all are at the Whirlwind in Platinum Park at three o'clock. However, do not let them know where they are being taken or for what purpose."

"Easy enough, since I myself don't know," the inspector tartly replied. "What did you have in mind by that question about universal joint?"

Frost was already on the way out. His long stride kept him a jump ahead of the pungent fumes that trailed him.

VI.

CONEY ISLAND expected a huge turn-out on this, one of the final Saturdays of the season. The concessionaires revised their estimates upward when the day broke hot and sticky with a humidity almost at the saturation point. But their most lavish hopes fell short of reality when the metropolitan dailies carried pictures and lurid accounts of the skeleton rider.

The spectacular nature of the occurrence, the wide publicity given it, and the natural drawing power of Coney Island combined with the discomfort of the heat wave to lure one of the greatest throngs within memory to that popular resort.

From early morning, the subways were jammed. By noon, more than five hundred thousand human beings had flocked around the beach, board walk, and amusement centers. By mid-afternoon, it was clear that between 1,500,000 and 2,000,000 visitors would swamp all facilities.

The figures in the waxwork museums looked as though they would melt from the heat. Barkers grew hoarse shouting their cause and trying to outshout rivals. Every time a hula dancer or a strong man, a midget or a leopard woman appeared in front of a side show, a dense mass of humanity washed around the bait.

The swirl of energy centered around Platinum Park. It was experiencing the largest single day's take in its existence. Hundreds and thousands waited in line at each of its forty-one attractions. It took strength and patience to get anywhere near the merry-go-round, until special guards had to be called out to keep the line moving and preserve order of a sort.

Just before three o'clock, a most alluring young woman suddenly appeared in front of the Magic Hall.

There was a cluster of people around the Whirlwind which, like all the others in Coney Island, claimed to be the highest and fastest roller coaster in the world.

Inspector Frick and his plain-clothes detectives had done their work well. They had quietly rounded up Barburg, Moss, Variss, Jepson, Markey, Madame Serpa, and Hermes, all of whom watched with various reactions as Professor I.V. Frost calmly climbed into the front seat of the coaster car, with a package in his lap. No one else rode with him. Not long before he took his seat, he vanished beneath the supporting framework of the roller coaster with another package, which was missing when he returned.

As he sat down and the operator started to push the control stick, Moss broke from the group and waddled toward him. "Why do you waste our time?" he complained. "All these people waiting, with cash tickets already. Maybe I go with you, yes?"

"No."

"Is there something wrong in my wanting to go with you? I'll go along for fun, yes? Such a business!"

The professor squelched him. "I ride alone."

Frick, who had jumped after Moss in an effort to head him off, tried to act now as peacemaker. "It's his affair after all, Ivy. If he insists on going along, I don't see that we have much right to stop him."

"If he wishes to take the risk and responsibility, that is his funeral, not mine," Frost retorted. "Operator—contact!'

Moss seemed undecided over the professor's cryptic comment, and while he wavered, the coaster car gathered momentum, slid down the preliminary dip, caught in the grooves of the endless belt for the first high climb that would launch it on its way. The slightly baffled watchers saw it creep to the top of the incline and poise, heard it thunder down the first cliff.

It shot to the next crest, slowed with the drag of the safety brakes, hurtled on another giddy dive. The roar and rolling clatter, one car shooting with one occupant only, developed an uneasy tension in the group who watched. They waited for something to happen, and nothing happened. Or they seemed amused, but only Frost genuinely enjoyed the episode. Or they looked bored, anxious to leave.

The car thundered down the last, long decline and curved into view again. Frost's hair whipped in the breeze. His features expressed a keen relish. He leaned forward enthusiastically, an almost happy gleam in his eyes. Frick felt disappointed. It just wasn't in character for the professor to amuse himself at the expense of others. This was child's play, when murder had to be solved.

Frost made no move to climb out. "Great! I'm going around again!" he exclaimed.

THE CAR got under way. Moss, fidgeting nervously, suddenly bounded across the platform and leaped into a rear seat as the coaster car slid off. Inspector Frick made a vain dash after him, shouted angrily. Moss looked back, grinning.

Frost turned around and spoke curtly, but whatever he said did not reach Frick above the clatter of the mechanism. The car went up the steep haul. Moss faced the professor, then clambered over the intervening seats until he sat beside Frost.

As the coaster car reached the crest, Frick thought he saw a smolder in Frost's aspect, a glance that was tenseness, command, and anticipation. Moss waved his pudgy arms in expostulation. The car plunged from view with a crescendo velocity.

The deep bass note of its highest speed at the lowest depression began to rise as the car shot up the next ascent. It flashed into sight again on the second mount, hurtled toward the brow. Frost was leaning forward against the power of momentum, his hands gripping the crossbar. He had turned his head slightly, and seemed to be issuing orders to Moss, but his gaze remained intent upon the track.

Suddenly Moss stood up. The car leaped to the peak of the ascent. There was no drag of safety brakes. It did not pause in its wild rush. It rocketed from the tracks and its own momentum hurled it a dozen feet skyward. It crashed clear of the wooden railing.

The mysterious awareness of tragedy brought a hush over the crowd, a silence of magnetic tension. Frost, rising like a predatory bird from the car, made a futile grab for Moss. Moss, crazed with fear, fought him and leaped for the torn railing. He resembled a huge beetle as he sprawled for a moment with arms and legs threshing. He missed his aim by a wide margin, hurtled earthward beyond the scaffolding.

To Frick's horrified gaze, the body of Frost plummeted after Moss, in the wake of the plunging car. There came a terrific crash; and with that fatal sound, the tension broke; a murmur surged up from the crowds; then the scuffle and scrape of countless running feet, as thousands upon thousands swarmed toward the scene of the crash.

VII.

AS JEAN MORAY watched Ivy Frost prepare to enter a coaster car of the Whirlwind, resentment that she had felt earlier began to boil inside her. Frost was only using her as a tool, a means to an end, as he had done numerous times before. She might be an efficient aid, gifted in many ways, but still he treated her as an assistant only. He did the thinking, and she followed orders. And now, as always, he had set the stage. Perhaps she also served who only stood and waited, but Jean grew quite unreasonably rebellious as she thought about it, and worked herself into an angry mood.

Why should she merely follow orders? Why not act on her own initiative for once? Frost had specified the Magic Hall, therefore it must possess special significance. It was time she threw off this high-handed domination.

All at once, she knew that she was not going to stand in the background and watch Frost put on a show. Her expression altered with the spirit of mischief and determination.

She deliberately turned and started for the door to the Magic Hall.

"Hey, lady, get in line. There's lots of folks ahead of you," the ticket collector protested.

"There were," she corrected with and impudent smile. "I'm Miss Moray, Frost's assistant, on special duty about the murder."

"Oh. Well, you'll have to wait a minute anyway. There's somebody inside now."

"How does it happen that only one person at a time is admitted?"

"Well, it's like this: When the Magic Hall first opened, we used to let folks in by the dozen, but they got all mixed up, bumped into each other, busted the mirrors, and raised a general rumpus. It's a tricky place. You've got to watch yourself. So the owners finally made it a rule that only one person or one couple could go through at a time."

A bell rang. The ticket man asked: "How much time do you want?"

"Just a minute or two."

She walked through, but dallied in the entrance hall. A series of six preliminary mirrors lined one side of the corridor to the Magic Hall. She looked at her reflection in the first one. The glass, warped to height, showed her incredibly tall and thin. "Good gracious! Is that I?" she exclaimed to herself. She hastily passed on.

In the next panel, with horizontal concave and convex curves, she saw her figure weirdly distorted. She pouted wryly at this monstrosity.

The fourth mirror brought new disillusion to the figure of which she was proud. It was a convex glass in which she saw a caricature whose beadlike head and feet expanded at obtuse angles toward a waist line that was yards broad.

The next panel reversed the preceding image. She wrinkled her nose. "I don't like you. I haven't liked any of you so far," she declared emphatically, pointing a finger straight at her reflection.

The passage now made a right angle turn. Following it, she entered the Magic Hall and halted, amazed and fascinated by an optical illusion of extraordinary imaginative effect.

The room itself, while scarcely more than eight feet in height, covered a fairly large area, whose original size proved difficult to estimate accurately, because of the mirrors and the room's odd shape. Aside from the floor and ceiling, the room was a dodecahedron, each of its twelve sides a mirror, and each mirror faced by an opposite.

Jean's true image, caught in one mirror and reflected to the mirror opposite, bounced back again; and thus tossed between mirrors multiplied to infinity and diminishing to infinity in all directions, presented her with her receding counterpart in countless hundreds and thousands whichever way she looked. And with the illusion of multiple identity came the illusion of tremendous vistas and immeasurable distance; for the mirror walls reflected themselves and flung each other into ever departing remoteness.

She realized with apprehension that she had lost the true location of the exit.

She took a step forward, and all the thousands of her counterparts in all the thousands of receding chambers took the same step, creating another fantastic panorama. She watched throngs of identical Jeans walk among throngs of identical halls; but in all that repeated and multiplied movement, sound was absent. The comparative silence intensified the phantasmal, eerie nature of the experience. She looked at ghosts. Her eyes ached and her senses lost awareness of actuality.

A PORTAL began to open, a thousand portals. Quick unease came over her, when she tried in vain to fix the precise location of the mirror that was pivoting. Perfect indirect lighting did away with highlights. It was difficult to discern the glass. A feeling, inexplicable but profound, of something about to happen, some impending terror, made her heart beat faster. The portal, the countless portals, opened farther and pivoted shut in a cascading torrent of sliding mirrors. The portal, the countless portals closed.

A thin, cadaverous man, Barburg, slumped against a mirror somewhere. He was dead; a dagger protruded from his heart, and scarlet stained his shirt. His dead eyes stared at her, and panic descended, for the corpse in hosts and hordes was everywhere, reflecting in all the mirrors and halls even as her own image. She was surrounded by an army of dead men, their eyes glaring at her even in death. There were thousands of Jeans, and every Jean accompanied by a corpse.

She ran into glass and bruised herself. She felt along the smooth surface, and the thousands of other Jeans felt along the walls of their separate, unending prisons, a panorama as terrifying as it was strange. Then she stumbled against the corpse, and it slumped lower, sprawling on the floor. The contact made her whole being shudder. She felt curiously anæsthetized, as though each nerve had been tied in a separate knot, so tightly that she could not scream. She watched, in a sort of conscious nightmare, while all the duplicating and receding images of the dead man slumped lower in all the other halls and upon countless floors.

Pushing with all her strength against the mirror in front of which the corpse lay, she forced it to pivot far enough for her to slip through. The murderer might be waiting outside, but a live man was preferable to a dead one.

She paused with quick apprehension in the dark passageway, but heard nothing to indicate the presence of any one else. She drew a small fountain-pen flash and a flat automatic from the pockets of her slacks. The thin beam poked around and picked out a door. She opened it carefully and let out a little yip when she saw the altogether too lifelike gorilla. People passing looked at her idly. She heard a barker at one end of the inclosure. To her right, the curtain was partly pulled back from a booth labeled MADAME SERPA, and among other things she saw a fine collection of daggers like the one that had killed Barburg.

What would Frost do under the circumstances? She thought of several moves—to enter Madame Serpa's stall, to ask passers-by if they had seen any one come out of the door, to look around for clues. After a few seconds of indecision, she pocketed her automatic and went back to the corridor. There were two more doors, she found, an eastern entrance to a crowded dance floor, and a western exit to the open parts of Platinum Park, where other visitors went their way.

While Jean was walking along the corridor, her light crossed the point of a brad protruding from the wooden side. Billions of brads were never so royally decorated as this one, for it wore a crown of crimson, and a couple of drooping strands. One of the threads was dark-gray, and the other so blue as to look black. Jean detached them from the drop of blood. She looked at them, and slowly a half-satisfied expression came over her face. She snapped the threads and tucked one set away. The other she carried in her left hand and trotted around to the front of the Magic Hall.

"Don't let any one else in," she told the ticket collector. "There's a dead man inside—Barburg, one of the owners."

"Go climb a tree," he scoffed.

Jean flared up. "Go look for yourself. Then go climb a couple of trees!"

She hurried toward the Whirlwind. It surprised her that the roller coaster was not running, but crowds were running toward a single objective. Excited tumult filled the air. None of the group she expected remained on the loading platform of the Whirlwind. Its second ascent showed a jagged rip high above the ground.

VIII.

INSPECTOR FRICK bucked the rush with a skill born of war and riot experience. He heard piercing whistles cut through the uproar. Alert policemen were already summoning assistance and sending in for the riot squads. But Frick remembered his duties only with an automatic instinct. All his anxiety went for the welfare of Ivy Frost. He caught sight of the splintered coaster car, and near it the still, crushed form of Moss. Swept on in the tide, he got a fleeting glimpse of the mechanical and human débris.

Toward him worked a dynamic figure that towered above the throng and elbowed it aside.

"Ivy! How—"

Frost stopped him. "I had a hand parachute. I expected this. The parachute was strong enough for two, but Moss lost his head and committed incidental suicide."

They made headway against the surge. Frick asked: "What happened? How did the accident come about?"

"It didn't happen. It was deliberately planned. A wedge-shaped obstruction had been planted between the tracks. Operating from a distance, the murderer sprang it above the level of the tracks as the car approached, and the car simply catapulted off. The murderer was in that group on the loading platform. The wiring from the wedge ran along the framework of the roller coaster to one edge of the platform."

"But why didn't it work the first time you went around?"

"Obviously, because some one in the party happened to be looking at the murderer. He could not act without being noticed until general attention was focused upon me in the coaster car. But as soon as he acted, the stage was set for him to trap himself. He is in that group, and cannot get away without immediately drawing suspicion. In addition, I placed my assistant where she could clearly watch the actions of all concerned. And, finally, I concealed a miniature motion-picture camera to photograph the scene and show the murderer at work."

They broke free of the main jam and headed for the platform. Frost glanced at it, asked with a harsh challenge in his tone: "Where is the group? I gave specific instructions for it to be kept there intact until I had finished my operations."

The inspector squirmed uncomfortably. "Well, Ivy, you didn't tell us what you were up to. You didn't say that this was the trap."

The professor drawled with biting sarcasm: "And if I had made such an announcement, do you seriously delude yourself into believing that the murderer would have made any move? The whole success of the trap depended upon its being known to none but myself."

"But nobody knew what you were up to. There didn't seem to be much point to it. I suppose the others got tired watching, or swept aside when the crowd went wild."

Jean Moray, flushed from running and excitement, scampered toward them.

"And what did you see?" Frost inquired.

"Barburg—murdered—in the Magic Hall!" she gasped.

Frick, with a startled expression, sprinted away. Frost said: "What did you see on the platform of the Whirlwind?"

Her eyes opened wide in guileless innocence. "Why, how could I see anything on the platform when I was finding a corpse inside?"

Frost carefully drew out a very long cigarette which he lighted and inhaled. Rian came out from among the roller-coaster supports, carrying an object that he was examining with open curiosity. He didn't see Frost and Jean until he was within a few paces. Then he looked up from the object.

"Uh—hello! Look what I found hidden down there. Some bird must have been taking pictures and went off and forgot his camera. Ain't that the nuts?"

Frost mused softly, meditatively: "I arranged a perfect trap, but the suspicion is dawning upon me that I observe a perfect mess."

If he had gone into a rage, or unloosed a blistering barrage from his extensive vocabulary, he could not have achieved a more excoriating effect. Frost surveyed the collapse of his plans with an Olympian serenity. The human causations may have interested him briefly, but he showed no inclination to waste time on unprofitable regrets or to linger among the ruins.

Rian muttered, "Uh, is something wrong?"

"I'll take my camera, if you don't mind. Did you happen to notice the actions of any of the suspects before you began your tour of exploration and discovery?"

Rian reddened, thought hard for a few moments. "Well, Barburg was standing near me, and I heard him say something about going to see about a cracked mirror. That was while you were riding the roller coaster. I didn't pay much attention because I saw something flash in the sunlight under the scaffolding or whatever you call it, so I went down there to have a look and found the camera."

"And while you were gone, Barburg walked to his death in a passageway behind the Magic Hall. Who told Barburg that a mirror was cracked?"

"Search me, I don't know." Rian raced after Frick.

Jean handed Frost one set of the threads. "This is the only clue I found. They were caught on a nail in the wall."

THE PROFESSOR studied the strands with analytic eyes, absorbed as though reading the pages of an informative text. "It is impossible to predict the value of these," he judged. "I will have Frick round up all the suspects again. That may take hours, and meanwhile they have ample opportunity to change socks and clothes.

"Even if the murderer was brought here immediately and confronted with the evidence while still wearing the fabrics from which these came, the circumstance would be cause for suspicion rather than conviction. He could claim that he had walked through the passage before the murder. Unless several reliable witnesses can be found to testify that they saw him go into the passage shortly before the murder or come out immediately after, the threads will not be of major help.

"It would be difficult to locate such witnesses even by public appeal, if they exist; and if found, their testimony as to time and identification could be invalidated by any competent criminal lawyer during cross-examination."

Jean said contritely: "I'm sorry about the roller coaster fizzle. But the way it turned out, it was a good thing I went inside the Magic Hall."

Frost uttered truths without reproaching her. "I assigned you to the Magic Hall primarily to watch the Whirlwind and to obtain direct testimony against the murderer. From the spectacular nature of Reisenham's death and with the assistance of several other deductions, I knew that he would utilize equally prominent media for further operations.

"The roller coaster and the Magic Hall were the most suitable for his plans. If what I anticipated took place at the Whirlwind, you were in a position to support my deductions. If the other alternative occurred in the Magic Hall, the identity of the murderer would be solved by elimination of all the suspects at the Whirlwind.

"Unfortunately, since human beings do not possess an extra eye in the back of the head, it was impossible to watch simultaneously the roller-coaster tracks and the group on the platform, aside from attempting to save Moss' life. The discovery of murder is but a starting point. The major importance lies in prevention and solution of crime."

The professor hiked off toward the Magic Hall, a veil of abstraction in his eyes.

Jean, watching him leave, tried to guess what new processes of thought occupied his attention. It was curious how readily Frost managed to penetrate into the minds of other people, and how difficult it was to estimate what went on in his head.

Jean had very positive ideas in view, but it was a testament to the force of Frost's character that she wasted many seconds staring after him and attempting to figure him out before she started putting her own theories into action.

Then she hastened out of Platinum Park and got into her roadster. Traffic was heavy pouring away from the city, but the incoming stream a mere trickle. She drove mainly with the intention of going places and doing things in a hurry. A lovely smile and an enchanting face work wonders. She got by with some petty violations of traffic laws, at practically no delay. She felt quite pleased after each demonstration of her devastating influence upon the male of the species. These demonstrations almost recompensed her for her failure to make a dent upon the unyielding armor of Frost.

She wove in and out through traffic, found the accelerator an interesting toy to play with, got a kick out of some fancy driving. She did not take chances and was by no means a reckless driver, but her assurance and nimble dodging left many a frazzled nerve in her wake.

Jean reached Manhattan and headed for a specialty shop on Fifty-seventh Street. She stopped there for several minutes, came out wearing over her halter a lustrous blouse decorated with an artful green figure which she had not intended to purchase, but which she couldn't resist the moment she saw it. She continued uptown to the West Seventies.

The address she halted in front of was a narrow brownstone house five stories high, of former dignity but now in its decline. She walked up the steps and looked at a row of corroded buzzer buttons and weathered cards. One of them bore the name: Ginger Lary.

Jean didn't press the buzzer because the door, though shut, was unlatched. She climbed two flights and went along the corridor to a rear room. She listened, dropped a hand in her pocket and felt the reassuring cool grip of the automatic. She rang the room bell.

NOTHING HAPPENED. She waited an interval, rang again more insistently. She heard the muffled sound of running water which ceased, then a door closed. She repeated the ring after another brief pause. She didn't hear the footsteps she expected, but a key turned and the door opened a little. "Who is it?" a voice called in slightly annoyed tones.

Jean pulled out the automatic and shoved hard on the door. "Stick 'em up! Fast!"

The surprised occupant of the room reached for the ceiling, her warm, brown eyes big with respect for Jean's pistol. "Ginger" Lary was a couple of inches shorter than Jean. She was slim, had rich, wine-dark hair, thick and soft, with mahogany hues and highlights. All her coloring was vivid, from hair and eyes to skin as duskily golden as a ripening peach. Her features had a natural attractiveness with soft, rosy lips, a short and truculent nose.

"What do you want?" Ginger asked indignantly "Who are you and what's the gag?"

"Get dressed! We're going places."

"Oh, we are, are we? Guess again."

Jean said: "You're wanted in connection with the murder of Leo F. Barburg at Coney Island this afternoon."

Slowly the color drained from Ginger Lary's cheeks; her eyes grew frightened, stricken. She was young but looked weary and older. Her arms dropped to her sides. A mask of defeat and despair altered her face. All at once she flung herself on a studio couch, sobbing into her arms, her shoulders quivering.

A lot of thoughts swirled through Jean's head at that moment. Ginger Lary was no hard-boiled gun moll or gangster type. She didn't resemble an adventuress wise in the ways of the world. She was just a good-looking kid who had got herself into a jam. In spite of her original intentions, Jean's sympathy went out to her.

Without further ado, Jean marched across the room, sat down beside the bowed figure, and put her arm around Ginger's shoulders. "Come on, Ginger," she urged gently, "spill it."

IX.

THE SUN was setting. It hung low in the west, a ball glowing red through the haze and murk of the atmosphere. Mugginess lingered on in Coney Island. Attendance had fallen off from its peak, but sweltering multitudes still thronged the beach and board walk.

They taxed the facilities of all the amusement centers, with the single exception of Platinum Park, which was closed to the public. The fickle crowds that had promptly flocked into it after discovery of the skeleton rider, had just as promptly flocked out of it after the Whirlwind disaster.

The wildest sort of rumors circulated—that the police were suppressing information about other deaths, that every device in the park had been tampered with and turned into a dangerous instrument of destruction, that corpses were buried all over the grounds, that even to enter the park meant a risk of life. The police finally cleared the park of visitors and closed it as a precautionary measure.

The group clustered in the manager's office at Platinum Park suffered from the heat like every one else, except for Frost who, as he towered above the others, appeared indifferent to such minor topics as weather and temperature. Frost was speaking to those assembled.

"At the heart of this mystery stands the new attraction called the Werner Turner. It has a direct connection with everything that has happened here, from the disappearance of Reisenham to the murder of Barburg. When I first arrived here this morning, I reached this conclusion by means of logic, analysis, observation, synthesis, and deduction. The facts had to be tested by theory, and the theory tested by facts.

"The Werner Turner bears the given name of Reisenham, but from all evidence, Reisenham was a business man purely and simply, without an inventive streak in him. His name might have been a front for the other partners; but by a single question I found out that they were likewise devoid of mechanical aptitude. They lacked knowledge of so elementary a principle as the universal joint. The making of money seems to have been their main interest.

"I wired to Washington and discovered that Reisenham had patented the Werner Turner early this year. That fact immediately raised a question: How did Reisenham who was not an inventor hit upon so profitable an invention? The answer is, he didn't. From this point on, all other answers clearly ensue and the problems explain themselves."

"I don't see that they do," Inspector Frick said, after waiting for Frost to proceed.

"Isn't it obvious? Some one else invented the Werner Turner. He either did not have the funds to patent it, and brought his idea to Reisenham, or Reisenham overheard him explain the principle and nature of his invention. In either case, Reisenham got there first and received the patent rights. The inventor, realizing what had happened, appealed to Reisenham; and we may be sure that Reisenham was deaf to such appeal.

"Judging by the success of the attraction here and at other amusement centers to which rights have been leased, a fortune is involved. The royalties this year alone should amount to more than half a million dollars. There was little hope for the inventor to prove his claims and obtain legal redress. If he lacked funds to patent his invention, he certainly had no money to hire high-priced counsel and fight his case through the courts.

"He decided to take his own revenge. He made an appointment with Reisenham in the basement of the repair shop. Here occurred an unforeseen twist that proved greatly to the inventor's advantage.

"The inventor probably made the appointment by telling Reisenham that he had another new idea in mind; but the inventor actually intended to threaten Reisenham or kill him if a share in the royalties was not forthcoming. Whether or not Reisenham believed the inventor is immaterial, for Reisenham himself had reached the conclusion that only death would put an end to the inventor's persistence.

"Thus, neither one cared to be seen going to that appointment. Reisenham must have used some simple disguise such as dark glasses and mustache when he entered Platinum Park through the adjoining side show; only thus can be explained Reisenham's reasons for and success in getting to the shed without being recognized the night he disappeared. Keeping the appointment resulted in his death. The inventor stuffed the body behind a pile of old doors and lumber slanted against a corner of the room.

"The body was not discovered the following day. For one thing, the shed is only in occasional use and at irregular intervals. Days and weeks sometimes lapse before any one has a reason for going to it. Any one who did enter it the day following the murder saw nothing unusual, partly for the excellent reason that the inventor had smeared tar over the bloodstain on the floor."

"You didn't tell me that before!" Frick exclaimed.

"You didn't ask me," Frost retorted. "The inventor may have secreted himself in the shed again the night after the murder, carried the body to the excavation while the workmen were elsewhere, and covered it loosely with sand; or he may have waited till a subsequent occasion, and reopened the spot. He needed very little time. The morning crowds would obliterate any traces of his work in short order; and no one who did notice the patch would attach the least significance to it. The precise hour and evening that he worked are immaterial. It should be remembered that Variss was off duty on both those nights; but when on duty thereafter, his schedule of hourly inspection was common knowledge to every one concerned.

"This procedure, however, would require that the body be interred, disinterred at a later date, and part of it reinterred at still another date—a highly improbable sequence with highly probable risks of discovery. The alternative is that the inventor simply left the corpse in the shed basement. He expected it to be found, but it was not. At this season, repair work is held to a minimum because the whole park will be overhauled when it closes for the winter. Consequently, no one used the shed.

"As the days passed, with Reisenham officially listed among the missing, the inventor must have thought often about the hidden body; and gradually his original plan assumed a new shape. His vengeance would go farther. The corpse had not come to light; he himself would make it emerge into the open, but in such a manner that it could never be identified, so he thought.

"Reconstruction of his actions would, I presume, present a terrifying picture to many minds. I can visualize him returning to that dark basement, aware of the corpse rotting in a corner, forcing himself to approach that gruesome form. The hatred that impelled him onward must have been so powerful that it brushed horror aside.

"I will not enlarge upon the details. The evidence tells the story. Modern scientific methods make it difficult to destroy identifying characteristics of a body. Even corpses immersed in water for months, or in the last stages of decomposition, have been identified through dental work, scars and marks, hairs, deformities, fingerprints, etc. But the very thoroughness with which Reisenham's body was reduced to a skeleton had the reverse effect. It simplified identification, as I have already shown."

MADAME SERPA'S face had a greenish tinge. Hermes, the magician, squirmed uncomfortably. Markey listened, soberly intent.

Frost continued: "Having the solution and knowing the identity of the murderer now, I would ordinarily have turned the information over to the police for whatever action they chose, since this was not one of my private cases. At the request of Inspector Frick, I went on, for there remained the problem of apprehending the inventor. He had done his task so thoroughly that there was no objective evidence to incriminate him, and the circumstantial evidence incriminated a great many other persons. I therefore led him into a trap of his own devising.

"While surveying the park, I noticed the wire on the Whirlwind framework. I deduced for various reasons that he never intended to operate the device he had installed. It would have been discovered during the next periodic inspection. The mere fact of its existence would have so alarmed the public as to cause a heavy loss in attendance not only at the Whirlwind but in all of Platinum Park.

"I made my plans and took a ride on the roller coaster. The murderer by then knew that I was closing in on him. It was I whom he feared. If he could do away with me, he probably would never be caught, for his was a mental determination that would never crack in a police grilling. And when Moss made the fatal blunder of jumping into the car, the murderer had what he thought was a golden opportunity to round out his vengeance at one blow."

Frost lighted a cigarette and inhaled deeply. "In order to make his own plans, the murderer had to know long in advance what I would be doing and when. What he did not know was that he alone among the suspects had the knowledge. The others first heard of it only when they were rounded up and brought to the platform of the Whirlwind," Frost said, with a sardonic glance at Sam Variss.

All heads turned. There was an instant's silence before Variss spoke, in a tired voice: "You win. You've told it all except for a couple of things.

"The night Reisenham came down to the basement in the shed, I didn't know he was armed. I intended to threaten him first, though he had stalled me along so many times I was mad enough to kill him. While we were arguing, he told me to get some papers he'd left on the ground floor, and like a dumb cluck, I started off. Then it struck me as being queer so I turned around and the skunk had a pistol with a silencer attachment.

"Naturally, I moved fast and my one shot finished him. Then I found out that his pistol had jammed as those with silencers are likely to do. That explained something that bothered me—why I'd been taken off the Werner Turner and put on night duty. Reisenham had gotten to hate and fear me almost as much as I did him. He made it easier for himself if it came to a show-down.

"I didn't drag the body to a corner. I stuffed it in the big boiler and put the cover on, where I wish it was, still.

"This afternoon, on the platform, I whispered to Barburg that a mirror was cracked behind the Magic Hall. Tell him anything that costs money and he jumps to see how much it'll cost. The second time you started around, Barburg was leaving. People were moving around and the group breaking up. It was easy to walk to the end of the platform and kick the button because a couple of others walked by there, too. Then I—"

There was a commotion at the door. In walked Jean with her prize. Ginger Lary ran across the room like a frightened faun, and Variss folded an arm around her protectively.

X.

FOR ONCE, even Frost seemed surprised. Inspector Frick was a study in consternation. A hum of voices and questions arose. Jean stamped a foot imperiously. "Shut up! All of you! I'll do the talking now and you can do it later!"

The vehemence of her command silenced them. Jean rattled on: "I've a lot of things to say and I'm going to say them now. In the first place, I just hope you bring a murder charge against Ginger Lary, the girl over there, for Barburg's death. You can try from now till doomsday and I'll bet dollars to roses you never get to first base with any jury I ever heard of.

"She's the real reason Reisenham died before he expected to, and, personally, I think it was a grand idea. If you want some real crooks, you'd have to go a long way to beat Reisenham, Moss, and Barburg. They're cheap frauds.

"Ginger and Sam Variss were going to get married this spring. They had a lot of plans when Sam got royalties for his invention. He didn't get any royalties because Reisenham stole his idea and patented it. So Ginger and Sam didn't, because it's a hard grind when you get only fifteen or twenty dollars a week as a night watchman. I gather that Sam's a sort of quiet soul, hasn't many friends, and doesn't talk about himself, which is why nobody seems to have heard of Ginger.

"Anyway, Ginger was in the passageway back of the Magic Hall. She had a blackjack and a dagger that Variss stole from Madame Serpa.

The dagger was for protection. She was to hit Barburg with the blackjack and knock him out. Variss said he would see to it that Barburg went into the passageway. Variss knew that Frost was closing in on him; but, obviously, Variss couldn't be at the Whirlwind platform and in the passageway at the same time. That would throw the whole case open again. And Ginger and Variss had an agreement not to see each other for a month after today.

"The idea went haywire because it worked too well. When the roller coaster went off, everybody started for the wreck. No one paid much attention to any one else; but if Variss hung around the platform of the Whirlwind, he'd be conspicuous because he'd be alone.

"Ginger figured Barburg would be blinded from sunlight when he stepped into the passage, but he wasn't. He must have had eyes like a cat. He dodged the blackjack, made a dive for her, and started choking her. She stopped fighting at that stage and let him have the dagger. She was scared and figured it was his life or hers. Barburg staggered against the mirror and it swung. She closed it and ran. That's all there is. This whole mess would never have happened except for Reisenham's meanness. He was the real criminal. He got exactly what he deserved and I'm glad!"

The inspector fidgeted. When she halted for lack of breath, he shifted her attention: "Do you mind telling how you plucked this woman out of thin air?"

"I didn't. In the scuffle with Barburg, Ginger kicked and a nail tore her skirt and hose. She didn't know it at the time, but I found the threads. The rest was easy. They were high-grade and handmade. I can't tell you how I knew. You get to know fabrics by feeling them. And a woman on Ginger's mission would dress to be inconspicuous in darkness. That's the only reason she'd wear a dark-blue skirt and gun-metal hose. About the only place I know of that has things that feel like those threads is an Irish store on Fifty-seventh Street, so I went there and asked, and I was right."

Frick looked openly bewildered by her line of thought. "What made you think that the threads came from a woman's apparel rather than a man's?"

It was Jean's turn at being stumped. She blinked her eyelids, taken aback. "It just didn't enter my head that there was any question about it," she confessed. "The moment I saw them, I wondered why any woman would wear such a color combination."

Frost strode toward the door. As if awaiting his signal, the others began a bustle of various activity. The inspector hurried after him, caught up with him outside.

"Wait a minute, Ivy," he implored. "Miss Moray is right. We have enough to indict the two, but getting a conviction is another matter. If this comes out in court the way it stands, there's a good chance they'll beat the chair or maybe win acquittal."

With a note of finality, Frost stated: "Ethics and punishments are not for me to decide. My interest lies in the solution of crime, the detection and apprehension of criminals. All aspects of the mystery have been clarified."

The professor was gone.

Jean climbed into her roadster with a feeling of utter content. She didn't know what his mood or attitude was. But she hoped she had got under his skin. Her face wore the contented smile of the cat that licked up all the cream.

GIANTS IN THE VALLEY

A curious dullness filmed Beta's eyes. A thick, guttural snarl rattled in his throat; a brittle snap cracked sharply—

ONE COLD MORNING in November, when a piercing wind that seemed laden with frozen needles swept from the Hudson, Jean Moray dashed from 11 to 13 State Street at her customary hour of nine.

Professor I. V. Frost would not be up yet. He seldom rose before noon, because he seldom retired before dawn.

Jean let herself in and collected the morning's mail. There was always a large stack. To-day she counted five parcels and picked eighteen letters off the floor where they had been pushed through the door slot. As she straightened and looked at the fat, placid Buddha which squatted benignly in a niche at the end of the hallway, she stiffened.

An eye hung in mid-air.

For a moment, in the dim light, she thought that it was a living, human eye, but when she looked closer she found that it was artificial, brilliantly realistic but, nevertheless, artificial. It hung suspended on a wire from an overhead light fixture and turned with a slow, unpleasant motion as though watching her. Gradually it became still again with the subsidence of the air currents caused by her entrance.

She did not disturb it, since it might have been placed there by Frost himself, but she could not imagine why. Puzzled by the presence of so unexpected an object, she entered the book-lined room that served for the reception of clients. From a pedestal in one corner, the bust of immortal Socrates faced a seventeenth-century portrait of Bacon.

Jean received another uncomfortable shock. On the table was lying an eye with a chill, gray, impersonal stare. The slitted yellow eye of a giant cat reposed on the telephone stand. The tiny, black, beady eye of a snake occupied the mantel. A reddish hawk's eye brooded beside Socrates.

Wherever she turned, she found eyes, artificial eyes of animals, birds, reptiles, and human beings. They were as disconcerting as if they had been real.

Jean went about her work efficiently, but now and then she caught herself glancing up at those mechanical eyes whose baleful gaze seemed to follow her every move. When curiosity and unease got the better of her, she walked into Frost's private laboratory. She found more eyes—eyes everywhere—unobtrusively placed so that it came as a distinct shock each time when she looked into an obscure corner and suddenly discovered an eye staring back with a cold, eerily lifelike gaze.

She walked on into the museum. This was a fairly large room of shelves and glass-topped displays which contained objects salient to every case that Frost had handled. Here was the sword that had severed the hand of the green man, the thyratron tubes of the pipeless organ that had thundered doom to the brides of the rats, the catapult that had hurled liquid, air-frozen corpses from an East River roof.

The monkey carved of ebony, whose interior had been hollowed for the great raw diamond of the artist of death, rested here, a dagger from the Coney Island murders, and the surgical kit that had created a second Nick Valmo.

In a cage, still squawking stridently, was the plumed parakeet that had originally plunged Jean Moray into peril which first brought her to Ivy Frost.

HER EXPLORATIONS ceased at this stage. She knew of more pleasant games than hunting for eyes. Whether she found them or not, the effect on her nerves was just the same.

She returned to the library and went through the mail. Four of the parcels cotained a book, "Keys to Melanesia"; some herbs from Tibet; crystals and pure extract of vitamin E, andromin, pituitrin, dinitrophenol, and thyroxin; and an exposure meter.

The brown paper of the fifth and heaviest package bore the lettering in rough capitals: "I.V. Frost, State St., N.Y. C." There was no return address, and no clue to its origin. Even the postmark had blurred illegibly.

When the thought occurred to Jean that it might contain a bomb, she handled it gingerly and with new respect. Frost had made enemies. A crank or crook might well have chosen this method to get him permanently out of the way. Yet she had never heard of a bomb in the shape of this package, which was about two feet long by five inches wide and five deep.

She finally decided it would be safe at least to remove the outer wrapper. As she was unfolding the paper, she discovered on its inner surface another address, that of the American Museum of Natural History. She studied the paper's folds and creases. The lettering of the two addresses was similar, but they could have been the product of different hands. It looked as if some one had prepared the package for mailing, and some one else had opened it, reversed the paper, and written Frost's address. Why?

The parcel contained a plain wooden box with a slide cover. She removed this and then pulled out some excelsior stuffing. A large, unlabeled, and tightly stoppered bottle came to view. It inclosed, preserved in a fluid, presumably alcohol, an animal specimen. Her early trepidation gone now, and curiosity again foremost, she lifted the bottle out and stood it upright so that she could examine it against the table lamp.

Her expression of interest slowly turned to one of repulsion. The bottle, some twenty inches tall and four in diameter, imprisoned a loathsome little monster of a species unknown to her. At first glance she took it to be a white snake or eel because it was so long and smooth. Then she judged it a saurian when she noticed its three pairs of tiny feet. Next she guessed it to be a rodent, because of its sharp ears and pointed snout, the rat tail fully as long as its body, and the minute pink digits of its feet.

It had no hair or fur. The body was as bald and slimy as a worm. In the end, she confessed herself at a loss to classify the thing. Moving the jar had imparted to the specimen a lazy swaying. It quivered in suspension, on the verge of becoming alive. Perhaps it was alive, preserved in a solution like that used for the artificial heart. She investigated no further. Frost was welcome to the pale little nightmare.

The matter of the miscellaneous eyes and the queer specimen weighed on her as she sorted the mail. Her attention drifted from an anonymous letter that threatened Frost with a variety of picturesque but improbable deaths—What did the eyes mean?

There was a second letter from a firm of attorneys asking Frost to intercede on behalf of a wealthy playboy awaiting the electric chair at Sing Sing.

"Certainly I could intercede," Frost had told her after the first letter. "There is one detail forgotten by the chap and therefore not in the hands of his attorneys which would win him a commutation of sentence if not a new trial. But why should I bother? He is guilty; the law has sentenced him, and I see no reason to resort to legal trickery for its own sake. Request declined." This second appeal would probably not even gain a reply from him—What was the thing in the bottle?

A large munitions company offered him his choice of a lump sum in six figures annually or a per unit royalty for the rights to a new type of silencer that he had patented, a silencer for machine guns and rapid-fire small arms; but the same mail brought a dictum from the war department that the invention would be declared Federal property and a military secret, with equitable compensation. Again she wondered who had sent the bottle to Frost, and why.

THEN the correspondence struck lighter vein! Somebody in the Bronx had lost a pet pigeon, and wanted to know if Frost wouldn't please track down the footloose squab. Jean couldn't figure out how he would react to this one. He might dismiss it with annoyance; or it might appeal to him, because of its oddity and the difficulties involved.

The ring of the doorbell startled her. She listened but heard nothing to indicate that Frost was up yet. She walked swiftly into the laboratory and pressed buttons whose functions Frost had explained. A panel slid open from the back of the hallway Buddha; light glowed, and the telescopic eye above the doorbell brought her the features of a stoop-shouldered and irritable-looking man. Shell-rimmed glasses did not conceal his light-blue eyes. His lips were thin, dyspeptic wrinkles lined his face, and he wore a patch of tape on his long lower jaw.

Jean spoke into the annunciator. The stranger's voice, muffled and anxious, floated back. "Is this the residence of I.V. Frost?"

"Professor Frost is not at home now."

"The devil with Frost!" the stranger exploded. "I don't care whether he's here or in China! All I want is my specimen."

"What specimen?"

"Damned kids got hold of a package I sent out to be mailed and changed its address. Where is it?"

"Who are you?"

"The name is Wlwlwl."

The sound was an unintelligible mumble. Jean said, "Speak louder, I didn't catch the name."

"Wlwlwl!" the stranger roared. "Young woman, you're a confounded imbecile! Do I have to stand here shouting all day? Here's my card. If you'll kindly look at it, perhaps in words of one syllable I can drive home what I'm here for into that empty pod of yours!"

Jean furiously closed the contacts and went out to the hall entrance. Murder was in her eyes. She jerked the door open.

"By gad!" Mr. Wlwlwl gasped. "By gad but Mr. Frost—"

"Professor Frost," Jean corrected him icily.

"Mr. Frost has remarkable taste in his—ah—personnel!" the visitor exclaimed. "A looker if I ever saw one. Stunning! Amazing! I marvel that he can keep his mind on his work! Or does he? Does he have a mind? Do you? But then you wouldn't need one. It's too bad you don't."

In a voice as soothing as a panther's pur, Jean retorted to the volcanic visitor, "Perhaps I can supply what you lack."

He blinked at her for a moment. "Bravo! An excellent reply! You take me aback, yes, indeed you do. Do you mean that you can give me the specimen which I most certainly lack? That would be the charitable view. Or do you imply that you possess the charm that is absent from this frame? An unkind observation, but I dare say well taken. Come, come, this is getting us nowhere. Madam, my card!"

Uncertain whether to be angry, flattered, or amused, Jean glared at him with hostile wariness.

"I have a coat on and I shiver," he complained. "Alas, I can see that we will never be friends because I do not enjoy standing in a cold wind. Do you do this often? If you catch pneumonia, I might send you carnations, if you don't recover."

She was so worked up that she had forgotten about the weather. She felt the cold now, and noticed the lead-dull sky. Rain or sleet was in the wind. She looked at the card in her hand. The light was poor and the pasteboard almost as unfathomable as its owner. She would have had difficulty reading its microscopic printing under the best of circumstances. When she brought it closer to her eyes, the writing did not even look like English. The words were blurred and ran together and her hand trembled with cold. She shifted her gaze to her shivering fingers and watched them till they relaxed. But then they refused to hold the card and it began to slip away. She went after it, eyes fastened on the Lilliputian script, but it receded farther and farther, and the card grew as dark as the printing, until there was nothing but darkness.

II.

HER HEAD ACHED. When she tried to move it, flashes of pain and fire tormented her. She breathed pure oxygen, followed by stinging fumes that made her gasp. Her eyelids were glued shut.

"Easy," came a vaguely familiar voice. "You'll be all right in a minute."

The rocket-streaked darkness became lighter and gradually turned into a ceiling. She again tried to open her eyes and discovered that they were open. She felt muddled. Something about a card kept floating hazily through her drift of impressions. She was lying on a couch, and after a slight struggle got herself erect.

"That's better," said Frost. His thin nostrils quivered; a bright glimmer was in his eyes, and his features were eagerly attentive. "Now tell me what he took."

"Who took what?" she mumbled, trying to collect her wits.

"That's what I'm asking," the professor chided her. He looked very long and gaunt as he stood peering down at her. "How did he divert your attention—with the old calling card or personal message trick? I'm surprised at your succumbing to so elementary a ruse. I'm almost as surprised that he didn't kill you while he had such a fine opportunity."

"Is that all it means to you?" Jean flared, white with anger. "Maybe I was careless, but if you knew how it happened—and suppose I didn't recover—"

"But you did, and I know how it happened," Frost calmly interrupted her.

Jean intended to bounce up and walk out, but the room reeled, and she remained seated.

"Good," Frost approved. "Get mad. The more furious you become, the sooner you will be yourself. In as much as you seem to doubt the truth of my assertion, let me refresh your memory. As you did not know, I went out last evening for a walk. While strolling down Riverside Drive, it occurred to me that I had never completed a pedestrian circuit of the island of Manhattan. I recommend that you duplicate my performance some day, in stages if necessary. If you keep your eyes open, you will discover a number of interesting, unusual, and surprising features. The tour, by the way, required somewhat over sixteen hours, but the time could be considerably shortened by omission of pauses to investigate special districts.

"Returning here at one o'clock, I find you unconscious in the hallway. The obvious conclusion is that you met some one at the front door. Your attention must have been diverted for a few seconds in order for the gas pellet, concentrated carbon monoxide, to be broken virtually under your nose. It is unthinkable that you would casually submit to such treatment, but there were no signs of a struggle. A logical and effective method of diverting any person's attention is to present him a card or letter of tiny and illegible writing that may or may not be the language he knows.

"I next made a rapid survey of the library, but none of my possessions had been disturbed. I noticed that you had not finished opening mail that arrived in the first delivery, whereas a couple of letters from the second delivery lay in the hall. The time of the occurrence was thus fixed at between eight thirty and eleven, roughly ten o'clock.

"Upon the table I found shreds of excelsior. Of four packages visible, two had contained no stuffing; one was packed with matting, and one with wood shavings. I am left with the inescapable conclusion that a package is missing. I am left with the additional inference that the package went astray when it came here and was reclaimed by the sender or his agent. The drastic means he employed confirms either the great value or the complete worthlessness of the contents. Which was it?"

"You aren't human. You aren't anything but a detached brain that figures things out. You don't need anybody or anything. If the world blew up under you, all you'd do would be to look on and guess how it happened and decide how it would end," Jean accused hotly, bitterly. "It doesn't matter if I get a raw deal. It wouldn't bother you if you came home and found the place in ashes. You wouldn't worry if you were sunk in cement at the bottom of the sea. You'd only go on figuring how it happened and why and a way out, and if there wasn't a way out, that wouldn't faze you either!" She stormed from the room.

Unfathomable light stirred in the depths of Frost's black pupils; his eyes brooded, and as he stood facing the door through which she had vanished, his features held a strange contrast. There was a frown on his forehead, and a crooked smile on his mouth. He removed a long cigarette from the container on a stand at his elbow. He was inhaling deeply when his assistant returned, her lovely face erased of emotion, repaired of make-up, and restored to the guileless innocence of a summer morn.

Frost asked, "Which was it?"

"Neither great value nor complete worthlessness—just queer," Jean replied, looking at him with cool, hazel gray eyes. She explained what had happened.

Frost grew increasingly restive throughout her story. He insisted upon a detailed description of the creature in the bottle. When she finished, he was smoldering with nervous energy.

"I anticipate meeting your visitor. I shall be disappointed if he is not a decidedly different kind of villain. As for the freak, it may be of little worth in itself, but it is the key to a world in creation, to life haphazard."

"Life haphazard?" Jean echoed, puzzled.

"Our coming guest will explain; and if the visit is much delayed or the explanation insufficient, we will force the answers in our own way. There is a challenge here the like of which I have never met, and rarely heard. We shall meet the wisdom of the future in the cradle of to-day, and wrest from time the shadows of things to come. Those who would be lords of a new realm and re-create both animate and inanimate life—"

THE RINGING of the bell stopped the flow of words that had begun to encroach upon the mystic's province. Jean hadn't the least notion of what he was talking about or what his statements meant. She watched Frost's tense, lean figure as he strode to the window and peered through its shutters.

"Take it," he ordered. "Don't bother with the safety checks."

He cocked an eye at Socrates into whose stone face was chiseled the dream and thirst for knowledge that have obsessed wise men through all the latter years of history. Frost's face stood out in profile as Jean left the room; and she felt that surely the same compelling need for knowledge was the power that drove him, and the source of power.

When she opened the door, her heart skipped a beat, and everything tangible and real seemed to be slipping away from her. She experienced that inner panic which comes of facing an alien personality wholly beyond the dictates or control of reason.

It was raining now, a cold, steady drizzle blown in gusts and flung in eddies by the fitful wind. Against that gray background, she saw a middle-aged woman with bedraggled hat and soaked coat. She must have been attractive once; but now her skin was as gray as dust, her lips distorted and crawling and writhing slowly over her teeth, and a madness in her eyes. They were sultry eyes, like dark-red flames, and there was no indication that they saw or comprehended Jean. The woman dwelt within a far world of her own. She carried a bundle wrapped in newspapers, carried it as though it was a baby, and marched past Frost's assistant.

Jean recovered from her petrified state and shut the door. She could think of nothing to say. Instinctively she felt pity, but with that emotion went fear. She followed the woman into the library. The woman laid her bundle on the table. From the angle where Jean stood, she saw Frost's reflection in the mirror above the mantel. The woman looked up and also saw the mirror, and then in a sobbing fury flung herself at it, beating it, hammering it, pounding wildly.

Frost sprang after her in a flash, tore the mirror from its hanging, and turned it around. The woman whirled toward him, fists raised, but suddenly they dropped to her side, clenching and unclenching. She glared at him, the sultry fire in her eyes grown hot and feral, raindrops sliding from her nose and chin. She turned and paced around the four sides of the room, her head turned toward the walls, as though she were searching for spies hidden behind the books and buried inside the wall paper.

"It is gone," Frost suddenly stated in a matter-of-fact voice, but clearly and sharply.

His words penetrated the barriers of madness that separated the visitor from reality. She whipped toward him, her eyes glowing cinders, less raging. "Gone? You got it?"

"It was taken away."

"Oh." A pause. "I didn't take it away." A pause. "What was it? I didn't have time to find out. Was it pretty?"

Frost shook his head.

The woman began laughing. She laughed in a high, mirthless, and bleating falsetto. She laughed so hard that the tears crept from her eyes. "Of course it wasn't pretty! Nothing is pretty at New Eden." She stopped laughing. "Alpha isn't pretty either. I brought you Alpha."

"Who or what is Alpha?"

The woman squinted at him, crying now. "Alpha is dead. Alpha has been dead a long, long time. Only Beta is left."

"What did Alpha die of?"

"They said Alpha fell from a tree. They lie. They killed Alpha. I saw them. They didn't know I saw them. Alpha was trying to eat one of them." A cunning look came into her features, the look of a she-wolf. "They buried Alpha. I waited. They watched me day and night but I waited for years. They thought I was knitting sweaters. I was knitting sweaters but I fooled them—oh, a piece here and a snip there, until I had the rope knitted so I could get over the wall. I dug Alpha up before I left."

Frost lighted another cigarette but not for an instant did he take his glance away from the woman. Her eyes locked with his, and the compelling intensity of his gaze drew random admissions out of the mysterious and strangely populated kingdom of her mind. Frost exhaled an island of spicy smoke. "Why did you come to me?"

"I once overheard Santelle say that you were somebody he never wanted to run up against. He said he wouldn't go near State Street unless he had to. I remembered the name and the street. You will stop him, won't you?"

"How did you know what I am?"

"I don't know what you are. I sent the package here. I was afraid Santelle would find out. Last night I got away. I walked miles. It took me all this time to get here."

She suddenly stopped and turned her head a little, as though listening to voices that whispered in her ear. The red embers faded from her eyes, to be replaced by the vacancy of distance. A slow, secret smile changed her mouth. She listened, and listened on to inaudible voices, hearing things where Jean found only a stifling silence, and seeing visions afar. She was alone with phantoms. She had entered a trance that imprisoned her, or liberated her, beyond reality.

Frost said softly, "Call the hospital."

Jean obeyed.

The woman gave no sign that she had heard; and when she was taken away, she went without protest and without indication that she knew what was happening.

Frost waited with restrained impatience, in a silence that gave his assistant the jitters, until the visitor was gone. Then he pounced upon the bundle and ripped the papers off. Inside, and with particles of soil among them, lay a pile of bones. To Jean, it seemed to comprise the skeleton of a small creature. The skull looked almost human, almost simian, yet neither, and was far too large in proportion. The cranium had been crushed.

III.

JEAN could not understand Frost's nervous tension. If this was murder, it was murder of years gone by, and who can account for the vagaries of madness? Very little in the woman's irrelevant statements meant anything to Jean, yet Frost was a dynamo of suppressed energy. He put the bones aside after a thorough scrutiny. His eyes were glittering eagerly.

Jean complained, "Nothing ties up with anything else. First it's a freak in a bottle, then a lunatic comes after it. Next another lunatic turns up and leaves us a bag of bones. I don't see what's to get excited about. You can't make sense out of nonsense."

"Quite the contrary. The whole riddle is now perfectly clear. I know where we are going, what we will find, and who and what we will encounter. But as it happens, the very truths that I have interpreted will afford us our greatest difficulty. Deducing the enigma and unraveling the facts were a fairly simple process for analytic and synthetic reasons. But demonstrating the truth will involve obstacles of a peculiarly dangerous kind.

"Miss Moray, this is one adventure in which you need not participate. I recommend that you remain here. No logical mind can foresee or entirely prepare for the crazed whims, the fantastic improvisations, and the irrational complexities of being detached from the patterns of life to which we are accustomed."

Jean said, "I'm in on this. I've a score to settle."

"Every safeguard I can devise may not be enough," Frost warned. "The rational mind, no matter how brilliant or analytic, is at a disadvantage when thrown against the phantasmagoria of unreason. Logic is a system. Insanity is a lack of system. Neither can meet the other on its own ground. Neither can anticipate the other. And when logic must deal at the same instant with counterlogic and with irresponsible fantasy, the odds are against reason."

"I'm still in," Jean stated, simply.

"Then you must be prepared to forget all your concepts of the plant and animal kingdoms. You will be plunged into a nightmare. Humanity will take on a new and perhaps appalling significance. Evolution will turn into a myth. You will see the infancy of to-morrow's world, but an infancy weird and as yet uncontrollable.

"There is time for you to take a quick lunch. Do so. Then bring up some grenades from the munitions storeroom, and while you're about it, a quart of whisky from the wine cellar. Pick out something good, but not the best—four-year-old bonded rye will do. When you return to the laboratory, you will find a suit that looks somewhat like a skiing outfit. Don it."

Frost strode into the laboratory.

An hour afterward, when Jean had finished her tasks and was taking the suit that Frost had provided, she overheard him answering the telephone. "Yes. . . . Discharged ten minutes ago? In care of husband, S. D. R. Gant. . . . Fine. Thanks."

In the late afternoon, the *Demon,* Frost's own specially built automobile, left the basement garage and purred out of the driveway of 13 State Street. Sodden skies made the air almost as murky as night, and headlights winked through the cold drizzle that swirled upon autumnal gusts. Rain splashed against the windshield. Little streams trickled down under the twin half moons of the wipers. Upper Manhattan swiftly faded behind them, and Frost took the span of the George Washington Bridge. The pavement was a wet menace.

"I'm enjoying the conversation," said Jean. "It's so witty, so informative, so stimulating." She looked at him from the corners of her long-lashed, innocent eyes.

"I knew you would appreciate its scope," Frost agreed. "Words unspoken are often of far greater significance than the ones we use. It takes a connoisseur to savor the eloquence of silence."

"I can't say that I enjoy being mistress of nothing at all. If I went around collecting silences, I'd have nothing to talk about."

"A splendid undertaking!" Frost approved. "Nothing is one of the most impressive concepts in the entire range of physics, mathematics, and the physical universe. It is a symbol that no philosopher can do without. Only a most obstinate, timid, or ignorant person would eliminate the concept of nothing from his life; but at life's end, it would overtake him, overwhelm him, and engulf him in its closed circle. I heartily approve of your project, Miss Moray. In itself, it is sufficient for an intellectual lifetime."

There was no suggestion in Frost's voice that he was spoofing her.

Jean toyed with a cigarette. Frost followed the Palisades for a few miles, then angled away from the Hudson. The rain was falling harder now. The dead leaves in the woods were soggy, and the naked trees glistened wetly. They were following a macadam road that wound across hills and dipped into hollows.

"Some day," said Jean with a sweet slur, "I hope a tiny little emotion gets into you. It would probably curl up and die of toxic poison right away, but just the same I'd love to see it happen. Or else you'd corrupt it with arguments until you convinced it that it wasn't an emotion after all but just a hunk of cold logic that tried to masquerade as something else."

"When emotion is reason, logic is murder," Frost stated with oblique succinctness.

Jean was still wondering what he meant by that one when he halted, his headlights shining on a gate across a private road. He got out and, lifting the gate by its "No Trespassing" sign, moved it aside. Jean ran the car through, and Frost shut the gate.

THE DIRT ROAD he now followed was narrow, grass-covered between the ruts, and miry. The trees were so close that branches frequently hit the windshield and top of the car. Darkness had fallen, but the blackness hardly seemed much denser than the murk of the afternoon. That road wound uphill, and the car slid and lurched on a couple of steep grades.

Jean tried again. "Why did you send her to the insane ward?"

"In order for Santelle to get her out as fast as possible."

The answer surprised her. "I don't get it."

Frost explained, a trifle irritably, "Santelle sent a specimen to the museum. He didn't want his connection with it known, but he did want it in reputable hands to support claims that he intended to make subsequently. Doubtless he has already sent other material to the museum. The staff there is composed of scientists, not criminologists. They would have some but not much interest in where the thing came from. Santelle gave the package to some one for mailing, but before that person took it away, Santelle's wife—Mrs. Gant—re-addressed it. Santelle's messenger later must have made some comment on the package's destination, and he realized what had happened.

"He came after the package and retrieved it. Under no circumstances did he want an investigation made of New Eden, least of all by any one who was connected with both science and criminology. But meanwhile, Mrs. Gant had escaped, taking with her far more damaging evidence. Santelle, the instant he discovered this, notified the police that she was missing. It was a shrewd move. He told them that she was insane, which was true, and that she had stolen an animal skeleton, which was a half truth.

"I sent her to the hospital as a psychopathic case, name unknown, which automatically notified the police, which brought Santelle hot after her. But she no longer has the bundle. Santelle knows now where it is and what it will lead to, and that knowledge will force him into the open and on the offensive."

"Who is this Santelle?"

"Santelle D. Rae Gant. When I last heard of him, some fifteen years ago, he was a brilliant young biochemist who inherited wealth and suddenly went into retirement."

Jean, after a few moments' thought, shifted the subject. "Why are there eyes all over the house? Did you put them there?"

"I suppose every man has the prerogative of collecting what his fancy dictates. Some prefer postage stamps; others prefer miniatures, or snuff-boxes, or butterflies. Why not eyes? Or, for that matter, screws, or samples of paper, or pottery beads, or—"

The car rounded a curve and Frost stopped abruptly. The headlights shone on a tree fallen across the road. Frost slid over Jean. A pistol equipped with silencer gleamed in his hand. Things happened too fast for her to follow. "Lights off!" She flicked the switch at his command.

The right door opened and slammed. For an instant all was blackness and rain. Then orange flame flashed beyond the fallen tree, and she heard a rapid, coughing stutter. Bullets screamed off the left side of the *Demon* and made cracked-glass dimes on the windshield. There were a couple of faint pops from the right, so faint that she could hardly hear them, but the yellow-red flashes ceased. Darkness and rain, till a cone of light played beyond the tree, and followed the tree as it left the road.

IV.

FROST returned. The headlights of the car infringed on the tree, and the motionless figure beside it, a sprawled figure with its hands clamped around a submachine gun. "Dead," said Frost. "Through the heart. A big brute who looks like an ex-pug or a strong-arm specialist. Nice set-up. If he'd got us, they would have gone free on the plea of suspected highway robbers who refused to halt, in case our bodies were found, which might not have occurred for years, if ever."

"What made you wise to the ambush?"

"The winds with which I am familiar do not chop trees down. A driver facing such an impediment would normally climb out the left door, and offer a fine target against the headlights. The incident should suffice to answer your question about the eyes. You wanted a reason. There it is. If you think that eyes are always watching you, you will always be ready for any emergency."

The road dipped downhill. A half mile farther, a wall of concrete and boulders at least ten feet high appeared on their left and stretched ahead indefinitely. Iron spikes curved out from the top of the wall, with barbed-wire entanglements.

Frost stopped the car and issued swift orders. "We get out here. Walk on until you come to a gate. Ring the bell. When some one answers, grow hysterical. You were waylaid and your friend was killed and the man who waylaid you was killed. You need help and you want to notify the State troopers. Give me your automatic. You'll be safer without it for the next few minutes. You are beauty in distress."

Frost took some things and disappeared toward the wall. Jean began trudging along the road. There was almost no grade now. The area inclosed by the wall appeared to lie at the bottom of a valley. Her hiking shoes grew caked with mud. Rain pelted her but the suit shed it. The suit was warm and of iron-tough fabric.

The darkness was so black that she would have been filled with forebodings if she had been by herself. Even the knowledge of Frost's presence could not wholly stifle the fear that comes by night to the lone traveler in the forest and in a strange place. Her rôle acquired realism. The beam of her flashlight wavered along the wall.

She hurried, breathing harder, until a massive gate leaped out of the blackness. The wall continued beyond it. She rang a rusty bell button again and again. The rain-swept gloom pressed down on her with rustles and whispers. She was cold of face and hands, and scared.

The door swung open. Light dazzled her eyes. "Well!" rumbled a huge voice. "What the hell you doing here?"

"I've got to get to a phone!" Jean gasped. "I was driving with a friend—we stopped a while—some one held us up—shooting started—they're both dead; they've killed each other—"

"Well, I'll be damned!" came the voice, startled, and like a bass drum. Jean deciphered the outlines of a figure as tall as Frost, but built like a barrel. The voice changed. "Well, now, ain't that too bad! Come in, lady, we'll take care of you right away. It's just too bad it happened but—"

"But don't you understand? They're dead! Call the police! There must be State troopers around!" Jean cried wildly. "I've got to get help! They're lying back on the road and I couldn't get the car to start! I've been running and running to find a house!"

"State troopers? Sure, we'll take care of all that. Now, now, take it easy, beautiful. I got a rod in my paw, just in case. Walk right in and we'll fix you up." A hand the size of a baseball glove yanked her rather than helped her through. Her teeth clicked. The door grated shut.

The hand guided her. "To the right and we'll—"

The giant toppled backward and crashed on the ground. A pistol flew out of one hand; a flashlight spilled from the other, as he clawed at the rope that was strangling him. A new light sprang out to reënforce Jean's. The man flailing the ground was a giant, a mountain. His hair came halfway to his little eyes. He had a square mass of flattened features for a face. He must have weighed two hundred and thirty.

Frost's hands, slender and with beautifully tapered fingers, flashed into the light with a hypodermic. The man-mountain saw it coming and tried to roll over. The hypodermic plunged into his wrist. He tore at the rope. His face darkened; veins bulged. A merciless light dazzled his eyes. Gradually his struggles weakened and became of curious slowness. With a deft motion, Frost slipped the rope off. Breath returned to his lungs then in deep gulps. He flopped around on the ground in futile efforts to rise, but his arms and legs seemed to be unmanageable. Paralysis overtook him. He lapsed into coma.

Frost's flashlight picked out a stone hut. He dragged the man toward it, the cumbersome body helped along by the mud that greased its passage. The door was unlocked. He pulled the man inside. Jean followed. Three cars were parked in the garage. Hauling his victim to a heating pipe that ran from floor to ceiling, Frost looped his arms behind his back and handcuffed his wrists around the pipe.

A ROW of spike-tipped javelins stood in a corner. Frost hefted one of them, his eyes frowning. The shaft was six feet long.

A combination bedroom-living room lay left of the garage. In its rear, a door at right angles to the one from the garage opened onto a refrigerator—a room-sized refrigerator—with whole carcasses and slabs of meat hanging on hooks!

Frost picked some receipts off a spindle and leafed them. "Astonishing, and perhaps illuminating," he murmured.

"What is?"

"That a household of seven or eight persons, or even ten, should require an average of fifty pounds of meat per day!"

He returned to the garage and stared thoughtfully at the unconscious giant. "Our friend down the road was six feet tall. This one is six feet four. If the others are built in proportion, they must have Gargantuan appetites—but fifty pounds of meat per day! Hmm. In case you did not notice, hooks curve inward from the top of the wall, as well as outward. The barbed wires carry a charge of electricity sufficient to stun. That wall was designed not only to prevent intrusion, but also to stop anything inside from getting out."

After another glance around the garage, he started to leave. Jean heard a throaty growl. Frost dropped to the ground and slammed the door behind him in Jean's face. A great weight crashed against the door. A series of dull *pop-pops* instantly followed. Jean jerked on the door.

Frost was just rising. She could not see his face. "All over," he announced. His light played upon a dog of such size as she had never dreamed existed. It was still kicking in death throes, its jaws, neck, and body pierced by bullets.

It must have been four feet from nose to rump, built like an English bull, but with the legs of a hound, and baring with its last foaming snarl an ugly set of jaws capable of ripping a man's throat out or biting an arm through. It was coal-black. It weighed at least seventy pounds.

"They come large around here," Frost said softly. "Better keep your automatic ready." He returned the weapon to her and refilled his own.

The night was made of rain and wind and—warmth.

"That's queer." Jean sounded perplexed. "I was shivering before and now I'm so warm I'm uncomfortable."

"A network of heating pipes is embedded in the soil. The space within these walls never experiences snow or the temperatures of winter. Get ready for something of a shock."

He shifted his flashlight along an arc. It shone upon a solid mass of vegetation—colossal violets as tall as a child; orchids the height of a man; vines that had developed spikes instead of leaves; black roses; a crazy jumble of growths and hybrids that belonged nowhere on earth, not even in tropical jungles. It looked as though all the freaks and abnormalities in the botanical kingdom had been assembled in this one place.

Only a general impression registered upon Jean, however. She might have received a shock, but the picture had scarcely formed before it was driven from her mind. Unlike most women, she had, up to then, had no particular aversion to snakes and worms. From that moment on, she developed a horror of them that never completely left her.

The cone of light passed across a body lying at the edge of the luxuriantly evil vegetation—the body of a man with skull crushed. He was thickset, powerful, not as tall as the other two, but even broader and heavier, as cushioned as a wrestler.

Nestling along the ground and at right angles to him lay a gigantic and avid worm. The long, dark shape was as big as the dead man. Fur tufted its fat segments. A horny head moved slowly among the pulp.

In the depths of the wilderness, a screaming ululation rose to staccato quavers and sank into gurgles as of some one drowning or trying to talk through blood.

V.

"TAKE the light," Frost snapped. He faded back toward the garage. The shrieking subsided, left the night to wind and rain. The monstrous worm raised its head, turned toward the light, and swayed slowly. It reared its forepart. Ridges of locomotory flesh palpitated on its underside. It made a clicking with its horned beak.

Frost's gaunt figure leaped into the light. He inserted a javelin under the worm and heaved it yards away. He rammed the steel tip home. The worm writhed, its fat folds tumbling and threshing convulsively. Soft fluid pulsed out in fitful gushes. The worm was dead, but so low in the scale of evolution that it might squirm for hours before the muscular reflexes ceased. Though nauseated, Jean forced herself to advance.

Frost was bending over a patch of loam beside the corpse. He looked at shoe prints, whose clear outline the rain had already destroyed. Among them, filling fast in the steady downpour, lay the mark of a bare foot, a dozen inches in length, narrow as a lath, and with six webbed toes. The professor looked at the marks with an air of abstraction. They had become unrecognizable blurs when he dragged the corpse off and stowed it in the garage.

Upon his return, he plunged into the weird vegetation. He made no comments, whatever conclusions he had reached. If he knew the identity of the dead man, what had killed him, and why, he kept the knowledge to himself. He made no effort to shade the flashlight. As nearly as Jean could tell, they were following a dimly outlined path. She kept close to Frost, a feat not difficult because he advanced like an actor in a slow-motion picture.

The occasional trees and dense lesser greenery dripped moisture in a warm and steamy atmosphere. The cone of light traversed grass as large as ferns, ferns that bore flowers of irregular shape and numerous variety, tall, thick stalks capped by unexpected moss or leaf clusters or pods or immense blooms, and bushes from whose blossoms rose stems that ended in different flowers, fragile or sturdy, exotic as orchids, of overpowering fragrance, and with gorgeous hues.

There were parasitic growths, vines that throttled trees, and mushrooms that sapped the life of broad-bladed reeds. Some of them quivered with eerie sensitivity when the light reached them. It was as though the plant kingdom had gone mad, species imitating species, until there was no longer any characteristic feature to distinguish a flower from grass or a fern from a bush, or even one flower from another flower or one grass from another grass. Some specimens were prodigies in size, others dwarfed or warped fantastically.

The vegetation pressed so close to the path that they were forced to push aside branches and stems. The ground was soggy. The air had a strange, wet smell of things in growth and death, in full flower and final decay. The night was full of sibilance—patter of rain, swish of grass and leaves, sound of creatures astir somewhere in that mystery-shrouded blackness.

The beam swung upward to warn Jean of a low branch. Another worm, a vast, dark, mushy blob, lay along the branch, its weight causing the dip in the bough. Frost did not disturb the worm. Jean ducked under it, sick with loathing and fear that the enormous slug would descend upon her. The worm stirred. Its hard mandibles clacked against wood as its head turned. Then it was behind her.

A little mewing broke out all at once. They came in a rush—tiny balls like kittens, but with leonine heads. They were no larger than mice, but they swarmed at Frost and Jean with raking claws and spitting, savage "meows," and bloodthirsty jaws.

Frost trampled them. They bit at the fabric protecting Jean. They vainly tried to hook their claws into her ankles and clamber up her legs. She stifled revulsion. Following Frost's example, she kicked them and squashed them. They scrabbled in dozens, ravenous fiends of fury, until the path became lumpy with their carcasses.

The remaining horde suddenly changed goal. They turned cannibal and attacked their fallen with the same ferocity that they had attacked the human beings. Near by sounded a slithering and rustling. Were the colossal worms already creeping toward the feast? Or did other menaces prowl to the commotion? What had Frost said earlier? Something about evolution discarded, something about a nightmare. It was a scene from another planet, or the demented processional of delirium.

Frost strode past the creatures. Jean shuddered as her feet trod humps that were not soil. The thin yowling faded behind, and again the darkness filled with the rustle of leaf and branch, and the murmur of rain. The vegetation became sparser. They approached a clearing. Off to their right, fingers of blue-white brilliance hung above the ground.

"Wait here," Frost whispered, and slipped away with his flashlight extinguished.

He disappeared so quickly that Jean had no chance to protest. The automatic clenched in her hand gave small aid in soothing her nerves. She had been in a number of tight spots on various occasions while assisting Frost with cases. Sometimes she had been as cool under fire as the celebrated cucumber. Sometimes she had given up hope of getting out alive, and once or twice she had been filled with panic such as the night when she first glimpsed the green man. But she had not previously been in the state of ragged jitters that now hit her.

BACK THERE in the rain and darkness lay two dead men, and alien vegetation, and fabulous worms, and cat creatures. She momentarily expected a new attack from one or more of the perils uncovered. And what of the thing that had screamed so weirdly? What sort of monster would emit so inhuman a cry? Whence came the strange footprints? And what unimaginable other horrible entities roved through the black depths around her?

A leaf trailed against her ear. Startled, she brushed it away. It recoiled and clung to her ear affectionately. This time, to her consternation, it refused to be brushed away. She tugged before it pulled off with a faint plop. Her ear tingled. She put her hand to it and risked a quick flash. A drop of blood smeared her forefinger.

Toward her swayed a long-stemmed plant with huge, glossy leaves and a single flower. The blossoms, cup-shaped, held concentric rings of soft little feelers that palpitated outward ready to fold inward upon whatever morsel they could get, the chosen delicacy being Jean's ear. She stifled a gasp and shifted her stand away from the carnivorous plant.

The minutes seemed endless. She imagined a thousand terrors around her, from vicious creepers and crawlers to murderous blooms. If anything ever happened to Frost when a mess like this trapped her—

She started nervously when Frost drawled in a low tone, "Toward the lights. The way is clear except for ground stuff."

She found it impossible to keep as quiet as he managed. She swished grass and bushes, but the presence of other sounds made absolute stealth unnecessary.

In front of them loomed a building with a foundation of stone masonry. From waist height to its peaked roof, glass panes walled it, like a greenhouse. Long drapes curtained the windows, but through the aperture between each pair a blue-white dazzle poured. Inside, upon a smaller and regulated scale, grew plants akin to those from which they had just emerged. Bed after bed contained well-tended flowers, shrubs, and vines in all stages of development. Scarcely a one bore more than a rough resemblance to any familiar variety.

Santelle, owl-eyed, was peering at a mound of loam heaped beside a bed in process of formation or destruction. With Santelle stood a husky bruiser in striped jersey and overalls. Did any one in the vicinity, Jean wondered, fail to top six feet or two hundred pounds? This one had the shoulders of a stevedore, a slim waist, and close-cropped head. His jaw stuck out; his forehead leaned back; his flat cranium made an acute angle at the rear of his skull, and the base of his skull slanted parallel with his face.

While Jean absorbed the scene, Frost had attached to the pane a device linked to a small ear phone

"Take it," he whispered. "I'll follow their lips."

Voices, low but clear, came through the earpiece.

"Enough for to-night. You can finish the bed to-morrow. I may do it myself. Never mind, Fritz. Are the bulbs ready?"

"Yeah."

"What about that last litter of mice? Did any survive? Of course not. Well, we'll try again."

"The one without legs and two heads is still feeding. Six pounds and a half it weighs already."

"It does? The little rascal! It's wonderful, Fritz, wonderful, or don't you feel that way about it? No, you don't. You're just a pig-headed Dutchman. No matter. Science will immortalize us both when we publish our results. Do you want to be immortalized? Come, come, speak up. You don't care, is that it? I thought so. Stubborn to the last. Ah, well, Fritz, my fame and my genius will be ample for us both. Right? Don't answer, no, please don't—"

Santelle poked his head around so suddenly that the shell-rimmed glasses slid a half inch down his nose. He peered at the floor. A trapdoor banged. A new figure straightened up—the giant whom Frost had left narcotized and shackled in the garage!

Frost murmured, so dimly that Jean had to fill in words, "Not thirty minutes past, I gave him enough morphine to anæsthetize the average man for twelve hours, yet here he is! A phenomenal case! He must have the constitution of a rhinoceros, the vitality of a turtle, and the strength of Hercules!"

"Slug!" the stoop-shouldered Santelle exclaimed impatiently. "What are you doing here? Why aren't you at the gate? Answer me instantly! No, don't talk. Haven't I told you repeatedly that I don't wish to be disturbed? Yes, I have; oh yes, I have. Yet you pop up here like a confounded jack-in-the-box. Come, come, what is it, or are you tongue-tied?"

"Slug" growled. "Quit beefing. The thin guy and the gal got by. I'd have been here sooner only he give me knock-out drops or something, only they wasn't much good. I ain't even groggy."

"Indeed? He must be a very sly person, oh my, yes, quite an eel. I trust our pleasant pets in New Eden give both of them a juicy welcome. If not, we will take them as they come. We are superior in numbers and defense, not to mention brains. My brain, that is. Fritz, warn Hake and Strafey. Away with you; begone, at once!"

Fritz, descending through the trapdoor, sank from sight.

The instant that he moved to obey Santelle's command, Frost murmured in Jean's ear, "Watch till I return," and melted into the rain-washed blackness.

VI.

FOR a hundred yards, the professor ran as though upon a cross-country dash in broad daylight, his long legs flying. He came to a small stone house like the one at the entrance to New Eden. His actions here became rather puzzling. He raced to the side of the house and found a window with a grille of steel bars. He pushed the barrel of his pistol between bars and smashed the glass pane inside.

He dashed around to the front of the house. After a few moments of swift, methodical work, he opened the door. He promptly felt for a wall switch and flicked the lights on, leaving the door ajar.

The gas that he had left seeping through the window upon his previous tour of reconnaissance had accomplished its invisible service and dissipated. Another of Santelle's husky troop lay sprawled on the floor beside a tipped chair. Frost straightened the chair and sat down. In his eyes, intent upon the floor, hovered a coldly sardonic glint.

The trapdoor swung up almost as soon as Frost had taken his position. Fritz's head popped through. "Hake and—"

Frost drawled, "Were you looking for some one? Come right in." His pistol aimed at the exact pupil of Fritz's left eye. Consternation, the thought of trickery, and watchful submission followed in quick succession across the man's angular face. He unfroze his position and climbed through.

"Put your gun on the table," Frost ordered.

A gleam entered the big Dutchman's steel-blue eyes.

"Don't take the chance!" Frost warned. "Your face is your traitor. It tells your intentions before your brain has issued the command."

Fritz tossed his automatic on the table.

The professor removed its clip. "Now, precede me, and carry out the rest of your mission precisely as though nothing had caused the least interference. If other ideas occur to you, you might also imagine how uncomfortable you would be with bullets reposing where your heart was."

With respect and without enthusiasm, Fritz led the way. They went down a ladder and along a narrow tunnel, until they reached a second ladder. Fritz climbed first and pushed the trapdoor open.

"Strafey," he called, "Santelle says to—"

Fritz kicked backward. Frost took the kick on both forefingers and

Fritz catapulted into the room. Strafey, a new member of the beef-and-brawn trust, had an automatic halfway up when Frost shot with careful deliberation.

One of those unexpected accidents to which firearms are subject resulted. Frost's bullet nicked the curved-over tip of the middle finger in Strafey's gun hand, smashed through into the clip, and detonated a cartridge. The weapon ought to have burst. Instead, the slug tore through the butt and neatly removed two thirds of that same middle finger. Strafey dropped the now useless automatic. He tied a handkerchief around the finger. There was no more expression on his coarse, bristly jowls than if a mosquito had stung him.

Fritz got up in a daze. Two powerful, compact batteries in Frost's pockets connected with needle tips in his gloves. Fritz probably wouldn't have understood even if the professor had chosen to explain. He did not choose.

"Let us rejoin the somnolent Hake, and see whether we can awaken him," Frost suggested dryly.

They looked like a parade of giants as they traversed the underground passage. Fritz, in the lead, just cleared six feet, with a hundred and ninety pounds of solid bone and muscle. The middle position fell to Strafey whose impressive height topped Frost by two inches. Strafey must have weighed at least two hundred and fifty. He was the hugest of all in this nest of superbrutes. Frost strode in the rear. He was six feet four, but his gauntness made him look feeble by comparison. Fritz and Strafey did not think so, however. An implacable will and a relentless purpose dominated Frost's glittering pupils.

In the first stone hut Frost took the weapon of the unconscious Hake. Then he addressed his two prisoners, "Bring him back to life."

The two stared as if somebody was crazy. Fritz said, "First you knock him out, now you want him brought to, yeah?"

"Badly phrased, that is the thought."

They laid to with a will. They went to work in a manner that would have turned the ordinary mortal into morgue material. They slapped him up and whacked him down. They bounced him on the table for exercise. The pats they gave his head would have split a normal skull. They poured gallons and buckets of water upon him. They tried pulling his arms and legs out of their sockets. They kneaded his flesh, hammered his chest, and sat on his stomach. When they ran out of fresh ideas, they started over again.

After a while, Hake muttered, "Lemme be. Quit playing, guys, I'm sleepy."

They worked on him some more. They grabbed a towel and did their best to rub the skin off his chest and back. When they smacked his muscles, it sounded like packing crates hitting cement.

Hake finally sat up. "All right, if you're gonna be like that." He jerked Strafey's ankle. Strafey landed with a crash. He stuck a thumb in Fritz's eye and shoved him over on his back. Then he lay down mumbling.

"That's enough." Frost stopped the roughing. "He's coming around."

Strained silence lasted for fifteen minutes. Hake breathed in stertorous mumbles, then he got up, shook his head violently, opened his eyes, and snarled, "O. K. What's the play?"

Frost glanced at his watch. "Time's up. Clear out of here. If you had the sense, you would flee the grounds. You won't. Santelle can supply you with new weapons."

"Huh?" Strafey glowered.

Frost's voice became harsher, impatient. "Get out."

Fritz cursed. "We might as well rush him. He's gonna pick us off when we hit the door."

An egg-shaped object suddenly rested in Frost's left hand. "I will most assuredly annihilate the three of you if you delay much longer. You may recognize this object as a hand grenade. The notion of heaving it into your midst appeals to me strongly."

Strafey and Hake jammed in the doorway, but Fritz butted them outside.

Frost brought out the key that he had appropriated when removing the unconscious Hake's pistol. He went through a door at the rear of the room and up a short flight of stairs. He used the key on another door which was massive enough for a bank.

MRS. GANT stopped pacing around the room like a caged animal. Her eyes leaped out like crimson embers in the glow of the flashlight. Frost turned a switch outside the door.

The sultry hatred in her eyes dimmed when the illumination came. "You sent me back here. You kept Alpha. What do you want?"

Frost's sentences sounded eerie. They had a hard, mechanical, hypnotic timbre. "The door is open and you are free. The day has come.

The way is yours. Here is the gun, which holds seven shots. Here is a hand grenade. It works like this—

"I am your friend. Jean Moray is your friend. Jean Moray is the young woman who was with me when you came. She, too, has helped you. She is here at New Eden. Do not harm her. If you harm her, she cannot help you. Jean Moray and I give you freedom. Walk out. No one will stop you. When you are out, you are free. The automatic will shoot seven times. The grenade will blow up once. Do not use the grenade until you must. It can wreck this house. It can blow the wall open. It can kill us all. Save the grenade. Use it when nothing is left."

For an instant, as Frost intoned the words, the hot, mad flame left her gaze. Pure, enraptured, joyous exaltation replaced it. That unearthly expression graduated into calmness. Sanity, grave, unsmiling, and forlorn, lingered for a tick of time.

Then the sullen haze thickened in her eyes, and she paced toward him with the wariness of a jungle cat. She took the weapons that Frost held out for her. She walked down the stairs, not fast, not slow, in unhurried purpose. Frost's expression, introspective, brooding, and inscrutable, remained until the darkness infolded her.

He returned to the other stone hut. It had no second floor. In its rear, however, he found a door, steel-studded, and more ponderous by far than the one that had imprisoned the woman.

When he opened it, a fetid odor assailed him, a musty and nauseating animal stench. Concrete stairs led downward. Stone walls inclosed the passage. He began descending, stealthily, his features so grim and taut that they seemed chiseled in marble. He twisted his head a little in the attitude of an intent listener. He heard ghosts of sound, like barely audible breathing and skin rubbing stone. The noisome smell grew stronger and more intolerable.

The stairs ended in the corner of a basement. Frost reached the bottom of the flight. He paused, crouched forward with every muscle tense, and leaped into the den. He whirled, keeping his back to the wall.

The basement, twenty feet square by twelve feet high, had accumulated through years débris that turned it into the lair of a beast. The walls dripped slime. Dirt, filth, bones, shreds of fur and flesh littered the floor ankle-deep. Restlessly roving feet had trod the rubbish into a hard-packed, uneven surface.

The instant that Frost entered, the dweller of the den sprang from its lair, low in the far corner. The power behind its pounce hurtled it all the way across the room with its webbed talons curved into claws. The electrical jolt that Frost gave it sent it twisting aside. It uttered a shrill, raucous, gurgling roar, hideously different from any sound that ever poured from animal throat or human voice. It rose on all fours, knelt on its haunches, and stiffened to its full height, a monster as appalling as the ogres of legend.

Even Strafey, the biggest of Santelle's thugs, would only have reached to its shoulders. From its soles and its long, webbed toes to its matted skull it stood seven feet tall and more. It had the general form of man, but shaggy, bluish gray fur covered every exposed inch of its body. The fur, hanging from its ears, its face and forehead, its nose and throat, completely obliterated whatever features it possessed. Only its eyes could be seen. They bulged, ash-gray, and as large as oysters.

In spite of its colossal bulk, the creature moved with the sinuous ease of a snake, the litheness of a jaguar. Swaying slightly, it glowered at Frost with pale and vacant eyes. For a timeless interval, they stared at each other within striking distance, equally taut and equally wary.

Perceptibly Frost's right arm started lifting until it pointed to the flight of stairs. The gaze of the monster followed his motion. In a chill, brittle tone, Frost commanded, "Beta, go!"

It listened to the words. It did not look at Frost again. Suddenly it became a Juggernaut in action. It took the steps in silent bounds. A great gray phantom, it fled into the darkness.

Frost drew out one of his special cigarettes, lighted it, and inhaled deeply, once. He crushed the cylinder under a heel before he strode upstairs.

VII.

WHILE Jean Moray listened and watched through a slit between the greenhouse drapes, Santelle complained, "You've been drinking again, Slug. Yes, indeed you have. I can tell it by your breath. If I catch you drinking again on duty, I will not chide you. Oh, certainly not. I will discipline you severely. I warn you, most severely."

Slug growled, "Aw, pipe down. It wasn't enough to hurt a flea. I didn't feel so hot when I come to so I took a couple of fingers. It couldn't have been no more'n a pint."

"A pint! Do you measure with the fingers of Thor? By heaven and salamanders, you must be drunk! You are drunk. Don't contradict me; you are. Soon you will be unable to speak clearly, but that is of no consequence; you never could. You haven't yet told me what happened. What happened? Must I drag everything out of you by questions in order to obtain an answer? Answer!"

"I dunno what happened. I heard the Tommy going like sixty down the road. I figured Mike was giving 'em the works. The next I know the bell rings. I figure it's Mike, but it ain't; it's the dame. She's a fast worker. She pulls a sob story so I get her inside and—kerplunk! Just wait'll I get my hands on that skinny guy!"

Santelle objected, "Then they must have killed Mike. Didn't I tell you to get a good man, didn't I? Of course I did. I asked you to obtain for me the services of the very finest killer available. And what do you do? You supply me a duffer, a nincompoop, a common idiot who, no doubt, let himself be murdered in cold blood."

"He was a good guy," Slug insisted. "He probably ain't no more, but Mike Mohood was one of the best trigger men there is. He knocked off a dozen guys I know of around New York. He worked in Kansas City and Philadelphia and Chicago and San Francisco and nobody ever made a rap stick. Something must 'a' gone haywire. I wanna know why Rafferty didn't back my play up like you said he was gonna. Where is Sig? Why wasn't he around for the fireworks?"

"He was, but in no condition to participate," Santelle answered. "Sig Rafferty is no longer with us. He lost his head— Oh, quite literally. Slug, you must never be careless with Beta. It is a mistake that you can make but once. Not twice or thrice, mind you, but once. Sig was not a little careless, but stupendously careless. I did not dream that a human being could be so careless. Or perhaps I compliment Sig too highly by calling him a human being. We will not argue the point; it is a small one, I assure you.

"Beta cracked his skull magnificently. Hah! Do you know what it sounded like? No, no, of course you don't. I will tell you: It sounded like a skull being cracked. I drove Beta back to his den, but Sig is still lying between the wall and the garden. I quite forgot about him. Dear me, my memory is becoming dreadfully lax. That reminds me—no, stay here, I will only gone for several jiffies."

Santelle scurried to the trapdoor and popped out of sight. Slug fished a pack of cigarettes out. He lighted one with a match that he scratched on his thumb nail.

Ten minutes passed and Slug was on his second fag when Jean heard steps near by. As she ducked and turned, light flooded her.

"Not a word! Quiet!" Santelle hissed. "Into the greenhouse with you! Hurry!"

He snatched her automatic, extinguished the light, and, holding her wrists behind her back, shoved her ahead of him. She enjoyed kicking his shins until Santelle pushed her face down into the grass. Inwardly raging, she gritted her teeth. To have been trapped so simply made her doubly angry because Frost had told her to await his return and she had assumed that Santelle's footsteps were those of the professor.

As they entered the greenhouse, Santelle crowed, "Now we have you. The others will take care of Frost. Excellent! You thought I didn't know you were outside the window but I did, indeed I did! It was most considerate of you to wait until I reached the garage and returned through the garden. A pretty garden, is it not? Don't answer!"

Slug flung his cigarette away. "So Angel-face is back again! Ain't that just too bad? Lemme spank her down. I'd kinda like her to remember me."

"Slug, you are by no means a gentleman. You must improve your manners, truly you must. Tie Miss—er—what did you say the name was?"

"The name is Glbglb," Jean mimicked.

"Indeed? A very odd name. Slug, tie Miss Glbglb's arms. Tightly, yes, tightly, behind her back. Careful. She keeps her temper in her heels."

When Slug had finished, Santelle approved. "Very neat. You should have been a hangman, Slug, it would have been capital work for you. Back to the garage with you. Away; do not argue! We have them now but we must take every precaution to see that they cannot get out so easily as they got in."

Slug left in sullen humor.

SANTELLE eyed Jean. "My dear, did I tell you that you have a very unusual and remarkable beauty? You please me too much, even if there is some grass upon your nose. Leave it there. It is quite becoming because it is unexpected. I could use you, my dear. Would you like to serve the cause of science? Neither Alpha nor Beta proved quite the success I had hoped. They were lamentable in some ways. Oh, not in all, not in all; nothing but success has ever attended my efforts. But more can be done.

"Will you marry me? No, I can see it in your expression. You disappoint me. I was afraid that you did not have intelligence to compare with your beauty. But as I have made it happen, nature can be changed. Are you surprised? Yes, you are, but I decline to argue. No matter. You will have to change your mind, and if you do not"—Santelle glanced at the new, unfilled flower bed—"then I fear that beauty must return to Mother Earth! A useful but depressing thought. I would much prefer having a Gamma and a Delta to follow Alpha and Beta."

With his mouth open to begin a new sentence, Santelle stopped talking. His long lower jaw moved up as he closed his lips. Wrinkles gathered above his eyebrows. "My memory tricks me; it does in the most unfortunate manner. Now where can Fritz be? It must be a half hour since I dispatched him. I wonder could he have stopped to talk with Hake and Strafey. But no, they have nothing to talk about and know nothing to say. Would they need his help? No, not unless they were trying to think, in which case he could not help them. I have it! He returned while I was gone, and Slug neglected to inform me. I will have words with Slug, a great many words and—"

Strafey, Hake, and Fritz erupted into the greenhouse, all jabbering in unison.

Jean stared in open astonishment at the huskies. She had never before seen at the same time and place so many strapping specimens of brute male strength as New Eden boasted. But time to think was lacking. From that moment, incident and violence followed each other so swiftly that the avalanche raced ahead of her.

Some one shouted that Frost had taken their weapons. Santelle, a sneer of supreme annoyance on his face, began to upbraid them. Fritz brushed him aside and lumbered from the greenhouse into another part of the building. He returned with an armful of automatics and a submachine gun as well as extra ammunition. Hake and Strafey each got two of the smaller firearms. Fritz kept the Tommy for himself.

High, mirthless laughter shrilled outside. It stilled the voices of all within for the fraction of a second. Hake growled, "That's Libby! He must 'a' let her out!"

"Don't get excited; don't be alarmed; no harm done!" Santelle exclaimed. "We'll—"

A wild, gurgling roar answered the woman's laughter.

Strafey cursed savagely. "Beta's loose!"

Santelle chirped happily, "Splendid, perfect; nothing could be better! That means Frost is dead! If he went into the den, Beta would never let him out alive! Fritz, attend to Libby. Hake and Strafey, get Beta back into his cell. I'll take care of the lights." He dashed out of the greenhouse.

The three had only begun to move when glass crashed. One of the drapes billowed and parted. The broken pane framed a face in whose eyes the sultry red flame now burned fiercely.

Fritz swung around, the submachine gun nestling in his arm, his elbow crooked.

"She's got a gun!" Hake yelled.

Spitting flashes came from the broken window. Fritz jerked, again and again. He took a step toward the window. The Tommy wabbled in an ever larger circle and stuttered fitfully. Glass tinkled and crashed. A little red worm started crawling down the woman's cheek. Fritz staggered drunkenly.

"Watch where you're aiming that Tommy!" Hake screamed and dove. The twisting submachine gun blasted him in mid-air. He was dead when he hit the floor. Fritz couldn't see. Fritz didn't know what he had done. Fritz lurched to one knee, tried to get up, and crashed on his side. His left fist hammered the floor dumbly.

The lights went out inside the greenhouse. Illumination like daylight flooded the grounds around it. Santelle scuttled back.

The mad face at the window vanished suddenly, mysteriously, as a though a giant hand knocked it aside, or an invisible current swept it away. A whole section of glass and framework burst inward carrying with it two of the ceiling-high drapes. They billowed downward through the blackness. They provided another mantle for Fritz and Hake.

Through the opening, and outlined against the bright glow made luminous by the rain, stepped a great gray monster. Yellow flashes flared in the greenhouse. All at once the lights outside extinguished and illumination filled the greenhouse. A congealing hand seemed to clamp down on Jean's heart with intolerable pressure. For the first time in her hectic young career, Jean flopped in a dead faint.

Strafey was a good shot. He had a good target. The target was too big—so big that he couldn't decide on the vital spot. He hit the target, *smack, thud, smack, thud.* The great gray shape came on.

"Beta! Beta! Beta!" Santelle screeched over and over. The wild face appeared at the windows again. A hand crept up with blunt-nosed automatic. Santelle, frantic, sprinted off in erratic jumps. The hammer clicked upon an empty clip.

Strafey used up one weapon, cursed, and flung it in the shaggy face. It caromed off the forehead. The gray shape came on. Strafey had a second weapon aimed point-blank when webbed talons plucked him from the floor in a mighty heave. His feet swung up toward the roof and completed a circle. When he slammed flat on the floor, there was a dull thump and two distinct, sharp cracks.

Driblets and patches of scarlet stained the monster's head, shoulders, and chest, and dyed its fur in widening patches. It turned and squinted with pale, colorless eyes at the unconscious girl.

"Beta!" called the woman at the window, and more loudly, *"Beta!"*

VIII.

SLUG LONNERGAN sat with his chair tilted against the wall so that he could cover both the entrance and the trapdoor, at the gateway to New Eden. He held an automatic ready. Glass from a broken bottle glinted at the base of the wall. Loud footsteps sounded outside. Slug had his gun pointed at Frost's waist when the professor walked in with a quart of whisky in his hand.

Frost stopped in the doorway and looked surprised. "Now how in the world did you manage to get free?"

Slug roared, "Blow me down if it ain't the skinny guy ready for his medicine! That's a hot one!" The brute's flat face twisted in a scowl. "I got a notion to let you have it now, tying me up that way. Ain't you got no better sense? As soon as I come to, I heave and the bracelets snap."

Frost observed with grave admiration, "You must be a man of great strength."

"I'm the strongest guy there is! I can bust bracelets like string! See that?" Slug stuck his left wrist out. A red weal marked it. It carried a steel circlet with the link twisted and shorn. "You're gonna pay for that. I'm gonna bust every bone in your body. I'm gonna break your wrists first. Then I'm gonna smash your nose and the rest of you. I can do it and I'm gonna do it and I'm gonna get a kick out of doing it!"

"I felt a little nervous after all the excitement," Frost said. "I thought a dash of whisky would be good for me. I was after a glass, but I fear I made a mistake coming in here unprepared."

"Fella, you sure did. No hard feelin's, unnerstand, but I'm gonna break every bone in your body! Say, is that a full quart? Santelle busted my last bottle. Say, what's the idea? Doped, huh? All right, wise guy, down with it! Go ahead, swallow!"

Frost tore the seals off and tipped the bottle. Slug watched with narrow eyes. "Stop!" he roared. "Put that bottle down!"

Frost set it on the table. Slug tilted forward in his chair and got up. "Have a chair!" He waved in mock politeness. Frost walked over and sat down while Slug circled around to the table. Keeping his gaze on the professor and the automatic steady, he lifted the bottle with his left hand. Close to half a pint gurgled down his throat before he set the bottle down.

"Say, that's swell stuff! I didn't no more'n kill a pint when Santelle pulls a fast one. He comes here and smashes the rest. That guy's got a nerve. Maybe I'll bust him too after I bust you up." He glared suspiciously at Frost. "You think I'm drunk, huh?"

"Not at all."

"I am too! I'm as drunk as a fool! I'm drunk as a hoot-owl! I'm gonna get drunker and then I'm gonna bust you to pieces. You're a sap! You wouldn't have come back here like you did if you wasn't a sap!"

"I'm afraid you're right," Frost agreed wryly.

"You're crazy! It took brains to put one over on me, so you ain't a sap, but I got the drop on you." Slug tilted the bottle for another huge swallow.

"I really ought to be leaving," said Frost.

"No you won't! I'm gonna kick you out when I get good and ready! I'm gonna kick you out and tear you to pieces. You'll like that, won't you?"

"No, I'm afraid I won't."

"Yes you will! You got to like it because you're gonna take it!"

"You might let me fortify myself. My bottle seems to be only half full now. The speed with which its contents disappear alarms me," said Frost, seeming anxious.

"You don't need nothin'. You ain't seen nothin' yet. Just wait'll I finish it off and start workin' on you. If I wasn't gonna bust you up, I'd feel kinda sorry for you."

"Don't feel sorry for me."

"The hell I won't! You're such a lousy dick I gotta feel sorry for you! You go and get yourself killed before you find out what it's all about. Santelle's a sap. He's the biggest sap in the East for letting that pet of his get so he can't handle it. But you're a bigger sap. You're the biggest sap in the whole damn country because you don't even find the answers before I knock the stuffin's out of you, only you're so damn skinny I guess you don't have much stuffin's."

"I know the answers. I know them even better than you do. There is nothing which you could tell me that I do not know already."

"You're crazier'n a bedbug! I can tell you what it's all about and I'm gonna, see? It's like this—"

"Save your breath."

"SHUT UP!" Slug yelled. "Shut up and keep your trap shut! When I talk, you're gonna listen and like it! Santelle knows a lot about science even if he is a sap, see? He's got a lot of junk here. He found a way of messin' up seeds so they grow cockeyed. He tried it out on animals and they turn into freaks like nothin' you ever laid eyes on, only he can't make 'em come out the way he wants. They get extra legs or don't get any at all or they're little shrimps or they grow to whopping size."

"Yes, yes, I know," Frost drawled.

"Sure you do! I'm tellin' you!" Slug roared. He took another gulp sufficient to paralyze most men. "Y'know, I kinda like this stuff. You ain't got another bottle, huh? It don't seem so strong but it tastes all right. A hundred proof. I guess it's pretty good. I bet I could get plastered if I had enough. Oh yeah, I was tellin' you what it's all about so I can bounce you off the wall.

"Santelle decides to let Alpha and Beta grow up without any help. They gotta live by themselves and learn whatever they can any way they can. He don't know what they'll turn into, but he's gonna find out and keep a record. Alpha and Beta was twins. Libby thought they was just freaks, but it pretty much broke her up. Then she found out about the dope or whatever it was Santelle used and she went nuts.

"Santelle wouldn't kill her and he was afraid to send her to the bughouse so he locked her up. Beta's only twelve now and look at him! Alpha was killed four years ago. Santelle used to let 'em run around by day. Alpha cornered him like he meant business and Santelle lost his head. He had a crowbar and smashed the brute. At that, Santelle just about lost out.

"That scared him plenty. The way Beta's growin', he's gonna get so big nobody could handle him, so Santelle has to hire the huskiest guys he can find. He has to pay us plenty. He has to get tough guys and crooks because they're the best ones to keep their traps shut. They don't talk. The first stuff I told you I got from Fritz. Fritz has been here longest because Santelle had to have somebody to help him and take orders right from the start. The rest of it I found out myself. Santelle has Alpha on the brain. He's afraid he's gonna have to take a murder rap if it leaks out. He don't want no one to know nothin' about the joint. He thinks he's gonna change plants and animals. He thinks he's gonna start a new race. He's nuts! He's a sap, that's what he is! Any guy who figures he's helpin' things along by turnin' out a bunch of apes like Beta is just a fancy dope. I'd just like to see Santelle—"

"I believe he is standing in the doorway behind you," Frost observed.

"What do you take me for, a bigger sap than you are?" Slug yelled. "Even if he was, it wouldn't make no difference—"

"You talk too much; indeed you do—oh much too much," Santelle complained. He held a bundle of papers under one arm and an automatic in his right hand. "I've expostulated with you, Slug, about your thirsty tongue and now I find it wordy. You are drunk. You must be drunk or you would have heard the shooting. No matter. You will hear it now—"

Slug Lonnergan, in spite of his bulk and the quantity of whisky he had absorbed, whirled around with savage speed. No speed could have been fast enough. Santelle's first bullet caught him in the arm and he took the next two in the chest. He couldn't get his own gun up as he staggered toward the flaming automatic, yet his finger tightened and slugs gouged the floor at Santelle's feet. Santelle stepped back as the body toppled.

Santelle aimed at Frost.

Frost snapped, "Santelle, with age you add stupidity to madness."

"Oh no, I add success to genius. I will not argue the point with my inferiors, certainly not; it is self-evident. I will merely say that it is self-evident, since you will not have time to realize its truth. You should not have come here, really you shouldn't. Your death is my gain."

"Slug expected to kill me and did not. You hope to kill me and cannot."

"You boast. I find it a most disagreeable trait except in the case of such authorities as myself." Santelle came forward.

"What authority?" Frost's voice dripped biting scorn as corrosive as acid. "You are not a scientist, because you are unable to tolerate failure; you lack the integrity to admit that your experiment was a failure; you have not the courage to start anew, and you cannot control your work.

"You are not a genius, for you have created nothing that will endure in the imagination of mankind. You are not a scholar, since you were unable to profit by the results of your research. You are not a wise man, because your strongest defenses were the outposts of New Eden, and your weakest its center which contained your most precious secrets. You are not a foolish man, in as much as you understood the difficulties you faced and prepared to meet them."

FROST'S WORDS became the summation of unalterable fact which is the sentence of doom. "But you have become psychopathic to a degree where your perspective nullifies the validity of your actions. You have preserved New Eden, its occupants, and its life at all costs. You committed psychological murder, so to speak, by driving Libby to insanity. You killed Alpha in order to preserve and further your work. You killed Sig Rafferty because he blackmailed you and threatened to talk. You expected the rain to support your alibi. No rain can erase the signs of a terrific struggle. Rafferty had been hit on the head again and again. Yet the grass was not trampled or the soil torn—"

"You have a small skill in perception," Santelle conceded. "If you had developed it you might have lived. I disposed of Sig, oh my, yes, quite completely. Slug here could have demolished him in one blow. I was compelled to use several. What is one or ten when the result is the same?"

"What is one or seven when the result is the same?" Frost stated with brief ambiguity. He stood up. "Your hatred of the logic that annihilates you is so strong that you abandon precaution. You fired six bullets into Slug. You have one left in the clip. Which will it be? I, who face you, or Beta who has just entered behind you?"

Santelle's face grew cunning. "Ah, no, I refuse to be tricked; positively I do. You are a very clever person, Mr. Frost, but not nearly so clever as I am. Will I turn around? Indeed I will not. You can talk. Beta cannot. Beta obeys when I command, but I find you most obstinate and recalcitrant. Your demise meets with my full approval; I might even go so far as to say my enthusiastic approval. Now—"

Mighty, webbed talons clamped around Santelle's throat. He left the floor as though hurled from a springboard. The jerk swung his arms downward. The papers scattered. His finger tightened convulsively on the trigger, and the shot grazed the creature's leg.

A curious dullness filmed Beta's eyes. The great, gray monster swayed slowly, its shaggy fur wet with rain and blood. A thick and guttural snarl rattled in its throat. A brittle snap cracked through the air, and Santelle's head lolled foolishly.

"Beta!" shrilled a voice from the darkness outside.

Like an automaton, the creature pivoted and padded away. It staggered uncertainly, with slow, ponderous tread. Santelle dangled a foot from the ground. Dumbly clinging to its burden, it tottered into the night.

Frost lighted a cigarette and exhaled pungently acrid smoke. He picked up the manuscript, strode out of the room, crossed the garage, and stood in the doorway.

Flame split the darkness with a momentary blast that only suggested the shapes of objects blown asunder.

Frost's face was inscrutable as he hiked to the greenhouse. He worked briefly on Jean Moray, but she remained dead to the world. He carried her out.

He was breathing harder by the time he reached the entrance to New Eden. Her weight dragged heavier with each step. He trudged along the road. When he came to the *Demon,* he looked weary.

With miraculous timing for one in a faint, Jean suddenly opened her eyes, looked up at his face, and murmured, "I think I'm all right now." She climbed into the car, while an expression of complete disgust briefly altered Frost's features.

The car gathered momentum. Jean watched Frost from the corners of her eyes. She finally decided it was safe to speak without drawing a caustic reply. "I don't understand why Mrs. Gant attacked your reflection in the mirror but not you in person."

"She didn't. From the angle at which you stood, you saw my image. She, in her position, was almost facing the mirror. She saw her own reflection. The violence she displayed was one of the important factors that led me to deduction of the truth. She tended toward having a split personality without being wholly irrational. For a rôle that she had played unwittingly, she hated her image, and tried to destroy it as a vicarious substitute for suicide. Since she did not kill herself when she had the opportunity upon escaping from New Eden, she must have hoped for vengeance and lived for it."

"Was that why you armed her and turned her loose?"

Frost shrugged for reply.

Jean asked, "What was that—that gray creature?"

The professor, with a far-away look, answered indirectly, "Santelle hoped to be the prophet of a new day. He made a discovery along whose same lines scientists are now engaged in research. Briefly, it has been learned that X rays, when turned upon the seeds of plants or the germ cells of plants or animals, produce hereditary mutations. They create new varieties and species by altering the genes and chromosomes. Thus far, however, no way has been found to control the changes. Freaks and monsters result as often as useful mutations.

"Santelle stood at a threshold that he could not cross. If he had succeeded, he would have been possibly the greatest man who ever lived. He would have been the master of a new creation. He would have had power to alter the characteristics of every existing species of plant and animal life. He would have been able to speed up evolution and create new species. He would have brought supermen into being. He would have dominated human thought and radically altered the course of human affairs. As it is, he will achieve a measure of posthumous recognition through publication of his records upon New Eden. Yet it is doubtful whether science will ever reach the goal to which he aspired."

"Why not?"

"How can it be reached until experiment points the way? Who would knowingly and willingly submit to such experiment? Would you? If you were married and given the opportunity, would you run the risk of having children who were abnormal in the hope that they would be prodigies or supermen?"

"Why yes," said Jean unexpectedly, turning her head toward Frost with a demure smile upon her lips and approval in her beautiful, guileless face. "You haven't given me much time to think but I believe I will accept your offer."

Frost's answer could not conceivably be termed anything but a snort.

BONE CRUSHER

Frost's tone was one of lofty condescension:
"You are mad—not brilliantly mad but hopelessly—"

THE DAY BEFORE, he had told her to take the morning off and amuse herself as she saw fit. He gave no reason. He seldom bothered to explain unless he had to, and not always then.

"He" was I.V. Frost, professor of various sciences who became bored with the stuffy atmosphere of classroom routine and retired in order to indulge his eccentric whims whenever he chose and to specialize in the solution of crime enigmas. He was an unlovely and improbable detective, because nature and the laws of chance could scarcely have produced a thinner or taller scarecrow, a bleaker visage, a more complex personality, or a more inhumanly logical mind.

He was neurotic and given to moods of ascetic isolation. He worked in bursts of furious nervous energy at infrequent intervals. He didn't like run-of-the-mill murders, robberies, swindles, and other material in the ledger of crime. He refused more cases than he accepted. No one had ever been able to figure out any consistent basis for his fees.

He had presented bills ranging from one cent to two hundred and nineteen thousand, eighty-seven dollars, and sixteen cents. The only times he made an appearance before noon were those when he had been up all night. He never resorted to disguise because nothing short of a series of major operations could have made him less striking in appearance.

"She" was Jean Moray, his heart-wrecking assistant. It had taken her more than a year to obtain even this scant information about Ivy Frost. With the reticence of a clam, he shut himself off from close human contacts by invisible but none the less strong barriers. It was not so much that he loved his own company as that he found little stimulus from most of the genus homo; and rather than be bored by other people, he preferred to bore himself.

So she thought, though she was never sure. Frost had a habit of sliding out of one category and into another about the time she was certain she had him pinned down. His attitude kept her in a state of turmoil.

Just because the ivory tower stood so aloof, she tried the harder to break it down, with woman's unerring resentment against whatever ignores her. Yet the closer she got, the more hesitant she became. It would be fatal if his existence grew indispensable to hers, while hers remained a matter of supreme indifference in his life.

What emphasized her irritation was his blithe disregard for her beauty. Jean Moray bore not the least resemblance to a movie star. She had a genuine and distinctive beauty, exotic because of her high cheek bones and wide-set, greenish-gray eyes, the graceful and tempting curve of her lips, and a slightly better than streamlined figure.

She left her parcels at 11 State Street, and shortly before noon admitted herself to the mansion at 13. It was characteristic of her that she arrived during the morning, since Frost had told her not to arrive during the morning.

THE USUAL MISCELLANY of mail had been shoved through the letter box into the hall. She scooped it up and deposited it on the library table. She stared with disapproval at the eyes, some human and others of the bird or animal kingdoms, which Frost had placed in various corners. He asserted that their presence kept him alert by giving the impression that he was always under the surveillance of hostile eyes, but if that was his real reason, she deemed it insufficient. The eyes, even though artificial, gave her the jitters. She longed for an excuse to crack them or toss them on an ash heap.

Glancing into the laboratory, she saw no sign that Frost had used it this morning. She was about to attack the mail when a faint but tempting aroma wafted from the kitchen and reminded her that the time had come for a modicum of pabulum. Jean had a healthy appetite which she tortured in order to preserve her faultless topography. She was a Spartan against her inclinations.

When she entered the kitchen, she saw Frost's long form slouched over the stove. He looked somewhat sinister, as though preparing a poisonous brew. Whatever his task, it absorbed his attention as fully as if he were making a microscopic analysis or a test for bloodstains. A great assortment of jars, cans, packages, and containers lay upon the table. He was intently watching a pot in which a fluid of gelatinous consistency simmered, and which gave off the appetizing aroma that had attracted her.

Jean looked on. Finally, when Frost continued to refuse to recognize her presence, she asked with a mixture of pique and curiosity, "What's that? It smells delicious."

"Soup," he answered laconically, without turning his head.

"What kind? I don't seem to know it."

"Bird's-nest soup."

"Bird's-nest soup? What a strange name! What's it made of?"

"What do you suppose it's made of—vegetables and beef?" Frost drawled with a trace of impatience. "Oddly enough, it happens to consist of precisely what its name would imply—a bird's nest. It is a particular kind of bird's nest found in cliffs along the coast of China—"

"Ugh!" Jean wrinkled her nose. "Don't bother about any more details. Bird's-nest soup, indeed! I'd as soon eat snakes!"

"Help yourself. There's a jar of snake snacks on the table behind you," Frost blandly replied. "They're quite good, a bit reminiscent of smoked eel."

"They don't interest me."

"They would if you were hungry enough." Frost paused in his labors after seeing that the broth was simmering properly. "Your attitude, Miss Moray, is characteristic of a surprising percentage of Americans. I doubt whether any other country than ours has so many baseless prejudices, such arbitrary likes and dislikes, such fads and fashions in diet. One year calories are the rage; then it's raw foods or vegetarianism; now vitamins appear to be in demand. Perhaps the timidity of civilized man, with respect to food, is merely another manifestation of human nature's inability to expand. The species shows infantile monotony in the sameness of its diet."

"I can't make head or tail out of that. You speak in contradictions. First you say people go in for all sorts of experiments, then you say they don't have variety enough."

"Precisely. They confine their experiments to the foods to which they are accustomed. If they want to gain weight, they consume more potatoes and desserts; if they want to reduce, they go in for lamb chops and lettuce; if they desire vitamins, they soak up milk and fruit juices.

They simply vary the proportions that familiar foods have had in their diet. They seldom venture farther afield or seek uncommon viands.

"For instance, there is a richly flavorous Chinese pheasant in one of those tins behind you; another contains preserved mango; among the rest you will find dried abalone, pickled squid, a Thuringian blood sausage, Hawaiian breadfruit, South American peccary, powdered alligator eggs, ewe's milk cheese that is almost able to walk, dried locusts that—"

"Locusts!" Jean yelped.

"Why not? They are considered a delicacy by Arabs and tribes of North Africa. American Indians in the western deserts have considered them a dietary staple in the past. Why should civilized man be squeamish? Cattle eat grass; man eats cattle, and eventually grass grows luxuriantly from man, doubtless to fatten other cattle for later men, ad infinitum. Locusts live on vegetation; why shouldn't man regard them in the same light as cattle? Why should he object to them when he accepts snails, squids, sea anemones, crabs, and similar scavengers whose diet if closely scrutinized would not exhibit nearly the same happy results as that of the locust? In truth—"

THE SHARP ringing of the bell interrupted him.

"Take it," said Frost. "I am not to be disturbed except for a matter of peculiar and exceptional novelty."

For an interval after his assistant's exit, he regarded the broth with a brooding eye. His features stood out in profile like those of some lean, predatory bird about to strike. His nostrils quivered as he sniffed the aroma of the simmering pot. He cocked his head sidewise in an attitude of keen attentiveness. He sighed, fished a long and pungent cigarette from his pocket, lighted it. He exhaled an island of smoke as though to submerge the delicate scent of the quondam bird's nest, which he left untasted as he strode out of the kitchen.

He met his assistant at the door.

"Oh, I was just coming after you," Jean said.

"So I observed. Her story had better be a good one."

"Her story? Why, how did you know—"

"What are ears for if not to hear, or eyes, if not to see, or a brain, if not to employ it at least once in a great while for the purposes of ratiocination and deduction?"

The caller nervously twisted a handkerchief as they entered. A rather plump but attractive brunette of thirty, with a narrow forehead and full cheeks, looked uncertainly between Frost and his assistant as though she hardly knew what to say.

"It's about my husband, Arthur Kaliters," she blurted. "Dr. Yungrud thinks he's going mad. He, my husband, that is, claimed he saw a man pull his hand off a few days ago and then the next day a strange woman followed him around eating lighted cigarettes, and then another stranger swelled up and down like a balloon—"

"Where is your husband?" A spark had begun to kindle in Frost's eyes.

"I don't know. You see, I talked to Dr. Yungrud by phone yesterday and he told me to spend the night away from home because Arthur was developing a persecution complex and he wanted to find out if that would help any. Then I saw Arthur and told him I had to see my parents last night, but he didn't seem much interested. Then this morning I got all upset—I haven't been home yet—but I'm sure that oily psy—psychia—"

"Psychiatrist."

"I'm sure he's got some terrible hold over Arthur or maybe there's a whole gang mixed up in it—and the other crazy things that Arthur says he saw—"

The telephone rang. Jean lifted the receiver and listened. She turned to Frost. "It's Inspector Frick of the homicide bureau. He wants to know if you can come right away to the corner of Woodroad and Haven—"

Frost pursed his lips. "Woodroad and Haven? That undeveloped marshy section where the city is only now beginning to lay down a decent road? Hmm. It must be homicide, of course. But Frick would not summon me merely to view the body of another gangster taken for a ride. And the city is paving an extension," Frost mused. He lapsed into silence, but gradually a crooked smile touched his features.

"Tell Frick that I know what he wants me for, that I am already pursuing the investigation along lines of my own, and that I am sending you out to survey the scene. Tell him to delay the work of removal until you arrive."

Mrs. Kaliters clutched at her throat all at once. Her face had gone white and strained. "My husband—"

Frost flicked ashes in the general direction of an already overloaded tray. "Possibly. I think not. Miss Moray, when you finish your examination of the—sights—at Woodroad and Haven, join us at the Kaliters' residence."

"Which is at—"

"Woodroad Avenue—1701," Mrs. Kaliters volunteered.

Frost raised his eyebrows in a quizzical glance.

II.

ACROSS the light snow that had fallen during the night, a single line of footprints marched up the sidewalk toward the house at 1701 Woodroad Avenue.

"That's amazing," Frost observed.

"What is? The footprints? They're just an ordinary set."

"That's the amazing factor. It is past noon, yet last night's snow has not been removed, and only a single set of footprints extends toward the house. None return."

"What's wrong about that?"

"Where are the prints of other members of the household? The postman's tread? Tracks of callers and delivery clerks?"

Mrs. Kaliters stooped, then hurried toward the house. "They look like Henry's steps—"

"Henry?"

"Jenkins, the butler. He has a long, narrow foot. I told him to take the night off and he evidently came back this morning."

Frost stopped her at the door. "Wait until I return."

"Why? I must go in. Arthur may—"

"Wait," said Frost with a cold, inexorable command. "I shall return in a few minutes."

Without a backward glance, Frost hiked around the side of the house. His unbuttoned coat flapped in the wind. Hatless and barehanded, he seemed oblivious to cold and indifferent to winter. He trailed sparks in his wake, sparks that rode with fumes as stinging as particles of ice.

He stopped to examine a series of tracks underneath casement windows. The long, narrow footprints of the front sidewalk marched away from the windows toward the hedge that surrounded the house and lot. Another set of footprints, broader and shorter, extended from the hedge to the window. Among them was a swath about a foot and a half in width with two deep grooves in its center. The swath also lay between the windows and hedge.

Frost circled the house. There were no other prints; just the long thin ones that went in the front door, the same ones that started under a side window and went to the hedge, a squatter set that began at the hedge and advanced toward the window, and the indeterminate swath.

Frost returned to the casement windows and pushed them open. He stepped through as they swung inward.

The dark-haired, fleshy man sitting at a desk did not speak. He had once been handsome in an arrogant fashion. He was no longer very pretty. Few men are when their eyes have popped out from the force of a bullet through the temple.

Frost walked to the front door and opened it. "Bad news," he announced with what seemed brutal brusqueness. "Your husband is dead—murdered."

Color drained out of Mrs. Kaliters' face and turned it into putty. As she fainted, Frost broke her fall and eased her to a hall settee. He then put in a call to the homicide bureau and left a message for Inspector Frick.

He returned to the man whose eyes had popped out. The man sat at a solid-walnut desk covered with plate glass. The glass was clean except for the ring left by a tumbler. There was no tumbler. There were only a few microscopic splinters, sharply curved and thin. A .45 rested beyond the man's finger tips. Frost broke the chamber and discovered two bullets. On the floor he found an empty shell and across the room the slug that had killed.

In front of the dead man lay a batch of closely scrawled papers. For a suicide note, it was of exceptional length. The manuscript read:

> My Darling Cory:
>
> It is evident that I am on the verge of madness. I can tell it by your eyes. I can see it clearly in Dr. Yungrud's attitude. I know it on the basis of the queer hallucinations that have obsessed me for the past week. I could go on, and end my days in a sanitarium. That is unthinkable for a man of my wealth, position, and vanity. I could hope for recovery. That would mean nothing to me since I would always face the specter of relapse. The only solution is final and complete—the way out.
>
> Forgive me. I prefer to act upon my own initiative rather than yield to the ministrations of others. I leave you fairly

well provided for. Whatever grief you may feel will disappear in time. I loved you neither well nor wisely, but perhaps in death I can compensate for what I did not offer in life. So be it. I satisfy my own will by the taking of my own life; perhaps I give you the freedom I suspect you want; in any case, I break an intolerable dilemma.

Dr. Yungrud has not said it in so many words, but he plainly believes me to be the victim of a persecution complex. Years of subconscious fears have brought it on. You know the nature of some of those fears. Possibly you have guessed or suspected the others. I list them here to show what havoc I have caused and to explain why I feel justified in ending my existence.

Twelve years ago, before I married you, I led the more or less irresponsible life of any young man with more money than was good for him. One night, after a wild party, I was arrested for drunken driving. When I sobered up, I found myself facing much more serious charges. I had run down a pedestrian named Samuel Reagin who was maimed for life as a result of his injuries. I had left the scene of the accident. It took all the influence I had to get out of that jam. I escaped a prison sentence but lost my driver's license and was put on probation. I forestalled a damage suit by settling out of court through my attorneys. The sum was considerable. It amounted to a conditional trust fund of $100,000. During life I agreed to pay the income from this fund to Reagin.

Two years later, I became involved in an affair with Mona Lita, a nightclub hostess. I wrote several compromising letters and appeared in some highly indiscreet snapshots. The infatuation might have lasted, but about that time I met you and dropped Mona. There were scenes. She threatened to cause plenty of trouble. I don't know if she was genuinely fond of me or simply took me over the hurdles for what she could get. At any rate, to ward off a breach-of-promise suit for which she had ample grounds, I made a settlement. I established another limited trust fund similar to the other. While living I agreed to pay her the income, conditional upon her remaining single. If she wanted, the $100,000 and income thereof were to revert to me.

Four years ago I got myself into another bad jam, the worst of them all. That was the time I had an argument with the caretaker one night after I'd been drinking too much. The upshot was the struggle in which he received injuries to which he succumbed some months later. I established a trust fund like the others for his widow, Mrs. Limmer. Since there were no witnesses to the altercation, charges were finally dropped. What no one knew was that there *had* been a witness: the butler, Henry Jenkins. His testimony could easily have sent me to prison for a considerable term. I boosted his wages by the simple expedient of establishing a fourth trust fund in his name.

Not long after, I began wondering about my sanity. Temper, mistakes in judgment, and whisky had cost me my reputation and a large, part of my fortune. I finally went to a psychiatrist, Dr. Yungrud, to be psychoanalyzed.

Of course, I told him all the details he wanted to know and which I could remember about my life. His fees seemed exorbitant, but too late I saw what a hold over my life I had given him in case he chose to violate my confidences. The matter never came into the open, nor am I positively sure that such thoughts occurred to him. At any rate, up went another trust fund, the income ostensibly and actually serving as an annual retainer for Dr. Yungrud's services in lieu of any and all other claims or fees.

Through the depression, the rest of my fortune shrank rapidly. For the past year financial worries have weighed heavily on me. In the event of my death, you would not find much to rescue out of the wreckage, except the insurance which I managed to keep paid up. That $100,000 is practically all that is left. Yet other things have recently convinced me that it would be better to make my exit and leave you with that moderate security rather than try to struggle along by borrowing on the insurance to a point where my death would leave you with nothing.

These recent events were the hallucinations that again raised doubts about my sanity. Yungrud has not been able to offer me much consolation so far. I am afraid he believes as I do.

A week ago, I went out for exercise one evening. Snow began to fall. I enjoyed watching the flakes come down and stayed out longer than I intended. When I strolled toward home, it was quite dark, except for the street lamps. As I approached the last of these, on the corner nearest here, I became aware of a large, bulky man standing at the edge of the patch of illumination cast by the lamp. When I passed him, he seemed gigantic. I felt uneasy and unconsciously hurried my steps. My uneasiness persisted. Some instinct warned me that he was watching or stealthily following me. I risked a glance backward as I turned in at our gate.

He was looking toward me. The hat pulled low over his forehead kept his features in shadow, but his eyes burned with an unnatural intensity. With a slow, deliberate motion, the more horrible because he did it as casually as you or I would rub our eyes or brush our hair, he seized his left hand with his right. He tugged and twisted, with his gaze still fastened on me. He pulled his left hand off as if it were so much cheese. Dark drops dribbled toward the ground. He lowered his glance as though his attention had been distracted. Wasting hardly a second on what he had done, he strode off in the darkness, the stump of his left arm thrust into his overcoat pocket, while the left hand remained clutched in his right palm.

My face must have been white when I entered the house. I remember you telling me I looked as if I had received a shock. I started to tell you the truth but you gave me the queerest look and asked me if I wasn't feeling well.

I took a stiff drink of brandy and retired but I couldn't get the picture out of my mind. I was positive I had seen what I thought I saw. I was equally positive that such things simply do not happen in life. Then the only explanation could be that my grasp on sanity was slipping. Finally I dressed and went out again. I walked to the light where I thought I had seen the occurrence. I found dark stains, then partly covered by the falling snow.

I made an appointment with Yungrud the following afternoon after a sleepless night and after the encounter had preyed on my thoughts all morning. At that time he said I was worrying too much and needed a rest. He recommended a sea voyage.

It was a gray day. When I reached home in the late afternoon, I returned to the lamp-post to find out if there was some obstruction or other that might have caused an optical illusion.

A plainly dressed woman, with a pale face, was standing there. I only intended to give her a passing glance, but in that glance I saw her put a lighted cigarette to her lips and work it into her mouth. She gulped it, swallowed it. While I watched, she opened her hand bag and took out another cigarette which she lighted and ate. I was so hypnotized and spellbound that I forgot myself. I must have watched her for several minutes, during which time she did away with dozens of cigarettes.

When I couldn't stand it any longer, I walked up to her. She began to back away with a very peculiar expression on her face as if she was afraid of me.

I said to her, "Pardon me, madam, but I've been watching you for some moments. I'm at a loss to know why you are consuming cigarettes. Would you mind telling me?"

She continued to back away, still with that strange expression on her face, and said, "I don't know what you mean. I don't smoke. You've been staring at me while I was powdering my nose. If you don't go away, I—I—" Then she turned around and ran off.

It was probably a mistake to mention that happening to you. It upset you as much as the other one. It caused me far more trouble, and after a night of bad dreams, I decided to spare you the details of any further hallucinations that might pester me.

The next day I went to a firm of private detectives. I had some idea of having them keep a man at my heels. When I explained what was wrong. they suddenly lost interest, and told me in so many words that what I needed was a doctor, not a detective.

I then made another appointment with Yungrud. Perhaps their advice worked out for the best on the whole. I still had hopes that there might be some reasonable explanation for what I had seen. But if an unbiased observer failed to substantiate me and saw nothing of what I saw, my last shred of faith in myself would be gone forever.

Since those first two experiences, I have had several more, culminating in last night's grotesque development. I did not tell you about those in between, nor is there any purpose to be served by enumerating them here now. They would only distress you. However, I was so shaken by what I witnessed last night that I blurted out part of it to you before I regained control of myself. Since you heard part, I might as well tell the rest.

I had dinner with friends in town last night. They were going to the theater but I begged off from that and took a taxi at Times Square. I thought the long ride home would do me good but it did nothing to settle my upset mind. I paid off the driver and watched him roll away. When I turned toward the gate, I saw a small man standing by the lamp-post. He was not much bigger than a pygmy. For some reason, his presence disquieted me strangely. Perhaps it was because he stared so fixedly at me. I took a few steps toward the gate, then, moved by an unaccountable impulse that I now heartily curse, I looked in his direction again.

He was fully a foot taller than he had been a few moments before. I felt as if hands were crawling over my scalp. I closed my eyes and shook my head vigorously in an effort to clear it. When I ventured another glance at the stranger, he was still staring fixedly at me, but now he was as tall as I am, and visibly growing taller. A sudden horror overwhelmed me and I broke for the house. I ran up the sidewalk but when I reached the porch, the demon of perversity made me risk another glance. The man was as little as when I had first laid eyes on him; and he was trotting down the street at a leisurely gait.

While I looked, his head began to revolve like a hideous knob on a pivot until it completed a half circle, so that I saw a face where the base of his skull should have been. He walked off, his eyes fastened on me, his features rising outlandishly above his back and shoulders. I watched him and the head that had revolved till he passed out of sight in the darkness. His slow, nonchalant gait, hardly any faster than a worm's progress, gave me unspeakable chills. I don't know why, except that it was so utterly sinister and had something of fatal finality in it.

At that moment, I made my decision. I could go on and wait until I saw monsters swarm around my bed. I could eventually go to an institution and find my world peopled with creatures that pulled their limbs off at random or changed their shape and size. Or I could end this gradual deterioration before it reached a more malignant stage. For that reason, I was secretly relieved when you told me this afternoon that you were spending to-night with your family. I intended to give Jenkins the night off but you seem to have anticipated me by giving him the order yourself. I prefer to be alone when I let the curtain fall upon my life.

Now that you know the circumstances and the reasons for my act, I hope that you will forgive me. In a financial sense, and perhaps from the standpoint of happiness or well being, you will be better off without me. As for me, I am glad to be free of the burden of care and worry.

Arthur.

III.

A BELL interrupted Frost's reading of this curious message. He skimmed the last pages and replaced the manuscript on the table. He went to the door to admit his assistant.

Jean glanced at the motionless figure of Mrs. Kaliters who was still lying on the hallway settee. "What happened to her?"

"Nothing. She fainted when I told her her husband had been murdered."

Jean mustered as angry a glower as she could to her unnaturally white face. "You told her—as bluntly as that?"

"Of course. A hysterical woman would have been a liability. And the shock was a blessing that gave her a respite in oblivion before she faces disagreeable realities once more. I take it you did not have much success in identifying the corpse?"

Jean looked as if she was going to be ill. "Ugh! They'll never identify it or even get it to look like anything human. You should have seen Inspector Frick's face."

"Inspector Frick's facial prowess may be of interest to students of physiognomy but will scarcely serve to advance the solution of two murders."

"Two?"

"Certainly. Did you think I meant the corpse you examined when I mentioned the murder of Arthur Kaliters? His body lies here. The gruesome thing you saw was some one else."

A fleetingly suspicious inflection came into Jean's voice. "You were out there?"

"No."

"Then how do you know what I saw?"

Frost said impatiently, "Deduction, more or less pure and comparatively simple. Inspector Frick telephoned a request that I come to the corner of Woodroad and Haven. That is in an undeveloped part of Greater New York where a good roadbed of asphalt is only now being laid down.

"Frick would not summon me except for homicide, homicide with some striking or distinctive feature. A gangster taken for a ride? No. Merely the body of some one killed elsewhere and dumped there? No. Why, there? Because the city is building a road. What is essential to the construction of an asphalt road that could be profitably used in connection with murder, and which would have a spectacular touch or leave a mark of originality? A steam roller. How would a steam roller serve? By making such unrecognizable pulp out of a body that identification would be virtually impossible."

"Some day," Jean prophesied, "somebody will come to you with a queer story and without budging from the laboratory you'll deduce who was killed and how and why and where and all the rest of it. Then what'll you do when you get the analysis of crime down to such a fine art that there isn't anything exciting in it any more?"

Frost appraised her with scientific impersonality. "I might try my own hand at homicide. I can think of several ingenious methods for making you an object of deep controversy among coroners. But you haven't post-mortemized the object at Woodroad and Haven."

Jean edged away from him slightly. She didn't quite relish the detachment he showed or his readiness to assist her demise. "There isn't much to say. You've already guessed what I found. I got out there and met Frick and the rest of the squad. When I left, they were still trying to figure out what to do about it.

"Woodroad Avenue used to be a dirt road running through flat, marshy land. Cheap apartment buildings have started to go up around there recently, which I suppose is why the road is being improved. But for half a mile square there aren't any buildings. The cross streets are being marked out and paved for a short block on each side of Woodroad. The avenue has been paved as far as Haven Street. That's where they left the steam roller last night. There isn't a watchman. There isn't any one around there at night to steal anything. The body would have been found sooner, but the paving job was halted while they cleared snow off the main streets.

"One look made me ill. What there was was practically part of the pavement. The steam roller had been run over the body several times until it got as flat as the asphalt. It was just a sort of red, gooey carpet. You couldn't tell its age, sex, or size. There weren't any clues to identify it or indicate who left it there. The police were wondering how they could remove it to the morgue and what could be done about it if they succeeded."

"Were there any articles of fiber, metal, or clothing?"

"No."

FROST PERSISTED. "None whatever?"

"Absolutely none. Good grief, what a way to die!"

"That was neither the place nor the method of death," Frost corrected her.

"That isn't what the police thought."

"It's what they *will* think. I confess myself a trifle disappointed that you have not made an obvious deduction."

"Indeed?"

"If there was no fiber or metal, the victim was not bound or tied to a stake in the roadbed, yet the clothing had been removed to prevent identification. If he had been alive and conscious, he certainly would have been rendered helpless. Since he was not trussed up, he must have been unconscious. Since it takes time to start a steam roller, time in which an unconscious person might awaken and escape, he must have been dead.

"If dead, why the additional mutilation? Of many reasons possible, there are only two probable: a frightful hatred that persisted beyond death; or the desirability of having a missing person stay missing instead of being identified dead."

"Who's missing?"

"My dear Miss Moray! Several hundreds of the thousands of persons who annually disappear in these United States are never heard of again."

"You don't know who's missing and a corpse can't be identified and the murderer didn't leave any clues. That's just splendid? Maybe it would be a good idea to grow onions. The private detective business doesn't seem to be doing so well these days."

"Pardon me, but I do know who is missing and I propose to identify the corpse by identifying the killer through the clues that he carried away with him."

"You mean the clothing?"

"Certainly not. He will have destroyed it. I mean the clues that he does not know about. Read the suicide message which names the killer and his motive. Taking into consideration the factors in this room and surrounding the second corpse, you can easily reconstruct the entire crime."

Frost began opening drawers in the desk and rummaging through the contents. He found bundles of canceled checks which he flipped through rapidly. From time to time, he laid one aside until he had abstracted more than a dozen. They bore dates of irregular intervals during the preceding four years, were made out to "Cash," ranged in amount from $100 to $1,000, and had been uniformly indorsed by "John K. Enrique."

He next went through a telephone directory and jotted down several addresses. When he finished, he looked at them with an air of slightly cynical detachment. He glanced at his watch and asked, "Miss Moray, are you very good at hitting a target by throwing things at it?"

"Sure, if it's a big enough target," said Jean modestly. "I used to play kitten ball a good deal. Why?"

"Excellent. Get some bricks, golf balls, or whatever object you can manage best. At precisely four o'clock, be outside the residence of Mona Lita at 2761 Woodlawn Avenue. Choose a rear window and smash it. Don't wait to see the results. Drive to the home of Samuel Reagin at Woodlawn and One hundred eighty-seventh Street. At five o'clock, you will be making inquiries of him concerning his knowledge of Arthur Kaliters and Henry Jenkins. You will be a private investigator employed by Mrs. Kaliters. Then return to 13 State Street."

"But those are some of the people for whom he set up the trust funds. According to the conditions he made, they would lose out by his death. Why them?"

"Kaliters was a trifle careless with his English. 'While living' and 'during life' may have meant either that the trust fund was to last as long as Kaliters was alive, or that it should operate during the life of the beneficiary."

"Isn't there anything worth its face value in this case?" Jean complained. "Even the simplest statements suddenly turn out to have a double meaning."

"The murder does offer some neat problems in deduction," Frost admitted, "but the answers are by no means difficult. The murderer has shown a certain amount of cunning. It will be interesting to watch him trap himself."

FOOTSTEPS fell heavily on the porch as the police arrived, and Jean hurried on her way. She was not detained a moment, for the department was indebted to Frost and his assistant for the solution of many a puzzling mystery.

Fifteen minutes later, Inspector Frick of the homicide bureau exclaimed, "Confound it, Frost, what right have you to turn a lunatic suicide into a murder case?"

"Arthur Kaliters was a vain man. He started to commit suicide, but he would not have chosen and did not employ a pistol. Examine the pupils of his eyes and you will find them contracted. He took an overdose of sleeping tablets and washed them down with a tumbler of water which at that time stood on the desk. You will find some splinters there. They are too thin and too sharply curved to have come from a broken table glass. They are, however, of the precise thickness and curvature of the ordinary commercial tube that contains ten tablets of veronal.

"Also, notice the checks made out to 'Cash.' The indorsement 'John K. Enrique' is an obvious anagram of Henry Jenkins."

Frick's face lighted up. "I get it. The butler had been blackmailing

Kaliters for additional hush money. Kaliters was probably pretty well stupefied by the time the butler got home to-night, and started a quarrel during the course of which Jenkins shot him."

Frost tapped a cigarette. "And how do you account for the mysterious footprints? The set which leads toward the house, but does not lead away, and whose owner is nowhere within the house?"

"That's easy," Frick explained. "A burglar got into the house, or else was standing outside the window and saw the murder. Whichever it was, Jenkins killed him too and dragged the body off. Jenkins' footprints run from the window to the hedge. The broad trail was made by the body and the parallel grooves are where the heels dragged.

"Say! I've got a hunch that *that's* the body the steam roller ran over! Jenkins drives off with the body intending to dump it somewhere. This place is on Woodlawn Avenue. He passes the stretch where they're putting in a new road, sees his chance, and not only gets rid of the stiff but makes damn sure it won't be identified.

"Ivy, this is one case we've cleared up in short order. It's practically in the bag already, don't you think?"

"Why, yes, I do," said Frost innocently.

"I thought so. We'll get a confession out of Jenkins as soon as he's brought in. I'll have a pick-up sent out over the teletype system right away. What's your hurry? Where you going?"

"I seen no reason to remain since you seem to have the problem well in hand here. If you should want me later, you'll find me in my laboratory."

"Maybe I'll drop around about six unless you're too busy."

"I will only be hunting for half dollars and putting peas in walnut shells," Frost drawled absent-mindedly as he departed.

The pure blank essence of noncomprehension had a field day on the inspector's features.

IV.

THE RAVEN-HAIRED angel of the reception room in Dr. Yungrud's suite was tall for a woman and profitably attractive for his clientele. She knew her business, his business, and everybody else's business, which knowledge, judiciously stored away in her memory, kept her well supplied with such absolute essentials as mink coats and platinum watches.

She was typing file cards with neatness, precision, and a minimum expenditure of energy when the door opened. She watched with considerable interest the entrance of the ghost of Hamlet, grown a good deal taller and more inscrutable during the centuries since Shakepeare's day.

Said the specter, "Tell Dr. Yungrud that I will see him."

"Have you an appointment?"

"No."

"Dr. Yungrud's office hours are from ten to twelve. Other hours are by appointment only."

Frost observed in a matter-of-fact tone, "Dr Yungrud's ignorance concerning the fundamentals of his profession is exceeded not only by the stupidity of his schedule but also by the general atrophy of what may once have been his intelligence."

Miss Raven-hair took an instant liking to the gaunt stranger but suppressed the inclination to laugh. "When would you like an appointment and what is the name?"

"The name is I. V. Frost. The subject is murder. The appointment will be immediately. My business cannot wait. Dr. Yungrud's amorous indulgences can."

The receptionist became the epitome of dignity and hauteur. "Dr. Yungrud's time is extremely valuable. I'm sure he will not care to hear insinuations—"

"My dear young woman, surely the deduction of the obvious should occasion neither resentment nor surprise. When I note that his last visitor was feminine, that the appointment began an hour and a half ago, that it has not yet terminated, that your glance strayed just now toward the door to his private office and afterward to the clock, and that a knowing smile then flitted across your face briefly, I would be a traitor to logic if I failed to infer the facts."

Without another word, Miss Raven-hair rose and walked to the door marked "Private." She rapped ostentatiously, returned to her desk to pick up some file cards that she did not need, went back to the door, and knocked again. She took a little time to pat her hair and smoothed some invisible wrinkles from her dress. A few additional seconds were required to brush imaginary lint from her cuff before she turned the knob and closed the door behind her

Hardly a minute could have lapsed before she came out into the reception room again with her features molded into stony determination. Her expression changed swiftly as she found herself alone. Her intended utterances died unspoken. She walked across the room and opened the main door, but there was no one outside.

With an almost imperceptible shrug, she resumed her seat at the desk. She had encountered queer people before. Doubtless she would be exposed to many another unfathomable character and meaningless occurrence so long as she held an occupation that entailed contact with aberrations of the mind.

She felt, however, a persistent impression that the room had somehow changed. From time to time she looked up from her work as the illusion continued. Not till half an hour later did she realize that Dr. Yungrud's dark-blue overcoat no longer hung upon the rack. It had been replaced by a black one.

AT EIGHTEEN, Mona Lita had been a sloe-eyed siren of the night clubs who would have "wowed" the foot-loose citizens if she had possessed something besides sex appeal. She wowed them anyway on such occasions as she had the opportunity, but she couldn't quite make the grade against Broadway's cutthroat competition. Her titian-haired beauty was relegated to the lesser forms of piracy—hat-check girl, cigarette vendor, occasional line work.

At twenty-eight, Mona Lita had magically become an ash blonde with a softer figure that had collected a few more pounds. Her financial worries had been taken care of by the generosity of one Arthur Kaliters. That security provided her with a sybaritic sort of existence that was more hectic than healthy.

She arose well before mid-afternoon. With a Scotch-and-soda pick-up and a shower out of the way, she permitted herself a frugal breakfast of tomato juice, a pair of eggs, a half dozen crisp slices of bacon, several toasted English muffins with jam, and three cups of black coffee.

Thereafter she lolled around in lounging pajamas and smoked one cigarette on top of another while wish-dreaming through an assortment of movie magazines. At three forty-five the doorbell rang and she lazily sighed for a maid. She didn't keep a maid. She didn't believe in servants because they found out too much about you.

When she got around to answering a subsequent ring, her eyes grew big as she tilted her head to look up at one of the longest and most impressive men she had ever met. He wasn't good-looking but he had strangely compelling black eyes and an inner drive that she felt like a solid impact. She knew magnetism when she met it because it was her own specialty. For that reason, she maintained a wary reserve, especially when she learned who he was and why he had burst in upon her.

She tried out her personality, but for once it didn't work. She might as well have made overtures to the Sphinx. She gave the simplest and most uninformative answers possible, but had the irritating conviction that Frost knew her answers before she spoke and read her mind before she herself was aware of what was rattling around in its great open spaces.

The interview progressed to her complete dissatisfaction. When, at four o'clock, a loud crash and the tinkling of much glass heralded the demise of a rear window in her flat, she bounced to her feet as though the sofa had spawned a brood of full-grown lobsters.

"Allow me to investigate," Frost volunteered with undue alacrity.

"No, no, you mustn't; stay here! My bedroom—it's a sight—I'll be right back—wait here—it can't be anything serious!" she flung back breathlessly as she lost both mules in an effort to depart faster than her gleaming legs were willing.

"Well, if you insist," Frost temporized, but she didn't stop to hear whatever else he may have said.

There was ruin in her bedroom. Some one had chosen a devious method of presenting her with a brand-new baseball for which she had no conceivable use. It occurred to her that children do not play baseball in winter, and when she peered out the window she was indeed unable to find any youngsters within eyesight.

The cold draft chilled her. Nettled, she slipped into a mandarin robe and returned to her visitor. He had vanished. A man so tall and gaunt could not easily have concealed himself in the apartment, but she nevertheless went through its limited hiding places. While thus engaged, she discovered a hundred-dollar bill. It reposed on the shelf in a closet from which every single pair of her gloves had been removed.

Mona poured herself a bigger and better Scotch and soda.

FROST noiselessly eased himself over the window sill and drifted across the room like an animated shadow. From below came the murmur of voices—the caressingly musical tones of Jean Moray, and the husky answers of Samuel Reagin. He listened at the door for a few moments. The voices were too muted by walls and distance for words to be distinguished.

On a bureau he noticed a photograph of Reagin. It showed a dark-haired slim-waisted man of indeterminate age who wore a weary mustache. His arms were long for his body and the lines of his shoulders made a square. Frost took the picture in at a glance on his way to a closet, where he remained for several minutes.

He emerged with a coat and trousers from Mr. Reagin's wardrobe. Mr. Reagin did not yet know of his good fortune, but he was the possessor of a hundred-dollar bill that would purchase a couple of suits like the one that Frost had just collected.

The professor again listened at the door. The far-away hum of voices continued, about equally divided between the crystal-clear inflections of Jean and the throatiness of Reagin.

Frost moved toward the window. It closed soundlessly behind him.

He walked to his car which he had parked two blocks off and drove to his laboratory. When he came out ten minutes later, he carried a black valise with as much gingerly respect as though it contained a nest of bombs.

It had been a gray, gloomy day to which the early dusk of winter now added its shroud of darkness. Frost drove out Woodlawn Avenue to the filled-in marsh around Haven Street where the new road was being constructed.

A raw wind blew across that open stretch. There was no traffic. The traces that remained of the gruesome discovery which had been made in the vicinity earlier in the day would have passed unnoticed except by a trained observer. Frost examined the roadbed, the construction materials, and the steam roller. For a quarter of an hour he busied himself on the scene. He tossed the empty valise into his car when he left.

Returning to 13 State Street, he spent some time in the laboratory with his collection of wearing apparel: the overcoat, suit, and gloves. Afterward he walked to the table in his library, where his indulgences took an odd turn. A bust of Socrates on a pedestal in one corner of the room faced an old etching of Bacon on the opposite wall. Between them stood Frost with an array of silver coins.

His hands and fingers possessed a graceful beauty that belied the rest of his appearance. He used them nimbly now. At first the coins slipped and tinkled occasionally on the table, but the longer he practiced, the more swiftly and magically they vanished as though they had never existed, or sprang into view seemingly from nowhere, or multiplied at a rate that would have made a banker envious.

More than an hour lapsed before the ring of the telephone interrupted his pastime. The voice he heard was that of Jean Moray, and she began excitedly, "I'm back at Woodlawn and One hundred eighty-seventh—"

"I'll be right over." Frost cut her short and hung up.

A thin, sardonic smile altered his expression for a moment. He lifted his eyebrows questioningly toward Socrates, who continued his imperturbable stare into the eternity of stone.

V.

FROST had a mechanical device when he slipped around the side of the house, but when he faded away from a window, it was no longer with him. A light burned in a front room, but the blinds were drawn. Reversing the usual custom of mankind, he chose to enter the house by way of its attic, and without troubling to notify its owner.

As he completed his descent, the window with which he had tampered shattered with a brittle *crack!* At the sound of the crash, Frost was across the lower hall to the door of a darkened room. His right hand came up while his left reached out and flicked a light switch. The room filled with amber illumination.

"Hold it," Frost drawled.

The man who was sidling toward the broken window, where the shade had begun to flap in the draft, froze in his tracks, his back toward Frost. An instant fraught with deadly potentialities ended on the thud of the pistol that he let fall from his hands before he pivoted to stare down the muzzle of Frost's revolver.

Samuel Reagin had not changed greatly in the years since the photograph on his bureau upstairs had been taken, except that he was smooth-shaven now and his hair had thinned. He possessed eyes of a light and unearthly blue whose curiously blank tranquillity seemed to belong to another world.

In a voice of throaty timbre, he asked casually, "What made you anticipate the trap?"

"All life is a trap for which the skeptic is always prepared."

"The young woman would profit by your foresight. By the way, you will find her in the front hall, bound and gagged. No doubt she would breathe better free of the rug that appears to have wrapped itself around her."

"No doubt she would," Frost agreed.

"I'll be glad to assist her," Reagin murmured taking a step forward.

"As you were," Frost snapped. Not for an instant did his gaze shift. "Having endured the discomfort this long, Miss Moray will not mind a few minutes more of it."

"I do not regret the drastic measures since I object to unnecessary intrusions into my private life. I would gladly do the same for you, I don't mind saying."

"Perhaps you will have the opportunity," Frost answered cryptically. "However, it should not be an utter surprise for the murderer of Arthur Kaliters and Henry Jenkins to find his life subject to considerable scrutiny and intrusion."

"Do you often experience these hallucinations? I might find your talk amusing but for its painful implications."

"Then you will appreciate even more the painful implications of another hallucination that I've recently enjoyed," Frost retorted. "The hallucination is remarkable because of its inescapable and extensive realities. One of these is my possession of a suit whose ownership can be traced to you. A second is the presence on the coat sleeves and trouser cuffs of oil-and-grease spots and sand, gravel, and cement particles. A third is the factual demonstration I can give, proving that these have been on the fabric for not longer than two days. A fourth is that this precise combination of markings and insignia can be traced to the particular steam roller at Woodlawn and Haven, and to none other.

"It is possible for a murderer to avoid leaving a single clue at the scene of his crime, or to avoid carrying a clue away with him, but it is impossible to commit murder and to avoid both. Your mistake lay in the second phase. Disposal of the body and preventing identification are the fundamental problems that face all murderers. You employed an ingenious method in attacking these difficulties, but the crime was far from perfect. There are no master minds of crime, and the so-called perfect crime exists only when the investigators are at fault or err in the interpretation of facts that test their theories.

"Permit me a cigarette."

THERE WAS no change of expression in Reagin's strangely colorless eyes. They seemed dreamy and disinterested. "Your facts uphold your theories, I'm afraid, but I'd like to know how you ever arrived at the theories. I'm at a loss to account for their basis."

"Simplicity itself. I merely proceeded from the impossible to the rational."

"A rash procedure."

"A statement of truth," Frost set him right. "There were two starting points in the suicide message left by Kaliters. It would have been equally feasible to work forward from the beginning, or to progress backward from the end. I chose the second course.

"The last part of his message dealt with his alleged visions. Either he was unbalanced, or he was sane. He was not a psychopathic case, because he wrote with a logical sequence and impartiality of observation that are foreign to the unhinged mind. He had worries, fears, doubts, and neuroses, but not many more than the majority of mankind.

"What he saw could then be accounted for either on a supernormal or a normal basis. Supernatural realms may exist, but I have found nothing in my experience to support such a belief. On a normal basis, it was exceptional for him to have even one of the experiences he described. It is unthinkable even under the laws of coincidence that a gang of magicians and sleight-of-hand artists, comprising at least two men and one woman, had chosen him as their victim. The multiple experiences, therefore, became reduced to the single source of a man or a woman. A man was indicated because female impersonation is vastly easier than male. The hand-removal and cigarette-devouring illusions are effective even on a stage and in bright light; they must have been weirdly impressive at twilight and during the ordinary course of life to a man who was already in an upset, nervous state.

"The clue that exposed the whole plot was the clue of the man who grew taller and shorter by a matter of several feet. That is an illusion that could not be accomplished by a tall man, because a tall man cannot arbitrarily reduce his height. It could be done by a short man, but only by one means. Out of this ensue all my other deductions, including the origin and motive of your crime. Even the clue of the man whose head revolved was unnecessary for the solution, though that feat, which is physically possible but so difficult that it requires seven years of daily practice, automatically eliminated the later suspects from my considerations."

Reagin's pale, vacant eyes continued to stare at Frost unblinkingly. There was a moment's strained silence before he spoke, in a tone of indifference, "Apparently I'm not as clever as I thought I was. And yet the police regarded the suicide note the result of dementia. You ought to have done the same. You carry your stubborn persistence to unpleasant extremes.

"Well, that's that. You're right. Twelve years ago, I was struck and severely injured by a car that Kaliters drove. His settlement took care of me for life. I had no need to work for a living or to worry about the future, but all the months that I lay in the hospital before I recovered, I alternated between bitter despair and gnawing hatred. As it was, I lost both legs in the accident that almost cost me my life.

"While recovering, I whiled the time away in various fashions. Among the books given me to read I found one on amateur magic. I practiced some of the simpler tricks until I became adept. Then I got more and more interested in the subject, and as the months dragged I began to scheme for revenge. Ultimately I intended to kill Kaliters, but the possibilities of optical illusion fascinated me. I found out by experimenting on the nurses at the hospital that even simple tricks like swallowing the thermometer and pulling it out of my ear upset people badly when they weren't expecting it. It caught them off guard.

"Revenge became a sort of obsession with me. The longer I waited, the sweeter it became, and the longer I practiced, the more expert I became at one mystifying illusion after another.

"I learned everything I could about Kaliters and his affairs. I made myself familiar with his life. I had all the time in the world and I took as much of it as if I were spending years in preparation for a concert début. On numerous occasions I shadowed him. There was no possibility of his recognizing me, because the only glimpse of me he ever had was the night of the accident when he was too drunk to remember anything.

"AFTER I left the hospital, I found that modern ingenuity had made available artificial arms and legs that were nearly as efficient as real limbs. They were more satisfactory in some ways. They didn't ache or pain or cause trouble. I could run and walk and jump as well as before. I could drive a car and swim. The substitute limbs were adjustable so that they could be lengthened or shortened. I had a special pair made with a much greater extension range. I tried them out one evening on some youngsters who were playing in a lot. I scared them half out of their wits. They all ran away when I suddenly grew two feet taller.

"When I finally launched my campaign against Kaliters, other circumstances favored me. He was a weak, spoiled sort of person. He got himself into serious trouble more than once. He squandered the money he had inherited and has lately been despondent over financial matters. When I began my work, he thought he was losing his hold on sanity.

"The night he was killed, I parked not far from his house and walked over to it."

Frost said, "The tracks in the snow enabled all the correct deductions to be made."

"Not to the police. At least I succeeded to that extent. There was no one home. I entered the house through a side window. There was an illusion involving a gun and a rope that I intended to use for my climax. It would have finished Kaliters if I had been able to use it. But he had already determined on suicide, and had begun writing a long note as soon as he was home. I watched him take the poison tablets, and gloated as his life started to ebb away. A full hour of sweet satisfaction and revenge should have been mine before he reached a state of coma and death. The drugged torpor was under way when that infernal servant returned.

"The fool instantly saw the situation and ran toward the telephone. I had to step out and stop him. With the gun aimed, I made him face the wall. Then I slugged him with the butt and finished my program by killing Kaliters. It appealed to me that Kaliters was dying by his own hand and that I could have the thrill of murdering him while still making it look like suicide, but if any suspicions were roused, Jenkins would take the blame. When I left, his shoes were on my artificial limbs.

"He was too heavy for me to carry, so I hauled him on my spare, which is merely a board support equipped with rollers. Beggars often use them to arouse sympathy by pushing themselves along the sidewalk. I've always had one with me since a time a few years ago when my first set of limbs was destroyed in a fire and left me helpless for a couple of days. As for the rest—"

"Stick 'em up! Drop that gun! *Drop it!*" shrilled a voice from behind Frost.

With utterly untypical alacrity, the professor obeyed. "A woman, an automatic, and the jitters scarcely present the best combination for logical action. Obedience becomes a virtue," he dryly remarked.

A serene and beatific glimmer entered Reagin's pale blue eyes. "Pure logic carried you far, but it didn't carry you far enough," he exulted as he tied Frost's hands. "Mona was a little late but she always comes through. Where you made your mistake, Frost, was in figuring that because I had the compelling motive, I worked alone. You can't find out everything by logic alone. There was nothing to show that Mona and I were engaged at the time of the accident. You didn't know that we already played Kaliters for a sucker years ago. We set up the old badger game and it worked to perfection. He actually fell for her and she took him for breach of promise. Then we were secretly married, which was a great joke on him, because according to the terms of the settlement, Mona's income was to stop the instant she got married. That was another motive for getting rid of Kaliters. Sooner or later he'd have found out the truth, and that would have ended half our graft."

"Can it be possible?" Frost's voice had a peculiarly ironic and exasperating meekness, as though he was enjoying a private jest. "It would seem that I made a fatal mistake. Obviously there is no other course for you to follow now except to dispose of Miss Moray and myself. I trust your method will be swift and painless. I would not care to undergo the same fate as Jenkins."

"That's the funny part of it," Reagin muttered, his pale eyes placid. "I like the idea of sending Jenkins some company. When you two are out of the way, the cops'll never catch up with us. I'll enjoy watching the papers to see if they ever identify what's left after the steam roller is through."

VI.

THE WIND blew in piercing gusts, but a different chill made Jean shiver. Her eyes strayed from the massive bulk of the steam roller where it loomed in the darkness and turned with mute appeal toward Frost. Tape over her lips prevented her from speaking. She felt numb, for there was nothing that Frost could do for either of them now, and it was too much to hope for some miraculous intervention of fate.

She lay in the direct path of the steel monster. Frost sat closer to it. Somewhere in the darkness beyond stood the car that Mona had driven while Reagin watched with a pistol in hand during the ride out. Mona stood at one side, here, holding the weapon while Reagin moved toward the controls.

"Let 'em have it if they start squirming," said Reagin. "Don't shoot to kill—just make 'em stay put."

"Years of brooding have made you mad," Frost stated in a tone of lofty condescension. "Not brilliantly mad, but hopelessly and irretrievably insane."

"The trouble with you now is that you're in no position to appreciate the hand of an artist," Reagin answered.

"My dear fellow! If you appreciate the hand of an artist you should revel in the knowledge that the dictaphone I planted in an upstairs closet made a complete record of your conversation with and capture of my assistant. The second dictaphone outside the broken window has recorded your confession," the professor blandly retorted. "By reckless driving, you may possibly manage to reach them before my good friend Inspector Frick of the homicide bureau."

Mona let loose a stream of furious profanity. Reagin turned his head toward her, his voice plaintive. "Please don't display your temper so, my dear. Pay no attention to any attempts to rattle us. We will find out later if he is bluffing. For two or a dozen murders, we can only die once. Their tune will change as the engine of death rolls down upon them."

"Perhaps it will never reach us," Frost, suggested, an odd inflection coloring his words.

Reagin stopped short and stared at him. A vicious flame had begun to kindle in the pale-blue eyes. He hesitated, took an uncertain step toward Frost, then hastened to the steam roller and prowled around it. He seemed to be deliberately restraining his movements while he pursued a sort of leisurely tour of investigation.

Jean watched, puzzled and helpless. He examined the controls. His figure bent and she heard scratchy sounds. The cold wind had so numbed her face that every time a muscle twitched her skin chapped. Uncomfortable though she was, the last minutes passed like seconds before Reagin reappeared. He paced slowly, carrying a small box from which wires dangled. He walked away into the darkness. When he came back, the box was missing.

His eyes had grown strangely hot, as though a coal burned somewhere at the back of their surface blueness. He stood above Frost like a snake about to strike. Whether from cold or anger, his teeth ground.

"So you had it all fixed, didn't you? Just enough explosives to kill the pilot while you and that snooping dame would be protected by the front roller. If you hadn't spoken, I'd have started the steam roller and blown myself to smithereens. You're clever but you aren't clever enough. You talk too much. Now I've spoiled your little scheme and your work has gone for nothing. I find myself developing a violent dislike for you. You'll pay by giving me an extra pleasure.

"Mona, see that they lie down and keep their feet pointed toward the steam roller. I want them to watch it creep on. I want them to feel it and see it as it works toward their knees, crushing them, inch by inch. Tear the tape off her mouth so she can make more noise."

Jean clenched her teeth as the tape was ripped off. She expected a twinge of pain that did not come. If Mona's jerk had cut her lips, her nerves were too chilled and deadened to respond. She wondered if she would receive no more sensation when the tons of steel bore down.

Frost did not answer Reagin. Whatever reaction the killer may have hoped for—chagrin, a plea, despair—failed to materialize. Frost might as well have been a carved image for all the interest he showed in the proceedings.

Reagin's features became sullen as he once more started for the steam roller. His figure merged with its mass.

Minutes slipped by. The headlights of a late auto drifted along Woodlawn Avenue a hundred yards distant, but Jean recognized the futility of attempting to summon help. No driver would stop at this hour in such a lonely stretch for a cry in whose origin and sincerity he would have no reason to believe. The auto sped past.

A kind of cold shock raced through her as she realized that the ponderous black mass had begun to move. Terror had no opportunity to build up inside her, or to demolish her control. Her consciousness had only registered the unalterable fact that the juggernaut was launched upon its bone-crushing, irresistible course when a mighty hand clutched her heart.

The world exploded in flame and flying metal and human débris. The ground erupted under the middle of the steam roller and dissolved its central structure to shards. Things flew overhead and to each side but the front roller protected her from the blast. Mona, lifted from her feet, took a backward jump that left her stunned yards away. Jean's ears roared like a cataract.

In the denser blackness that ensued, and as her senses recovered, Jean felt her bonds being cut. "How—what—"

"Up," Frost ordered, helping her to her feet. "You're all right. By this time you ought to know that nature presented me with supple hands and fingers that I can almost tie into knots. I've never met the rope or wire from whose bond I could not free myself. This way. You'll find the little lady already seated in the car. She is getting nasty about some bracelets she hasn't worn before. To others we will leave the task of assembling Reagin. I gave him enough outs and warnings but he insisted upon operating the engine. His mania doomed him. Even so, I believe he would have thanked me, if he could, for sparing his vanity the humiliation of court and an asylum or the chair."

Several miles later, her circulation restored and her normal spirits returning, Jean looked out the window. "This isn't the way to 13 State Street."

"But it is the way to police headquarters, where our guest will no doubt be received with enthusiasm—and to Chinatown."

"Why Chinatown?"

"Its restaurants are open virtually all night."

"So are lots of restaurants that are much nearer home."

"Unfortunately," drawled Frost, "none of them specializes in bird's-nest soup."

927

PANDA

The snub-nosed automatic swung up, spurted flame—

"SUCH A BUSINESS!" said Mrs. Appeldorf, who was as round as a bushel basket. "Nothing but grief it makes for me. Sometimes I think I leave this city. Elsewhere I am better off, yes? Two weeks now I have my Home Delicatessen and it gives trouble, trouble, always trouble.

"First those nasty young men come to me and say I should hire them. 'For why I should hire you?' I say. 'I have a clerk already yet.' They say, 'We will protect you.' I tell them, 'I am all right. I do not need protection. Go away, shoo, else I call a policeman.' They make faces but they do not frighten Mrs. Appeldorf. I shoo them out. That is good. I do not like them.

"Then I go off one afternoon to shop. When I am back, I find people standing around, lots of people, policemen, and an ambulance all waiting. I rush inside. Peter, who worked for me ten days already, and a good boy he was but slow in the head, he is dead. The police say he climbs up to reach something on the top shelves. He loses his balance and falls. It is not enough that the stupid one comes down on his skull. But no, a five-pound can of tomatoes lands on his nose and that is the end of Peter. Such a pity.

"So this morning I am busy in my shop when two men come in and ask me, 'Is it that you have a license for Oscar?' I tell them, 'But no, should I?' They say, 'Very well, then you must get one. We are from the city. We will take Oscar away until you buy a license.' I tell them, 'I will buy a license now. How much?' They say, 'Oh, no, you must go down and apply for a license. We will take Oscar away now and write you a letter about this.' I cry. Five years old now is Oscar and never before has he been away from me a day even.

"They go off with Oscar. All day I wait and what happens? Nothing happens. Finally I call the city offices and ask, 'Where is my Oscar?' They do not know what I am talking about, the dumb-bells. Then tonight comes a telegram messenger, only he does not bring me a telegram. He has a note. It is a piece of paper folded over and pasted. There is no envelope. I sign for it and the messenger goes away. The note says—"

Frost interrupted her. "Did you bring the note with you?"

"But no. I put it in a kettle of hot water. It disappears, *poof,* like that!"

Professor I.V. Frost, who, sprawled down in an overstuffed chair, had been listening with a rather bored attitude to the woes of his midnight visitor, suddenly sat up. He lifted the cover from a teakwood box at his elbow and extracted a poisonous-looking cigarette that emitted dense, curiously fragrant fumes as he lighted it and exhaled.

His assistant, Jean Moray, watched him speculatively. That habit of his, which he appeared to indulge only when a problem presenting some unusual feature came to his attention, invariably fascinated her.

The thin height of Frost, his gaunt features and moody black eyes that were generally lackluster, acquired a mysterious energy when something stimulated his interest. Then he toyed with cigarettes of his own blend and impregnation. His splendidly modeled hands were in violent contrast to the rest of him, for nature had bequeathed him only that one touch of beauty in a frame otherwise distinguished for its eccentricities.

All the beauty resided in Jean Moray, who was too beautiful in her own original and individual fashion. But Frost, to her constant exasperation, remained unique among men in his indifference to her. He didn't dislike her. He didn't seem to have any feelings about her. She was just a tool, an efficient instrument that served his purposes at times.

SHE emerged from reverie to hear Frost ask, "Do you mean that the writing vanished when you put the note in water?"

Said Mrs. Appeldorf, with a helpless flutter of her hands, "But yes, the writing goes, the paper goes, everything goes. It melts, just like that, like—like salt. The water turns dirty."

"Why did you drop the note in water?"

"Because it said I should. I only do what it tells me. Now it is gone. Such a business. I am so excited thinking I will get my Oscar back, I do not read the note very carefully, but I remember what it says. The note tells me how Oscar is fine; he is being taken care of; his expenses are very heavy though, and I can have him back when I pay the bill for his board. It comes to twenty thousand dollars."

"Twenty thousand dollars!" Frost raised his eyebrows.

"That is much money, but I have thirty thousand dollars in the bank. I love Oscar. He is all I have. I will pay that to get him back with me again. The note says I will receive a telephone call, and hear Oscar's voice, and know that he is alive.

"The note is not signed. It says that if I put the note in hot water, a secret sign in invisible ink will come out, so I will know who I must pay the money to, but that the rest of the note will fade. Ach, the untruthful ones. I do as they say, and what happens? There is no secret sign. Nothing comes out. Instead, the writing fades, the paper melts, and what do I have then? I'm asking you. Nothing.

"So then the telephone rings and a voice asks, did I receive the note, and I say yes. The voice asks, did I put it in water, and I say yes. Then I hear my Oscar and I know he is all right. Then the voice tells me I should get the money from the bank to-morrow, and I say it is well. The voice says it will speak to me again when I have the money ready. If I go to the police, it is all off and Oscar will die. I promise I will not go to the police as I want my Oscar back.

"You are not the police. Did I do wrong to come to you? It is all a very strange business. I only want my Oscar back. I remember Mr. Ransome who got into trouble once and you save him. He stops at my Home Delicatessen many times. One day he tells me how you help him. To-night I call him up and he tells me to come see you right away. He says you will bring my Oscar back without I should pay twenty thousand dollars. Yes?"

"I think so," said Frost ambiguously. "My fee, in this case, will come from another source. Don't worry about that. But who, or what, is Oscar?"

"Oscar, my brave, my pet, my big baby, he is like a son. Five years I bring him up and now they take him away from me. Oscar is a panda."

"A what?" asked Jean, puzzled.

Frost's eyes became still more animated. "Which variety—the common or the giant?"

Mrs. Appeldorf explained, "What you call giant, a big one."

"Let us start at the beginning. Where did you obtain this remarkable pet?"

"My husband, Wilhelm, he brings him back from Asia five years ago. We have no children. Wilhelm thinks maybe I like a pet. I name him Oscar, he is such a funny fellow. I love him like a baby almost. Wilhelm, he is a merchant, an importer; he travels much. Last year he dies and all I have is Oscar and the insurance—fifty thousand dollars. It is very lonely by myself. Two weeks ago I read about delicatessen for sale, and I think how much better it is to have store, busy all the time, and Oscar there with me. So I buy the delicatessen. It has place to live above it. I move there with Oscar."

"What's the address?"

"My Home Delicatessen? It is 927 Willough Street."

"Were you accustomed to keep Oscar in the store or in the apartment?"

"Both. He is very tame, no trouble."

"On the day that you left Peter in charge of the store and returned to find him dead, do you recall where you kept the panda?"

"I leave him tied to chain in corner of my store."

She started to ramble on, but Frost silenced her with a frown. "That's enough. Go straight home. Do your living quarters face the street?"

"The day room is on the second floor in the front, yes."

"Stay in it for the next hour. Keep the lights on and the curtain up. Move around every few minutes. Be at your bank the minute it opens in the morning, nine o'clock sharp. Take a telegram messenger with you. Draw out ten thousand dollars in one-hundred-dollar bills, put them in an envelope, address it to me at 13 State Street, and give it to the messenger to deliver. Then go back to your shop and continue business as usual."

"Ten thousand dollars? Ach, such a lot of money for a fee—"

"It isn't a fee," Frost retorted impatiently. "You'll get it back, and Oscar as well. On your way!"

FROST lifted a receiver from its cradle and dialed a number. He obtained an answer almost immediately. "City desk, please." An interval of seconds, then, "Bordon? Hello, Fred. Frost calling. . . . I'm fine, thanks, but dispense with the pleasantries. I want some information in a hurry. Who's king in Willough Street Section? I don't mean the official political boss, necessarily, but the actual holder of power. . . . Sam Lee Radek? You're sure? An odd name. Thanks."

He hung up and dialed another number as Jean was entering. He had a longer wait this time before a sleepy voice finally growled, "What the hell you mean callin' at this hour, whoever the blazes y'are?"

"Pete Ransome, I deduce," Frost drawled. "Your language remains as picturesque as ever, neither time nor custom staling its infinite variety. Ivy Frost calling, in case your mnemonic faculties have not already informed you."

"Gee, boss, why didn't you say it was you? I'd 'a' known it by them six-bit words if you'd gimme time enough. How you doin'? I ain't heard from you since the time I took the big box out of your place an' then—"

"Yes, yes," Frost cut in.

Pete was big, ugly, dumb, honest, and strong as a water buffalo. Frost had once saved his life by proving that he simply did not have brains enough to commit a murder by using spoiled antitoxin serum. Pete always admired him for that, and never missed a chance to repay Frost on the rare intervals when the professor could use his services.

Frost, who had been turning the leaves of the telephone directory to the "R's," stopped at the page headed "Rac-Rad" and said, "Can you get dressed in a jiffy? Good. Go out and hunt up a phone a few blocks away. That's just so the call won't be traced to you. Then call this number—yes, write it down—and say to whomever answers, 'A woman has been killed at 927 Willough Street.' "

"Gee, is that right? Say, you don't mean that nice old lady who—"

"Pete," Frost chided, "I sometimes wonder what nature put into that peculiar lump that is attached to your shoulders. No one has been killed. Nevertheless, in fifteen minutes call the number I gave you and say that a woman has been killed at 927 Willough Street. Keep your voice gruff. Do not answer any questions, or say anything more. Hang up as soon as you have made the statement. Got it? Then go back to your home and stand by. You may hear from me again within an hour. Have you your truck handy?"

"Yep. It's right outside. I c'n start in a second."

"Fine. If you don't hear from me within the hour, return to the arms of Morpheus."

"Huh?" But Frost had hung up.

HE VANISHED into his laboratory and came out a few minutes later with a valise that he was closing. A glance at the clock showed two twenty

"Miss Moray," he commanded, "buy or rent a giant panda, whichever proves feasible, and have it here before nine o'clock."

"But what," Jean wailed, "is a giant panda? For the last half hour I've been hearing about the beast whatever it is, and I still haven't the slightest idea if it looks more like a monkey or a giraffe. You want a giant panda. All right, I'll get one if there's any to be had. But just how am I supposed to recognize the beast if I see one?"

As though the chain of his reflections had been broken, the faraway aspect faded out of Frost's eyes. "The panda is a rare animal found among forests on the hills of inner Asia. The panda is about the size of the ordinary domestic cat. There is a giant variety, however, that sometimes attains a length of six feet and a weight of over three hundred pounds.

"In general appearance, it resembles a black bear, but its head is more like that of a raccoon or fox. It has dark fur around the eyes as if it wore spectacles. The fur of its legs and around the shoulders is mahogany-brown, so dark that it looks black. On its head, back, and sides, the fur is a light-tan.

"The moment you have obtained or made arrangements for the delivery of a specimen, make a list of restaurants, beer parlors, and delicatessens in the vicinity of 927 Willough Street. If I am not back before seven a. m., take a blank check to the proprietors and buy a store, any one will do so long as it is within a block of Mrs. Appeldorf's Home Delicatessen."

"Buy a store? What for?"

"And also buy a tattooing outfit. There are a number of so-called tattoo parlors in the Bowery where you should be able to obtain the needles and pigments."

Her eyes wide and astonished, Jean stared at the professor.

Frost said abruptly, "I can't take time to explain now. Here's a hundred dollars. Wrap it up in some yellow copy paper, put it in a plain envelope, type the address, and mail it to Pete Ransome to-night.

"One more thing: Get a quantity of fresh bamboo sprouts or young plants."

"To eat, I suppose," Jean ventured with poisonous sweetness.

"Precisely." Then he was gone.

II.

FROST left his car parked around the corner from the Home Delicatessen.

Light shone through the two front windows of the narrow building at 927, on the second floor. After a few minutes, the figure of a woman crossed both panes in silhouette. Frost stepped into the shadows of a doorway on the opposite side of the street. Dirt, pieces of paper, bits of rubbish skittered on the wind. Frost did not again turn his gaze toward Mrs. Appeldorf, who continued to follow the instructions he had given her earlier.

He had been standing there for ten minutes when the headlights of an automobile traveling at high speed shot into view several blocks distant and turned along Willough Street. The car decelerated as it approached and rolled to a stop not far from the professor. A chunky man with a dark hat pulled down over his forehead got out of the driver's seat and sauntered along the sidewalk. The silhouette of Mrs. Appeldorf crossed the windowpanes again.

"Well, I'll be damned!" muttered the chunky man. "What the hell is Charlie's idea sending me on a wild-goose chase?"

He pivoted toward the sedan.

A long, hollow snout, gleaming bluish in the glow of the street lights, jabbed into his side.

"Keep going," Frost ordered in a cold, quiet voice. The man kept going until he reached the vehicle. Frost deftly removed a snub-nosed automatic from a side pocket of the man's topcoat. The man whirled in a lightning move and bounced his skull on the barrel of Frost's gun.

"That's all," Frost snapped. "The next time you try a fast one, you won't have a chance to think about it later. Not ever."

The matter-of-fact threat in his words carried conviction. The chunky one, in spite of stars and rocket flashes that paraded through his head, acquired a healthy fear of the gaunt and forbidding specter at his side. Frost removed another gun from a shoulder holster and a knife from an inner pocket. He pulled a third pistol from a side pocket of the car, then motioned the disarmed captive into the driver's seat. He himself slipped into the rear seat with his valise.

"I don't believe I caught the name," said Frost.

"Meyer Drubin—*awk!*" His hands flew to his throat as a noose dropped around it.

"Hold off—you won't be strangled, yet," Frost warned him ominously. "This is merely insurance against reckless driving. I am holding the loose end. It's a silk cord that will stand a five-hundred-pound pull. The moment you make a false move, I jerk, and you're finished. I'm going to lie on the floor—keep your eyes to the front! If you adjust the windshield mirror, you will see a small tube at your shoulder. That's one end of a periscope. I'll be watching you, your driving, and the road. Now drive back to the garage."

Drubin's face was moist as he threw in the clutch. The silken noose, flesh-colored, almost invisible, lay like a circlet of fire, a tight fire of doom around his throat. The car jumped, wabbled, picked up speed.

"Come, come," rose Frost's annoyed voice from the rear. "If this is the best you can do, I may dispense with your services now rather than later."

The sedan steadied and purred on. Drubin's knuckles were white from the tensity of his grip on the wheel.

DRUBIN drove for ten minutes before he came to a red brick building with an old wooden sign, that creaked in the wind, hanging outside. The sign read: "Venda Garage, 24-Hour Service." A steel drop door closed the driveway that was its sole entrance and exit.

Drubin stopped with his headlights flooding the door and honked several times. The door slid up. As Drubin drove through, he heard a rear window lowered. The car rolled up the ramp. A pale-faced man with a stubble and wearing greasy overalls waved at Drubin, then turned to lower the door into place.

His glance flicking to the mirror, Drubin saw Frost's arm go through the open window. The hand held a weighted bag on a thong. The bag came down, *bop!* on the night attendant's skull. The attendant half turned. His eyes were quite blank, but his face had a sort of idiotic, foolishly happy grin as he slumped to the floor.

Drubin parked the car. Frost rewarded him by handcuffing his wrists to his ankles and taping his mouth. The professor then climbed out, walked back to the garage attendant, knelt beside him, and felt his pulse. The man was breathing irregularly, and moaning a little. Taking a phial from his pocket, Frost unstoppered it and waved it under the attendant's nose for a few seconds. When Frost replaced the bottle, the man's breathing had become slow and regular.

Frost finished closing the door. He surveyed the garage, which was not large. The dozen cars lined up filled most of the area. Room remained for only two or three more vehicles. For a garage of such modest pretensions in an out-of-the-way district like Venda Street, the automobiles maintained a surprisingly expensive average. Nearly all were new models and five of them custom-built.

The lift interested Frost. It was big enough to take the biggest car with room to spare. Gun in hand, he ran it up one flight. The second floor held a rack of tires, besides accessories, tools, and repair equipment. It also inclosed a small truck, freshly painted and with a number of parts newly replaced.

The top floor was partitioned. Of the four separate rooms, one contained files, ledgers, and miscellaneous débris, one had a table with ash trays and glasses on it and a cuspidor and several chairs around it as well as a telephone on a stand, while the third sported a bureau and cheap four-poster bed.

THE LAST ROOM contained only two items, but those two of a kind that probably had never before enlivened the presence of any garage. They comprised a cage, and the occupant thereof, one giant panda. The beast blinked as Frost turned the lights on. It had a grotesque appearance, with the dark fur around its eyes lending it a scholarly aspect as though it wore spectacles. Its raccoonlike face seemed both wise and childish. Oscar was about five feet long and had a beautiful, fat tummy. He was a rather attractive animal, who looked at the visitor very much as if he were expecting Frost and merely waited to see what would happen next.

"Hello, Oscar," Frost greeted him gravely.

"Haroof!" said Oscar.

Frost walked over and inspected the cage, It had no casters. He tried to budge it, but it resisted his efforts. Cage and animal must have weighed at least three hundred and fifty pounds. He hiked out of the room.

"Hraw!" Oscar sounded plaintive.

Frost waved a genial hand at the creature. "My friend, I agree with your sentiments, but inasmuch at nature did not endow me with quite the amount of super-herculean strength that I venture to say resides under your fuzzy exterior, I will need a measure of assistance."

"Gr," Oscar grunted and sat back on his haunches.

Frost returned to the room with the table and chairs, took the telephone, and called a number. On the first buzz he got an answer.

"Hello, Pete, Frost calling again. Thanks for making that phone call."

"Gee, how'd you know I done it already! You a mind reader?"

"That's right. But here's something else. Take your truck and drive to the Venda Garage at Venda and Eighty-ninth. When you get there, use the elevator. On the top floor you will find a cage with an animal inside it. It's heavy—weighs at least three fifty. Can you manage it alone?"

"Sure. I'll haul it along the floor an' down the elevator. I once heaved a four-hunnerd-pound casting up to a platform. It busted the platform, but that wasn't—"

"I know it wasn't your fault. Excellent. When you've done that, drive to my place at 13 State Street. If my assistant is not there, leave the cage at the bottom of the garage runway."

Frost hung up and went back to the panda. "Oscar, you are about to go for a ride. Until then, dream that you are basking on top of a bamboo in Asia."

"Waw," Oscar growled.

Frost turned out the light and descended to the main floor. He dragged the unconscious attendant out of sight, took the shackles off Drubin, and removed the tape. He prodded him to a telephone in the cubicle that served as the office.

"Call Charlie," he commanded, "and tell him that Mrs. Appeldorf is very much alive."

Drubin obeyed, his enthusiasm visibly increased by the black orifice at the end of a pistol that pointed directly at his forehead. Frost made him hold the receiver away from his ear far enough for both to listen in.

"Yes?" responded a suave voice.

"It's Drubin. That tip-off was a fake. Maybe you better check on it if you can. Nobody's dead at the Willough Street place, or at least the old lady's still kicking."

"It took you long enough to find out. Why the delay?"

"Aw, I just got held up getting to a phone. There ain't anything open around there this time of night. That all?"

"That's all."

Frost returned to the car that Drubin had driven and trussed his prisoner as before. From his valise, he then took out a camera and a holder with a flash bulb. He returned to the top floor just long enough to waken Oscar to a blinding flood of light while the camera shutter clicked.

III.

IT WAS almost four when Pete Ransome drove his truck into the Venda garage. The door was up. Pete didn't wonder why. He didn't see any one in sight. He didn't find an attendant and didn't look for one. The garage was strangely deserted, but Pete went straight to the lift as soon as he saw it.

When Frost gave orders, Pete obeyed in his dumb, dogged, faithful way. His actions would have been the same if he had found twelve dead men sitting at the wheels of the twelve cars, or if the garage had been swarming with police or bees. Somehow, Frost would have made it all right, pulled him out of a jam, turned a mess into apple pie. Frost always seemed to have the right dope. Pete didn't worry because Frost was the brainy guy to figure things out.

Pete went up to the top floor and prowled around until he found a cage with a very queer animal inside. The animal growled, *"Wruf!"*

"Shut up, you!" Pete muttered. "You look like somethin' I dreamt of the time I ate a hunk of bum cabbage."

"Rr-r-rr," rumbled the beast.

Pete grabbed the cage and hauled it along the floor. It grated and the occupant squawled. Pete got it down to ground level where he gave it a quick heave. The muscles on his shoulders and the veins in his neck corded, and his face turned the color of liver. The cage landed on the back drop of the truck. Pete shoved it inside and closed up. Oscar protested some more. Pete climbed into the driver's cab and the truck clattered off.

When Pete was out of the way, and no longer in need of protection from any surprise intruder or unexpected attack from the rear, Frost got up from the floor of Drubin's car. He closed the garage door. Next he hauled the unconscious night attendant back to the spot where he had originally collapsed. After photographing the scene, he took a snap of Drubin, lying bound and helpless.

He restored the used flash bulbs and photographic equipment to his valise, but took out a coil of tough, thin rope and a kit of tools. He carried them to the top floor, climbed a series of iron rungs in the wall next the elevator, and pushed open a roof hatch cover.

After walking completely around the roof, he fastened the rope to the steel grate over a drainpipe in a rear corner, tested it, then dropped the coil over the roof's edge. Next he spent five minutes remodeling the fastening of the hatch. When finished, he descended several rungs, lowered the hatch cover over his head, slipped the inside catch into place, and pushed. The hatch cover went up. Though apparently still fastened securely from the inside, the cover could now easily be raised by any one on the roof.

Frost finished his business in another ten minutes, returned to the ground floor, got into Drubin's car, drove out, and stopped only to close the door behind him.

ALMOST half an hour after he had left, the attendant began to mumble and thresh around. He opened his eyes and sat up. Gingerly he felt his head as if he didn't expect to find it. His actions were uncoördinated like those of some one suffering from a bad hangover. At length he managed to get to his feet and give the automobiles a onceover.

"My Lord," he said bitterly, "the next time I lay eyes on that Drubin rat I'll plug him before he knows what hit him."

He staggered toward the office telephone, then changed his direction and rambled for the elevator when a new thought struck him. He rode to the top floor, let out some additional profanity upon finding Oscar among the missing, and hurried to the phone.

When he drew an answer to the number he dialed, he barked into the receiver, "Charlie? It's Murse calling, yeah, from the garage. Get a load of this! Drubin drives in about an hour ago and lays me out cold.

"Wait a minute before you start yelling! No, I didn't see him do it; he worked too fast; he just got past and I was closing the door when he slugged me. That ain't all. The cage with the whatchamacallit's gone. It's a plain, raw double cross and you tell me who's it. . . . Naw, I guess he thought I was dead or he'd have put some holes in me. I just came to and started looking around the joint."

"But Drubin couldn't manage that heavy cage alone!"

"Sure, I know, somebody's got to be in on it with him. They could've cleaned the whole place out while I was on ice. They had plenty of time. Naw, I don't know what else they took."

MEANWHILE, Frost had driven back to 13 State Street. He found Oscar where he had told Pete to leave him. He stowed the car away, rolled a crate carrier outside, tipped the cage against it, and wheeled Oscar into the garage. Even with mechanical aid, the exertion proved strenuous, and Frost's features set in grim lines. He inhaled deeply from one of his special cigarettes before he went up to his laboratory.

A typewritten sheet of paper was propped conspicuously on a table. It read:

> Memo:
>
> Attention Professor I.V. Frost:
>
> 1. You are now the proud owner of a giant panda, male, four years old, by courtesy of the Zoölogical Importers Supply Co., Staten Island, to be delivered by 8,00 a. m. to-day, C. O. D. $850.
>
> 2. Two dozen young bamboo trees will be sent by Horticultural Specialties, Inc., Yonkers, about 7:00 a. m., C. O. D. $240. (N. B. I looked in the encyclopedia and found that Pandas eat bamboo foliage.)
>
> 3. The advertising office of the *Times* informed me that the B. B. B. Beer Parlor-Lunch Counter at 907 Willough Street has been offered for sale a couple of times recently. I phoned the owner, Mr. Grossen. He will be pleased to sell for $4,200 spot cash. I have an appointment with him at 8:00 a. m. to close the deal. (How's that for fast work and using the brain that you once referred to as my molecule?)
>
> 4. If Pete Ransome doesn't get a hundred dollars in the morning mail, blame the United States postal service, not me.
>
> 5. I am now going out to try and buy a tattooing outfit. While I'm about it, I think I'll have Ivy Frost in the middle of a nice big broken heart with an arrow sticking through it done in beautiful blues and reds on my left forearm, as a tragic warning to mothers never to let their daughters become assistants to criminologists.
>
> (Signed) Jean Moray.
>
> P. S. 6. I'd hope the panda bites you except that the poor thing would either break all its teeth or probably catch blood poisoning and die.
>
> J. M.

A fleeting smile chased across Frost's face as he finished reading the note. He crumpled it up and began developing the films he had taken at the Venda garage.

IV.

WHEN Jean Moray blithely sauntered into the library reception room of Frost's residence shortly after five in the morning, she carried a tattooing outfit. She was tired but did not show it. She looked as fresh as the proverbial daisy-and far more appealing.

She found Frost sitting like Buddha upon an ottoman with an air of serene detachment while he alternately blew smoke rings and sipped thick, black coffee from a cup on the table beside him. He rose the moment she entered.

"Leave the tattoo outfit here. We're going to abandon an automobile."

"Does it take two to do that?"

"I do not propose to waste an hour laboriously taking subways, els, and taxis back from nowhere. Moreover, we have my own automobile to collect."

"Some night when you get absent-minded and let me have an hour's sleep, I'll be so surprised that I'll lie awake thinking about it."

"You can sleep later in the morning and afternoon. You'll need to. There's a good deal of work ahead of us."

"There's a lot of work behind us."

"Including this sleeping beauty," Frost agreed, as he opened the garage door and indicated Drubin.

Adjoining the basement garage, which was part of the mansion on State Street, and directly under the front porch, lay a stone-walled cell barred by a massive steel door with a grate in it from the rest of the garage and cellar. A dim light illuminated the cell. In one corner, Oscar crouched on the bottom of his cage, and upon a cot lay Drubin quietly snoring.

"Who's he?" Jean asked.

Frost explained.

"Why's he sleeping?"

"Part of a grain of morphine somehow seems to have found its way into his system," Frost remarked. "I can't imagine how he came to be so careless."

"Yes, you look terribly, terribly regretful," Jean retorted in a voice too liquid and musical to be anything but sarcastic.

Frost sped Drubin's sedan up the ramp.

"Why don't you hire a butler or a couple of employees to do some of the routine work around the house and on cases?" Jean complained. "It seems to me a waste of time for us to bother getting rid of one auto and finding another."

Frost shrugged almost imperceptibly. "The best way to get anything done is to do it yourself. The more servants involved, the greater the risk of leaks and errors, and the larger the amount of information that they must necessarily possess concerning their employer. He plays the strongest who plays alone and takes no one into his confidence. If I could be in several places in different guises at the same time and doing a variety of things, I would be quite content, until I became bored.

"But since life is not so constituted that any given individual can subsist devoid of contacts with society, I made a single concession to independence. Until such time as you leave my employ or suffer an unfortunate demise, I will make no other such concessions."

JEAN'S EYES glinted with green lights. "I like the nice, cold, casual way you speak of the most disagreeable topics. *Br-r-r,* don't you think it's a bit chilly? I wonder what they would find if they ever opened your head. Probably a lot of stalactites hanging from the roof and long rows of cubby-holes each with a neat little fact or piece of logic rolled up in a blue ribbon and tucked away. And on the floor there'd be a couple of tiny dried-up wisps. Those would be the emotions that tried to worm their way in but died of starvation before they ever had a chance."

"Emotion nullifies reason."

"Of course it does," Jean said in hot exasperation. "That's the fun of it! Don't you ever get sick of facts, and logic? Haven't you ever wanted to kick them overboard and say, 'to hell with them, I'll do any crazy old thing I think of just because I want to, and not for any particular reason'?"

"All psychological motivation reduces itself to the truism which you imply." Frost smiled. "People, including myself, always do what they want to, whether the action be murder or marriage or both. Emotion may be reason, in a sense, but reason is never emotion."

Jean pulled a pack of cigarettes from her purse and lighted one. Inwardly, she was in a mood to commit mayhem. Against Frost's imperturbable exterior, sometimes laconic, sometimes mystifying, but always aloof, she had tried with all the wiles she knew to make a dent, in vain so far as she could determine.

If he had despised her, she could have rationalized his attitude so that she felt flattered. If he had loved her, she would either have responded or felt the glow of another triumph in the history of her conquests and promptly lost interest. But the complete indifference he displayed, his failure to realize that beside him sat one of the most delectable and desirable sirens in all the metropolitan area, was a reaction that she had never before elicited from the male of the species.

Shrewd enough to realize that her present tactics weren't succeeding, she changed the conversational trend as skillfully as she could.

"Where do emotion and reason fit into the story of Mrs. Appeldorf, her panda, the note that dissolved, and the rest of it? I didn't see much to go on, yet you said hours ago that it was all perfectly clear. It isn't."

"Both inductive and deductive reasoning, analytic logic and synthesis, when properly balanced, point to the solution. The facts are there and need only be tested by a true theory. The problem presents one perplexing feature, however, that makes a full and complete solution difficult."

Jean tossed her cigarette away. "I don't follow you."

"Consider the facts in their chronological order: Mrs. Appeldorf and her husband are a childless couple. Five years ago he presents her with a rare animal, a pet I venture to say such as no one else in all America possesses. That unusual creature serves to furnish her with a sort of compensatory mechanism. She has something that distinguishes her from other women. She lavishes upon it the affection that they would devote to a child. It becomes, to her, like a child, and as such obtains an emotional value out of all proportion to its intrinsic worth."

JEAN sat up straighter, turned her head a trifle to look from the corners of her long-lashed eyes at Frost. "You know too much about feminine emotions. And you're not a psychiatrist. Where did you learn all this?'"

Frost replied impatiently, "Observation, reason, and answer follow each other. To continue, Mrs. Appeldorf becomes a widow; her affection for the panda correspondingly increases, but time also hangs heavy on her hands, and two weeks ago she purchases a delicatessen. She moves into a district where she is a total stranger and takes the panda with her.

"She is visited by a couple of thugs who ask her for money. Her innocence of the vermin whose racketeer methods mulct small tradesmen, and her inherent honesty, are such that she refuses their demand.

"Several days later, she returns and finds her clerk a victim of accidental death. And thus the police listed the murder."

"The murder?"

"Certainly. Consider all the circumstances. The thugs left empty-handed. When racketeers do not obtain their demands, it is a common practice for them to indulge in physical assault upon the proprietor or his employees. One beating is usually sufficient to insure payment of the dues for 'protection.' To make clear to you what happened, I will explain it as it happened, though part of the truth is dependent upon deductions derived from events that transpired later.

"At least one thug, and perhaps two, returned to the store to repeat their demand. Peter, the clerk, was alone. Peter, whether he knew of the previous visit or not, could do nothing without Mrs. Appeldorf's consent. He was beaten.

"One of his assailants was Meyer Drubin. Whatever they hit him with, probably the butt of a gun or a piece of lead pipe, proved fatal. In desperation, they hastily tried to make it look like an accident, and their imaginations were so limited that they did the simple, natural thing, perhaps the only thing that could have saved them.

"They pushed Peter behind the counter, spilled cans from a top shelf, and dropped a heavy tin of tomatoes on his forehead. To die in such a fashion would be so freakish and ignominious that it would seem like a pure, accident, and hardly any questions would be raised. The police might have asked, Peter would only be reaching to make a sale to a customer.

"The customer did not report the accident. Why not? Because there was no customer, therefore no accident, therefore Peter was murdered. The police probably didn't even reason that far, because clerks always find shelves to straighten, goods to stack up, supplies to rearrange in their spare time, and so on.

"But in making their get-away, they passed the panda which, excited by the turmoil, clawed Drubin. They could not kill or harm the panda in retaliation without at once giving evidence of homicide. Yet the very mark of the panda's claw upon Drubin was circumstantial evidence of manslaughter if the police happened to pick him up. It was a queer dilemma which they could not stop to solve. Any moment a customer might enter. They had to leave Oscar unharmed and get away from the store.

"Yesterday, the panda was stolen in broad daylight by two men posing as city departmental employees and taken away in a truck, outfitted at the time as a city-owned vehicle, later repainted and remodeled, and now standing on the second floor of the Venda Garage."

It all seemed so simple, so inevitable, when Frost explained it, yet Jean had not been able to make the pieces fall into place herself.

FROST CONTINUED, "With the panda in their possession, the racketeers could have killed it or held it till Drubin's wound healed and then turned it loose. Instead, Mrs. Appeldorf received a ransom note.

"Why?

"No ordinary racketeer could have known or guessed her devotion to the pet and her willingness to pay the sum demanded for its return. The racketeers were part of an organization that operated over a wide area. She was new to the district. Yet some one knew how much she cherished Oscar, some one in the Willough Street section learned of her pet almost as soon as she arrived.

"That some one knew the racketeering group and could work with them and through them. That some one could find out how much she had in the bank. The average crook would not be sufficiently well-read to have information that would enable him to send a self-disappearing note. The only person who would fit these and a few other necessary qualifications which I won't enumerate must be not only a resident of but a power in the district. He is Sam Lee Radek, who, at least, showed exceptional astuteness in using casein."

"Casein? That's a protein solid found in milk, isn't it?" Jean interposed.

"Yes. In the last year or two it has been extracted and manufactured into various substances and articles more interesting as curiosities than of commercial or practical value. Casein has been processed into flat sheets like paper which can be written upon by pencil or type, but not the usual inks. I expected to see it figure in kidnaping cases long before now."

"It's perfect," Jean exclaimed.

"For this purpose, yes. One of the great problems facing the criminal not only in kidnaping cases but in other types of blackmail is the extortion note. Handwriting, typewriting, paper, fingerprints, postmarks, watermarks, and numerous other such clues are of immense value. Yet paper made from casein, if immersed as when Mrs. Appeldorf obeyed instructions, will dissolve almost instantly. All clues are destroyed. The victim will remember the gist of the note, but not a shred of evidence remains to help the authorities.

"Sam Lee Radek hit upon one of the most ingenious devices that has ever come to my attention. He utilized it perfectly to serve his ends. With such shrewdness, he might have made a fortune in business, whereas his career is nearly finished.

"Locating the stolen panda, and testing the truth of my deductions, were simple matters. The panda must have been held in a garage because it was removed in a truck in the view of witnesses who might have noted the license number or become suspicious. The truck obviously was disguised for the occasion, and, of necessity, must lose its identity as swiftly as possible. The change could only be made in a hurry and with comparative safety in a garage, while the same building would serve admirably as a hiding place for the panda.

"I told Pete Ransome to phone Radek and report that a woman was dead at 927 Willough Street. If Radek were among those guilty, as I suspected, and if the report were true, and if the woman were Mrs. Appeldorf, then he no longer had any chance of collecting a dollar in extortion money. He had to investigate the rumor immediately. He could not go himself because of the possibility of an ambush or trap implied by the mysterious telephone call. He would phone the leader of the racketeers. For the same reasons, that gentleman would not go out in person, but would send an underling, which was precisely what I wanted."

Frost stopped beside his own automobile which he had left parked around the corner from the Home Delicatessen. The streets were gray now with cloudy dawn. He told his assistant to take the wheel of the *Demon* and follow him. He drove Drubin's sedan miles away, abandoned it on the Brooklyn water front, and got out to take the wheel of his own car while Jean slid from the driver's seat. Frost headed back toward 13 State Street.

"I see it now." Jean spoke as though there had been no interruption. "Drubin steals the panda; Radek needs the money. Willough Street is just an average district. Radek, for all his control over it, can't get much in the way of graft. Drubin has to steal the panda to protect himself against a manslaughter charge, at least till his wounds heal, and Radek steps in to use the panda for purposes of extortion."

"Correct it to say that Drubin stole the panda on orders from higher up. That would be the head of the racketeering mob, the man called Charlie."

Jean's forehead acquired puzzle wrinkles. "Well, I don't see where the difficulty lies. You've recovered the panda; you have Drubin, and Mrs. Appeldorf will get her Oscar back without the necessity of paying out $20,000."

"There's nothing to prevent them from stealing the animal again, or killing it. She will probably be harassed by strong-arm tactics until she pays a weekly fee for 'protection,' like other storekeepers in the district. She has almost no legal redress. The kidnaping laws cover human beings, not animal pets. Yet the theft of her panda caused her as much grief as a kidnaping would to the average family.

"In several ways, this is a most peculiar case. On the surface, we've already solved it, but, actually, the solution thus far has scarcely touched the deeper roots, the persistent sore spots, the sources of all the trouble. Our next and harder task is to launch a chain of events by activating a focal point or two so that the whirlwind is reaped."

"How are you going to do that? What happens next?"

Frost evaded a direct answer. "I have never had cause to believe that clairvoyance was among my talents."

V.

AT EIGHT O'CLOCK in the same morning, Jean met Mr. Grossen. At eight fifteen, ownership of the B. B. B. Restaurant and Beer Parlor had passed to "Mary V. Jennay." The preliminary bill of sale duly signed, Grossen confessed, "You should make money on the investment, but not much, you understand; the times are not good, and people do not spend like they used to, but a leetle profits every week, that is good."

"I'll make things hum," Jean promised.

Mr. Grossen fidgeted, clasped and unclasped his hands, finally looked at the toes of his well-worn shoes and stated, "Mr. Radek, he is the boss around here."

"What of it?"

"Well, it's good to know about him. You know how it is, if something goes wrong, you get in a leetle jam maybe, he fix it. He knows every one by name. You drop around to see him some day, huh?"

"No, I won't. I don't care who he is."

"Then I call him up, Miss Jennay, and tell him I sell the store to you. You do not mind that?"

"Do what you like about it."

Jean took the keys with her. Still following Frost's instructions, she waited till ten minutes of nine before going to the newly acquired shop. By then Mrs. Appeldorf was on her way to the bank to draw out the $10,000 as Frost had told her, so that Jean had little likelihood of a chance encounter with her.

On first glimpsing the property, Jean figuratively turned up her nose. It was a narrow shop with a frontage of not more than twenty feet. Rather poorly kept, it looked third-rate. It contained, principally, a long counter divided into two sections, a short one for sandwich service and coffee, a larger one for beer. There were a number of high stools and a few small round tables with chairs made out of barrels.

She unwrapped a flat, thin parcel she had been carrying and removed a cardboard sign. She put the sign in the front door between glass pane and an inside curtain. The sign read: "CLOSED—OPEN SOON UNDER NEW MANAGEMENT."

To the right of the door lay a display window and shelf. A shoulder-high horizontal rod and curtain separated the shelf from the interior of the shop. The window was dusty. All in all, the layout proved not only adequate, but of some extra help for the purposes of the Frost-Moray combine.

Jean took an unobtrusive position in a chair at the front, where she could look out of the space between the wall and the end of the curtain that backed the window display. She could see without being seen. She sat there for nearly half an hour before Mrs. Appeldorf waddled by toward the Home Delicatessen.

A minute or two later, a sedan halted across the street about midway between the B. B. B. Restaurant and the Home Delicatessen. A man sat at the wheel, a man of whom Jean could discern only broad shoulders and a moon face. The man did not get out. He looked as if he was waiting for a friend.

JEAN returned to the inner sanctum and idled time away by rearranging some glasses, straightening chairs, and otherwise examining the shop. She was still so engaged when there came a knocking on the door. She went to it and unlocked it. A soft-spoken stranger, who might have been an insurance salesman except for his smoky eyes, pushed his way in.

"The store isn't open for business yet," Jean objected.

"That's all right, sister, make mine a beer."

"I said the store wasn't open and meant it. I just bought it and I'm trying to decide about redecorating it. I don't even know if there is any beer."

"Are you the new owner?" He sounded suspicious.

"Yes."

The stranger looked at her. "My name's Harry," he said. "Maybe you'll get to know me."

"I don't want to know you."

"You might find it worthwhile. I'm here on business. I might be able to save you money. You're planning to open and run the place?"

"Yes."

"Then you ought to join the ROPA."

"The what?"

"The ROPA—Restaurant Owners' Protective Association. It'll only cost you ten dollars a week and I'll be around every Monday. We see to it that you aren't bothered, if you get what I mean. You're protected from anything happening to you."

Jean kept silent for a few moments, as though thinking hard, then looked up with big, innocent eyes and said, "Oh, I see what you mean. Well, I guess it's a good idea to join."

"Smart's the word for you," Harry approved. "With your looks, you ought to double business here, and that's where maybe you and I get along better. Naturally, if business picks up, the cost of protection is higher, and would have to go up to twenty or maybe twenty-five bucks. But they let me do most of the field work, so if I don't say anything, naturally the cost doesn't jump. In the long run, it's worthwhile being nice to me."

"I'm sure it is. I suppose it would be best for me to join right away, before the store is open for business, even?" Jean took out a ten-dollar bill.

"That's right. Now we'll see that nothing happens to you. Protection—that's us." He eyed her again, then turned to leave.

"What about a receipt?" Jean called.

He looked back with pitying astonishment. "We just don't bother about them. Don't worry. You won't have any need for one."

Jean returned to the window after he had left. The sedan with the moon-faced driver still remained across the street.

She waited a half hour, closed the store, determined that she was not being followed, and returned to 13 State Street.

Searching for Frost, she found quite a variety of other things. The laboratory looked more like a greenhouse or part of a tropical forest, because young bamboo trees had been stacked everywhere. On one table lay almost-dry prints of scenes from films that Frost had exposed at the Venda Garage. Beside them lay $10,000 in hundred-dollar bills.

Hunting through the mansion for the professor, she finally found him in the cell under the front porch. That impregnable fortress now contained, in addition to Drubin, not one giant panda but two, both of whom Frost was feeding in alternation the leaves and tender branches of young bamboo trees.

THE PANDAS, in separate cages, munched the foliage and from time to time growled or sniffed suspiciously at each other.

"Turn 'em loose," Jean suggested. "We'd probably have the battle of the century on our hands. The menagerie seems to be doing well. If the detective business is turning into a zoo, why not add a few more lovely specimens? An aardvark, for instance—I learned that one from cross-word puzzles—and a sacred ibis, or maybe a sea serpent."

"Why not that big rat scampering across the floor just behind you?" Frost added to her suggestions.

Jean jumped about five feet with an involuntary and not very ladylike "Damn!"

"Never assume that something is true merely because some one says it is true," he drawled. "A moment's reflection should have told you that my back was largely toward you, that the feeding of the pandas occupied my attention, and that I could not possibly be in a position to know whether a mouse or a rat or nothing was at your heels.

"Remember Nick Valma, who came to us with a bizarre narrative that in itself was true, except that the gentleman speaking did not happen to be Valma, who was already murdered. If I had said that a mummy was chasing you, doubtless you would either have paid no attention or fainted on the spot, but because I made a statement that might easily have been well-founded, you acted as if it was a matter of fact. Eternal challenge, the open mind at all times, the position of the inquirer and skeptic are essential for the discovery of truth.

"What did you learn at our beer parlor?"

"Mrs. Appeldorf is being shadowed by a man with a round face. I'd recognize him if I saw him again. Up to the time I left just before noon, he was still sitting at the wheel of a sedan parked across the street from the store. The racketeering organization is known as the ROPA—short for Restaurant Owners' Protective Association. They're certainly fast workers. I hadn't been in the store two hours before the collector came around, an insufferable weasel who calls himself Harry. The store is listed for ten dollars a week for protection. I paid the first installment."

Frost fed another sprig of leaves to Oscar while the second panda growled. "Good work. As the old melodramas would phrase it—the plot thickens with a vengeance. There are several hundred small restaurants and beer parlors in the Willough Street district. The ROPA must be collecting upward of $5,000 a week, more than $250,000 annually.

"Miss Moray"—and Frost's expression was again coldly sardonic from appreciation of some unspoken jest—"call the Armored Car Trucking Corporation, hire a car with two husky guards in addition to the driver, and have it stop here at five this afternoon.

"If the prints in the laboratory are dry now, put one set of the pictures into the most freakish envelope you can find and address it by hand to the district attorney. Do not mail it until after five o'clock, however. Now get some sleep, and come to the library at four thirty for final instructions."

Jean shook her head in mock despair. "It used to be criminology, then it became a menagerie, and now it's chess or a sort of guessing game. It's a new system of mathematics. What do two and two make? Did I hear you say four, my friend? No, no, they make a lot of sausage. Good night, one and all; we must leave you now."

She trotted upstairs and carried out Frost's orders. With them attended to, she lay down on a settee for a moment's rest and in five seconds was deeply and dreamlessly asleep.

SHE AWAKENED to a touch on her shoulder and sat up. "Come into the laboratory," said Frost. It was four thirty p. m.

He led the way, but she paused long enough to repair her makeup, don a new complexion, and comb her hair. When she entered the laboratory, she saw Meyer Drubin, stripped to the waist and lying face down on a metal table, his wrists handcuffed behind him. On his shoulder a group of five distinctive scratches several days old was healing. They were unmistakably the mark of the claw of a panda.

"When those heal," Frost remarked, "the case against our prisoner would be difficult to prove. Therefore, the tattooing outfit, so that blue pigmentation will preserve the evidence of guilt indefinitely."

For several minutes then he talked, issuing instructions while she listened attentively. At a quarter of five, she nodded understanding and hurried out of the house to carry out those strange instructions.

Frost returned to the laboratory, unfastened the handcuffs after putting the tattooing outfit away, and shook Drubin roughly. "Put your shirt and coat on. You are a marked man now in all senses of the word. After a while, I'll free you, but if you, by some miracle, should escape beforehand, keep away from all your former associates."

Drubin dressed sullenly. Instead of restoring the handcuffs, Frost tied him with a length of rope. The doorbell rang when he had finished. He found that the armored car ordered by his assistant had arrived.

Ten minutes later, having sent the armored truck on its way, Frost hiked to the second floor and entered a closet. Kneeling on the floor, he pressed a button and surveyed the laboratory directly below him.

Drubin, straining and twisting, had almost completed the task of freeing himself from the knots and bonds that Frost had deliberately left slack. While the professor watched, Drubin got up and hurriedly glanced around. He ran to a table and stuffed Mrs. Appeldorf's $10,000 into a breast pocket. He snatched his own loaded automatic which lay beside the money. He scooped up the pictures of himself and the Venda Garage—the third and final set that Frost had printed—and stuffed them into a hip pocket. Then he cautiously tiptoed across the floor, opened the door slowly, and continued along the hall corridor.

He made a clear get-away. Frost, a peculiar, mirthless glitter in his black eyes, watched Drubin jump into the first taxi he met.

The professor descended, got his own car out of the garage, and drove away.

VI.

MRS. APPELDORF finished wrapping some pumpernickel for a customer. She made change for a dollar bill, watched the purchaser depart, and leaned her plump arms on the counter. She sighed heavily. It was almost six o'clock, but not a word had she heard from the kidnapers of her beloved Oscar, not a call had come from I.V. Frost, and nothing did she know about the fate of either Oscar or the $10,000 she had sent the professor. She looked wistfully at the corner where she sometimes kept the panda. It was lonely without Oscar.

As she leaned there daydreaming, she heard a commotion out front. She looked toward the door. A big armored truck, a veritable fortress on wheels, had stopped at the curb. Two strapping huskies emerged. They waited till the driver covered them with a sub-machine gun that could pivot in almost any direction. Then they went to work.

Mrs. Appeldorf was both curious and alarmed. She began wringing her hands. "Such a business! It gives me aches in the head."

The two guards unlocked the steel door, hoisted a big cage, and marched heavily into the store.

Mrs. Appeldorf screamed, "Oscar! My little pumpkin! Is it that they bring you back safe, yes?" She rushed around the counter as the men entered.

"Where do you wish us to leave this?" asked the man in front. "It's heavy, whatever it is."

Mrs. Appeldorf peered into the cage. Her excited welcome changed to a look of keen disappointment. She shook her head at the panda. "This is not my Oscar. It looks like him, it is very much like him, but no, it is not Oscar.

"I don't know anything about Oscar," the guard politely replied. "Will it be all right to set this on the floor? Our instructions were to deliver this here." They set the cage and giant panda down and departed.

"Oh, oh, oh," wailed Mrs. Appeldorf. "I think I go mad! First they take my Oscar, then they send me this one! All over we have to get acquainted, now!"

The guards climbed into the truck; the driver resumed his seat, and the fortress on wheels rolled off.

THE moon-faced man in the sedan across the street stepped to the sidewalk and headed for the nearest drug store. His face was white with suppressed rage. He entered a telephone booth and dialed with vicious jabs at the finger slots.

When he received a connection, he snarled into the mouthpiece, "Charlie? . . . Jake on the wire. Talk? . . . O. K. Listen to this and like it: I tailed the woman to her bank this morning. She drew out a lot of dough—I don't know how much, but it was plenty—then she pulled a fast one, gave it to a telegraph messenger who was waitin' there, and came out. My orders were to keep her in sight, so I followed her. I don't know where the guy went and there wasn't a chance to phone in about him.

"I followed the dame back to her store. I've been sitting here all day. And now what the hell happens? An armored car drives up and delivers that damned beast—two guys and another covering them with a Tommy. I couldn't butt in. There wasn't any point tailing the truck. You couldn't pry information out of that armored-car company even if you used dynamite.

"By all the squirts in jail, that dame paid out the ransom money right under my nose so I couldn't find out where it went, and she got the beast back in a way I won't be able to find out where it came from. We're up against one hell of a smart play. It's a cinch she didn't dope it out herself, and neither did Drubin, so what's the answer to that one?"

A series of explosive sounds came over the wire.

"O. K., chief, it sounds screwy, but I'll do it."

He emerged from the booth and scanned the sidewalks as he slowly approached the Home Delicatessen. The nearest pedestrian was a dozen yards away from the store. He sauntered inside and pulled his right hand out of his coat pocket. The snub-nosed automatic swung up, spurted flame in rapid staccato crashes. The giant panda leaped and howled, spun madly around and around.

The moon-faced man sprinted from the store. Seconds later, the sedan was a vanishing streak.

Mrs. Appeldorf ran over to the cage. She didn't pursue the fugitive or try to stop him. It was characteristic that she instinctively tried to help the animal. The panda was beyond aid, slaughtered by seven slugs, all direct hits.

Onlookers gathered magically, excitedly.

A new commotion arose out front. A fortress on wheels stood at the curb and the same two guards who had delivered the panda marched in again. They hoisted the cage between them.

"Wait—wait—" Mrs. Appeldorf cried hysterically.

"Sorry, lady, our orders were to return in ten minutes and take the cage out again."

"But it's dead! It's dead—"

"I don't understand it any more than you do. As far as I'm concerned, it's the goofiest job we ever had. But orders are orders."

The guards carried the dead panda outside and stowed it inside the armored truck as carefully as if it was a million dollars in currency. The witnesses watched the performance in stunned silence. The guards took their positions, the truck gathered momentum, and until it disappeared it was the object of bewildered glances.

VII.

CHARLIE GINO, who had organized and made the ROPA what it was, left the nominal offices of the company on Fourteenth Street and sped to the Venda Garage. Bull-necked, heavy-jowled, black-haired, he never looked more than casually like a human being. As he drove toward the garage, murder lurked in his eyes.

He went to the conference room on the top floor, where the business of the ROPA was actually transacted, and where the sinister alliance of mobsters and the shadowy shapes behind political figureheads found a mutual clearing house.

He had barely arrived before Jake burst in. Jake elaborated his earlier report and told of killing the panda. He ended by asking, "What was the sense of that? It looks like a screwy play to me. Why'd you tell me to turn the heat on the animal?"

"The cops picked up Drubin's car on the Brooklyn water front this morning. They think he's been taken for a ride and dumped somewhere else. They're looking for him dead, and are liable to pick him up alive. If they searched him and found those scratches, somebody'd be sure to think of the Appeldorf dame and her panda and the 'accidental' death of that Peter guy and that would tip off the whole works. Now, with the beast dead, she'll either get rid of it to-night, or the garbage collectors'll haul it away in the morning."

While Charlie was talking, Harry entered and delivered the day's collections. Murse, the night attendant at the garage, came up to report before taking over his job.

And while the four conversed Meyer Drubin came into the room.

There was a sudden terrible silence. Murse's eyes narrowed to ophidian slits and his hand crawled toward his left armpit. Jake and Harry shoved their chairs away from the table. Gino got up slowly like a slow-motion picture, his face dark and savage.

"You dumb bonehead!" Gino snarled. "I suppose you came back to tell us it was all a mistake? You didn't lay Murse out cold. Oh, no. Somebody was hiding under the back seat and just reached out and tapped Murse on the head. Just like that. Then they tapped you and swiped the beast and took both of you off." Gino's harsh, froglike croak grew thick with furious sarcasm.

Drubin stopped short. "Sure, that's it; I was just gonna tell you."

"He was just going to tell us!" Gino mimicked. "Isn't that too touching? I suppose next you were going to tell us you didn't know a damn thing about how the beast got away?"

"Say, what's eatin' you guys?" Drubin set his jaw. "I didn't even know it was gone."

"He didn't know the beast was gone." Charlie Gino mouthed the words. "The poor dear lamb will now tell us he's been tied up and tucked away all this time. He didn't help fix up a tricky double cross. He didn't split ten grand to sell us out for the twenty grand we had all sewed up. Somebody else did the dirty work and Meyer just now manages to make his get-away and come rushing back to tell us all about it. Is that it?"

"Sure, sure, that's the way it was." Drubin scowled. "It happened like this. This bird I never seen before cops me in front of the old lady's store and ties a rope around my neck and makes me drive in here and—"

Charlie howled, "What do you take us for, a bunch of dopes and suckers?" He turned to Murse. "Did he have a rope around his neck?"

Murse blurted viciously, "Like hell he did. I'd like to see anybody drive with a rope around their neck. Nuts! I could cook up a better yarn than that in no time. Drubin, you rat, you double-crossed us. Even if it all happened the way you claim, it still doesn't give you an out.

"That's the way it would have to happen if you got in on a double cross and tried to make it look like you were in the clear. Who'd you split the ten grand with? Radek? I suppose you figured we'd swallow your line of hot air. You two would have the dough; we'd be sold out; you'd be in with us again, and then—"

"I don't know what you're talkin' about!" Drubin shouted. "Do you mugs think I'd be sap enough to show up here again after a double cross? I'd take a run-out to Frisco!"

"And that would be a dead giveaway. Oh no, you wouldn't. You had to take a chance on coming back here because you knew you'd be rubbed out whenever we caught up with you. Shut up!" Gino roared, "It was Radek, wasn't it? Sure it was! He calls up early this morning and yells his head off about a woman killed at the Willough Street place. He tells me to send some one down to take a look. Now get this, you fathead, because it's the last thing you're gonna hear.

"Radek knew that you and Murse were the only ones in the garage at night, so it would have to be you that went out, so Murse would be left alone. So Radek met you at the Willough Street place, and rode back with you. The two of you tapped Murse and took the panda and collected the dough. You abandoned your car in Brooklyn and Radek hid you out, probably tied you up so you could wiggle loose after a while and then you'd come busting in here." He stopped only because he ran out of breath.

"No, no, you got me wrong!" Drubin screamed. "Look, I can prove it, I got it here—" His hand dived for his hip pocket.

A PISTOL appeared in Murse's right hand as he jerked it from the shoulder holster. The flaming spurts made dark dimes on Drubin's face. He folded forward flat on his stomach, his hand still twitching around the hip pocket. The reverberating crashes died away, and the odor of burned powder bit through the air in the room.

Charlie Gino walked around the table and knelt beside the dead man. "Well, I'll be damned! He wasn't going for his gat after all! Oh well, he'd have got it later anyway."

He fished through Drubin's pockets and drew out a pack of bills that he hastily counted. "Ten grand! Gee, can you tie that! The dope was still carrying the ransom dough! He couldn't have had a chance to split it yet."

He continued his fishing, and brought out a group of pictures which showed the giant panda in the Venda Garage, Meyer Drubin lying bound in a car, Murse lying unconscious on the floor.

Furrows of perplexity darkened Gino's brutish features. "Here's a queer one. I don't make it. Where did Drubin get these and why's he carrying them around?" An idea hit him and his temper began to rage again. "I get it. A double double cross. The punks not only sold us out for ten grand, they took pictures to prove Drubin couldn't have done it. They framed an out for Drubin to put him in the clear.

"If he'd had a chance, I bet he'd 've told us he swiped these. And then we'd have been blackmailed by Radek or whoever he was working with to buy these pictures back! As long as the scratches didn't heal on Drubin, his pal could hold these over us and threaten to turn them over to the cops if we didn't come across. Of all the set-ups I ever heard of, this takes the cake! We sure got rid of Drubin just in time." One by one he burned the photographs with matches.

"Murse, you get on the job downstairs. Tell the day man, Snyder, to stick around a while longer. No, send him right up.

"Harry, you and Jake dump Drubin in a sack. Put some metal junk in with him and take this gun along. Put him in a rumble seat. Then Harry, you and Snyder drive out and sink him in the East River. Sink the gun somewhere else. Get busy."

Ten minutes later, while they still had not quite ended their activities, the speaking tube in the wall behind Gino's chair made hollow sounds. He swung around and listened. Amazement, suspicion, fury, and reluctant acquiescence successively altered his expression. "O. K., send her up in a couple of minutes."

He faced the others, barked, "Take the sack, all of you, and put the stiff in the end room. Shut the door and stay there till I tell you what next."

An old rug covered the few small blood spots that had resulted from the murder. Gino's henchmen carried the bulky gunny sack down the hall and into another room.

Charlie Gino leaned back and lighted a black malodorous cigar whose fumes erased the lingering, acrid odor of gunpowder.

THE ELEVATOR DOOR rumbled. Heels clicked in the hall. At

a brisk, businesslike gait, Jean Moray entered. "I'm looking for Charlie Gino."

"That's me. What do you want?"

"Twenty-five thousand dollars," she coolly replied.

"Keep on wanting it. Who are you?"

"The name is Jennay. I—"

Gino's eyes slitted. "Jennay? Jennay. I've heard that—say, you just bought a store at 907 Willough Street, didn't you?"

"Yes, but we haven't time to discuss that now. I don't want this twenty-five thousand dollars as a gift, you understand. I have something to sell."

"Yeah? What?"

"A giant panda."

Charlie Gino hesitated for a barely perceptible instant. His eyes smoldered, wary. "I don't want to buy, whatever it is."

"It's a dead panda. I'll sell it for twenty-five thousand dollars spot cash."

Gino's fists pounded heavily on the table. "You—you—" He choked.

"Don't lose your temper. You look unpleasant enough as it is. This panda that I am offering for sale is dead because it has seven bullets in it. They're what makes it so valuable."

A heavy-caliber pistol seemed to jump into Gino's right palm. "You're a looker, kid; you're one of the classiest I ever saw; but you're just about through. You've put your foot into it, and you're either going to come clean right now or you'll never get out of here to tell about it."

Jean didn't flinch by the quiver of an eyelash. With supreme assurance and poise, she went on patiently as though talking to a child. "You don't seem to understand. My, what a terrible temper you have! You see, I keep this dead panda in an armored car downstairs. If I am not down there within ten minutes—only eight minutes to go, now—the guards have orders to drive to police headquarters and deliver this dead panda to the police."

Gino croaked, "I don't give a damn what you do with it!"

"Don't you? But that isn't all. About an hour ago, I mailed a set of photographs to the district attorney. The photographs were taken in this garage. They show a live panda. Naturally, when the police get a dead panda, and a picture of a live panda in this garage, and a picture of a man tied up and another man knocked out, why, they are going to be extremely interested, don't you think? I wouldn't be surprised if they came up here to look around and they might even reopen investigation into the accidental death of a clerk in a certain delicatessen where a panda was a pet.

"Six minutes to make up your mind."

Gino snarled, "Are you cuckoo? If the stuff's in the mail, I'd be a sucker to pay you twenty-five grand for the animal."

"Oh, no. You see, if you buy the panda, then I will go to the post office and have the letter recalled."

"Huh? You can't get a letter back after it's mailed."

"Oh, yes, you can. Call the post office and find out for yourself."

Thirty seconds later, Gino put the receiver down and muttered, "You win on that one."

"Of course. Four minutes left. So, if you decide to buy this panda, this is what will happen: You give me the twenty-five thousand dollars. We go downstairs and the two guards get out of the truck. I climb in with the driver. The guards open the back and take this panda out and leave it here. You send somebody along either to ride with us or to follow us and we drive to the post office.

"We must be there before eight p. m., because after that the proper official won't be there until eight in the morning and that would be too late. It's now almost seven thirty. The letter I mailed is in a very peculiar envelope, so that it will be easy to identify and to stop delivery on it. I forgot to tell you that one of the pictures in the envelope is a photograph of Meyer Drubin's back. It shows the mark of the claw of a panda.

"Three minutes." Jean tapped her foot.

Gino made no effort to conceal his black anger as he pulled a pack of currency from his pocket. "Here's ten grand." He opened a safe in the wall and took out another sheaf. "There's the rest."

"Coming down with me?" Jean asked carelessly.

"Get out! A guy named Jake will take care of you."

He walked to the elevator and called Jake out of hiding, whispered, "Tail the dame to the post office, see if she orders a letter called back from the police, then keep on tailing her and find out where she goes."

Jake got into the elevator. Charlie glowered at Jean as the door closed.

"Good-by, Mr. Gino. My, what a perfectly awful temper you have!" Jean gravely called back.

When the armored truck rolled off, Jake was following it and the dead giant panda lay in the garage. Gino sent Snyder and Harry away to dispose of Drubin's corpse. "When you finish, come back and get rid of the damn beast. And maybe there'll be something else to haul out."

He waited till they had gone, before lifting the telephone receiver and dialing. After a short wait, "Radek? I got something to talk over.... Yeah, it's important. At the garage. Make it snappy."

VIII.

PEOPLE sometimes took Sam Lee Radek for a Slav, and sometimes they took him for a Eurasian, but whatever they thought of his nationality, they always had a tendency to remember him in association with lard. He was not fat, but his features looked dark and oily. He was not in poor health, but his hands exuded perspiration with unpleasant persistency. He never lost his temper, but his restraint was a curious mixture suggestive of worms, iron, and espionage.

After the phone call from Charlie Gino, he began bandaging his right hand and continued swathing it until it was almost the size of a ham. He put it in a sling and had trouble adjusting the sling so that his arm rested comfortably. The moment it was set to his satisfaction, he went out and took a cab. Naturally he could not drive his own automobile by one arm alone. He gave an address a couple of blocks from the Venda Garage and walked the rest of the distance.

In the conference room, Charlie Gino grunted, "You made pretty good time. What happened to your hand?"

"Infection. What's on your mind?"

"Plenty." He spoke sullenly, without removing the cigar from his mouth. "A while ago, I bought a panda."

"I saw it downstairs."

"It was dead when I bought it. I paid twenty-five grand for the carcass."

"Why?"

"You ought to know."

Radek leaned his good arm on the table. Strang will-o'-the wisps were tumbling around the back of his pupils. "Charlie, you're a liar and a poor one at that." His voice sounded even but the flecks in his eyes danced.

Gino slowly got up.

Radek's voice had a gentle, dreamy quality. "You didn't *pay* twenty-five grand for that panda. You *took* ten grand for it. And then you killed it. And you haven't had a chance to dump it yet."

Charlie Gino looked purple, as if he was going to explode from internal pressure.

Radek went on in the same soft, casual voice. "This was my play, Gino, and you gummed it, sold me out, for a measly ten grand. Why the double cross? Isn't your racket big enough for you any more? Is it power you want now? Do you think you can step into my shoes? What were you going to do with the panda? Frame me?"

Gino's answer came in a husky, trembling rattle from the force of his wrath. "What was *I* going to do with it? Why, you crazy ape, what are you trying to pull? How the hell did it get here if *you* didn't send it? You brought this kid in from outside and planted her in a store next to the old lady's place where she could spot everything and get hold of the beast as soon as Jake killed it. Try and get around that."

Radek murmured, "It was you, it must have been you, who called me early this morning, Charlie, and I fell for it. I called right back and told you to look and see if a woman was dead at the Willough Street place. And that gave you the chance to go down and arrange to sell me out.

"You thought I wouldn't get wise, because it was I who told you to go down there. Your punks did the dirty work. You've got the organization. You could swing this. I suppose your rats were to plant the panda in my place while I was here, but I came too soon, so this part of it fizzled?"

Gino bellowed, "Why the hell would I do that?"

Radek persisted, "I'm telling you. Is the twenty-five grand you mentioned the pay-off? What I'm supposed to shell out so you'll destroy the carcass? Or else it's to be planted on me? Id have a sweet time explaining away a dead panda with a lot of slugs in it, wouldn't I?

"Maybe I could prove I wasn't anywhere near the woman's store when the clerk got bumped off, but it would all come out in the wash, Charlie, and then it would be curtains for me. I'd be through as a power in this district, and I wouldn't dare tell what I know because your killers would put me on the spot if I did.

"And I can't raise twenty-five grand. You know that, Charlie. You know I needed twenty grand, but I didn't get it. You got ten grand and now I'm in a nice jam. I can't pay to have the carcass destroyed, and I can't afford to have it found. The only thing—"

With just a sudden, quick breath indicating his inarticulate fury, Charlie Gino hurled himself across the table, his hands reaching for Radek's throat, his face muscles convulsing.

A muffled sound boomed out, and the end of Radek's bandage disappeared, and wisps of smoke curled up while his arm jerked a little. What at first gave the impression of a third eye appeared on Gino's forehead. He was dead when he sprawled on the table, but Radek for a second or two kept aimed at him the small automatic that he had bandaged into his right palm.

"THAT'S THAT and good work!" A cold, sardonic voice snapped from behind Radek. "Keep your hands high!"

Radek spun around, the automatic flaming as he turned. He saw a tall, gaunt, forbidding specter in the doorway, a specter with ruthless eyes as hard as black diamonds. There was a pistol in his hand.

Then something hit Radek's shoulder and the arm went numb, and he reached with his left hand to tear the automatic from its bandages, but a red hole suddenly made its appearance on his wrist and he watched it with fascination when he found he couldn't move his fingers any longer.

"You can't get away. Murse is downstairs. Where did you come from?" He heard himself muttering, but even as he talked, what sounded like the wail of police sirens rising and falling and rising again beat into his ears.

"The name is I.V. Frost, and, if there were need, I would depart in the same manner that I arrived an hour ago, by way of a rope from the roof to the ground." Frost took a strange-looking device from his pocket. "Snyder and Harry only went a block with Drubin's corpse before I shot a serrated steel disk from this weapon. The disk sliced off a piece from one of their bullet-proof tires and the car hit the curb where, unfortunately for them, a policeman came over to investigate.

"There was some gun play. Snyder is dead, Harry and the policeman wounded, and the radio squads warming around will require considerably less than five minutes to find out that the car came from this garage.

"Always observe facts carefully, then interpret them accurately, then substantiate them by a theory that supports them and which in turn they support," Frost drawled.

"Meyer Drubin thought he was tattooed, hence would always bear the mark of his crime, hence must rely on the power and protection of Gino's organization. I don't suppose it even occurred to him to take his shirt off and hold a mirror to his back. I pressed the blunt head of the tattoo needle against the scratches, and, because Drubin expected the worst, he imagined he felt the pricks of the needle point.

"Gino bought a dead panda for twenty-five thousand dollars. It apparently never entered his head, or yours, that there could be more than one giant panda in existence, and perhaps he did not know that all fully mature pandas look alike with the same peculiar markings and characteristics.

"He was not once told that he was buying a specific panda named Oscar. He was merely offered a dead panda, and his own imagination convinced him that it had a different identity. It was quite worthless save for whatever nominal sum it might have commanded had it been stuffed and mounted in a museum.

"By now, my assistant has stopped delivery of a letter addressed to the district attorney and containing some photographs taken here. But those pictures are no longer of any particular value. Jake may still be following Miss Moray, and may have discovered her identity, for all the good that knowledge will now do him.

"And it all happened," Frost mused, "because Oscar was a panda."

MRS. APPELDORF was closing up the Home Delicatessen for the night when an armored car rolled in front of her store and stopped. Two guards got out, opened the truck, and hoisted a cage between them.

The front man muttered, "Somebody is crazy as a bedbug. It'll be me if we have to bring any more of these things here." Aloud he asked, "Where do you want this one, lady?"

"Oscar! My brave, is it you?" cried Mrs. Appeldorf.

Oscar woofed, *"Haraw!"*

THE LUNATIC PLAGUE

Towing the inert figure, Jean stared frantically at the onrushing lights—that brought death.

THE BIG BLACK police limousine nosed toward the curb, stopped in front of 13 State Street. From it emerged a man of slender stature, scarcely more than five feet six, whose truculence and erect bearing suggested former military service. He was reddish of face, with graying hair, but carried his forties like twenties.

Inspector Frick, in charge of the homicide bureau, ran a large white handkerchief across his forehead as he walked toward the stone mansion.

In the smoky haze that passed as atmosphere, the outlines of buildings shimmered. The tall apartment houses lining Riverside Drive seemed outlined in flame against the sun and shaken by tremors of earth. New York was suffering one of the annual heat waves that made seven million people wonder why they'd ever arrived at or stayed in that infernal congestion of dirt, detestable odors, torrid humidity, and air, street, and harbor pollution.

Inspector Frick punched the bell under a brass plate, green with verdigris that almost concealed the name: I.V. Frost.

He heard no bell ring, no sound, but after perhaps ten seconds the door opened magically and Frick walked in. He had made many visits to Frost in the past, but he never failed to be impressed by the quiet efficiency of the different inventions and scientific discoveries that Frost utilized.

The door closed behind the inspector. He cocked an eye resentfully at the Buddha that squatted in a niche at the end of the hallway. He disliked the inhumanly human eye that turned in mid-air with a slow, unpleasant motion. He could not imagine why any one would collect artificial eyes as a hobby. Frost may have been serious or sardonic when he once remarked, "The eyes I place around me are a constant reminder of the steady vigilance needed for all emergencies."

Frick sighed when he entered the library.

The professor's streamlined assistant, Jean Moray, looked up from the desk at which she sat, and waved him to the laboratory.

Some men snub the fates that favor them. Frost, an eagle in his solitude, lived purely for the thrill of the man hunt, the pursuit of knowledge, the application of logic and science to the solution of crime. At no time had he shown awareness that one of the most desirable of unattached sirens served him. Jean Moray's exotic style of beauty and alert mind made her a distinct asset.

He entered the laboratory. Frost sat on a stool at one of the tables. With his great height and thinness, his ascetic face in profile against a window, he looked like a specter or the incarnation of a bird of prey.

A low hum, persistent, steady, droned from the table. Approaching closer, Frick saw a mass of steel armor casing around what resembled a dynamo.

Frost, engrossed in it, drawled, "What's the difficult problem now? I'll listen while you talk. Unfortunately, the centrifuge will require my attention for a few minutes."

The inspector asked in a slightly nettled tone, "What makes you think I'm not just paying a social call? You haven't even looked at me."

"Your own reply, if nothing else. I might remark that one does not necessarily scrutinize perfume in order to detect its scent, or peer at an egg to ascertain its taste, or stare at a radio set to determine its tonal qualities."

"True enough. Also, I can took at your machine without getting any idea what it's for."

"The centrifuge? This particular specimen, an improved model, which I started two hours ago, has reached a speed of 300,000 r.p.m. It works somewhat on the principle of a cream separator. There's a quartz observation piece and a light-beam reflector to watch what happens. At present the cell contains several drops of blood from which the red coloring matter, hemoglobin, has filtered out."

"What good is it?"

"It permits the measurement of molecular structures, and the separation of a liquid into the components. It may lead to new discoveries or processes; it may prove of help in crime detection. Thus far I've tried it out on blood, alcohol beverages, saline solutions, and cellulose compounds.

"You haven't yet stated the purpose of your visit."

"Confound it, Frost, you always have some new gadget or curiosity that takes other people's minds off their business, and then you complain because they forget what they came for," the inspector protested. He added with seeming irrelevance, "Did you ever hear of a plague of lunacy? Is there such a thing as an epidemic of insanity, or contagious madness?"

WHILE the inspector spoke, Frost's right hand had been moving toward the control of the centrifuge, but it stopped before reaching its objective and darted toward a pocket of his leather jacket. It came out with a long cigarette. When lighted, the cylinder sent up fumes of pungent aroma. So far as the inspector knew, that gesture was Frost's only invariable habit. He never smoked, unless a knotty problem aroused his interest, and he never smoked anything but the excessively long cylinders which he manufactured himself.

Frost stated, "Insanity as such is not communicable in the sense that various diseases are. However, some infections result in mental derangement, and the person contracting an infection of that kind could loosely be said to have caught insanity as a secondary product of a primary disease.

"Mob hysteria, war fever, lynch-gang fury, and other mass demonstrations have been considered proof by several psychologists that mental disorders can be contagious, but other authorities have challenged the conclusions. In meanings rather than words, there has not yet appeared the slightest evidence that lunacy can be epidemic, or that a normal person can catch it from a victim of insanity."

"I was afraid so. Just the same, the whole town's gone crazy in the past week. A couple of queer cases started me thinking yesterday afternoon; I spent all of to-day on an investigation, and now I've got a collection that reads like the records of a lunatic asylum. Listen to these:

"About a week ago, on August 3rd, the riot squad had a call to Fifth Avenue and Sixteenth Street during the noon hour. A jam of hundreds surrounded an elderly chap who was pushing a peanut up the sidewalk with his nose. The crowd, of course, jeered and kidded him.

"He refused to call off the act. The police arrested him on charges of disturbing the peace. Then we found we had dynamite on our hands, or a lemon, depending on how you look at it. The man turned out to be Harmin, president of the big White Trust Co. Nobody in the crowd or the riot squad had recognized him, fortunately, and we squashed charges. A couple of evening papers carried the story, but they didn't know Harmin's identity.

"Do you know what he said when we asked him why he pushed a peanut up the street with his nose? Harmin made the silly answer, 'Oh, I thought it was a jelly bean.' " Inspector Frick snorted.

"On August 5th, the homicide squad had a run in Queens. A girl went up in her private plane, and jumped overboard—without a parachute. Her plane crashed a mile away. If you remember the headlines, she was Paula Van Wyke, heiress to the Van Wyke coffee millions. She had everything she wanted, everything to live for. A host of activities took up all her time. Popular and attractive, with plenty of dates, she had fallen in love recently and set the wedding for next month. There simply wasn't any reason for her to commit suicide by diving out of a plane, but she did."

II.

THE INSPECTOR continued: "Before nine a. m. on August 6th, radio cruisers answered a call to the main offices of the Oil Products Co. When the first of the clerical staff arrived that morning, they found the rooms littered with frogs—hundreds of them—hopping all over the place. Nobody would admit anything about how the frogs got there. Nothing was stolen and no other damage done. We decided that some disgruntled employee had caused the trouble, but to-day I learned that the office manager, a fellow named Gildreth, received an order to take a compulsory three months' leave of absence to recover from a nervous breakdown. He's already at sea. Though other officials won't talk, they evidently consider him to blame for the frogs.

"On the day following, at about two o'clock in the afternoon, the next incident happened. Suspicious actions by a well-dressed, distinguished-looking man attracted the attention of a patrolman on duty in Central Park. The man carried a dazzling lamp—in spite of the bright sunshine. He walked along slowly with the lamp aimed at his feet. The patrolman went up to question him.

"He said he was looking for a million dollars.

"The patrolman didn't believe him and asked if he'd lost cash or securities.

"The man blurted, 'Oh, I didn't lose anything, I was just looking to see if I could find a million dollars.' Then he said the darkness made it impossible for him to see without the torch. He claimed to be the society sportsman, Elerton, but had nothing to prove it. The officer arrested him for observation.

"At headquarters, they allowed the man to make a phone call. His secretary came down soon after and identified him as Elerton. Elerton refused to explain his goofy stunt. He wouldn't commit himself one way or another when they offered him an easy 'out' by asking if he'd paid off one of those freak bets you sometimes hear about."

Frost lighted a new cigarette from the butt of the former as the inspector turned another page.

"The evening of August 8th, a Saturday, saw a good crowd at the Plaisir, one of the Broadway night clubs. Most of them don't do much business on week-ends in summer, because the people with money go to the country or travel abroad, but the Plaisir picks up what's left, besides the out-of-town buyers and tourist traffic. It's a theater, made into a restaurant with the usual stuff—cover charge, extras, floor show, etc.

"It's one of the places we keep a plain-clothes detective on duty.

"That night he watched arrivals in the lobby for a while, and talked a little with the hat-check girl at 11:30. Her name is Loy Loris, or at least that's what she calls herself. The detective then gave the rest of the premises a looking over and drifted back to the entrance around midnight. Then he stood by a palm plant and kept an eye on the hat-check booth.

"This girl, Loy Loris, is a black-haired beauty who probably just missed being a featured entertainer. She wears a costume; white satin trousers and a scarlet silk blouse with a gold heart on it. She looks stunning in it.

"Well, she had taken the blouse off. She wore a circlet around her throat. Tied to it by a piece of thread, an oversized fishhook hung at her breast. The detective figured it for a new stunt by the management—until he saw her search all the stuff that had been checked.

"He walked over to make the arrest.

"She asked on what grounds.

" 'For larceny,' he explained.

"Loy Loris protested, 'Oh, I didn't steal anything. I put a dollar bill in each of the hats!'

"The detective investigated, though he didn't believe her, and by the shades below, that's exactly what she had been up to! While they chewed the rag, a man came in alone, a fellow who'd been there often, a ward politician named Mike Hoolan.

"Hoolan said to the girl, 'I didn't wear a hat so I'll check this two-dollar bill, but I want some change.'

"The girl took the bill. She unfastened the fishhook and gave it to him. She said, 'Here's your change.'

"Hoolan's hands started trembling. He pricked his thumb, but finally managed to put the fishhook in his pocket. He turned around and went out. Loy Loris picked up her blouse and got into it.

"The goggle-eyed detective couldn't drag a word out of her. Before and after that one incident, she acted normal. The management didn't like it. They almost fired her, but after raising a fuss they let her stay on."

FRICK turned to another page. "Yesterday afternoon, August 11th, the last of these things happened—but first I'll have to go back a little. The night before, a radio cruiser, drifting along Greenwich in the produce-market district, spotted a man fidgeting on a street corner. He loitered around, seemingly ill at ease. The cruiser circled the block.

"As the two patrolmen drew near him a second time, ready to question him, a thin, swarthy figure popped out of the shadows and blasted away three times. The first man died before he hit the sidewalk. The officers got the killer, but couldn't find the gun. They combed the vicinity, and later squads of police searched every inch within blocks. They didn't locate the weapon.

"During the half-block chase to catch the killer, he either tossed the gun to an accomplice hidden in one of the dark store entrances he passed, or he slung the gun away and it landed on one of the trucks going by.

"The murderer was Gus Berber, a gangster and racketeer whose power has been growing recently. But here's the fantastic part: The pockets of the dead man contained nothing except two wet, dead goldfish. Berber claimed he had never laid eyes on the man before, couldn't identify him, happened to stroll by through pure chance and tough luck, and had no connection whatever with the murder.

"We identified the dead man later through an appeal to the missing persons bureau from his wife.

"She told us he received a telephone call about nine that night; it seemed to upset him. He went out a while after, for an hour's walk, so he explained. She grew worried when he failed to return by midnight. She couldn't account for the goldfish. It developed that he had gone to his room before leaving the apartment. He removed everything in his pockets and took two goldfish out of a bowl.

"I know; I know it sounds crazy, but that's the way it happened," the inspector insisted as Frost sat up straighter with an expression of what he mistook to be skepticism. "The murdered man was Fitzroyd, the orchestra conductor. So far as we've learned, Berber and Fitzroyd actually were complete strangers to each other.

"We quizzed Berber the rest of that night and all the next morning, without making a dent in his story.

"His lawyer went to Judge Hagerman in the afternoon for a habeas corpus writ. Judge Hagerman made an astounding ruling. He ordered Berber's release on the ground of lack of evidence. Two police officers eyewitnessed the murder. They didn't lose sight of the killer for a second during the chase. They caught him cold. But, said Judge Hagerman, they couldn't show a motive and they hadn't found a weapon. By their own admission, Berber must have had a gun; but, since he didn't have a gun, he couldn't be the killer. We couldn't charge him or hold him for trial until we found the gun and linked it by fingerprints or serial numbers to Berber."

Frick unconsciously tightened his right fist and beat the knuckles against his left palm after he laid the portfolio aside.

"There they are, Ivy. If you can make sense out of them or throw light on them you'll do us a favor that I, in particular, won't forget. It's a mess. The very fact that we are the police hampers us badly here. We can't file charges against most of the persons involved. We can't use pressure to make them talk. They obstinately refuse to admit anything.

"I spent all of to-day gathering these reports. I've personally seen a few of the people concerned, I got exactly nothing out of them. I've an idea the episodes are all linked together, but how and for what purpose I don't know. Of course, it's possible that there's no connection between them, but if there isn't, they're the most incredible set of coincidences in my experience. Otherwise, it looks to me like a plague of lunacy."

"Neither coincidence nor lunacy." Frost glanced at a clock. "Five minutes of six. By to-morrow morning at this hour, and perhaps sooner, I'll have the mystery solved."

AN AIR of doubt crossed the inspector's face. "Aren't you stretching your optimism quite a bit? How could you even begin to get around to all these people in twelve hours?"

Frost lifted his eyebrows. "I have not the slightest intention of bothering myself with the individuals concerned."

"But damn it all, how can you say that?" Frick checked the names off on his fingers. "There's the financier, Harmin, who pushed the peanut with his nose. Paula Van Wyke, the heiress, dived out of a plane. The business executive, Gildreth, specialized in frogs. The society sportsman, Elerton, used a high-powered torch to hunt for a million dollars in broad daylight. The hat-check girl, Loy Loris, wore a fishhook for a necklace and gave it away as change to a politician named Hoolan who checked a two-dollar bill because he didn't have a hat. The orchestra conductor, Fitzroyd, kept a couple of dead goldfish in his pockets when shot and killed by a gangster, Gus Berber, who didn't even know the victim, and whom Judge Hagerman freed on a phony technicality.

"For all I know, a lot of other queer things that don't figure in these reports may have happened. What more could you ask? Where the dickens can you start if not with the facts?"

"What results did the police achieve when they started with the facts?" Frost asked pointedly.

Inspector Frick came as close to flushing as he ever could, but he made no answer.

The professor continued, "No, the difficulty is that your portfolio does not involve enough people. The lunatic plague must spread, or be made to spread, even farther." He opened the switch of the centrifuge, but the drone continued. It would run for hours under momentum.

Frick began, "if you manage to clear up any part of the mystery that—"

"The whole sequence is perfectly clear already, but the most important detail remains to be filled in."

"If deduction took you that far, why not all the way? Why don't you just think a while longer and tell me everything?"

"You credit logic with the powers of magic, but in pique, I suspect, rather than from belief," Frost retorted. "Deduction is only one of many faculties and resources necessary for the solution of crime problems. To the best of my knowledge no murder case has ever been solved without the use of deductive processes.

"On the other hand, I am not acquainted with any homicide that pure deduction alone has solved, not excepting Poe's celebrated story about the Marie Roget case. I have heard it called a masterpiece of pure deduction. It's nothing of the sort. Analysis, synthesis, logic, the examination of evidence and evaluating it, the obtaining of material data and suggested courses of action are all in the narrative.

"I dislike the term, 'the scientific method,' for there are several scientific methods and the phrase only lends itself to confusion, but it serves for a guiding description to the modern technique. Deduction may identify a murderer, but it will never catch him. Fast action must bring the killer to justice."

"What do you propose to do?"

"Visit the Grand Central Terminal, and possibly the Pennsylvania Station."

"The Grand Central! Are you pulling my leg? What on earth can the Grand Central possibly have to do with an epidemic of lunacy?"

"Gold lies where you find it," Frost murmured.

The inspector looked bewildered when he departed. Frost walked out of the laboratory with him, while Frick's glance lingered for a moment on the highly interesting facial beguilment and enticing contours of Jean Moray's topography. A visit to Frost had this one redeeming feature. When the professor's meaning eluded him, he could always feast his eyes upon Frost's charming assistant.

III.

"DID YOU record the conversation?" Frost asked.

"It's on the dictaphone roll." Jean Moray looked too ravishing to be human, but her beauty was wasted, she saw with resentment. She eyed him, a malignant hope nestling inside her that some day she would pierce his impregnable armor.

The moment that Inspector Frick left, the professor's bearing changed in a subtle, indefinable manner. His figure somehow radiated a flow of invisible power, of will thrusting toward a definite though unexplained goal.

He ordered crisply, "Call police headquarters and give the desk sergeant this message to be placed as a memorandum on Frick's schedule. Say that I.V. Frost will see him tomorrow at ten with important developments pertaining to the lunatic plague."

"But he was just here. Why didn't you tell him then?"

"I've no intention of seeing him at ten with regard to anything."

Jean lifted the phone receiver. She had long ago found it futile to ask questions when Frost chose to speak in contradictions. While she carried out his instructions, she noticed him flip the pages of the telephone directory.

He jotted down numbers, went into the laboratory, returned with a device like a small microphone that he handed her together with the list of numbers. "Now call these and in each case say, 'The job was well done. That's all. There won't be any more.' "

"What's the mike for?"

"Speak through it. It's a voice filter. The listener will be unable to determine whether you are male or female, young or old."

"And the numbers?"

"Are those of the surviving members of what we may call the lunatic band. Repeat to them only the message I gave you, and ring off immediately."

Frost vanished into the laboratory again.

A half hour later, after Jean finished the last call and the last of the Arabic scrawls that formed her special preference in shorthand, Frost reappeared as though she had made an audible signal.

She reported, "The telephone laid some eggs. Naturally, I didn't have time to find out anything, since I wasn't supposed to talk. If you want the illuminating answers, they include, 'Say that over again,' and 'Huh?' and 'Who are you?' and 'Thanks, but—' and 'Oh, yeah? What the—' "

"Ah!" Frost exclaimed. "That's sufficient."

"For what? Scrambled eggs? Or am I supposed to rest in the dark like a sort of incubator tray?" Jean flared.

"If you could achieve it, that would be a fate not without strong merits," Frost said with enthusiasm. "I refer, of course, not so much to the tray itself as to the contents thereof which, in darkness and warmth, under controlled temperatures, commence the cycle of generation that produces—"

Hot argument hovered on Jean's lips, but before she could interrupt or Frost finish, the doorbell rang. Frost broke off his discourse abruptly.

"Handle the interview. When it's over, get to the basement garage as fast as you can, take the *Demon,* trail him or her, as the case may be. If you work at top speed you should manage it with seconds to spare. Keep your eyes open. You're going to race with death but you'll be safe inside the car. If anything causes you to lose sight of the quarry, stay in that vicinity, wherever it is, and tune in on the short-wave micro-set. Its four-mile range ought to be ample. If you don't hear from me by nine o'clock, return here."

He hiked off, his long legs carrying him out at a pace that would have meant a brisk trot for the average man.

JEAN WALKED to the front door. When she opened it, utter astonishment stilled her for an instant. The visitor brushed past her and into the reception room. Jean recovered from her amazement and followed close behind.

The visitor, a young woman in her early twenties, wore a costume the like of which Jean at first thought she had not seen since college days when sororities pledged and hazed the annual crop of yearlings. On second thought, Jean decided she'd never seen the like of that costume anywhere.

The caller stood a couple of inches shorter than Jean, with a fuller figure and a face attractive in a sort of pointed fashion—a thin, pointed nose, a chin that ended with a tiny, pyramid tip, a mouth with a distinct point on the upper lip.

The girl wore a mule with a white pompon on her left foot, an alligator-skin sandal on her right. One stocking was sheer and flesh-colored; the other open meshwork and black. For a hot, muggy evening, she chose to wear a fur coat, unbuttoned. Underneath it lay exposed generous areas of skin around her only other garments. Upon her head, however, perched a monstrously ugly hat, festooned with a long feather—a hat so hideous and unsightly that it must have survived from the 1890s.

Her left hand clenched an object. She had shoved her right loosely into a pocket of the fur coat.

This bizarre apparition said, her voice toneless, "I'd like to see Professor I.V. Frost."

"I'm sorry, he's not in," Jean lied with perfectly convincing innocence. "I'm his assistant, Miss Moray. You can speak freely, and I'll give him your message when he comes back. What is your name?"

"It doesn't matter. He doesn't know me. I won't be here again. I only wanted to give him a present."

"A present?" Jean instantly became suspicious, watched every gesture the woman made. "What for?"

"I don't know. I was told to get it and deliver it to him in person, but if he's absent— How long will he be gone?"

"I've no idea. Perhaps hours."

"I can't wait that long. Then I might as well leave it with you. You'll be sure to give it to him?"

"Of course. What is it?"

"A goose egg."

The woman opened her fist, handed Jean a big white goose egg, turned around, and walked out.

IV.

JEAN took the egg by automatic response. The outer door closed before the spell upon her broke and she remembered Frost's instructions. She had no time to waste on the bewildering visit and the preposterous present. Fleet-footed as a faun, she sped to the basement garage and dived inside the *Demon.* It purred up the ramp. The car that had brought the woman already rolled well on its way down the street. Jean almost lost it at the corner. She watched for the immense bonnet, then picked out the characteristics of the sedan with a keen eye, and thereafter had no trouble keeping it in sight.

Traffic was fairly heavy. The hour of dusk had come, with the sun just set and the street lights going on. Jean noticed another occupant in the front seat of the car ahead. A man, but so far as she could tell from the back of their heads, they did not talk to each other.

The sedan rolled down Broadway, past Times Square, and on all the way to Union Square. At Fourteenth Street, the woman stopped and got out. She pulled the fur coat tightly around her. Oblivious to the stares of pedestrians, she hurried into a tobacco shop where she entered one of the telephone booths.

She emerged a minute later, returned to the driver's seat, and drove off just before a policeman reached her. The officer hesitated, with the air of investigating nonsense afoot, shrugged his shoulders, and moved away as Jean picked up the trail again.

It led uptown back the route it had previously followed. It continued toward the uppermost regions of Manhattan.

The towers and skyscrapers of the midtown area, and the tall apartment buildings of the residential section on the upper west side faded into the dusk behind. Houses began to appear, then vacant lots, as the trail cut in toward the Bronx.

They traveled along Culver Avenue now. Jean flashed by an intersection where a parked auto had its wheels almost flush with the avenue. By the rear-view mirror she saw the headlights that swung around in her wake.

Her heart grew tight. Her glance flicked alternately between the sedan ahead and the car behind, until she confirmed her fears. She had ceased to be the hunter, had become the hunted, and the pursuers drove hot after her, the headlights looming ever larger as they closed the gap.

She pressed her foot on the accelerator. The *Demon* hummed a song of vast power and sailed away like a rocket. The feel of the magnificent machine in that swift pickup restored her courage. The vehicle was a masterpiece of engineering, specially designed and built for Frost after gangster bombs destroyed his previous model. A mobile fortress with punctureproof tires, steel armor, incased motor and gasoline tank, bulletproof glass, the *Demon* possessed many other features built in to Frost's specifications. She had once seen the speedometer touch 120 on a ten-mile straightaway before deceleration for a curve became necessary.

These thoughts flooded her for the few seconds that the *Demon* gathered momentum. The sedan seemed to stand still as she bore down on it. She lifted her foot.

THE JAWS of a trap threatened her. If she outran the pursuit, she must also race away from the sedan. If she kept her distance behind the sedan, she would be overhauled.

She put her faith in the *Demon* and in Frost. Tight-lipped, she held her relative position.

The dark limousine came on like a thunderbolt, swung out to the center of the road, drew abreast of her. A sudden gasp burst from her throat. She vaguely realized she had stopped breathing these last tense seconds.

The sinister snout of a gun, the barrel of a gun with a double grip and a drum that resembled a canister for motion-picture films, poked through the narrow, rear ventilation window. It spewed flame in spurts and flashes.

Even the completely closed *Demon* was not soundproof enough to conceal the vicious *ta-ta-ta-ta-ta-ta* of the submachine gun, though it sounded deceptively faint and far away. Fractures like dimes and quarters bloomed on the windows. Jean ducked her head. The crackle of lead against glass tortured her ears. She heard the whine of slugs that smote steel.

The firing ceased. She watched the limousine, saw the gun withdrawn. The *Demon* had come through, she thought, but as she exulted, the other car forged ahead and edged in. Pressed toward the curb and a crack-up, she stepped on the brake.

The limousine cut over more sharply.

Her gray-green eyes acquired the glint of ice. She pushed the accelerator violently. The *Demon* leaped as though sprung from a catapult, hit the limousine with the power of a pile driver. The jolt flung Jean against the steering wheel. The limousine slued, wabbled crazily, smashed a wheel against the curb across the road.

The *Demon* itself swerved, not because the impact had deflected its ponderous weight, but because Jean's grip slackened from the letdown. The car angled away from the roadbed. She straightened it out, scanned the avenue ahead.

The sedan had disappeared.

Her ribs ached. A glance at the rear-view mirror showed figures piling out of the limousine. Jean turned at the next corner. She crisscrossed the neighborhood in a futile search. She switched the shortwave set on but heard nothing. Finally she drove back toward the scene of collision and parked a few blocks away.

Of all the events crowding the past hour, she remembered most vividly the moment when the limousine drew parallel with her and the snout of a submachine gun slanted toward her, while the faces of three painted, grotesquely grinning clowns pressed against the windows.

V.

FROST closed the laboratory door at 13 State Street after ordering Jean Moray to interview the unknown client who had just rung the bell. He left the house and strode to the sedan parked in front.

He entered as casually as if he owned it, but sprawled down on the front seat. A woman's bag rested there. He scrutinized the contents, which consisted of currency, a handkerchief, and female stuff such as the inevitable lipstick. The dashboard compartment contained nothing. One side pocket yielded a .28 automatic. He found an old shopping receipt wadded down in a corner of the other pocket, below a hunk of waste and some road maps.

Frost had barely finished the swift survey when the door handle turned and a fantastically garbed young woman climbed in. Her eyes narrowed. Frost sat upright.

"What are you doing here? Get out of my car!"

"Good evening, Miss Kelsey; allow me to introduce myself. I am Professor I.V. Frost. I suggest that you drive away from here instantly."

"Of all the nerve! What do you mean by—"

"Get started."

She slammed the door, produced and turned the ignition key, and whipped out the automatic.

"A pretty thing," Frost murmured. "Tear-gas pens are useful, too, when they are loaded."

Her finger quivered on the trigger.

"Fire if you wish. Perhaps the gesture will relieve your nervous tension. I assure you that I'm in no danger since I took the liberty, and the pleasure, of removing the clip."

She jerked the trigger. Empty clicks sounded. She swung the barrel toward him. His fingers stopped it—fingers whose long and tapered beauty suggested the hand of an artist or feminine grace but the force of that grip reminded her of nothing so much as steel cable.

"Drive on!" Frost commanded.

She set her head forward, her eyes smoldering in her pale, pointed face. "Are you going to get out?"

"Eventually, yes; certainly not now."

"I left a present in the house for you. Why don't you go look at it?"

"Later."

"It's a goose egg."

"I'll counter with a cross."

Her brows wrinkled. The statement puzzled her. She glanced at him from the corners of her eyes, then threw the car in gear.

No word passed between them on the way down Broadway to Union Square nor did she volunteer information. If she noticed the auto that trailed her, she paid no attention to it.

Frost did not attempt to follow her when she stopped and used the telephone booth of a tobacco shop.

SHE RESUMED driving. Miles slipped behind them. They cut across upper Manhattan toward the Bronx. As Patricia Kelsey turned off Culver Avenue to a cross street, the mirror reflected spurts of flame from an auto that had swept alongside the big car keeping pace with them.

"There ought to be a law against people shooting off fireworks," Pat Kelsey stated indignantly as she reached another corner and turned again. Her knuckles whitened from her clench on the steering wheel; her mouth trembled.

"There is. There's also a law against shooting off firearms, but it has not prevented a good many thousands of marble slabs from being erected over the recipients of successful target practice."

Patricia ran the car up a private driveway and into a garage adjoining a large house surrounded by well-trimmed lawn and shrubbery.

She went around to the front of the house, Frost at her side, and found the door locked. She looked surprised, hesitated with indecision, then rang the bell.

A middle-aged man of substantial and prosperous appearance answered it. His pointed chin gave him a vague facial resemblance to Patricia.

His eyes gaped astonishment. He stared at the pair confronting him. "Pat!" he exclaimed. "Why are you running around in that—that— Words fail me. Is it some costume party you didn't tell me about—"

The girl ran past him without a word. He whirled, cried "Pat!" again, but she did not reply, He watched her flight until the bang of a door told that she had locked herself in a room.

He seemed on the point of following her but finally turned his attention to Frost. He glanced up the five inches that separated him from the professor's gaunt and towering length. "I don't recall having seen you with my niece before, Mr.—er—er—"

Frost introduced himself.

"Indeed?" exclaimed the other. "A private investigator? Did Pat request your services? Or has she been up to mischief? I don't understand this. Will you come in? I am Dr. Kelsey—Dr. Herbert Kelsey."

In the living room, Frost declined the offer of a drink but lighted one of his own aromatic cigarettes. "At what time did your niece leave this house?"

"I've no idea. She was not here when I arrived from my office downtown. That must have been at six thirty or so. Why do you ask? What significance does it have?"

Frost gave a scant outline of the circumstances under which Patricia had come to him.

Dr. Kelsey shook his head. "A goose egg, you say? Strange, to say the least. I confess I'm baffled. To the best of my knowledge she's never before done anything like it. When she's calmer I'll try to find out what she means by such absurd behavior."

"You may succeed where the police must fail, though I doubt whether you can elicit the slightest information from her. Let me know immediately if you do."

"Why should I succeed? Oh, I see. Because I'm a physician and, like lawyers and ministers, entitled to confidences. As it happens, medical men rarely treat members of their family, except for minor ailments and emergencies. They summon other physicians as a rule. I am no exception. I feel certain that Pat's case will simmer down to a mere prank or a feminine emotional explosion. In that event I will notify you. If a serious nervous disorder or mental disturbance indicates its presence, it would need therapeutic treatment, not the police.

"But why the police? I understood you to be a private investigator. Surely the police would not interest themselves to any extent in the case of a young woman who chose to wear unconventional clothing while making a visit. Granted that she brought a goose egg to you, a stranger. If you won't take offense, you yourself are just as unconventional in your tobacconary preferences. What it all amounts to—"

The ringing of a bell interrupted him. He crossed the room and lifted a telephone receiver. "Dr. Kelsey speaking."

He listened for a full half minute. His face grew perplexed. A knot of muscle collected on each jawbone. "But good Heavens, think of my practice, my reputation! Why, I can't possibly—"

After another pause, he answered slowly, "Oh, I see." He dabbed a handkerchief at his forehead.

He listened again and ended with, "Very well, then, I'll expect the call."

Grim wrinkles lined his face, He put the phone down. Oblivious to Frost, preoccupation with other thoughts making his eyes vacant, he picked up a decanter of sherry. He poured out a glass which he drank in rapid sips. He twirled the glass and murmured, "I must prepare for an urgent case. Suppose you phone me to-morrow."

Frost, already on the way out, flung a terse acknowledgment over his shoulder.

VI.

IN THE SHADOW of a retaining wall at the nearest intersection to the Kelsey residence, Frost took the mouthpiece of the micro-set from his pocket. "J. M.," he broadcast softly.

The voice of Jean Moray instantly replied. He sent her directions to meet him. A couple of minutes later the *Demon* rolled along and Frost slipped from his concealment.

Seated beside his assistant, he listened to her narrative, asked, "Did you recognize any of the three clowns?"

Jean sniffed. "You wouldn't recognize even your best friend if he painted his face up. How could you? But I can identify one of them by something else. The machine gunner had the thumb and little finger missing from his left hand. There can't be many men in the city with that special deformity; the only one I know of is Three-fingered Lefty, who's supposed to get paid by Gus Berber. How did you get here so quickly?"

Frost drawled, "I rode in the car that you trailed."

Her eyes glinted sparks. "And you just kept on riding while three killers did their hardest to put lots of nice cozy bullets inside me? That was sweet of you, so thoughtful and considerate, Or maybe you think I'd look better if I was ventilated like a Swiss cheese?"

"Your escape proves that you kept your wits. The *Demon* protected you from serious danger," Frost said nonchalantly. From a compartment at the base of the seat he took out two bundles, one of which he handed to her. "Slip into this bulletproof cloak. You'll need it later. Leave the hood off while you're driving, but put it on when you get out. Keep your pistol ready.

"While I talked with Dr. Kelsey, he received a telephone call. He will become another victim of the lunatic series during the next hour. Follow him if he goes away from the house. If he doesn't, and if he receives a visitor who seems eccentric for any reason, follow the visitor instead. Whichever it is, don't let him out of your sight. Notice particularly other persons that you may encounter.

"There's a miniature camera here that takes clear pictures, even by moonlight. If the subject does anything that attracts attention, photograph the crowd.

"I'm going to Grand Central Station now on another line of investigation."

"What a life!" Jean sighed, and turned the full force of her glance upon Frost. "Here it's a beautiful summer evening, and I broke a date with one of my favorite scoundrels in order to chase all over town and get shot at, where as we would have been dancing on a roof garden now, and later he'd have made love to me and—"

Frost eased himself out and closed the door. Jean smiled a contented smile, hoping she had irked him. His inscrutable expression, as he vanished around the corner, did not leave her a single clue.

She lolled behind the wheel of the *Demon* after Frost's exit. Nothing happened for the first half hour. Minutes passed until, at 9:15, a long, sleek roadster slid up to the Kelsey residence. The driver, its sole occupant, stepped out.

Jean's eyes bulged for the third time that evening. She instantly recognized the newcomer as April Holley, one of the most talented of rising screen actresses. April defied classification because she changed her personality, her make-up, her style, and her appearance for every role. She radiated in abundance that indefinable magnetic quality which separates the creative from the imitative artist.

THE DARKNESS and the distance at which Jean sat made it impossible for her to determine more than that April, in real life, seemed about five feet four and possessed a marvelous figure. She walked with a sinuous glide that floated her along. She wore a one-piece bathing suit of some pastel shade that caused Jean trouble in deciding where the fabric began and ended.

April merged with the shadows of the porch.

She came down the steps a few minutes later clinging to an arm of Dr. Kelsey. She said something. He appeared ill at ease. In startling contrast to her scanty raiment, he had donned full dress, including top hat and gloves. Not until they reached the roadster did Jean discover the reason for his nervousness. He walked barefoot. He had omitted shoes, socks, and spats. The unadorned feet obviously caused him extreme self-consciousness.

The roadster picked up speed. Power aplenty lay under its hood. It rivaled Frost's *Demon.*

April drove expertly but at reckless velocity toward Brooklyn. She jumped traffic signals, careened around corners, shot along thoroughfares. Jean found herself pressed to keep pace with the queerly dressed pair who streaked away. She dropped a dangerous distance behind on occasions; at other times she followed in their exhaust.

The flight continued to Coney Island. The roadster turned along the ocean-front drive and halted beyond the board walk's limits.

Dr. Kelsey stepped out of one side, April from the other. The screen actress carried a bucket. The doctor balanced a long-handled fork of close-set tines on his shoulder. They marched across the beach. They waded until the water reached their waists.

April held the bucket while her companion began digging for clams.

A few late fugitives from the metropolitan heat wave watched the performance with growing curiosity. New arrivals strolled over. A knot of spectators assembled.

Jean, parked a few dozen yards behind the roadster, lowered a window. The faintest of stars flecked the misty darkness. She heard the pounding surge and retreat of the Atlantic. The salt wetness of ocean filled the air. With Frost's camera, she took a dozen pictures of the spectators.

When the pair emerged, April looked fresh from the dip, but Kelsey's ruined outfit clung to him soggily. He dripped pools of water.

They met the law as they started up the sands. A member of the beach patrol dispersed the crowd. Another confronted April and her companion. The tone of his voice indicating that he recognized the screen star, he spoke, "You'll have to dump those clams back."

"Why?"

"It's against health regulations, Miss Holley. You can't eat 'em. The water's polluted and they're bad. What's the idea, anyway? Is this a publicity stunt?"

"We're on a scavenger hunt. It's a sort of game," Kelsey volunteered.

"I don't know anything about that, mister."

April said, "Take the clams. Throw them back. Eat them. Do what you want with them."

A hysterical edge suddenly altered her liquid accents. She thrust the bucket at the surprised officer and unceremoniously fled to her roadster like a frightened nymph from the sea. Kelsey pattered after her. He barely had time to jump on the running board before the roadster leaped away.

Instead of returning to the city, April followed the South Shore road and sped up Long Island. The congested sections and suburbs slipped behind. She drove at her former reckless speed and again Jean found it a hard task to keep the roadster in view.

AN HOUR passed. April was still streaking northeast and had reached a lonely, deserted stretch when headlights of a distinctly bluish tinge winked from far ahead. At this spot several hundred yards of flat, sandy soil covered with low bushes and clusters of weeds separated the road from the ocean. Hilly ground sloped on the landward side.

April braked the roadster to a violent stop.

An eighth of a mile behind, Jean slowed down. By the faint farthermost glow of her headlights she saw Kelsey descend and slam the door shut.

The roadster swept onward, went into high gear, made a right-angle turn. Jean took a sharp breath. Things happened so fast she couldn't comprehend them.

April drove straight for the ocean. The roadster bumped and jerked; its velocity mounted, it became a blur that tunneled the moonless darkness.

Kelsey whirled, stared, started to run after it. He shouted again and again, then hesitated and looked toward the bluish lights of the auto bearing down on him.

Jean stepped on the gas, switched her lights to flood, and angled toward the sea. The long beam picked out the sleek roadster, April's face, wild and desperate, unwaveringly awaiting the ocean. Her car must have been hurtling above sixty miles an hour when it smote the Atlantic with a hiss and a great splash. The waters closed over it.

April did not come to the surface.

Frost's *Demon* hummed a song of thirsting power as Jean shot it across the waste land. The *Demon's* weight and reserves kept it under control. She flung it true to the mark. She was dimly aware that the blue headlights had outlined Kelsey and that he held his hands high. The lights blinked off.

"Watch him; watch him!" Frost's words echoed through her mind.

"Let him be killed," her instincts commanded. One or the other—the man or the trapped, drowning girl—she couldn't manage both. Her nerves screamed to the rasp of rubber on sand as she swung the *Demon* broadside to the sea.

"Come up, come up, you've got to come up!" Jean implored aloud.

April did not rise to the surface.

Jean leaped out. Tongues of evil flame blossomed on the road. "They're killing him; they're killing him," she thought feverishly. Then hornet buzzes filled the air and slugs screeched off the *Demon*. Two stinging blows hit her through the bulletproof cloak as she darted around the *Demon*. She realized all at once that she—and not Kelsey—was the target. The shock sobered her. She had no time for battle or rage or anything but rescue of the drowning girl.

She reached the seaward side of the *Demon,* its body protecting her from the bullets. The extended burst of machine-gun fire, the spray of lead, ceased as she tore the cloak off. She kicked her shoes away, slipped out of her dress with a lithe motion at hectic speed, and flashed to the water.

A good swimmer, she shattered all her past records. A long crawl stroke cleft the surface, carried her beyond the spot where the roadster had submerged. She dived, came up a minute later for a gulp of fresh air, dived again. In eighteen feet of water she found April slumped over the roadster's wheel. She hauled the girl free, pushed for the surface.

She couldn't tell if April still lived. She used her right arm to keep the unconscious head above water, stroked out with her left arm.

The blue lights winked on, pointing toward the *Demon*. They began to cross the waste land, faster and faster. The vicious flames spurted anew. Jean went under. Her heart thundered. She swam until exhausted, came up for air, found she could touch bottom. The red flashes had ceased, and no bullets clipped the water around her, but the bluish headlights raced closer.

"Come out of it; wake up; hurry, you've got to help me make it!" she pleaded to the limp girl, but there came only a horrible gurgling rattle for answer.

Dismay filled Jean; she remembered that the nearest doors of the *Demon* were locked from the inside. It would do her no good to reach it ahead of the bluish lights. She would have to run into the open, face their murderous glare.

Splashing for shore, towing the inert figure, Jean stared frantically at the onrushing lights that brought death.

VII.

AFTER FROST had told his assistant to watch the Kelsey residence, he walked several blocks before he found a cab.

It dropped him at Grand Central Station. Frost joined the usual small rush of commuters who spent the evening in town and began an exodus around nine o'clock. The hands of the station clock stood at twenty minutes past the hour.

Frost went directly to the office of the station master.

A bent old wisp of a man with the gloomy face of a chronic hypochondriac sat back in a chair with his feet on the table. He had to spread them to see who came in.

He looked even more woebegone after he sighted Frost. "No, I'm not glad to see you." His voice rasped thin and shrill. "A fine friend you are. I don't see you for months on end, only when you got something you want to get out of me. The answer is no! Why don't you throw away that old leather jacket? I bet it would stand up if you threw it in a corner. I bet it's got so many acid stains on it now that you could boil it and get enough stuff out of it to win a war."

"Glad to find you in such good spirits, Mac," Frost greeted him cheerfully. "As a matter of fact, you're looking worse. You've probably convinced yourself that you've added arteriosclerosis, gout, and neuritis to your long list of fancied ailments since I last saw you."

"They aren't fancy ailments and anyway you're wrong. It's my hearing that ain't what it used to be. I'll be deaf in another—"

"Perhaps, but that will require six months to prove, whereas I cannot devote even sixty minutes to what I'm here for.

"On each side of the station there's a bank of steel lockers."

"Oh, sure, you mean the parcel locks. You interested in them?" MacDonald took his feet off the desk and perked up his ears, his face a little less mournful. "They're quite a gadget—automatic, you know. You open the locker, put your parcel in, and chuck a dime through the slot so you can get the key out. Then you lock the door and walk away. The key is your check, but you have to use it inside of twenty-four hours. What about it? Is this for one of your cases?"

"Yes, and a tough one. Is the mechanism such that a depositor could return within the time limit every day, insert another dime, and thus retain exclusive occupancy for as long as he wished?"

"Sure."

"Do you keep duplicate keys?"

"We don't have anything to do with them. The lockers are made by an outfit called Locker-Tite. It owns them and rents the station space. It has its own service man who comes around every morning to collect the dimes and see that the empties work O. K. They know me. Want me to call them? There's a man on all night."

"Find out if they list the individual receipts; if so, whether any lockers have yielded daily payments for the last two weeks. Get the numbers."

MacDonald lifted the telephone receiver and dialed. He absentmindedly toyed with a pencil while seeking the information. His thoughts kept straying back to a period two years ago when, as a locomotive engineer, he had driven his passenger express around a curve and piled it into a line of freight empties that were being sidetracked. He received critical injuries, but survived to find himself fired, then tried and convicted on charges of criminal negligence, involving manslaughter. He testified that the signal light showed green. The company experts found it in perfect working order.

The freight crew testified it had been set for red. MacDonald's stoker couldn't testify about anything because he died in the wreck. Frost read a full account of the circumstances, stepped in, and demonstrated how the light values could have been deliberately reversed by either of two methods. He found a few clues on the site and suggested a new line of investigation that produced the real criminal and exonerated

MacDonald. Incapacitated for heavy work, the pilot asked for, at Frost's suggestion, and received the job of station master.

MacDONALD hung up. "Here are your numbers. The first three boxes in the top row of each bank have been used every day. No. 27 is the only other locker that collected dimes the past two weeks. Hey, wait a jiff—"

Frost, disappearing through the door, called over his shoulder, "I'll be back in a minute."

He scanned the lockers as he strode past them to No. 27. Before he reached it, he took out several flat, blank keys which were coated with wax, and selected one. He inserted it, twisted it gently, and withdrew it. The action required scarcely more than a second.

He returned to MacDonald's office and, over the station master's voluble protests, perched himself on the desk. He studied the marks on the wax coating of the key, clipped the soft metal with a scissors that had nippers as tiny as a line on an oyster fork and thin like a razor blade, then used a small file to polish the edges.

MacDonald complained morosely, "There goes my job. Before my eyes he makes a key to open a box in my station with hundreds of witnesses. It isn't enough that I'm going deaf; he makes me a party to a larceny. And the jails are so drafty I'll probably catch pneumonia."

"You'll live to be a hundred," Frost prophesied.

"I'll live to be hunted? Who's responsible for that?" he cackled and launched a dissertation on deafness that never caught up with Frost's ears or his heels.

Frost inserted the key in Locker 27 and opened the door.

Inside lay a miscellany that would have supported the yellow tabloids for years. The nest could spawn blackmail, extortion, breach of promise, fraud, scandal, and murder. It included incendiary letters, forged checks, a pistol, I O Us, memoranda, pawnshop tickets, records of crooked business deals, proof of bribery, wax disks, clinical case histories, a diary in feminine script, and other items.

The documentary group, though not large, involved famous names, some in lesser ranks of society, others of unknowns. But the extensive photographic collection made it seem anæmic.

The picture studies comprised at least fifty, a miniature camera, equipped with telephoto lens, had obviously taken most of them from a distance. Many were of a nature to make the orbs bulge on even a veteran censor. The back of each snapshot bore the name of the subject. Single letters cut out of newspaper print and pasted together spelled the names.

Harmin, who pushed the peanut with his nose, had once written an angry letter that read like a threat of violent physical assault, and which could still bring him a prison sentence. A photograph of Kelsey and a woman could more than wreck his career. Gus Berber, before he had a police record, killed a man of whose murder he was never suspected. Gus later wrote the full details to a woman companion in a burst of incomparable stupidity and boastfulness. That confession, in police hands, would enable them to send him on the long road, perhaps even the last mile.

All the persons whom Frick had mentioned a few hours earlier appeared in the data by name or by photograph.

"Thanks for finding us the evidence. We'll take it now," ordered a voice at Frost's elbow.

He turned around. Seven plainclothes detectives, whom he did not recognize, ringed him in; at least a dozen more streamed toward him from all directions, the wail of a police siren rose outside, and a wild uproar swept through the station as the passenger traffic diverted to the scene of disturbance.

VIII.

JEAN, hampered by the dead weight of April Holley, struggled through the shallows to reach shore ahead of the blue lights. She breathed convulsive gasps. Her pulse hammered in her throat, temples and ears. She staggered out of the water, trembling and flushed from her exertions. She hauled the relaxed form to the running board, snatched up the bulletproof cloak.

There was no time to don it. She held it in front of her as a loose shield and darted around the rear of Frost's *Demon*. The long garment protected all but her legs below the knees as it flapped against her body. Then the machine gun snarled its savage chatter again; messengers of death winged the air. She didn't know how many bruises she received—half a dozen at least—from the impact of pellets that flattened on the fabric. Her ribs started aching once more.

She twisted the door handle. The cloak slipped, and her heart gave a great bound. It stopped entirely during the fractional instant that the headlights mercilessly flooded her. Then the door swung and slammed, and the bitter pills screamed off Frost's fortress.

Jean's heart raced wildly now, uncontrollably. She slid across the seat, snapped the opposite door open, tugged at April's body. She didn't look to see what the blue lights did. She couldn't look. She had to get that inert weight inside.

"Frost!" her lips whistled his name, and more loudly, *"Frost!"* Always before the professor had materialized like a magician, a phantom, at her moments of greatest need, but he was not here to help her now. She dragged April's head and torso into the car, worked madly to bring up the trailing legs.

Wraithlike figures slid around the *Demon,* one at each end; cold-eyed killers with pistols rising. Their faces made only a blur on her consciousness as they sped toward her. She stuffed the girl's ankles and feet toward the foot rest, yanked the door fast and clicked the lock. Her hands flew to the wheel.

Both men leaped on the running board. She put the *Demon* into high instantly, with the last drain upon its reserves which Frost had ordered her never to attempt except under fear of death.

The *Demon* took a mighty leap, like a plane catapulted on its way. The men grabbed with flailing arms, but no human strength could have resisted that prodigious thrust. The *Demon* drove forward with the power of a battering-ram. They bowled off into darkness, both of them, and Jean fought to head the *Demon* away from the sea. It purred across the sand, turned, streaked for the road.

Only then did she permit herself a glance at the rear-view mirror. She saw the blue lights crawl toward the pair. They picked themselves up and jumped into the car. It gathered speed. The blue lights circled toward the road, but away from the *Demon,* heading northeast.

JEAN STOPPED at the pavement. She felt the actress' heart, found a faint, perceptible beat. Jean pulled, panted, shoved, and toiled with a heroic determination. She got April's head down on the front upholstery and her legs dangling on the back floor so that her body made a jackknife. Jean kneaded the girl's lungs. Water purled from the bloodless lips. April's breathing grew regular between spasms of coughing.

Jean scanned the road. Far ahead crawled red tail lights, preceded by a milky glow. No other vehicle intervened. Jean threw the *Demon* into gear and started overhauling those far lights. It might be a wild-goose chase, but blue paper can color white light, and blue filters can be torn off white lights by a moment's work.

She swiftly narrowed the distance from the far tail lamp. She didn't know if it was the right car or if it contained Kelsey. She had lost track of Kelsey. The flying tail lamp offered the only action she could take.

April no longer needed emergency treatment. She ought to have hospitalization to guard against pneumonia, but Jean counted on finding aid at one of the towns ahead long before the time it would take to drive back to New York.

April trembled, began to push her hands against the seat. When she regained consciousness she climbed weakly in front and relaxed. The exertion brought a fit of coughing.

"Take it easy," Jean advised. "You're safe now."

"Why did you do it?" Despair undertoned the question.

"That's what I ought to ask," Jean retorted. "Why did *you* do it?"

April caught a corner of her lower lip between her teeth, made no reply.

Jean, after a sidelong glance, confessed herself unable to pigeonhole the character of the young actress. She sensed a personality complex, changeable, elusive. April Holley, in real life, proved the same enigma that had made her screen portrayals fascinating. She presented a problem, difficult to analyze, not because of pose but because of her genuine self. Even her eloquent violet eyes told little. Terror, curiosity, resentment, any of a dozen reasons might have caused their expression.

Jean changed the subject. "Somebody's going to pay for a perfectly good dress and practically brand-new shoes I left back there on the beach."

"I'm sorry. I'll—"

"Forget it. I didn't mean it that way. Driving barefoot doesn't exactly soothe my soles. Can you reach the pocket behind you? It ought to hold a pair of sneakers."

April turned and rummaged, brought them forth. Jean put them on with difficulty. With equal difficulty, April helped and tied the laces. "Do you carry extras of everything?"

Jean smiled. "Hardly. The sneakers are handy in summer time. The cloak will have to do for a dress when I get out.

"You'll find cigarettes in my pocketbook, but I don't think you ought to smoke now."

"Thanks." April drew one out and lighted it. After a minute she asked, "Where are you driving?"

"Frankly, I don't know." Jean introduced herself, added, "I know your name, of course. As far as tonight's concerned, don't worry. It won't reach print. And you'll see the end of the lunatic plague."

April looked puzzled.

Jean explained, "Ivy Frost will stop it. I can't say how, but he will. If you don't happen to know about Frost, he's a scientist who taught at universities for a good many years until academic life bored him. He had done research for crime detection laboratories among other things. When he resigned his professorship, he returned to private life as a specialist. Now he's one of the best. He won't touch run-of-the-mill stuff. Most of his cases spell murder. Even then it takes a strange mix-up or something bizarre to get his interest."

April, who had turned her head while Jean spoke, said irrelevantly, "You've got a strong personality of your own. Unusual. And looks enough. Have you ever tried Hollywood? If you want to come out some time—"

Jean shook her head. "Definitely no. Right now I hold about the most exciting position in the country. Maybe I won't live long at it but it produces more danger and thrills in a week than Hollywood could in a year. It makes living intense, hectic. It's packed full of hazards, but they're worth it."

Jean abruptly suppressed further comments she intended to make and silently called herself names. She wasn't getting information; she was giving it. True, she had idly chattered to put the girl at ease but she saw now that no one could control April. When the actress' nerves exploded and she wanted to drown herself, she instantly went ahead. Rescued, she had already forgotten the incident. Ill from exposure though she might be, she had certainly nursed Jean into admission of facts.

APRIL HOLLEY smiled wanly, her large purple eyes cherishing a secretive glow. Perhaps she had guessed what thoughts upset Frost's assistant.

Jean's answer died on her lips. Her attention jumped past April. It shifted because the car ahead turned off the road and ran up a short driveway to a bungalow that loomed dark against the sea beyond.

Jean continued driving, saw other isolated cottages, and around the next bend encountered the main cluster of a summer colony. No lights showed. The clock on the dashboard indicated 12:45. She parked off the road under a clump of poplars.

A quandary stumped her. She couldn't take April along. She feared that the actress might grow inquisitive about the *Demon,* or cause damage, or give way to an unpredictable whim if left behind in Frost's car. Every second's delay reduced her chances of learning what went on at the bungalow, if the occupants of the car were what she expected.

She took the ignition key, a pistol, flashlight, the cloak and hood. "Wait here," she told April, "I'll only be gone a few minutes."

April curled down on the seat. "Wake me when you get back." She closed her eyes.

Jean didn't know how to take the gesture and didn't stop to watch. The long cloak over her, she returned to the cottage.

It stood five or six hundred feet from the sea, with a ragged lawn that rolled down to the beach sands. The shadowy outlines of bushes, saplings, and young trees loomed against the ocean and sweep of sky. The mild, rhythmic wash of waves whispered upon the air. The sea was the calmest she had ever seen. That she could observe so much surprised her. A strange darkness prevailed. Without moon, and with the stars hazed out, the night held a mysterious, impalpable glow. She saw masses but not details. The warm, wet air made her uncomfortable.

The car, all lights off, rested at the road front of the cottage. A single square of illumination streamed from a window on the seaside. She heard clinking, hammering sounds. She was cautiously moving forward when the noise ceased. The light vanished.

Jean stopped dead still. A few seconds later came the thud of feet on the stoop, the click of doors opened and closed. The headlights beamed; the engine caught, and away rolled the auto.

Jean sped to the darkened window, swept the room with her beam.

Kelsey lay on the floor, spread-eagled, each arm and leg handcuffed to a spike. A big bruise welted his forehead.

Summer cottages seldom have doors or windows locked. Jean pulled the hood over her head, then raised the window and listened. She heard nothing.

Once inside, she knelt over Kelsey. His heart beat strongly. His captors had probably donated the bump on his head just to make him manageable. And when he wakened, he could die slowly, with no chance whatever of freeing himself.

She tested a spike, found it solidly embedded. She couldn't do much by her unaided efforts. She stood up.

"Hold it!" a harsh voice grated at the window.

She snapped the flashlight out, jumped for the door. At the same instant, the overhead light flooded the room.

"Stop where you are!" came a husky bark from the doorway.

Jean half turned to bring both in view, her mind racing, desperate. The two killers who had been bowled off the running board of the *Demon* had caught up with her.

The one at the window started coming in.

"Back or I'll shoot!" Jean ran for the window.

He came through. Two spurts exploded from her pistol. She saw him jerk. The effect was astounding. Feet on the sill, he leaped toward her, arms outflung. Too late, too bitterly, she realized that his powerful build represented not muscle but a bulletproof jacket. Her third shot hit the ceiling as the weapon flew out of her hand.

Pinioned from behind, she saw the second man pick up her pistol. His left hand lacked thumb and little finger.

"Nice work, boys."

Gus Berber drifted through the door jauntily. Gus looked like half weasel, half eel. He ripped the hood off Jean, cooed, "I thought so. When you lam from a joint, you don't have to keep on going. So we came back to see the pretty mouse. It's curtains."

"Three-fingered Lefty" scowled. "You mean it?"

"I mean it."

"Here?"

"Naw, down the road. Leave the guy to wiggle loose all by himself. Take her for a ride. Then tie up what's left and dump it in the sea."

"What's against the dame? Listen, Gus, you losin' your mind? You gave us screwy orders early this evenin'. Put paint on our faces and go some place and shoot a certain party if they tailed a certain party." Lefty snarled, "I didn't know who she was then. Next you give us screwy orders to put blue lights on our car and go to hell-and-gone and pick up a guy and bring him here. Sure, you were with us, so what? So here we are and the dame's such a knock-out I been wonderin' where I saw her. Now I know. She works for Frost."

"What of it?"

"What of it!" squawked Lefty. "Remember what he did to the Blake mob? And cleaned out the ROPA? And a lot of others? Gee, that guy's poison. Bump off the dame? We'd never even get a chance at court! He'd pick us off in just about the time it takes to tell!"

"The order stands," said Gus, softly—very softly. "It's the works, unless you want—" He left the sentence unfinished.

Lefty glowered, took a nasal breath, subsided. "O. K."

"That's better. I'm still running this show."

Jean's eyes widened.

A bluish muzzle crept over the window sill. Violet eyes and a flushed, reckless face bobbed up. "Drop your guns! I'll shoot the runt first! Turn her loose!"

"April!" Jean screamed. "Bulletproof vests. Shoot at heads!"

A fist clapped over her mouth.

Lefty spun for the window, his finger taut on the trigger.

IX.

FROST SMILED at the host of detectives who thronged around him in the Grand Central Terminal. A beatific expression lighted his features, as with secret, supreme appreciation of some cosmic jest. He drawled, "Life is sometimes inspiredly lunatic. One detective can catch twenty killers, but it takes twenty detectives to catch one detective. Get Inspector Frick down here."

"Any minute now," said the nearest man. "He left orders. We notified him the second you barged into the station."

The siren stopped wailing. The detective squad went to work to disperse the mob. Inspector Frick bustled through the hurrying commuters. He seemed both uneasy and self-satisfied as he approached the professor.

Frick ventured, with a half apology, "We caught up with you this time, Ivy. When I left you this afternoon I ordered twenty detectives placed here and another twenty on duty at the Pennsylvania Station. What have you got there?"

He glanced at the cache hastily, whistled, "Phew! We ought to clear the mystery up in short order after we work on this stuff and the experts go over it."

"They'll never see it!" Frost snapped tersely. He shut and locked the door.

"See here, Ivy—"

"Let's settle it outside, in your official limousine."

Frost strode off. The inspector issued a rapid order to the captain of the detective squad, then chased after the retreating figure.

Inside the automobile, Frost explained, "Headquarters will never see the material in that locker because I'm going to destroy it!"

"You can't do that!"

"I can and will. That assortment merely accounts for the lunatic plague. I could have told you as much this afternoon. I located the horde partly to verify my deductions, and partly in the hope that it might supply a lead. It doesn't. It offers not the slightest clue of any value to capture or identify the criminal.

"With twenty detectives and control of the station you can forcibly transport the stuff to police headquarters over my objections. If you do, I withdraw from the case and I can assure you it will never be solved. If you don't, I'll make the identification before to-morrow noon. I'll guarantee unquestionable proof of his guilt."

"We can reach the same result by analyzing the stuff."

"You won't get anywhere by analyzing the whole lot!" Frost answered impatiently. "There's a phrase that's lost its meaning from over-use, but it certainly applies here. We're up against a fiendish mind. You won't find one single fingerprint in all that pile. You won't obtain a solitary clue though you examine the letters and photographs from now till doomsday. You can question all the individuals concerned, threaten them, prosecute them, and you'll draw an absolute blank for all your efforts. Why? Because even they haven't the faintest idea who's guilty, and if they did they'd never talk because they'd face worse ruin."

"They'll face it and like it. They'll talk!"

"Why wreck the lives of a hundred in a futile search for one? They're no better and no worse than any average assortment of humanity. I've never met the individual, male or female, who didn't possess a flaw or a skeleton somewhere in the closet.

"Hasn't it occurred to you that the locker contains numerous prints, but no films? Where are the negatives from which those prints were made? On the basis of your recital this afternoon, logic at once told me that too many of the lunatic cases existed even for coincidence, therefore, they must be purposive, a common link must unite them; yet the persons involved in each scene had no personal acquaintance with those connected to other cases. Nor did fantastic behavior form their point of similarity."

"I told you they didn't connect."

"Ah, but they did. All the victims proved alike in their refusal to talk, their failure to offer any explanation whatsoever for the performances.

"Why did they refuse? Because they must have been commanded to silence. Why would they indulge in humiliating or even murderous actions and offer no defense? Because they acted under compulsion and possessed a deeper fear of the consequences if they failed in the least detail.

"What could account for such an intense fear? A combination of two reasons, and two reasons only. Each individual had a skeleton in his closet, some past offense against society or some folly committed, of which evidence existed. Some one owned that evidence, but the victims did not know his or her identity.

"Starting from those premises, deduction solved a little more than the basic pattern of the mystery. Many persons of prominence were already involved. The sword unquestionably hung over the heads of others. It would be physically impossible for the criminal to obtain overnight a wide variety of evidence that damns a large group. Therefore, he must have accumulated it over a period of time. Unlike the average blackmailer, he did not strike immediately, or strike for cash. The passage of years would make it still harder for the victims to trace his identity."

FROST EMPHASIZED. "He bided his time and struck. Now do you see the full magnitude of his scheme? What a terrific menace he is? He's cunning, ruthless, infinitely resourceful. No suspicion would fall on him, but if it did, no evidence proving his guilt must be found. Therefore, he would not keep the material on his premises. Yet he needed access to it day and night during his campaign of terror. Therefore, he would not store it in a bank safety-deposit box. Where could he put it? In a public lock box. From available sites he would choose the railroad terminal because of its size and traffic, with less likelihood of any one noticing him. But if the police found that box, they would get no clue to his identity, and he would preserve a substantial part of his power by storing the films elsewhere.

"They are his reserve. They lie in a safe-deposit vault rented under an assumed name at a bank."

"I'll put a hundred detectives to work! I'll have them comb every box in town if it takes months!"

"And he'll know every step you take! There's a leak in your own office. I found that out before I laid eyes on the locker. My assistant phoned a memorandum for your desk. Within an hour the lunatic plague—in the shape of a weirdly costumed woman—made its appearance at my residence. If you didn't announce your purpose at your office, no one could have foreseen your visit to me. Therefore, the memorandum. Through his hold over one police official, the criminal would learn the contents of the note. He would either stop his activities then or issue a thumb-at-his-nose gesture."

"A police official could trace the call!"

"Not the way this crook works. The official goes to a specified public pay booth at a specified time every day. There he receives a call from another pay booth and makes his report. He is then given the number and location of another booth, and the time to be there the following day, and at the hour is called from still a different public booth. Each booth is one of a large group at a busy place.

"Frick, the preparation of years went into this mess. Ordinary methods won't smash the plan overnight. Bank authorities won't coöperate with you on such a wholesale scale for a search based on a hypothesis. In any event, by the time you located the vault, the safety box would be empty and the films stored somewhere else. You'd only get a fictitious name and perhaps a vague, useless description from the guard."

"There must be a way! We've got to run him down,"

Frost drawled, "How? There are seven million suspects in this area, and no tangible clues. Any person already involved, living or dead, and any name or person figuring in the locker contents may be guilty of the lunatic plague."

"What!" The inspector gasped incredulously.

"Perhaps that's the most brilliant stroke. I'm convinced, for reasons too long to detail, that he deliberately included evidence which incriminated himself, so that he would automatically be eliminated from suspicion."

"Well, I'll be damned!" Frick exploded, his red face redder still from the flare of anger. "Does he think he's going to make a monkey out of us?"

"My dear inspector," Frost snapped, "that is exactly what he's doing. He had the insufferable egotism to compel one of his victims to bring me a goose egg, he's so supremely confident that the combined results of our work will total precisely zero." Frost glanced at the dashboard clock.

"When they bring him in," Frick threatened, "I'll tell the boys to work on him all they please if it costs me my job!"

"And if they never bring him in?"

Frick made no answer.

THE PROFESSOR continued: "Furthermore, some of that evidence came into his hands by a method that either deliberately framed innocent persons, or made it impossible for victims to know until now that it existed. The picture of a doctor and a woman patient could ruin them both, but you won't learn anything by quizzing them. Why? Because the criminal could have picked his name at random from a directory, rented an office across from his in another building, and waited days or weeks to get that one snap with a telephoto tens. As a matter of fact, it's only a routine physical examination such as any doctor makes hundreds of times, but it looks bad, very bad.

"You might locate the office used by the photographer. Later tenants would have obscured all trace of his occupancy, years back, under an assumed name. The rental agent at this date could hardly give much useful information. The guilty one may even be dead already."

"How the deuce can you figure that?"

"Fitzroyd, the orchestra leader, if responsible for the plague, could have issued a whole series of orders to different victims for them to carry out at future dates. He could have made the appointment at which Gus Berber shot him. Berber, on suspicion, may have determined to kill whomever he met on the chance that he was dealing directly with the man in whose power he lay. Fitzroyd, in advance, would order Judge Hagerman to free any suspect accused of a murder to occur that night at a certain locality. Fitzroyd may have planned to kill Berber, and the tables turned.

"Fitzroyd didn't have any gun on him," Frick protested.

"Neither did Berber. I believe that Berber planted one of his own men in a darkened doorway as an extra precaution. When he fled, he tossed the gun to his accomplice. And while the police chased Berber, the accomplice had ample time to frisk the dead man's pockets. The fact that Fitzroyd had a couple of fish in his pockets when taken to the morgue is no proof at all that they did not contain other items at the moment he fell.

"In that case, Berber's gang would have the key to the locker, would discover the contents, and be able to force his release even if Fitzroyd hadn't given instructions to the judge. I leave you to imagine how the lunatic plague would sweep on under the loving hands of Berber's gangsters.

"Gus Berber may be the criminal we seek. He could have accumulated much of the material in the locker through his various racketeering and vice connections.

"And neither Berber nor Fitzroyd may afford the answer. Consider then the dilemma that faced Berber. If he didn't kill Fitzroyd as ordered, he would go to the electric chair when the terrorist sent the incriminating record of a past murder to the police. If Berber did slay Fitzroyd, he would face the chair for that crime."

Frick insisted stubbornly, though with less conviction, "The dragnet will get him sooner or later. We'll make people testify. We'll salt him away for the rest of his life."

"Will you? On what charges? Blackmail? So far it does not appear that he's exacted a dollar of tribute. As the mystery stands, I see no grounds to convict him. A good defense attorney could demolish the prosecution's case because of its tenuous and hypothetical nature.

"Yet he killed Paula Van Wyke, Fitzroyd, and perhaps others as surely as if he drove a dagger into their hearts. His crimes are the more monstrous because he compelled others to accomplish the act and assume the burden of guilt. He's perfected his method and technique to such a degree that he enjoys virtual immunity from the law. In some respects he has originated a new kind of crime."

"There aren't any new kinds of crime." Frick scowled.

"Aren't there? I'd call this compulsory lunacy, or forcible performance, or murder by remote control. Libel and slander are on the statutes, but what law covers personal damage to yourself by your own crazy behavior? If we don't stop him and trap him fast, he'll establish a secret, one-man rule of terror over a hundred or more persons in all walks of life. He'll have the power of a dictator. He'll be an invisible god, controlling puppets. What he will do then is limited only by the wildest imagination. Anything; everything; wholesale homicide; blackmail on a scale of millions; whatever he wants to do." Frost looked at the clock again.

The inspector was silent for a moment. He didn't doubt any longer. Frost had painted a deadly picture. "Frost, you can do things we can't. Red tape and politics don't bother you. This thing has got to be stopped. Pass me the word and I'll get all the men and equipment you can use. If there's a way I can help you—"

"There is. Lend me this auto."

"Hm?" Frick exclaimed.

"That's all. I need power, speed, and perhaps the siren now. My own *Demon* is, unfortunately, in use."

Frick opened the door. "Want the chauffeur? He's inside."

"No. Be at your office after two A.M."

The limousine swung out and away.

X.

AT THE COTTAGE on Long Island, Lefty spun toward the window, his automatic pointing.

"Hold it!" drawled a cold, implacable voice from the doorway behind Gus Berber.

The instant that Frost spoke, Gus screeched. Whatever his words were, the roaring fury that swept the room drowned them.

Lefty continued swinging toward the window; his gun spat flame; but the explosion sounded like the echo of Frost's shot. Lefty swayed. His eyes peered stupidly at the spot on the wall where his bullet had plowed. He pitched over, a hole through his temple.

Gus Berber yammered and twitched as the window unloosed a spray of red flashes. April's wild shooting smacked his vest, thudded on Frost's cloak, took Gus once at the skull. Gus leaned against the wall, a curious look of surprise entering his face. His body sagged, and his face sagged into idiotic vacancy.

The third gunman released an arm to fire, tried to hold Jean for a shield with the other. She twisted, flung herself aside, stumbled sprawling over Kelsey. The second and final blast from the long-barreled pistol that Frost carried punched a piece of the gunman's face through the back of his head. By some oddity of reflex, his finger tightened and two more bursts spewed from his automatic. The slugs flattened at the level of Frost's knees. The gunman toppled.

Frost mourned dryly, without regret, "Not quite as I planned. However, the young woman's intrusion did not alter the results. I would suggest that she indulge in extensive target practice for the future, and wear more adequate protection."

April sprang across the sill, shivered from reaction. "I've never had so much excitement!" she cried hysterically. "That's why I became an actress. Nothing ever happened to me; I had to pretend all the adventures I wanted! I couldn't wait at the car. I found the gun there and came here, just hoping that—" She slumped in a complete faint.

Jean got up. "Ivy! If you'd reached us a minute later!"

Frost corrected her. "I was here before they arrived."

"But what—how could you have guessed?"

"I didn't guess; I knew. It's Kelsey's cottage. He had a picture of the place in the living room of his home. Give me the outline of what happened to you."

He listened to her résumé. His eyes suddenly glinted. "Splendid! That clears everything. Get the *Demon* and drive it here. Frick's limousine brought me but it's safely hidden where he can send for it tomorrow."

Frost went to work. By the time Jean returned he had freed Kelsey and restored both Kelsey and April.

Jean drove the *Demon,* April again at her side. As it gathered momentum Jean asked, "Where shall I stop first? Hospital or 13 State Street?"

"Neither. Police headquarters," was Frost's laconic answer.

Dr. Kelsey frowned. "Is that necessary?"

"It is, to stop you and the lunatic plague."

"Are you serious? I've no idea what you're talking about. You've killed the men who assaulted me. Is it something to do with them?"

"They died because I don't care for professional killers, and I particularly dislike individuals who try their marksmanship on my valuable assistant. I settled one score there. But they weren't acting on their own initiative. Berber had received orders from the nameless voice, the invisible threat—which was you! Now I am going to settle that score."

"GREAT SCOTT, man, look at what they did to me! I would have died if you hadn't rescued me!"

"What they did was also at your order and for the sole purpose of exonerating yourself from suspicion. You wouldn't have died or even suffered severely. When you remained missing, your niece would look here first of all. Or you may have left orders with some other victim to come to this cottage to-morrow."

"You're building mountains out of pure moonshine and utter nonsense!"

"By no means. You committed two errors—one trifling and one serious. The first consisted of including your niece among your victims. You did it because of the relationship. Knowing her habits and whereabouts, you could always use her for an emergency, as you did to-night. The weakness lay in ostensibly putting two members of one family under the same menace. If innocent, they, alone, of the victims would best be able by comparing notes to identify the criminal. If not innocent, one must be the criminal himself.

"The second error damns you. Miss Moray noticed it and by truly brilliant deduction, without my aid, arrived at the identical conclusion which I had also reached. When she entered the cottage, she did so not to free you but to bring you to justice.

"You put on an act at Coney Island to prove yourself caught by the lunatic plague. When you emerged from the water with Miss Holley, a policeman stopped you. Farther up the island waited a car with blue headlights to carry out the rest of your commands. You could not risk arrest because then Miss Holley could not keep the appointment.

"You volunteered the explanation that the pair of you were on a scavenger hunt. It meant nothing to Miss Holley. It meant everything to Miss Moray. All other victims gave no explanation for their behavior. They were under threat. No threat hung over you. Only you and you alone could offer a reasonable account of a fantastic performance."

"Bah!" Kelsey replied. "I'm perfectly willing to go to a police station. I'll not only face your foolish charges, I'll collect a nice fat sum for false arrest."

"You're not going to be charged," Frost stated.

"It's about time you changed your mind. Besides, you saw and heard for yourself the telephone call I received in your presence. I'll have to admit now that I'm one of the victims and you've seen how the voice works. If you don't catch him fast I'll be ruined."

"You mistake me," Frost answered dryly. "That telephone call was not a coincidence. There are no coincidences in your plan. I can explain every detail and show how each came about through your deliberate plotting. You took the incriminating photograph of yourself and a patient. You put the camera on the window sill of your office and snapped the shutter by pulling a thread.

"I repeat, I am taking you to police headquarters, but you will not be arrested, or charged, or tried." Frost's voice took on a hint of scorn and sardonic approval. "Inspector Frick is waiting for me. He will instantly commit you to the psychopathic ward at Bellevue for observation. Alienists will examine you. Within a month, you will leave to spend the rest of your life in an insane asylum."

A tense, protracted silence seemed only to deepen as Kelsey's breathing grew audibly hoarser.

Frost drawled, "I could tell you now most of your method, what started you off, how you operated, where you obtained some of the incriminating evidence, how you even forced some victims to bring you others. I shall leave that for the alienists."

Kelsey shouted, "You can't; you can't; you can't do that to me! I demand that I be arrested! You've got to place charges against me!"

Frost shook his head. "You're not a criminal genius, Kelsey. You're not a superbrain. You're nothing but a superlunatic, a dangerous maniac.

"What the alienists find when they are finished with you will be of interest to abnormal psychology, but not to the police. Your cell will be padded. There you can keep your delusions of grandeur and power to yourself. You can dream of terrorizing cities and nations. Your delusions won't annoy any one. You can pretend that you hold under your control every one who is stronger or more powerful or more important than your own warped little self. Your ego has already carried you from irresponsibility to madness. Possibly the alienists themselves will not be able to predict the final stages of your dementia."

Kelsey whipped a handkerchief from his breast pocket, patted his face. Something passed between his lips, and his teeth crunched. The odor of bitter almond drifted off on the currents of air washing through the car. His body twitched with almost instantaneous death.

"The easiest way out, for him." Frost shrugged, to April's horrified gasp. To Jean he said, "You can turn off the dictaphone now."

Her hand clicked a switch that she had touched when she started the *Demon* at the cottage.

Frost murmured, "I promised I would counter with a cross."

"What do you mean by that?" Jean asked.

"When he sent me a goose egg, I remarked that I would counter with a cross. And X marks the spot—

"Make it the morgue!"

KILLER'S

BAIT

"Are all the black imps of Hell under your thumb, Frist, that you should know—"

THE SUN, descending toward the western horizon, cast lengthening shadows across the ground. The rays filtered through oak and maple, from which the winds of autumn had already begun to strip the dry leaves of gold, flaming scarlet and tawny. They rustled in scattered heaps. The afternoon was warm, but held an implicit prophecy of colder days to come.

The human intruders formed only one of the incongruous elements in that quiet forest setting.

They had made their way over an old and almost obliterated dirt road through a part of the Catskills in lower central New York. Hills rose in the distance above the ranks of thinning trees. The party had halted at a barbed-wire barricade.

The odd feature of this barricade was that it stood ten feet high—too high for a man to go over, and so tightly interwoven that he could not go through without hopeless entanglement and laceration. The trees had been cut away from that fence years before. The young second growth had not yet risen high enough to offer aid in defeating the barrier.

The wires could be cut, if a trespasser wished to commit suicide by electrocution. At every ten yards a metal sign warned:

NO TRESPASSING
DANGER
HIGH-TENSION ELECTRIC
WIRES

The barricade extended as far as the eye could see in both directions. It had no break, no door. It completely inclosed some three square miles of forest, including a small lake and ponds along the course of a brook. The property belonged to I.V. Frost, a former professor who had turned to the private investigation of crime, and particularly murder in its more unusual phases, when classroom routine became boring to him.

A tall, gaunt figure, six feet four in height, with a thin, ascetic face and saturnine features, he towered over the rest of the group. The group, with one exception, consisted of newspaper reporters and photographers. They represented the nine New York City papers and three press associations.

The exception—the fourteenth member of the party—was Jean Moray, Frost's assistant, secretary, aid, and co-worker in the solution of crime. She was distinguished from the rest of the group by the fact that she alone stood on the other side of the wire fence. A long folding ladder that Frost had just taken down and stowed away in his big, specially built automobile indicated how she had crossed the barrier. Having crossed it, she was now marooned, until such time as Frost or some one else chose to return and help her out.

"What's wrong with this picture? It's too good to be true," muttered one of the photographers as he adjusted camera and bulb.

"Not at all. Miss Moray and I merely had a slight difference of opinion," said Frost airily.

"Yeah? It certainly must have been a slight difference, to make you go to all this trouble," came the sarcastic reply.

"There is a consideration involved, I admit. Since pure discussion and argument did not provide an answer that either of us would accept, we made a wager. Miss Moray is about to fulfill, or rather try to fulfill, her part of the wager. It is a foregone conclusion that she will lose."

"If I do, it'll be because of death. That's the only thing that can stop me," she retorted, her voice cutting the air, and musically, liquidly clear in spite of her resentment.

"How much is the bet?" asked a reporter.

"At odds of one thousand to one, I have wagered ten thousand dollars to ten that she cannot survive a week in the forest without the aid of a single product, invention, or necessity of modern civilization."

"What does that mean?"

"It means that she will start without clothing, without cosmetics, without wearing apparel, including hairpins and jewelry of any kind. She will have no matches, no magnifying glass, no pocket lighter, nothing by which to make a fire. She will have no gun, knife, ax, bow or arrow, or any other weapon by which to kill game. She will have no thread, fishhooks, spear, flashlight, or explosives.

"Yet her own ingenuity must enable her to survive. Under the terms of the wager, it is not sufficient that she merely remain here for a week. She could easily survive, simply by living on dry berries and the spring waters of the brook. She must kill or cause the death of at least one animal, catch a fish more than ten inches long, construct some sort of shelter against storm and cold, and build a fire."

A BRIEF HUSH fell over the group. Each, in his own way, tried to visualize himself undertaking the same venture—a modern Adam, a twentieth century Eve, and not among the Garden of Eden, but turned loose in the forest primeval. The wager, except for its news value, had no appeal to any of them, soft city dwellers that they were, accustomed to the conveniences and comforts of metropolitan life.

One of the photographers introduced a grim note. "What about wild animals—bear and deer? They can both be pretty dangerous."

"There are none within this tract."

"Snakes? What about rattlers?"

Frost shrugged imperceptibly. "They may exist. I have not been to this property for several years, though I've owned it for a long time. I cleared it of poisonous reptiles and dangerous wild animals the last time I visited it, at which occasion I also had the barrier erected."

"It's really electrified?"

"Yes. For this occasion, at any rate. The current is not ordinarily turned on, despite the signs. Few hunters ever reach this remote region, and the signs are sufficient to deter them."

"Then the current is turned on from outside the fence?"

"Yes, but only I know the location of the switch. The box containing it, and the cables that supply the power, are buried. It would be impossible for any one else to locate them except by pure chance, one in millions."

"So she's really and positively going to be stuck here for a week and can't get out if she wants to?"

"It isn't as final as that. There is a short-wave radio set at a designated spot inside the inclosure, whose location she knows. If the going becomes too strenuous, she can send out my call letters, and I'll come to her rescue. I rather expect to be summoned to-night."

"Not by me," Jean declared. "I wouldn't use the set even if six pink elephants and all the gunmen in America swarmed over the place."

"At least you won't have to worry about pink elephants. There aren't any," said a reporter flippantly.

Frost said, "I have seen a pink elephant at the corner of Broadway and Forty-second Street in the heart of New York City."

"Yeah? That must have been one rip-snorting bender that you were on. What was it doing?"

"I didn't ask it. The elephant had been painted pink for advertising purposes; a guide rode upon it, and it carried two large printed sheets. I might remark that only the rash ever make categoric denials of the possible truth of even the most fantastic of alleged occurrences.

"I have seen a red snowfall, a blue sun, and rain fall on one side of a city pavement while bright sunlight shone on the other side of the street. I know a man who is still living though he broke his neck several years ago. In Minnesota there was a cow, may still be for all I know, that had a small glass windowpane on its belly, whereby observers could watch it digest food. There was an aviator during the World War who fell out of an open cockpit when his plane began to loop, and who fell back into the same cockpit when his plane reached the bottom of the loop.

"Nothing that I have yet encountered in fiction is more fantastic and incredible than life itself."

The flip reporter preserved a wise silence.

Another asked, "What'll she do about scratches or if she breaks an arm?"

"Even bandages and medicines are products of modern civilization. But, of course, there is no need for her to go through with the wager. She can withdraw now rather than run the risks to which she will be exposed."

JEAN looked impatient. "When you're ready, I'm ready. I'm not backing out now or later, or at any time before the week is up. It isn't often that I get a chance to collect ten thousand dollars in a nice, juicy lump. You can start making out the check."

"There's nerve for you," muttered somebody under his breath. "More power to her; she's a better man than I am. Two nights in this forsaken spot and I'd have a case of the screeching heebie-jeebies."

"Me too," said Ron Macardi, the *Messenger's* reporter. He was a sallow, weary-looking, flaxen-haired individual with circles under his eyes. "Maybe I'd tackle it in the summertime, when you could pick berries and nuts and lie in the sun—but the first week of October—"

Frost looked at his watch. "This is your last chance to call the bet off," he said to Jean.

Jean began undressing. She was hardly conscious of the low babble of voices, the occasional phrases that reached her ears. She had doubts, serious doubts, about her ability to meet the terms of the wager, but no matter what came she would not admit the humiliation of defeat. There was very little logic in her method, but plenty of emotional resentment. She had let herself in for trouble. She would take the consequences, and win. She heard, vaguely, voices and comments.

"I don't know how that face missed Hollywood—"

"Golly, what legs—"

"There's a figure that would stump Einstein—"

And Macardi's languid drawl, "I kind of like the scenery around here. Hey, it's a gyp! She's wearing a bathing suit."

Frost smiled slowly. "I conceded the brassiere and tights. It's the scantiest suit purchasable in New York."

II.

JEAN FINISHED, packed her things neatly in an overnight bag, and tossed it with considerably more force than necessary over the fence toward Frost. Two of the news hawks dived for it, and the sounds of their skulls cracking as they collided brought a wicked smile to her face.

She waved an offhand farewell, turned, and drifted between the trees. She looked like a druid or hamadryad of olden times, her body lithe from healthy living, her skin deeply tanned, duskier than gold, more than nut-brown from soaking up the sea and the wind and the sun's heat all summer long. The fawn-colored bits of cloth she wore were almost invisible. The *svelte* sophistication that she often assumed melted away from her. Just before she vanished, a gleam of light reflected from her gray-green eyes, and her face in profile held an elfin, pagan quality.

The forest grew still again as the faint rustle of her receding footsteps died away.

Frost led the way to the cars. The *Messenger's* faithful servant murmured, half to himself, "I think there's something screwy going on. People make freak bets, but they don't make one like this, not at this time of year. How's the gal ever going to build a fire? Without matches or a magnifying glass, she's sunk on that score alone. Oh, well, she only stands to lose ten bucks."

The professor drawled, "Rays of the sun shining through a single raindrop or drop of dew have started forest fires. Sunlight focusing through bits of crystal-clear quartz has launched other disastrous fires. Flint, friction and compression are at her disposal. I am familiar with at least two additional methods by which she can build a fire without the aid of either matches or a magnifying glass."

"O. K., O. K., skip it. But it's a cinch she can't catch a fish without a fishhook or bait."

"On the contrary, she can close both ends of one of the shallower pools with branches. Then she can wade in and use another branch or her hands to toss a trout out, if she's patient enough. And that by no means limits the ways open to her."

Macardi looked skeptical. "Even so, how's she going to kill an animal without a weapon?"

"She can make her weapon—a trap net with a weighted branch and a vine noose, for example, baited with fish. Or, if her aim is sufficiently expert and luck is with her, she might kill a squirrel or a rabbit with a rock."

"Yeah, and she might wear herself out throwing rocks at squirrels and never hit one," Macardi answered, an edge in his weary voice. "And she might run herself ragged chasing bunnies all over the landscape without ever coming within a mile of one. So what's she going to do about shelter? Find a nice big crow's nest up a tree and pretend she's a bird?"

Frost made an astonishing answer. "Why, yes, I believe she's quite likely to do so."

"Huh?" grunted the flabbergasted Macardi.

Frost did not elaborate his mysterious statement. The party reached the autos, split into the same groups as when they had arrived, and headed for Quinquogue, where the reporters stopped to phone the story to their respective papers.

They built their copy around "A Modern Eve," "September Morn for Ten Grand," "Miss Robinson Crusoe," and "Girl Gets Bare

$10,000—Maybe," as their fancy dictated. The story earned several sticks of type in the conservative dailies. It was made-to-order feature material for the torrid tabloids.

FROST leaned against the door of his car as the cavalcade started up again for New York.

Macardi paused, fished for a limp cigarette, eyed the professor warily. "You wouldn't be sticking around here now, would you?"

"Why?"

The jaded news hound wet the tip of the cylinder. "Kind of a nice setup. As soon as we're out of sight you feed the gal or get her out—just like that. Oh, well, it's none of my business and it's hot till the lid comes off."

"There's no law against your staying here," said Frost. "You, or any, or all of you can cover the scene as long as you wish."

"I don't like the way you said that."

"I don't care what your likes or dislikes are."

"You know damn well we can't stick around. Editors are funny that way. They want about six more stories every day than we can handle. You're good at guessing. There's an answer—so what?"

"One's profession is a matter of choice. Change yours if you don't like it."

Macardi's eyes turned sullen. "That's another sour crack. You're a dick, Frost, a private dick. I know you've cleared up some tough cases that stumped the cops. That's neither here nor there. I've got an idea crawling around in the back of my head. The idea is that there's a whole lot more to this than you've let on.

"I can't see you going through all this business of a freak bet and payoff to some dame, even if she is your assistant, unless something else got under your skin—something big. How about it? Want to let me in? It's no secret that murder cases are the only ones that interest you. Is that what this is?"

"I was afraid you'd get on the trail of the real story," Frost replied with mock regret. "As a matter of fact, you're right. Sh, keep your voice down! It happened like this: A high official of the State department came to me this morning. He was disguised as the British ambassador. He told me that the Crown Prince of Bavaria, who was traveling incognito in the garb of a Hindu maharaja, had been slain by a poisoned cucumber at the hand of the pretender to the throne of Anjuria, who, cleverly made up as an American Indian chief, had however neglected to remove his patent-leather shoes and gloves—"

Macardi stalked off in disgust. "Nuts! That's no way to wangle an even break in the news."

"I have not the slightest interest in the attitude of the press. For or against, makes no difference to me."

Macardi stopped and turned. "We don't have to run the story."

"That's your business, not mine."

"But you sent out word to the editors that it was going to happen. We got orders to cover it. How come, if you don't care one way or another about publicity?"

"It would have leaked out eventually. Rather than play favorite with one newspaper, I preferred to give them all an equal opportunity to make as much or as little of the episode as they deemed best."

"Hey, Macardi! What's keeping you? We can't wait all day," some one shouted from the car ahead.

"O. K., coming," he called, and sauntered away from Frost.

The professor climbed into his car, and sent it drifting past the sedan where Macardi was trying to squeeze a seat for himself. The reporter glanced up, yelled, "I thought you said you were sticking around this burg!"

Frost slowed his machine long enough to fling over his shoulder, "I made no such statement. That was an assumption on your part which I neither affirmed nor denied."

Macardi bawled something else, but it was lost to the winds as Frost pushed his specially built car into the accelerating surge of its colossal power. It easily overtook the other cars and fled away from them like a rocket, dwindling and vanishing far ahead as they vainly tried to keep pace.

Once out of their sight, Frost took to side roads in a circle back toward the site where Jean Moray thought that she was partaking of a wager.

She was. But that streamlined and highly seductive young queen of the wilderness did not know that Frost had made the wager solely to use her as bait—live, human bait—killer's bait for a homicidal maniac.

III.

EARLIER THAT DAY, when the cool dawn of an autumnal morning had scarcely arrived, the jangle of the telephone roused Frost from the bed into which he had just turned. He lifted the receiver, listened intently for a few moments, then sprang up and dressed hurriedly. He pulled the old leather jacket, without which he was rarely seen, around him as he strode from the room.

The "Special," never reluctant to start, purred alive at his touch, rolled up the ramp of the basement garage in his mansion at 13 State Street, and coursed the still, dusky streets like a phantom. He turned into Central Park at Ninety-sixth Street, swung left, and halted a short distance farther on.

Leaving the Special, he hiked across lawn and pushed his way through shrubbery.

A blue-coated figure glanced up at him, said, "Say, how did you get here so fast? I just discovered the poor bloody creatures. It isn't a minute since I put in a call for the homicide squad. By the soul of me, not a radio car here yet, but my own eyes tell me it's the devil in person I see. Are all the black imps of Hell under your thumb, Frost, that you know about bloody murder before it happens?"

"Not quite, Grogan," Frost smiled briefly. He did not volunteer to explain that Pete Ransome, a big, dumb, brawny and loyal truck driver whom he knew, had made the recent phone call. Pete was driving through Central Park to make an early delivery when he noticed, from his high seat, that the park had a rather dreadful decoration behind a cluster of shrubbery. He informed Frost, leaving it to the professor to handle such incidental matters as notifying the police. Pete's few contacts with the police had been highly unpleasant. As it happened, a patrolman had made the discovery before Frost arrived at the scene.

The first dead man sprawled face up. His head, beaten to an unrecognizable mess, looked like the pulp of some horrible fruit. He was expensively dressed. Thirty feet away, upon the same winding footpath, lay the second corpse, doubled up, hands clenched over the abdomen and smeared with blood. The body was that of a younger man who had been shot once through the heart at point-blank range. A small mustache adorned his lip. He wore old, frayed clothing.

Frost examined the corpses intently, but moved aside as the homicide detail arrived and went into action. Some distance from the first body, where the murderer had evidently tossed it away, he picked up a wickedly weighted blackjack, capable of felling a giant. Strands of hair clung to its bloody surface. He turned it over to his old friend Frick, inspector in charge of the homicide bureau, who had just arrived on the scene.

A far-away look of abstraction brooded in Frost's inscrutable eyes. He smoked one cigarette after another, long, pungent cylinders of his own making that emitted a singularly spicy aroma.

THE INSPECTOR, a crisp and usually truculent little man who made up for his lack of stature by efficiency and a sort of bulldog determination, finished his study of the scene. He turned toward Frost, hesitated, then interrupted the reverie with, "What do you make of it?"

Frost countered, "What are your findings?"

"It's pretty obvious that the first man was slugged and killed, with robbery the probable motive. His wallet is gone. I wouldn't call it premeditated homicide. The second man evidently came on the scene as the killer was escaping, and got shot so that he would never be able to identify or testify against the killer. The killer threw his blackjack away because he knew it's impossible to trace them, because he didn't want to be caught with it in his possession, and because he didn't want to get blood on his pockets or clothing. He carried the pistol off because guns are easy to trace. He had to take a chance on being caught with it."

"What else?"

"This makes it bad. The bigger man is Elisha Funk, the million-a-year real-estate operator. The other chap seems to be an unknown named A. Carrovo or Carnovo, as nearly as we can make out from a dirty piece of paper in his pocket. There's a new angle. Might be a disgruntled tenant who got kicked out and developed a personal grudge against Funk."

"So he slugged Funk, and then conveniently got killed by some other footpad on the prowl?" Frost suggested dryly. "That leans a little too heavily on the laws of coincidence. Could you describe the killer?"

"Not very precisely, except that he must be a tall, powerful brute, because Funk stood about six feet and must have weighed around one eighty. A little fellow can't get force enough or accuracy enough to take a chance on slugging a much taller man. So the killer is at least five feet ten, and around one sixty to two hundred. Is that the way you figure it?"

"No. To begin with, robbery wasn't the motive."

"Funk's wallet is gone."

"Even if the wallet had contained several hundred dollars, it would have been mere pin money compared with the five thousand dollars, at least, that the ruby ring on Funk's left little finger is worth."

"The robber might have overlooked it."

"He could hardly have overlooked the equally valuable pin that is in the knot of his victim's tie. No, the wallet was taken to make robbery appear to be the motive.

"Furthermore, Funk has a bruise on his left shin bone; dirt and gravel are ground firmly into the palms of both hands, and both kneecaps are slightly bruised. From these and other indications, it is perfectly obvious that, as he was strolling along, he met the murderer. As they passed each other, the murderer tripped Funk, who put out his hands to break his fall, but did not succeed well enough to prevent his knees from getting bruised. Now what has happened to your picture of a tall, thickset murderer? A short, slightly built man could have tripped the victim just as easily, and finished him off with the blackjack."

"Why? What motive would there be in that?"

Frost shrugged, "No motive."

"You mean a homicidal maniac? It has to be that if there isn't a motive."

"Possibly. Motive may be all-important to the legal machinery of the Western Hemisphere. In other parts of the world, like the Far East, where human life is cheap, motive is comparatively unimportant. It frequently does not exist to any degree that we would think sufficient.

"Our murderer is definitely homicidal, but not a maniac. I've been expecting something like this for a long time. The wonder to me is that such a case has not come to my attention before."

FRICK looked puzzled. "I don't know if I follow you. The hardest cases that come our way are those in which somebody gets bumped off accidentally during the course of a holdup. They're tough to crack, because the victim and the murderer are unknown to each other, and there usually isn't the slightest clue or even a single witness. About the best we can hope to do is round up the known lush workers and stick-up gangs and try to pin it on one of them. Half the time it's just pure luck when we succeed. Is that what you mean? There've been several of these stickup murders, most of them with brutal violence, the past year. They're all still open cases."

Frost said, "I wish you had called them to my attention before."

"Why?"

"Because I could have saved some of those lives. Frick, you're facing a new and ruthless kind of murderer—one who likes to kill, but who is not a maniac. One who is clever enough never to choose a victim or to plan his crime in detail. He's a killer who strolls in isolated spots, but who never frequents the same spot twice—and who kills for the sheer lust of killing, in almost complete safety, under conditions that leave the police no clues.

"To-night there was an unexpected witness. Funk must have been killed about midnight, as he was walking through the park. Carrovo also took a late stroll, and saw the killer, if not the actual murder. The slaying of Carrovo is probably the first crime for which the killer had a logical motive: a murder to conceal murder. And by that act he gave away the whole pattern of his personal make-up, his method of operation, the way his mind works, and how he can be trapped."

"That's more than I can see." Frick sounded belligerent, on the defensive.

"Broadcast to the newspapers that you are searching for a one-armed Eurasian, six feet two inches tall, a religious fanatic, who has green eyes, wears earrings, and is well known to foreign police authorities. From clues discovered at the scene of the crime, you consider him the chief suspect."

"A green-eyed, one-armed Eurasian who wears earrings?" Frick echoed incredulously. "He sounds like something out of a nightmare. There certainly isn't any such freak in our records. What country does he come from?"

"He doesn't exist," Frost answered impatiently. "He's a figment of my imagination. Nevertheless, broadcast a description of him and let the newspapers play it up."

"Why?"

"Because I'm going to get a new pair of glasses."

Frick turned red. "Of all the crazy gibberish—what the devil has any of that got to do with these murders? A new pair of glasses—you don't even wear spectacles."

"Therefore, when I buy a pair, they must necessarily be new," Frost answered with maddening calmness, and impeccable logic. "These murders will be in to-night's headlines. The same papers will carry an entirely unrelated story concerning my assistant."

He strode off, leaving a sorely perplexed inspector.

Frick stared glumly between the retreating back of Frost and the corpses headed for the morgue, under the red, rising sun.

IV.

JEAN MORAY skipped blithely up the steps of the mansion at 13 State Street. She had recently returned from a month's vacation. Being a perverse and willful person, she took September for her vacation, and spent it in Maine and Labrador, because nobody else went there at the same time. She had enjoyed herself climbing precipices that were the bane of aviators, and swimming in waters that would have frozen the whiskers of a walrus.

The case of Mrs. Appledorf's panda was almost forgotten with the summer's heat. Memory of the lunatic plague, the last of Frost's adventures that she took part in, had faded with the dog days of August. Nothing exciting had yet happened since her return to duty.

The eye in the hallway gave her the creeps. It was an artificial, human eye, suspended from the ceiling. It turned with a slow, unpleasant, lifelike motion in the draft created each time that she entered. It fascinated and repelled her. Frost collected artificial eyes for a hobby. He distributed the eyes of mankind, the animal world, fish, and the kingdom of birds all over his mansion. He also kept a grim museum containing one object essential to the solution of every case that he had accepted.

Jean swung into the reception room. Stacks of books lined it. A bust of Socrates on a pedestal faced an antique etching of Bacon that graced the opposite wall. Midway between them lolled Frost, in an overstuffed armchair, his long legs stretched out to an ottoman, a pot of villainously black coffee at his elbow.

He eyed her with the contemplative and detached curiosity of a scientist watching an insect specimen on a pin.

"What's new? Or should I say, what's wrong?" she asked. "You've seen me before, so it can't be curiosity. If you were working on a case you'd be smoking one of those atrocious weeds; but you aren't, so it can't be business. That leaves what—something else?"

"Nothing of much interest to tell you."

Jean perked her ears. "Tell me what?"

"I doubt whether it would hold your attention."

"I don't know if it would or not. I can't tell till you let me in on the secret."

Frost handed her a newspaper clipping. The clipping was dated October 4th. She assumed it to be of the current month or year. Frost didn't tell her that it had come out of his files, and had originally been published in 1931.

He remarked, "The month does not seem to have produced an interesting specimen of the fine art of murder for us. In the absence of crime, the article struck me as opening up a fertile field for exploration of a different sort."

She read the article carefully. It was a Sunday supplement feature built around the theme: "What ten things would *you* choose, if you knew you were going to be wrecked on a desert island?" The article gave the answers of different explorers and travelers, who were unanimous in their choice of a magnifying glass and a knife as two of the ten essentials.

Jean said, "It seems like a silly sort of argument. You don't have time to choose anything when you're shipwrecked. The real test would be to find yourself stranded without anything to help you along. Even then, under any average set of conditions, you'd probably survive. Almost every year there's a new story about somebody getting lost in the woods and being found alive weeks later."

Frost shook his head. "I doubt very much whether any one accustomed to the luxuries and conveniences of modern civilization could last a week in the woods without them."

Jean said, "I'd bet about a hundred to one that I could do it, and without very great hardships."

Frost said, "Do you think so? I'd put it the other way around and change the odds to a thousand to one that you couldn't last for a week. Without food, clothing, matches, weapon or shelter—how could you survive?"

"I'd take you up on that if I knew of any place where I could go through with the bet."

FROST sent a quick glance over her from head to foot. "I'm inclined to make it a real wager. I have such a place in mind."

"Where?"

"A piece of property covering about three square miles that I own in an isolated spot some miles up-State from Quinquogue. It's completely inclosed by a barbed-wire entanglement."

"That's the first I've heard of your owning any such place."

"I dare say there are a good many things about me that haven't yet come to your attention," he answered with laconic brevity. "How does the exchequer stand?"

She opened the desk, looked at the bank books. "There's just short of seven thousand dollars in the savings fund and a mere one hundred forty-six thousand dollars in the checking account."

"Very well. If you are so confident of your ability, I will wager ten thousand dollars against ten dollars that you can't last out a week on that estate, without resorting to a short-wave set that I will place on the property, to summon aid."

"It's a bet. When do I start?"

"To-day."

"I'm practically ready now."

"There's one further condition. I'll notify the press of the wager, so that it may become a matter of public record."

"So much the better. It's only once in a lifetime that I'll get a chance to win ten thousand from you, and do it in such a way that the whole world will know about it. I'll get a bigger kick out of that than I will out of actually winning the bet."

"If you win the bet. Of course, if you fail, the shoe will be on the other foot. You may not find it as easy, pleasant, or profitable as you seem to think. In that case—"

"I'll do the worrying, when the time comes."

Frost looked at his watch, got up. "I'll take a run out to the place now, to make sure that it's as I left it a few years ago. I'll be back before noon."

It was not yet eleven when he returned from the trip, looking well satisfied. Jean had spent the interval trying to figure out a way of doing a little gypping on the side. She had every intention of smuggling a few matches into the place, and of taking some sort of weapon, such as a knife or small automatic, with her, but hadn't been able to work out any feasible plan before Frost got back.

She thought of putting a water-tight phial of matches in her mouth, but decided that the difficulties of speech would give away that little piece of double-dealing. It might be possible to hide a few matches in her rich mass of honey-dark hair, but Frost more than once had demonstrated that his eyes were as penetrating as X rays.

Jean Moray became distressingly afraid that she would have to fulfill the wager on a strictly honest basis and performance.

Frost completed his preparations and notified the papers. Toward one o'clock, the procession to Quinquogue got under way.

V.

JEAN MORAY grew increasingly apprehensive as the hour of sunset came nearer. She had been worried enough since Frost and the reporters went away shortly after four. The blithe assurance with which she had undertaken to be a prisoner for a week inside the electrified barbed-wire inclosure turned rapidly to dismay as she faced the hard realities.

Roughly timing herself by the sun, she guessed it to be at least five o'clock before she chose for camp and shelter the leeward side of an enormous flat-topped boulder not far from the stream. On the following day she expected to build a rude lean-to of branches against it, and a bed of leaves—or else to put weighted branches on top of the boulder, so that they would extend over her head as a roof of sorts.

But before bed and shelter, before food even, came fire. She quenched her thirst in the clear water of the brook. There were plenty of hickory nuts, but she wanted them toasted. She found some dried currants but didn't care much for them. She stirred up grouse, squirrels and rabbits, none of which seemed particularly anxious to get out of her way; and in the shallow waters of a pool a few hundred yards downstream from her camp she saw brook trout and perch.

She was hungry, but not hungry enough to want those animated delicacies served raw.

Fortunately for her, the mosquitoes and gnats had already ended their season. She was not so lucky with regard to deer flies, a few of which took a notion that her topography might prove succulent. They got mashed for their pains. Scraping off what was left of them made her skin crawl. Jean was learning all over again what she had forgotten since her scout and woodcraft days: that nature in the raw is absolutely indifferent to human life, and that the struggle to survive is a deadly, unceasing battle.

Yet she enjoyed the experience in a perverse fashion. It was a relief to be away from crime, bloodshed, murder, and the baffling mysteries that she had lived with ever since she became Frost's assistant. The fence made her safe from intrusion. Except for fulfilling the conditions of the wager, she had a week's vacation, an interlude, a primitive, elemental existence ahead of her. She would be too busy for loneliness. Only the darkness of night frightened her. She must have fire for comfort, for warmth, and for cooking if she caught anything to cook.

There are too many ways to start a fire in civilized communities. She discovered anew how hard it is to build a fire from the materials of the wilderness, and what difficulties must have stood in the way of man thousands of years ago, before he found the precious secret.

She had no steel or metal to strike against flint, or flint against rock. She had no matches or magnifying glass. She could not make a compression-tube artifact without tools. There were only two methods that she could think of: she could collect dry moss and leaves, and strike rocks until she was weary in the hope that eventually one of the occasional sparks would ignite the tinder; or she could look for a piece of quartz or other crystalline rock that might serve as a focusing agent for the sun's rays. As a last resort, she could try to short-circuit the wires of the fence.

Splashing along the stream, and bruising her feet on many a sharp stone, she picked up and discarded dozens of translucent pebbles before she obtained one that looked promising. It was irregularly shaped, about the size of her palm, and roughly concave on one side. The action of running water had worn it down, smoothed it, polished the surfaces, until she could not tell whether it represented a piece of quartz or the glass fragment of a bottle smashed by some picnicker long ago.

She climbed to the top of her big boulder to get the rays of the westering sun. Her tinder consisted of an array of dead leaves, old moss, and powdery rotten wood upon a fan-shaped branch.

She got the crystal into focus, and waited, anxiously, impatiently, as the sun sank lower. The air grew more chilly. The forest became, in a curious paradox, both noisy and quiet: the brooding silence that represents the absence of man and civilization; the faint sounds of gurgling water and complaining crow, of whispering leaves and the woodchuck that scurries, which are always audible below the seeming and deceptive hush of nature.

THE PUNK turned brown, black. The sun hung at the horizon. She blew gently, steadily, saw the black turn to a red glow like an ember, and issue a wisp of smoke. She fed it and breathed upon it, nursed it along. The glow spread. A pungent, acrid odor seeped out. She blew harder. The sun went down.

She nourished the flame from the rotten wood to the moss, from the moss to the leaves. She lifted the branch and carried the burning pile to the site below. Once she slipped. Half of her prize sifted away. Twilight thickened on the ground. She shivered in the cool air, and shrank from the darkening trees. The brook gurgled and splashed ominously.

Jean got the fire to bedrock, piled on weeds and twigs and more leaves, so that the fire grew strong. Its crackle drowned the murmuring splash of the brook. The dancing flame made patterns on the fringe of the forest, but the illimitable dark blanket of night crept closer.

"Get up!"

The sudden command startled her like a gunshot. She sprang to her feet and whirled around, shrinking back to the boulder.

She saw the vaguely gleaming reflection of a rifle barrel. Beyond it—a figure clad in boots and hunting breeches, shirt open at the collar, a slouching, angular figure with unkempt hair and a stubble of beard.

The same voice snarled, "What the hell you doin' here? Go on, scram!"

"What are you doing here?" Jean retorted indignantly. "Scram yourself! How did you get over the barbed wire?"

"Climbed over."

"You couldn't. It's electrified."

"You're crazy. It wasn't when I come over this afternoon. I been around here often. I climb over whenever I feel like it, see? Now beat it! Women are pi'z'n to me. They're worse p'iz'n when they try to start one of these here nudist camps. Go home and put some clothes on, an' then stay home."

"I'll do nothing of the sort! You've no right to be here or talk to me like that! Get off this property!"

"Shut up! I came here to get me a deer, an' I'm gonna get me a deer."

"It isn't the season."

"What the hell do I care if it ain't the season? I wants me a deer; I goes and gets me a deer, see?"

"There aren't any deer here,"

"I'll find out for myself. Now scram!"

He strode forward, trampled out her fire, began kicking and scattering the embers. "What's the idea buildin' a fire here? You want to set the woods a-burnin'?"

Jean Moray stooped, picked up a chunk of rock the size of her fist, and flung it, The action was not one that she had thought out in advance. Her temper got the better of her. She put the idea into effect as soon as it occurred to her. Like the majority of impulsive actions, it worked perfectly, whereas a deliberate plan would probably have failed.

The rock made a clunk on the man's skull. He toppled over with a thud, like a poleaxed steer, and sprawled in the dying embers.

Astonished at her unexpected success, Jean darted forward. Sticks and pebbles that she could no longer see bruised her feet. She knelt beside the stranger, tugged his body off the coals, and beat out the smoldering spots on his clothing. He breathed in gasps. A thin red worm of blood crawled down his temple, which had already begun to swell.

Jean slid the rifle aside and snapped the safety catch.

She hurried back to the remains of the fire, yelped as she stepped on a hot spark, and grabbed up the first stick she could find with her fumbling hands. The last afterglow was fading from the sky. She raked the sparks and flickering embers together, tried hard to get the fire going again but saw with dismay the final spark wink out. She dropped to her hands and knees, blew hard. A puff of dust arose; ashes swirled into her face and eyes; but the fire was definitely and completely out.

Hot and grimy from her exertions, ready to commit mayhem on the detestable stranger, she stood up. Maybe his pockets would yield matches or a flashlight. She turned around just in time to see him roll over to the rifle and get shakily to his feet.

"I'll learn you better'n to heave rocks at me!" he roared.

VI.

JEAN went downhill like a frightened fawn, as the hunter fumbled with the safety catch. She darted among the oaks and hickories, stumbling through the darkness. The rifle crashed. She could not tell whether he had shot into the air or toward her general direction. She heard threshing sounds! Then she had reached the stream and began following it. The sounds of the intruder died away.

She walked in the brook until she reached the broad, shallow pool, which she swam across. On the opposite side, she again followed the stream until, after another hundred yards, she reached a smaller, deeper pool.

Jean listened, heard nothing except the nocturnal whispers of the forest. She emerged from the water. The air was chilly, and almost as black as a coal bin around the pool, though overhead shone the most brilliant array of stars she had ever seen.

She found herself strangely weak and shivering, as she stood on the margin of the pool. The black waters stretched away, swirling and sinister, to the farther blackness of the forest. Reaction set in, and the fear that she had not had time for during the excitement and flight. The realization dawned on her that she was alone, defenseless, and cut off from escape by electrified wires—not only cut off, but locked in with a stranger whose favorite field of endeavor seemed to range between the violent and the homicidal.

A mass of split and fissured granite jutted along one side of the pool. She climbed slowly to the top. It would be as good a place as any for a breathing spell, and no one could approach without making a clatter of warning. For the first time, it occurred to her that her nudity gave her one marked advantage: she could travel far more silently on bare feet than could a man wearing boots, even if he followed the stream.

She pulled herself to the crest of the ledge.

A dark shape moved in front of her, bulged upward, a blob against the gloom. She could not wholly stifle the involuntary gasp that tightened her throat.

"Come right in. Never say Macardi forgot to stand up for a lady," a voice slurred out of the darkness. "I've been looking for you. I've been looking for you all over. I looked under the leaves, and you weren't there. I looked up the trees, and you weren't there. I looked in the pool, and under the rocks, and, so help me, you weren't there either. You weren't anywhere. So I sat here with a bottle. It's a hell of a good bottle, and there's two more—or it was a good bottle. Where was I— Oh yeah, wanna drink?"

"No."

"No?"

"No."

"Kind of a monotonous conversation. You sound sort of plastered. Funny. Oh, well, I'll try again. Wanna drink?" Macardi tilted his head.

"If any one's drunk, it's you!" Jean cried, and added venomously, "Ivy might at least have told me that this mountain retreat was a public reservation. How did you get in?"

"That's a secret," Macardi began, and coughed violently as some of the whisky paused at his esophagus. "I knew there was something fishy here, so I came back to see what. And I brought a stepladder with me. Who's dead?"

"Who's dead?" Jean echoed blankly.

"That's what I said. You're the most monotonous dame I ever talked to," Macardi complained. "Don't you know any words? Do you just go around saying what somebody else said? That's a hell of a life. Who's dead, killed, murdered, butchered? Frost only handles murder cases; so this is murder. Who's been killed and who did it? Catchee on? Does this have any connection with the two stiffs found murdered in Central Park this morning?"

"I don't know what you're raving about!"

"Oh, nuts—"

"Nuts to you!"

MACARDI took the bottle from under his arm, muttered to himself between sips, "She is completely ga-ga, otherwise known as ku-ku, and likewise batty-batty. She wouldn't be just plain ga, or ku, or batty, on account of she repeats everything. So she's a goof and that makes her a double goof. And I ditched the party and came back here all by myself to get a nice hot inside story. Phooey! O. K., sister, save yourself the trouble, skip it. I'll say it for you. Phooey-phooey. How's that?"

"I saw one man a while ago who was detestable. You're impossible!" Jean put all the scorn she could muster into her voice.

"So that's the way it is?"

She couldn't see his facial expression, but his tone indicated a leer on the owlish side. She blurted, "Are you going to go away and stop bothering me? If not, I'll leave."

"Don't go away. Stick around. It's kind of lonesome in these parts. What's this about another guy?"

"He has a rifle. It works."

"I thought I heard somebody cough a while ago. Thought it was you. Guess it wasn't. You know, I kind of like the way you wear your hair."

"You can't see it in this darkness!"

"But I'd like it if I could. Even if I hadn't smelled a murder I'd come back. Did anybody ever tell you you're beautiful? Well, you are. You get fed up in my racket, after you've seen about a million people—average folks and cranks. They all look worse than the million average folks and cranks whose stories you barged around after last year. I don't know why I stick it out. I guess I'm a sap.

"But you're a prize. This Frost knows how to pick 'em. So I came back. Only I couldn't find you; so I park myself here to keep an eye on things, and then you come along and climb right smack into my lap—practically. Life is wonderful.

"I'd like to kiss you. How about it? Here we are and maybe—" He staggered toward her.

Jean side-stepped, turned, cut the air in a quick dive. She had a moment of dread suspense. If rocks lay below her, or shallow water—

She arched under the surface, then up, gulped a breath of air, and swam underwater again. The second time she came up, she heard a terrific splash behind her, and wild yells. She resorted to the Australian crawl. When she splashed ashore, she still heard a commotion on the opposite side. She listened until convinced that Macardi had managed to flounder out of the pool.

"Come back here, you fool! I've got matches, pistol, fishhooks—everything!" Macardi's husky voice bawled across the water. "What's the big idea running out on me like that? Haven't you got any sense at all? You can't win this cock-eyed bet without a little help somewhere! Come on back! There are still a couple more bottles. Oh, nuts, what the hell am I yelling at her for? Pipe down, Macardi, and dry off before you catch a nice case of—hic—pneumonia. Where's that bottle? If she took it with her, I'll—hic—"

The rest of his words sank into a subdued and barely audible mumble. Jean stopped listening. She moved cautiously away from the pool toward the deeper gloom of the forest.

VII.

THE GROUND sloped higher. Jean halted, completely at a loss over what course to follow next. During the few hours of daylight she hadn't had time to explore more than a small part of the estate. She had no idea about the lay of the land ahead.

The air, perceptibly cooler, became uncomfortable except when she kept herself warm by constant movement. But the darkness had grown too intense for her to distinguish more than the shadowy bulk of things. Her feet ached. She had already scratched her legs numerous times. Ravines and pits might lie ahead for all she knew. Every step brought the possibility of rousing some animal, or perhaps stepping on a snake—

Jean shuddered. Unlike the majority of her sex, she had never feared snakes or worms until the night some months earlier when she had accompanied Frost to that nightmarish valley of giants called New Eden. Among other pretty specimens, it had contained worms six feet long and as thick as a man's body. She thereafter developed a strong horror of all soft, slimy things that crawled or glided.

She hated to go ahead into the unknown terrors of black night. There would be no moon and starlight could not penetrate the forest. She was equally reluctant to go back and run the risk of further encounters with the reporter—who liked the dreams that are distilled from grain—or the hunter who didn't mind poaching and who considered women to be poison.

Neither did she want to remain on the spot she occupied. She had no means of building a fire, and no covering for warmth. Already she felt goose flesh rising. But she obstinately refused to make her way to the short-wave set and send out a call for Frost. Yet the conditions of the wager had become intolerable, now that two strangers had crossed the barrier. It would be impossible to exist for a week under such a constant strain.

Jean at that moment mentally cursed all mankind. It was unlike Frost to have slipped up in his plans. Macardi's words came back to her. What was it the reporter had said—something about a couple of murders? She hadn't read the day's papers. Had Frost quietly gone ahead, using her for some greater design of his own, without giving her an inkling of his intention? She tried to recall her conversation with him that morning. As best she could remember, it had been she herself who suggested the wager and volunteered to go through with it.

Idle thinking got her nowhere. She looked up through a break in the trees, saw the brilliant, frosty myriad of stars that blazed across the whole vast sweep of the heavens. Against the canopy of night the trees flung their dark branches and remaining leaves. It struck her that visibility upward made a decided improvement over ground vision, which was about zero.

Again she acted on impulse. She chose the closest promising tree trunk, whose lowest branch she could just touch by standing on tiptoe, and started shinnying up it. Her sense of humor began to reassert itself. She felt slightly ridiculous. She formed a mental, inglorious picture of herself climbing up a tree, and managed to smile in spite of her exertions.

THE TREE, a maple, served her well. Not too big for easy ascent, and not too young for safety, it rose for fifty or sixty feet. After hauling herself up to the lowest limb, she found the branches frequent enough for fairly quick progress. She went up about halfway, and stopped to rest in a crotch as comfortable as wood can ever be.

"Hello! How do you like it up here?" called a smooth but disagreeable voice from the surrounding darkness.

Jean nearly fell out of the tree from pure shock. She gripped the branch tightly, peered above and below at the blobs that represented neighboring trees. She breathed softly, made no answer.

"Hello again!" came the voice. "I expected to find you sooner. Now that you're here, can't you talk?"

This time she was able to identify better the direction from which the words issued. She made out a dark lump that moved at about her same level on the trunk of a tree some thirty feet distant.

She hesitated, finally spoke up, "Is that you, Macardi?"

"No. Is he the chap who goes in for bottles?"

"Are you the hunter?"

"I suppose you could call me such. If you mean the person who shot off a rifle a while ago, no."

"For goodness' sake," she wailed, "how many people are there in this alleged piece of private property? Every time I turn around somebody leers at me. It's a nightmare. I get away from one, and another pops up. When did you come? And how? Who are you?"

"My name is Carson Goll, if that means anything to you."

"Carson Goll— Oh, you're the big-game hunter who got kicked out of membership in the Explorers' Club for conduct unbecoming a sportsman. What was it, now? I remember—using dumdum bullets on even small game. And weren't you supposed to have pumped a dumdum into some native porter who disobeyed you?"

"Your memory is painfully accurate. As to how I got here, I drove out on a motor cycle and climbed a tree. I had a weighted rope that I slung over the wire fence. The weighted end knotted itself around a tree inside the inclosure. It's a trick you learn in the tropics. I hooked the other end around a tree outside the fence, and came in hand over hand. Then I untied the knot, let the rope slacken until the hook fell loose, and pulled the whole rope over with me. It's the same way that I'll leave, and there'll be nothing to indicate that I was ever here.

"I arrived near sunset, after I read about your interesting wager in the evening papers."

A shiver of fear ran through her—a sudden, strong fear that refused to subside. She could not account for it. Something in the voice of the man, some threateningly murderous undercurrent to his suave words made her tense.

"What made you go to all that trouble? Why did you come?"

The calm, smooth response sent nervous creeps writhing over her. "I originally came here to kill you."

"Why?" She began fighting for time, to keep him talking, stave off action while she sought some means of escape.

"That's a long story. Briefly, I've always derived pleasure from killing, watching the blood spurt and the animal fall. That was years ago when I hunted game. The sport finally grew tame. Then the Explorers' Club deprived me of membership. I determined to go after bigger game. Society didn't seem to approve of me. But I was smarter than society, because I took my revenge in a way that society couldn't cope with.

"I'VE KILLED about a dozen times, so far. I choose victims with whom I'm not acquainted, in isolated spots where there aren't witnesses, under circumstances that don't leave clues. The stupid police of society haven't caught up with me. They never will. They aren't even aware yet that a single man is methodically killing whenever the mood is on him and the occasion warrants. They have the dozen murders down in their records, all unsolved, all listed as slain while being robbed. It amuses me."

"It sounds fascinating—in the same way as looking at a snake." Loathing filled Jean's normally musical voice. Was there any way that she could get to the short-wave set and summon Frost, she wondered? Aloud she added, "The first man I saw here proved detestable, the second impossible. You're horrible, unspeakably horrible. What made you change your mind?"

"About killing you? I don't know that I've changed my mind. The circumstances are different, since I discovered that two more people besides you and me are on the premises. I might kill you, as I first planned. The other hunter will doubtless electrocute himself when he tries to cross the barbed wire. The reporter will be too drunk to know what happened. In that case, the police are likely to assume that the hunter killed you, and accidentally killed himself while trying to escape, or that the reporter killed both of you.

"This is really much more promising than my last success. I killed a couple of strangers in Central Park last night. I bought the day's papers to read about the crime. Do you know what the silly police are doing? They're looking for a one-armed, green-eyed Eurasian who wears earrings. I laughed out loud when I read that. It's the wildest, silliest guess on their part that ever came to my attention. The same paper carried a story about your bet. It was a wonderful opportunity."

Jean desperately estimated her chances of dropping to the ground—hoping that the branches would break her fall—so that she could lose herself in the forest.

The merciless voice said, "Don't try to escape, my pretty bird. You will be just as lovely in death as in life."

"How do you know what I look like?"

"Why, after I got into the grounds, I used my binoculars from here. I saw you build a fire. I was going to approach the fire after dark, but, as you know, other events altered my plan."

"Do you make allowances for everything?"

The voice sounded more arrogant, proud. "Naturally. For instance, I wouldn't attempt to kill you from this spot, because you and I both are so situated that a direct kill by one shot would be well-nigh impossible, unless pure luck favored me. But you can't escape. You can't get to the ground before me. The rope is at my side, tied to a branch and dangling to the ground. I can slide down to it in a couple of seconds, faster than you can fall."

THERE WAS no way out, she thought, fighting to keep a note of panic from her tone. She must keep him talking, talking, even though it would do no good that she could see. Frost had betrayed her, used her as deliberate prey, left her no loophole. And by no conceivable means could he possibly come to her aid now, as he had always done before at her moment of greatest need.

"My ears are attuned to the jungle," Goll called to her. "Even if you got to the ground, you would be no better off. The patter of your bare feet would sound as loudly in my ears as the tread of hobnailed boots in yours. I've listened to the soles of native runners all over the world. I'll hear you and track you down when you think you're as silent as the wind. That's the way I planned it. I wanted to hunt you down, over a period of days and nights, as you fled through the woods. But the other two here have changed all that."

"You're mad!"

"That's what society would say, but as it happens I'm much too shrewd in my method to be crazy. Go ahead and yell for help if you wish. I like to hear people scream and beg for mercy before I kill them. It's music that's sweet to me. And it won't do you one single bit of good.

"Macardi has probably passed out by now. The other hunter is far away. I'd hear them approach long before they got close enough to help you. There's no one you can count on. There's nobody but us—the hunter and the hunted, the living and the dying. Come, come; why don't you cry as loud as you know how?"

Jean compressed her lips. She wouldn't give him that small satisfaction. She shifted her position, ready to drop and run. All the odds lay against her, but she had no other choice.

"So you won't yell? Not that it makes much difference. I recall another victim who made no sound, either. That happened when I was taking a cruise to Cuba, last winter. Late the night before we reached Havana; I was standing astern, watching the ship's wake, when another passenger came on deck and sauntered to where I leaned on the rail. I never have known who he was.

"I watched for an opportunity, waited till he hung over the rail, staring at the silvery-red path that the moon made over the ocean. I turned as if to go below, stooped, and grabbed his ankles. I gave him a quick heave, and overboard he went before he knew anything had happened. I watched him come spluttering to the surface a hundred yards astern. I think he was getting ready to let cut a shriek when a big fin cut the water—and down he went again.

"He came up once more, farther away, in the path of moonlight, but acted queerly. I imagine he was missing an arm or leg by that time. I believe there were two or three fins around him, but I couldn't be sure. Maybe he howled. He was so far away that I couldn't have heard. The fins cut the water toward him again. Something pulled him down suddenly. That was the last I saw of him."

Sick with horror at the cold-blooded, monstrous brutality of the story, Jean Moray swung downward. She took the chance in a thousand—anything to escape from the range of that voice, to stop its inhuman and corrupt ferocity.

The dark blob on the other tree dropped to the ground like a plummet, straightened itself upright.

Carson Goll stepped leisurely toward the maple, a revolver in his hand. "Did you think I spoke in jest when I said that the rope hung to the ground? Or when I remarked that murder gave me keen pleasure? Or when I promised to kill you? My dear, my lovely bird about to fall from the nest, I assure you that I meant every word of it."

Jean Moray stared down, paralyzed by the sight of the gun barrel rising toward her—

VIII.

I.V. FROST turned aside from the old dirt road before he arrived at the fence that surrounded his country acreage. He ran the Special into the woods where it couldn't be seen from the road.

Emerging from the automobile, he carried only three articles with him—a pair of spectacles, a pistol of excessively long barrel, and a map printed on paper so translucent as to be almost transparent.

In the hush of late afternoon, he strode swiftly ahead. He had smoked two of his curious cigarettes, and carefully extinguished the butts under pebbles, before he reached a spot at the edge of the barbed-wire fence. The spot had nothing to distinguish it from any other patch of ground.

He dropped to his knees beside a chunk of granite, and tugged at the rock. It swung back on a hinge buried below the soil. With a handkerchief, he dusted off the exposed surface, which consisted of a metallic plate. The plate was approximately a foot square. Directional beams of light crisscrossed it, so that it resembled a sheet of draftsman's or mathematician's paper.

The plate was a television grid that recorded on a small area the far more widely spaced directional beams operated by the electrified barricade around his property.

He placed the translucent map over the metal grid. The map contained a topographical outline of the land inside the fence.

One of the light lines blinked out. A line crossing it blinked out. Only a human being standing upright could interfere with the circuits. By those lines, it was possible to determine the position and direction of movement of any person inside the inclosure.

Frost took out a pencil and began tracing on the map the path that the subject followed.

Another group of lines on a different section of the grid began to break. He started a second pencil tracing.

Shortly after six o'clock a third set of interruptions began at the margin of the grid, well away from the other two.

Very close to sunset, a fourth line of progress developed on the vertical and horizontal lines at a corner of the plate.

Frost charted all four tracks. It was no difficult feat, since the directional beams on the small surface before him represented the area of his estate.

THE NIGHT grew darker and more silent. His attention remained glued to the grid. For another two hours, oblivious to the falling temperature and his cramped position, he watched the drama of convergence and separation which the plate recorded in its impersonal fashion.

The four tracks signified that four persons roamed within the inclosure. The lines gave no clues to the identity of those four individuals, yet Frost suddenly went into positive action as though everything was plain and definite. He removed the paper, opened a switch at the side of the plate. Electricity stopped flowing through the wires of the barricade. The crisscross of lights upon the grid vanished. Frost moved the granite rock back into back into position, towered upright.

He climbed through the fence, restored the electrical current by another concealed switch.

He donned the glasses, which fitted closely around his eyes—as closely as goggles. They were glasses of unusual appearance, with lenses much thicker than the ordinary type.

Before he put them on, the forest had presented itself as a great, black, indistinguishable mass. After he wore them, the forest sprang magically into strange and fantastic clarity.

The spectacles reacted to infra-red light. Infra-red light is always present in the atmosphere, but is not visible to the human eye. The electrified fence emitted additional infra-red rays.

The spectacles altered the values of light and darkness, transformed the landscape into a weird, phantasmal scene. The sky glowed with ghostly radiance, in which the stars stood as black dots. The leaves and boles of trees turned pale white, in an ebony setting. The ground lay clear, shadowless.

Frost took the long-barreled pistol in hand, went swiftly forward. He made faster and easier progress than would ever have been possible under the best conditions of bright sunshine and perfect vision. The spectacles and the infra-red light gave supervision, with all objects standing out in hard, naked outline.

He moved purposively toward a bleak mass of rock near the stream. The jagged pile towered gauntly above the neighboring terrain.

From that vantage point, he raised the pistol toward a point approximately six hundred feet distant. Jean Moray, descending the maple tree, looked like a product of nightmarish imagination. The infra-red spectacles turned her hair colorless, made her body seem Negroid black against the unnatural paleness of the tree.

At the foot of the maple stood a man, whose hands and face looked likewise Negroid, and who seemed to be wearing snow-white clothing. His black hand clutched a white automatic.

Frost sighted carefully, fired. The sharp crack of his pistol received an answer like an echo, as the white automatic in the hands of the stranger belched a black cloud of smoke upward toward the girl in the tree.

IX.

JEAN MORAY, staring with hypnotic intensity at the gun that Carson Goll pointed at her, stiffened involuntarily to the sound of a pistol shot. The killer jerked. She wondered why the bullet didn't hurt her. Then his automatic roared, and the slug whined several feet away from her, smacked a branch, ricocheted off through darkness.

Carson Goll brought his weapon back into aim. Again the pistol cracked. He sank slowly upon one knee, his automatic flaring wide of the mark. Fury and venomous hatred contorted his features. His left shoulder turned numb; all feeling went out of his left arm, and his right leg refused to support him. Sitting upon the ground, he tried once more to bring down his prey. But before he got the gun trained upon her, the pistol blazed for the third time. Eternal darkness smashed from his heart to his brain, as a leaden pellet lodged in his heart.

Jean Moray continued to stare, stunned, incredulous. She saw the final flash of pistol fire from a spot a couple of hundred yards distant. She knew of no marksman in the whole world who could shoot with such phenomenal accuracy at that range in pitch blackness.

She heard the tread of approaching steps. She was afraid to clamber down, lest it be the hunter who hated women.

Then a towering, familiar figure emerged from the wall of blackness, and she gasped, "Ivy!" Whereupon, for the second time in her life, she passed into an ignominious faint.

She returned to consciousness, found herself lying on the ground. Frost was inspecting the corpse of the dead man. "Feeling better?" he drawled. "You very nearly committed harakiri. You took the precaution of fainting folded over a branch, fortunately, but hereafter I would suggest that you pick a somewhat more substantial medium for your moments of oblivion. Tree climbing was never one of my favorite sports."

She sat up, as angry as she had previously been grateful. "And who's responsible for that? You certainly got me into a fine mess! Where'd you come from?"

He explained briefly, added with a touch of regret, "I'd like to have taken him alive. I deliberately winged him with the first two shots. Those were warnings, his chance for an out. He didn't take it. The case is closed."

"I still don't understand how you could have figured out the identity of four people just by looking at a crosshatch of lines."

Frost said, "That was one of the most fascinating instances of pure deduction that has yet captivated my imagination. I know the exact spot at which you had entered the estate, and your line of direction, hence I had no difficulty identifying your position, since I reached the grid scarcely more than a half hour after I left you.

"But a second person was already within the inclosure. That second person must have been a poacher or hunter. But he could not have come with any knowledge of your presence, for the story had not yet gone out to the newspapers. Furthermore, one of the lines pursued an erratic course, such as would be made by a person surveying unfamiliar land. The other line, much more direct, followed the stream, as a hunter naturally would.

"When the third line appeared, the story had reached the newspapers, but no one could possibly have seen it and come here from New York in that short period of time. Yet the newcomer got safely over the fence; therefore he must have known that it was electrified; therefore he must have been one of the reporters. I would even go so far as to state positively that it was Macardi."

"YOU'RE RIGHT," Jean admitted.

"When the fourth line appeared, plenty of time had elapsed for the story to appear in the newspapers, and for the killer to come after the bait. But there was no danger, and no necessity for action, so long as the line representing the killer and the line representing your meanderings remained well apart. The moment your line turned and advanced toward the spot where the killer had taken his stand, I acted. Though I saw none of the four persons, I could identify each and follow events as closely as though I had been an eyewitness. And when the time came for me to take part in the game, the spectacles more than equalized the disadvantage of being at a distance.

"Are you ready to call the bet off?"

Jean got up. "Call the bet off? Certainly not. I've won the bet. I'm going back to town with you. You can make me out a check for ten thousand dollars right now."

Frost turned, stared at her with some surprise. "Indeed? And on what basis do you make the claim? Under the terms of the wager, you agreed to spend a week here."

Jean smiled. "Ah, but you didn't specify a week of seven days. I've lived an entire month during the hours I've been here."

"But you didn't land a fish."

"I landed Carson Goll, who was the biggest fish of all, and much more than ten inches long. Man is an animal. By your own admission, I brought about his death. He was both a fish and an animal."

"You amaze me. Am I to understand that you managed to build a fire?"

"I kindled a flame in the heart of Ron Macardi, a fire whose light lured him back here as irresistibly as a moth."

"Your points are taken with as much poetry as truth. Granting them, there yet remains one more consideration—the matter of constructing a shelter."

Jean's voice took on a triumphant spirit. "I can't think of any better protection and shelter against a rainy day than the check for ten thousand dollars which you are going to make out, payable to me."

"Well, I'll be damned!" Frost exclaimed.

Still wearing the spectacles, he sat down on a stone. He took out a check book and fountain pen, rested the book on one knee, and began writing a valuable piece of paper. The check looked fantastic by the infra-red light: white ink, flowing upon jet-black paper.

STOLEN
FROM THE
MORGUE

"Stop it! Stop it! You're dead—damn you!"

THE BUZZ of the house bell brought Jean Moray two thirds awake. She reached out and pressed the switch of a table lamp. The electric clock read 4:10. "Damn!" she muttered.

The bell buzzed again, its echoes dying away in the silent house with ghostly effect. She shivered. The radiators, hot as they were, could not wholly ward off the cold. One of the worst winters on record had hit New York.

The bell rang once more. She slipped mules on, pulled a silk robe around her pajamas, trotted downstairs. The motion awakened her fully. She paused long enough to look at the indicator, which told her what sort of caller to expect, then continued to the door. When she opened it, a gust of subzero wind smote her, chilled her wrists and ankles, drew a veil of ice over her from hair to soles, through her inadequate garments.

"Special delivery for I. V. Frost," said the man. "Sign here; it's registered. Hell of a night."

Jean took the pencil he offered and scrawled a wavy, indecipherable line. "Do you really think so? I'd hate to be caught in your idea of an arctic blizzard."

Jean banged the door before she opened the letter. She scanned it, frowned, and after another "Damn!" used the private wire to Frost.

"Yes?" came the professor's drawl almost immediately.

"A special delivery for you. It's about some teeth stolen from a corpse in the morgue at— Wait a minute till I find the postmark and—"

"Bring it up."

Jean heard his click. She stated softly, but with feeling, to thin air, "Go climb a tree. Go jump in a lake. Bring it up? Come down and get it. Ivy, something's really going to surprise you some day. Its name is Jean Moray. It has the patience of an elephant, and everybody else but you thinks it's practically the last word in streamlined 'It.' You don't, yet. But I'm going to break down the walls and the shells you keep around you if it takes years. Then it'll be my turn to give the cold shoulder and you'll get a notion of what a real iceberg is."

Jean shivered, drew the wrapper closer around her cold shoulders, opened the door.

She scampered up the steps of 13 State Street. In the corridor, full of crisp energy from the dash, she completely forgot to notice the eye. Frost collected artificial eyes. He always gave a different reason for adopting so curious a hobby. The eye in the hallway, which happened to be human, also happened to have a distressing habit of swaying with a creepy, terrifying slowness every time the outside door was opened.

She paid no attention to it as she passed underneath the thread by which it hung.

A LIGHT in the reception room attracted her. She glanced in. Frost, slouched down in an armchair, had his long legs stretched out to an ottoman. He wore the old leather jacket and corduroy trousers that Jean would like to have thrown away or buried, so rich were they in acid stains and chemicals.

He was blowing rings of aromatic smoke toward a bust of Socrates that graced a pedestal. The smoke came from a cigarette three times the length of standard brands. The indirect light from a floor lamp turned his features inscrutable, which they always were. He had the air of a man who had been meditating for hours upon an abstruse intellectual problem.

Jean said, "As long as you were up, you might at least have volunteered to come after the letter."

"I've been here only since you set foot on the porch. I was asleep at the moment you called."

"Well, you could have told me to take my time."

"You could have come at your own leisure. I said nothing about imperative haste. I merely told you to bring the letter."

Jean, by a strong effort, suppressed the exasperation that threatened to surge out of her. Frost was right. She hated to admit it. So she refused to admit it. "Here's the letter. You shouldn't sound so snappy when you aren't in any particular hurry. It's below zero. After all, pajamas and a sketchy suggestion of a wrap-around aren't much to be wearing in this weather."

"True. You ought to dress more warmly," Frost agreed tersely and took the letter.

Jean narrowed her eyes. He was absolutely inhuman at all the wrong times. Here she stood, alluring, tempting, from her soft mass of hair that held all the lush, mellow colors of a superb rye whisky, to her green eyes and immaculate complexion, her high cheek bones and languorous lips, the figure that would have tantalized a sculptor for Diana or Aphrodite, if he could have kept his mind on the work.

But she felt that she might as well have been a wooden image or a stuffed specimen in a museum, for all the impression she made on Frost. The only occasion when he appeared to be aware of her existence was when he had a specific use for her, solving crime and murder. In his last case, he had deliberately made a wager with her, and set her up as bait to snare a kill-crazy murderer, while she wandered around like Eve in the wilderness. He had shot Carson Goll, the killer, she had won the bet, but she had remained deeply resentful ever since, because he had not told her and she had not guessed the real purpose behind the wager.

Frost looked up from the letter. "Is that still bothering you? It shouldn't. You played your part admirably. Indeed, without your essential assistance, we could neither have caught nor killed the late biggame hunter, Carson Goll."

There was a sardonic glint in his black eyes as he resumed his perusal of the letter. Jean eyed him wrathfully. He had an uncanny faculty for reading her thoughts, though neither she nor any one else had yet succeeded in guessing his. Sometimes he chose to tell her the processes by which he deduced the nature of her thinking, and sometimes he volunteered nothing. This was one of the occasions when he didn't explain.

THE LETTER told of a peculiar occurrence. It read:

> If you have forgotten my name, I was one of your students ten years ago when you were still teaching. I've followed your work to some extent since you turned to murder mysteries for a profession, or is it a hobby? Anyway, I've kept up with a few of your successes that the papers reported.
>
> I don't know if I'm mixed up in a murder case or not. Whatever it is, there's something damned queer going on around here—right smack under my nose, as a matter of fact.

I've been the night superintendent in charge of the county morgue here at Northport for the past couple of years. My predecessor on the job, Will Graeley, simply disappeared. Not a trace of him has been found. I didn't know him personally, and I don't suppose that has anything to do with what I'm going to tell, though it might.

Northport is a fair-sized town, population a couple of hundred thousand or more, I guess. It's mostly on the coast, but it goes inland a mile or two toward the hills. The morgue is modern and big, bigger than they really need. There are refrigerated drawers to take care of a hundred stiffs. I don't know if it was built so large because of political extravagance, or to make extra jobs. Maybe they figured on getting prepared for any emergency. Anyway, that's beside the point. Only once since I've been here have we had more than ten stiffs cooling, and sometimes there isn't a single one.

I'm here alone at night. For some reason or other, most of the bodies come in during the day. Once in a great while we get somebody killed by a hit-and-run driver, or murdered in a holdup by night. As I say, I'm the whole works at night, but there are eight people altogether on the two day shifts, which last from seven in the morning to nine at night. Bradman is the other keeper in charge; then there are two clerks, and four attendants, besides a cop in plain clothes, that the police department keeps on deck. At least three of the eight are always here. So you can see it would be pretty hard, impossible I'd say, to pull off any dirty work during the daytime. Which is why I'm the goat, I suppose.

An old duck by the name of Billings was brought in a few nights ago. He'd already been dead a couple of days when found in a vacant lot on the edge of town, miles from where he had any reason to be. It looked as if he'd been slugged, robbed, and dumped out there. Darn near all his teeth had been knocked out, and the funny part is that the cops couldn't find even one of them. Relatives claimed the body yesterday.

I didn't think much more about it until to-night, when the Thompson brothers landed here an hour apart.

There's quite a story behind them. They had a violent quarrel when they were in their teens or twenties. It's supposed to have been over a woman, and they both lost out. I don't know how true it is. Their jealousy or rivalry or whatnot turned to hatred, and for the last fifty years they've been living in the same big one-room cabin. They drew a line in the middle that neither would cross. They wouldn't speak to each other, and they wouldn't speak to any one else. Neither would leave the cabin alone. When one went out, the other came along, marching silently aide by side. When they had to buy stuff, they wrote the order on a scrap of paper. They lived on the income from a trust fund that brought them just enough to barely live on. A queer sort of death-in-life. They both grew full beards and long hair clear down to their shoulders. They looked like prophets or fanatics or something.

Well, around midnight the police brought in Blythe Thompson. A patrolman had heard cries, rushed to investigate, and found him dying behind a sand dune on the beach. He was dead by the time the radio car arrived. They brought him here, not knowing at first who he was. I identified him right away. The police left to notify his brother, Goodall Thompson.

About ten minutes later, the night bell rang. I went to the entrance, but didn't see any one. That was the last I knew for a while. I got two bumps on my dome, one where I was slugged, and one where I hit when I fell. I don't think I was out more than a few minutes. Nothing was taken from me. I couldnt figure out why any one would slug a morgue keeper. Most people, especially crooks, don't want anything to do with morgues. I looked around and couldn't find anything wrong.

An ambulance brought Goodall Thompson in half an hour. The cops had gone to the brothers' cabin and found him there dead, shot through the heart by a .45. They found a .45 beside him. It had blood on the butt. They figured that Goodall had clubbed his brother to death on the dunes, went home, and killed himself in remorse.

I noticed that Goodall's beard sagged where his mouth would be. I took a look. His teeth were gone. They had either been removed years ago, or else he wore false teeth and didn't happen to be wearing them when he died. But the cops looked around the cabin and didn't find any false teeth.

That gave me a hunch, so I pulled Blythe out on his tray. He didn't have any teeth either. If my life depended on it, I couldn't swear whether either or both or neither had false teeth or no teeth.

But there is not the slightest question about identifying the two bodies. From the looks of things, somebody may have knocked me cold just to see if Blythe Thompson had any teeth, or steal them if he wore false teeth. And stealing them to delay identification would be nonsense; the legend of the brothers was well known. Both died violent deaths less than an hour apart. I don't agree with the police theory, but I'm in no position to contradict them.

> Three in a week with the teeth missing. That's past coincidence. I can't make it out.
>
> Does it interest you? I'd be glad to hear from you if it does. There's no chance of a fee, of course, so forget it if you're busy.
>
> Tirus L. Morgan.

"Ah, here's where we make a small fortune," Frost mused aloud, "and where I recover considerably more than the ten thousand dollars paid to you, plus other expenses which were lost on the last case."

"I beg your pardon?" Jean furrowed her eyebrows. "Do you by any chance happen to refer to the letter I brought? I seem to remember that it very definitely stated that there would be no reward or a fee."

"So it did," Frost agreed. "Nevertheless, I detect the advent of a pleasingly fat addition to the balance in the checking account. Get the long-distance operator, for Tirus L. Morgan at the county morgue in Northport."

Before Jean could take the receiver from its cradle, the telephone bell rang. Frost reached out a hand whose slender, tapered fingers and whose beauty were distinctive in his otherwise gaunt form. He neatly plucked the instrument from her grasp and drawled, "Yes?"

Over the wire floated the operator's voice, "Just a moment, please; here's your party. You may go ahead now," followed a second later by a deeper voice, "Hello! Hello! Is this Professor I.V. Frost? . . . It's Tirus Morgan calling, from Northport. Say, did you get a special delivery I sent you? . . . You did? Good. Listen, can you hop the next train up here? Something else has happened. Listen to this—"

Frost listened. He heard a heavy thud, a crash and clatter, then silence, ended by a click. He jiggled the receiver. "Operator, try to get an answer from the county morgue at Northport. . . . Yes, I know I was just talking to that number, but we were cut off. Keep on trying for the next fifteen minutes. If you don't draw a response by then, stop trying."

II.

FROST HUNG UP, his eyes alight with an intense black glitter which was characteristic when a problem compelled his attention. "Four murders brought home to us, within a few minutes—"

"Four?" Jean interrupted, on a rising inflection.

"Billings, the Thompson brothers, and now either Morgan or some one who pretended to be Morgan. Other murders already committed or about to be committed for the same purpose are a distinct probability. That was the reason I told you to reach Morgan by long distance to warn him. We're going to Northport. Be ready in a quarter of an hour."

"Morgan? You were just talking to him and were cut off."

"I don't know whom I was talking to. The fact that he claimed to be Morgan is no proof that he was. However, he stopped speaking. Most persons do," Frost added dryly, "when their skulls have been cracked open."

"But even so, the roads are blocked from yesterday's blizzard. A car can't get through. The trains won't be running, or else they'll be hours late."

"I was not aware that I had mentioned automobiles or trains."

"Well, the planes certainly won't be taking off in this weather."

"Mine will."

Jean exclaimed, "Yours will! I didn't know that you owned one. I've been with you now for two years and I never before heard you mention a plane."

"I am not responsible for the state of your ignorance. Neither have I found it wise policy to inform any single individual of the full scope of my activities, interests, and connections," said Frost before he hiked into his laboratory.

Jean had no time to think of a crushing retort. She hurried out, accomplished a miracle in quick changing, and was ready almost on the dot. Since Northport lay in New England, and the temperature flirted with subzero marks, she chose skiing togs.

The morgue had not answered Frost's call within the limit he specified. He used his specially built car to reach the hangar, and drove over icy pavements, snowdrifted streets.

Less than an hour later, while the dull gray of dawn struggled to pierce a sky blanketed with lowhanging, dark clouds, his monoplane *If* took off from its jersey landing field. It carried some bundles that Frost had assembled from the choice and varied supplies that stocked his laboratory. Jean didn't ask the nature of their contents, and he didn't volunteer the information.

The field dropped away; the *If* banked and straightened northeastward, bucking erratic head winds. The low ceiling, the pea-soup clouds and fog a mile thick, were bumpy. At 11,000 feet, the *If* found smooth flying. Jean looked at the unfamiliar array of meters, instruments, and controls with envy. Frost handled the *If* easily. She mentally decided that she, too, would next master the art of flying.

"Why did you call it the *If*? That's an ominous word for a plane."

"My name, and consequently my initials, were gifts concerning whose reception I had very little to say," Frost answered obliquely.

Jean silently damned her own obtuseness. Of course—I. F. for Ivy Frost. The *If*—an unlucky and unlikely name for a plane—and yet the reason for it proved absurdly simple, like many of Frost's explanations.

She made light of her lapse. "If the *If* doesn't fail us— Dear me, I can see that conversation is apt to become confusing. When the *If* lands us at the morgue— My goodness, that sounds worse.

"This case looks like tooth trouble. Why would any one commit murder over teeth, or if not that, why would he go to such lengths to steal teeth from a corpse? Prevention of identification doesn't seem to be the answer."

FROST spoke without turning his head, so that she had to lean over to hear him above the drone of the motor. "Many explanations are possible. The teeth may have been stolen solely to lay a red herring in the path of investigation. They may be wholly devoid of significance. On the other hand, they may have been taken for their intrinsic value, if they were false or filled teeth. More than one person has had diamonds set in dental caries, and has thereby acquired a dazzling smile.

"Again, no one may have stolen the teeth. Remember that Morgan referred to all three corpses in terms of age. Old people often wear sets of false teeth, or are toothless, and are prone to lose or misplace the artificial teeth. We have no information as to whether true teeth were knocked out by violence, or false teeth are simply missing. A dentist might conceivably murder some of his patients, and remove all traces of his dental artistry in order to prevent suspicion from falling on him.

"Each dentist stamps his personality and identity upon his work: the tools that he uses; the method of treatment that he adopts; his technique; his care and thoroughness or his perfunctory approach; the proportion of gold, silver, amalgam, porcelain, and cement in his fillings; his extraction or preservation of dead teeth; his orthodontia, bridgework, capping; his surgery on impacted teeth; all are clues to characterize him positively."

"I asked for a little light. I got a sunburst that's blinding," said Jean plaintively. "Which answer is the right one, if any? Can the facts be determined as yet, or have you managed to develop a logical sequence out of the skimpy material?"

"Yes. I have. Far from being skimpy, the material is exceedingly rich." Frost's tone and expression told her nothing and, she decided, were deliberately noninformative.

She leaned back, relaxed into a more comfortable position, and lapsed into silence. From time to time she turned a quick, covert flash from the corners of her eyes at the bleak profile of Frost. His gaze did not waver from the course, though his faculties seemed centered inwardly upon a mental problem.

Jean did her make-up over twice on the trip, with a great deal of painstaking fuss, and adding fresh, guileless radiance to her eyes on the first experiment, for innocence.

The pilot kept the *If* upon a straight course.

Jean's second new face toned the general effect up toward sophistication, and emphasized the seductive appeal of her mouth.

Frost continued to peer ahead.

There was a dram of exciting new perfume in her hand bag, a perfume subtle, provocative, and insidiously pervasive. She touched the stopper to the lobe of each ear.

"Belair's *Idée Enchanté* is a rare and distinctive essence," said Frost, without turning his head. "So rare and distinctive that a blind man in a crowd could visualize the wearer. An able-bodied man in an open field or forest at night would have no difficulty locating and murdering the wearer, if his intentions lay along such unpleasant lines."

Jean used a kerchief to rub off and absorb the perfume. She was on the verge of deep and violent impulses. But she would keep on trying to find the location of Frost's Achilles heel, if he had one. His armor had thus far proved impervious to all onslaughts. On her own dates, away from her duties, she devoted much of her efforts to sidetracking ardent males of the species. She was confident that she had no reason for trying to make an impression upon the professor except the thrill of conquest.

Striking in appearance, almost grotesque, he lived like a solitary eagle or a lone wolf, self-sufficient, an island universe. The situation was a challenge to Jean to force herself into dominance or importance in his existence. But it always seemed to be Frost who dominated the picture and who bent the wills of others toward the goals that he planned. The dilemma had existed since she first met the professor.

AS the *If* began dipping toward the cloud banks below, where Northport should lie, she ventured to ask, "How will you know where to land? Suppose there's no field—"

Frost cut her short. "I phoned the municipal airport while you were dressing. It's ready for us. I also phoned an advertisement for the final morning edition of the Northport *Citizen,* and reserved a suite of rooms at the Northport Arms Hotel for you.

"Immediately after we land, go to the hotel. You ought to reach it by nine o'clock or shortly thereafter. The rush will begin at nine thirty and—"

"What rush?"

"A deluge of applicants responding to the newspaper announcement. I'll give you a list of questions to ask each applicant. You will also have $5,000 in new five-dollar bills which you are to distribute one to every person interviewed."

"When on earth did you get $5,000 in brand-new currency at four thirty in the morning?"

Frost said, with a touch of impatience, "From the large sum of cash that I always keep on hand for emergencies.

"I am launching a whole series of events to-day. The climaxes will come in a rush to-night. Hold interviews at the hotel suite from nine thirty this morning to three thirty this afternoon. You won't have a chance to analyze the index cards very thoroughly as they are filled out and turned in to you, but you should be able to offer a few general observations about the drift of information. I'll phone you between noon and one o'clock. I'll stop at the hotel at four o'clock."

"But what sort of people will I interview, and on what subject? What's it all about?"

"The best answer is the one that you will discover for yourself," said Frost blandly.

The *If* lost altitude steadily, cut through the cloud soup, emerged from a ceiling of 700 feet, with visibility less than a half mile in thin ground fog. The municipal landing field, flood-lighted, lay at the south end of Northport. It was covered with hard-packed snow, an icy, smooth expanse which the *If* made a perfect landing upon and slid across.

Frost added a few minor instructions to those he had already given Jean while they were coming down.

She wondered, as she climbed out, if he ever forgot an important detail. Her chain of thought started from the fact that two taxis were at the field, and obviously expecting them.

Frost whirled away in one taxi, with a wave of his arm in her general direction, while she was still collecting the bundles and packets that he had dumped on the seat beside her in the second taxi.

III.

THICK FROST covered all except the double-glass observation panels in the taxicab. Piles of snow lined the streets. The windows of stores and houses glittered with icy patterns. Flakes of snow swirled on a congealing wind that crackled out of Canada.

The taxi drew up in front of the county morgue, a big, gloomy stone structure that might be less dismal in summer when the trees and shrubbery around it were blooming, but whose depressing nature was intensified now by the naked trees and snow-banked hedges.

Several persons on the way to work, with mufflers and mittens, overcoats, overshoes, and ear muffs, saw a tall, gaunt specter stride up the steps. They wondered why he was so foolhardy as to go hatless in such savage weather. Two patrolmen in a passing radio car, one of the dozen that Northport boasted, noticed him hesitate at the closed but unlocked door before he went in.

He was a man of distinctive individuality that they couldn't easily forget. Unmistakably I. V. Frost, he belonged in New York. Their province was Northport. They resented the presence of outsiders, but orders compelled them to continue their leisurely cruising.

During Frost's momentary pause, neither pedestrians nor police saw him slip a paraffin-coated blank strip of soft metal into the keyhole and twist it. He withdrew it, dropped it into a pocket, and entered.

The atmosphere of the morgue, ordinarily somber and grim, was tense with excitement. The two men arguing at the desk in the outer office, one seated, the other perched on an edge of the desk and swinging a leg, lapsed into silence as Frost strode toward them. In the great, drab, gray repository beyond them, where the tray receptacles for the unidentified dead stretched away in long and oppressive banks, three more men clustered, talking and gesturing.

"Good morning, Mr. Bradman. The strange disappearance of the late Tirus L. Morgan is not as mystifying as it would seem. I hope that your friend, the detective, will agree with me."

The man in the chair, middle-aged, with graying hair, a thin mouth, and the flinty features of rock-ribbed New England, got to his feet. He stared up at Frost. "Yes, I'm Bradman. Now explain yourself. I have never seen you before. How did you know who I am?"

"The air of authority belongs to the superintendent in charge," Frost drawled.

The second man, equally thin-lipped, but more ruddy of face and more blunt of figure compared to the lank Bradman, squared around. "I'll second that, stranger. How do you happen to know me? And then do some fast talking. The news hasn't had time to get around that Morgan disappeared."

FROST lighted one of his pungently spicy cigarettes. "The police detective, like other persons, carries the marks of his profession in his gestures, motions, appearance, habits, and voice. Allow me to introduce myself—Professor I.V. Frost. I happen to have been the last person talking to Morgan at the moment when his earthly existence was suddenly and most unfortunately terminated."

"You're right. I'm Serle of the detective squad. Go on talking. What makes you think that Morgan's dead?"

"What makes you think that Morgan has vanished?" Frost countered.

"All we know is that he's gone. He wasn't on the job when the day shift arrived this morning, but the place was locked up, and his keys were hanging on the outside door. A woman he's been going with called because he hadn't shown up for a breakfast date and she was alarmed. Then we found a note in the typewriter to the effect that the job was driving him crazy, and that he decided to light out before he wound up in State Asylum."

"Any one can type a signature," Frost said.

"How do you know it was typed?"

"Because dead men can't write their signatures."

"Spill it. You know a lot more than you've told us."

Frost gave a quick résumé of Morgan's letter and subsequent long-distance telephone call.

Serle argued, "It sounds like a mess to me. I've got a notion that Morgan really did skip out. He faked the act about being cut off in the middle of talking to you. That would be a cinch. So, of course, he wouldn't pay any attention to the phone ringing when you were trying to get him on the wire again."

"I'm inclined to agree," Bradman spoke in a reedy, nasal voice. "We examined the interior of the morgue. There was no sign of a struggle. Nothing is missing."

"Except Morgan," said Frost pointedly. "And can you now give me a logical motive why Morgan went to such elaborate lengths to summon me ten years after he, and then merely as a student, had last seen me?"

"It does seem unlikely, to say the least," Bradman admitted. "Neither do I understand his references to teeth. I fail to see what possible importance they have."

Serle shook his head. "It seems reasonable to me. In the first place, if any teeth are missing, Morgan likely took them himself. In the second place, if he wanted to disappear, it would be a good idea to make people think he was dead. And in the third place, he might have got hipped on the subject of teeth. You can't expect folks with mental quirks to act sensibly. When they're going crazy, they act like they're going crazy."

Frost retorted, in ironic vein, "Your system of deductions is truly the most wonderful that has ever come to my attention. You have now established that Morgan acted deliberately, for sane reasons best known to himself. You have also determined that he was mentally irresponsible, and that he acted upon irrational motives. I will soon be led to believe that Morgan was not one man. He was a couple of supermen."

BRADMAN raised the hand of peace in a ministerial gesture. "Come, come, let us not descend to personal aspersions. We have no cause to believe that anything drastic has happened. We have only Morgan's communications to you, his note of farewell to us, and his absence. It will be time to entertain more serious convictions when he returns, or when his body is found. Doubtless one or the other, will occur before the day is over."

"Right," Frost tersely agreed.

The keeper of the morgue pursed his lips for a moment, then, "I think he'll be found alive. If he had been killed, the chances are that the body would already have been discovered."

"The body may never be discovered," Frost contradicted him.

The Northport detective scowled. "What are you talking about? It's the hardest thing in the world to get rid of a corpse. They've been left up in trees, and the buzzards called attention to them, or else they were found when the leaves fell off in autumn. They've been buried, and they came to light when rains washed the dirt away or somebody plowed them up or a dog started rooting around. They've been dumped in lonely gullies, where a prospector or hiker came across them. They've been sunk in lakes and rivers, and eventually they came to the surface."

"True." Frost nodded, exhaling a cone of fragrant fumes and crushing the butt out. "Nevertheless, dozens of individuals disappear every year and are never seen again."

The morgue superintendent asked, "Just what do you mean? First you agreed with me that Morgan would be found to-day, then you said we might never locate him."

"I know of one safe, even extraordinary, hiding place where his body would not otherwise be found for years. I expect to find him there. I know of one other hiding place where his body could never be found. I will not look for him there in case he is not where I think.

"One of my cases," Frost continued, "involved a man named Nick Valma. I found him in five pieces, each piece heavily weighted with scrap iron, at the bottom of a lake. Here, however, we have the entire Atlantic Ocean opening before us. That is the second of the hiding places to which I referred.

"Eastern gangsters from New York to Boston are believed to have disposed of certain victims by a similar method. They are said to have added a refinement of torture, by setting the victims' feet in pails of wet cement, waiting for the cement to harden, and then dumping the victims overboard alive and helpless.

"If Tirus L. Morgan has been slain and dropped into even the shallowest, smallest cove on Northport harbor, the search for him may as well be abandoned. A fleet of divers could work offshore for years, pass within fifty feet of him many times, and never locate the skeleton. Not the least attractive feature of such disposal is that the murderer can always find the remains if he should desire, simply by making note of his alignment between any two landmarks and his approximate distance from shore."

SERLE struck a match to a cigarette. "Br-r! It's cold enough outside and it's bad enough being in a morgue. Why bring up such nasty ideas? I hope you're wrong about Morgan."

"If you mean you hope that he is not at the bottom of the Atlantic Ocean, I agree with your sentiment. I should regret his taking a secret, or a fortune, or both to the grave."

"What secret?" Serle demanded.

"What fortune? Nobody takes a fortune to the grave!" Bradman exclaimed.

"Indeed?" Frost lifted his eyebrows. "I seem to recall that vast sums in jewelry, precious metals, and valuables have been found in Egyptian, Grecian, Roman, and Incan tombs. It is a matter of speculation how much gold and silver in dental fillings, and how much jewelry like brooches, rings, and personal ornaments, have been and are being buried every year in the graves of our own civilization."

"What of it?" Serle asked bluntly. "If Morgan was worth even a small fortune, that's proof of his insanity, or he'd never have kept hold of a punk job like night super in the morgue. Anyway, the only money he had was what he earned."

"I know nothing about the state of Morgan's finances," said Frost. "I merely remarked that I would regret it if he took either a secret or a fortune, or both, with him."

"There you go again about a secret," complained Bradman. "What kind of a secret?"

"That is a matter worth investigation. When Morgan talked to me, he seemed excited, and was on the verge of disclosing information. It must have been a development that occurred just prior to his telephone call. Were any corpses admitted to the morgue last night?"

"No," replied Bradman. "We checked up on that when we opened up this morning. The procedure, when discovery of a body is reported to the police, is for the Northport Hospital to send an ambulance on the off chance of finding a spark of life left. The ambulance then routes the corpse here. There was no record in the filing index of a delivery last night. We called the police and the hospitals to verify this."

Serle cut in, "You sidetracked us, Frost."

"So?"

"You mentioned a couple of spots where you thought you might lay your hands on Morgan if he's dead, as you seem to expect. You told us about the second of those spots, the Atlantic Ocean. You said you wouldn't bother hunting there. You also said you believed you'd find Morgan in the other hiding place. But, do you know, you somehow forgot to mention what that other choice of yours was?"

An odd, mirthless twist of the lips made Frost's expression more stern than Bradman's. His eyes acquired a bleak intensity, an unholy grimness. He turned, walked swiftly into the morgue proper.

Bradman and Serle, left silent by the compelling power of Frost, and by the sinister purposiveness of his actions, followed him. The three other men who had been grouped in the storage room stared, broke up their conference, and drifted over to watch.

One by one, Frost pulled out the trays at the end of the long row of vaults. He inspected the subject with a quick, piercing scrutiny, and slid the drawer shut. A muffled thud punctuated each inspection as the receptacle slid back into place.

A strange, strained silence enveloped the figures surrounding him. They were all hardened to the gruesome duties that their work entailed. Yet their breathing became more audible, distinctly harsher, as Frost opened and closed the drawers.

There were six corpses registered in the filing index at the outer office. There were six corpses briefly described and tagged upon the end drawers of the morgue. All six corpses were in their allotted positions, and slid out in all their stone-cold blindness for the light to flicker upon before they retreated into the darkness and confinement which were prelude to their oblivion.

The dampness of the air absorbed the underlying and ineradicable smell of disinfectants, death, decay, autopsy, preservative fluids, alcohol, formaldehyde. The tables for post-mortem examination gleamed dully from the morgue lights high overhead. The silence increased, so that the scuffle of shoes and the rustle of a man's arm on his sleeve spoke with a whisper of thunder.

Frost pulled out the seventh, eighth, ninth, tenth trays. All empty, as they should be, they rolled back with a more hollow echo than attended the loaded receptacles.

There were four trays to a deck, twenty-five decks to receive the dead, and every receptacle just as chilled, as coldly refrigerated, as though it preserved a body unidentified.

The thirtieth slide *did* contain a body. There was no question about identifying the specimen, however. The specimen was grotesquely convulsed in premature *rigor mortis.* The specimen had a fracture of the skull. Bloody froth, congealed on the lips, called attention to the fact that all thirty-two teeth had been knocked out and stolen away. The specimen had quite obviously recovered consciousness after it had been stuffed into the drawer. But the specimen had been too weak to break out, and refrigeration had done the rest.

The specimen had died in burial alive at the morgue.

The specimen was Tirus L. Morgan.

IV.

THE NORTHPORT ARMS, up to the minute of Jean's arrival, had been a staid, respectable, conservative hotel. Built thirty years ago, it had changed only its plumbing and some fixtures as concessions to modernity. Its lobby was spacious beyond all need, with a ceiling two stories high, from which four crystal chandeliers of immense size and elaborate ornamentation dangled upon chains of brass. A dark-blue, plush carpet, somewhat faded and worn by the tread of a generation, completely covered the floor. The sofas, davenports, armchairs, and overstuffed rockers preserved the substantial and genteel elegance of an earlier decade.

Even the registration desk swept through a semicircle of noble and impressive scope. Behind it puttered a manager of bewhiskered dignity, but amiable and leisurely in his expansive way.

There were eight other persons present—five men and three women, all exuding well-fed contentment and smugness—when Jean Moray blithely walked in shortly after nine o'clock. Her skiing outfit created a sensation that her figure and her piquantly sophisticated face added to. Five men perked up and came to life with drools of anticipation. Three women turned stern-lipped and haughty, with disapproval.

The manager eyed her regalia askance. "Why, yes, Miss Moray, a suite has been reserved for you, but our guests are—ah—a trifle, shall we say, inclined to be—"

"Oh, you mean they're conservative?" warbled Jean with her most provocatively winsome smile. "I understand. Of course, it's natural that they would be jealous of others like us who are young or attractive or important. Isn't it nice to be envied?"

Mr. Whiskers beamed all over like a one-man sun. "Let me show you to your suite, Miss Moray. The boy will not be back for a few minutes and I am sure you will not want to waste your time waiting. Oh, it's no trouble, I assure you."

Five pairs of eyes looked wishful, and three pairs hardened with reproof, as the manager escorted Jean, the loveliest and most exotic beauty who had yet graced the hotel in the years of its existence. He took her to her rooms, fussed about to see that everything was satisfactory, and finally returned to the desk with a new jauntiness.

JEAN had just time enough to get cleansed and settled before the rush began, promptly at 9:30. The advertisement that Frost had ordered for the final morning edition of the Northport *Citizen* read, as she quickly discovered from the applicants who had clipped it out of the Personal Notices column:

> A brand-new five-dollar bill will be given to every man and woman past 60 who will answer a brief questionnaire. Apply between 9:30 and 3:30 to-day only. Suite 409-410, Northport Arms Hotel.

Jean left the door of Room 409 open. She sat at the writing desk in the other room, with the connecting door likewise open. In the drawer she stowed away the five-dollar bills that Frost had given her, in ten piles, one hundred bills to each packet. The bundles of index cards she arranged on top of the desk.

At first she interviewed the applicants singly, but the waiting throng swelled so rapidly that she saw she could never complete the task by the hour set. She adopted a speed-up system, summoning them in groups of twenty, distributing the cards to be filled out, and reading the questions aloud. Mr. Whiskers at the main desk was a trifle flustered by her sudden request for two dozen sharpened pencils, but filled the order in a few minutes.

The questions were no more curious than the group that responded to the advertisement.

Old men, old women, in their 60s, 70s, 80s, 90s, even a few that seemed to have passed the century mark, hobbled, limped, tottered, or rolled up on one leg, two legs, three legs, and in wheel chairs. Most of them were shabbily dressed, and some evidently had come from poorhouses and homes for the elderly. All the infirmities of age were represented in that group. Ear horns and a couple of ear phones vied with crutches and canes. Able-bodied friends led more than one blind man, and wheeled more than one invalid or paralytic.

Jean for a while found them a pathetic lot, and then developed a deep sympathy for these lives in the twilight of their existence. She had not expected so big a rush—nearly a thousand replies to the advertisement. She did not believe that there could be many other old people in Northport, except those who were economically secure, or who had not read the paper. When the rush was at its peak during the noon hour, she experienced a feeling akin to horror that civilization could flaunt, in a city no larger than Northport, so many lives that had nothing left to anticipate and little means of brightening the days that remained.

There was one little old woman with tiny red eyes and a pinched, starved face who burst into tears when she received the crisp bill. She clutched it in a hand like a bird's claw.

"What will you do with the money?" Jean asked kindly.

The old woman said, "I know I won't live out this winter. I have no relatives, no friends, no money. I'll buy as many pots of flowers as I can. I'll watch them grow and bloom. I want them around me, all bright and growing, when I'm not here any longer. I'll talk to them. I'll know them all by name. They will be my new friends, my young friends, my very own."

Jean watched her as she plodded out. Suddenly Jean had an emotion of insensate rage that she couldn't define, a thickening in her throat, an impulse to smash something, anything, she didn't know what. It was gone as swiftly as it came, under the pressure of work to be done.

She thought during the early interviews that it was the money that counted most to these aged individuals, but she learned that such was not the case. The woman who wanted flowers, and a few others who needed the money for compelling reasons, were exceptions. Most of them needed money, it was true, but curiosity had activated others. The point that mattered to most of them was that this opportunity provided an adventure of tremendous excitement in their barren lives. Some one had taken an interest in them. Some one wanted old people, not youth. Some one was willing to pay them money just for answering a few questions. They were starved for even a little attention from a world that had forgotten them. It was an event that would furnish them with endless material for chatter and memories in months to come.

THE QUESTIONNAIRE that Frost had provided was simple. Each applicant was asked: Have you ever had any teeth filled, or artificial teeth made? What dentist, or dentists, performed the work? In approximately what year, or years, was the work done? A few statements as to age, identity, and sex rounded out the list.

The index cards came in so fast that Jean had no opportunity to do more than scan them. From comments and remarks that were dropped, however, she gleaned a few nuggets of general interest. One was that tooth cavities, dental caries, seemed to develop more frequently in youth than in age. The majority of the applicants who reported fillings also reported that the larger part of the work was done in their early life, except for replacements. She also picked up the information that a number of them had patronized one Dr. Paul Sorokin, who died suddenly of heart failure in the 1890s. His practice had been taken over by a Dr. Fleming, to whom most of the patients had gravitated. Dr. Fleming, in turn, had died years ago.

One old man, surprisingly brisk and spry in spite of his wizened face and great age, cackled, "I'm 92. I'm going to live to be 102, by fiddershins and fiddlesticks. So it's my teeth you want to know about? I've got 'em all except one that Dr. Sorokin filled and later pulled.

"Do I remember him? I should say yes. He was a rare one. He had a face like a goat, what with his little white Vandyke dribbling down from his chin. But a good man, a good man, always puttering around with things, he was. It's a wonder he ever built up a practice, but he did.

"I guess he had enough money so he didn't have to worry. He had a few wealthy patients, but he seemed to spend more time on folks who couldn't afford to pay. He did just as good work for them, too, except that he didn't use gold in making *their* fillings. At that, he'd sometimes use silver, and he knew he'd likely not get a dollar for it.

"He was married, and when he died, peacefullike, it was in bed, of heart failure. They said he'd leave his wife fixed for the rest of her life, but come to find out he wasn't wealthy at all. She sold his practice and good will to Dr. Fleming. But Fleming wasn't much interested in poor people who couldn't afford to pay, so he kind of let it slide, all except the ones who had money. I guess Fleming was all right; he made a nice living.

"Mrs. Sorokin died a few years after her husband. She even sold his sailboat before the end, but she had plenty to last her the way it turned out, because she didn't last long. Fleming died, too. I guess it must have been twenty years back. I disremember what took him off. I guess it was a stroke."

He kept on mumbling his recollections as he left.

The procedure with the applicants, though fatiguing, had a peculiar fascination. Jean, on several occasions, got the conviction that she was living on a planet where no birth had occurred for decades, and where the aged inhabitants waited without hope for the day of oblivion. At still other times, she felt hemmed in by the unreality of a vivid dream.

Nevertheless, she didn't forget lunch, which consisted of a sandwich and a Scotch and soda sent up on a tray. She munched and sipped while the interviews continued. She didn't pause in the routine and block registrations, even when a reporter came along to get a feature for the evening edition of the Northport *Citizen*.

He was an enthusiastic reporter. In the presence of a dozen witnesses, he told Jean that he was married, that she was the most beautiful creature he had ever seen, and that he would gladly run off with her and abandon his family. When he got tired of asking her for a date for the evening, he worked around to the feature story.

Jean, following Frost's instructions, readily admitted that the professor had engineered the scheme. His reason, she glibly explained, was that he had made a private wager about the average number of dental caries per individual that would be found in any given age group. Even if he paid out $5,000 during his investigation, he would still win a larger sum if his contention was correct. Jean was sorry that she couldn't give any more details. The reporter jotted a few notes and went out, after declaring that he couldn't live without her.

Shortly after he left, Frost called. She cleared the room while she talked to him. It was ten minutes before she resumed her work. Frost made her repeat verbatim the garrulity of the nonagenarian who had rambled at length about Sorokin, boats, Mrs. Sorokin, and Fleming.

"Ah! That's what I wanted. It's the missing piece!" Frost exclaimed when she finished.

"What is?"

She heard the click of Frost's receiver. The meaning of his comment puzzled her throughout the remaining interviews.

Jean was ready to call it a day at 3:30. Against her desires, she dallied beyond the hour that Frost had set. She was glad that she did. Five stragglers arrived, and each one of them left with the promised reward.

She closed the doors as her watch flirted with the hour of four. Only a few dozen bills were left of the thousand with which she had started.

V.

WHEN FROST brought the corpse of Tirus L. Morgan to light in the county morgue, it was he himself who broke the inertia that enveloped his audience in stunned silence.

To the detective, Serle, he snapped, "Notify police headquarters. You know best your own procedure. Comb the neighborhood for witnesses who may have seen some one leave the morgue between four and seven this morning. Try to find the missing teeth—"

One of the attendants looked sick. "Imagine getting all your teeth knocked out!"

Frost answered, "The blow on the skull felled Morgan. His assailant stuffed his unconscious figure in the nearest receptacle. The teeth were hammered out while he lay on the slab. Morgan regained only partial consciousness, not enough to feel pain, if that's what bothers you. He died within fifteen minutes of the attack."

Bradman, the keeper of the morgue, protested, "But why? Why take his teeth? That is nonsensical brutality!"

Frost shrugged. "So it would seem. Do any of you possess knowledge on the condition of Morgan's teeth?"

The Northport detective, on his way to telephone, heard the remark. He slowed and half turned. "I have. I'll save it." He continued on his way.

One of the attendants blurted, "I don't like Serle. Never did. I've had sandwiches and coffee with Morgan a couple of times. He had good teeth I told him he could pose for tooth-paste ads. He laughed and boasted that he never had any tooth trouble."

"Ah!" Frost's eyes lighted. "That explains a great deal, and also adds another perplexing feature to a riddle that's already mystifying. The more I see of this case, the better I like it. Your name? Crandall! My assistant will send you a slip of reading matter that you can endorse and cash."

Frost started out of the morgue.

Bradman dashed after him, with an anxious plea. "Wait, wait! This puts me in a very unfortunate position. The police are sure to quiz me—all of us. It may affect our jobs."

"Forget it. With every one in the same boat, it won't make a particle of difference."

Bradman looked puzzled as the professor hurried into the freezing, crackling outdoors. Serle interrupted his telephoning to bawl at Frost, who didn't take the trouble to pause in his stride or to answer.

It was nearly ten o'clock when Frost left the morgue. The ground that he covered in the next six hours and the stops that he made would have baffled the most analytic observer, besides defeating the most skillful of shadowers.

At four o'clock he had himself announced at the Northport Arms Hotel and walked in on Jean Moray. While listening attentively to her detailed report, he skimmed through the pile of cards that she had collected.

Again his jet eyes gleamed. "This is excellent corroborative material. It all dovetails now. To-night you're going to keep vigil in a graveyard."

"A graveyard! In zero weather? What for?"

"Both Fleming and Sorokin are buried in Oak Grove Cemetery. The actions that I launched to-day will come to a head to-night in the cemetery, the morgue, or both."

"I hope you aren't expecting them to come out of their graves."

"Why, yes, I am confident that one of them will. However, if you object to a vigil in the cemetery, you can go ahead and choose the morgue instead."

JEAN looked far from enthusiastic. "I never heard a worse set of alternatives—the cemetery or the morgue, indeed! At that, I've come so close to landing in them both so many times since I started playing this dangerous game with you that I suppose I might as well see what my future home looks like. Well, I guess it had better be the cemetery. At least the population there is safely underground, in spite of what *you* think. I'd hate to have to peek at the ones in the morgue. What have you been doing all day?"

Frost told her of his adventure at the morgue. "Since then, I've covered considerable territory. From old files of the Northport *Citizen,* I found the death notices of the two dentists and their burial grounds. Oak Grove Cemetery is a large tract. I located the two graves, and made a chart that should enable you to find them easily, even after dark.

"I visited real-estate companies, and examined records in the Northport city hall. Sorokin lived in a beach cottage at Bay Cove, which cottage is now occupied by Detective Serle, and his wife. Fleming had a house farther north on Crystal Bay, which is now owned by the superintendent of the morgue, Bradman.

"I made a trip to each and learned about a remarkable duplication of events. Will Graeley, you may recall from Morgan's letter to me, disappeared two years ago. He was the night keeper of the morgue before Morgan. Mrs. Serle reported that one night, when her husband was on extra duty, she received a telephone call that he had been injured. Naturally, she rushed away to the designated spot. The call was a decoy. During the hour of her absence, the cottage was thoroughly ransacked."

"Did the burglar steal anything?"

"Nothing at all from the cottage. But a horseshoe was removed from the tool shed."

"A horseshoe!"

"Exactly. With hundreds of dollars' worth of rings, small jewelry, and cash in the cottage, the intruder chose to carry off with him a horseshoe as his entire loot."

Jean's face turned blank. "That's too preposterous for comment. What in the world can it possibly have to do with teeth and murders?"

Frost lighted one of his special cigarettes with keen zest. "That strange burglary occurred just a few days before Graeley vanished.

"I then talked to Mrs. Bradman. It seems that early one evening, a couple of years ago, she received a telephone call to the effect that her husband had been injured. Naturally, she rushed away to the designated site. The call was a decoy. During the time of her absence, the house was thoroughly ransacked. The sole object missing was a horseshoe that had hung above the front door as an omen of luck."

"Another horseshoe? Why, it's incredible!"

"The second burglary likewise took place just prior to the disappearance of Graeley. When the Serles bought Sorokin's cottage, they found the horseshoe in the tool shed. When the Bradmans purchased Fleming's house, the other horseshoe already hung above the door. The horseshoes obviously formed a pair that had become separated.

"That evidence alone is insufficient to determine whether the horseshoes originally belonged to Fleming or to Sorokin. However, you learned from one of your elderly visitors that Sorokin was fond of puttering around with things. On the basis of that information, plus a deduction or two, I know that Sorokin enjoyed pitching horseshoes, and that he constructed a pair of his own, suitable in shape, size, and weight for his particular technique."

FRANKLY BEWILDERED, Jean stated, "This muddle is becoming crazier than the lunatic plague we got mixed up with several months ago. Next, you'll be telling me that Sorokin's interest in amateur sailing is important."

"Highly important," Frost agreed to her further perplexity. "Though Bay Cove is partly frozen over, Sorokin's mooring marker sticks above the ice. The Serles still use it occasionally in warm weather to anchor their own small motor boat, and that's worth noting.

"It's also worth noting by the afternoon papers that the morgue will remain closed for a few nights, until the city council decides either to appoint some one for the vacancy or to keep the morgue permanently closed by night."

"I'm glad I chose the cemetery!" Jean exclaimed fervently. "It's probably the first time in history that any one was glad to choose a cemetery, but as against holding the fort in a morgue—give me the great outdoors, cemetery or not!"

"And by the way," Frost added, "I rented a cottage for a month."

Jean perked up. "A month? If it's going to take that long to find the answers, I'll have time to spare for winter sports—skiing, skating, ice boats, bobsleds—"

"If you wish to remain here, you doubtless will," Frost answered dryly. "I detest cold. I am returning to New York on the *If* to-morrow morning."

"But the cottage— If you rented it for a month—"

"I may not use it at all. I am simply preparing for all emergencies. I also wished to convey the impression, in case the rental reached the attention of others, that I was planning a long sojourn and expecting slow progress. As a matter of fact, the puzzle is now entirely clear. My work will be finished well before dawn. All that remains is to catch the guilty one."

"A small detail, but an important one," said Jean with a flippant touch. "What now?"

"A modicum of pabulum," Frost drawled. "It occurs to me that I have neglected breakfast and lunch. There is not quite an hour to spare. I refuse to go out again in this abominable interspatial cold until necessary. I'll have an à la carte order sent up. What would you like?"

"What are you having?"

Frost got the chef on the wire. "Oysters on the half shell, hors d'oeuvres, ripe and stuffed olives, clam chowder, assorted nuts, broiled lobster with drawn butter, lettuce and tomato salad with mayonnaise, a porterhouse steak medium to rare with grilled mushrooms, *julienne* potatoes, hot mince pie, Roquefort cheese and crackers, a large pot of strong coffee—Pernod if you have it, otherwise Drambuie—and poppyseed rolls."

"All on one tray?" queried the kitchen.

"Certainly not. Send the incidentals on one tray and the principal courses at intervals of ten minutes."

Jean objected, "I don't know if I want any of those things. You shouldn't have ordered before I made up my mind."

Frost said tersely, "I'm waiting for you to make up your mind. That's my order. What would you like for yours?"

Jean curled herself in a chair with a plaintive wail. "Nature is a mean old fraud. I have a figure to keep. I keep it by watching my diet, sometimes. You don't give a damn. You eat what you like. You sleep when you like. You do what you like. You smoke and work as hard as a demon when you like. And it doesn't seem to make any difference. You're always your unusual self, whatever that is. There's no justice.

"I'll have eight Scotch and sodas. Tell them to send one up every fifteen minutes for the next two hours."

VI.

THE DRIVER of the taxi, when Jean found one, was astonished to hear, "Go out Seabluff Road."

"How far?"

"Till I tell you to stop."

Jean glanced at her platinum wrist watch, a gift from some wealthy young would-be Casanova whom she had refused a date immediately after she met him. She didn't recall his name. He had sent her the watch to weaken her resistance. She returned the watch by the same messenger, without explanation. It came back by the same messenger, with a note to the effect that it would keep on coming back until she made a date. The donor never again laid eyes on the watch, or Jean. The watch showed a few minutes of ten.

Northport slept. The street lights, glittering frigidly, became more infrequent, and then ceased as the cab went inland. The headlights slanted along ice-sheeted pavement, reflected from high-banked mounds of snow that lined it in the city proper. They reached more sparsely settled country. The snow walls grew less massive, but the drifts higher. The State plows had pushed the snow aside for clearance, but the open fields gave full scope for blizzards to pile the flakes deep in every hollow and to the top of many an evergreen.

Jean saw a ghostly, weird world of white, broken by the gaunt, black boles of trees. There was no moon. There were no stars. The cloud fog still blanketed the sky. There was only the white tape of road winding upward between interminable banks of snow, fields of snow, and the naked trees.

"Sure this is the right road? It's a long way between stops out here," the driver ventured.

"Keep going."

The cab slid on in a wilderness of bleak and icy loneliness. Jean lighted a cigarette, inhaled a few puffs, and tossed it away. It tasted flat. The heater in the cab couldn't wholly dispel the tang of the crackling air.

"Stop here. What's the fare?"

"A dollar ten, miss. But there's nothing around here. Just the cemetery ahead, no house for a mile."

Jean handed him a bill and a half dollar. "Keep the change."

"I'll wait if you like."

"Thanks, but I'll ski back."

The nonplused driver watched her get out with the skis she had brought. He mumbled something about "Damn fool. Women these days ain't what they used to be." But the rest of his views upon the opposite sex went back to town with him.

It was black out, and bitter cold. Jean carried the skis while she continued along the roadbed. Visibility ended at less than twenty feet. She could see clearly for only a step or two. The cold air would have braced her, made activity both a sharp pleasure and a necessity under other circumstances. Now she felt utterly alone, with vast solitudes all around, and the spooky promise of the cemetery ahead. It was the toughest assignment that Frost had yet given her. But the other choice, the morgue— Jean shuddered. The .38 that she carried gave her scant comfort.

A grove of oaks made its appearance to her right, an array of giant sentinels. They marked the edge of the graveyard. Remembering the landmarks that Frost had pointed out on the diagram, she kept on for another five minutes. Then she floundered through a drift, donned the skis, and began gliding into the cemetery.

THE SNOW had not drifted nearly so much inside Oak Grove Cemetery, presumably because of the great windbreak of trees that encircled it. But ripples and furrows had built up in the lea of all tombstones. The snow, firmly packed and dry, made for perfect skiing.

Jean was as scared as she had ever been. The blackness of night, the powdery whiteness underfoot, the eerie silence, intensified after a bough creaked or soughed in the merciless cold, keyed her nerves. And everywhere gravestones rose at all angles, in all sizes and shapes. She stopped to get her bearings several times. Some of the headstones were so ancient that the wind and the rain and frost had stripped their inscriptions of legibility. Not even a name remained of some one whose life may have possessed importance to himself or to his period generations before.

It was desolate and uncannily terrifying ground, however hallowed.

From the void ahead came, suddenly, a peculiar sound, as of wood smiting metal. Jean's heart turned a somersault. She froze to immobility. The sound repeated itself many times, and ceased. She strained her ears. For better hearing, she lifted the lined, open-faced hood that protected her head; but silence prevailed.

The sound had come from the direction of the two graves that Frost had told her to watch.

Her heart began beating faster as she stealthily advanced. The graves of Sorokin and Fleming could not be many yards ahead. Rustles and slithers, creaking and crackling noises—these she heard; but they represented the snow that scurried and the trees that swayed.

The peculiar sound started again, a dull *whack!* Jean froze, listening. The sound came at regular intervals. This time she varied her technique, and continued skiing onward while the sound covered her approach.

When the sound stopped again, she stopped, too.

Some one—for a purpose that she dreaded to visualize—had entered the graveyard. That some one was very near to her, but completely hidden by the blackness. She waited, her nerves aquiver, for the sound to resume.

She heard a dry whisper, a faint crunch retreating across the snow. The new sound tantalized her. It seemed as if the other sensed her presence, and hurriedly left. Jean, both alarmed and given a faint new courage, waited, breathless. The sounds had all stopped. Only the dismal bleakness of her surroundings was left.

She glided onward, slowly, straining her ears.

A distinct click gave her brief warning, preceded by a fraction of a second the eruption of blinding flame from the ground not ten paces ahead. The concussion hit her as she tried to fall flat. Impressions flooded her. She saw dozens of tombstones illuminated, while the grave of Sorokin blew up from the blast of dynamite. Chunks of frozen earth and blocks of ice bombarded the vicinity. She saw a figure crouching over a portable electric detonator beyond the danger zone. She thought she caught a fleeting expression of surprise when the glare outlined her presence.

One of the hurtling lumps felled her, and a short oblivion blotted out the scene.

Jean opened her eyes to a cone of light that played into the fresh crater. Sorokin had risen from his grave. She remembered Frost's prophecy, which had become gruesome reality. The flashlight flowed over the fragments of a casket and body buried decades before. The grisly inspection lasted several minutes.

Jean struggled to rise. It was not the explosion that still numbed her, she discovered. Her hands and feet were tied.

The flashlight swung toward her, covered her from head to foot, then turned away. It retreated a long distance, halted, and came back. Jean found herself hoisted onto a sled. The grave of Sorokin vanished amid the blackness and mystery behind. Headstones marched by. Her bonds, the cold, and her bruises defeated her attempts to wriggle free.

Her captor unceremoniously dumped her in the back of a sedan, wedged her firmly on the floor. The engine coughed. She listened to the purr of the motor, the clanking of chains on ice. Her hands and feet grew numb, though the air seemed warm. Time lapsed in a haze of timeless unreality. A half hour, an hour might have passed before the sedan stopped.

The driver hauled her out, fixed her, skis and all, upon the sled. He added heavy wrenches and tools to the bonds on her feet. He began pulling the sled. Jean couldn't figure out what was happening until the sled hit ice, and slid swiftly across a smooth expanse. Then she knew.

This was the end, the pay-off. Her assailant had taken her to one of the partially frozen coves along the Northport coast. Thinner ice, then freezing water, lay ahead. Jean stared skyward. She couldn't help herself. She couldn't do anything. She felt oddly numb, as though in a trance or a state of suspended animation. At the last moment she would waken from this hideous dream.

The towman gave a powerful tug to the sled. It shot across the fringe of ice, crackled at the edges, and plunged in. Pulled by the weights on her ankles, Jean Moray plummeted to the bottom.

VII.

JEAN GASPED, filled her lungs with air just before sinking. The shock of icy water upon her face brought her wide awake. Her mind worked on a hair trigger. But there was no escape, now, for the water would soak and tighten her bonds. She could hold her breath for two minutes at most. She had perhaps five minutes of life remaining.

It was a horrible way to die, trussed, heavily weighted. The killer could have rendered her unconscious before drowning her. That he didn't showed deliberate, sadistic cruelty.

She hit bottom, to her surprise, in a couple of seconds or so. The water was scarcely fifteen feet deep. So near the surface, and yet it might as well be miles. She swayed from the effort of her struggles, like a human flower growing upon the ocean bed. The water, soaking through her clothing, began to spread a final numbness all over her.

A glow spread around her, and she wondered if her vision had already begun to record the hallucinations of dying. Her breath bubbled away, when she could restrain her muscular reflexes no longer. Her empty lungs clamored for air. She gulped a mouthful of water, tried with frantic, panic-driven terror to stave off the inevitable.

There was no way out save the way of bitter destiny. Her lips parted, as her tortured lungs burned for air. The salt water gushed—

Then cool, fresh air, floods of pure air, and a weight upon her shoulders. Half in a daze, she doubted this strange new dream that beset her. It couldn't be—and yet she inhaled cool, clean air, and the water bubbled at the level of her shoulders, but rose no higher.

Something tugged at her wrists behind her back. She felt a quick jerk. Her hands were free. She raised them to feel, to steady, to convince herself of the reality of the diving helmet that rested on her shoulders. She felt a pull at her ankles, then they, too, were free. The shimmering light played over her, turned away, and, under its new direction she saw a figure incased in full diving suit.

It was Frost. It could only be Frost, but by what incredible miracle of anticipatory deduction he had been able to foresee and to prepare for her rescue was beyond her grasp.

She followed his lead. Some twenty yards toward shore, he performed a puzzling action. She noticed a heavy chain swaying loosely. The links had been newly severed from a large ball anchor. Frost grasped the ball by the short length of chain still attached to it, and dragged it with him.

She wondered where the fresh air came from, until she made out the bulge of an oxygen tank on Frost's shoulders. There was, she discovered, a similar tank at the base of the helmet she wore and clamped tightly to it. At this shallow depth, pressure from the tank easily counterbalanced the water pressure, prevented the level from rising.

Solid ice made its appearance above them. She was fast becoming paralyzed from the cold and exposure. She watched Frost stoop, advance a few steps farther, and hammer at the ice. He broke through. Seconds later, she bobbed up beside him. Four feet of ice walled them in the hole that Frost had cut earlier that night. An inch of ice had formed on the surface again during his absence.

He hoisted himself out, leaned down, and hauled Jean up. With a powerful wrench of his fingers, he removed his own helmet, while Jean simply stooped and let hers fall off.

FROST grasped her hand, started running across the ice. Her wet garments began to freeze instantly in the zero cold. Frost ran her until she panted for breath, trying to keep up with his long legs, until her circulation flowed again and her pulse throbbed. They reached shore, and still Frost set the pace, plunging through snow and darkness.

A darker blob loomed ahead of them. Frost took the steps of the cottage in a jump, flung the door open.

It was blessedly warm inside, but Frost hurried her to another room. In the fireplace burned the embers of the fire that he had kindled several hours earlier. Frost tossed more kindling wood on, and chunks of seasoned birch and pine. The fire began to blaze higher, to crackle more hotly. Jean dropped in front of it.

"Oh, m-my b-b-but I'm c-c-cold," she chattered. "I've n-n-never b-b-been so c-c-cold in all m-m-my l-l-life!"

"There's a blanket on the sofa behind you. Take a drink of this." Frost handed her a bottle.

The drink that she swallowed burned its way down, a welcome stimulant. Frost said, "I'll be back in a few minutes," and strode out.

He returned to the pit in the ice, donned his helmet, and retrieved the anchor ball. He heaved it up after hard work. Once free of the water, it proved far too heavy to carry. He dragged it along the ice to shore, and finally to the cottage. He returned for the two helmets, and when he was again inside the cottage, he removed the diving suit.

Frost plucked from a pocket one of the long, sharply aromatic cylinders that he indulged in whenever he was working on a problem, and inhaled with relish. His features bore an animated expression. He appeared to be highly pleased with the progress of events.

He entered the main room. "How are you feeling—well, I'll be damned!" he exploded.

Things of feminine origin festooned the region of the fireplace. They hung from the backs of chairs, from the mantel, were spread on cushions, dangled even from a piece of string that Jean had found and tied between the backs of two chairs. The garments already gave off steam. Little pools of water drying on the floor indicated where they had first been wrung out. And in front of the fire sat Jean, happily toasting herself *sans* blanket.

"Hello!" she called cheerfully. "I'm practically recovered. Now tell me some bedtime stories."

"You'll compromise me yet," Frost reproved her.

"I hope so!"

"I'm off in a minute. There's an important item on the schedule. It's time to clip the wings of our blood-thirsty playmate."

"Not without me!" Jean said hotly.

"You're in no condition to go out."

"I'm perfectly all right! It won't take fifteen minutes more for my things to dry out. It wasn't my fault that I slipped up. You can't tell what a dynamite blast will do, even if you're prepared for it. I've a personal score to settle. I'm going to be in on the finish. But tell me, how did you know where to find me?"

"Simple enough," Frost explained. "The killer must be either Bradman or Serle. I determined that by a series of deductions based upon the evidence at hand earlier to-day. I watched the way their respective minds worked, and implanted upon them both the procedure to follow if you fell captive.

"The killer had to work fast. The obvious spots for tossing you into the brine were the end of the ice beyond the protruding spar of Sorokin's mooring marker here in Bay Cove, and at the end of the ice beyond a finger of land projecting into Crystal Bay. You will remember that both are actually fresh-water ponds above the high-tide line."

"But how did you know which it would be?"

"By knowing definitely the identity and psychology of the killer. It fitted into my plans perfectly, since I intended to dive for the anchor ball in any event."

JEAN THOUGHT HARD. "It must be Serle. He lives in one of the cottages here. Naturally, he'd do it at his own back door, where he could keep an eye on developments."

"Not necessarily. Bradman might choose this site with equally good reason, in order to divert suspicion from himself if the body should ever be found."

Jean took a deep breath. "That's as close as I ever want to come to the finish."

"The only real danger lay in losing your head. You didn't, or the ending might have been different. Of course, I studied charts of both bays to-day. Nowhere in either of them is the water more than twenty feet deep. Otherwise I would have made different plans."

"What's the importance of the anchor? And who's 'it'—Bradman or Serle?"

"You'll find out soon enough," Frost promised. "Are you still determined to see the finish?"

Jean got up with alacrity, felt the flimsies and the woolen ski suit. "They're almost dry. I'll give them about five minutes more."

Frost issued some instructions, handed her an automatic to replace the one that her assailant had removed. "Start out in ten minutes," he told her before he left.

The moment she heard the door close, Jean permitted herself the luxury of a wry scowl. "I'm going to get you yet, Ivy. Just what the dickens does a girl have to have or do to make you interested? Good gravy, aren't youth, beauty, and brains enough? What more do you want?"

The outer door opened. Frost's voice floated along the hall and echoed into the room with a sardonic undertone. "Don't waste your time on such fruitless speculations!" The door closed again.

Jean Moray looked the picture of consternation. She was a moderately chastened young woman as she started to dress. After this, she would keep her thoughts to herself. But Frost was good at identifying her purely mental processes, too, she had learned on more than one occasion.

VIII.

MIDNIGHT had passed when Frost reached the entrance to the morgue. Not a single person was out on the frozen, shrouded street. He tried the door, found it locked. The key that he had made from the impression he took upon his first visit fitted perfectly. He twisted it and slipped inside, closing the door behind him.

Chill and desolate silence reigned in the morgue. Frost sent a pencil of light ahead as he strode directly toward the main room. The grim, awesome atmosphere seemed to disturb him not a bit. The beam of light played across dissection tables for post-mortem examination, across the concrete floor, and came to rest upon the vaults that held the unidentified dead.

Once before, Frost had pulled out the trays, and studied the human débris in cold storage. He began at the beginning, with methodical thoroughness, and brought the same bodies into the circle of his flashlight. The loaded shelves rolled back with a ponderous thud. The empties returned with a hollower sound.

He went down the line. Thirty, forty, fifty, sixty, the slabs came out and slid into position. Working swiftly along the rows that had never been used, he finished each inspection in a few seconds.

The ninety-fourth tray was heavy.

It required a stronger effort before it yielded. At first glance, it appeared to contain a solid, irregularly shaped block of what resembled old Roquefort cheese. A thick shroud of mold had developed from the central material, completely incasing it, and overcoming refrigeration by inevitable time. The mass had a vaguely human appearance in outline only.

Frost did not touch the mold-embedded corpse, or linger over his gruesome find. He started pushing the slab back into place.

A light suddenly coned around him. "Hold it! Reach for the ceiling!"

Frost obeyed, turned around with a deliberately insolent nonchalance, as though in a matter-of-fact situation that he had expected. "You didn't come back soon enough for Will Graeley."

"I came back soon enough to get both Graeley and you."

"Ah, but twice the risks are required to dispose of two bodies."

The hard voice from the darkness growled, "That's my worry."

"And a large one you'll find it," Frost retorted grimly. "When I exposed the body of Morgan this morning, I expected the police to recall the mysterious disappearance of Graeley two years ago, to examine all the trays here, and to make this discovery themselves. Evidently Graeley was of so little importance that the police had forgotten about him. Therefore, the killer would return to-night, perhaps his last opportunity, and remove the forgotten corpse before the police did think of investigating.

"By the way, I found what you have been hunting for the past couple of years."

Hoarse, strained breathing came from the darkness. "The hell you did!"

"Ah, but I did. And, of course, when you shoot me, you will automatically kill your last hope of learning where I've hidden it."

"I'll burn you and break every bone in your body till you tell!" the voice threatened.

And Frost drawled, mockingly, "A process that will take time. And time is a precious commodity of which you have little to spare and none to waste to-night."

A false confidence entered the voice. "You're bluffing."

"Think what you will."

A TENSE SILENCE, then, "If you really found it, lead me to it and I'll let you go."

"Your promise," Frost declared evenly, "is not worth the breath you waste upon it. Two years ago, Will Graeley, by virtue of his position and his knowledge of the elements, made a discovery that promised to lead to a fortune, except that his working hours were at night, the very time that researches should be made. He took you into his confidence. Your greed made you kill Graeley, take what he had already found, and continue the hunt alone.

"You ransacked your own home when you burglarized the houses in which Fleming and Sorokin once lived, in which Bradman and Serle now live. Your selfishness was so absolute that you did not even want your wife to share your discovery. You were looking for a clue, a map, a diagram of some sort, aside from the horseshoe. Time passed. You learned that the Thompson brothers owned full sets of artificial teeth made by Sorokin. You killed them to get those teeth. You had evolved the rather fantastic, but by no means impossible, theory that Sorokin had left the clue concealed in a hollow filling, or in a false tooth. You wanted the teeth for their own sake.

"But Morgan became suspicious. He made the same discovery that Graeley had originally made. You killed Morgan before he could communicate the information to me. You knocked Morgan's perfect set of teeth out solely to throw investigation off the track."

"You don't know what it's all about!" jeered the voice.

Frost continued imperturbably, "When I was here this morning, I left a suggestion that much wealth goes to the grave. I knew that the idea would irresistibly seize you that Sorokin had taken his secret with him. But you would need to dynamite the grave in order to open it in this weather. But that would serve two purposes—even if you didn't find what you were seeking. You could remove Graeley's corpse from its now dangerous hiding place here, dump it into the same grave with Sorokin, and shovel the snow and chunks of earth back in. The graveyard is far from habitations. The explosion would pass unnoticed. The vandalism might well not be discovered until spring.

"And why did you go to such lengths of murder and violence?" asked Frost rhetorically. "Greed, overwhelming greed, was the motive."

"Yes? Greed for what?" snarled the voice.

"For platinum. Pure platinum, so worthless when it was first on the market in the latter half of the nineteenth century, before it came into demand as a precious metal, that Sorokin used it only on his poorest patients, and flattered them by telling them it was silver. Pure platinum, so cheap that he made horseshoes out of it.

"And he died without realizing its future value. Your mistake lay in thinking that he became aware of its rising price, and secreted the remainder as a private hoard. You imputed to him the motives that would have guided you.

"But I found it, where it has reposed in almost full sight for all these decades."

"I'll get it! I'll kill you and find what you've done with it if it takes weeks!" the voice shouted.

FROST STIFFENED. "What's that? Why, Miss Moray, what are you doing here? Why do you look so strange?"

The cone of light did not waver off Frost, but the eyes of the man holding the flashlight widened with the quick flash of fear. His gaze shifted, his finger taut on the trigger of the weapon that he held in his other hand. A smaller, thinner light slanted upward on the face, only the face, of Jean Moray, glistening, haggard, ghostly pale as death.

"Stop it! Stop it!" shrieked the voice. "You're dead, damn you!" The gun in his hand roared flame and thunder.

But the light had flicked out, just before he shot, leaving only darkness where Jean's face had been, and her own automatic fired first, at a point behind the flashlight.

The flashlight wabbled. The killer's shots went wild, ricocheting. He slumped, sprawled on the floor.

"Good timing!" Frost approved. He turned on the overhead lights.

"Tell me—where—" gurgled the dying Bradman.

"The hollow ball anchor at the bottom of Sorokin's mooring marker in Bay Cove," said Frost. "The anchor, though heavy, wasn't heavy enough to suit him. Sorokin simply filled it with the rest of the metallic powder, and put a lead seal on. It contains about two hundred and fifty pounds of pure platinum. And that means approximately two hundred thousand dollars by to-day's prices. I wish this was 1919."

"Why?" asked Jean.

"Because the price of platinum has fluctuated widely. It has sold above three hundred dollars an ounce in the past, compared with to-day's price of around fifty dollars. Then the value would have been one million two hundred thousand dollars."

BLOOD IN THE GOLDEN

CRYSTAL

**There is a red mist is the golden crystal—
red mist of blood, danger, sudden death!**

THE TWO CANDLES shed scarcely enough illumination to reveal the table upon which they stood. The dark, unpolished surface was otherwise bare, except for the crystal ball that rested between the tapers. A yellowish tinge pervaded the sphere, which looked as large as a bowling ball, and opaque. It was impossible to determine whether a layer of gold leaf inclosed an ordinary crystal, or whether the glass itself possessed the yellow hue.

Madame Futura extinguished the candles. Just before they flickered out, their dying light wavered upon her oily face and hands, upon the gypsy kerchief that swathed her head, upon the voluminous blouses, skirts, and petticoats she wore. Like many of her tribe, she had a plump figure, with a small face and thin hands that gave her a witch's appearance.

Opposite the fortune teller sat a black-bearded man, facing the crystal. He wore a dark, ill-fitting suit—shabby but neat—that emphasized his muscles. He was tall—at least six feet in height—and must have weighed close to a hundred and ninety pounds. He exhibited the physical perfection of a football player in top form. His age was uncertain. He might have been past twenty, or not far from forty. His eyes, walnut-brown, held a glint that was at times hard and mocking, at others shy and naïve.

The candles went out. Impenetrable darkness lasted for a few seconds, till a faint glow began to swell within the crystal. The glow grew stronger, became a swirl of milky mist, and then a golden pulse that shimmered around the surface of the sphere, welling outward from its heart and subsiding again. The black-bearded man strained his eyes intently at the golden crystal, fascinated by the shapes and forms of light that drifted through the sphere.

Madame Futura began speaking, her voice toneless, monotonous. "Light and darkness divide your life. I see swift changes ahead, good fortune and bad. A great crisis is coming. It is almost upon you. There is red mist in the golden crystal—red mist of blood, danger, sudden death. And there is a cloud, a black cloud. It is passing away. It has been there for—ten—yes, for ten years. It is passing away to-night, to-morrow, into the red blood of battle."

The voice droned on, eerie, impersonal, translating the fateful prophecy of the crystal. At times it stopped, remained silent for a minute or longer, while the golden light pulsed and dimmed in the sphere. Then the hum of the air-conditioner vibrated through the room. The hum remained constant, but the black-bearded man concentrated his attention on the voice whenever it resumed.

At the end of an hour, the golden light glimmered down inside the crystal ball and died away. A match sputtered, and Madame Futura re-lighted the candles.

The black-bearded man put his palms on the table and shoved himself to his feet. He pulled a crumpled five-dollar bill out of his pocket. Madame Futura stared at the now dull and opaque crystal. The visitor tossed the bill on the table, but she made no move to take it.

She was still peering into the sphere when he strode across the room and went out.

AT THE ENTRANCE of the building, whose weather-beaten brick front and deeply worn steps still bore traces of a former elegance, he halted long enough to turn up his coat collar. He pulled his hat down. A March wind lanced the street with invisible needles of ice.

He hurried along the walk. The clock in a drug-store window showed a few minutes past eight. Street lamps shone upon an almost deserted pavement. The few pedestrians paid no attention to him. Bearded men and queerly dressed misfits were no rarity in the Village. Even Vann Street, out-of-the-way and on the fringe of Greenwich, had no time to pause for human oddities.

He stopped at a diner, ordered a double hamburger and a glass of milk, which he topped off with a piece of pie. When he had finished, he pulled out the stump of what might once have been a pipe, though in its present state it looked more like a hunk of impure carbon. He wedged tobacco tightly into the bowl until the pipe would scarcely draw. When he lighted it, it made a sucking, gurgling sound.

A truck driver, lustily sawing away upon a chop, turned his head. "You better bury that thing."

"Maybe I will—when you bury that chop where it belongs—with the rest of the fossils."

"Black-beard" paid his check and walked out. A slight commotion among the outer layer of whiskers was the only sign that he may have been smiling.

It was a quarter of nine when he reached the subway kiosk and trotted down the steps. He dropped the pipe into a side pocket. An early edition of the morning *Call* was being placed on the news stand. The top of the page screeched "Extra!" He glanced at the headline, stopped in his tracks so abruptly that some one hurrying behind collided with him. He fished a handful of small coins from his pocket, paid three cents for the paper.

Riding downtown toward South Ferry, he read the scanty details. Two words occupied the upper half of the tabloid's front page:

HACKETT SLAIN

Underneath was a file picture of the dead man, inset on another file photograph showing him at a desk in his home, with a rough X marking the spot where his body had been found. The story on Page 2 read:

> State Highway Commissioner Francis L. Hackett was murdered early this evening in his home off Gramercy Park. He was shot through the head at close range.
>
> Police discovered the body at 7:35 p. m. The body was still warm. It is believed that Hackett met his death between 6:45 and 7:15.
>
> As this dispatch is being written, the body has not yet been removed. Some of the highest officials of the police department are at the scene, including Police Commissioner Seefurth. Hackett's residence is completely surrounded by a heavy guard.
>
> The crime is one of the most sensational in the city's history. Hackett was regarded as gubernatorial material by his party for the 1940 election. His rise to power has been phenomenal. A district party worker up to 1930, he was elected State representative in that year, a State senator in 1932, and last year was named highway commissioner.
>
> Hackett's wife died a few years ago, leaving him without heirs.

The account continued along the usual lines, about the police having an important clue in their possession, the nature of which they refused to divulge; with an early arrest promised; and suspects being questioned.

Black-beard read the story avidly and took the paper with him when he got off at the Chambers Street station.

He climbed the stairs, but before leaving the kiosk, stopped to haul the carbon-coated stump of pipe out and relight the dottle. The pipe wheezed and gurgled. He walked into the face of a wild wind, his head down.

AFTER a couple of blocks, he turned, hurried a few yards farther and turned again into a darkened doorway. Inside, a single bulb dimly outlined a flight of stairs.

The hallway above, when he reached it, showed eight doors. A man in front of a door at the rear was knocking on it.

Black-beard made for that door.

The other man twisted his head. He was shorter than Black-beard and meek of appearance. He wore glasses and carried a fat brief case.

"What do *you* want?" Black-beard shifted the pipe around to a corner of his mouth without removing it.

"Do you live here?"

"What if I did?"

"I have here any magazine that you want—"

"I don't want any magazines."

"Any magazine you can name. I've got it. A single copy or a year's subscription."

Black-beard said in his deep, bass voice, "You're working the wrong district, buddy. I'd buy a lot of magazines if I could, but I can't afford it. That's all there is to it. Nobody else that lives here can, either. Better move uptown."

"There's a snappy number here," urged the agent. "You won't find it on the news stands. Just take a look at it. Take your time—" He opened the flap of the brief case.

"No dice. I can't use anything you've got."

Black-beard shoved the salesman aside, took out a key and unlocked the door. He pressed a wall switch. A lamp on his bureau shed a soft light. Black-beard, by the reflection in the mirror above the bureau, saw the solicitor still behind him and preparing to follow with further arguments. He slammed the door and listened till he heard footsteps go down the hall.

He took a step forward, halted. He unbuttoned his overcoat mechanically, tossed it on the cot that served as his bed. His hat followed. His eyes searched every corner of the room. The pipe, fuming its last, trailed strong odors as he approached the bureau.

One of the drawers stood ajar. He looked down at it, frowning. He peered around the room, into a cheap wastebasket, and back to the rickety bureau. He pulled the drawer out. He stared at it for several moments, an uncertain, puzzled expression in his eyes. He tugged at his beard with his left hand, while his right reached into his hip pocket and then dived for the drawer. He was conscious of more footsteps in the hall.

The door suddenly sprang open. Black-beard flicked his glance toward the bureau mirror. It reflected the open door, two detectives with drawn revolvers, behind them a bluecoat, more police—and the tramp of footsteps in the hall.

A hard voice clipped the order, "Drop that gun! Hands up and keep 'em up! Thor Peterson, you're under arrest for the murder of Highway Commissioner Hackett and—"

II.

BLACK-BEARD pulled his hand out of the drawer. It clutched a pistol. He fired instantly at the lamp on the bureau. The room was plunged into darkness—darkness and fury. Spurts of yellowish-orange flame from the doorway answered his single shot again and again. The mirror shattered with innumerable tinkles of glass and the bureau rocked as slug after slug ripped into it. The .45s riddled the spot where Black-beard had been standing, but Black-beard wasn't there any longer. He had dropped the pistol after the first shot and leaped sidewise.

For a fraction of a second, his figure loomed large against the almost imperceptible light that filtered through the window from the outside. He plunged head-first, taking glass, frame, and then the sash, caught by his flying heels, along with him.

It was a second-floor window. He came down, hands outstretched, broke his fall with his shoulders, tumbled across the areaway. The yawning window behind him spewed tongues of hell. The explosions crashed and boomed back and forth between the walls of the areaway. Bullets smote concrete, screeched off ash cans.

He vanished across the areaway, through the rear entrance of a group of tenements on the next street and across the street into still another section of ramshackle buildings. For three blocks he took to the dark hallways, the unlighted courts.

With a cautious survey of the street upon which he found himself, he began running, fleet as a deer, keeping to the shadows and the protection of warehouses. He reached the subway kiosk, dived down as a radio car came sirening onward a block distant.

There was the rumble of an approaching express train. Black-beard dropped a nickel in the turnstile and sauntered to the rear end of the platform. The express rolled in, stopped with clanks and a whish of opening doors. He stepped inside. The doors began to close.

Two blue-clad figures raced down the steps, pounded for the turnstiles, cleared them in a jump—as the express got under way and picked up speed. Black-beard watched them through the glass panels on the door. Without wasting a second's time, the pair turned and raced back up to the radio car.

Black-beard breathed a sigh of relief and leaned against the door. A young couple stood by the door opposite. The girl looked at him, started to say something and collapsed in a dead faint. Her companion's eyes bulged; his face turned whiter; his lower jaw drooped until his mouth hung agape.

Black-beard lowered his eyes. A big red worm was crawling down his coat. The worm came out of a hole in his upper left shoulder, near the collar bone. The worm had no end. It kept on crawling out, crawling out, as though determined to reach all the way to the ground.

He gave the young couple his back to watch—but that didn't help, because another red worm was crawling from a hole shoulder-high.

The train thundered into Fourteenth Street. The moment the door began to open, Black-beard hurled it wide with a sweep of the arm and leaped out, pushing passengers aside as he raced across the platform. Two figures—the inevitable two figures—detached themselves from the throng and closed in on him. No guns drawn—they couldn't be used among so many innocent bystanders—the detectives made the point of a V to cut him off at the turnstiles.

There was a double tackle, a triple collision—and two figures sprawled backward, bounced upon the platform. Black-beard went through a turnstile and up the stairs like a one-man cyclone. A babel rose behind him, a medley of cries—that ever-ominous sound, the bay of the mob in pursuit.

An electrical bolt seemed to run ahead of Black-beard from person to person. The descending line of passengers turned hostile. A fugitive was escaping—with police at his heels and a swelling crowd at theirs.

"Kill him! Kill him! Don't let the lousy bum get away!" bawled a white-haired, red-faced elderly gentleman in the midst of the pack. A solid phalanx of five lined up at the top of the stairs to block the exit against Black-beard.

He hit the group with a hurtling body smash. They all crashed down on the sidewalk. Black-beard got to his feet first, simply because he was on top. He sprinted for the taxi at the head of the line, piled in, snapped at the driver, "Give it the works. In about two seconds flat, you're going to be mobbed."

THE STARTLED DRIVER sent the cab leaping ahead. Men jumped on the running boards. Black-beard slid the windows down, punched the unwelcome boarders off.

The taxi careened around the corner and zipped up Seventh Avenue. Behind swelled the siren of a radio cruiser. The wail of sirens filled the night. They rose on all sides, in all directions. The whole city seemed swarming with squad cars and prowl patrols.

The taxi outdistanced one pursuer. As it was settling into a normal speed like any other taxi, a cruiser cut in ahead from a side street. The taxi swerved, careened against traffic into the one-way street to avoid a collision. There was no backing out. The prowl car swung around, picked up the trail. The taxi hurtled on.

The taxi driver yelled, "Where to?"

"Uptown! State Street!"

The taxi swung off the one-way street, began weaving and cutting through traffic. On Forty-second Street, it turned and headed for the west-side express highway.

Black-beard couldn't find his pipe. "Got a cigarette?" he asked the driver.

"Sure. Here."

Black-beard didn't light the cylinder. He pushed it through the forest of beard and chewed it. The cigarette disappeared.

The driver said, "I guess we're in the clear now. Did you eat that thing?"

"I like 'em better'n lollipops."

The driver lapsed into silence. The fare was plainly a nut. Minutes passed before he volunteered, "The next is State Street. What's the number?"

"The address is No. 13."

"Did you say 13? This sure looks like your unlucky night."

The taxi squealed to the curb in front of a stone mansion. Black-beard pulled the last bill out of his pocket and flipped it to the driver. "Keep the change. And scram!"

The taxi was rolling before he finished.

III.

AT THE SOUND of the house bell, Jean Moray turned away from the table where Professor I.V. Frost was bending over the eyepiece of a microphotographic outfit. She walked swiftly to a wall cabinet and opened it.

"A bearded man. He's been shot!" she cried out.

"The door release. Get out the first-aid kit!" Frost snapped, already halfway out of the laboratory. Jean's fingers touched a switch. The outer door sprang open instantly, and Black-beard stumbled into the corridor.

She had the kit ready when Frost came back, the stranger beside him.

Frost went to work after a quick glance that sifted the stranger from head to foot. "A flesh wound. The bullet entered from the back and came out between the clavicle and the second rib. Your shoulder will be painfully sore for some days, but you are little the worse off. We'll just have time to dress the wound before the police arrive."

Dismay crossed the bearded man's face. "The cops—you called 'em?"

"Not at all. The driver of the cab that brought you will notify the police as fast as he can."

The stranger blurted, "How do you know— What—"

Frost cut him short with, "No time to analyze deductions now. Tell me, why did you spend the past few years at a variety of occupations, ranging from lumberjack to knight of the road, but suddenly abandon the outdoors within the fortnight and come to New York?"

"Because I can't forget," came the puzzling answer.

Frost finished dressing the wound, lighted an exceptionally long cigarette of pungent fragrance. His eyes acquired the luster of polished ebony. There was a new intensity to his interest, a concentration of will, the force of a driving intellect. He asked a strange question: "How did you spend the morning of January 21, 1926?"

"I left home for high school at eight twenty. I had to hurry because I was going to be late. I met Jim Hawkins on the way. He was late, too. We were afraid of old man Schipp, our English teacher. He always made a nasty crack about anybody who was late. When Jim and I got to the classroom—"

"What was the lesson for the day?" Frost asked.

"We were reading 'The Merchant of Venice.' "

"Do you remember the opening lines of the third act, Scene II?"

> "Act III, Scene II. Belmont. A room in Portia's house.
> Enter Bassanio, Portia, Gratiano, Nerissa, and attendants.
> "Portia: I pray you, tarry: pause a day or two
> Before you hazard; for, in choosing wrong,
> I lose your company: therefore forbear a while.
> There's something tells me, but it is not love,
> I would not lose you; and you know yourself—"

Jean Moray listened with astonishment and open incredulity. It was beyond belief that any one, on the spur of the moment, could recall his exact, detailed movements during a day selected at random more than ten years ago. But what could the stranger gain by glib fabrications?

The violent, persistent ringing of the house bell again broke out. She moved to the wall cabinet, exclaimed after a few moments, "The police!"

"Go to the door and open it in one minute," Frost ordered.

Jean strolled out of the laboratory. The ringing continued, angry, impatient. She paused to admire herself in a mantel mirror. At the end of the designated interval, she opened the front door. The officers and a third man confronted her.

THE NEAREST of the three stated the obvious fact, "We're the police. There's a dangerous killer in here somewhere."

Jean said sweetly, "Of course. He's in the laboratory right now."

The officer drew his revolver, started forward. "Which way to the laboratory?"

"I'll take you. You'll find Frost working on some microphotographs."

"Damn Frost! We're not after him!" the officer said.

"Oh, you don't want to see Frost, then?"

"I don't give a hang about Frost!"

"Well, I'll tell him so," said Jean. "Though this all strikes me as being pretty silly. Good-by."

"Listen, miss," the officer growled, "there's a black-bearded guy went in here. Isn't that right?" He nodded his head toward the third man, a cab driver.

"Sure, sure, that's right. This guy is leaking blood like he's been shot. He has a black beard all right. He tells me to let him off here and I do. I watch him while I drive away. He gets up to the door. I see the door open and he goes in. A tall, thin guy comes to meet him. Then I get out of range and the door closes. I beat it for the cops like I just told you."

Jean eyed him with interest. "It must be wonderful to have such a vivid imagination. Is it always a black-bearded white man with a bullet hole? Or do you sometimes see a white-bearded black man with an arrow stuck through him?"

The officer hardened. "Quit stalling, miss. This man we're after is dangerous. He's wanted for the murder of State Highway Commissioner Hackett."

Jean gave a perceptible shrug of her shoulders. The laboratory smock that she wore concealed the seductive lines of her figure, but emphasized the piquant sophistication of her face. She stepped aside. "You men certainly have one-track minds. Go talk to Frost about your black-bearded bugaboo, or whatever you call it."

The policeman's jaw muscles tightened, but he made no comment as he and his companions strode into the laboratory.

"Hello, what can I do for you?" Frost asked. He was swabbing a cut on the back of his left forearm, and about to bandage it. A razor-sharp scalpel, with a red smear, lay on the table.

The officer in the lead looked with instant suspicion at the blood-stained cotton, the iodine and adhesive tape. "Where'd all that blood come from?"

"From you," Frost retorted.

"From me?" the officer repeated blankly.

"Your confounded pummeling on the door disturbed me just as I was slicing a couple of hairs from my skin for microphotographic purposes. It happens to be my blood, but it came from your exasperating and violent assault upon the doorbell. What is it that you wish?"

"We want a black-bearded guy with a bullet hole in his chest."

Frost seemed greatly amused. "Indeed? Yours is a singular, a fanciful, request. I can offer you quite a variety of chemicals, tools, and mechanisms from my supplies here, but I am fresh out of black-bearded men with bullet holes in their chests."

"As sure as my name's Donergan"—the jaw clamped harder still—"we'll search this house, if we have to keep the place surrounded for a month before we get a search warrant."

"You won't need one. Miss Moray, show the gentlemen through the house from attic to basement. Open any door, any closed space, that they may wish to examine. Allow them to tap the walls and measure distances," Frost stated with imperturbable calm.

"O. K.," Donergan said briefly.

Frost resumed his position at the microphotographic apparatus. The two officers and cab driver filed out with Jean Moray. Five minutes later, the doorbell again proclaimed its existence.

Frost opened the wall panel, looked at the image of a quiet, scholarly man who waited on the front porch. Frost went out of the laboratory in long strides, an eddy of smoke in his wake.

WHEN he opened the door, the stranger urged in smooth, quiet tones, "I'm selling subscriptions to magazines, also single copies. I've got all the latest numbers here and some you don't see on most of the stands."

Frost asked, "Let me see your identification cards."

The agent promptly brought out a wallet, from which he extracted several cards authorizing Curtis R. Kane to solicit subscriptions for various publications.

Frost flipped through the cards, handed them back. "Try another time. At the moment I appear to be having difficulties with the police who, amusingly enough, labor under the strange belief that I keep my domicile supplied with black-bearded men featuring bullet holes in their chests."

Mr. Kane looked perplexed, as though uncertain whether to smile or to sidle away. "Er-r-r—"

"Good night," said Frost, closing the door.

He returned to the laboratory with a far-away air of abstraction.

Ten minutes later, Donergan & Co. made their reappearance.

Frost glanced up. "I take it you had no luck in your quest?"

Donergan looked black. He stood there scowling for a moment. He honestly didn't know whether to take the taxi driver's statement at face value, or if he should rely on the lack of results of the search as favoring Frost's attitude. "There never was a place got a better frisking than this one—"

Frost remarked, "Did you try the refrigerator and the radio console?"

A glint came into Donergan's eyes. "That's two we skipped. We'll take you up on that right now." He motioned his partner back toward the kitchen.

They opened the refrigerator, stared at its neat array of comestibles and tapped its inside walls. They left it, went out into the reception room and worked upon the radio cabinet until convinced that it provided room for nothing more than the unusual radio innards. Then they marched back into the laboratory.

Donergan stared hard at the taxi driver. He shifted uneasily and protested, "Say, it's all true like I told you. It took me maybe a couple of minutes before I found you cops, see? Maybe this guy slips the other guy out in those couple minutes. Maybe—"

"Skip it," Donergan grunted, and to Frost, "Got any idea who this bird with the black beard is?"

"I haven't the least idea."

"You better have, in case be just happens to turn up around here. His name is Thor Peterson. He's wanted for the murder of Highway Commissioner Hackett, earlier this evening. He's the hottest potato in the East right now."

"What makes you think him guilty?"

"He was seen entering Hackett's place around six thirty to-night. Hackett was shot some time between six forty-five and seven fifteen. The body was found along toward eight. Soon after eight we got a definite lead on Peterson. A detail went down to the place where he rooms. They got there just after Peterson, caught him red-handed. He was taking the gun that fired the two fatal shots out of his pocket to hide in a drawer. He was also hiding part of the cash and bonds he'd stolen, which was his motive. Hackett kept a large amount in a safe that was rifled. That's all. It's an open-and-shut case, except that Peterson shot the light out and dived through the window, leaving the gun and loot behind. They winged him, but he got away. That finishes him.

"This is the longest speech I ever made," said Donergan earnestly. "There are a thousand men combing the city for Peterson right now. The alarm's gone out over the six-State teletype. If you think you can help Peterson beat the chair, guess again. If you help him at all, you're through as a private dick in this burg. You'll be bucking the whole police department every move you make."

"The principle of coöperation is an excellent one," Frost drawled.

"Sure, only some people don't do what they say." The Donergan jaw clamped pointedly. "I got an idea Peterson is still in this block. His luck has held out all evening. It won't hold out forever. The shape he was in, he wouldn't have been able to get away from here between the time the taxi driver dropped him and called us."

"So?"

"So I'll tell you what you'll find out fast enough anyway. We're searching this whole block. We're planting men in front of every building. If Peterson is here, he'll never get away. No matter what you do to him, or how he changes his looks, we'll get him."

Donergan & Co. filed out.

IV.

JEAN MORAY accompanied the police and the hack driver to the door, watched them for a few seconds as they walked toward the waiting prowl car and taxi.

The wail of sirens rose above the muted evening murmur of the city. It was as Donergan had promised: officers in uniform on the corners of the block where Frost lived, plain-clothes detectives piling out of other cars to cover the entrance to every building.

Jean closed the door. She got back to the laboratory just in time to see Frost enter it from the opposite door, which led to the kitchen. And sauntering alongside the professor was Black-beard.

"Where did you hide him?" she asked. "They went up on the roof, looked down the chimneys and searched every possible spot. They drew a blank."

Frost smiled thinly. "I told them where to look. Did you watch when they opened the refrigerator?"

"Of course."

"What happened?"

"They tapped the walls of the refrigerator, and they all sounded hollow, which was natural, since the machine stands in an alcove."

"Didn't that impress you as being extraordinary?"

"Certainly not. Why should it?"

"Because," said Frost, "there is a narrow space occupied by kitchen equipment on each side of the refrigerator. The unit stands a foot or more off the floor. And, of course, there is open space above it to the ceiling. But it is backed against the wall, and, therefore, tapping the inside rear of the refrigerator should have produced a solid sound. When the police heard a hollow echo there, they should have instantly been suspicious. The unit is built in two parts. The whole interior can be made to slide out, leaving only the outer shell and exposing entrance to a shallow second alcove large enough to hold a couple of men."

He shifted, his attention to the fugitive. "Now tell me your story from the beginning."

Black-beard took a seat on the edge of the table. "To begin with, my name is Thor Peterson—"

Frost instantly shot back, with irritation, "That isn't your name."

"What makes you think it isn't?"

Frost commanded, "Either tell the truth or I'll drop the case where it stands. Thor Peterson could not possibly be your real name, for several reasons, including your physical characteristics and pigmentation. I've already told you that you spent recent years in outdoor occupations, and only returned to New York within the fortnight. I say returned, advisedly. I will go further. You left the city by running away. You ran away because you faced a problem you couldn't cope with. You hated your home life and your surroundings so much that you changed your name, in part or in whole. You made a complete break for a different life."

Black-beard stared at Frost as if he were a magician. He gasped, "Say, I went to a fortune teller tonight. She told me a lot of stuff that's true, but she didn't hit the nail on the head the way you do. Why did I run away?"

"Because you are the proud possessor, and also the luckless victim, of a condition known among psychologists as identic memory."

"Huh?"

"I questioned you a short while ago upon the events that happened during a day selected at random from your past life. You told me, in detail, what happened. You quoted, word for word, a portion of the text of 'The Merchant of Venice.' You didn't give the gist of the text. You gave the exact text, as though your mind instantly conjured up a photographic picture of the page of the open book, from which you mentally read. That is identic memory.

"Only a few rare individuals among mankind have ever possessed that remarkable talent. Macaulay is believed to have been one of them. It isn't too late yet for you to achieve a brilliant success in life. Now, will you tell me your story?"

"GEE!" exclaimed Black-beard fervently. "All my life I been wondering what was wrong with me, and you're the first person that told me."

"A competent psychiatrist could have told you the same thing, if you had taken the trouble."

"Only I didn't, because I don't know what that word means."

"Psychiatrist? A specialist in mental hygiene. Your education has certainly been erratic."

"I'll tell the world it has. O. K., here goes. My real name is Thor O'Larry. I was the only child of Irish-Scandinavian parents. I had a hell of a time from the start. I'd get perfect marks at school. Then the teachers would accuse me of cribbing and cheating. So they'd flunk me. Then there'd be more hell to pay at home. I didn't have to study much, because I memorized a page the second I saw it. So the family told me I was a lazy pup and likely enough I cheated in exams, because I didn't study enough to know anything.

"Result was that when fifteen, I hadn't got past first year of high school, but I knew more than anybody else in school and should have been up to college. I couldn't stand it any more. I knew something was wrong, but I didn't know what. I came to hate the whole business. I simply ran away from home, school, and city. I changed my name. I wouldn't look at another book. I was big for my age, so I got by in tough spots and I set out to make myself as tough as they come."

"Just a minute," Frost interrupted. "What did your parents do? Were they well off?"

"Anything but. Oh, I suppose dad made two or three thousand a year. He was a glass blower. He melted glass over a flame and blew it into all sorts of fancy shapes. He sold them to art and gift shops all over town. He made a fair living at it, but he certainly didn't get rich."

"Your parents are both dead?"

"I found that out when I got back a couple of weeks ago. They've both been dead for several years. I went out and saw their graves. It got me down. I guess I kind of expected to see them, though I never wrote or saw them after I ran away.

"That was in 1927. Like you say, I could remember everything that ever happened to me. My mind is a sort of long motion picture. I remember the pages of all the books I've read, all the places I've been, all the streets and store windows I've seen, the whole works. One trouble was that I naturally remembered all the mistakes and errors, too. I'd always write down misprints that occurred in whatever I was asked to quote. It was automatic. I could straighten it out if I was given time to think about it, but it damned me with the teachers. Far as they were concerned, that proved I cheated. Identic memory, huh? Wish I'd known it then.

"ANYWAY, I skipped off in 1927. I washed dishes. I worked in harvest fields. I dug ditches. I threw broncs in the West. I've been in plenty of jails for vagrancy raps. At times I've slept on the ground. I've shipped on freighters, lived in the logger camps. I never held a job more'n three months. Then I moved on. I didn't know what I wanted, so I drifted around and tried just about everything. But I did get as strong as a bull. I haven't lost a fight in the past six years.

"I steered clear of cities, until I got a strong yen to see the old place and came home a couple of weeks ago.

"I took a furnished room down along the North River. Then I looked around my home district, the Village. Everything had changed. There was hardly anybody I knew and nobody recognized me after ten years and wearing a beard. But I saw Hackett one day. Dad used to know him. I stopped him, asked him a few questions."

"Did you know of his prominence in politics?"

"Not till to-night. If I had, I wouldn't have bothered him. He was bowled over when I told him who I was. He couldn't believe it at first, said my folks had given me up for dead long before they themselves died. But I finally convinced him I was Thor O'Larry. He asked me to come over to his place when I got around to it, as he wanted to tell me something.

"I went to see him about a week ago. He told me that after my folks had gone he took care of what they left, mostly personal stuff like clothing which was packed away in a few trunks, and some furniture. I said I didn't want the things; he could do what he liked about them. He next gave me seven hundred and fifty dollars which he had collected. Part of it was money owed to dad by various gift shops, and part was what he got by selling stuff on hand when dad died. He said dad had several times told Hackett to watch those things for my sake.

"Hackett asked me to get in touch with him again to-day. I did. I saw him about six thirty to-night. He said he had a good job for me, but first he wanted me to see this fortune teller who was so good, and find out if the stars O. K.'d it. Hackett always did go for palm readers and crystal gazers. By the way, he got on to Madame Futura in the first place because he sold her a tricky golden crystal that dad had made one time after I ran away. It was among the stuff left at the end. Hackett sold it for two hundred and fifty dollars and seemed to think he'd pulled a fast one on Madame Futura.

"Getting a fortune teller's O. K. sounded kind of goofy, but I liked the idea, being told what would happen to me, so I went to see this Madame Futura."

"Did you kill Hackett before you left?"

"I've never killed anybody." Then O'Larry recited the reading that he had received while the golden crystal glowed, and his discovery by newspaper headlines that Hackett had been murdered.

FROST told his assistant, without shifting gaze from O'Larry, "Call Madame Futura and ask her at what time she cast the future of a black-bearded man to-night."

Jean glided toward the phone.

"So you don't believe me? Faith, it's wasting m' time I am." The trace of a brogue and bitterness crept into the O'Larry voice.

"Far from it. The matter of timing may prove to be the difference between life and death. Madame Futura may be able to furnish you with an iron-clad alibi, if the minute of Hackett's death can be fixed."

"Ya. I'm not ready to enter Valhalla yust now," said Thor with a Scandinavian accent.

Frost drawled wryly, "Your speech passes with disconcerting ease, to say the least, between English and American, plus Irish and Scandinavian variations. I hope that you never find occasion to use all four in one breath."

"Lord!" cried the young giant. "Why take a crack at my tough luck just because I didn't receive the advantages of higher education, ya?"

Frost lifted his eyebrows in quizzical horror.

Jean returned. She said, "Laugh this off. Madame Futura saw her client some time around seven and eight. She can't say whether before seven till after eight, or after seven till before eight. She doesn't wear a wrist watch and doesn't keep track of time. Her readings usually last from a half hour to an hour."

Thor O'Larry muttered, "Won't I ever get the breaks? That cooks my goose, I guess."

"Forget it!" Frost snapped. "Go on with your story."

"Well, all the way back to my room I was wondering why anybody would want to kill Hackett. Then, at my door, I met this guy selling magazine subscriptions. I got rid of him—"

"Describe his appearance," Frost ordered, a quick gleam in his eyes.

O'Larry answered with a perfect description of the Mr. Kane who had called on Frost.

O'Larry continued, "I got inside my room, and I knew right off that it wasn't the way I left it. I saw it the way it should have been, but a bureau drawer was out a half inch. I went over and hauled it open. The seven hundred and fifty dollars that Hackett had given me was still there—but so was another pile of bills, and a couple of bonds that I'd never seen before. So was a pistol. I pulled a handkerchief out of my hip pocket and picked the gun up. I just had time to notice that it had been fired twice. Then the cops flocked in; I shot the light out and dived through the window."

"Wait here. I'll be back in less than an hour," Frost said abruptly, and motioned to Jean Moray.

In the hallway he told her, "Watch O'Larry. Don't let any one in till I return. That impetuous young man is apt to do something more impulsive than wise. He'll be shot on sight if he tries to leave the house. His brain is one in millions and his life has much too great a potential value for him to be killed now."

V.

FROST climbed into his custombuilt special and rolled up the ramp from the basement garage. He swung along State Street, turned into the west-side superhighway, and raced downtown.

He drove straight to police headquarters, hiked in, asked for Inspector Frick of the homicide bureau. Almost immediately he was talking to that crisp official, who carried a surprising amount of dignity in spite of his small size. He stood nearly a foot shorter than Frost. He was an ex-army officer.

The inspector looked surprised, wary. "I was about to call on you, Ivy."

"I thought as much. That's why I'm here."

"I suppose you know that your street is completely blockaded."

"But Hackett's secretary isn't there and never has been, to the best of my knowledge," Frost retorted.

Frick's stiffish manner turned to bewilderment. "Hackett's secretary? What do you mean by that? I didn't know he had one."

"Perhaps he didn't, in the ordinary meaning of the word. But look for a man who saw Hackett regularly, stayed in the background, and posed as Hackett's private secretary when third parties were present. If I were you, I'd have him picked up for questioning."

"What does he look like?"

"Never having seen him, I can't say, except that he's no taller than you are and very little heavier than either of us."

"You're sure he's a man?"

"Positive."

"Name?"

Frost shrugged. "The answer to that is beyond the scope of pure deduction. I could find out by taking time to investigate, but time is a valuable commodity to me right now. Your organization can uncover that useful knowledge soon enough."

"I don't see what earthly purpose will be served. We've got an open-and-shut case against Thor Peterson for the murder of Hackett: direct evidence, circumstantial evidence, motive, everything."

Frost stated rather than inquired, "Isn't it a fact that an anonymous voice gave you the tip-off leading to discovery of Hackett's body, and also suggested where you might go to find the killer?"

Frick's expression betrayed him before he answered. "What difference would it make?"

"The anonymous tip-off is always a matter for suspicion. The speed with which this murder has supposedly been solved, and the chain of evidence and circumstances which are altogether too pat, should be cause for skepticism. Let me make a suggestion: Investigate the golden crystals!"

"Investigate the golden crystals? What the deuce are you talking about?"

"Perhaps you've driven along State roads and noticed the row of small glass hemispheres that follows the center line of the highway upon curves? They're popularly called golden crystals."

"I've not only seen 'em, I've bumped across 'em. Useful gadgets for night driving. The headlights of your car shine on the surface of the things and make 'em sparkle, so you can follow the curve of the road more easily. They make for safer driving. And they don't hurt tires," Frick added. "What about them?"

"They might be a cause of violent death. Hackett's murder, for instance."

"See here," said Frick belligerently, "are you suggesting that I chase around the highways squinting at those blasted gadgets in order to find Hackett's killer? What am I supposed to do—look for his picture in one of them? Wait a minute—"

"I can't stop any longer," Frost said over his shoulder. "I've given you a pair of important leads. I'll toss in another for good measure: Fortune tellers are an interesting class. You might find it worthwhile to have your future prophesied.

"I'd also suggest that you order your men to refrain from shooting when they capture Thor Peterson. He's unarmed. He's already been shot once, which is going to be an embarrassing matter for the police when Hackett's real slayer is caught."

The inspector's face was a battle ground for expressions ranging from consternation and bewilderment to hostility and stubbornness, as Frost vanished.

THE PROFESSOR took the wheel of his special and drove back to 13 State Street. When he was still a mile away, the sound of sirens suddenly shrilled in the distance, above the city's murmur. Frost's car flowed faster through the stream of traffic, turned and shot into State Street.

The detectives had vanished from the entrances to the different buildings. The radio cars had likewise gone.

Frost parked his car in front, dashed up the sidewalk and steps. The interior of the house was strangely quiet, except for a thumping sound in the kitchen. Frost made for it.

Pinned to the kitchen door was a scribbled note:

> Sorry I had to do this. She didn't want to let me get away. I've got to go. I remembered something which means I have to act right away.
>
> Thanks for the help. I'll be seeing you if I get out of this jam. My going this way, the cops won't be able to gang up on you or make any charges stick if they knock me off.
>
> Your doll is a beauty. Tell her I said so. St. Peter must have been sleeping on the job when she took French leave of Paradise. Or maybe the devil had more to do with it, the way she fights.
>
> Thor.

Frost read the note at a glance, pushed the door open.

Jean Moray was making the thumping sounds. She made them by managing to tilt backward and forward upon the chair to which she was tied and gagged. Her normally gray-green eyes were flaming with wrath.

VI.

THE FURY in Jean's eyes diminished a trifle when she spied Frost. But Frost followed a plan of action that intensified her emotion. He ran toward Jean—and beyond her. He hiked into the laboratory, surveyed it quickly, walked over to a row of carboys.

He went out of the laboratory, climbed all the way up to the roof. A flashlight in hand, he studied the surface of the roofing for a minute, in the face of a freezing wind.

Last of all, he returned to the second floor and looked at the washbowl and floor of the bathroom.

When he descended, the ghost of a smile haunted his expression. He freed his assistant in short order.

Her voice quivered, hot with wrath. "Why didn't you do this five minutes ago? If I sat here dying, I suppose you'd run for a pair of scales to find out if I weighed any less after death than before. Then you'd get out a monograph on how much my soul weighed, with footnotes and cross references—"

"An interesting idea. It's been done, but there's not nearly enough data upon bodily loss of weight at the time of death," Frost agreed. "The possibilities—"

"So it doesn't make a damn bit of difference to you that I'm tied up and hurt and wrecking my wrists and ankles and teeth trying to get loose—"

"The fate of Thor O'Larry—"

"I hope he rots in prison! I hope the police give him the prize third degree of all time!" Jean cried. "What thanks do I get for trying to help him? After you left, he moved around and finally went upstairs. He called down to me. I followed him up. He pointed at something in a closet. When I went over to look at it, he gave me a push. Hard. He slammed and locked the door. I sprang the lock from inside by the electrical release and was out before he knew it. But that fraud is made of steel springs. He carried me down here—and that was the finish. I kicked his shins all the way. I hope they develop gangrene! If the shooting I heard means that the police have put some new ventilation in your pretty Thor O'Larry and his fertile imagination, I'll stand up and cheer!"

"This sounds more like a case of love at first sight than—"

Jean stormed, "Love at first sight? Are you crazy? What makes you say such things? If I ever lay eyes on him again—"

"In that case, I need not bother to mention his fate. Forget about that. Now, the next thing I want you to do—"

"What happened to him?"

"It's of no importance. I want you to—"

Jean asked imperiously, "Did he get away?"

"He acted with more determination than reason," Frost made a guarded answer. "He used rough tactics for your own sake. He had to leave. He wanted to make it appear as though we hadn't aided him. He wanted us to resent him openly, for the special benefit of the police."

"That's different. What happened to him?"

"He trimmed the beard off and shaved—"

"Good!" Jean exclaimed fervently. "That was the ugliest shrubbery I've seen in a long time."

"He borrowed an overcoat of mine. He took one of the larger experimental balloons out of stock and a tank of helium. He carried them to the roof, where he inflated the balloon until its lifting power about offset his weight. Then he jumped. The police saw the shape rise, the wind sweeping it up Riverside Drive. They began firing, but he landed and made a safe escape."

"How do you know?"

"More radio cars are sirening their way to this vicinity. A man hunt doesn't grow larger for a dead quarry. And minus that identifying beard, O'Larry is not apt to be so easily recognized or captured.

"How would you like to have your fortune told?"

"Fine. Go ahead. Do you read palms?" Jean thrust out her hands.

"YOU'RE a bit premature in your assumption. Madame Futura is the person I have in mind."

"Better still. I've never had my fortune told. It's something I'd certainly like to know."

Frost gave her a curious look, and in his eyes, for an instant, she thought she detected a light of profound sympathy, of profounder knowledge with a somber undertone. "Are you speaking seriously?"

"Of course. Wouldn't *you* like to know the future?"

Frost answered slowly, "No, most emphatically I would not. I have no desire to foresee the least part of the future."

Jean was openly puzzled. "Why not?"

"Because," said Frost in a dreamy, introspective, visionary tone far different from his usual voice, "knowledge of the future would be utterly worthless for any practical purpose. It could never be used. It could never serve as a basis for action. You could never profit by it, or take advantage of it. It would be dead knowledge, knowledge that destroyed itself."

"I don't follow you at all. I don't see why."

"Let me give an illustration. Suppose you foresaw that you would die in an automobile accident upon May 1st. In order to avoid that fate, you stay in your bedroom during the whole of May 1st, and continue to live."

"That's exactly why I'd like to know the future!" Jean agreed enthusiastically.

"Ah, but in that case, you do not alter the course of destiny. You merely demonstrate that you do not know the future, because you do *not* die upon May 1st as you had anticipated, and therefore, it makes no difference what you do upon May 1st. If you know that you are to die upon May 1st you *must* die on May 1st in order to make your knowledge truthful. If you survive beyond May 1st, your presumed knowledge is false. Now do you see what I mean?"

Jean nodded wryly. "I see it, only I wish I didn't. This is one of those times when I feel like saying, 'Damn all logic'! It's like wanting something—and yet—"

Frost shrugged. "I doubt whether there is a more universal desire in the hearts and minds of all mankind than the wish to know what is coming, and to foresee the events of tomorrow. Accompanying that dream is another universal belief that such knowledge could be utilized for profit. But if a successful attempt was ever made to use that knowledge, the knowledge would instantly become false. I would find neither excitement not satisfaction in solving murder mysteries, if I knew in advance what the answers would be. All the stimulation lies in the process of discovering truth and reaching a solution."

"Well, I wish I knew what this one is all about. Hackett's murder, and O'Larry, and fortune tellers, and a glass blower, not to mention the magazine agent—"

"—and Hackett's secretary," finished Frost. "It's all perfectly clear now, though it required a fairly long series of deductions. We'll have it over with inside of an hour. Go to Madame Futura. Have her cast your future. Notice carefully every detail of what happens."

VII.

FROST hiked out of the kitchen. The myriad questions that Jean wanted to ask died on her lips. From past experience, she recognized Frost's purposive driving energy and knew the futility of trying to delay or impede its progress.

She got her coupé out and drove toward Greenwich Village. Without pausing, she managed to extract a cork-tipped cigarette from her purse and ignite it by the dashboard electric lighter. She inhaled a couple of times and tossed the cylinder away, almost intact. Then she put her mind to the business at hand.

Frost had seemed entirely confident about solving Hackett's murder, but Jean grew more confused as she tried to analyze the factors. If O'Larry hadn't killed Hackett, who had? The secretary that Frost mentioned? In that case, where did Madame Futura fit in? As a partner of the unnamed secretary, or through some hold that she had over him?

If O'Larry was the goat of a frame-up, what could be the motive? And what part did the magazine solicitor play in this muddle? His unobtrusive appearance twice, at highly climactic moments, seemed to indicate something more than pure coincidence. Was it he who had planted the evidence against O'Larry and who, trapped as he was leaving O'Larry's room, pretended that he had just arrived to sell magazines? That might well account for his later trailing of O'Larry to Frost's residence. It would also suggest that the agent had some connection with Madame Futura, because the evidence damning O'Larry was planted during, or shortly after, his visit to the fortune teller.

Jean was dissatisfied with her theories. She felt that they had only produced a nest of dubious goose eggs, when she arrived at Vann Street. Madame Futura lived at No. 248.

Jean turned into the street. As she approached the block where the fortune teller lived, she saw a figure enter that address. The man resembled the description Frost had given her of Kane, the subscription agent. Jean ran her car to the curb and parked a little beyond the building.

She hurried back, entered the lobby just in time to catch a fleeting glimpse of the same figure vanishing through the right-rear apartment on the ground floor.

Jean looked at the names alongside the apartment bells. Madame Futura occupied 1C, which Kane had just entered. She tried the main door, found it locked.

In quick succession, she pressed the buzzers to the top-floor studios—5A, B, C, D. The latch clicked.

She opened the door, glided down the hallway to Madame Futura's apartment. She listened at the door, but heard nothing. She raised her hand, knocked twice.

The door opened like magic, so instantaneously that she stuttered. "I— Are you Madame Futura? I'd like my fortune told."

"Won't you please step in?" the woman asked.

IT WAS very dark in the entrance. Jean saw no light except the golden glow inside a large crystal ball that stood on a table at the far side of the room. She took a step forward, saw, too late, the crumpled figure that had been concealed by the opened door.

She stopped instantly. Quick as a panther, Madame Futura grabbed her by the arm, yanked her, sprawling, into the room.

Jean got up, tugging at her automatic. She had it in her hand when Madame Futura, with amazing agility for one of her substantial build, pounced upon Jean. Madame Futura didn't try to snatch Jean's automatic. The fortune teller had a .45 revolver in her hand, brought the butt down once.

The automatic relaxed in Jean's grasp. Her wealth of luxuriant hair cushioned the blow, saved her from unconsciousness. Dizzy with pain, she watched the walls of the room reel, saw the fortune teller pick the automatic out of her nerveless fingers. As in a dream, she watched Madame Futura haul the inert figure—was it Kane, the magazine solicitor?—across the floor into another, much smaller, room.

The fortune teller returned, and while Jean tried in vain to make her paralyzed limbs obey, she felt herself lifted, carried to the same room. There was a click, and cold steel locked her wrists behind her back. This was a nice fortune, she thought.

A light went on. Jean saw that Madame Futura had a black eye, a raw bruise on one cheek. Overturned chairs, a bunched rug, gave further evidence of a struggle. It hadn't come from Jean's brief resistance. The magazine agent had evidently given no resistance whatever; he must have been felled the instant he got inside the door. He was still unconscious. There was a third figure, likewise handcuffed and stretched out on the floor.

It took her several moments to recognize those clean-shaven, happy-go-lucky features. Thor O'Larry was unexpectedly goodlooking without the atrocious beard. He had the appearance of an adventurer, a rover. Jean felt positive that when he recovered consciousness, there would be in his eyes the laughing light of a certain irresponsible deviltry. He had evidently put up a stiff battle before Madame Futura blackjacked him. Blood trickled from two big lumps on his head.

Madame Futura finished tying the legs of her three victims. Jean, seeing better as the waves of pain subsided, found herself in a small kitchen.

The fortune teller closed the door through which she had hauled the three. She turned the gas jets of the stove on, lighted them. She produced a phial and loosened the stopper. A whiff of cloyingly sweetish fumes came to Jean.

Madame Futura said softly, "Chloroform will make you sleep. And while you sleep, the gas flame will burn up the oxygen in the room and give off carbon monoxide. You will die painlessly of carbon-monoxide poisoning. I'll be back in a couple of hours to remove the handcuffs and rope. The police, no doubt, will find the bodies in a few days or a week. They'll also find themselves with a baffling riddle on their hands. But they'll never find Madame Futura."

She bent over O'Larry, waved the phial under his nostrils. His breathing, which had been stertorous, uneven, became slow and regular. She repeated the motions on Kane, until he, too, sank into deeper slumber. Last of all, she knelt beside Jean.

Jean squirmed, twisted, flung her head sidewise. The fortune teller smiled a little, forced Jean's cheek against the floor. The fumes were sapping her resistance, floating her will off into a vague and cushioning blankness. Only a few seconds more. It would be an easy death, a pleasant one, a painless oblivion—the wrong way to die after all those hectic, exciting adventures with Frost—

VIII.

THE SECOND DOOR to the kitchen—the rear door—sprang open. "That's enough. Hold it!" snapped a harsh, implacable voice.

Madame Futura dropped the phial, the fluid spilling on the floor. Like a cat she whirled, side-stepped, the .45 leaping up with her hand in a continuous flow of motion.

She fired a wild shot that hit the stove. For another shot had preceded hers, and she had half spun as she pulled the trigger. The pistol slipped out of her grasp. Her right arm hung useless. She stooped, clawed for the weapon with her left hand.

"As you were!" clipped the same hard voice. "Or I'll put another through your left shoulder."

Madame Futura glared with hot, savage eyes, the eyes of a trapped animal. Her hand drew back from the weapon.

"That's better," Frost drawled, stepping into the room and kicking the pistol aside. "Now release my assistant. She appears to be the only one of the three with partial consciousness. The others may as well wait."

While Madame Futura sullenly obeyed, using her good hand, Frost dropped towels to smother the chloroform.

"Now, into the next room," Frost ordered, and marched her out.

During the minutes that they were gone, Jean breathed some spirits of ammonia that she found on a shelf. The sharp fumes helped clear her head. She had begun to feel more her normal self when Frost returned, prodding a man a foot shorter than he was, and of medium-heavy build. There was something familiar about the newcomer, his small face and hands—

"Madame Futura!" Jean exclaimed.

"And also Hackett's missing secretary," Frost added. "Otherwise known but little publicized as Johnny Jones, which isn't his real name either, but that's of no importance."

"Now it's all perfectly clear," Jean commented sarcastically. "Would you mind telling me by what giddy process you made sense out of this mess?"

"It was logic, not a giddy process," Frost retorted. "I found it highly fascinating, while it lasted, to analyze O'Larry's story, which served as the basis for a long series of deductions. I am pleased to announce that they have now been supported by facts.

"The starting point was Kane, the magazine agent, who came to O'Larry's door and to mine at crucial moments. Obviously, Kane was trailing O'Larry closely. Kane could have been a private investigator, an insurance-company detective, a city detective, or a Federal agent. There was no reason for the first three types to shadow O'Larry. Neither was there any apparent reason for a Federal agent to shadow him. Therefore, Kane was on the trail of some other person, and checking up on that other person's life so thoroughly as to investigate even his associates and the people with whom he came in contact.

"O'Larry had chiefly been in contact with Hackett. But Hackett was entirely occupied with city and State affairs and would hardly be violating Federal laws. Therefore, Hackett was under scrutiny for the same reason that O'Larry was. Both had a common contact with only one other person. That person was Madame Futura. Therefore, the person whom Kane was directly investigating must be the fortune teller, Madame Futura."

"Well, it begins to sound easy enough. I don't see why I didn't figure it out," Jean complained to herself.

"Obviously, a close relation existed between Madame Futura and Highway Commissioner Hackett. But there was no reason why he should spend much time in her quarters, and she would be so picturesque a visitor at his home that she would attract widespread attention. On the other hand, it would be absurd to postulate a go-between who spent much time dashing back and forth between Madame Futura and Hackett. Therefore, Madame Futura must represent some one in disguise, some one who had established the character to hide behind, but who stepped back into real life on the occasions when he saw Hackett.

"Such was the picture when Thor O'Larry suddenly returned after a ten-year absence, during which he had been presumed dead. His parents were dead. By O'Larry's own words, Hackett was bowled over when O'Larry stopped him on the street one day. Hackett voluntarily gave him seven hundred and fifty dollars. There was no need to, since O'Larry plainly expected to inherit nothing from his parents. Therefore, Hackett must have had another motive. He must have wanted to appear as a benefactor, in order to prevent O'Larry from making inquiries.

"Therefore, O'Larry's parents must indeed have left him something worthwhile. What could it be? His father was a glass blower. He had died several years ago—at which time Hackett suddenly began his rise to power, and became State highway commissioner.

"What articles of glass would have patentable features and be of value in connection with roads and motor vehicles? Safety glass was a possible answer. Nonglaring glass, or glass that polarized light was another choice. The third was a glass projection that would serve as a road marker and guide."

Jean exclaimed, "The golden crystals!"

"OF COURSE. O'Larry told us that Madame Futura's crystal was one that his father had made. It was a large, golden crystal. The State highway markers are small hemispheres of patented design and construction. O'Larry's father had designed the golden sphere and invented the golden crystals."

"I shouldn't think there'd be much money in them," Jean strenuously objected.

"In a State of this size, at least one hundred thousand crystals would be needed on the initial order to mark all the curves and turns on State highways. At two dollars each, the order would amount to two hundred thousand dollars. A twenty-five cent royalty on each crystal would amount to twenty-five thousand dollars. And that is just the beginning.

"The roads are cleared by snow plows during the winter months. The plows efficiently remove the snow, and just as efficiently trim the crystals off with neatness and dispatch. Which means that at least ten per cent and possibly above twenty-five per cent of the glass hemispheres must be replaced every spring—a further royalty of two thousand five hundred dollars to six thousand dollars or more.

"That total represents just one State. Multiply the figures by the number of States using the crystals and you begin to get impressive figures. Add Federal highway construction, and you get additional hundreds of thousands, plus bribery of influential officials, which is where Johnny Jones originally entered the picture.

"Kane undoubtedly was on his trail in connection with certain large sums that are generally believed to have changed hands in connection with governmental contracts specifying installation of the golden crystals. That part of my deduction cannot be substantiated until Kane awakens."

"Save yourself the trouble," Jones muttered. "You're calling the shots. Keep on calling 'em. The manufacturers gave me fifty thousand dollars to put in the right hands. I did. I got a fat cut. But the thing leaked out. I went into hiding when I heard the G-men were getting hot. I'd met Hackett. He got the royalties that were supposed to be held in trust for the O'Larry kid. He used the money for political power. And when he got that, he pushed the gadget that brought him a two-bit cut on every number. Golden crystals went into all the State roads as soon as he became highway commissioner."

"They have a legitimate purpose," Frost resumed. "But when O'Larry returned, Hackett saw his world about to crash. He stalled for time. Then he decided that O'Larry must be put out of the way. He arranged for the visit to Madame Futura. Madame Futura was to kill O'Larry in return for a split on the royalties.

"But Madame Futura saw a chance to take all—Hackett had more than two hundred thousand dollars in cash and bonds on hand in case he had to leave the country suddenly. Madame Futura did not kill Thor

O'Larry. She made an elaborate prophecy on one of the new, hour-long records. When the lights went out, she departed by the back way. The hum of air-conditioning apparatus was a great help in the deception. Across a wide table, and dazzled by the glow of the huge sphere, in black surroundings, O'Larry took the voice as genuine.

"Madame Futura became Johnny Jones, slipped out of the other apartment—"

"What other apartment?" Jean interrupted. "You might give us a vague idea of what—"

"I'll explain in a minute. Johnny Jones killed Hackett while Hackett waited alone in his study under the very conditions that he had prescribed. He was waiting to receive a message from Madame Futura. He received it from Johnny Jones in the form of two bullets through the head. Johnny took the cash and bonds, went down to O'Larry's room where he placed the gun and a small portion of the loot. He tipped the police off to Hackett's murder and to O'Larry as the chief suspect.

"He returned to his apartment with time to spare. When the reading ended, he turned the light out, slipped into his former position, and was there at the finish. You'll notice the black drapes around the chair back in a sort of niche in the main room. It's hard to see the chair in ordinary light, impossible by the light that emanates from the golden crystal."

JOHNNY JONES said sourly, "I bet it wouldn't work on you. The O'Larry kid is near-sighted, only he don't know it."

"Johnny Jones would cease to exist thereafter," Frost went on. "Madame Futura would flourish, until O'Larry had been killed by the police or executed for Hackett's murder.

"Unfortunately, O'Larry survived and came to me. But while I was away on a short absence, he took French leave. He remembered something. I would venture to state what he remembered— He recalled that at the end of the crystal gazing, some feature of Madame Futura's garb, possibly her headgear, differed greatly in position or arrangement from what it had been at the start of the reading. O'Larry suddenly realized that he had only a voice to indicate her presence. Therefore, he would immediately return to Madame Futura's apartment for a show-down.

"Kane would be at his heels. Therefore, I sent my assistant, so that she would either break up the party, or be a source of further delay. Madame Futura was being driven out of the built-up character that she had expected to use. And she couldn't become Johnny Jones, who was wanted already.

"I had reached the conclusion that Johnny Jones and Madame Futura could not be seen frequently in the same apartment without arousing suspicion. Therefore, there must be an adjoining apartment occupied by Johnny Jones, while Madame Futura held forth in the other. The most satisfactory layout would be one where two buildings backed up against each other, with a ventilation shaft between them.

"After my assistant left, I drove here, circled the block, and discovered that such a layout prevailed. I entered the building behind this one and took the liberty of investigating the apartment that backs up to Madame Futura's. I had intended to await the flight of Johnny Jones, but since it was entirely possible that he might bear unkind thoughts of O'Larry, Kane, and Miss Moray, to a point of doing them bodily injury, I straddled the ventilation shaft, which is merely two feet wide, and came through the bathroom window."

Jean turned the battery of her eyes on Frost with what she hoped was soulful admiration.

"Are you ill?" asked Frost, in a tone that she couldn't identify as either solicitous concern or raillery.

Jean sniffed.

"Release the others," Frost ordered Johnny Jones.

He obeyed.

Frost watched him, and when the work was finished, the professor glanced at Jean, drawled, "In view of the fact that they may continue to sleep for some time—"

Jean darted forward suddenly. "Ivy! Behind you! Jones!"

Frost turned leisurely, "Jones? Why, I rather imagined that he might take the opportunity to skip out while my back was turned. The rear door, the bathroom, and by now he must be vanishing through the ventilation shaft to the other apartment."

"You let him get away?" Jean exclaimed, disappointed.

"He had no time to take his loot, which is in this apartment and which, of course, rightfully belongs to Thor O'Larry. Also, I neglected to inform him that before I entered the adjacent building, I phoned Inspector Frick and told him to watch the entrance of that building for the murderer of Hackett who would emerge in a great hurry—"

From the near-by street, the blasting of gunshots crashed out through the night. The explosions lasted for only a second.

Frost said, with a shrug, "That was the out for Johnny Jones. I don't think he made it."

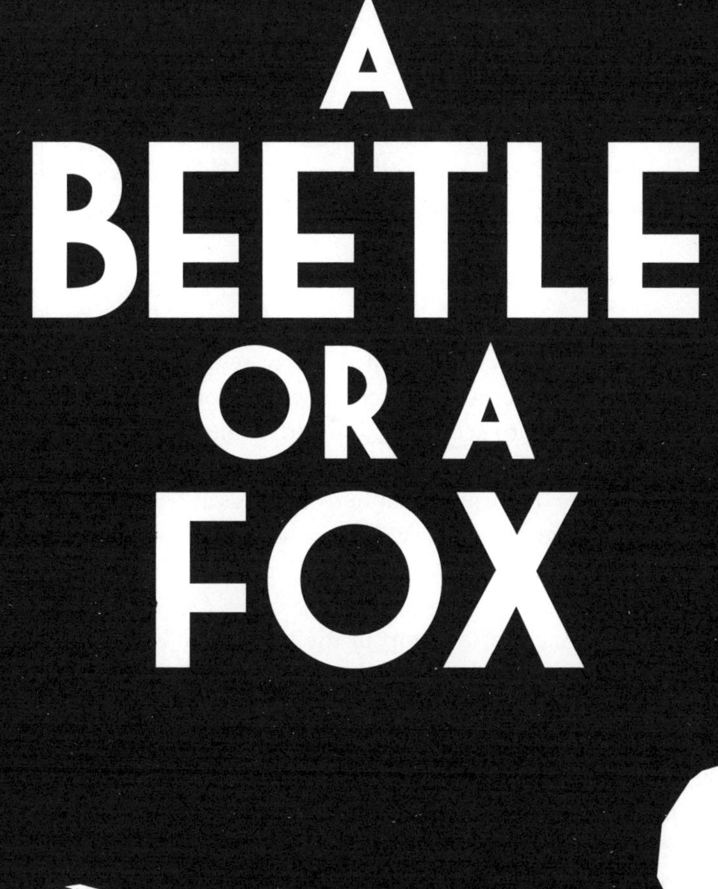
A
BEETLE
OR A
FOX

**Frost stood—looming above the mad crowd like a lone sentinel—
Then—slowly—calmly he drew out a long, pungent cigarette—**

SALLY PATTERSON had a way with her. It was an intangible something that attracted customers and made them want her to sell them things that they didn't need. She was tall and slim and willowy. She had mahogany-dark hair, big brown eyes, and such a sunny disposition that her smile was as refreshing as a spring breeze. But her good figure was the chief asset that had caused the personnel bureau to assign her to the Beach Accessories Shop in the department store.

The Beach Accessories Shop in itself was artfully persuasive. It reminded the public that far more than a mere bathing suit was necessary for swimming purposes.

Sally drifted among the displays like part of them. She looked as though she had just changed from a bathing suit, or was about to slip into one.

She had been exceedingly busy all morning. Friday was always a heavy day, and Friday in June meant the usual week-end rush. By eleven o'clock, her thoughts already strayed toward the lunch hour and the brief relaxation it would afford.

She was bending over a counter, making a memorandum on a sales pad, when, out of the noise and bustle of shoppers, there fell on her ears, in the voice of a cultured Englishman, the most astonishing request that had ever been made of her.

"I say, excuse me for intruding, don't y' know, but I would like to buy a jolly old beetle or a fox."

Sheer force of habit made Sally finish writing the word she had begun. Then she straightened with a start of blank surprise. He was, she saw, an honest-to-goodness Englishman. He wore a monocle. He was dressed in cutaway and striped morning trousers. He wore a carnation in his buttonhole. He was rather thin, not much taller than Sally herself, and he conveyed an air of breeding and culture. There was just a trace of snobbishness in his manner. It could have been offensive in some one else. It seemed a natural part of him. In fact, Sally found it rather pleasant.

At first resentful because she thought he was making fun of her, Sally suppressed the flip retort that sprang to her lips. "What was it you wished?"

"I would like to buy a beetle or a fox."

SALLY had heard him correctly the first time. He wasn't mocking her. He didn't look addled in the noodle. He appeared as casually sincere as though he was pricing a garment.

Vastly perplexed, Sally said, "I'm afraid you've come to the wrong place. Hadn't you better try a zoo or a circus?"

"No," said the Englishman. "You see, I really don't care whether the beetle or the fox is alive or dead."

"I see," said Sally, though she didn't see at all. "Well, perhaps you could get a stuffed one at a shop where they specialize in stuffing animals."

The Englishman patiently explained, "It doesn't matter whether I have the genuine animal. An imitation will serve as well. I simply want a beetle or a fox."

Sally had a sudden, insane temptation to blurt, "Why don't you go out fox-hunting or go catch yourself a beetle?" But such was not the tactful way to handle difficult customers.

Sally asked, "It must be a beetle or a fox? Nothing else would do?"

"It must be a beetle or a fox."

"Life-size?"

"The size is of no consequence. It can be very small or very large."

"Have you a special material in mind? Would it be all right if it was made of cloth?"

"The material does not matter," the Englishman spoke suavely. "It can be made of gold, silver, steel, wood, plaster, porcelain, or rags. It can be made from any substance. I do not care whether it is carved, cast, handmade, or poured. I merely wish to purchase a beetle or a fox."

"I believe we can take care of you if you want to leave an order," Sally volunteered.

"I have no time to leave an order. I desire the creature now. I must have a beetle or a fox to-day."

"I'm afraid we can't accommodate you," Sally answered. "As it happens, we do have a beetle and a fox but—"

"Excellent! May I see them?"

"—but they're not for sale. They just came in this morning. They're part of our special display of beach novelties."

"Not for sale?" echoed the Englishman. The monocle slipped out of his eye. "That seems jolly strange, don't y'know. Why do you put them up if they aren't for sale?"

"Well, we use them for backgrounds and exhibits. They'll go into permanent supplies and be used from time to time in other parts of the store. But they wouldn't be what you want. They're much bigger than life-size. They're practically giants and they're very grotesque."

"Oh, I say, there must be a way to purchase them," protested the Englishman. "I think I would fancy them, rawthaw."

"But they're not for sale," Sally insisted stubbornly. "As a matter of fact, there was a fellow in earlier this morning who wanted to buy the entire display when we were finished with it. He didn't say anything about beetles or foxes, but he wanted the lot. I asked Mr. Corri, our section manager, about it and he said emphatically no. The display is considered part of store fixtures."

"By Jove, there must be a way to purchase the beetle or the fox," the Englishman repeated just as stubbornly. "I say, could I jolly well look at the old blighter?"

Sally snickered. "Wouldn't Mr. Corri love to hear you call him that?"

The Englishman didn't smile. "I meant, d'you mind if I look at the beetle and the fox in your bally old show?"

"Of course you can. It's over this way," said Sally, stepping out from behind the counter. In a kind of sinuous glide, she floated her way down the aisles, whisked around tables and drifted between shoppers. By some miracle of poise, the Englishman stayed at her heels, his faultless tailoring, even to the restored monocle, surviving the crowd.

Sally stopped at a tableau that was roped off.

"By Jove, it's priceless. I say, who had the devilish ingenuity to think of that?" exclaimed the Englishman.

THE TABLEAU was a glorified beach scene as it might exist in some mythical land of Cockaigne. Surrounded by a variety of small items that the department store wished to hoist off onto a suspecting public, a group of gay young things rode off to sea. The mermaids were ultra-sophisticated dummies displaying the latest in bathing suits. Their steeds were a seal, a beetle, a fox, a swan, and a turtle. The steeds were smartly stylized, whimsically proportioned and oversize.

A very strange thing happened. The fox moved, drawing his forepaw back. Sally blinked her eyes and stared hard. The mermaid in a yellow halter and blue trunks astride the fox slipped sidewise on her mount.

"My goodness!" exclaimed Sally. "She's going to fall off!" Sally hastily stooped under the rope and ran to the tableau.

The fox jerked its leg back suddenly. Sally looked on, pop-eyed. She regained her wits just in time to rescue the wax mermaid.

"E-e-e-e-e!" squealed the shrill voice of a woman with nervous jitters, who was watching the exhibit. "It moved! It's alive! It's coming after us! *E-e-e-e-e!"*

"Stop that horrible caterwauling, you silly awss!" complained the Englishman peevishly. "Cawn't you see that the beast is merely a stuffed imitation? Besides, did you ever hear of a fox the size of a jolly old goat?" Which magnificent logic was lost on the neurotic female who squealed again because the fox lifted his forepaw all the way up to his chest.

Sally called faintly to the carpenter who was putting finishing touches on the far corner of the exhibit, "Jack, come quick!"

The carpenter hurried up.

"Something—is terribly wrong," Sally gasped. The carpenter took the wax model from her arms and put it aside.

She pointed to the fox.

The carpenter looked at the fox that had moved. He rubbed his chin, undecided what to do. The fox shuddered as though ready to leap across the room. And with that motion, the carpenter's mind was made up for him. He pounced upon the inanimate brute and laid him on the floor.

"Something's inside, probably a rat," he muttered and hauled a knife from his pocket. Forgetful of his surroundings, he worked with matchless speed and folly. He slit the line of sewing on the inside of the foreleg, and pulled out a handful of stuffing.

There did not rush out, however, a rat. In fact, nothing rushed out. The unmistakably human hand and arm exposed simply stayed there. But whether by another spasm, or as a result of the carpenter's slash, the thread ripped farther. The head of the fox suddenly bounced up to hang limply on its neck, and the face of the dead man sprang into full view. His nose was simply a hole where the bullet had entered his brain. Very cold, and very stiff in post-mortem rigor, the body experienced another cadaveric spasm that shook the fox.

A sort of nightmarish shock paralyzed Sally. She couldn't tear her gaze away from that gruesome face with its blank, staring eyes. And yet she was conscious of something intolerable, insufferable, about to explode.

She managed, by a queerly detached effort, to turn her back on the dead man and the fox. Her will and her body no longer seemed related to each other. She had difficulty in walking. She wondered vaguely if she was going to faint.

Then the department store, which prided itself on being the largest establishment of its kind in the world, spawned a major riot upon its second floor where the beach accessories were located.

There was the sound of a shot. Something hit Sally, and she heard another shot. The Englishman miraculously had a pistol in his hand. There was a moment's electric silence, followed by shrill, panicky riot on the part of the several thousand customers on the floor. Every one near the corpse and the shooting fled in a screeching babble. Every one at the far ends of the store endeavored to rush in to see the cause of disturbance. A table tipped over with a crash. Whole rows of items were swept from counters. The panic was on.

Sally slumped to the floor. She was aware of an extraordinarily attractive girl with a streamlined figure who coolly fought the crowd and dashed up. She had an automatic in her hand as she knelt beside Sally.

Things got blurred. Sally was vaguely conscious of a dark, swarthy, sleek little man with a peculiarly evil smirk, who allowed himself to be swallowed by the crowd. Sally saw an extraordinarily tall and gaunt-faced stranger of the late thirties or early forties plunging his way into the crowd. Of the Englishman there was no trace.

Things went black for Sally—

II.

JEAN MORAY knelt beside the inert figure of the sales clerk. At first glance it looked as though Sally Patterson was dead or dying in the midst of a welter of gore. But she had only been stunned, grazed by a bullet that furrowed her temple. Jean snatched a smart new neckerchief that one of the wax dummies was sporting and applied it to the wound. It stopped the flow of blood.

Professor I. V. Frost had started to plunge through the rioting mob of shoppers but halted short. Store detectives had begun to make their appearance, but their shouts and bawled orders merely intensified the uproar. For the time being it was virtual suicide to try stemming the stampede of hysterical humanity

Frost stood, looming above the crowd like a lone sentinel brooding upon the tide at his feet. With automatic motions, he extracted a cigarette of exceptional length and pungency, and lighted it while his gaze was fixed far down the aisles toward the distant escalator that ran to the main floor. He watched for a few moments, then turned away suddenly and strode up to the astonishing fox, with a quick side glance at the unconscious clerk.

Jean said, "It's a surface wound. She'll be up and around by to-morrow, with plenty of publicity and attention to repay her for the damage. But why did the Englishman shoot her? That was the most cold-blooded assault I've seen in—"

Frost cut her off. "The Englishman made no attempt to shoot her. He did not shoot at all."

"But I heard two shots—"

"Right now," Frost retorted dryly, "there are doubtless a hundred wild witnesses who could be found to swear upon ten thousand Bibles that the Englishman tried to murder the poor girl and, failing in the attempt, tried to murder the nearest person to him. As a matter of fact, a singularly repellent little individual, with many of the characteristics of a rodent, pulled an automatic and shot at the Englishman just as the corpse came to light. The Englishman started back with an expression of dismay, and the bullet intended for him hit the innocent bystander, the clerk.

"The Englishman knew instantly that he was the target and whirled around, drawing a pistol. That sudden movement saved him a second time, the bullet thudding into the wax model over there. Look closely and you can see the hole it made.

"The Englishman then sprinted down the aisle with the dark little fellow hot on his heels. It was quite a spectacle. The Englishman had the advantage of a quick start and got into the thick of the crowd where further shooting was out of the question. The little chap had the advantage of inconspicuous size, which enabled him to slide more easily through the mob.

"In many ways," Frost drawled with all the relish of a master at chess watching a couple of champions at work, "it was one of the oddest races I've yet witnessed, and run off under adverse conditions that made it well-nigh impossible to progress. In spite of obstacles and handicaps, the two reached the finish line, otherwise known as the escalator."

"And you let them get away?" Jean exclaimed, incredulous.

"Of course."

"But if they got through, you could have made it, too!"

Frost remarked offhand, "I'll pick up the trail instantly when I wish to. I know exactly where to find them. I must confess that I am not one who derives enjoyment or profit from pitting my energies against the combined fury of several thousand females. There was a keener intellectual satisfaction in watching the performance of the fox and the hound, so to speak. The Englishman reached the escalator well in the lead. He made good his escape. The expression of baffled rage on the face of the dark pursuer, when he came to the top of the escalator, would have done credit to the best villain in Hollywood."

He stooped over the wrecked display. The face of the dead man leaped out, garishly grotesque, from the covering fox. Frost scrutinized the corpse quickly, turned his attention to the seams where the stuffing had been put in before the fox was sewed together, and pulled out a handful of the stuffing, which he thrust into a pocket of his leather jacket.

Frost straightened up. "There's nothing more to be done here. Follow me," he snapped tersely, and began hiking away from the exhibit. Eddies of spicily pungent smoke swirled behind him, and Jean fleetingly wondered by what deft magic he always managed to produce one of his long, specially made cigarettes which he used only when his mind was stimulated by a hard problem. She rose, leaving Sally to aid already on the way.

THE SIRENS of radio cruisers and the gongs of riot-squad cars converged on the department store. A plain-clothes man materialized from the passing throng and blocked Frost's way.

"Get back there, you! Nobody leaves till I say so."

A sardonic smile hovered on Frost's lips, and the glint of a cold amusement glittered in the depths of pupils so dark as to seem black.

"My dear fellow, I would say that a thousand-odd witnesses are already streaming down the elevators and escalators. Surely the departure of two more can make little difference."

"Get back till I find out what's going on here!"

"You'll find a dead man in fox's clothing. He isn't going anywhere," Frost said acidly, and added, "but I am. If you have any further complaints, tell them to Inspector Frick of the homicide bureau. He doesn't relish delays in the solution of murder cases."

"Why in blazes didn't you say you were working on the case? Say, who are you?" began the detective, but Frost and Jean had already eddied away upon the retreating tide.

Frost said blandly to his assistant, "As a matter of fact, Inspector Frick certainly does not relish delays in the solution of murder cases. Isn't it unfortunate that our late inquisitor was so careless as to leap to the immediate conclusion that we were part of the police force, and that we were on official duty?"

"Very unfortunate," Jean agreed sarcastically. "I can't imagine what put that idea into his head."

She saved her breath then. She needed it to fight through the crowd and stay at Frost's heels. The going became a nightmare. One hysterical woman, jammed against Frost by a sudden surge backward from people ahead of her, began pounding him with her fists as though he was personally responsible for all her discomfort.

Frost looked down at her with a quick and curious expression, partly of disgust, partly of annoyance, a little of the scientist studying a beetle on a pin, a mixture of tolerant understanding, and more of an implacable drive onward to his own objectives, which couldn't be bothered or halted by so small an impediment as an emotional female.

The glass in a show case shattered; a scream rose. A clerk stood leaning over a counter, with an air of silly bewilderment. Somewhere a child was vociferously howling for its lost mamma, and a dowager with hat rakishly awry glared ominous threats at all who jostled her.

THEN they were through the mob, riding down the jammed escalator, and across the lower floor, and out to the streets as bluecoats and detectives swarmed through all entrances.

"Gosh!" Jean gasped. "That's the worst riot I've seen!"

"Your life will be a quiet one if this is the limit of your exposure to humanity running loose," Frost flung over his shoulder. "That was merely a disturbance of the mild variety. I take it you've never been at the scene of labor troubles, or racial disagreements, or witnessed the films of war records and civilian populations in the times of unrest abroad?"

"Good heavens, no!"

Frost shrugged. "I hope you are never exposed to those perilous matters. I wish that humanity itself could cease to be afflicted by such cancerous growths. And yet, it is plainly a logical development that vast explosions of human passion are only the exhibition on a large scale of the desires, hatreds, loves, and other emotions inhabiting the individual. There is a murderer in nearly all of us."

They reached the door of Frost's car, parked a block away.

Jean looked innocently straight ahead, but she was watching him from the corners of her eyes. "Really? The explosion of all the emotions in some men I've met wouldn't be noticeable except at a meeting of deaf-mutes."

Frost took the wheel. He answered with instant enthusiasm as he swung the car into traffic, "Your simile could be improved. Emotional outbursts are of little use at such a gathering because they can be artificially and successfully simulated. No, when a group meets, and is accustomed to express its ideas by lip movements and manual gestures it—"

"Excuse me while I powder my nose," said Jean, opening her purse. "I didn't mean to interrupt, but would you mind telling me what this is all about?"

"At the usual meeting of deaf-mutes, the customary procedure is as follows—"

Jean tapped her foot on the floor board. "When I want to learn about *that,* I'll read a book at the library. This affair of the beetle and the fox is—"

A far-away look came into Frost's eyes. He swung the car around a corner toward Fifth Avenue. "The beetle and the fox. Yes, it's a most peculiar puzzle."

Jean finished with the lipstick and started in on a compact. "Puzzle? It's like hash—you can't tell what's in it. This morning at ten thirty you—"

"Ten twenty-five," Frost corrected her.

"—you appear at a phenomenally early hour, take a cup of horribly black coffee, and glance at the front page of the New York *Daily Blah.*

You suddenly sit bolt upright. You put a phone call through to your crony down at headquarters, Inspector Frick, and ask him about the hijacking of a truck. Then you whisk me out in a terrific hurry and we pile into the *Demon* and you drive downtown like a speed racer. To what? To the department store.

"We sprint for the second floor just as hard as we can, and you tell me to circulate around the Beach Accessories Shop, which I do, and this follows. Why? What for? A dead man. Who is he? What started you off on his trail? I looked at the front page of the morning *Blah,* but I couldn't find a darn thing worth a second glance. As for that business about the truck that was hijacked, it happens nearly every day in the year without causing you to break out in such a rash of activity."

III.

FROST expertly tooled the car into Fifth Avenue. "An ordinary hijacking would indeed fail to elicit my further interest. But this was no ordinary hijacking. Far from it, it was of the essence of the extraordinary. Do you happen to recall the details?"

"Clearly, but I don't see anything unusual about them," Jean insisted. Her thoughts flashed back to a brief crime report at the bottom of the page:

THUGS HIJACK, ABANDON TRUCK

Driver Slugged

His suspicions aroused by the actions of a man attempting to enter a parked truck on West 16th Street shortly after 2 o'clock this morning, Patrolman T. J. McCarthy investigated. The man claimed to be Michael Higgins, driver of the truck. He asserted that a car forced his truck to the curb shortly before midnight. Three men slugged him, bound him inside his own truck, and drove off.

Higgins said he managed to free himself from his bonds after a long struggle, when the truck stopped. He exhibited bruises, ropes and a gag to substantiate his story.

The truck was abandoned at almost the precise spot where it had been hijacked. A careful search disclosed that its load of merchandise was intact. Police are unable to account for the mysterious hijacking. It is believed that the thugs may have chosen the wrong truck, or were frightened away before they could remove the contents.

"You profess to see nothing unusual in that report?" Frost drawled. "Three men drove off with a truck and its kidnaped driver. If they had chosen the wrong truck, would they have bothered to return it to the spot where they seized it? Or if they were frightened away from their loot, would they have had the leisure to drive the truck back?

"I should say that they would promptly abandon the truck wherever they happened to be. But since they did return the truck, they must have done so for a reason, in order to carry out a premeditated plan. They wanted to leave the truck at the site of the hijacking so that, with no apparent damage done and with none of the merchandise missing, the police would have no incentive for making more than a superficial investigation, if any.

"They succeeded. But why had they taken such pains? Because there must have been something in the merchandise that they wanted. The driver to the contrary, they must have made some change or altered the merchandise.

"I immediately telephoned Frick and asked him for the report on the crime. The truck belonged to the Borough Transport Co. It was delivering a shipment of forms for use by the department store in displays. The same issue of this morning's paper contained an advertisement of the store featuring a new exhibit in its Beach Accessories Dept., opening to-day."

"It's funny I didn't think of that," said Jean. "I see it now. The three hijackers drove the truck somewhere, ripped open the fox, put the dead man inside, sewed it up again, and drove the truck back to where they seized it. But why such elaborate pains?"

"Not so elaborate, considering the difficulty that every murderer faces in disposing of the victim," Frost drawled. "You simply haven't reasoned the steps out far enough. The three thugs obviously wanted to conceal the corpse in a place where it would not be found for several days. They expected that after the display was taken down in a week, it would be sent to a storeroom, as customary, where the body might not be found for months or years.

"But they had reckoned without *rigor mortis.* Post-mortem spasms and muscular contractions brought the corpse to light."

"WHERE we came in on the finish, or rather the middle. You certainly have a talent for discovering disagreeable affairs, even when they don't fall into your lap," said Jean. "Now that you managed to find a corpse without too great difficulty, what are you going to do about it? Did the dark man and the Englishman just happen to be around? Who is the dead man?"

"One at a time," Frost protested. "Nature did not endow me with a dozen tongues. The identity of the dead man remains to be learned, but it must possess a special importance or the murderers would not have taken such odd and extreme measures to attempt to conceal him for a long time.

"The dark man may be one of the three thugs, but for logical reasons that I'll explain in detail—"

"No, tell me the simple facts."

"The dark man is the one who gave orders to the three to hijack the truck. He supervised the opening of the fox and the disposal of the body. He went to the department store and tried to buy the entire display. You may have overheard the clerk say so. That effort was solely to make sure that the exhibit was not for sale at any price, and that it would go into dead storage.

"But having learned what he wished, the dark man loitered around. Why? He was still not satisfied. He thought that something might go wrong. It did. An Englishman appeared on the scene. The Englishman very definitely knew that either the beetle or the fox contained the dead man. And yet, if you recall the Englishman's questions, he phrased them in such a way as to make it appear that he had only a general interest in beetles and foxes, and that he had no idea his request would or could be granted.

"The Englishman knew more than he admitted. Therefore, he was either present when the dead man was put inside the fox; or one of the three hijackers subsequently tipped him off. Since the latter alternative is incredible for various reasons, it follows that the Englishman must have been present during the stuffing process, and that he came to the store either for the same reason as the dark man, or for just the opposite reason."

"The opposite reason? You mean to buy the fox and remove it with the corpse? That sounds queer. Why wouldn't he notify the police? Or was he one of the murderers who later broke away from the rest?"

Frost shrugged. "The question is an interesting one. Let us hope that the answer is equally interesting."

Jean wore a light frown. "It may be interesting, but as far as I can see it will be a nuisance and an expense without much chance for a fee."

"I hope so," Frost agreed.

"You—did you say you hope so?" Jean echoed. "You don't want to be paid for plunging into a murder mess?"

"Exactly."

"Well, if you're going in for charity work exclusively, I'd better start looking for a new job pretty soon."

Frost replied, "The net profit on all the cases we handled last year, due chiefly to the platinum horde we recovered, was over $200,000 after all expenses were paid. That is the maximum of profitable operation."

"So now you refuse to take any more fees? Well, you ought to be able to clean out the profit in a year or two," Jean prophesied.

"Not at all. But the Federal and State income taxes take such a high percentage from all sums beyond that figure," Frost informed her, "that I would rather take additional cases and decline a fee than accept the fee and turn it over to tax agencies. It pleases me to achieve the dual purpose of avoiding excessively heavy taxation and at the same time contributing my share toward the gratuitous solution of problems for those who are deeply in trouble."

JEAN tamped a cigarette of a popular brand on her thumb-nail. She wondered if she would ever fully understand the character and motivations of Ivy Frost. Sometimes he exasperated her; sometimes he fascinated her strongly; but seldom did he seem to have more than a casual awareness of her. Instead of finding her a strikingly exotic beauty, he treated her as a capable assistant.

He was, she noticed, flinging quick glances sidewise left and right at irregular intervals. Occasionally he slowed the car without apparent reason. She studied the people on the sidewalks. She tried to follow his gaze as it swept the towering citadels of stone, the enticing show windows, and the famous mercantile establishments that lined Fifth Avenue.

"If you're looking for the Englishman or the one you called a rodent, isn't this a haphazard way to go about it?" she ventured to ask.

"Yes, indeed."

"You can hardly expect to drive blithely around in the hope of finding either of them."

"That's precisely what I am doing."

Jean complained morosely, "In one breath you admit it's a hit-or-miss method, then you contradict yourself."

"This would be a highly uncertain method of locating the Englishman if it were a matter of chance encounter," Frost explained, "but it isn't. I am expecting to meet him because I am expecting to reach his destination at any minute."

Jean pondered silently for a block. She racked her brains trying to imagine what business could possibly have lured the Englishman to Fifth Avenue after his encounter with death in the department store. The monocle? He might have lost it. If so, he would try to replace it. On Fifth Avenue? There were numerous opticians' shops. It was a distinct possibility, but she couldn't recall what had happened to the monocle during the excitement.

Finally she asked, "Just where are we going?"

Frost's answer made her gasp. The professor casually remarked, "We're going through a wedding ceremony."

Light dawned on Jean. She made a beautiful recovery and beamed at him maliciously, "This is terribly sudden. I wasn't prepared. I'm thrilled to pieces, but couldn't you wait? It will take a little time to get the license, and we really ought to announce our plans, don't you think? And prepare for a large reception afterward?"

For the first time since she had known him, Frost looked ill at ease. He removed the cigarette with a muttered "Damn!" as his fingers accidentally brushed the glowing stub. Jean flattered herself that his face for a moment was rather richer with unaccustomed color than usual.

Frost said, "The Englishman was dressed for a morning wedding, a fashionable one. He is bridegroom, best man, or usher. I am looking for the church."

"And here it is!"

The exclamation was involuntary. She saw the reason for his drive along Fifth Avenue, lined as it was with numerous churches between the marts of trade. The churches were the edifices in front of which they had slowed. Now they had arrived at another church, but in front of this one a canopy extended over the sidewalk; an organ peeled; and every pew was occupied.

IV.

"OBSERVE the time, eleven twenty," said Frost. "Observe also the air of subdued nervousness among the attendants and especially the receiving usher. In view of the fact that eleven o'clock is a customary hour for morning-wedding ceremonies, would you not say that the conclusion is inevitable that an unexpected delay has occurred? A delay such as the failure of the bridegroom to arrive on time. I believe that I will wait here for our missing Englishman."

"Good enough." Jean settled lazily back, prepared for an indeterminate breathing spell.

She was rudely disillusioned. Frost ordered crisply, "While I'm waiting, go inside, talk to the bride, and obtain what facts you can."

"But I don't even know who the bride is!"

"This is an excellent opportunity to find out. It's one of those special occasions for which I need an assistant of your sex," Frost replied. "You can tactfully manage to draw the bride into privacy, whereas a man, a total stranger, would have an exceedingly difficult task under these circumstances. I urge you to make all haste. I'm expecting quick and quite possibly violent developments."

Jean slid out of the *Demon* and walked up the steps of the church.

The receiving usher looked at her with questioning eyebrows. "Are you a friend of the families? May I see your invitation?"

"Take me to the bride. I must talk to her right away. I have a message for her," Jean stated.

"If you will give me the message, madam, I will see that it is delivered to Miss Bradbury."

Bradbury—Bradbury; the name touched a vaguely familiar chord in the back of Jean's memory, but she was not able to identify it immediately. "I must see her personally. The message is highly important. It concerns the bridegroom. There has been a slight accident and a further delay may be necessary before he can get here. The name is Miss Moray." Jean wore just the right degree of anxious determination.

The usher wavered for a moment, then summoned another usher. "Miss Moray has a personal message for Miss Bradbury. Will you see that she delivers it?"

Jean felt a trifle annoyed. The atmosphere was too full of politeness and ceremony and stuffy formalities. A fashionably dressed congregation filled the pews. Whatever they thought of the inexplicable delay, there was no sign of unrest or impatience. They waited in fashionable quiet for the fashionable vows of what was no doubt a fashionable young couple.

It seemed to Jean that even she was being fashionably led to what surely would be a fashionable reception room. She was wrong only to the extent that the occupants thereof showed definite signs of anxiety and worry. The usher whispered to the bride; the bride looked over at Jean, and then the bridesmaids, who were a lavishly gowned and sumptuous array of smart young beauty, looked over at Jean. Finally the remaining principals of the ceremony looked over at Jean, the last to look being a portly gentleman unmistakably the bride's father.

JEAN MORAY looked coolly back at them all. She was admiring the bridal gown and making mental notes of what the other girls were wearing, when the bride detached herself from the group and floated up to Jean. A little hum of studiously polite conversation arose and every one politely pretended to be ignorant of the intrusion. The bride led Jean into a smaller room and closed the door.

"I am Janice Bradbury," said the bride. She had a spoiled, rather hectically willful face and nervous hands, but she made a stunning appearance. Jean had no time to notice more than her greenish eyes and red hair as richly dark as Bing cherries, drawn back and coiffured in a Grecian mode. For the name now meant something to Jean—Janice Bradbury, air woman and eldest daughter of the Bradbury Corp., which was a leading producer of planes, motors, and air equipment.

"You wanted to see me? Ronald—something has happened to him? Who are you?"

Jean made a guarded answer. "I'm Jean Moray, Professor I.V. Frost's assistant. You may have heard of him, an ace specialist in solving crime cases. The Englishman has been involved in a mix-up that might be fairly serious."

"Ronald? Sir Ronald Weatherby? Involved in a crime?" The bride-to-be appeared incredulous. "Why, that's impossible. Surely there must be a mistake. He couldn't. Where is he?"

"He's on the way." But Jean purposely avoided saying where he was on the way to. "Just who is he that you're so positive he couldn't be connected with an unpleasant affair?"

"Sir Ronald? Why everybody knows who he is. He represents a large private firm abroad—"

"What firm?"

"I can't say exactly. I never asked. But he travels all over the world."

"Has he been here long, in America?"

"He arrived only yesterday for our wedding. Why do you ask? What has happened?"

"He landed only yesterday? And yet you found time to make all these elaborate preparations for the ceremony?"

"He was last here two months ago. We made all our plans then. Naturally, we have been in constant communication with each other."

"Can you think of any reason why he might have gotten into trouble? Are you acquainted with a very small, dark, dapper man whom he knows?"

"There is no such person to my knowledge. Sir Ronald avoids trouble as much as possible. What in the world brings you here? What are you leading up to?"

Choosing her words carefully, and releasing only the outline of facts, Jean minimized even those. "There was a commotion at one of the leading department stores a short while ago. Sir Ronald happened to be present when a pistol was fired which inflicted a slight injury to a bystander. He was not directly responsible, but in the excitement that followed he attracted attention. You know how these unfortunate accidents will develop. He left with imperative haste. No doubt he will arrive soon, at least Frost is outside expecting him."

Janice Bradbury said, "Professor Frost is outside here? Then he must be expecting more trouble. Wait for a few seconds. I'll return almost immediately."

SHE OPENED and closed the door. Jean found no opportunity for extensive reflection about her next move. The bride-to-be glided back in much less than a minute.

"Take me to Frost," she commanded.

Jean raised the objection, "But you can't leave the church at this stage of the proceedings. It simply isn't done."

"It's going to be done."

"But it's highly unconventional. It's not at all the proper thing. What will the wedding guests think when they see you out at the curb talking to a private detective? It might create a small disturbance."

"Oh, darn convention!" Janice burst out with vehement feeling. "It's no time to argue about matters of form. Ronald is nearly half an hour late. I'm by no means satisfied with the statements you have made. I absolutely insist on speaking to Professor Frost."

"Well," Jean temporized, "I suppose it could be arranged. Why don't you wait here for us? It will only take me a minute to dash out and bring him in."

"I want to find out what's going on. Professor Frost wouldn't have come here in the first place merely to see whether Ronald made his scheduled appearance. Frost can have no personal interest in our wedding plans. I have an absolute right to know what Professor Frost is up to and what he has on his mind."

Jean thought, "Janice, you may have a right, but if you find out what goes on in Frost's mind, you'll be the first person to do so." Aloud she said, "Won't it be awkward making your way past the guests and attendants?"

"We don't need to. Follow me."

Janice Bradbury led Jean Moray through a different door, into a study room, and then down a short corridor to a side exit that was evidently the private service door.

They emerged around the corner and hastened to Fifth Avenue. The pedestrians in sight stared with unmitigated curiosity at the bride-to-be, but Janice Bradbury evidently believed that the stares of the populace were of no consequence so long as she successfully avoided causing whispers among the throng inside the church.

"Now which way? Where is Professor Frost?"

Jean took charge and steered her ahead toward the *Demon,* which was parked about a third of the way down the block.

As they drew near it, Jean noticed that Frost was peering ahead with a peculiar intentness. She looked toward lower Fifth Avenue but saw nothing unusual. Yet Frost continued to stare fixedly, and appeared unaware of their presence as they reached the big vehicle.

Jean opened the door. At the same moment, Frost's hands flew to the controls. The car, thrown into gear, quivered with incipient motion. Frost abruptly slammed on the brakes, or Jean, halfway in, would have been hurled aside.

"In! Quick!" he barked. "Get in or get out!"

Jean stared at him in amazement.

V.

AT THE MOMENT his assistant trotted up the steps of the church, Frost had shifted his gaze to the rear-view mirror in his automobile. He lowered his glance on occasions to sweep the avenue ahead, but concentrated most of his attention on the mirror. It commanded a full range of traffic for perhaps a block uptown behind him, as much as could reasonably be expected in a crowded street like Fifth Avenue.

The wedding ceremony apparently held no interest for him. He did not give the church the benefit of a single appraisal after Jean Moray had left him.

Five minutes passed. The traffic signal changed at its slow intervals—two minutes of green for Fifth Avenue, one minute of red for the crosstown cars.

The signal was on yellow, preparing for red, and Fifth Avenue traffic was slowing accordingly, when a taxi squealed to a stop by the curb at the intersection behind Frost.

The Englishman clambered out, hatless, but with the monocle in place, and as debonairly perfect in attire as though he had never been near a scene of shooting and had never fought his way through a mob of wild shoppers.

"I say, old chap, this is close enough, don't y'know. I'll stroll to the bally church. A nip of fresh air will be good for me, and all that sort of thing."

He pulled a bill from a wallet and waved it at the cabby.

The hackman asked, "Are you the guy gettin' stitched?"

"Haw-haw-haw, very droll, I must remember that!" The Englishman turned away, beaming. "Oh, by all means keep the change. The ride was worth a goodish tip."

The cab rolled on.

The Englishman looked puzzled. "Stitched? Stitched? How quaint! I wonder what the silly bloke meant. Possibly a reference to tattooing. Curious people, these Americans, to go around inquiring of each other whether they have been tattooed. Can it be the newest fad?"

So musing, the Englishman paused, waiting for the light to change to green, and crosstown traffic to stop whisking in front of him at what seemed a frightful speed.

A sedan rolled around the corner, hugging the curb. The Englishman stepped back. The sedan stopped squarely in front of him; the rear door popped open, and he found himself unhappily eyeing what looked like a tremendous orifice, being the business end of an automatic in the hands of a slate-eyed fellow who snapped harshly, "Come on, climb in. Make it snappy or else you'll—"

"Oh, but I say, I cawn't, really I cawn't," exclaimed the Englishman. "I'm jolly well late for my wedding, don't y'know, and it isn't cricket."

"Get in!" growled the voice behind the pistol.

Sir Ronald Weatherby was painfully conscious of the fact that, though several other pedestrians stood near him waiting for a change of light, not one of them noticed the menace. To all intents, a car had stopped to pick him up, and he was merely entering at his leisure.

"Come on or take it!" snarled the voice. There was no doubt whatever about what the "take it" meant.

"You Americans have the oddest habits!" complained the Englishman. "I am quite able to walk to my wedding without the aid of an armed bodyguard."

"You ain't going to no wedding," jeered the voice, and asked of the driver, "Did yuh ever see such fancy togs? Ain't he the lady-killer?"

The Englishman obeyed the ugly command of the automatic. The door slammed shut behind him. The sedan picked up speed as it rolled toward Sixth Avenue.

A MATTER of seconds only had sufficed to cover the whole episode from beginning to end. Frost, watching the Englishman's reflection in his rear-view mirror, and seeing the sedan block him from view, swung the *Demon* into motion. At the same instant, the door opened and Jean Moray was entering. Frost stopped the car before it rolled an inch.

"In! Quick!" he barked. "Get in or get out!"

Jean stared at him in amazement. Janice Bradbury opened the rear door and started to enter.

"Close those doors!" Frost snapped.

Janice stepped forward, there was a tearing sound, a jerk, and her bridal train was thoroughly enmeshed in the door handle.

"Oh, I'm caught!" cried Janice.

Jean sprang to her aid, and between them they managed to untangle the feminine finery in less time than it would take to cross a street.

Frost said dryly, "The Englishman has just entered a sedan. It's rapidly disappearing, in case you're interested."

"Take me to him!" Janice gathered the train of her gown and seated herself, while Jean slammed the door.

The *Demon* leaped forward with a jerk that snapped Jean's head back hard. She was feeling it gingerly to make sure it still belonged to her when she was flung violently against Frost as the car careened around the corner and shot toward Sixth Avenue.

But the sedan was gone. It had vanished during those precious seconds when Jean and the bride-to-be tangled with Frost's plans. He wasted no time in a futile cruising around the district.

Janice began to sniffle.

"Forget it," Frost drawled. "It was one of those unfortunate occasions that no one can foresee or avoid. The only difference it makes is that instead of trailing the sedan to its destination, I'll find the destination and meet it there."

"But how, how?" wailed Janice. "Ronald is gone and m-my wedding is a m-mess and it's m-mostly my fault!"

"Do something about that!" Frost flung at Jean as he stopped in front of a drug store. He dashed inside to a phone booth and dialed a number that he had jotted on the back of an envelope earlier that morning. The number was listed to the driver of the truck that had been hijacked.

When the connection was made, he asked, "Michael Higgins? This is to complete the report you made on a hijacking last night."

"Say, what more do you want? I told you cops all about it."

"Do you recall any unusual sounds that you heard while the three thugs were driving the truck?"

"Huh? Well, you gotta remember I was tied up inside. I couldn't hear much. Except there was a kind of *whooshin'* sound that lasted quite a while. Oh, yeah, and I heard it again later. Does that mean anything?"

"Watch yourself. Be wary of visitors. Your life is in immediate danger."

"Whatta yuh mean?"

His question went astray, for Frost had hung up and was hiking back to his car.

Under the able ministrations of Jean Moray, Janice Bradbury had recovered her poise and once again looked the part of enchanting bride-to-be.

Frost ordered, "Miss Moray, take a taxi down to 126 North Street as fast as you can get there. Michael Higgins, driver of the hijacked truck, lives there. Keep your automatic ready for use. I want a complete report of everything he remembers concerning the assault."

Janice settled back in her seat.

"I haven't time to return you to the church," Frost stated.

"I won't return without Ronald."

Jean slipped out. "Is that all?"

"Call me at State Street the moment you have the information." To Janice, Frost said, "You simply can't walk away from a ceremony in which you are a principal."

Janice watched Jean enter a taxi that sped her off. Janice answered "Oh, yes, I can. I left your assistant when we were in the church long enough to tell my father to take charge of postponing the ceremony if I wasn't back within a few minutes. Ronald is in trouble. My place is with him."

"Confound it, I refuse to accept the responsibility for your private life."

"You can't help it," that headstrong young modern flatly declared. "You seem to be sure of finding Ronald. I'll stay with you till you do. I've got a much greater interest in him than you have."

Frost stated with equal flatness, "I have a crime to solve. It will be a serious handicap if you persist in your obstinacy. I can hardly conceive of more arresting raiment than bridal clothing. In the vicinity to which the chase is leading, you will be more conspicuous than a white elephant in Times Square."

"That's not very complimentary," Janice reproved him, "but you're taking me to Ronald."

Without wasting time on further protest, Frost sent the *Demon* rolling and drove uptown at a sure but hair-raising clip. They made a spectacular contrast—the professor with his gaunt, spare figure, and the bride-to-be in the lavish array of silk, lace, and flowers that were to have adorned her wedding. Frost asked a few pointed questions about the Englishman, but kept silent with regard to his own plans.

The midtown region swept behind them, then the apartment buildings lining Riverside Drive, until Frost turned a corner and halted in front of the mansion at 13 State Street.

VI.

WHEN Jean Moray left Ivy Frost and Janice Bradbury, she hailed a taxi. It swerved to pick her up. She climbed in with, "See how fast you can get to 126 North Street."

"I gotcha, miss."

The cab sailed for lower Manhattan.

Left mentally breathless by the swift turn of events, Jean tried to puzzle out a sequence for them, without noticeable success. The key figure was evidently the Englishman, but she found it hard to visualize him as the head of a criminal band. And yet, the very fact that he had been present when the dead man was hidden inside the fox certainly did not argue for his innocence.

The identity of the dead man was another puzzle. He might be a person of peculiar importance, as Frost had asserted, but he was neither famous nor influential nor wealthy. Of that she felt positive. The arm and hand that protruded from the stuffing of the fox were well-muscled, with strong, rough fingers, the hand of a man accustomed to manual labor. In all probability he was a workman whose name would mean nothing when it became known, and who would be remembered solely for having been the unfortunate center of a bizarre crime.

In that case, what importance could the dead man conceivably have, except the possession of special knowledge which he had been slain to suppress? The theory seemed valid, but would an ordinary workman be likely to be blessed with either the brains or the opportunity for acquiring knowledge so valuable that it led to murder?

Jean temporarily dropped that line of speculation. She was due to face Michael Higgins. In spite of the truck driver's apparent innocence, had he been a participant in the plot? Had he deliberately allowed himself to be kidnaped, with a full understanding of the purpose intended?

She turned her attention to the buildings as they approached North Street. It was in an older part of Manhattan, on the west side, about halfway between Fourteenth Street and the Battery; a district of warehouses, garages, small manufacturing concerns, wholesalers, and dilapidated residential buildings of three or four stories' height.

No. 126 was an ancient brick structure of small apartments. It looked uninhabited, and probably was almost empty during the daytime, while its occupants scattered to their respective jobs.

JEAN paid off the taxi and walked into a small, grimy vestibule. Soiled name cards were attached to the dusty mail boxes. Michael Higgins was the proud owner of No. 3. Jean tried the hall door. A lock of prodigious dimensions proclaimed its metallic strength, which went for naught because nobody had taken pains to see if the catch was working. It wasn't. Jean opened the door and entered a dimly lighted corridor. Therein clung a musty smell that had doubtless developed and ripened over a period of decades.

Apartment 3 was on the ground floor at the rear. Jean stopped and listened at its door. She heard nothing. It seemed well nigh impossible that anything could happen or that any one could be inside the room without being heard outside, so badly did the door set in the jambs.

Jean knocked loudly.

There was no answer.

Somewhat puzzled, she knocked again. Frost had expected Higgins to be here waiting for her. But Higgins must have acquired some different notions of his own. Still, Frost had told her to keep her automatic ready for trouble.

She tried the door. It, too, was unlocked. Jean stayed to one side with her eyes fixed on the space at the hinges, as the door opened a few inches. No one was attempting to hide behind the opening door—an old trick that Frost had taught her to guard against.

She opened the door wide, but saw no one inside. It was a poorly lighted, cheaply furnished room, with a bed in one corner, a table, and a few chairs.

Jean closed the door behind her.

An astonishing thing happened. One of the chairs leaped straight off the floor and crashed toward her. She ducked, but the flying mass hit her arm and the automatic clattered away. A man blossomed from the spot where the chair had stood.

"Well, I'll be—" he burst into a startled oath. He was not prepared to find the intruder a woman.

Light dawned on Jean. He was Michael Higgins, on guard for reasons best known to himself. "Michael Higgins! I've come from Ivy Frost—"

The light proved a dud. Jean found herself in a furious battle that ended with cold steel pressing her.

"That's better, kid," growled the man with the gun. "Turn around."

Jean heard ripping, tearing noises. Then pieces of cloth clung affectionately to her mouth, absorbing and stifling all the good words inside of her, and she found herself all at once possessed of an amazingly erudite range of blood-curdling epithets. More strips of cloth wooed her wrists into quiescence behind her back. And more strips came to dwell upon her eyes, shutting off the light of the world. And finally her ankles were bound.

She was lifted and dumped into a bag or sack of some kind. She heard the door open. She was carried out and dumped again. There came a sound of gears meshing, and then the motion of a vehicle.

Jean dwelt in a little world, dark, stifling. It seemed that eternities passed before the car finally stopped, eternities of cramped limbs and insufficient breath and hot anger, with futile tugging at the bonds that confined her. A half hour? An hour? It was impossible to estimate time.

AGAIN she was lifted and carried.

Then voices: "So you got Higgins?"

"Nope"—that was the voice of her captor—"it's a dame. She's working for a dick. Higgins must 'a' got warned off; he didn't show in."

"A woman! Why did you bring her here?"

"Aw, pipe down, Savoldi. I hadda do it. She's a hell-cat if ever there was one. Higgins was gone and I couldn't leave her there to spill the beans."

"So you brought her here to spoil everything? Reaver, I told you to take care of Higgins while we went after the blasted Englishman. You let Higgins go and you bring a strange woman instead. Turn her out."

Jean felt herself tumbled and pulled. The eye bandages were removed.

A great many impressions then crowded upon her restored vision. She was in an amazingly long, wide room. It contained rows of empty steel shelves, hundreds of crates in assorted sizes, whole racks of rifles, high explosives, shells, machine guns, and other munitions to supply a small army.

In front of her stood Savoldi, the sleek, dapper little man who had precipitated the riot at the department store. Around him were three henchmen, including her captor. They were the trio, she decided, that had hijacked the truck.

And bound to a chair sat Sir Ronald Weatherby.

Savoldi shouted, "Now it's a mess we can't get out of! It's poison she is! It's poison!"

"You only get the chair once if it's one murder or a dozen."

Savoldi howled, "You fool, you fool, you'll have the cops and the G-men and private detectives swarming down on us!"

"Oh, stop having a fit. You should 'a' thought of that before you bumped Tonson off. That was one smart brain storm, I don't think. Putting the guy in a fox where he wouldn't be found in a year. Blah. He waltzes out the same day."

Savoldi screamed, "Could I help it? It was fate; it was a crazy accident! It was a great idea even if it didn't work!"

"Sure. Now get a great idea about how we're going to get rid of these two."

Jean listened to the charges that hurtled back and forth. She was patiently working on the strips, even though she saw no way out of the room except through the door by which they had entered. The shed had no windows.

While studying the door, her eyes suddenly stared. A cold shiver ran over her. Black smoke was seeping under that door. She watched it thicken, curl up.

"Hey, what's she looking at?" Reaver shouted.

All four spun to face the only entrance.

"The place is on fire!"

Savoldi scuttled to the door, yanked it part way. An ocean of smoke boiled through, shot with a solid wall of flame.

Savoldi slammed the door.

"The emergency exit! Quick, before it all blows up!" Savoldi bawled, sprinting to a far corner of the shed.

"What'll we do with the girl and the Englishman?"

"Let 'em cook!"

Jean and Sir Ronald stared at the vanishing four, while the volume of smoke grew thicker and flame danced.

VII.

FROST dashed into his laboratory at 13 State Street, hauled out of his pocket the wad of stuffing that he had removed from the fox, and busied himself with microscope and chemical solutions. His attention was wholly absorbed by his work. For all the notice he took of Janice Bradbury, that attractive bride-to-be might have been another specimen in a test tube.

Utterly incongruous with her surroundings in her bridal attire, she watched Frost for a few moments, then inquired, "Why do you keep that horrible eye hanging in the hall entrance, and those other eyes in your library?" She referred to artificial eyes of man and animals that Frost had placed at various points.

He answered without looking up, "They focus my attention. They distract the attention of visitors. And they are constant reminders to be ready for any emergency because there are always watching eyes by day and by night."

Janice Bradbury looked dubious. She didn't approve of having unpleasantly realistic eyes strewn about one's home.

A cabinet caught her gaze. She glided over to it and examined its astonishing array of objects; a platinum horseshoe, strands of human hair, exploded cartridges, a counterfeit cent, signed statements, the bones of a rat, a paper with a pile of greenish mold, a golden amulet, a broken hypodermic needle, a silk stocking with a run, a phonograph disk, and dozens of other items.

"What is all this junk supposed to represent?" she asked in a disapproving tone.

Frost answered with a trace of irritation. "If you are referring to the display cabinet, the material consists of one important item or clue essential and pertaining to the solution of every criminal case that I have accepted. Rather than keep a voluminous file, I find that a single object is sufficient to inform me of all questions relative to the problem in which it figured. A trained student who has completely mastered analysis, logic, and deduction, should, by studying any one of those items, be able to reconstruct the complete, original problem."

"What a macabre hobby!" exclaimed Janice.

"Indeed?" Frost's voice had a caustic edge. "It occurs to me that a bridal gown would be a noteworthy addition to the display as the central feature of my most recent case."

Janice replied with considerable heat, "Why, the very idea is an outrage! If you must add to your gruesome collection, you could do worse than choosing a—than putting a little—"

"A monocle or a fox? Either would be fully as pertinent as the bridal gown. Perhaps I shall," Frost murmured indifferently.

Janice eyed him, uncertain as to how to interpret his comment. Frost went on working. She drifted away from the cabinet, stood looking on at his procedure for a short interval, and finally asked with consuming curiosity, "How long are we going to be here? Is that necessary?"

"Absolutely."

"I don't see what good it does to poke around a handful of wadding."

Something like the suggestion of a sigh came from Frost. "This is the shortest route to Sir Ronald Weatherby."

Janice looked baffled.

FROST EXPLAINED, "He is being taken to the same spot where a truck operator was driven last night. That man, Higgins by name, did not see or know where he was taken, but twice he heard a prolonged *whooshing* sound, as he described it. That sound marked the departure and return of the truck through a tunnel. The only one within range is the Holland Tunnel. The truck was driven to Jersey and back. Thus I know the approximate location of the spot."

"That doesn't necessarily follow. Jersey covers a large area."

"But only two hours elapsed between the time Higgins was kidnaped and the time he freed himself and found himself back at West 16th Street. While he was a captive, a certain fox was opened, a process that took at least a half hour. Allowing a half hour for the drive each way, and a half hour for Higgins to free himself, the time is accounted for. Therefore, the site I am seeking must lie within fifteen minutes' driving distance from the Jersey exit of the Holland Tunnel, since fifteen minutes are needed for the drive from there to West 16th Street."

"That still covers a good-sized area."

"Watch!" Frost touched a match to a tiny fleck on the wadding. The speck flared up.

"Smokeless powder," Frost said, as though that explained everything. "Now notice this." He dropped a few strands of wadding into a clear solution that immediately turned yellow. "That's part of a test disclosing the presence of sulphur in the wadding.

"That waste rested on the floor of the building where the fox was operated upon. The wadding picked up grime that is characteristic of the purposes for which the building is used. I have now learned that it is a storehouse for explosives. It is situated so close to a factory which gives off sulphur gases in its smoke that the wadding has become impregnated with sulphur. Now we have the spot narrowed down to a very limited range."

Frost went into his library, took a massive folio from the shelves, spread it out on a table.

The volume contained maps. Frost stopped at the page he wanted. "This is an industrial map of New Jersey, showing the position of factories and their chief products. Within the fifteen-minute range of the Holland Tunnel, these are the only three using large quantities of sulphur, and this"—he indicated one of the three—"is the only one which is near a munitions depot."

He closed the folio. From his laboratory supplies he selected several objects of a miscellaneous nature that puzzled Janice, who asked, "What do you need those for?"

Frost answered, "I may not need them. They are preparation for whatever set of circumstances prevails when we reach our goal. Miss Moray was to have phoned me but has failed to do so. My personal interest in the case is now quite as important as yours." With which illuminating comment he hastened outside to the *Demon,* stowed the objects and Miss Bradbury therein, and sent the car speeding down the west side.

Midtown Manhattan flowed behind them, then Fourteenth Street. Frost drove at the maximum of safe speed, the *Demon* humming a song of vast reserve power as it skimmed ahead of car after car.

They reached the Holland Tunnel. Janice became conscious of a peculiar sound that was aptly described by *whooshing.* She studied the smooth, flowing sides of the tunnel, and quickly found the reason for the *whooshing.* At regular intervals there were narrow setbacks or alcoves in the walls, and the reverberating sound of a passing vehicle made a distinct *whoosh* when the waves bounced out of the recesses.

They emerged in Jersey, and Frost headed away from the urban area. Ten minutes of fast driving brought them to a grimy factory whose chimney belched smoke with an acrid, stinging bite. Frost drove on to a low shed that covered acres of ground. It was a shed of curious appearance, completely without windows or doors except at one spot that evidently served as a tiny office, and one other that was a loading platform.

Frost drove along a blank wall of the building. "Ah, the emergency exit," he murmured and stopped. He climbed out, did something to the lock, and returned to Janice.

"The lock seems to have jammed for some mysterious reason," Frost announced blithely. "I'm afraid that any one inside really wouldn't be able to use the exit now. However, the combined efforts of three or four husky men would burst the door from its hinges. I would be sorry to see that happen. Miss Bradbury, would you relish a part in capturing the abductors of Sir Ronald?"

The gleam in her eyes was almost unholy.

Frost handed her a strange contraption that resembled a hand fire extinguisher. "Stand by the door. The moment you hear pounding from within, use this." He showed her how to manipulate the gadget and hastened back toward the office entrance, carrying a couple of objects under one arm, and with his right hand on the automatic in a side pocket of his leather jacket.

Underlying the grim aspect of his mission hovered a fleeting expression, as though Frost was deriving a secret, sardonic amusement from some abstract jest.

VIII.

SAVOLDI slipped the catch off the inside emergency door and plunged toward the outer door. He turned the knob and heaved. Nothing happened. "Hey, the outside door's stuck!" he yelled.

The three at his heels drew back to hurl themselves against the barrier to escape.

But Jean Moray, her eyes glued on the office door, saw it spring open. A gaunt, familiar figure erupted through the flame and smoke. Frost crossed the room in long strides. He flung the inside door of the emergency exit shut and locked it. A frantic beating and pounding commenced from the four who were trapped.

"And that is almost that," Frost drawled. He returned, and while cutting the bonds of Jean and the Englishman, listened expectantly.

The shouts of the four changed to choking gasps and coughs.

"Miss Bradbury seems to have done a good job of spraying the nausea gas," Frost murmured approvingly.

"I say, old chap, don't y'think we jolly well had better leave before the place blows up? I don't fawncy that, really I don't," said the Englishman.

"Oh, *that,*" said Frost with a careless wave of his hand. "Merely chemical smoke and flaming gasoline on a cloth curtain, saturated. Effective for trapping rats and eliminating the possibility of gun play."

"How the deuce d'you do it? I say, where's Janice?"

"She is on the way."

Jean interrupted. "Let me get this straight. The dead man inside the fox—"

"He was Benjamin Tonson, my half brother," the Englishman answered simply. "He was employed here by the Savoldi Export Co. I really don't know much more. I arrived yesterday for my wedding. Benjamin communicated with me. He seemed most upset, oh, definitely, don't y'see. He insisted that I come to this beastly place at midnight, but the chap wouldn't say why. It was dashed irregular.

"When I arrived, I saw a truck outside. I passed by a window and saw a light. I looked in. I thought these blithers were playing a silly game. Would you believe it? I saw them sewing up their jolly old fox. It was amazing, no end. But one of the chaps saw me. By Jove, I didn't know I could sprint so fast. I came back later, but they had all left. Benjamin didn't come.

"This morning I phoned the beastly place. I was told that Benjamin had resigned his position. It all sounded deucedly queer, don't y'know. I began to think about the men sewing up the fox. I remembered the name on the truck; the Borough Transport Co. I wangled the destination of the truck out of the owners. Then I went to the department store to find the fox. I didn't have much time, don't y'see, what with my wedding and preparing to sail for a honeymoon tonight. I say, what *is* the pip of the orange?"

Frost countered with, "You're agent for a private munitions firm abroad. You buy arms in quantities?"

"We purchased three million pounds—fifteen million dollars' worth—from this company last year."

"That purchase from the Savoldi Export Co. is the answer," Frost stated.

THE ENGLISHMAN turned huffy, "Oh, I say, you cawn't make such insinuations; it isn't cricket. We paid for supplies that were delivered. There was no bribe of any nature, if that is what you fawncy."

Frost shook his head. "There are some rather cryptic records in the outer office. Savoldi made a profit of five million dollars on that transaction. But he didn't pay a Federal income tax on that sum."

"Why the old bounder!" exclaimed the Englishman.

Frost smiled thinly. "Offhand I can't say what the tax would have amounted to, but $2,000,000 would be a rough guess. And Benjamin Tonson, the man in the fox, was killed because he learned about that unpaid tax. He was intending to inform the Federal tax officials."

"Oh, that's preposterous! What would he gain? There was a prospect of his arousing extreme displeasure on the part of his employers."

"That is very likely the reason why he wanted to talk it over with you," Frost said. "He was afraid he might be killed because he knew the type of men who were his employers. They learned of his intentions, perhaps by seeing him take an interest in the firm's scanty records and having him shadowed. They killed him before he could use his valuable information."

"I see," said the Englishman. "I don't quite understand why Benjamin took such a risk."

"Because the Federal income-tax bureau has a custom of paying ten per cent of such recovered tax evasions to the informer. Ten per cent of $2,000,000 is $200,000. That is what Benjamin Tonson would have profited by his fatal knowledge."

"Most interesting, most distressing, yes, really," said the Englishman. "I wonder where I could find one?"

"Find what? An income-tax evader?" asked Jean.

"A justice of the peace," said the Englishman, adjusting his monocle. "I say, is one allowed to be married in this bally old State of Jersey?"

SKELETONS, INC.

**Charles Partho—believes he will be slain by a dinosaur—
because he sleeps in a sarcophagus—but he is, really, quite sane—**

THE VISITOR who came to I.V. Frost that warm summer evening had a singular name and a remarkable appearance. He presented his card with a sweeping flourish. The card read: "Alexander Partho Hendiadis." The man who bore this impressive name was nearly as long and as thin as Frost himself.

Hendiadis looked surprisingly like an old-fashioned cartoon of a blue-nose reformer. He wore a black suit with black gloves and a black silk hat. He had a stern face. His head was bald on top, but around the sides ran a fringe of long hair that curled outward in a ruly manner. Mr. Hendiadis was a very couth person with a freshly scrubbed face and a wart on the tip of his nose. His coat pockets were oversize; the right pocket had a tremendous bulge; and the bulge squirmed every now and then in a way that made Jean Moray's skin crawl. It was as though Mr. Hendiadis carried a pet rat around with him.

Frost glanced at the card, then gave his visitor one all-encompassing look that took in every detail of his clothing, appearance, and habits. From long experience Jean Moray knew that Frost, after a quick, penetrating examination, learned more of a client's life and background than some one else could find by a week of research.

Frost, whom his friends nicknamed "Ivy," was a former professor at the Atlantic Institute of Technology and other universities. He had become bored with the academic routines in the search for knowledge, and had adopted a far more exciting profession. He became a specialist in the solution of murder mysteries, preferably those with a bizarre twist whereby his distinctive talents of logic and deduction enabled him to make bold moves that were beyond the scope of ordinary police routine.

He overcame the usual police antagonism to private investigators partly by ignoring it, partly by sheer force of personality, and partly by being so completely indifferent to publicity that Inspector Frick's homicide bureau in nine cases out of ten took full credit for the cases that Frost cracked.

He owned three mansions at 9, 11, and 13 State Street. His laboratory, office, and residence were at 13. No. 11 had been given over to the use of his assistant, Jean Moray. She had never been inside of No. 9 and did not know what it contained.

The professor dropped the card of Alexander Partho Hendiadis upon an end table. Jean watched Ivy rather than the visitor. Frost idly fixed his gaze upon a bust of Socrates that graced a pedestal on one side of the library-reception room, opposite an old print of Bacon that hung on the wall.

The visitor announced, "It is with extreme reluctance that I have forced myself to take this step. The matter is not one for the police. I distrust psychologists, who would be unable to cope with the trouble, in any case, if it proves serious. Therefore, I seek your assistance. Having learned of your successful exploits upon several occasions, I believe I can entirely trust you."

Frost listened with lackluster eyes, profoundly disinterested. "What is your problem?"

"It is no problem of mine, I can assure you, except indirectly. It concerns my cousin, Charles Partho, with whom I have been living for many years. We are the last members of our families and have no near relatives, I should explain. For that and other reasons, we have been more like brothers than cousins."

Frost's great lack of interest seemed to grow still more complete. "Indeed? What problem faces Charles Partho?"

"He is convinced that he will be slain by a dinosaur."

FROST suddenly sat up and reached a hand out to lift an exceptionally long cigarette from a container at his elbow. Jean Moray breathed a faint sigh. It was the gesture for which she had been watching. Frost never indulged in those sharply aromatic cylinders except when a puzzle stimulated his faculties.

"Slain by a dinosaur? Yes, it would be possible," Frost agreed, to the vast perplexity of Jean Moray. "Your cousin is an eccentric, of course."

Mr. Hendiadis looked astonished. "How did you know that? But he is quite sane, quite sane, make no doubt about it, even if he does choose to sleep in a sarcophagus."

Frost lighted the cigarette and blew out an island of fragrant smoke.

"He sleeps in a sarcophagus and expects to be slain by a dinosaur? Your remarkable cousin excites my curiosity. Why does he believe he will be killed by a dinosaur?"

"Because he sleeps in a sarcophagus," was the surprising answer. "Charles Partho is a man of contradictions. He has superstitious beliefs, though his mind, in general, takes a rather scientific bent. For some time he has been positive that a dinosaur will kill him. However, that does not worry me nearly as much as the green mamba that almost poisoned him a week ago."

"A green mamba!" Frost exclaimed. "Where did he get that tropical central African snake in New York?"

"He really didn't get it. It came to him," said the lank Mr. Hendiadis.

"That's an ambiguous statement. Precisely what do you mean when you say the snake came to him?"

"I'll explain in a minute. But I warn you that there may be nothing to all this. Nothing, in fact, seems very surprising to me after Skeletons, Inc."

"Skeletons, Inc.? Who or what are they?"

The visitor answered, "Why, they are hundreds and hundreds of skeletons, naturally. What else could they be?"

"They could be bone meal," said Frost with a touch of acidity. "What is the purpose of these skeletons?"

"Well, you can't exactly say that a skeleton has a purpose," said Mr. Hendiadis lamely. "A skeleton is—well, it's just a skeleton. Anyway, I don't know much about it; I just happened to mention it offhand. That isn't what I wanted to see you about."

Jean Moray listened with increasing amazement. When a stranger bearing the name Alexander Partho Hendiadis brought forth a story involving death from a dinosaur, a man who slept in an Egyptian burial coffin called a sarcophagus, a virulent green mamba from Africa, and a mysterious horde of skeletons, that was news even among all the fantastic and bizarre cases that had passed through Frost's hands in the past. And when the visitor, in addition to his odd name and appearance, carried in the pocket of his coat something that squirmed and writhed, Jean found herself both fascinated and repelled.

The thrill of danger, and hazardous adventure on the border line of death, had been constant since her first association with Frost. But excitement bred a thirst for more in that insatiable young woman.

Jean Moray had a perilous beauty. Hers was an exotic face, with langurous lips, high cheek bones, wide-set, gray-green eyes, and hair the color of mellow rye. She had a seductive, streamlined figure. She was as changeable as a chameleon. Sometimes she adopted the marks of ultra-sophistication, while at other times she affected a naive simplicity of manner. But her perilous beauty never changed. Frost had frankly told her at the outset that he had a definite use for her striking attractiveness. It focused and diverted the attention of others at critical moments. More than once when she had been trapped by killers, she had escaped after they had delayed action a little solely because of the spell exerted by her physical beauty, a thin margin of time that was sufficient for Frost to spring to her aid.

All men responded to her sex appeal, except Frost. And whether through pique or perversity, she had grown to want him above all others, the one man she couldn't have.

Hendiadis was no exception. The glances he flung at her were intended to express stern disapproval, because Jean always took pains to wear as little clothing as possible, out of self-respect and admiration for her figure. But underneath his apparent rebuke lay an obvious desire.

"YOU SEE, it's like this," he said, addressing himself to Frost but with his gaze straying toward Jean, who sat ostensibly taking notes with one leg crossed over the other. She did take notes at times, though all conversations here were recorded automatically on a concealed dictaphone. Hendiadis found it a trifle difficult to concentrate on his story. His eyes kept sliding up and down the silken expanse of Jean's limbs, from her lovely ankles to her knees.

"Well, continue." Frost sounded brusque.

"Well, it's like this," the visitor repeated. "My cousin, Charles Partho, bought the sarcophagus more than a dozen years ago, at a time when many Egyptian tombs were being discovered and opened. This is a big one. It is seven feet long inside. It weighs at least half a ton, being cut out of solid stone. It gives off an aroma of faint perfume, of spikenard and myrrh. That fragrance has not materially lessened during the fifteen years that Charles has slept in the sarcophagus. He claims that it induces him to sleep better.

"He has always been something of a collector. We own the whole brownstone in which we live. It is as full of specimens as a museum. We had a heated argument when he bought the dinosaur and brought it home. He had it mounted in the library, which was the biggest and indeed the only room in which it could be installed. The thing stands about fifteen feet high and is twenty-five in length."

"To what species does it belong?"

"Tyrannosaurus Rex—the king of the dinosaurs," answered Hendiadis. "I didn't object to the sarcophagus, and I didn't object to the broken Greek vases and African masks, or the totem pole and the big stone image from Easter Island, or the Chinese ceremonial robes and the medieval armor, or even the human skeleton. Charles brought them all home at one time or another. But I most decidedly objected to having the bones of that colossal monster, the giant dinosaur, occupying a good half of the room. However, I became accustomed to it, if not reconciled.

"Then, about a month ago, Charles dreamed that he was going to be slain by a dinosaur. He didn't confide the details of the dream to me, simply the main point. He often spoke of the legendary curse that afflicted the discoverers and defilers of Egyptian tombs. As I said, he is superstitious. And while he refused to stop sleeping in the sarcophagus, as I urged him to, he got the notion that in some way he was going to be killed by the dinosaur as a penalty for having occupied what was formerly the coffin of an ancient Egyptian. He said it wouldn't do any good to stop sleeping in the sarcophagus. The damage was done. It couldn't be made either worse or repaired. Fate was fate and you couldn't change it. You know, the oriental idea of kismet and what not."

Frost prodded him with, "You haven't accounted for the green mamba. How did he acquire it?"

"Oh, yes, the snake. Well, it arrived a week ago in a box addressed to him, but without a return address. He asked me to open the package. I told him he knew well enough that I never opened other people's mail. It seemed to annoy him. He tore off the wrappings, and when he removed the lid, the snake lashed out like a flash of green lightning. I don't know how he escaped death. The fangs grazed his sleeve. He leaped back, and when the snake slithered across the table, he seized a poker and killed it. Then he pickled it in alcohol, put it in a glass jar, and set it on the desk, where he admired it every day in the morning light of the sun."

Jean shuddered at the thought of a man who would calmly preserve a viper that almost killed him. But the effect of the narrative on Frost was electrical. He bounded out of his chair with a curt, "Wait here. I'll return in a few moments," and hiked off into his laboratory.

Jean waited in astonishment.

Alexander Partho Hendiadis compressed his lips, then stated morosely, "I do believe I am wasting my time. It looks as if I came to the wrong place. The fellow does not even let me finish my story before he springs straight into the air and departs with the speed of a fleeing antelope. It would appear that I may as well do likewise."

He rose and reached for his black silk topper.

The laboratory door opened as Frost returned. To the average eye there would have been no change in his appearance; but Jean recognized the slight additional outline of a bulletproof vest that he had donned. He was fastening the old leather smoking jacket that he habitually wore. Before he looped the belt over, she caught the gleam of two small, dark disks, one on each side of his chest. They somewhat resembled a miniature camera.

"I'm sorry you couldn't wait to hear the rest of the story," began the visitor.

"I'll hear it on the way to your cousin," Frost said tersely.

"But why such haste? One moment you are listening intently, and the next moment you bound around like a water drop on a red-hot stove."

"For the excellent reason that I wish to interview your cousin while it is still possible," Frost stated with an ominous implication.

He led the way to the basement garage. His big, specially built car, which Jean had nicknamed *The Demon,* armor-protected and with bulletproof glass, rolled up the ramp a minute later. It swung into State Street toward the address given by Alexander Partho Hendiadis.

II.

FROST SAID, "Is your cousin afraid of the police?"

"No. Why do you ask? Oh, you mean because he didn't report the incident of the green mamba to them? How did you guess that?"

"Some deductions are too obvious to require explanation. Did neither of you deem it unusual to receive so deadly a gift in an anonymous parcel?"

Hendiadis appeared to find the presence of a lovely, tempting, and bewitching young woman at his side a source of distraction. "What's that? Oh, the parcel. Well, we often receive packages at home, though they usually come to Skeletons, Inc. Mail without a return address is uncommon, but arrives with sufficient frequency so that it doesn't attract any special interest.

"The box with the green mamba was mailed locally. We haven't the slightest idea of who sent the snake or where he got it. Charles was pleased to add a specimen of a fairly rare snake to his odds and ends. He decided it was sent as a mistaken practical joke, or else the sender by pure accident forgot to put his name on. Charles thinks that any day now he will receive a letter asking why he hasn't acknowledged receipt of the green mamba. That's one reason he delayed about telling the police.

"There was another reason. I'm not anxious to divulge it, but I suppose I'd better. It's simply that I—"

Jean gave vent to a sudden, startled cry of fright. She was sitting in the middle of the roomy front seat, with Hendiadis to her right. Something very cold, clammy, and horrible to feel was crawling across her lap. She glanced down, to meet the beady eyes and whipping forked tongue of a moccasin snake that was uncoiling from the pocket of the man with the Greek name. The writhing bulge which she had noticed earlier had more or less faded into the background of thoughts. She had guessed at a pet rat. The snake was too much to bear. Her lips parted.

Before she could utter another sound, Frost snapped, "Hold it, both of you! The snake is harmless, Miss Moray. Its poison ducts have been removed. But unless the owner keeps it under control I shall take great pleasure in making it just a smear upon the pavement."

With nervous haste, Hendiadis grasped the reptile behind its swaying head and returned it to the pocket. Jean's skin crawled from imaginary contact with the moccasin, even after it had been removed.

"If you don't mind," she stated, with as calm a voice as she could muster, but in cold rage, "you can drop me at the next corner. I flatly refuse to work on a case that means having snakes crawl over me."

"I'll drop the case before I'll drop you," Frost retorted just as bluntly.

It was the warmest admission she had ever heard him make. The unexpected promptness with which it came gave her a pleasant tingle that partly mollified her, and atoned for the liberties the snake had taken with her anatomy.

"I'm very sorry," Hendiadis apologized. "I was so concerned with my story that I overlooked Jasper. He's an inquisitive little imp, but harmless. I meant to warn you about him. Somehow it slipped my mind. I've had him about a year and have grown quite fond of him. I often take him out with a leash and a long cord, and let him slither through the park."

Jean opened her purse and grasped an automatic. "If I so much as see Jasper's hideous head again, I'll shoot. And I won't mind a bit if your legs get in the way."

Hendiadis hastily shoved one hand down over the pocket, made sure that Jasper was confined. "As you may have suspected by now, Jasper was the other reason why my cousin didn't notify the police after he received the green mamba in the mail. He knew that I had a pet snake. He thought that I might have been responsible for sending the mamba. He didn't accuse me outright, but he half believed that I had made an attempt on his life."

"I should think he would!" Jean exclaimed fervently.

Hendiadis looked unhappy. "Well, appearances were against me, and of course I would be his heir if anything happened to him.

"But last night I almost got killed by an accident that was peculiar to say the least. In the room with the dinosaur there is a desk that we both use, though not very often. Charles was fussing with the skeleton of the dinosaur. He asked me to get him a dust cloth out of the center drawer. I went over to the desk. But instead of going around it and seating myself in the chair to rummage for the rag, I leaned across the top of the desk and pulled at the drawer. It stuck. I gave it a yank. The drawer flew open. There was a muffled explosion. Splinters leaped from a hole in the middle of the drawer, another hole appeared in the back of the chair, and the bullet went part way into the wall.

"If I had been sitting in the chair, I would have been shot through the heart or chest.

"Charles looked as startled as I was. We kept a pistol in that drawer. We investigated and found that a pencil had been jammed against the top and bottom of the drawer, its lower end against the pistol trigger, and the weapon itself tightly wedged by various objects, so that jerking the drawer open fired the pistol. It could have been the result of an unfortunate accident. We hadn't used the drawer for a week or longer.

"But I began to wonder. The only person who would profit by my death was Charles, my heir. He had asked me to get something out of that drawer. Only the fact that I happened to lean across the top of the desk saved my life. I didn't openly accuse him, but he must be blind if he couldn't read my suspicion. On the surface, it began to look as if each of us was plotting to kill the other by devious methods. The whole business is bewildering. You can readily see why neither of us is anxious to call in the police. A strictly private investigation is needed."

THE BRIGHT LIGHTS of midtown Manhattan flowed by off to their left, as they followed the west side highway on down to the 23rd Street ramp, which Frost used to reach the Chelsea district where Hendiadis and Partho lived.

Frost asked nonchalantly, "Is Skeletons, Inc. a profitable business venture?"

"It will never make a million, but it does well enough. Why?"

"I'm interested in the details of a concern that specializes in such bizarre, if not morbid, objects."

"There's nothing morbid about skeletons. You get used to them like anything else. Why, Skeletons, Inc. was founded before the War by a man named Harry Bonaparte. It's an appropriate name. Besides, he has a cadaverous look. He's still part owner. In the post-War depression he had a hard time, but my cousin bought a half interest and the business continued. Then I came to live with Charles Partho; the crash of 1929 happened, and I possessed just enough money to rescue the venture. Now it's again paying well. Charles and I together own a three-fourths interest, while Bonaparte has the other fourth.

"As the name suggests, the firm deals in skeletons. I don't mean human skeletons, although we do keep them in stock, but skeletons of all sorts of animals, birds, fish, and insects from all over the world. If you're sufficiently interested, I'd be glad to have you come down, and bring your assistant with you, to look at our stock."

"No, thanks," Jean declined with a shudder.

"The prospect attracts me," Frost drawled. "Do you keep a large supply?"

"We have a whole floor, with several thousand skeletons always in stock. They are chiefly the common species of animals and birds, but we have a few rarities."

"What price do they bring?"

"Well, that depends on many factors such as condition, scarcity, demand, and so on. A human skeleton is worth one hundred and twenty-five dollars. That has been a standard price for many years."

"Where do you obtain the human skeletons?"

"From South America chiefly."

Frost wore a slight frown. "Indeed?"

"We pay fifty dollars to seventy-five dollars apiece for them. However, I doubt whether we import more than a dozen a year, for the demand is light. We have our suspicions about the origin of the skeletons, but we don't ask questions. We believe that some members of the native tribes think it a great lark to kill off an enemy or any convenient stranger and to dispose of his body, or skeleton, for a few dollars. However, that's no concern of ours."

Frost asked, "Where do the other types of skeletons originate?"

"We get them from everywhere, from field expeditions abroad, from amateurs, from museums. You can buy the mounted skeleton of a mouse for five dollars. A primate ape will run from ten dollars to two hundred and fifty dollars, depending on whether it's a small monkey or a gorilla. A fossilized dinosaur egg at one time fetched as high as ten thousand dollars, when the first few were discovered. Now the cost is much less, and it's constantly going lower as more and more eggs are discovered in central Asia. Likewise, the complete skeleton of a giant dinosaur, such as Brontosaurus and Tyrannosaurus, once brought ten thousand dollars and even more. The high price resulted not so much from scarcity as from the fact that it took the labor of several men a long time to excavate bones in the first place, and the labor of several experts a year or more to assemble and mount a complete skeleton.

"The price we pay is naturally much less than what we charge. We buy one type of chimpanzee at fifteen dollars and sell it for forty-five dollars. The margin of profit is necessarily large because we make only a few sales a day, though our territory literally covers the world."

Frost wore a far-away look of intense concentration. Jean decided that some detail in the narrative had struck a wrong note with him. That didn't surprise her, because the entire story and all the skeletons struck a wrong note with her. She heartily hoped that she would never be compelled to visit the display of Skeletons, Inc.

THE BIG CAR rolled to an easy stop in front of a brownstone house.

A middle-aged woman was ringing the bell with obvious impatience.

Hendiadis exclaimed, "Why, there's Mrs. Gillis, the housekeeper. What's she doing out here?"

Frost slid out of the car, the others at his heels, and took the steps in long strides.

The woman turned to Hendiadis. She complained, "A fine thing it is, sending a decent, hard-working woman out at this time of night on a wild-goose chase."

The man was flabbergasted. "What are you talking about?"

"You know very well. You phoned less than an hour ago. You asked me to meet you immediately at Times Square. There I went, bless my soul, and I waited thirty minutes. I didn't take my key. Now I've been trying to get in for at least ten minutes, but Mr. Partho has gone to bed and here you are coming along and asking me what I am doing here. A fine how-dy-do, I call it."

"I never phoned you!" Hendiadis insisted.

"I'm afraid we're too late," Frost said. "Get your key.

Hendiadis fumbled awkwardly with his left hand, his right still restraining Jasper, the moccasin snake. He got the key out and opened the door.

Frost plunged in. Jean got a quick glimpse of paintings and busts upon the walls, of books in cases and stacked on the floor, of mounted fish, seventeenth-century clocks, fifteenth-century armor, and antique coins. The place was a storehouse of objects from all ages and all parts of the world.

The professor entered a room that was lighted. It was a room fit for a palace, in its spaciousness. It had a desk, and cases filled with miscellaneous items. A green snake in a glass jar stood on the desk. The immense skeleton of a Tyrannosaurus occupied at least half of the room. But the skeleton had lost its head.

The head was imbedded in a human head, the head of a corpse.

Charles Partho had been killed by a dinosaur.

III.

MRS. GILLIS, the housekeeper, emitted a shriek; Alexander Partho Hendiadis developed a pair of goggle eyes and face as yellow as beeswax; Jean Moray fought the nausea that rose in her throat. Charles Partho had died a gruesome death. The heavy skull of the dinosaur, poised fifteen feet above him, had crushed his head to pulp when it fell upon him.

Frost bent over the body. He examined the remains with the swift, impersonal study of a scientist looking at a bacterium under the microscope.

He stood up and started to lift his arms toward the wiring that united the skull to the rest of the skeleton. He stopped suddenly when his arms were shoulder-high. He pulled a chair over and climbed up to examine the wiring. Jean wondered why he took such pains not to raise his arms high.

"Call the police," Frost ordered as he got down.

Jean notified the homicide bureau.

Frost drawled, "Start preparing an alibi. Charles Partho was murdered."

Hendiadis ran his tongue across his lips. Beads of sweat started from his forehead. His face grew almost green. "Murdered!" he echoed. "But—but it can't be! The skull fell on him. It was an accident! You can see how he stood under the skeleton!"

"No," Frost corrected him, "he was lying under the skeleton. He was already unconscious when the skull crushed his head. There is a bruise above the right ear, toward the base of his head, that could not possibly have resulted from the falling dinosaur's skull. Some one slugged Partho. His assailant was so well-known to him that he didn't expect an attack, hence the absence of any sign of a struggle. The murderer dragged his limp body under the mount and loosened the wiring. It didn't break or work free by itself.

"The killer performed his work so carefully that the police may write it off as an accidental death, even after a close examination. The skull of a dinosaur is an improbable murder weapon that would never occur to the average mind."

The skin stretched as tight as a drum on Hendiadis' face, making the bones stand out. "I didn't do it! I didn't!" he croaked in a strange voice.

"I merely stated the facts of death," said Frost. "I suggest that you prepare an alibi. The police will learn that you had a motive for killing your cousin, and that you had the opportunity. He died approximately an hour ago. You could have left him, telephoned to get the housekeeper out of the way, and returned to kill Partho. Then you could have come to me with your narrative, and have attempted to use your presence at my home as an alibi—especially if the police cannot fix the exact minute of death, as is likely to be the case.

"Furthermore, the police will believe that since you keep a pet snake, you were guilty of the attempt to kill him by mailing him a deadly green mamba. They will also believe that you reached across the desk and avoided being killed by the bullet, when the drawer opened, solely because of special knowledge. You knew the pistol was there and thus took pains to be safe. You knew it was there because you put it there. You made two previous attempts on the life of Partho. You succeeded on this, the third try. That's what the police will say before they lock you up on a murder charge."

"But I didn't kill him! I'm being framed!" Hendiadis squalled.

Frost snapped, "Get yourself under control. Let the police arrest you. You may have a hard time of it, but at least your life will be safe. There's something much more sinister underneath all this. I'm going after it. Where does the other partner of Skeletons, Inc. live?"

"Harry Bonaparte? He has a place on Washington Square South. Now that I think of it, you certainly ought to question him. He collects instruments of death."

"He collects—what?" Frost exclaimed sharply.

"Weapons and instruments of death. It's a hobby of his. He's made a specialty of tools that have been used by different countries and governments of all ages to inflict the death penalty. He has a bachelor studio full of the stuff: hangman's rope, daggers, knives, a guillotine, firearms, poisons, axes, medieval and oriental torture machines, chains, an electric chair, and so on."

The wail of police sirens shrilled closer.

"One more question," Frost asked. "Is there any one on duty at the offices of Skeletons, Inc. to-night?"

"The only employee we have is Paul. His last name is Luca but we all call him Paul, though he's getting white-haired and must be fifty by now. He started out with the firm when Bonaparte founded it. We really don't need him, there's so little work. We rarely ship or receive more than five or six skeletons a day. He is officially the superintendent in charge. Yes, you might find him on duty. He often works evenings unpacking and mounting fresh stock."

THE SIRENS came howling down the street. Frost tore out of the room, Jean Moray at his heels. They piled inside *The Demon,* which hummed a smooth song as it sailed away from the arriving radio-patrol cars.

Jean ignited a cigarette that her jangled nerves craved, but she took only a puff before tossing the cylinder away. The memory of the dead man with the snout of a dinosaur's skull imbedded in his brain lingered all too vividly in her mind.

"Did Hendiadis kill Partho?" she asked suddenly.

Frost side-stepped her question. "An almost ironclad case can be built up against him. There is no positive way in which he can clear himself. The only method whereby he can establish his innocence is the indirect method of definitely proving that some one else is guilty. What you have seen thus far is only the beginning. There's a far greater crime underlying the murder of Partho."

"What is it?"

"Watch it develop," Frost drawled, to Jean's exasperation.

She complained, "Goodness knows what more there could be. Hendiadis keeps a pet snake. Partho had the bones of an extinct monster, not to mention enough peculiar objects to supply a museum. They ran a skeleton factory. The skull of the dinosaur killed Partho. And now you're on the way to visit a fellow named Bonaparte, who has the pleasant habit of collecting tools to commit murder."

"It's a strange assortment," Frost agreed. "Everyone involved with the murder appears to be an eccentric pursuing freakish paths. The fantastic nature of this case makes it singularly attractive."

In spite of the warm night, Jean felt a chill at the back of her neck. There were times when she considered Frost inhuman. The cold, dispassionate intensity with which he bent his analytic faculties toward solving even the most hideous of murders seemed abnormal to her. He was like a perfect, impersonal machine automatically ticking off numbers until it invariably produced the correct combination and the one possible answer.

It was only a short distance from the brownstone house where Partho and Hendiadis lived in the Chelsea district to the colonial brick building on Washington Square that was the home of Harry Bonaparte. Frost covered the ground in less than five minutes.

Ten thirty had just passed when they stopped at the curb. Many fugitives from the heat still sat on benches or strolled through the park.

But the night grew late, and the number of loiterers lessened. There was no wind. The air had a sultry, sticky dampness, laden with grime and rank odors, unpleasant to breathe and disagreeable to feel.

Frost said tersely, "Wait here."

HE CLIMBED OUT and vanished inside the vestibule. Harry Bonaparte occupied the entire top floor of the four-story building. Frost did not ring the apartment bell. There had been lights behind curtained windows on the ground floor. Frost rang the bell to that apartment. When the buzzer clicked he hiked in, hastened down the hallway, and took the first flight of stairs before an apartment door opened on the first floor.

He heard a man grumble, "The next time those dratted lugs forget their keys and ring our bell, I'll raise hell with the management." A slam punctuated the words.

The ghost of a smile crossed Frost's face. He continued his climb.

He found the door at the top-story landing locked. Again he ignored the bell button. He listened for a moment, then took an oddly shaped tool from his pocket—a tool with many adjustable prongs. He inserted it in the keyhole, and after half a minute pushed the door open.

The apartment was dark. He closed the door behind him before pressing a wall switch.

The light showed a strange conglomeration of bookcases, cabinets with glass shelves, pedestals, and nooks, all occupied by daggers, knives, machetes, guns, and other death-dealing instruments. With only a glance at the assortment, Frost crossed the room and opened another door. He clicked a second wall switch.

The chief mechanical feature of the room, when the light went on, proved to be a guillotine that stood against a wall. The blade rested in the bottom groove, and the blade was red.

The head of a man held the middle of the floor. The eyes, wide open, stared straight toward the doorway with a blank idiocy. A little pool of blood lay under the severed neck. Drops of blood spattered a trail to the guillotine from which the head had rolled.

Most horrible of all was the body jammed against the base of the machine. The headless trunk had fallen in such a way that the great fountain of blood which normally spurts out after a decapitation had been bottled up. Only a few dark drops oozed from the wound that was sealed by the baseboard of the guillotine. But the fingers writhed and crawled with scratching sounds upon the floor, while the limbs twitched with slow, terrible jerks.

The skull of a dinosaur had killed Charles Partho. Harry Bonaparte had died under the blade of his own guillotine.

IV.

FROST'S FACE bore no expression when he examined the macabre remains. Only his eyes showed a black glitter, the light of an implacable will. He did not touch the head or the body, though he gave them a close scrutiny. He devoted more time to the guillotine.

Upon a desk in the same room he found a small, flat sheet of paper beside a typewriter. The short note typed on it read:

> To whom it may concern:
> I have done this because I killed Charles Partho. I killed him to make it look like an accident. I wanted to get back control of the business that he took away from me. I realize now that the police will not be fooled. They will never catch me. I have cheated the electric chair.

The note was signed with ink in a round, clear script: "Harry Bonaparte."

Frost studied the letters of typewriting. He ran a sheet of paper into the machine, typed a few lines, and compared the result with the letters on the suicide note. They tallied in every detail. The keys of that specific machine wrote the message.

Opening a drawer, the professor found the canceled stubs of checks, a lease, and other documents bearing the signature of Harry Bonaparte. He compared them with the signature on he death message. The ink was the same, and the signatures as nearly identical as is ever possible in the handwriting of one individual. Harry Bonaparte, beyond all doubt, had signed the note.

Frost went out. At the doorway he paused to throw the switch. The eyes of the head continued to stare at him with an idiotic vacancy. The mouth gaped, as though drooling with the thought that suicide was suicide, and that not even Frost could change it to spell murder. The rest of the body had stopped its horrible twitching. The hands came to rest with the fingers curled against the base of the guillotine.

Frost plunged the room into darkness. He strode across the adjoining room, extinguished its light, and locked the door to the apartment.

Descending the stairs, he encountered no one. In the vestibule he plucked from his pockets one of his long, acrid cigarettes. He cupped his hands to light it. The glow flickered on hands of distinguished symmetry and grace, hands with slender, tapering fingers and almost feminine beauty. They were the hands of an artist. Unpredictable nature, in an errant mood, had bestowed upon Frost's gaunt and forbidding build that one attribute of perfection.

He hiked into the hot summer night, a swirl of aromatic smoke eddying behind him. Heat lightning had begun to flicker in the west, accompanied by the rumble of distant thunder. The lightning flared upon a colossal bank of black clouds that soared upward toward the zenith.

FROST got into his car. He briefly told Jean of the appalling scene he had left.

"Well, that ends it," she said, relaxing. "Since Bonaparte killed Partho, the police can't hold Hendiadis on any charge. Let's go home and call it a washout."

Frost retorted, "The mystery is deeper than ever. I tried to reach Partho in time to prevent his murder, but he was killed. I made all speed over here. The murderer struck again before my arrival. I am going to catch up with him before the night is over. Harry Bonaparte didn't commit suicide. He was slain."

Jean exclaimed, "But I thought you said he left a suicide note typed on his own machine and signed in his own script!"

"I stated that I found such a note. I did not assert that he left it. He did nothing of the kind. The note was not written until after his death."

"I don't understand you. A dead man can't write his signature. If the signature is genuine—"

"It is," Frost drawled. "Nor was it traced from a previous signature. The trick is so simple that it hasn't occurred to you. The slayer recently asked for the signature of Bonaparte, with the pretext of adding it to an autograph collection. The murderer killed Bonaparte tonight and typed an alleged suicide confession above the signature. He handled the paper by the edges, or used gloves, so that only Bonaparte's fingerprints will be found on it.

"The first murder took place at approximately nine thirty, the second a half hour later, at about ten o'clock or soon after. The protracted muscular spasms were unusual, but not rare. They normally cease a minute or two after death, and thus would indicate that he died just before my arrival on the scene. The decapitation actually occurred at least thirty minutes ago.

"Could Bonaparte have operated the machine to cause his own death?"

"Easily. It will be virtually impossible for the police to establish a suspicion of murder. Only under a microscope could it be proved that the ink of the signature had dried thoroughly, while the ink of the typing remained still damp. But that distinction would not be sufficient to brand the note spurious or to warrant a murder investigation."

Jean shivered again. The snake that crawled on her lap, the head crushed by a dinosaur skull, now the head cut off by a guillotine—Was the night to be one long procession of horrors?

"How did the murderer persuade Bonaparte to put his head in the guillotine? Did he first tie him up?"

"No. Bonaparte's wrists and ankles showed no marks of abrasion. The killer used a device that invariably leaves signs upon the body."

"You contradict yourself, don't you?"

"Not at all. The slayer merely flung a silk cord or noose around Bonaparte's neck and half strangled him. As soon as the victim became unconscious, the killer removed the rope and dragged the body to the guillotine. There he placed the neck with the marks made by the cord directly under the blade. The falling weight obliterated the signs of strangulation. The severed head lost its blood content, and all traces of congestion vanished before they had a chance to become fixed."

"Can't the police make the same findings?"

Frost shook his head. "That was not a finding. That was pure deduction based on the absence of clues. The police proceed on the basis of obtaining clues."

JEAN thought hard. "Hendiadis could have killed Partho. He couldn't have killed Bonaparte, because Hendiadis was with us a half hour ago."

"Correct," Frost approved. "If the murderer is working alone, Hendiadis can't be guilty. But if the murderer has an accomplice, then Hendiadis leads the suspects."

"Which is the truth?"

Frost said, "I want you to stop at Skeletons, Inc. Take a taxi. The superintendent in charge, Paul Luca, may be there yet. Buy a spider from him. Make it as difficult as you can. The point is to stay there and forestall another attempt at murder. If the office is closed, you will be too late. In that case, hold the taxi and wait till I come for you."

"Where will you be?" she demanded.

"At a gambling den," Frost drawled with an air of preoccupation.

His casual answer ruined her poise. "You go to a gambling hall in this emergency? You think it all right for me to chase after skeletons while you enjoy the night life?"

"Yes." His replay was a model of brevity.

Jean didn't quite know how she found herself on a street corner hailing a taxi. Frost had slowed his car; the door had sprung open, and she was clambering out. It happened so quickly that she couldn't decide whether she had gotten out of her own accord or with enthusiastic impetus from Frost.

She watched the professor speed toward the Great White Way.

"A pretty kettle of fish this is," she thought. "The nerve of him, abandoning me in such a neighborhood at way after eleven. Any gentleman would have sent me to a gambling den while *he* chivalrously went spanking after skeletons. But not you, Ivy, my goodness no. I bet there isn't a fig leaf worth of chivalry in the inhuman mechanism that buzzes where your heart and brain ought to be. Chivalry—poo!"

A cruising taxi spied a most enchanting young vision, who was alluringly curved and who waved an imperious hand. Notions about a lovely damsel in distress warmed the cockles of the cabby's soul. He swung his vehicle to the curb.

The lush dream of beauty and temptation floated inside. Jean Moray warbled, "Go to hell and back—meaning Skeletons, Inc., East River and Front Street."

Sadly disillusioned, the driver scowled as he stepped on the gas.

V.

THE BUILDING at which Jean Moray arrived had been near the center of industrial New York long ago. But the swift expansion of the city during the twentieth century had forced business centers to move northward. The district, about midway between the Battery and

Fourteenth Street, now presented an aspect of decay and grime, with numerous abandoned structures, forlorn with the deterioration of age.

Jean paid the driver, gave him a quarter tip, and told him to wait for five minutes.

The storm sweeping out of the west had pushed vast masses of low, black clouds overhead and toward the Atlantic Ocean. Thunder came in almost continual crashes. Gusts of wind had begun to blow fitfully. An electrical center accompanying the clouds split the sky with giant rivers of flame. But only a few scattered advance drops of rain had thus far spattered down.

Jean scampered across the sidewalk and reached the protection of a doorway. The decrepit building that housed Skeletons, Inc. occupied a half block and stood five stories high.

A metal plaque with a list of the tenants informed her that the business she sought roosted on the second floor. She saw a flight of rickety stairs. The entrance door was so wabbly that she believed she could have demolished it with a good push, but the effort proved unnecessary. She found the door unlocked. For that matter, it was difficult to see how the door could possibly be locked, with its rusty, broken, antiquated mechanism.

She walked in and climbed the creaky stars. One flight up she paused in front of another door, but saw neither a bell nor a knocker. Without more ado, she tried the doorknob with the full and pleasant expectation of proving the entrance locked.

Much to her dismay, the door opened. She made a mental note of interest: though the door swung easily upon well-oiled hinges, it had massive strength. Solid steel usually does.

But the ponderous door exerted only a brief hold upon her attention, for the dim light from outside shone upon the mounted skeleton of an ape squarely in front of her. The leering thing looked on the verge of leaping at her, and she drew back with an involuntary start.

An overhead bulb far inside the room cast a reassuring glow. She entered, letting the door click shut upon its hinges. A musty odor pervaded the air—the dry, dusty smell that attaches itself to rooms long-sealed, and particularly to museums that are not too well ventilated. She saw windows on one side of the room, but the grime of years covered them. Moreover, they faced the rear, and were separated from the wall of an adjacent building by only a few feet. Sunlight never had a chance to enter.

The entire floor had been turned into one vast room. It contained a horde of bones—a storehouse and display of skeletons that comprised the animal world. In cases, upon daises, on shelves, in corners, against the walls, and even hanging from the ceiling, skeletons crouched, ran, climbed, lay down, and pounced in every posture imaginable. There were tiny, delicate bones of rodents, the larger frames of forest carnivores, and one grinning, human skeleton whose bones had turned brown with age.

She had encroached upon a fantastic realm of the fleshless dead. She stood motionless for seconds in the grip of paralyzing impressions. She clearly heard her own pulse, but not a sound else, save the muted and far-away crescendo of thunder. Nothing moved; nothing lived among that array of bones.

"Hello!" she called.

Her voice quavered away into the distant corners with a hollow, ghostly emptiness that brought goose flesh.

No one answered her call. Her voice died out in low echoes.

She began threading her way down the aisles, past cases, and between rows of skeletons. Her skin crawled. The musty odor tickled her nostrils. She overcame a nervous inclination to sneeze. Her footsteps pattered softly, with a dry rustle as of little, fleshless creatures rattling across the floor.

"Hello!" she called again. But the grisly echoes that went away and mocked her affected her as badly as the silence.

No voice answered her from that cavernous den.

JEAN MORAY was thoroughly scared. She stood still, ready to dash out of the place and its mysterious desertion. Then she saw an ordinary worktable with tools, mounting equipment, and an array of loose bones. For some reason the sight steadied her. The mundane tools indicated that, to those who owned the business, it was conducted upon the same basis as any other commercial venture.

Her spirit felt better, but her qualms and queasiness persisted. All the reassurance possible, with a dozen friends around her, would never enable her to feel at ease among skeletons, one or ten thousand.

Jean walked to the workbench. She noticed a door some yards away from it. She found herself tiptoeing. The door stood slightly ajar, showing dim light from beyond it, and stairs going down.

"Hello!" she spoke a third time, and listened to unearthly echoes mutter off into the corners.

As before, no answer came, but she heard a patter of steps in the regions below. They slowly drew closer, till the door moved wide open. A white-haired, ruddy-faced wisp of a man, clad in a laboratory smock, entered. He wore thick-lensed glasses, behind which his blue eyes blinked. His mind seemed to be preoccupied with Elysian fields afar. He squinted at Jean, took his glasses off and polished them, put them back on, and squinted at Jean again. He appeared surprised to find that she hadn't vanished. Visitors evidently upset him.

"Are you in charge here?" asked Jean.

"Yes, I am. Here is my card." He fumbled under the smock, ransacking one pocket after another. "Dear me, where can I have left the cards? I really do keep them somewhere. Possibly I left them in my day coat. I must remember to look. At any rate, I am Paul Luca. May I be of service to you? I presume you came after something?" His voice carried a gentle, reedy quality, as though long association with skeletons had dried out his vocal cords.

"I'm interested in spiders—that is, if you happen to handle them. I'd like to get a good specimen."

The blue eyes brightened. "Spiders? Yes, we have several in stock. A very fine specimen arrived only yesterday. Would you care to examine it?"

"If it won't put you to too much trouble.

"Oh, not at all, it's always a pleasure."

He took the glasses off, gave them a flick with a handkerchief, and restored them to his nose. Jean Moray was still there. Since no amount of manipulation made the illusion of a highly tempting young woman disappear, she must be a reality.

Luca sighed, turned around, and leisurely retraced his path out the door and down the stairs.

The frail old man was gone for at least five minutes before he returned carrying a small cardboard box. Jean spent the interval growing more and more acutely conscious of all the skeletons.

VI.

LUCA placed his pasteboard on the table and pried the cover off with loving pains. "See, isn't it a beauty?" he asked.

Jean looked at the biggest and most horribly repulsive spider she ever wanted to see. It was a huge tarantula, its framework nestling on cotton.

"Y-yes, it's a beautiful specimen," Jean agreed, stepping back from the hideous thing.

"It's a perfect specimen. You can have it for only two dollars fifty."

"I'm afraid it isn't quite what I want," she temporized.

"Oh." He sounded a trifle disappointed by her lack of enthusiasm. "Well, I'll show you another."

He restored the lid and carried the box off with more tender solicitude than was ever shown by a mother for a favorite infant.

Four or five more minutes passed, while he remained in the regions below. Jean spent the period wondering what lay down there. She recalled that the windows of various small shops and offices lined the front of the ground floor. Probably they were shallow. Skeletons, Inc. no doubt needed space and more space for the storage of its ungainly goods, and had expanded to include the rear half of the ground floor.

At that stage of her musings he returned with another little box. He announced with less zest than before, "This one is shopworn. Oh, it's a good average specimen but it hasn't the fine points of the first. Still, it will give excellent service for ordinary purposes. I can let it go at a dollar."

Jean couldn't think of any purpose whatsoever for a tarantula. She ventured a jittery glance at the second specimen. It was smaller than the first, but equally loathsome. She couldn't even be bothered to look at it long enough to find out wherein it was shopworn.

"I'm sorry, but they both are much too large for what I had in mind," Jean trilled as sweetly as she could.

A note of disdain altered his previously amiable manner. "Oh, well," he piped huffily, "if all you want is just a common garden variety of spider, I can let you have one of those for twenty-five cents."

"I'm sure that will be satisfactory."

Again he trotted off on his trek to the nether regions, leaving Jean with a feeling of success, if not satisfaction. Frost had instructed her to kill time in order to forestall murder. She was doing well, with the unexpected coöperation of Luca.

She listened for the sound of his returning footsteps when five minutes had passed. She heard only the now continuous far rumble of thunder, muffled by the walls of the building. The fact impressed itself that sound from the outside world had to be of deafening proportions before it could penetrate the realm of the skeletons.

Minutes crawled by, but the frail little man did not come back. Jean grew restless. The animal bones gave her the creeps. She fidgeted. A cigarette, nervously lighted and smoked with haste, burned to a stub. She ground it out on the table top.

Ten minutes passed, fifteen, and still there came no sight or sound of Paul Luca. A hazy fear was forming in her mind, a grim suspicion that she hated to admit.

Frost had told her to be on guard against murder. *What if Paul Luca had been murdered while she was waiting for him to return?*

She tried to reassure herself, but the host of skeletons frayed her nerves. She decided that he must be rummaging among the supplies, or that he had absent-mindedly forgotten where to find other spiders.

FIVE MORE MINUTES infinite time in departing. She started a second cigarette, but it tasted sour. She extinguished it after a puff.

What if Paul Luca had been murdered?

The question took irresistible hold of her imagination. Any activity promised relief from the tense, harrowing wait amid hundreds of skeletons. She drew the automatic out of her purse. Her heart pounded so loudly that she couldn't hear the thunder.

She walked to the doorway and called down, "Hello!"

The words drifted off with hollow reverberations. They died out. She received no answer.

Jean Moray, forcing a nonchalance that she did not feel into her voice, announced to emptiness, "Hello! I can't wait any longer! Good-by!"

She slammed the door behind her. Standing at the top of the stairs, she listened to the echoes wander off. No reply broke the tomblike solitude.

Carefully, she removed her slippers. She took the steps going down upon noiseless feet.

At the bottom, she face an eerie stretch of corridors, lined by dark rooms with doors open, closed rooms, and occasional skeletons. A series of overhead lights illuminated the main corridor.

Jean Moray tiptoed on, till she came to one more flight of stairs leading down to the basement. The fountain-pen flashlight in her purse served to illuminate some of the dark rooms. She saw shelves laden with bundles, cases piled on floors, and filing drawers that carried scientific labels.

She needed time. Time was lacking to search them all. Impulse drew her downward. Her silk-clad soles trod the flooring without a whisper of sound. The automatic remained tight in her grasp.

Ages passed before she arrived at the basement. The hum of a motor became audible. She wondered uneasily why a heating plant should be operating in the summer.

A single electric bulb glowed in the basement. She noticed bins and storage compartments. Above all, she spied the door from behind which the hum originated.

Jean Moray hesitated on the threshold. Her impulse to flee had become overpowering, filled with fatal lure and dread. But she had not discovered a trace of the mysteriously missing Luca.

She gingerly opened the door.

It was like opening the gates of madness and hell. She saw a boiler. Hot flame roared under it. Hissing, steaming water filled the cauldron to its brim. On the surface floated a thing that might once have been human. Boiled eyes transfixed her with a gaze the essence of blind horror.

Jean Moray opened her mouth to shriek, but her voice snapped in her throat.

Pure terror sent her flying up the stairs. She took the first flight, raced down the corridor, and ran to the display room. She scooped up her slippers without stopping to put them on. Still in her stockinged feet, she darted between the mounted skeletons. Fleshless grins mocked her from all sides. Ghostly presences haunted the ominous silence. Her racing limbs beat a swift pitapat upon the floor.

She reached the massive steel door and tugged at it. It did not move. She pulled with all her strength.

The door was locked.

The light went out.

HORRIFYING BLACKNESS blanketed her. She stood rigid in

an agony of breathless suspense. She felt suffocated. Her heart hammered like a wild prisoner trying to escape. She waited, tense, straining, in the smothering darkness and oppressive solitude of a tomb. Then, with infinite slowness and care, she set her slippers down, laid her purse beside them. She kept only the fountain-pen flashlight. Her right hand still clenched the automatic.

Jean began to drift along the wall. Afraid to use the flashlight and thus betray her position, she felt for obstructions with her toes. She moved in the direction of the windows. Not even the faintest ray came through them. The gloom was Stygian, impenetrable, absolute.

As suddenly as it had gone out, the ceiling bulb flashed on again. Jean froze.

A robed and hooded figure stood by the windows. A gloved hand rested on a wall switch. The other hand held a pistol.

Jean fired. The hooded figure staggered. She had scored a direct hit, but it did no damage. Bulletproof clothing, she thought bitterly.

The light blinked out after that single instant of electrical tension. The hooded figure did not return her fire.

She went through a living nightmare, a terrifying game of hide and seek, played in darkness among skeletons, with intermittent flashes of radiance. She circled toward the second door, the only other exit. The hooded figure obviously would shoot if she got close to the windows. She fired twice more when the light came on for split seconds, both shots hitting, before she stopped wasting ammunition.

The last time that the light burned, it found her only a dozen feet from the second door. It did not seem possible that the hooded figure would let her escape in this weird game of cat and mouse. Darkness descended again. She dashed for the door, fully expecting to find it locked or to meet a fusillade of shots.

She fumbled in blackness. The door opened. She streaked through.

Frightened and bewildered, she used the flashlight now as she fled down the steps. She ran along the corridor. Behind her sounded the tread of following feet. She could not bring herself to go down into the basement where that awful thing bubbled in the cauldron.

The corridor ended at a door. She opened it and darted inside. She found herself trapped in an empty room without windows. In panic, she extinguished her light, waited with taut nerves beside the door. When it opened, she would smash her weapon on the hooded head.

Timeless, eternal seconds ticked by. She had an insane impulse to fall sound asleep and forget this waking nightmare. She heard no sound. Her finger tips, touching the edge of the door, felt no motion from it. The hair-trigger suspense exhausted her. The urge to relax grew stronger. A cold stream of air blew under the door and tickled her toes.

Suddenly suspicious, Jean tried the door. It would not open. Her fingers had lost their strength. How had the door been fastened? By electric control? Her thoughts became dazed. Her mind issued commands that her body would obey. Then her mind began sliding off upon waves of billowing darkness and nausea. Not air, but odorless gas, was pouring under the door.

She slumped to the floor as consciousness faded. Her lips formed a whisper, "Ivy!" that died out into oblivion.

VII.

AFTER letting Jean Moray out of his car, Frost stopped at the next drug store and entered a phone booth. He called the home of Inspector Frick, head of the police department's homicide bureau and a friend of long standing.

The inspector himself answered instantly. His crisp voice snapped back, "Make it fast, Ivy. I'm going out on a case that just turned up."

"Examine the wiring on the dinosaur," Frost drawled.

A startled oath burst from the inspector. "What the devil are you? A clairvoyant? How did you know that a dinosaur is connected with the murder? Don't tell me you've already been there!"

"Right! Where can I find Sammy Lekner?"

"The night-club owner and operator of a gambling syndicate? The current bad boy of crime? We've been raiding his places without luck so far. You'll get him in his private office over the Ivory Club, if you reach it before twelve. After that he's in his Park Avenue suite. Why?"

"Thanks. Here's another murder for you." Frost reported the guillotine slaying on Washington Square.

Inspector Frick exploded. "What! A guillotine death there? Who—" But the professor had hung up.

Frost returned to his car and drove swiftly to the midtown Fifties, where night clubs bloomed thicker and shadier than blueberries in a pie. Summer crowds thronged Broadway and the theater district almost as densely as at the height of the winter season. But the small top crust of society, which had all the money, went off to cooler places for the summer, leaving the hot spots stranded with meager business.

The hat-check girl at the Ivory Club, having little else to do, stared at Frost with great interest, even astonishment, when he hiked in. He presented an utterly incongruous appearance in those sybaritic and modernistic surroundings for wealthy pleasure seekers.

"Check your hat, sir?" she chimed from force of habit, which was indeed a silly request since Frost didn't wear a hat.

Ignoring her, the dining room, and the floor show, he went upstairs. A thickset plug-ugly standing in front of a door wore all the characteristics of a bodyguard.

"Whattaya want?" he growled.

"Sammy Lekner," Frost said curtly.

"He's busy. Got an appointment?"

"Come along and see." Frost threw the door open. The bodyguard, uncertain and awed by the professor's towering picture of determination, drew a gun and followed him.

OILY-FACED, smiling, Sammy Lekner sat at his desk. The smile froze when Frost barged in. A sallow-cheeked man with hot eyes, who had been sitting on the edge of the desk, got up. His hand hovered at an armpit holster.

"What the hell are you doing here? Who are you?" Lekner demanded.

"The name is I.V. Frost. I want the answer to a question."

"I haven't got any answers for any private dick. Scram!"

"You haven't heard the question."

"I'm not going to hear it. I don't care what it is. I don't give answers to private dicks. Now beat it before the boys get sore."

Frost walked over to the desk. The sallow man slid around behind him to join the plug-ugly. His voice cutting thin and sharp as a razor, Frost whipped out with, "Keep your bogiemen under control, because if they're dead they won't do you a bit of good. The question that I want answered is this: does the underworld have connections with a man who, for a price, absolutely guarantees to dispose of a corpse so that no trace of it will ever be found?"

Sammy Lekner snarled, "Joe! Mike! Shove this louse out of here!"

"Stick 'em up, tough guy!" rasped a voice behind the professor.

Frost's hands went shoulder-high in lackadaisical manner. He stated evenly to Lekner, "You haven't answered my question. Remember, I warned you that dead bodyguards are of no use to you."

Lekner ordered furiously, "Give him the rough treatment, boys."

"Turn around! Get those hands up!" barked the voice behind him.

Frost turned and stared with darkly glinting eyes at the automatics in the hands of the two killers.

"Get those hands up or I'll kill you!" threatened the sallow-faced trigger man.

Frost's right arm shot up to its full length. A bullet burned a hole through the upper right side of his leather jacket. It smashed into the sallow-faced man. He staggered back, hands clawing at his heart, kept on staggering back, and hit the wall. He slid down until he was sitting on the floor. His upper trunk folded over. He was dead.

"You dirty—" screeched the plug-ugly. His gun roared—an instant after Frost shifted his position and reached his left arm high. The wire inside his sleeve pulled the trigger of the other disk-shaped gun on his left chest. The bullet smote the killer, whose own shot furrowed the floor.

He tried to raise the weapon.

Frost's arms dropped. He flicked a pistol from a pocket of his jacket.

Lekner was streaking for a drawer in his desk. "Gino! Gino!" he bawled.

A STEEL SNOUT poked through a slit in the wall back of Lekner. A chatter started, and Frost, though jolted, took careful aim at the slit. He fired once. The spitting cough of the submachine gun silenced. A shrill screaming began, turned bubbly, and ended with a slow, choking gurgle. A heavy thud from behind Frost marked the passing of the plug-ugly. The gun beyond the slit in the wall fell with a crash.

Sammy Lekner had a gun halfway out of the desk.

"I wouldn't try it," Frost advised him.

The gambler, after, one venomous look at the pistol in Frost's hand, let the weapon drop.

Frost said, "If you hire another machine-gunner, tell him to aim for the head always. It's harder to hit than the body, but a safer play. A face can't flatten a slug. Bulletproof clothing can."

He flung a brief glance at the corpses behind him. "I told you that dead bodyguards would be of no further use to you," he murmured.

A mad glare burned in Sammy Lekner's eyes. "I'll remember this: your life has an X in it from now on, the X that marks the spot where they find a stiff."

Frost paid no attention to the threat. His voice turned harsher. "I asked you a question. I want the answer—immediately."

Sammy Lekner said balefully, "O. K. You're dealing. There is a guy that gets rid of bodies. Remember a certain judge that disappeared a couple of years ago? He stopped some lead because he wouldn't make good on an I O U for fifty grand. But the murder would have made the city too hot for the parties that bumped him off. So they paid this guy two and a half grand to get rid of the corpse. That's his regular price. He's used whenever a ride victim is big enough so that the cops would blow the lid off the town. No corpse, no snooping cops. It's a cinch.

"That's all. There isn't any more. Ask me who he is—I'll tell you the answer. I don't know. I've never seen the guy. It's a long story. What it boils down to is that he contacted a certain bigshot three-four years ago by phone. He said he would get rid of inconvenient corpses. He said the next time a welcher went on a ride, we should put the body in a trunk with the two and a half grand, send it to a storage warehouse, and mail the ticket receipt to a post office general-delivery box.

"The people finally tried it. But they wrote down the number of the receipt before they mailed it. They called the warehouse a couple of days later. The trunk was gone. That's the way it worked. No questions asked; everybody satisfied.

"What the guy does with the stiffs, nobody gives a damn. Who he is, nobody cares—or knows. None of the stiffs ever turned up later, so the cops couldn't nail any charges, and the missingpersons bureau is still looking for some gents that ain't."

Frost said, "A good answer," and vacated the premises.

Outside, he saw no sign of disturbance. The noise of the gun play had not penetrated through the thick walls of Lekner's office.

When he reached the street, Frost found a deluge of rain whipping across the pavements. He dashed inside his car and drove toward the lower East side.

MIDNIGHT had nearly arrived by the time he reached the dark, antiquated building that housed Skeletons, Inc.

Parking the car, he selected a few items from the extra equipment that he had ordered installed when the machine was built. He did not, however, move toward the building entrance.

Instead, he slipped into a narrow alley that ran alongside the structure in the middle of the block. The rain poured down on his head and face. He went through a gateway. The alley made a right turn. It became a dead end behind the building, with just room enough for a car to back around in.

There were no windows on the ground floor. A steel door offered the only entrance. Frost took the oddly shaped tool that he had used once before that evening and attacked the lock. A minute went by before the mechanism yielded. Frost opened the door with extreme precaution, until the aperture barely sufficed to put an arm through. He flashed a quick light on the inside of the door.

A small, round mirror was imbedded in the steel.

Frost brought forth a pocket mirror larger than the one in the door. He held it in front of the imbedded mirror, opened the door wide, entered, and closed it. Then, with the same extreme care, he lowered the mirror.

The glass in the door served as reflector for an infra-red beam of invisible light. Opening the door would swing the mirror out of alignment, break the circuit, and sound an alarm. By holding a pocket mirror steady when he entered, Frost had kept the reflector and the circuit in uninterrupted working order.

There were other cells inside, all placed high enough so that rats and dogs would not set them off. Frost knelt. The faint trace of a sardonic smile on his lips, he made his way under the beams of dark light.

Using the same technique, he entered a storeroom that attracted his attention.

Seven grinning human skeletons lined the walls, each skeleton jointed and mounted. With a fine disregard of his macabre subjects, Frost examined the bones.

VIII.

FULL CONSCIOUSNESS returned to Jean Moray with an abruptness that made her blink her eyes at the smooth expanse broken by a globe opposite her. It took a second to realize that she was lying on her back, looking at the ceiling.

She heard movement near by, and the low hum of a motor. The mechanism, apparently in the next room, brought her a shuddering recollection of the cauldron and its contents.

She reached out an arm, but the arm wouldn't reach. She tried to get up, and found she couldn't.

Her wrists and ankles were tied. The surface on which she lay felt cold, metallic. A wave of horror swept through her as she realized that she was stretched on an object more like an operating table than anything else.

All her clothing had been removed. A sheet covered her nearly to her chin.

The hooded figure stood with back toward her, busy at a task that she could not fathom. She was experimentally testing her bonds when the figure turned around before she could shut her eyes. She now recognized a small electric furnace as the mechanism that had riveted his attention. Her clothing, including the slippers, lay in a little heap beside the furnace.

"Ah, so you have wakened, my dear?" came a gentle, dreamy voice.

"Luca!" cried Jean.

The hooded figure made a slight bow. "You will excuse the liberty, I am sure. I became suspicious about the innocence of such a beautiful young creature as you coming out in a storm to purchase a spider. I had work to do. I gave you a chance to go away. I hoped you would when I took so long to find the spiders. But you stayed on. The third time I came down here and watched your movements."

"Watched my movements!"

"Of course. There are a number of photo-electric cells distributed around. Every time you intercepted a beam, you broke the circuit, and a warning flashed on the diagram board over in the corner. You can see it if you crane your neck. I charted your course to the boiler room, before locking the outer door by electric control. The carbon monoxide then made you amenable. It is one of many useful supplies that have accumulated during my years of work. I could have shot you, but a shattered bone ruins the value, the perfection, and the innocence of a skeleton.

"Your purse yielded me your name, Miss Moray, and the fact that you are regrettably employed by a detective person who calls himself Professor I.V. Frost. Now that you have learned too much, I must add you to my collection of skeletons, I am sorry to say. It is a great pity for one so lovely to die so young."

"You can't do it!" Jean cried desperately.

"Why not, pray?"

"Frost won't let you! You'll be killed before you succeed!"

The hooded man protested, "Oh, I think not. You see, Frost cannot enter without my knowledge. No one can enter without breaking the circuit of the photo-electric cells.

"My dear child, you interrupted me at a most unfortunate time. Tonight I am reducing a corpse that a gentleman with a police record paid me to dispose of. When the body is ready, the flesh will be stripped from the bones and incinerated. Then I pulverize the bones of a legitimate skeleton from our stock, burn the powder in the electric furnace, and substitute the new skeleton in place of the old. Thus vanishes a body.

"I was about to begin the preliminary work of destroying all material evidence with regard to you. Would you like to watch the process?"

THE QUESTION was purely rhetorical. Not waiting for any answer, he walked back to the electric furnace.

"See!" he called, lifting her sheer hose—two dollars and ninety-five cents a pair, mourned Jean—and tossing them into the white-hot heart of the furnace, after rolling them up into a ball. The heat turned them to a cinder, to nothingness, in a moment's flash.

"And now these filmy things, then the dress"—ninety-eight dollars and fifty cents, Jean mentally wailed, gone in a quick, devouring flame—"and the slippers." They took longer, but mere seconds of that infernal heat turned them to carbon, to a puff of sparks.

Luca sighed. "What lovely flames they make, garments so fragile and shoes so fine. Now watch the more durable evidence melt away."

He tossed her initialed belt into the furnace. The suede burned; the clasp turned to a restless pellet of molten metal.

"Lost, one purse, in the fires of eternity," murmured the hooded figure, flinging Jean's hand bag to the incandescent field. It shriveled and passed. Compact, lipstick, mirror, coins, keys, the metal hinges, all hissed and bubbled as they degenerated to swell the dancing pellet.

"A pity," Luca commented. Her platinum wrist watch set with diamonds, the gift of a would-be Don Juan who never saw her again after sending that expensive bribe, crackled into the avid maw. The glass shattered; the strap carbonized; the case and works glowed, fusing with the molten metal globule.

"Last of all, the source of light, the dealer of death." Into the dazzling core sailed Jean's flashlight, followed by her automatic. The pistol resisted the longest of all the items, but it too reddened, turned soft, and finally liquefied.

The hooded figure chanted, like the high priest of a forbidden ritual ceremony. "Thus perish the garments you wore, even as life is consumed from the flesh. All the trinkets of betraying metal are welded into one anonymous lump. The identifying evidence is utterly destroyed."

Jean, twisting upon the table, made this her opportunity. She raised her bound wrists to her head, fumbled in her soft wealth of hair, and shoved her hands back under the sheet. The action took a few seconds while Luca faced the furnace.

Her hands grasped a thin, sharp blade, in a tiny case, that she wore concealed in her hair for an emergency like this. Frost had originally suggested the idea to her.

Luca watched the radiant fire. Jean awkwardly manipulated the blade, cut a finger, and winced. Then forefinger and thumb pressed the blade's edge against the cord. She felt it part.

The hooded figure turned around and moved nearer. "It is useless to struggle. Your death will be quick and painless, for I want a perfect skeleton as long as the job must be done. I may even give you a choice. Would you rather have pure carbon-monoxide gas? Or prussic acid? Or ten grains of morphine? Or perhaps—" His voice ceased abruptly. He was staring at the sheet.

A red stain had made its appearance from the cut on Jean's finger.

The sheet billowed up. He tried to dodge, but she flung the cloth over the hooded figure, at the same time shoving him violently. He lurched backward against the electric furnace. The smell of burning cloth rose.

Jean almost made it. She seized the blade, slashed the cord at her ankles, and sprang from the table.

A gun appeared in the hooded man's hand at the same moment that he bounded forward from the furnace, sweeping the sheet aside.

"That was a most dexterous move. My congratulations," he stated, a quiver in his voice.

Jean stopped dead still, sick with frustration, the blue ring of doom pointed squarely at her.

The voice continued, "I am afraid that I can take no more chances. You are altogether too reluctant, obstinate, and perverse. Much as I would like a perfect skeleton, I must forget my wishes for the sake of safety. I regret that I am compelled to shoot you."

IX.

"HOLD IT!" snapped a cold, menacing voice from behind Jean Moray.

A dozen instantaneous impressions crowded her mind. The hooded figure took aim; the door sprang open; an explosion from Frost's weapon beat the hooded figure's shot by a tick of time, the blast from Luca's gun sounding like an echo. The pistol spurted out of his hand, his wrist shattered by Frost's accurate aim. The bullet intended for Jean Moray spanged shrilly into the metal table.

"That's better," Frost drawled. To the ineffable delight of Jean, his face acquired a slightly rosier hue as his glance caught her.

"Dear me, you have an astonishing predilection for losing your clothing."

Jean snatched the sheet and wrapped it around her without too great haste.

The hooded figure irritably demanded, "I wish both of you would go away."

"We will," Frost promised, "after delivering you to safe-keeping in the hands of the efficient police."

"Oh, come, the police have no case against me. They can't do much simply because I prepare skeletons."

"True. And they will have a difficult task if they try to convict you for the murders of Partho and Bonaparte."

Luca snapped, "Are they dead? I can't say that I'm sorry, but the police can't prove anything against me. Why should I try to kill them?"

Frost said, "Several years ago you began disposing of bodies slain by gangster bullets. You dealt with Sammy Lekner, if not others. You did so for several reasons: profit, which amounted to a neat sum at two thousand five hundred dollars per corpse; a sort of perverse pleasure in exercising your ingenuity—the same satisfaction that a skilled craftsman or artist derives from his work; and a vicarious thrill from breaking the laws of society with impunity.

"Whether Partho, Hendiadis, or Bonaparte became suspicious of your midnight activity is beside the point. You determined to put them out of the way, partly because you wanted more complete freedom of action, and partly because you wanted sole ownership of Skeletons, Inc."

The hooded man declared, "That's ridiculous. I don't possess even a part ownership."

FROST WENT ON, "You sent a green mamba to Partho and fixed a pistol in a drawer hoping that Hendiadis would kill himself. You had free access to their home because you had known them for so many years. Both plans failed. To-night you telephoned to get the housekeeper out of the way, and went there to murder the two men. You found only Partho; but that was a lucky break from your standpoint. You killed him, then visited Bonaparte, slew him, and typed a false confession above a signature that you had previously obtained.

"You expected the police to take the suicide message at face value, or to accuse Hendiadis. Either way worked to your advantage. If the police built a case against Hendiadis, you would remain in possession of the business; and if the police let him go, you would kill him at a later time."

"Why?" Luca demanded.

"Because they owned Skeletons, Inc., but had no immediate heirs. With them out of the way, the business would be entirely yours simply by default. There wasn't any one to claim it."

"That's all very interesting as pure theory or deduction, but prove it."

Frost answered with a crooked smile, "I have no intention of proving it."

"Then I insist that you leave these premises."

Frost drawled, "The electric chair would be a quick, definite end that wouldn't dismay a mind of your type. Therefore, I will follow a different course. You will be charged with lesser crimes, including assault upon Miss Moray with a deadly weapon and intent to kill. You will go to Sing Sing for twenty-five to fifty years. Neither death nor freedom will be yours. You will spend the rest of your natural life brooding over your failure. You will spend it in confinement, with absolutely no control over you own existence, except prison regulations.

"That is the punishment which will—"

A flurry of movement suddenly shook the hooded figure. His uninjured arm darted to a pocket. It flashed up under the hood, and Jean distinctly heard the crunch of teeth upon a pellet.

Violent contortions seized the figure. Jean shuddered, turning her eyes away. It took Paul Luca a full minute to die.

Frost shrugged. "It was the best way out for him. His mind couldn't tolerate the prospect of a living death in prison walls. He could flirt with the electric chair, or get away scot-free with murder, but he couldn't bear the thought of the middle way—long years of punishment for minor crimes."

The professor's gaze shifted from the dead man. As he looked at Jean Moray, she thought she saw a fleeting smile.

"What are you laughing at?" she asked.

"I'm not laughing. I am a trifle amused by an idea that has occurred to me." His glance fell upon her lower limbs. "A hood and robe can make a sinister impression. So also can a sheet have a ghostly effect—but not when it is accompanied by ten pink toes."

ELECTRIC DEVILS

Ivy Frost drawled, "I arrived several minutes ago—but I waited until—"

I.V. FROST'S black eyes studied the visitor in a moment's glance that encompassed all details of her physical appearance. She wore very little make-up. Her black hair, coiled low at the nape of her neck, needed attention. She seemed to be a plain, unobtrusive woman who would never attract notice in a crowd or alone. Rita Merril—the name she had given—was carelessly dressed, too carelessly, for, with a little pains, she possessed the figure, features, and coloring to make a striking brunette beauty. Any average woman would have capitalized on those natural gifts.

Her listless, brown eyes looked back at Frost. She said indifferently, "Kyle Oberon wants to see you. I don't think it's anything you'll care to waste time on, but he's been so persistent I thought I'd better talk to you and get it over with."

"Who is Kyle Oberon?"

"A—a friend." She hesitated. "He used to be an engineer or something at the Marvelight Laboratory, busy with electricity and atoms. I don't know much about those things."

Frost suddenly sat up. A glint came into his eyes, which had previously been as lusterless as his visitor's. He took a long, specially made cigarette from a container at his elbow, lighted it, and exhaled a stream of acrid smoke. "The Marvelight Laboratory—that's the private workshop of the inventor and physicist Thomas Nicholas Thaddeus Hill, generally referred to as T.N.T. Hill."

"I believe so," said Rita vaguely. "Kyle used to mention him, but I never met him, and I've never been to the laboratory."

Frost prompted her, "You say Kyle Oberon used to be an engineer at the Marvelight Laboratory. Where is he now?"

"He's—" again she hesitated—"he's been in the State Hospital For

Mental Diseases the past few months. There was a bad accident after he lost his job. It affected his mind. He keeps raving about the blue devil and demands your help."

Every trace of boredom vanished from the professor. His face in profile looked vulpine, and his gaunt figure suggested a bird of prey about to swoop as he urged the woman on. "Suppose you start at the beginning. How long was Kyle Oberon employed at the Marvelight Laboratory? Why did he receive his dismissal and when?"

"I don't know when he first went there to work, but at the time I met him, about a year ago, he had the same position at the laboratory. I took it for granted he held an important place with a steady future. Though it's a small shop, you know, privately owned by Hill, and a staff limited to only a few assistants. Anyway, that isn't very important.

"I guess Hill just decided to cut down expenses five or six months ago. Kyle received a month's salary. He took the blow hard. I don't think the money mattered, but his work absorbed him. He hated to leave. He started brooding. One night he went out and didn't come back. The next day he was found lying outside of the fence that surrounds the Marvelight Laboratory. I forgot to tell you that it is in a secluded spot, entirely closed off by electrified barbed wire. Kyle had apparently tried to cut the wire to get inside. He received a severe shock and burns. He was unconscious when they found him. They took him raving to a hospital. He never became himself again, but tried constantly to escape, alternately yelling about a blue devil and imploring them to call you."

"Why did he pick my name?"

"He happened to read about your work on some case or other in a paper one time. I remember he remarked then that you'd be a good person to know if he ever got in a jam. It seems to have stuck in his mind even if he's not—what you'd call sane."

Frost asked, "Have you any idea what he means by this blue devil?"

She shook her head. "As far as I can make out, it's just the result of an electric shock. I suppose there was a big blue flash when it happened. His twisted mind has built it up into a blue devil. I see him once a week. I try to avoid the subject, but there's no avoiding it."

FROST SAID with an odd inflection, "It appears to be such a simple case of personal misfortune and accident that there is nothing to investigate."

"That's what I think," Rita Merril agreed. "There hasn't been a crime committed, or a murder. I don't see what good a detective can do."

Frost crushed the stub of his cigarette in a tray. "Did you ever hear of the Electric Devil?"

"No. What's that?"

"It's a mechanical robot devised by T.N.T. Hill several years ago. He displayed it at the meeting of one of the scientific academies. It operates by both radio remote control and electricity. The newsmen nicknamed it the Electric Devil because of its weird appearance and the variety of functions that it could perform in an almost human manner."

Rita murmured, "It's strange that Kyle didn't mention it to me."

"He may never have seen it. Hill hasn't put it on public display since that one occasion. I mention it because it was made of a bluish metal, stood about seven feet high, and might just as well have been called a blue devil as an Electric Devil."

"Oh." She frowned. "Then it's possible that Kyle might have seen it, and when he got the shock it so deranged him that he's all confused."

Frost shrugged noncommittally. "We're going to visit Kyle Oberon."

A faint spark of surprise or hope came into Rita Merril's eyes. "I hadn't made arrangements but I suppose we could see him to-day. I did this more or less as a matter of course, you know. I really hadn't expected you to show much interest."

"It's hardly a police matter," Frost agreed. "However, it gives me an opportunity to make the acquaintance of T.N.T. Hill, who is a legendary figure and so shy that few people have ever seen him. He was scheduled to address another scientific convention a month ago but sent a paper to be read *in absentia*.

"Just think of it, there is a man who is a wizard, a genius—at atomic physics, electricity and radio—with a score of inventions and discoveries to his credit, yet who has probably not even been seen by more than a half dozen persons in the last half dozen years. When he presented his Electric Devil, much discussion rose as to its potential value in war-time, but so far as is known, he did nothing more with it, and retired it to obscurity.

"His recent paper read to the Society of Electrical Engineers concerned the wireless transmission of electrical energy. It's a problem that many inventors have tried to solve because a huge fortune awaits the successful. If power could be broadcast like radio, if homes could be lighted by electricity flowing without wires from central transmitting stations, the whole vast, cumbersome system of wires, poles, conduits, cables, high-tension lines, and so on could all be done away with. The cost of electric power would fall; consumption would multiply, and a new industrial revolution would be launched."

RITA MERRIL looked perplexed. "I suppose so, but I didn't come to see you about Hill. I'm worried about Kyle Oberon, in the hospital."

Frost drawled. "I'm afraid my scientific curiosity and enthusiasm got the better of me. As you say, there's probably nothing that can be done for Oberon aside from the expert care of psychiatrists, but the case offers me an unparalleled opportunity for firsthand knowledge of a genius who is more than likely to stimulate my imagination. I'll talk to Oberon to satisfy him and you. If you don't mind waiting a few moments longer, I'll phone the hospital first."

He picked up the telephone at his elbow and asked for long distance.

Frost insisted on speaking to the superintendent in charge. The conversation lasted for only a minute, and from the professor's end was limited chiefly to one-word questions.

Frost replaced the receiver. He stated with expressionless features, "Kyle Oberon escaped from the State Hospital For Mental Diseases last night."

Rita Merril's eyes bulged. "What! How could he? He was in the dangerous ward with iron-barred windows!"

"He may be insane, but he engineered a remarkably ingenious coup. Somehow he stole or ripped out a section of electric cord. He rigged up an auxiliary circuit after removing the light bulb in his room. He called to a guard that his light bulb had burned out. The guard came over to investigate, put his hands on the bars of the door, and got an electric jolt that knocked him out. Oberon broke the circuit by pulling the wires loose with a handkerchief, took the guard's keys, and made his escape."

"Have they caught him?"

"Not yet. The alarm is out. He had but a few minutes' start, yet vanished in the darkness outside."

"What will I do now?" Rita Merril gestured helplessly. "What can we do until—"

"Go home. Wait for Kyle Oberon."

"Do you think he'll come there?"

Frost snapped, "He may find his way here. I'll notify you if he does. It's more likely that he will strike out for his home. Leave me your address."

She wrote a number down. "You'll really talk to him when you can?"

"Of course. But there is nothing to be done until some trace of him is found."

Rita Merril departed in the thoroughly listless manner of one who had no idea of destination in mind.

II.

THE MOMENT she was gone, Frost's air of impatience dropped away. He hiked back through the reception room and into his own private laboratory.

Jean Moray looked at him with questioning eyes. She had been out of sight there during the interview. She had just turned off the dictograph that recorded the conversation.

"You don't want me to trail the Merril woman?" she asked expectantly.

"No. That's what she half expects. She'll be off guard if she assumes that we accepted her story at face value."

"I didn't get a look at her," Jean reminded him. "I was only here listening. Is it a case worth your trouble?"

Frost drawled, "More than that. It's worth our lives."

A cloudy look entered Jean's gray-green eyes. She stared at him levelly, the curve of her languorous mouth unsmiling. "It didn't sound dangerous to me."

"It is. That woman was dressed for a part. She dressed too perfectly: hair loose, complexion undone, clothing awry, manner uncertain—yet she could be a lovely thing if she wanted to."

"You're very observant of feminine habits."

"They interest me only when deception enters. Rita Merril didn't want us to investigate Kyle Oberon. She hoped I would be so little interested that I would refuse the case. She knew before she came that Oberon had escaped. She hopes that if he makes his way here we'll pay scant attention to him. She did her best to stifle curiosity. She wanted to head us off."

"Then why did she come?"

"For the obvious reason that Oberon does want our help and is trying to reach us. He won't. He will be killed beforehand. But she—and they—were anticipating all possibilities. Furthermore, since she made it appear that hasty action was unnecessary, haste must be absolutely imperative."

"What do you mean by 'they'?" Jean asked.

"We're facing one of our hardest ventures," Frost answered obliquely. "T.N.T. Hill is dead, murdered. That's one mystery we must solve."

"Hill dead! Why I heard you say that a paper of his was presented to some scientific meeting only a month ago! You wanted to meet him. That's why the case appealed to you."

"So I told her," he admitted. "A paper of his was read in his absence. He probably prepared it months before but he didn't read it because he couldn't. I would have liked to meet him, and I may still do so, for it is sometimes profitable to make the acquaintance of dead men. The intricate, difficult pattern of a crime and of murder that may affect the course of history can be deduced from her story by logic alone."

Jean looked incredulous. "How?"

FROST ORDERED, "Call the State Hospital at Rocklyn again. Find out who signed the commitment papers for Oberon. If the address checks with the address left by Rita Merril, go there. By fast driving you should be able to arrive before she returns. The address she wrote down is Pelton, an up-State hamlet on the west side of the Hudson. Hill's Marvelight Laboratory lies several miles outside of Pelton, while the State Hospital at Rocklyn is about twenty miles east.

"Oberon may still be trudging his way from the hospital toward his home in Pelton. The house will be watched so long as he eludes capture or death. If the rest of the band found him and killed him while Rita was on her way here, the house probably won't be watched. Be wary, try to get inside the house. Watch Rita, and if she tries to leave stop her by any means possible."

"How can I get in touch with you if necessary?"

"I'll be in Pelton shortly after you. I'll locate you when the time comes. Before then I'll attend to several other items, including the tractor."

Jean frowned. "What tractor?"

"The new high-powered tractor that I'm going to buy," said Frost impatiently. "I also want our old friend Pete Ransome, the burly truck driver, to operate the tractor if its available."

"What on earth do you want a tractor for?" Jean exclaimed. "Are you going in for farm implements and the agricultural life?"

"A tractor is useful for other purposes than cultivating fields. It can serve well in connection with things above the ground," Frost gave a cryptic answer.

He strode out of the laboratory, an eddy of aromatic fumes beclouding his wake.

Jean Moray called the State Hospital For Mental Diseases. She learned that the commitment papers for Kyle Oberon had been signed by R. M. Oberon, who claimed to be his wife. R. M. could stand for Rita Merril. The address tallied with the address the woman had given Frost.

Jean divested herself of the smock. She got her coupé out and headed for the George Washington Bridge.

III.

IT WAS past noon when Jean reached Pelton, a mere cluster of old colonial mansions and farmsteads nestling in a valley whose encircling hills stood dark and thickly forested.

She did not care to arouse curiosity by asking directions in so small a community. Rita Merril might have arrived ahead of her, though Jean thought not. Many miles back she had passed a sedan speeding over fifty, whose single occupant, the woman driver, fitted the description that Frost had given her.

But it was unnecessary to ask questions. Pelton consisted of a few stores and houses strung along the main street, with three dirt cross roads that wound off toward the hills. On one of these a rusty tin arrow pointed, with the words "Marvelight Laboratory."

Jean passed by, took the third road.

More than a mile out of town she came to the Oberon tract: a white manor house perched upon a knoll, surrounded by woods and fields. A small orchard of crab-apple trees separated the house from the road and almost entirely concealed it. Jean drove on to the next bend in the road and parked her car in a side lane that evidently led to some farmer's pastures.

She walked back and followed the edge of the crab-apple orchard until she had a clear view of the house. It looked deserted, with all doors and windows shut.

Jean found a screen door at the rear hooked from the inside. With the butt of her automatic she poked a hole in the screen large enough to reach through and lift the hook. The inside door was unlocked. Jean smoothed the torn screen as best she could, fastened the hook again, and entered.

Utter silence prevailed. She listened intently, but caught only the rustle of leaves and the buzz of a fly.

She drifted through the rooms on the first and second stories, but discovered nothing to arouse suspicion. Returning to the kitchen, where she had originally entered, she suddenly heard the crunch of tires on the driveway alongside the house. The car stopped; a door slammed, and footsteps pattered up the back porch.

Jean sprang for a door that evidently led to a cellar. She barely got it closed behind her before she remembered that the screen door was locked. Some one rattled the door, muttered an angry "Damn!" and went around to the front of the house.

Jean had descended all the way to the cellar before footsteps sounded on the floor overhead. She found a long workroom that occupied the entire rear half of the cellar. A small window at ground level admitted enough light for her to see condensers, coils, rheostats, generators, and a host of other electrical equipment.

The footsteps started hurrying down the cellar stairs. Jean opened the door of a big steel locker, discovered old clothes inside, and promptly took her place among them. She had a fairly clear view through the ventilation slits.

INTO THE ROOM ran Rita Merril. She hastened to a table, flung a switch, and lifted the receiver of a telephone. Jean made a mental note of it: a private, direct wire that had no connection with any central operator or national system. Calls could never be checked or traced on this line.

The woman's voice rose, quick, breathless, "Pietru? I just got back. . . . What's that? You got Oberon? . . . Dead. . . . Well, that's a relief, though it's a rotten break it couldn't have happened sooner. I've wasted about six hours burning up the roads to New York. . . . Yes, I saw Frost and threw him off. He nearly yawned with boredom. No one tailed me, and we'll have the rest of the day, at least, free to finish up. . . . No, damn the luck, he turned out to know too much! He's smart, all right, and up to date on his physics. He's more anxious a meet Hill than to talk to Oberon. . . . I'm afraid he'll be out sooner or later. If we aren't finished, you'd better be ready to send him to whatever hell Hill and Oberon are wandering through. . . . Are you ready for another test? . . . Good. It's almost ten minutes to three now. Make it exactly at three o'clock. I'll be ready."

She hung up and hurried to a far corner of the room out of Jean's sight. Jean became uncomfortably warm in her crowded locker, but the ventilation grooves provided plenty of air.

Ten minutes went by before Rita again appeared. Then Jean almost gave vent to an audible gasp, for a marvelous transformation had altered the plain woman whom Frost had interviewed. Now she presented a radiant and perilous beauty, a bizarre, exotic splendor, weird, like a visitor from another planet.

Rita Merril had stripped, and donned a skin-tight, leaden-hued fabric or foil that sheathed her from head to foot. The concealment of fingers and toes gave her limbs a froglike appearance, intensified by the goggles she wore and the smooth covering that hid her mouth, ears, and hair, so that her head lost its distinctively human and feminine attributes.

Her body moved like molten, bluish metal. She seemed to flow with a liquid motion toward a small dais that stood apart from the rest of the room. Upon the dais rested a mechanism with tripod, pointer and rheostat. No wires led to the machine. It reposed upon the wooden basis with no connection to anything else. A series of upright metallic rods fringed the opposite side of the dais.

Rita Merril's lithe figure moved between the tripod and the vertical rods. She stood tense, expectant, her eyes fixed upon a wall clock. The minute hand crept up, and the hour of three chimed.

A vibrant thrill visibly shook her body. Then she stood as motionless as a statue.

A low hum rose from the machine, a drone that turned into a crackle, into light that sparked and danced at the tip of the pointer. With a sudden swift movement, Rita flashed a hand out and adjusted a dial as though tuning in a radio station.

The drone intensified. Blinding tongues and forks of flame roared from the pointer, leaping farther and farther toward the upright rods. The roaring became shattering thunder, until a steady flow of lightning flashes arced from the tripod to the rods. Dazzling rings ran the length of the rods. The rods turned red, white with infernal heat. In the center of play of those terrific energies, Rita Merril became a silvery devil goddess of light, for the electric torrent bathed her, hurled its bolts and flaming sheets around her, but left her untouched.

In one final burst of incandescent fury, the upright rods melted down into white-hot puddles; the machine and tripod collapsed with a red shower; the shrieking storm of power died away.

An after roaring deafened Jean's ears. Her eyes ached from the effect of that intolerable glare. She stared with awe at the blue-gleaming figure of the woman who should have been utterly consumed by fires of hell—and Rita Merril stepped down, proud, triumphant mistress over the lightning flashes!

SHE RAN to the telephone, stripping the metallic hood away from her head as she ran. Her ebony-black hair tumbled out in disorder, while her eyes shone with a fever of excitement. She lifted the receiver. Her voice rushed the words out in such frantic haste that they were almost unintelligible. "Pietru! You've done it! You've done it! We've won! I set the control at a three-foot range. I've never seen such perfect, awful hell! The rods melted; the machine blew up; you could have wiped out the whole house if I hadn't limited the range! And it didn't touch me! I haven't even got a blister! The suit is one-hundred-per-cent protection, but everything metallic in range goes blazing down to death! Pietru, we can equip our army with those suits and they'll never be touched! We can flood the enemy with an electric tidal wave and their guns, ammunition, barbed wire, men, everything with a scrap of metal will go roaring into oblivion!" Her voice broke off abruptly.

When she spoke again her excitement had cooled and her words had a more humble tone. "I'm sorry, Pietru. The fever of success swept me away. But don't worry, no one overheard; no one could possibly have listened in on a word of it. . . . All right, I'll be over as fast as I can make it—in about twenty minutes, after I change my things."

Rita hung up the receiver. Jean pushed the locker door wide and stepped out, automatic in hand. Rita whirled at the faint sound of Jean's soles touching the floor.

"Keep those hands high!" warned Jean in a tone ominous for all its silkiness.

The blue-sheathed arms rose to obey. For a moment an expression of almost silly befuddlement fleeted across the woman's face. Then it was gone, and she coolly returned Jean's gaze with a touch of supercilious disdain. "Would it be too much to ask the meaning of this ridiculous and melodramatic performance?"

Jean stepped forward. "Turn around and keep your arms up."

Rita started to swing. A glint in her eyes warned Jean—but not soon enough. A heavy tread came from the entrance to the room.

"Drop that gun or take it!" snarled a guttural voice.

Jean suppressed her inclination to fire. She might drop Rita, but she, in turn, would be a victim of the gunman. Inwardly boiling over the way in which the tables had been turned, Jean let her automatic fall.

The man sidled toward Rita. A short, thickset individual with Slavic features and a twisted ear, he reminded her of a toad.

"Who's that?" he demanded of Rita, jabbing a thumb toward Jean.

"I never saw her before."

"Got any idea who she is?"

The ecstatic glow had long died out of Rita's face. Now it became cruel with an evil, poisonous beauty. "The only person she could be is the assistant of that miserable scarecrow of a detective, Frost. I remembered Oberon raving that Frost had a good-looking assistant. *Pfaugh!* Frost's choice of an assistant seems to be about on a par with his alleged skill as a detective."

"O. K. Should we run her over to Pietru?"

Rita Merril's scornful answer dripped acid. "Why should we put him to the annoyance? She played a game. She knows the end. This house is going to be destroyed anyway. The corpse will be unrecognizable. Horvack, you are renowned for the accuracy of your shooting. Well then, fire!"

With no sign of emotion, the squat man raised his pistol a fraction of an inch and squeezed the trigger. To the accompaniment of a sullen explosion, a gout of orange flame spurted from the blue orifice.

IV.

FOR SEVERAL MINUTES after Jean Moray had driven away from the mansion at 13 State Street, Professor I.V. Frost busied himself making telephone calls. Then he dashed into his laboratory, collected several items, and stowed them in his specially built automobile.

The long, powerful car nosed toward the west-side highway. Frost headed downtown and crossed over to Jersey through the Holland Tunnel. Another twenty minutes of hard driving brought him to the hangar that housed his huge plane, the *If.*

Three men, a truck, and a tractor were already waiting for him. Two of the men had just delivered and unloaded a shiny new tractor, fueled for action.

The third man, a Hercules of modest brain power, was Pete Ransome whose life Frost had once saved, and who gladly proffered his brawny services whenever the professor needed them. "Hey, Ivy, this is one time I beatcha to the tape!" Pete grinned.

Frost waved at him and rolled the huge plane out by means of its mechanical track. He dropped the runway to the freight compartment, and with the other's help stowed his car and the tractor inside. The two vehicles filled the compartment. Frost wrote out a check for the tractor. The two truckmen took it and drove off.

Pete Ransome climbed into the cockpit beside Frost. With a roar, the airplane taxied across the field. Heavily laden, it rose slowly, cleared some telephone wires with scant feet to spare, and soared northward.

Averaging two hundred miles per hour, Frost sighted Pelton forty minutes later, and settled the *If* toward an open pasture a couple of miles southwest of the hamlet. The plane made a rough landing on a bumpy field, but rolled to a stop without accident.

"Ain't nature grand?" Pete yawned and stretched. He helped Frost unload the vehicles.

The professsor made a quick sketch of roads and landmarks as he sighted them from the air. He gave the map to Pete, with instructions. "Remember, timing is all important," he warned.

"I gotcha boss. I never drove one of them tractor babies before but watch me burn hell outta this road-eater."

"I hope not!" Frost exclaimed with a pained expression.

"Keep your shirt on," said Pete cheerfully. "Ya ain't used to the way us guys sling the lingo. Don't worry."

"Your elocution is on a par with your linguistic ability. Both are unique," Frost said, as he took the wheel of the *Demon*.

Frost's last glance of his muscle-ridged ally showed that worthy bouncing into the seat of the tractor alongside the gleaming streamlines of the towering *If.*

Markham's General Store graced the heart of Pelton. A small shop, it nevertheless offered a prodigious variety of articles ranging from sofas and threads to canned goods and hot-water pads. It was also the post office. Frost stopped at this characteristic American phenomenon and entered.

A DOUR, taciturn personage held forth therein. A complete absence of customers faced his solitary grandeur, but he didn't welcome the professor.

Frost wasted no time in skirmishing. "What's the way to the Marvelight Laboratory?"

The dour one's aspect turned openly hostile. "Stranger, just keep lookin' around and you'll find it, I reckon."

"I don't want to find it. I merely want to know the way to it."

The dour one ruminated, eyeing Frost warily. "You got business there?"

"No. But some faces are going to be permanently missing from that vicinity before I'm through."

The bleak eyes peered at Frost. They didn't change, but an indefinable thaw took place. Frost had made another ally, and the hostile suspicion previously directed against him became enmity against the crew of Marvelight.

Frost remarked offhand, "I understand they're all new faces at Marvelight."

"That's right, come five, mebbe six months. There was Hill. He never did show up in town much. He ain't showed up at all since he took on the new fellers. That suits us. Some of us ain't got much use for folks that treat their hired help that way. And there was Barton. He moved clean out when he lost his job. And there was poor old Oberon, who went out of his head. Things kinda changed after Hill put Pietru in charge. There's some queer-lookin' furreners up there now."

Frost drawled, "I wonder if anything unusual happened around this district last night, say within a radius of five miles."

"Well, now, I dunno. Let's see. Seth Abernathy claims he saw a kind of bluish light out Marvelight way this mornin' along about five when he was milkin' cows. Might that interest you?"

"It might," Frost admitted, adopting the chary indirectness of the villagers. "Other incidents might also give me notions."

"Well, now, it seems as how the high-tension wires north of town got busted. I hear they sent a crew down from the power company thirty miles off at Bingham to scout around. I reckon they ain't found the break yet. Funny thing is, there wasn't no storm in these parts."

Frost remarked, "Maybe they could use some help."

"I reckon they could."

Frost took an envelope from his pocket. "This ought to go out in the morning mail, unless the owner comes back for it."

"I kinda guess it'll get mislaid overnight, exceptin' the owner claims it," said the dour one.

Frost took leave without another word between them.

The Marvelight Laboratory where the bluish flare had been reported lay northwest. The broken power wire lay somewhere northeast. Frost drove northeast.

The power line cut straight across fields and up hills, often miles away from any road. Yet Frost took the first side road off the main highway and sped along its winding course. From time to time he glanced at the poles and wires in the distance. It had been obvious, from the repair car parked by the highway, that the trouble-shooters had struck across field on foot to locate the break.

The dirt road swooped closer toward the wires in hilly country. Frost spied a dark ant of a figure on the crossbeams of a pole against a distant hillside. He stopped at the nearest point and hiked into the woods. A quarter of an hour passed before he came upon the ground helper who passed remarks with his companion high in the cross arms. Both ceased work as Frost emerged from the forest. His ungainly length erupted like an apparition.

The professor called, "What's the trouble?"

The ground aid said, "I dunno. We just found the break. We're fixin' it. Ain't had time to look around yet."

Both men watched him, then resumed work as he plunged back into the woods.

Frost beat along the dense growth lining the ten-yard swathe of the right of way that had been cleared for the power lines.

Under a clump of prickly ash he found the body of Kyle Oberon, contorted, and with frightful electric burns.

His features grim, forbidding, he inspected the corpse and the neighboring ground with minute thoroughness. Before returning to his car, he called to the trouble-shooters to make a careful search of the woods. "You'll be surprised at what you find!" Acid truth lurked under that sardonic promise.

Frost drove back toward Pelton.

V.

JEAN MORAY stared wide-eyed at death when the squat thug Horvack fired. The scene burned upon her consciousness: Rita Merril, clad in the bluish metallic raiment that emphasized every wicked curve of her body, watching like a witch of evil doom; the still smoldering wreckage of the machine on the dais; the dark, expressionless face of the killer; the dim expanse of the cellar.

Horvack sighted and shot. But the blast from his pistol echoed a crash that preceded it by the fraction of a second. His bullet screamed wildly over Jean's head. His body jerked. A terrible grape sprang upon his brow. Reflex action made his fingers contract upon the trigger. Another bullet, from a dead man, howled along the floor. Horvack collapsed with a queer, whistling sigh.

Rita Merril leaped for the weapon that slipped from his fingers.

"Hold it!" came the harsh whiplash of Frost's voice.

She stopped abruptly, glaring like an animal at bay.

The professor strode into the room.

"Ivy!" gasped Jean, while murderous hate flamed into the eyes of Rita. "Another second—"

Frost interrupted her. "I arrived several minutes ago. I witnessed the last of the demonstration that Miss Merril kindly afforded us. Horvack's entrance might have been prevented, but only at the cost of serious risk to you."

Jean's heart again did a turnover. Aloud she said simply, "I'm glad."

"Here are handcuffs." Jean snatched the pair that he tossed. "Fasten them and hurry her along. We've an important appointment to keep."

Rita Merril complained, "I'm not exactly dressed to go out."

"The better for us," Frost answered coldly, but did not elaborate his enigmatic remark.

Jean handcuffed the furious Rita and marched her out to the *Demon,* which Frost had left parked not far from his assistant's coupé. Jean kept a hawklike guard over their prisoner in the back seat, while Frost drove on.

WHEN JEAN could no longer restrain her curiosity, she demanded, "What happened back there in the basement?"

Frost was silent for a brief interval. Then, "Electricity is a strange and mysterious power. Physicists can speak in terms of electrons, or positive and negative charges, or fields of force. Engineers can build dynamos and transmission lines. Utilities can sell electric production. But the fact remains that no one knows exactly what electricity is, or its precise nature. Its enormous possibilities have not even begun to be exploited.

"T.N.T. Hill had been experimenting with electricity all his life. He dreamed of making it work still more for the benefit of mankind. His goal was the wireless transmission of power. He came close to success, so close that it cost him his life. Invaders took him prisoner while he worked alone at night. They discharged his only two employees by means of an order they forced him to sign. They killed him and commandeered his laboratory. Pietru, the leader of the gang, and a well-known electrical expert in his native land, wanted that secret for sinister uses. But either Hill hadn't quite succeeded in his final step, or he refused to divulge it. The pirate band was compelled to continue experimenting."

"And to-day they were successful?" Jean queried.

Frost nodded assent. "The tripod was the discharge agent. The machine fed it tremendous quantities of electrical energy. But the machine had no way of producing that energy, nor did it have any visible connection with a source of supply. Therefore, however incredible it may seem, we are left with one inescapable logical conclusion that the machine worked on the principle of a radio, and received electric power by wireless from some distant transmitter. That transmitter must be at the Marvelight Laboratory."

Rita Merril breathed deeply, a long, inarticulate gasp of dismay.

The professor added, "I found the body of Kyle Oberon. Rita, the advance agent of the invaders, made the first contact with Oberon, won his affection, and used him to learn the secrets of the laboratory. After the slaying of Hill and the discharge of Barton and Oberon, she could keep a close watch on Oberon. Barton moved away.

"Oberon was killed this morning near the Marvelight Laboratory, but the gang didn't find the body until after Rita had gone to New York to interview us. The gang couldn't afford to run the risk of having the body found in or near the laboratory by inquisitive detectives. They carried the corpse miles away, snipped a high-tension wire, and abandoned the body with a pair of wire clippers. If the dead man was discovered, it would seem that the demented Oberon had climbed a pole to cut the wires, had been electrocuted, and his body hurled by the shock to a thicket many yards away."

"How was Oberon really killed?"

"I'll show you later," Frost prophesied grimly.

He had been following a backwoods road toward the north. All at once he stopped for no apparent reason, a quarter of a mile beyond the last crossroad. There was a stir in the underbrush near by. Pete Ransome lumbered into view.

"Gee, swell timin', boss!"

"Here she is," Frost answered, opening the rear door.

Pete hauled Rita Merril out.

"Gosh, is this the dame?" exclaimed Pete.

"Take your big paws off me!" Rita flared.

Frost said, "The instructions are clear?"

"To a T." Pete unceremoniously slung the metallic blue body over his shoulder. Rita kicked and struggled and twisted, but the burly truck driver ignored her flailings. They made a strange picture, the brawny six-footer, and the lithe, shimmering, weirdly clad figure of the woman, as they stood framed for a moment against the flaming colors of the autumnal woods in the deep silences of the wilderness. Then Pete carried his burden into the forest.

Jean shivered. She felt the play of ominous gathering forces rising to a climax.

Frost turned the car around, heading southward and westward.

VI.

WHERE the rusty tin arrow pointed with its almost illegible legend, "Marvelight Laboratory," Frost turned aside to follow a little used, winding road. He drove slowly, his eyes sweeping the way ahead. Two miles crept behind them. The road twisted around hillsides. More than another two miles farther ahead, in a shallow valley, Jean caught sight of a sprawling structure, a broad, low shed half hidden among trees.

The road dipped toward the valley. Frost negotiated a sharp curve. Not twenty paces ahead, a tangle of barbed wire blocked the road completely. On both sides rose the forest wall. There was no room to back around. Even to Jean's eyes it was plain that the wire barricade had been erected hastily and recently, stretched between two stout oaks.

"Fast work," Frost commented. "They're taking every precaution on the flimsiest suspicion. They must have gone into action the moment they spied my plane."

His hand flicked to a lever on the dashboard. At the same instant he stepped on the gas. The big vehicle, with a deep hum of power, hurtled forward toward the barbed wire like a black thunderbolt. Jean braced herself for the shock.

Motivated by the lever that Frost had pressed, the front bumper divided in two. The two halves swung upright and revolved. Where the bumper had been, there now stood two tough, sharp blades, two grinding shears.

The vehicle smote the tanglement with a force that snapped Jean's head. The wires twanged under the shears' bite, and the *Demon* ripped through the barrier.

A vast fountain of rocks, dust, and smoke spouted skyward behind the car. The rumbling roar of an explosion blasted the earth. The car careened wildly; the concussion bit it like the blow of a cosmic hand. Frost fought for control as the wheels lurched at the rim of a curve and a drop-off. Then it swerved back to the road while rocks and pebbles beat a hail upon the roof.

Jean looked behind. A great hole yawned where the barbed wire had blocked the road. She shuddered. If Frost had stopped—only bits of metal and human fragments would have remained of them.

She expected to hear the crack of rifle fire. But the reverberations of the blast rolled away. No one moved in the forest.

Jean, shaken and unnerved, lighted a cigarette, but tamped it out after a few fitful puffs. Her throat felt parched.

FROST put the car out of gear and let it roll of its own weight. The grade was steep enough to keep it moving at a fair clip. While still a mile from Marvelight, and when the automobile had nearly reached the bottom of the valley, Frost brought it to a stop.

He took a pair of binoculars. Five, ten minutes passed while he scanned the far side of the valley beyond the laboratory. Then he held the binoculars steady upon one spot, and finally passed them to Jean.

She glued her eyes to the glasses. There sprang into range, a couple of miles distant, a brand-new tractor chucking along the road. Pete Ransome bounced in the driver's seat. He appeared to be enjoying his ride. Beside him lay the woman in blue. Rita struggled now and then to roll off, but Pete firmly pushed her back into place.

Frost took the binoculars. The tractor swerved from the road, cut through young underbrush, and rolled across the fields toward Marvelight. A half mile area surrounding the building had been inclosed by electrified barbed wire.

Pete Ransome bumped the tractor merrily onward, closer and closer toward the wire fence. The scene looked peaceful, yet undercurrents of fateful tension brooded over the valley.

Plowing onward, the tractor crashed the wires. Sparks blazed; crackles of bluish flame sputtered from the broken ends and hissed off the tractor. But Pete and Rita, protected by the cushioned seat and insulation, escaped shock. The tractor, scarcely pausing, ripped a hole wide open through the barrier in a shower of ugly sparks.

The tractor made a loop inside the inclosure and lurched back toward the gap.

Suddenly blue light streamed from the laboratory. It struck the tractor. Instantly a dazzling flare enveloped it with the fury of lightning flashes. That intense, blinding blue tortured Jean's vision. The tractor glowed evilly red. The bodies of Pete Ransome and Rita Merril jerked violently. Two dark shapes were hurtled aside from that blue-and-red inferno.

Frost's features looked chiseled from marble as he lowered the binoculars. His voice sounded implacable as doom. "They play for keeps. Very well, Pietru, the stakes are death. I left a check for ten thousand dollars, payable to Pete's wife, with the postmaster at Pelton. I had hoped that the letter would not need to be mailed. But now—" He left the sentence unfinished. "Rita was to have been Pete's protection. The gang could not possibly have failed to notice her, yet it ruthlessly destroyed even its own member in order to prevent a single outsider from entering the grounds."

Jean frowned. "Pete and Rita were sufficiently insulated from the electric charge in the fence. Why didn't they escape from the blue light?"

"Because that was superpower, an electric flood sent by wireless transmission. You've had a glimpse at the future, and the future's warfare."

The professor snatched a valise from the floor of the car and strode off through the trees, Jean keeping pace by a brisk trot. She felt a little relieved that Frost had held the binoculars at the end. Even to her naked glance the spectacular flame that had destroyed the tractor had not entirely prevented her from glimpsing those black, gnarled figures—

VII.

IN THE HUSH and deepening shadows of twilight, Frost and Jean reached the wire barricade that surrounded Marvelight. The professor made a quick test; electric current, whether because of the gap that the tractor had ripped, or because power had been turned off thereafter, was no longer flowing through the fence.

Frost then performed a bizarre action. He set an alcohol burner on the ground and lighted it. He adjusted a reflector behind it so that it directed the heat inside the grounds of Marvelight. Rising, he lifted from the valise an extension arm of the kind often used on telephones. Jean, puzzled, noticed that the extension was made entirely of wood, and ended in a wooden hook. Frost took a stand ten feet away from the lamp.

"What's that for?" she demanded.

"Watch!" Frost said tersely, facing the wire tanglement, his gaunt figure tensed.

There came a stir in the vegetation beyond the wires. Leaves parted, and a luminous metallic arm rose into view, pointing toward the alcohol lamp and the reflector. A blue flame appeared at the taloned finger tips. A flash of incandescence enveloped the lamp, while the reflector burned red-hot. Frost shot the extension arm forward. It leaped straight for the mark; the hook caught, and the professor gave a violent tug. The hook broke, but down crashed a monstrous metallic figure. A jangling buzz whirred inside of it. The blue flame died down.

Jean only realized bow keyed up she had been when her breath emerged in a taut sigh.

"That is the blue devil that Oberon raved about," Frost drawled. "It's a perfection of the electric man that Hill exhibited several years ago. No doubt there are others spaced at intervals around the inclosure. The robot is a mechanical watchdog raised to deadly efficiency. It is equipped with a device sensitive to body heat, which can always be detected through any range of variations in atmospheric temperature. That is what killed Oberon when his deranged mind led him to try to break through the barricade. I set up the burning lamp and reflector so that the robot felt its heat before it had time to detect the heat of our bodies. You saw with what quick, accurate marksmanship it released its electrical charge at the source of heat."

Frost helped her across the dead wires. With awe she inspected the phosphorescent monster, which lay in the thick shadows like a fallen giant from some far planet. Its inhuman features, its frozen aspect and limbs of wrought metal fascinated her. Yet a simple push had wrecked that ingenious masterpiece of man's design.

THE PROFESSOR gave it not another glance. He strode into the woods toward the laboratory. Within sight of it, he handed the binoculars back to Jean. "Watch from here. Keep your automatic ready for a last stand—"

The professor left her and swung around toward the northern side of the laboratory.

A faintly discernible path ran toward the spot where Pete's tractor had opened a gash in the barbed wire.

Frost bent down for a few moments, then melted into the shadow of a willow clump. He held the loose end of a rope.

Minutes passed before a crackle of twigs arose, and soft footsteps grew audible. A man came walking from the direction of the burned tractor. He drew out a cigarette and lighted it by cupped hands, without pausing in his pace.

Frost tugged the loose rope. Fastened to a tree across the path, the length rose a few inches, tripping the man at the ankles.

He pitched forward, a gasp in his throat. Frost leaped from shadow, pistol ready. But fate had a gruesome whimsy. The man dived onto the side of his face, his body at an angle, before he could use his arms to break his fall. A sharp snap cracked out. The man's lungs emptied with a whistling sigh. They did not fill again.

Frost walked back to the laboratory. All senses keenly alert, he nevertheless strode positively, as though the grounds were his familiar habitat.

He headed for the entrance and calmly walked in. The late member of the Marvelight crew had not troubled to lock the door before going out to inspect the tractor's ruins.

A short passage and an office met the professor's gaze. Beyond lay the open door to a much larger room, evidently an experimental shop. Frost strode on through.

A great variety of electrical equipment, massively impressive and of intricate design, filled the laboratory. Its only occupant was a baldheaded man with pointed wolf's ears who stood, his back to Frost, resting one hand on a switchboard of many copperous levers. The hand held the largest switch in that giant control board.

"Is that you Voril? It took you long enough. What did you find?"

"The name is I.V. Frost," the professor curtly told him. "Your game is lost, Pietru."

VIII.

PIETRU kept his hand on the switch but turned far enough to peer at the professor. He wore thick-lensed glasses that gave him an owlish aspect, belied by the thin, cruel gash of his mouth and his eerily pointed ears.

He possessed a mind of quick comprehensions, for he answered Frost almost immediately. "The game is not lost yet, my friend. It is quite true that you could shoot me with the gun that you are aiming so well. But, living or dead, my hand would throw this lever, and *pouf!* The lightnings will rage and set off the explosives that have been placed to destroy this spot when I am through with it."

"You're through with it now," Frost snapped.

"But you cannot kill me without thereby causing your own death. You would not wish that to happen?"

"It makes not the slightest difference to me," Frost contradicted him. "Whether I die in the inferno you intend to unloose or whether I survive is beside the point. The point that matters is that I have solved a crime, and that your career is ended."

Pietru scowled slightly, chewed his lip. "I am afraid that you do not understand. You cannot escape unless I am permitted to live. If I die, we both die."

"Of course."

Frost's ready agreement shook the egoistic calm of Pietru. He peered more intently at the professor, and tried another tack.

"Perhaps you would like to learn the whereabouts of T.N.T. Hill—"

"Hill has been dead for months, murdered. His body is presumably buried under these grounds. I know that he is dead. Further proof is unnecessary."

Pietru tried again. "Hill discovered a priceless secret. There are many secrets that will perish with us if the laboratory is destroyed. Most of all there is that great principle underlying the wireless transmission of electrical power. It is a discovery that can alter the whole destiny of the world. It can shape the future of civilization."

"It could," Frost agreed, "but it won't. You would turn that knowledge into destructive channels. You think of it only as a method of waging warfare, of successfully attacking other nations."

Pietru argued, "The course of civilization will be set back a hundred years if this invention is lost. There is no other man alive who has Hill's genius."

"The war that you would launch would end civilization," Frost retorted. "Better a few years of peace and slow progress without the invention than the ravage of war with it."

Pietru said gently, "Each of us is born with a loyalty to his native land. We can try to disguise it but it remains with us."

"I don't question the sincerity of that statement."

Pietru resumed, "But in my country we had no such marvelous facilities for discovery and invention as you have here. We lack the natural resources, the educational opportunities, and the wealth. We are an old country.

"WHEN I first learned of Hill's experiments, I realized what power we would have if he was successful and if we could obtain the discovery for our sole use. Hill did not agree with us. He refused our offer. I understood his reasons, but the stakes meant far more to us. We liquidated Hill and assumed responsibility for carrying on his work. It had to be done here, of course, since we could neither duplicate his laboratory nor ship it abroad."

"I deduced all that," Frost interrupted coldly. "There are no unsolved mysteries left in connection with this crime."

"Except the mystery of how wireless transmission of electrical energy is accomplished," Pietru reminded him.

Frost shrugged. "I admit that I would enjoy learning the technical details to satisfy my curiosity. But my curiosity is utterly unimportant and irrelevant compared to the larger stakes at issue."

Pietru urged, "Think well before you act. My country is not rich like many other nations. Yet I can offer you wealth beyond your dreams if you will forget all this until to-morrow. Our work is finished. We can be gone before dawn. A million dollars in United States currency, and another million on the first day of every year."

"The accumulation of funds was never a major or even an important goal of mine."

"Perhaps women?" suggested Pietru. "Rita was lovely. A dozen, a hundred, as lovely or lovelier could be yours. The stakes are very high, I agree. The pick of our fairest flowers would not be too much."

Frost smiled thinly. "Such temptations fail to interest me. You're wasting time."

"Honors? Titles? Office? What would you demand? I have full power to grant your requests."

"I have none to make."

Pietru shook his head. "Every man wants definite returns from life, or seeks desired goals that lure him on. You cannot be an exception."

"Knowledge has been my only pursuit. That, and the mental stimulation of the hunt, the thrill of attacking a snarled, intricate problem for its essential solution, have given me all the satisfactions that I needed."

"I can hardly believe you," Pietru stated. "I do not understand you, or how you can be devoid of the passions and greeds and burning emotions that live in us all."

Frost began striding toward Pietru.

"Stop! Stop or I'll close the switch!"

Frost continued walking straight for the man with the pointed ears.

"You fool!" shrilled Pietru. "You are throwing fame, fortune, and life away! Every step brings death closer!"

The professor kept up his stride.

Pietru's hand jerked on the switch.

JEAN MORAY'S EYES ached from the strain of watching the Marvelight Laboratory through the binoculars. She had stared for long minutes at a lighted window. She saw the gaunt figure of Professor I.V. Frost enter the laboratory. He paused near the door. For many minutes longer he appeared to be carrying on a conversation with some one whom she could not see. Only a blur of syllables came to her ears at this distance.

Then she saw Frost start walking across the room, a strange, sardonic expression on his face.

Titanic lightnings roared through the laboratory. Vast cataclysms of flame and thunder like the explosion of a planet stunned her. Blue hell, incandescent, irresistible, burst through all the walls. A screaming, raging torrent of such terrible energies as she had never imagined inundated Marvelight. Myriads of blinding suns and stars engulfed Jean Moray—

She opened her eyes to the darkness of night and a cool breeze. She struggled to her feet with a rush of memory and a cry, "Ivy! Ivy!"

But only ashes and glowing red embers and a deep crater marked the site of the vanished laboratory.

ACKNOWLEDGMENTS

"Frost," Copyright © 1934 Street & Smith Publications, Inc., for *Clues,* 1934. Copyright renewed © 1962 by Donald Wandrei.

"Green Man—Creeping," Copyright © 1934 Street & Smith Publications, Inc., for *Clues,* November 1934. Copyright renewed © 1962 by Donald Wandrei.

"They Could Not Kill Him," Copyright © 1935 Street & Smith Publications, Inc., for *Clues Detective Stories,* February 1935. Copyright renewed © 1963 by Donald Wandrei.

"Bride of the Rats," Copyright © 1935 Street & Smith Publications, Inc., for *Clues Detective Stories,* April 1935. Copyright renewed © 1963 by Donald Wandrei.

"The Artist of Death," Copyright © 1935 Street & Smith Publications, Inc., for *Clues Detective Stories,* June 1935. Copyright renewed © 1963 by Donald Wandrei.

"Death Descending," Copyright © 1935 Street & Smith Publications, Inc., for *Clues Detective Stories,* August 1935. Copyright renewed © 1963 by Donald Wandrei.

"Impossible," Copyright © 1935 Street & Smith Publications, Inc., for *Clues Detective Stories,* October 1935. Copyright renewed © 1963 by Donald Wandrei.

"Merry-Go-Round," Copyright © 1935 Street & Smith Publications, Inc., for *Clues Detective Stories,* December 1935. Copyright renewed © 1963 by Donald Wandrei.

"Giants in the Valley," Copyright © 1936 Street & Smith Publications, Inc., for *Clues Detective Stories,* February 1936. Copyright renewed © 1964 by Donald Wandrei.

"Bone Crusher," Copyright © 1936 Street & Smith Publications, Inc., for *Clues Detective Stories,* April 1936. Copyright renewed © 1964 by Donald Wandrei.

"Panda," Copyright © 1936 Street & Smith Publications, Inc., for *Clues Detective Stories,* July 1936. Copyright renewed © 1964 by Donald Wandrei.

FIRST EDITION
2020

THE COMPLETE IVY FROST by Donald Wandrei was published by Haffner Press, 5005 Crooks Road, Suite 35, Royal Oak, Michigan 48073-1239.

One thousand trade copies—and a limited edition of one hundred numbered and slipcased copies signed by D. H. Olson, Raymond Swanland, and Stephen Haffner, with a facsimile autograph of the author—have been printed on 50# Domtar Earthchoice Tradebook Cream from Adobe Bembo and House Industries Neutra. The printing was done by Maple Press of York, Pennsylvania. The binding cloth is Arlington Cloth Black Vellum.

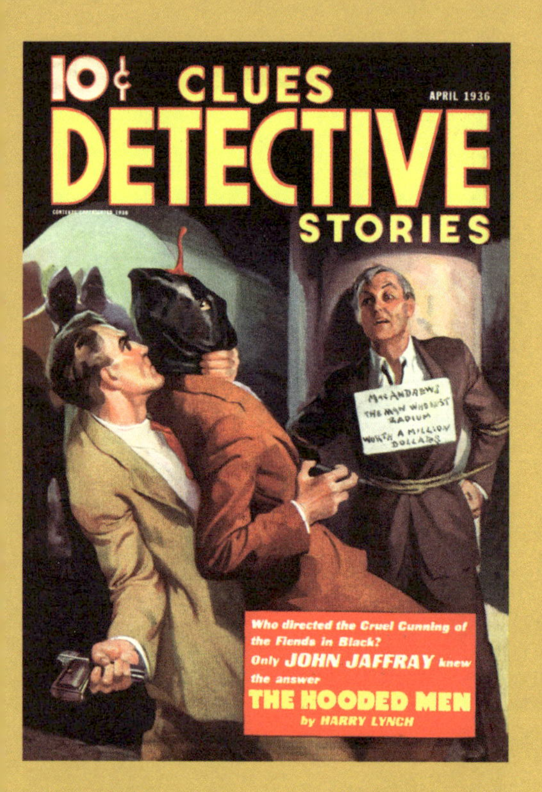

10¢ CLUES
APRIL 1936
DETECTIVE
STORIES
MacANDREWS
THE MAN WHO LOST RADIUM
WORTH A MILLION DOLLARS
Who directed the Cruel Cunning of the Fiends in Black?
Only JOHN JAFFRAY knew the answer
THE HOODED MEN
by HARRY LYNCH

★IVY FROST★JAFFRAY★EDDIE KELLY
10¢ CLUES
JULY 1936
DETECTIVE
STORIES
*PANDA
AN IVY FROST STORY
by
DONALD WANDREI
★★★ A 3-STAR ISSUE

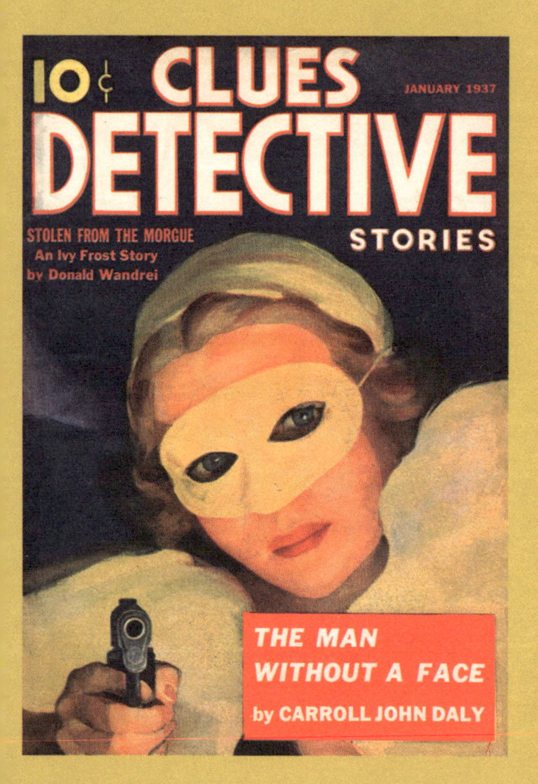

10¢ CLUES
JANUARY 1937
DETECTIVE
STORIES
STOLEN FROM THE MORGUE
An Ivy Frost Story
by Donald Wandrei
THE MAN
WITHOUT A FACE
by CARROLL JOHN DALY

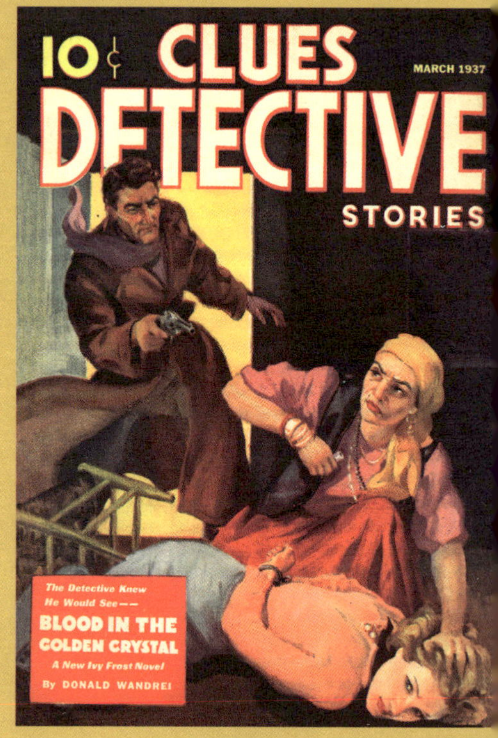

10¢ CLUES
MARCH 1937
DETECTIVE
STORIES
The Detective Knew
He Would See——
BLOOD IN THE
GOLDEN CRYSTAL
A New Ivy Frost Novel
By DONALD WANDREI